ISAAC ASIMOV
THE COMPLETE STORIES
Volume 2

ISAAC
ASIMOV

VOLUME 2

The Complete Stories

A FOUNDATION BOOK

DOUBLEDAY

New York London Toronto Sydney Auckland

A FOUNDATION BOOK
PUBLISHED BY DOUBLEDAY
a division of Bantam Doubleday Dell Publishing Group, Inc.
666 Fifth Avenue, New York, New York 10103

FOUNDATION, DOUBLEDAY, and the portrayal of the letter F
are trademarks of Doubleday, a division of Bantam Doubleday
Dell Publishing Group, Inc.

Library of Congress Cataloging-in-Publication Data
(Revised for vol. 2)

Asimov, Isaac, 1920–
   The complete stories.

   "A Foundation book."
   1. Science fiction, American.
PS3551.S5A6   1990   813'.54   90-3136
ISBN 0-385-42078-1
      0-385-42079-X (trade pbk.)

Contents

Introduction

In the first two volumes of my collected stories (this is the second), I have well over fifty stories printed, and there are still plenty more for future volumes.

I must admit that it fills even me with a kind of awe. I say to myself, "Where did I find the time to write all these stories?"—considering that I have also written hundreds of books and thousands of nonfiction essays. The answer is that I've been at it for fifty-two years without pausing, so what all these stories mean is that I've now gotten to be a rather elderly person.

Another question is, "Where did I get all the ideas for these stories?" I am asked that all the time.

The answer is that in the course of more than half a century of thinking up ideas, the process becomes automatic and, indeed, unstoppable.

I was in bed with my wife last night, and something or other spurred my imagination and I said to her, "I've just thought of a brand-new frustrated-wish story."

"What is it?" said she.

"Our hero, who is blessed with a plain wife, asks a genie to grant him a different, beautiful young woman in bed with him every night. He gets it on condition that at no time must he touch, caress, or even just casually bump the young lady's backside. If he does, the young lady turns into his wife. Each night, in the course of lovemaking, he finds himself unable to stay away entirely from the backside, and the result is that every night he finds himself making love to his wife."*

* Since my dear wife, Janet, is to me the most beautiful woman in the world—and she knows it—she did not take umbrage at this story, aside from telling me that I had a sick mind.

The point is that everything reminds me of a story.

For instance, I was going over a complex set of galley proofs of a book of mine when I received a call from an editor. He wanted a science fiction story in a hurry.

"I can't," I said, "I'm all wrapped up in galleys."

"Put them aside."

"No," I said, and hung up. Still, I couldn't help but think, as I hung up, how convenient it would be if I owned a robot that could do my galleys for me. At once I did put them aside because I suddenly had a story. You'll find it here as "Galley Slave."

My favorite story in this collection is "The Bicentennial Man." Just before we entered the bicentennial year of 1976, an editor asked me to write a story with that title.

"About what?" I asked.

"About anything. All I have is a title."

I thought. No man can be a bicentennial man, for we don't live for two hundred years. A robot might but he is not a man. So how about a story about a robot who wants to be a man. And I at once began "The Bicentennial Man." It ended by winning a Hugo and a Nebula.

Once, my dear wife, Janet, had a bad headache but felt it necessary to prepare dinner for her loving husband anyway. As it turned out, the dinner was an unusually good one and—being a husband—I said, "You ought to have headaches oftener." And after she finished throwing something at me, I wrote the story "Light Verse."

A fellow writer died young in 1958 and got a nice obituary in the *New York Times*. Those were early years and no one expected anyone to pay attention to science fiction writers in those days. I took to brooding. When I passed on to the great typewriter in the sky, would the *New York Times* make mention of that fact, too? Nowadays I know they will but in those days I didn't. So after I had brooded sufficiently over the matter, I wrote "Obituary."

I had an argument with an editor once, hot and heavy. He wanted me to make a specific change in a story of mine, and I did not want to make it—not out of laziness, but because I thought it would spoil the story. In the end, he had his way (editors usually do) but I got even by writing "The Monkey's Finger," which is a good description of what went on.

A woman editor once asked me to write a story about a woman robot, since all my robots had been (up to that time) men. I agreed with no trouble whatever and wrote "Feminine Intuition." What I remember best about the story was that I didn't quite get it through my head that the woman editor in question wanted the story for herself. I rather thought she was giving me generalized advice. Consequently, when I finished the story and a different editor told me he needed one badly, I said, "Here's one." And when the first editor found out, boy, did I get it!

Sometimes stories arise because other people make some casual remark.

Such stories as "Let's Get Together" and "Rain, Rain, Go Away" are examples. I don't feel guilty about lifting ideas from the statements of other people. They're not going to do anything with them, so why shouldn't I?

But the point is that stories arise out of anything. You just have to keep your eyes and ears open and your imagination working. Once during a train trip, my first wife asked me where I got my ideas from. I said, "From anywhere. I can write a story about this train trip." And I started writing it longhand. That story does not appear in this collection, however.

—ISAAC ASIMOV

Not Final!

Nicholas Orloff inserted a monocle in his left eye with all the incorruptible Briticism of a Russian educated at Oxford and said reproachfully, "But, my dear Mr. Secretary! Half a billion dollars!"

Leo Birnam shrugged his shoulders wearily and allowed his lank body to cramp up still farther in the chair, "The appropriation must go through, commissioner. The Dominion government here at Ganymede is becoming desperate. So far, I've been holding them off, but as secretary of scientific affairs, my powers are small."

"I know, but—" and Orloff spread his hands helplessly.

"I suppose so," agreed Birnam. "The Empire government finds it easier to look the other way. They've done it consistently up to now. I've tried for a year now to have them understand the nature of the danger that hangs over the entire System, but it seems that it can't be done. But I'm appealing to you, Mr. Commissioner. You're new in your post and can approach this Jovian affair with an unjaundiced eye."

Orloff coughed and eyed the tips of his boots. In the three months since he had succeeded Gridley as colonial commissioner he had tabled unread everything relating to "those damned Jovian D. T.'s." That had been according to the established cabinet policy which had labeled the Jovian affair as "deadwood" long before he had entered office.

But now that Ganymede was becoming nasty, he found himself sent out to Jovopolis with instructions to hold the "blasted provincials" down. It was a nasty spot.

Birnam was speaking, "The Dominion government has reached the point where it needs the money so badly, in fact, that if they don't get it, they're going to publicize everything."

Orloff's phlegm broke completely, and he snatched at the monocle as it dropped, "My dear fellow!"

"I know what it would mean. I've advised against it, but they're justified. Once the inside of the Jovian affair is out; once the people know about it; the Empire government won't stay in power a week. And when the Technocrats come in, they'll give us whatever we ask. Public opinion will see to that."

"But you'll also create a panic and hysteria—"

"Surely! That is why we hesitate. But you might call this an ultimatum. We want secrecy, we *need* secrecy; but we need money more."

"I see." Orloff was thinking rapidly, and the conclusions he came to were not pleasant. "In that case, it would be advisable to investigate the case further. If you have the papers concerning the communications with the planet Jupiter—"

"I have them," replied Birnam, dryly, "and so has the Empire government at Washington. That won't do, commissioner. It's the same cud that's been chewed by Earth officials for the last year, and it's gotten us nowhere. I want you to come to Ether Station with me."

The Ganymedan had risen from his chair, and he glowered down upon Orloff from his six and a half feet of height.

Orloff flushed, "Are you ordering me?"

"In a way, yes. I tell you there is no time. If you intend acting, you must act quickly or not at all." Birnam paused, then added, "You don't mind walking, I hope. Power vehicles aren't allowed to approach Ether Station, ordinarily, and I can use the walk to explain a few of the facts. It's only two miles off."

"I'll walk," was the brusque reply.

The trip upward to subground level was made in silence, which was broken by Orloff when they stepped into the dimly lit anteroom.

"It's chilly here."

"I know. It's difficult to keep the temperature up to norm this near the surface. But it will be colder outside. Here!"

Birnam had kicked open a closet door and was indicating the garments suspended from the ceiling. "Put them on. You'll need them."

Orloff fingered them doubtfully, "Are they heavy enough?"

Birnam was pouring into his own costume as he spoke. "They're electrically heated. You'll find them plenty warm. That's it! Tuck the trouser legs inside the boots and lace them tight."

He turned then and, with a grunt, brought out a double compressed-gas cylinder from its rack in one corner of the closet. He glanced at the dial reading; and then turned the stopcock. There was a thin wheeze of escaping gas, at which Birnam sniffed with satisfaction.

"Do you know how to work one of these?" he asked, as he screwed onto the jet a flexible tube of metal mesh, at the other end of which was a curiously curved object of thick, clear glass.

"What is it?"

"Oxygen nosepiece! What there is of Ganymede's atmosphere is argon and nitrogen, just about half and half. It isn't particularly breathable." He heaved the double cylinder into position, and tightened it in its harness on Orloff's back.

Orloff staggered, "It's heavy. I can't walk two miles with this."

"It won't be heavy out there," Birnam nodded carelessly upward and lowered the glass nosepiece over Orloff's head. "Just remember to breathe in through the nose and out through the mouth, and you won't have any trouble. By the way, did you eat recently?"

"I lunched before I came to your place."

Birnam sniffed dubiously, "Well, that's a little awkward." He drew a small metal container from one of his pockets and tossed it to the commissioner. "Put one of those pills in your mouth and keep sucking on it."

Orloff worked clumsily with gloved fingers and finally managed to get a brown spheriod out of the tin and into his mouth. He followed Birnam up a gently sloped ramp. The blind-alley ending of the corridor slid aside smoothly when they reached it and there was a faint soughing as air slipped out into the thinner atmosphere of Ganymede.

Birnam caught the other's elbow, and fairly dragged him out.

"I've turned your air tank on full," he shouted. "Breathe deeply and keep sucking at that pill."

Gravity had flicked to Ganymedan normality as they crossed the threshold and Orloff after one horrible moment of apparent levitation, felt his stomach turn a somersault and explode.

He gagged, and fumbled the pill with his tongue in a desperate attempt at self-control. The oxygen-rich mixture from the air cylinders burned his throat, and gradually Ganymede steadied. His stomach shuddered back into place. He tried walking.

"Take it easy, now," came Birnam's soothing voice. "It gets you that way the first few times you change gravity fields quickly. Walk slowly and get the rhythm, or you'll take a tumble. That's right, you're getting it."

The ground seemed resilient. Orloff could feel the pressure of the other's arm holding him down at each step to keep him from springing too high. Steps were longer now—and flatter, as he got the rhythm. Birnam continued speaking, a voice a little muffled from behind the leather flap drawn loosely across mouth and chin.

"Each to his own world," he grinned. "I visited Earth a few years back, with my wife, and had a hell of a time. I couldn't get myself to learn to walk on a planet's surface without a nosepiece. I kept choking—I really did. The sunlight was too bright and the sky was too blue and the grass was too green. And the buildings were right out on the surface. I'll never forget the time they tried to get me to sleep in a room twenty stories up in the air, with the window wide open and the moon shining in.

"I went back on the first spaceship going my way and don't ever intend returning. How are you feeling now?"

"Fine! Splendid!" Now that the first discomfort had gone, Orloff found the low gravity exhilarating. He looked about him. The broken, hilly ground, bathed in a drenching yellow light, was covered with ground-hugging broad-leaved shrubs that showed the orderly arrangement of careful cultivation.

Birnam answered the unspoken question, "There's enough carbon dioxide in the air to keep the plants alive, and they all have the power to fix atmospheric nitrogen. That's what makes agriculture Ganymede's greatest industry. Those plants are worth their weight in gold as fertilizers back on Earth and worth double or triple that as sources for half a hundred alkaloids that can't be gotten anywhere else in the System. And, of course, everyone knows that Ganymedan green-leaf has Terrestrial tobacco beat hollow."

There was the drone of a strato-rocket overhead, shrill in the thin atmosphere, and Orloff looked up.

He stopped—stopped dead—and forgot to breathe!

It was his first glimpse of Jupiter in the sky.

It is one thing to see Jupiter, coldly harsh, against the ebon backdrop of space. At six hundred thousand miles, it is majestic enough. But on Ganymede, barely topping the hills, its outlines softened and ever so faintly hazed by the thin atmosphere; shining mellowly from a purple sky in which only a few fugitive stars dare compete with the Jovian giant—it can be described by no conceivable combination of words.

At first, Orloff absorbed the gibbous disk in silence. It was gigantic, thirty-two times the apparent diameter of the Sun as seen from Earth. Its stripes stood out in faint washes of color against the yellowness beneath and the Great Red Spot was an oval splotch of orange near the western rim.

And finally Orloff murmured weakly, "It's beautiful!"

Leo Birnam stared, too, but there was no awe in his eyes. There was the mechanical weariness of viewing a sight often seen, and besides that an expression of sick revulsion. The chin flap hid his twitching smile, but his grasp upon Orloff's arm left bruises through the tough fabric of the surface suit.

He said slowly, "It's the most horrible sight in the System."

Orloff turned reluctant attention to his companion, "Eh?" Then, disagreeably, "Oh, yes, those mysterious Jovians."

At that, the Ganymedan turned away angrily and broke into swinging, fifteen-foot strides. Orloff followed clumsily after, keeping his balance with difficulty.

"Here, now," he gasped.

But Birnam wasn't listening. He was speaking coldly, bitterly, "You on Earth can afford to ignore Jupiter. You know nothing of it. It's a little pin prick in your sky, a little flyspeck. You don't live here on Ganymede, watching that damned colossus gloating over you. Up and over fifteen hours— hiding God knows what on its surface. Hiding something that's waiting and waiting and *trying to get out.* Like a giant bomb just waiting to explode!"

"Nonsense!" Orloff managed to jerk out. *"Will* you slow down. I can't keep up."

Birnam cut his strides in half and said tensely, "Everyone knows that Jupiter is inhabited, but practically no one ever stops to realize what that means. I tell you that those Jovians, whatever they are, are born to the purple. *They are the natural rulers of the Solar System."*

"Pure hysteria," muttered Orloff. "The Empire government has been hearing nothing else from your Dominion for a year."

"And you've shrugged it off. Well, listen! Jupiter, discounting the thickness of its colossal atmosphere, is eighty thousand miles in diameter. That means it possesses a surface one hundred times that of Earth, and more than fifty times that of the entire Terrestrial Empire. Its population, its resources, its war potential are in proportion."

"Mere numbers—"

"I know what you mean," Birnam drove on, passionately. "Wars are not fought with numbers, but with science and with organization. The Jovians have both. In the quarter of a century during which we have communicated with them, we've learned a bit. They have atomic power and they have radio. And in a world of ammonia under great pressure—a world in other words in which almost none of the metals can exist *as* metals for any length of time because of the tendency to form soluble ammonia complexes—they have managed to build up a complicated civilization. That means they have had to work through plastics, glasses, silicates and synthetic building materials of one sort or another. *That* means a chemistry developed just as far as ours is, and I'd put odds on its having developed further."

Orloff waited long before answering. And then, "But how certain are you people about the Jovians' last message. We on Earth are inclined to doubt that the Jovians can possibly be as unreasonably belligerent as they have been described."

The Ganymedan laughed shortly, "They broke off all communication after that last message, didn't they? That doesn't sound friendly on their part, does it? I assure you that we've all but stood on our ears trying to contact them.

"Here now, don't talk. Let me explain something to you. For twenty-five years here on Ganymede a little group of men have worked their hearts out trying to make sense out of a static-ridden, gravity-distorted set of variable clicks in our radio apparatus, for those clicks were our only connection with living intelligence upon Jupiter. It was a job for a world of scientists, but we never had more than two dozen at the Station at any one time. I was one of them from the very beginning and, as a philologist, did my part in helping construct and interpret the code that developed between ourselves and the Jovians, so that you can see I am speaking from the real inside.

"It was a devil of a heartbreaking job. It was five years before we got past the elementary clicks of arithmetic: three and four are seven; the square root of twenty-five is five; factorial six is seven hundred and twenty. After that, months sometimes passed before we could work out and check by further communication a single new fragment of thought.

"*But*—and this is the point—by the time the Jovians broke off relations, we understood them *thoroughly.* There was no more chance of a mistake in comprehension, than there was of Ganymede suddenly cutting loose from Jupiter. And their last message was a threat, and a promise of destruction. Oh, there's no doubt—there's no doubt!"

They were walking through a shallow pass in which the yellow Jupiter light gave way to a clammy darkness.

Orloff was disturbed. He had never had the case presented to him in this fashion before. He said, "But the reason, man. What reason did we give them—"

"No reason! It was simply this: the Jovians had finally discovered from our messages—just where and how I don't know—that *we* were *not* Jovians."

"Well, of course."

"It wasn't 'of course' to them. In their experiences they had never come across intelligences that were not Jovian. Why should they make an exception in favor of those from outer space?"

"You say they were scientists." Orloff's voice had assumed a wary frigidity. "Wouldn't they realize that alien environments would breed alien life? *We* knew it. We never thought the Jovians were Earthmen though we had never met intelligences other than those of Earth."

They were back in the drenching wash of Jupiter light again, and a spreading region of ice glimmered amberly in a depression to the right.

Birnam answered, "I said they were chemists and physicists—but I never said they were astronomers. Jupiter, my dear commissioner, has an atmosphere three thousand miles or more thick, and those miles of gas block off everything but the Sun and the four largest of Jupiter's moons. The Jovians know nothing of alien environments."

Orloff considered. "And so they decided we were aliens. What next?"

"If we weren't Jovians, then, in their eyes, we weren't people. It turned out that a non-Jovian was 'vermin' by definition."

Orloff's automatic protest was cut off short by Birnam, "In their eyes, I said, vermin we were; and vermin we are. Moreover, we were vermin with the peculiar audacity of having dared to attempt to treat with Jovians—with *human beings*. Their last message was this, word for word—'Jovians are the masters. There is no room for vermin. We will destroy you immediately.' I doubt if there was any animosity in that message—simply a cold statement of fact. But they meant it."

"But why?"

"Why did man exterminate the housefly?"

"Come, sir. You're not seriously presenting an analogy of that nature."

"Why not, since it is certain that the Jovian considers us a sort of housefly —an insufferable type of housefly that dares aspire to intelligence."

Orloff made a last attempt, "But truly, Mr. Secretary, it seems impossible for intelligent life to adopt such an attitude."

"Do you possess much of an acquaintance with any other type of intelligent life than our own?" came with immediate sarcasm. "Do you feel competent to pass on Jovian psychology? Do you know just *how* alien Jovians must be physically? Just think of their world with its gravity at two and one half Earth normal; with its ammonia oceans—oceans that you might throw all Earth into without raising a respectable splash; with its three-thousand-mile atmosphere, dragged down by the colossal gravity into densities and pressures in its surface layers that make the sea bottoms of Earth resemble a medium-thick vacuum. I tell you we've tried to figure out what sort of life could exist under those conditions and we've given up. It's thoroughly incomprehensible. Do you expect their mentality, then, to be any more understandable? Never! Accept it as it is. They intend destroying us. That's all we know and all we need to know."

He lifted a gloved hand as he finished and one finger pointed, "There's Ether Station just ahead."

Orloff's head swiveled, "Underground?"

"Certainly! All except the Observatory. That's that steel and quartz dome to the right—the small one."

They had stopped before two large boulders that flanked an earthy embankment, and from behind either one a nosepieced, suited soldier in Ganymedan orange, with blasters ready, advanced upon the two.

Birnam lifted his face into Jupiter's light and the soldiers saluted and stepped aside. A short word was barked into the wrist mike of one of them and the camouflaged opening between the boulders fell into two and Orloff followed the secretary into the yawning airlock.

The Earthman caught one last glimpse of sprawling Jupiter before the closing door cut off the surface altogether.

It was no longer beautiful!

Orloff did not quite feel normal again until he had seated himself in the overstuffed chair in Dr. Edward Prosser's private office. With a sigh of utter relaxation, he propped his monocle under his eyebrow.

"Would Dr. Prosser mind if I smoked in here, while we're waiting?" he asked.

"Go ahead," replied Birnam, carelessly. "My own idea would be to drag Prosser away from whatever he's fooling with just now, but he's a queer chap. We'll get more out of him if we wait until he's ready for us." He withdrew a gnarled stick of greenish tobacco from its case, and bit off the edge viciously.

Orloff smiled through the smoke of his own cigarette, "I don't mind waiting. I still have something to say. You see, for the moment, Mr. Secretary, you gave me the jitters, but, after all, granted that the Jovians intend mischief once they get at us, it remains a fact," and here he spaced his words emphatically, "that they can't get at us."

"A bomb without a fuse, hey?"

"Exactly! It's simplicity itself, and not really worth discussing. You will admit, I suppose, that under no circumstances can the Jovians get away from Jupiter."

"Under *no* circumstances?" There was a quizzical tinge in Birnam's slow reply. "Shall we analyze that?"

He stared hard at the purple flame of his cigar. "It's an old trite saying that the Jovians can't leave Jupiter. The fact has been highly publicized by the sensation mongers of Earth and Ganymede and a great deal of sentiment has been driveled about the unfortunate intelligences who are irrevocably surface-bound, and must forever stare into the Universe without, watching, watching, wondering, and never attaining.

"But, after all, what holds the Jovians to their planet? Two factors! That's all! The first is the immense gravity field of the planet. Two and a half Earth normal."

Orloff nodded. "Pretty bad!" he agreed.

"And Jupiter's gravitational potential is even worse, for because of its greater diameter the intensity of its gravitational field decreases with distance only one tenth as rapidly as Earth's field does. It's a terrible problem—*but it's been solved.*"

"Hey?" Orloff straightened.

"They've got atomic power. Gravity—even Jupiter's—means nothing once you've put unstable atomic nuclei to work for you."

Orloff crushed his cigarette to extinction with a nervous gesture. "But their atmosphere—"

"Yes, that's what's stopping them. They're living at the bottom of a three-thousand-mile-deep ocean of it, where the hydrogen of which it is composed is collapsed by sheer pressure to something approaching the density of *solid* hydrogen. It stays a gas because the temperature of Jupiter is above the critical point of hydrogen, but you just try to figure out the pressure that can make hydrogen *gas* half as heavy as water. You'll be surprised at the number of zeros you'll have to put down.

"No spaceship of metal or of any kind of matter can stand that pressure.

No Terrestrial spaceship can land on Jupiter without smashing like an egg-shell, and no Jovian spaceship can leave Jupiter without exploding like a soap bubble. That problem has not yet been solved, but it will be some day. Maybe tomorrow, maybe not for a hundred years, or a thousand. We don't know, but when it is solved, the Jovians will be on top of us. And it can be solved in a specific way."

"I don't see how—"

"Force fields! We've got them now, you know."

"Force fields!" Orloff seemed genuinely astonished, and he chewed the word over and over to himself for a few moments. "They're used as meteor shields for ships in the asteroid zone—but I don't see the application to the Jovian problem."

"The ordinary force field," explained Birnam, "is a feeble rarefied zone of energy extending over a hundred miles or more outside the ship. It'll stop meteors but it's just so much empty ether to an object like a gas molecule. *But* what if you took that same zone of energy and compressed it to a thickness of a tenth of an inch. Molecules would bounce off it like this—*ping-g-g-g!* And if you used stronger generators, and compressed the field to a hundredth of an inch, molecules would bounce off even when driven by the unthinkable pressure of Jupiter's atmosphere—and then if you build a ship inside—" He left the sentence dangling.

Orloff was pale. "You're not saying it can be done?"

"I'll bet you anything you like that the Jovians are *trying* to do it. And *we're* trying to do it right here at Ether Station."

The colonial commissioner jerked his chair closer to Birnam and grabbed the Ganymedan's wrist. "Why can't we bombard Jupiter with atomic bombs. Give it a thorough going-over, I mean! With her gravity, and her surface area, we can't miss."

Birnam smiled faintly, "We've thought of that. But atomic bombs would merely tear holes in the atmosphere. And even if you could penetrate, just divide the surface of Jupiter by the area of damage of a single bomb and find how many years we must bombard Jupiter at the rate of a bomb a minute before we begin to do significant damage. Jupiter's *big!* Don't ever forget that!"

His cigar had gone out, but he did not pause to relight. He continued in a low, tense voice. "No, we can't attack the Jovians as long as they're on Jupiter. We must wait for them to come out—and once they do, they're going to have the edge on us in numbers. A terrific, heart-breaking edge—so we'll just have to have the edge on them in science."

"But," Orloff broke in, and there was a note of fascinated horror in his voice, "how can we tell in advance what they'll have?"

"We can't. We've got to scrape up everything we can lay our hands on and hope for the best. But there's one thing we *do* know they'll have, and that's force fields. They can't get out without them. And if they have them, we must, too, and that's the problem we're trying to solve here. They will not insure us victory, but without them, we will suffer certain defeat. And now you know why we need money—and more than that. We want Earth itself to get to work. It's got to start a drive for scientific armaments and subordinate everything to that. You see?"

Orloff was on his feet. "Birnam, I'm with you—a hundred percent with you. You can count on me back in Washington."

There was no mistaking his sincerity. Birnam gripped the hand outstretched toward him and wrung it—and at the moment, the door flew open and a little pixie of a man hurtled in.

The newcomer spoke in rapid jerks, and exclusively to Birnam. "Where'd you come from? Been trying to get in touch with you. Secretary said you weren't in. Then five minutes later you show up on your own. Can't understand it." He busied himself furiously at his desk.

Birnam grinned. "If you'll take time out, doc, you might say hello to Colonial Commissioner Orloff."

Dr. Edward Prosser turned on his toe like a ballet dancer and looked the Earthman up and down twice. "The new un, hey? We getting any money? We ought to. Been working on a shoestring ever since. At that, we might not be needing any. It depends." He was back at the desk.

Orloff seemed a trifle disconcerted, but Birnam winked impressively, and he contented himself with a glassy stare through the monocle.

Prosser pounced upon a black leather booklet in the recesses of a pigeonhole, threw himself into his swivel chair and wheeled about.

"Glad you came, Birnam," he said, leafing through the booklet. "Got something to show you. Commissioner Orloff, too."

"What were you keeping us waiting for?" demanded Birnam. "Where were you?"

"Busy! Busy as a pig! No sleep for three nights." He looked up, and his small puckered face fairly flushed with delight. "Everything fell into place of a sudden. Like a jig-saw puzzle. Never saw anything like it. Kept us hopping, I tell you."

"You've gotten the dense force fields you're after?" asked Orloff in sudden excitement.

Prosser seemed annoyed. "No, not that. Something else. Come on." He glared at his watch and jumped out of his seat. "We've got half an hour. Let's go."

An electric-motored flivver waited outside and Prosser spoke excitedly as he sped the purring vehicle down the ramps into the depths of the Station.

"Theory!" he said. "Theory! Damned important, that. You set a technician on a problem. He'll fool around. Waste lifetimes. Get nowhere. Just putter about at random. A true scientist works with theory. Lets math solve his problems." He overflowed with self-satisfaction.

The flivver stopped on a dime before a huge double door and Prosser tumbled out, followed by the other two at a more leisurely pace.

"Through here! Through here!" he said. He shoved the door open and led them down the corridor and up a narrow flight of stairs onto a wall-hugging passageway that circled a huge three-level room. Orloff recognized the gleaming quartz-and-steel pipe-sprouting ellipsoid two levels below as an atomic generator.

He adjusted his monocle and watched the scurrying activity below. An earphoned man on a high stool before a control board studded with dials looked up and waved. Prosser waved back and grinned.

Orloff said, "You create your force fields here?"

"That's right! Ever see one?"

"No." The commissioner smiled, ruefully. "I don't even know what one *is*, except that it can be used as a meteor shield."

Prosser said, "It's very simple. Elementary matter. All matter is composed of atoms. Atoms are held together by interatomic forces. Take away atoms. Leave interatomic forces behind. *That's* a force field."

Orloff looked blank, and Birnam chuckled deep in his throat and scratched the back of his ear.

"That explanation reminds me of our Ganymedan method of suspending an egg a mile high in the air. It goes like this. You find a mountain just a mile high and put the egg on top. Then, keeping the egg where it is, you take the mountain away. That's all."

The colonial commissioner threw his head back to laugh, and the irascible Dr. Prosser puckered his lips in a pursed symbol of disapproval.

"Come, come. No joke, you know. Force fields most important. Got to be ready for the Jovians when they come."

A sudden rasping bur from below sent Prosser back from the railing.

"Get behind screen here," he babbled. "The twenty-millimeter field is going up. Bad radiation."

The bur muted almost into silence, and the three walked out onto the passageway again. There was no apparent change, but Prosser shoved his hand out over the railing and said, "Feel!"

Orloff extended a cautious finger, gasped, and slapped out with the palm of his hand. It was like pushing against very soft sponge rubber or superresilient steel springs.

Birnam tried, too. "That's better than anything we've done yet, isn't it?" He explained to Orloff, "A twenty-millimeter screen is one that can hold an atmosphere of a pressure of twenty millimeters of mercury against a vacuum without appreciable leakage."

The commissioner nodded, "I see! You'd need a seven-hundred-sixty-millimeter screen to hold Earth's atmosphere then."

"Yes! That would be a unit atmosphere screen. Well, Prosser, is this what got you excited?"

"This twenty-millimeter screen? Of course not. I can go up to two hundred fifty millimeters using the activated vanadium pentasulphide in the praseodymium breakdown. But it's not necessary. Technician would do it and blow up the place. Scientist checks on theory and goes slow." He winked. "We're hardening the field now. Watch!"

"Shall we get behind the screen?"

"Not necessary now. Radiation bad only at beginning."

The burring waxed again, but not as loudly as before. Prosser shouted to the man at the control board, and a spreading wave of the hand was the only reply.

Then the control man waved a clenched fist and Prosser cried, "We've passed fifty millimeters! Feel the field!"

Orloff extended his hand and poked it curiously. The sponge rubber had hardened! He tried to pinch it between finger and thumb so perfect was the illusion, but here the "rubber" faded to unresisting air.

Prosser *tch-tched* impatiently. "No resistance at right angles to force. Elementary mechanics, that is."

The control man was gesturing again. "Past seventy," explained Prosser. "We're slowing down now. Critical point is 83.42."

He hung over the railing and kicked out with his feet at the other two. "Stay away! Dangerous!"

And then he yelled, "Careful! The generator's bucking!"

The bur had risen to a hoarse maximum and the control man worked frantically at his switches. From within the quartz heart of the central atomic generator, the sullen red glow of the bursting atoms had brightened dangerously.

There was a break in the bur, a reverberant roar, and a blast of air that threw Orloff hard against the wall.

Prosser dashed up. There was a cut over his eye. "Hurt? No? Good, good! I was expecting something of the sort. Should have warned you. Let's go down. Where's Birnam?"

The tall Ganymedan picked himself up off the floor and brushed at his clothes. "Here I am. What blew up?"

"Nothing blew up. Something buckled. Come on, down we go." He dabbed at his forehead with a handkerchief and led the way downward.

The control man removed his earphones as he approached and got off his stool. He looked tired, and his dirt-smeared face was greasy with perspiration.

"The damn thing started going at 82.8, boss. It almost caught me."

"It did, did it?" growled Prosser. "Within limits of error, isn't it? How's the generator? Hey, Stoddard!"

The technician addressed replied from his station at the generator, "Tube 5 died. It'll take two days to replace."

Prosser turned in satisfaction and said, "It worked. Went exactly as presumed. Problem solved, gentlemen. Trouble over. Let's get back to my office. I want to eat. And then I want to sleep."

He did not refer to the subject again until once more behind the desk in his office, and then he spoke between huge bites of a liver-and-onion sandwich.

He addressed Birnam, "Remember the work on space strain last June. It flopped, but we kept at it. Finch got a lead last week and I developed it. Everything fell into place. Slick as goose grease. Never saw anything like it."

"Go ahead," said Birnam, calmly. He knew Prosser sufficiently well to avoid showing impatience.

"You saw what happened. When a field tops 83.42 millimeters, it becomes unstable. Space won't stand the strain. It buckles and the field blows. *Boom!*"

Birnam's mouth dropped open and the arms of Orloff's chair creaked under sudden pressure. Silence for a while, and then Birnam said unsteadily, "You mean force fields stronger than that are impossible?"

"They're possible. You can create them. But the denser they are, the more unstable they are. If I had turned on the two-hundred-and-fifty-millimeter field, it would have lasted one tenth of a second. Then, blooie! Would have blown up the Station! *And* myself! Technician would have done it. Scientist is warned by theory. Works carefully, the way I did. No harm done."

Orloff tucked his monocle into his vest pocket and said tremulously, "But if a force field is the same thing as interatomic forces, why is it that steel has such a strong interatomic binding force without bucking space? There's a flaw there."

Prosser eyed him in annoyance. "No flaw. Critical strength depends on number of generators. In steel, each atom is a force-field generator. That means about three hundred billion trillion generators for every ounce of matter. If we could use that many— As it is, one hundred generators would be the practical limit. That only raises the critical point to ninety-seven or thereabout."

He got to his feet and continued with sudden fervor, "No. Problem's over, I tell you. Absolutely impossible to create a force field capable of holding Earth's atmosphere for more than a hundredth of a second. Jovian atmosphere entirely out of question. Cold figures say that; backed by experiment. *Space won't stand it!*

"Let the Jovians do their damnedest. They can't get out! That's final! That's final! *That's final!*"

Orloff said, "Mr. Secretary, can I send a spacegram anywhere in the Station? I want to tell Earth that I'm returning by the next ship and that the Jovian problem is liquidated—entirely and for good."

Birnam said nothing, but the relief of his face as he shook hands with the colonial commissioner, transfigured the gaunt homeliness of it unbelievably.

And Dr. Prosser repeated, with a birdlike jerk of his head, "That's *final!*"

Hal Tuttle looked up as Captain Everett of the spaceship *Transparent*, newest ship of the Comet Space Lines, entered his private observation room in the nose of the ship.

The captain said, "A spacegram has just reached me from the home offices at Tucson. We're to pick up Colonial Commissioner Orloff at Jovopolis, Ganymede, and take him back to Earth."

"Good. We haven't sighted any ships?"

"No, no! We're way off the regular space lanes. The first the System will know of us will be the landing of the *Transparent* on Ganymede. It will be the greatest thing in space travel since the first trip to the Moon." His voice softened suddenly, "What's wrong, Hal? This is *your* triumph, after all."

Hal Tuttle looked up and out into the blackness of space. "I suppose it is. Ten years of work, Sam. I lost an arm and an eye in that first explosion, but I don't regret them. It's the reaction that's got me. The problem is solved; my lifework is finished."

"So is every steel-hulled ship in the System."

Tuttle smiled. "Yes. It's hard to realize, isn't it?" He gestured outward. "You see the stars? Part of the time, there's nothing between them and us. It gives me a queazy feeling." His voice brooded, "Nine years I worked for nothing. I wasn't a theoretician, and never really knew where I was headed— just tried everything. I tried a little too hard and space wouldn't stand it. I paid an arm and an eye and started fresh."

Captain Everett balled his fist and pounded the hull—the hull through which the stars shone unobstructed. There was the muffled thud of flesh striking an unyielding surface—but no response whatever from the invisible wall.

Tuttle nodded, "It's solid enough, now—though it flicks on and off eight hundred thousand times a second. I got the idea from the stroboscopic lamp. You know them—they flash on and off so rapidly that it gives all the impression of steady illumination.

"And so it is with the hull. It's not on long enough to buckle space. It's not off long enough to allow appreciable leakage of the atmosphere. And the net effect is a strength better than steel."

He paused and added slowly, "And there's no telling how far we can go. Speed up the intermission effect. Have the field flick off and on millions of times per second—billions of times. You can get fields strong enough to hold an atomic explosion. My lifework!"

Captain Everett pounded the other's shoulder. "Snap out of it, man. Think of the landing on Ganymede. The devil! It will be great publicity.

Think of Orloff's face, for instance, when he finds he is to be the first passenger in history ever to travel in a spaceship with a force-field hull. How do you suppose he'll feel?"

Hal Tuttle shrugged. "I imagine he'll be rather pleased."

The Hazing

The Campus of Arcturus University, on Arcturus' second planet, Eron, is a dull place during mid-year vacations and, moreover, a hot one, so that Myron Tubal, sophomore, found life boring and uncomfortable. For the fifth time that day, he looked in at the Undergraduate Lounge in a desperate attempt at locating an acquaintance, and was at last gratified to behold Bill Sefan, a green-skinned youngster from Vega's fifth planet.

Sefan, like Tubal, had flunked Biosociology and was staying through vacation to study for a make-up exam. Things like that weave strong bonds between sophomore and sophomore.

Tubal grunted a greeting, dropped his huge hairless body—he was a native of the Arcturian System itself—into the largest chair and said:

"Have you seen the new freshmen yet?"

"Already! It's six weeks before the fall semester starts!"

Tubal yawned. "These are a special breed of frosh. They're the very first batch from the Solarian System—ten of them."

"Solarian System? You mean that new system that joined the Galactic Federation three—four years ago?"

"That's the one. Their world capital is called Earth, I think."

"Well, what about them?"

"Nothing much. They're just here, that's all. Some of them have hair on the upper lip, and very silly it looks, too. Otherwise, they look like any of a dozen or so other breeds of Humanoids."

It was at this point that the door flew open and little Wri Forase ran in. He was from Deneb's single planet, and the short, gray fuzz that covered his head and face bristled with agitation, while his large purple eyes gleamed excitedly.

"Say," he twittered breathlessly, "have you seen the Earthmen?"

Sefan sighed. "Isn't anyone ever going to change the subject? Tubal was just telling me about them."

"He was?" Forase seemed disappointed. "But—but did he tell you these were that abnormal race they made such a fuss over when the Solarian System entered the Federation?"

"They looked all right to me," said Tubal.

"I'm not talking about them from the physical standpoint," said the Denebian disgustedly. "It's the mental aspect of the case. Psychology! That's the stuff!" Forase was going to be a psychologist some day.

"Oh, that! Well, what's wrong with them?"

"Their mob psychology as a race is all wrong," babbled Forase. "Instead of becoming less emotional with numbers, as is the case with every other type of Humanoid known, they become *more* emotional! In groups, these Earthmen riot, panic, go crazy. The more there are, the worse it is. So help me, we even invented a new mathematical notation to handle the problem. Look!"

He had his pocket-pad and stylus out in one rapid motion; but Tubal's hand clamped down upon them before the stylus so much as made a mark.

Tubal said, "Whoa! I've got a walloping lulu of an idea."

"Imagine!" murmured Sefan.

Tubal ignored him. He smiled again, and his hand rubbed thoughtfully over his bald dome.

"Listen," he said, with sudden briskness. His voice dropped to a conspiratorial whisper.

Albert Williams, late of Earth, stirred in his sleep and became conscious of a prodding finger exploring the space between his second and third ribs. He opened his eyes, swiveled his head, stared stupidly; then gasped, shot upright, and reached for the light switch.

"Don't move," said the shadowy figure beside his bed. There was a muted click, and the Earthman found himself centered in the pearly beam of a pocket flash.

He blinked and said, "Who the blasted devil are you?"

"You are going to get out of bed," replied the apparition stolidly. "Dress, and come with me."

Williams grinned savagely. "Try and make me."

There was no answer, but the flash beam shifted slightly and fell upon the shadow's other hand. It held a "neuronic whip," that pleasant little weapon that paralyzes the vocal cords and twists nerves into so many knots of agony. Williams swallowed hard, and got out of bed.

He dressed in silence, and then said:

"All right, what do I do now?"

The gleaming "whip" gestured, and the Earthman moved toward the door.

"Just walk ahead," said the unknown.

Williams moved out of the room, along the silent corridor, and down eight stories without daring to look back. Out upon the campus he stopped, and felt metal probe the small of his back.

"Do you know where Obel Hall is?"

Williams, nodding, began walking. He walked past Obel Hall, turned right at University Avenue, and after half a mile stepped off the roads and past the trees. A spaceship hulked dimly in the darkness, with ports closely curtained and only a dim light showing where the airlock opened a crack.

"Get in!" He was shoved up a flight of stairs and into a small room.

He blinked, looked about him and counted aloud.

"—seven, eight, nine, and I make ten. They've got us all, I guess."

"It's no guess," growled Eric Chamberlain sourly. "It's a certainty." He was rubbing his hand. "I've been here an hour."

"What's wrong with the mitt?" asked Williams.

"I sprained it on the jaw of the rat that brought me here. He's as tough as a spaceship's hull."

Williams seated himself cross-legged upon the floor and rested his head against the wall.

"Has anyone any idea as to what this is all about?"

"Kidnaping!" said little Joey Sweeney. His teeth were chattering.

"What the devil for?" snorted Chamberlain. "If any of us are millionaires, I hadn't heard of it. I know I'm not!"

Williams said, "Look, let's not go off the deep end. Kidnaping or anything of that sort is out. These people can't be criminals. It stands to reason that a civilization that has developed psychology to the extent this Galactic Federation has, would be able to wipe out crime without raising a sweat."

"Pirates," grunted Lawrence Marsh. "I don't think so, but it's just a suggestion."

"Nuts!" said Williams. "Piracy is a frontier phenomenon. This region of space has been civilized for tens of millennia."

"Just the same, they had guns," insisted Joe, "and I don't like it." He had left his glasses in his room and peered about in near-sighted anxiety.

"That doesn't mean much," answered Williams. "Now, I've been thinking. Here we are—ten newly arrived freshmen at Arcturus U. On our first night here, we're bundled mysteriously out of our rooms and into a strange spaceship. That suggests something to me. How about it?"

Sidney Morton raised his head from his arms long enough to say sleepily:

"I've thought of it, too. It looks like we're in for one hell of a hazing. Gents, I think the local sophs are just having good, clean fun."

"Exactly," agreed Williams. "Anyone have any other ideas?"

Silence. "All right, then, so there isn't anything to do but wait. Personally, I'm going to catch up on my sleep. They can wake me up if they need me."

There was a jar at that moment and he fell off balance.

"Well, we're off—wherever we're going."

Moments later, Bill Sefan hesitated just an instant before entering the control room. When he finally did, it was to face a highly excited Wri Forase.

"How is it working?" demanded the Denebian.

"Rotten," responded Sefan sourly. "If they're panicked, then I'm damned. They're going to sleep."

"Asleep! All of them? But what were they saying?"

"How do I know? They weren't speaking Galactic, and I can't make head or tail out of their infernal foreign gibberish."

Forase threw his hands into the air in disgust.

Tubal spoke finally. "Listen, Forase, I'm cutting a class in Biosoc.—which I can't afford. You guaranteed the psychology of this stunt. If it turns out to be a flop, I'm not going to like it."

"Well, for the love of Deneb," grated Forase desperately, "you two are a fine pair of yellow-bellies! Did you expect them to start screaming and kicking right off? Sizzling Arcturus! Wait till we get to the Spican System, will you? When we maroon them overnight—"

He tittered suddenly. "This is going to be the fanciest trick since they tied those stink-bats to the chromatic organ on Concert Night."

Tubal cracked a grin, but Sefan leaned back in his chair and remarked thoughtfully.

"What if someone—say, President Wynn—hears about this?"

The Arcturian at the controls shrugged. "It's only a hazing. They'll go easy."

"Don't play dumb, M. T. This isn't kid stuff. Planet Four, Spica—the whole Spican System, in fact—is banned to Galactic ships, and you know that. It's got a sub-Humanoid race on it. They're supposed to develop entirely free of interference until they discover interstellar travel on their own. That's the law, and they're strict about it. Space! If they find out about this, we'll be in the soup for fair."

Tubal turned in his seat. "How in Arcturus do you expect Prexy Wynn—damn his thick hide!—to find out about us? Now, mind you, I'm not saying the story won't spread around the campus, because half the fun will be killed if we have to keep it to ourselves. But how will names come out? No one will squeal. You know that."

"Okay," said Sefan, and shrugged.

And then Tubal said, "Ready for hyper-space!"

He compressed keys and there was the queer internal wrench that marked the ship's departure from normal space.

· · · ·

The ten Earthmen were rather the worse for wear, and looked it. Lawrence Marsh squinted at his watch again.

"Two-thirty," he said. "That's thirty-six hours now. I wish they'd get this over with."

"This isn't a hazing," moaned Sweeney. "It takes too long."

Williams grew red. "What do you all look half-dead about? They've been feeding us regularly, haven't they? They haven't tied us up, have they? I should say it was pretty evident that they were taking good care of us."

"Or," came Sidney Morton's discontented drawl, "fattening us up for the slaughter."

He paused, and everyone stiffened. There was no mistaking the queer internal wrench they had felt.

"Get *that!*" said Eric Chamberlain in sudden frenzy. "We're back in normal space again, and that means we're only an hour or two from wherever we're going. We've got to do something!"

"Hear, hear," Williams snorted. "But what?"

"There are ten of us, aren't there?" shouted Chamberlain, puffing out his chest. "Well, I've only seen one of them so far. Next time he comes in, and we've got another meal due us pretty soon, we're going to mob him."

Sweeney looked sick. "What about the neuronic whip he always carries?"

"It won't kill us. He can't get us all before we pin him down, anyway."

"Eric," said Williams bluntly, "you're a fool."

Chamberlain flushed and his stub-fingered fists closed slowly.

"I'm just in the mood for a little practice persuasion. Call me that again, will you?"

"Sit down!" Williams scarcely bothered to look up. "And don't work so hard justifying my epithet. All of us are nervous and keyed-up, but that doesn't mean we ought to go altogether crazy. Not yet, anyway. First of all, even discounting the whip, mobbing our jailer won't be particularly successful.

"We've only seen one, but that one is from the Arcturian System. He's better than seven feet tall, and comfortably past the three-hundred-pound mark. He'd mop us up—all ten of us—with his bare fists. I thought you had one run-in with him already, Eric."

There was a thickish silence.

Williams added, "And even if we could knock him out and finish as many others as there may be in the ship, we still haven't the slightest idea where we are or how to get back or even how to run the ship." A pause. Then, "Well?"

"Nuts!" Chamberlain turned away, and glowered in silence.

The door kicked open and the giant Arcturian entered. With one hand, he emptied the bag he carried, and with the other kept his neuronic whip carefully leveled.

"Last meal," he grunted.

There was a general scramble for the rolling cans, still lukewarm from recent heating. Morton glared at his with disgust.

"Say," he spoke stumblingly in Galactic, "can't you give us a change? I'm tired of this rotten goulash of yours. This is the fourth can!"

"So what? It's your last meal," the Arcturian snapped, and left.

A horrified paralysis prevailed.

"What did he mean by that?" gulped someone huskily.

"They're going to kill us!" Sweeney was round-eyed, the thin edge of panic in his voice.

Williams' mouth was dry and he felt unreasoning anger grow against Sweeney's contagious fright. He paused—the kid was only seventeen—and said huskily, "Stow it, will you? Let's eat."

It was two hours later that he felt the shuddering jar that meant the landing and end of the journey. In that time, no one had spoken, but Williams could feel the pall of fear choke tighter with the minutes.

Spica had dipped crimsonly below the horizon and there was a chill wind blowing. The ten Earthmen, huddled together miserably upon the rock-strewn hilltop, watched their captors sullenly. It was the huge Arcturian, Myron Tubal, that did the talking, while the green-skinned Vegan, Bill Sefan, and the fuzzy little Denebian, Wri Forase, remained placidly in the background.

"You've got your fire," said the Arcturian gruffly, "and there's plenty of wood about to keep it going. That will keep the beasts away. We'll leave you a pair of whips before we go, and those will do as protection, if any of the aborigines of the planet bother you. You will have to use your own wits as far as food, water and shelter are concerned."

He turned away. Chamberlain let loose with a sudden roar, and leaped after the departing Arcturian. He was sent reeling back with an effortless heave of the other's arm.

The lock closed after the three other-world men. Almost at once, the ship lifted off the ground and shot upward. Williams finally broke the chilled silence.

"They've left the whips. I'll take one and you can have the other, Eric."

One by one, the Earthmen dropped into a sitting position, back to the fire, frightened, half panicky.

Williams forced a grin. "There's plenty of game about—the region is well-wooded. Come on, now, there are ten of us and they've got to come back sometime. Let's show them we Earthmen can take it. How about it, fellows?"

He was talking aimlessly now. Morton said listlessly,

"Why don't you shut up? You're not making this any easier."

Williams gave up. The pit of his own stomach was turning cold.

The twilight blackened into night, and the circle of light about the fire contracted into a little flickering area that ended in shadows. Marsh gasped suddenly, and his eyes went wide.

"There's some—something coming!"

The stir that followed froze itself into attitudes of breathless attention.

"You're crazy," began Williams huskily—and stopped dead at the unmistakable, slithering sound that reached his ears.

"Grab your whip!" he screamed to Chamberlain.

Joey Sweeney laughed suddenly—a strained, high-pitched laugh.

And then—there was a sudden shrieking in the air, and the shades charged down upon them.

Things were happening elsewhere, too.

Tubal's ship lazed outward from Spica's fourth planet, with Bill Sefan at the controls. Tubal himself was in his own cramped quarters, polishing off a huge flagon of Denebian liquor in two gulps.

Wri Forase watched the operation sadly.

"It cost twenty credits a bottle," he said, "and I only have a few left."

"Well, don't let me hog it," said Tubal magnanimously. "Match me bottle for bottle. It's all right with me."

"One swig like that," grumbled the Denebian, "and I'd be out till the Fall exams."

Tubal paid scant attention. "This," he began, "is going to make campus history as the hazing stunt—"

And at this point, there was a sharp, singing pinging *ping-g-g-g,* scarcely muffled by intervening walls, and the lights went out.

Wri Forase felt himself pressed hard against the wall. He struggled for breath and stuttered out in gasps.

"B-by Space, we're at f-full acceleration! What's wr-rong with the equalizer?"

"Damn the equalizer!" roared Tubal, heaving to his feet. "What's wrong with the ship?"

He stumbled out the door, into the equally dark corridor, with Forase crawling after him. When they burst into the control room, they found Sefan surrounded by the dim emergency lights, his green skin shining with perspiration.

"Meteor," he croaked. "It played hob with our power distributors. It's all going into acceleration. The lights, heating units and radio are all out of commission, while the ventilators are just barely limping." He added, "And Section Four is punctured."

Tubal gazed about him wildly. "Idiot! Why didn't you keep your eye on the mass indicator?"

"I did, you overgrown lump of putty," howled Sefan, "but it never registered! It—never—registered! Isn't that just what you'd expect from a secondhand jalopy, rented for two hundred credits? It went through the screen as if it were empty ether."

"Shut up!" Tubal flung open the suit-compartments and groaned. "They're all Arcturian models. I should have checked up. Can you handle one of these, Sefan?"

"Maybe." The Vegan scratched a doubtful ear.

In five minutes, Tubal swung into the lock and Sefan, stumbling awkwardly, followed after. It was half an hour before they returned.

Tubal removed his head-piece. "Curtains!"

Wri Forase gasped. "You mean—we're through?"

The Arcturian shook his head. "We can fix it, but it will take time. The radio is ruined for good, so we can't get help."

"Get help!" Forase looked shocked. "That's all we need. How would we explain being inside the Spican System? We might as well commit suicide as send out radio calls. As long as we can get back without help, we're safe. Missing a few more classes won't hurt us too much."

Sefan's voice broke in dully. "But what about those panicky Earthmen back on Spica Four?"

Forase's mouth opened, but he didn't say a word. It closed again, and if ever a Humanoid looked sick, Forase was that Humanoid.

That was only the beginning.

It took a day and a half to unscramble the space jalopy's power lines. It took two more days to decelerate to safe turning point. It took four days to return to Spica IV. Total—eight days.

When the ship hovered once more over the place where they had marooned the Earthmen, it was midmorning, and the Tubal's face as he surveyed the area through the televisor was a study in length. Shortly he broke a silence that had long since become sticky.

"I guess we've made every boner we could possibly have made. We landed them right outside a native village. There's no sign of the Earthmen."

Sefan shook his head dolefully. "This is a bad business."

Tubal buried his head in his long arms clear down to the elbows.

"That's the finish. If they didn't scare themselves to death, the natives got them. Violating prohibited solar systems is bad enough—but it's just plain murder now, I guess."

"What we've got to do," said Sefan, "is to get down there and find out if there are any still alive. We owe them that much. After that—"

He swallowed. Forase finished in a whisper.

"After that, it's expulsion from the U., psycho-revision—and manual labor for life."

"Forget it!" barked Tubal. "We'll face that when we have to."

Slowly, very slowly, the ship circled downward and came to rest on the rocky clearing where, eight days previously, ten Earthmen had been left stranded.

"How do we handle these natives?" Tubal turned to Forase with raised eyebrow ridges (there was no hair on them, of course). "Come on, son, give with some sub-Humanoid psychology. There are only three of us and I don't want any trouble."

Forase shrugged and his fuzzy face wrinkled in perplexity. "I've just been thinking about that, Tubal. I don't know any."

"What!" exploded Sefan and Tubal in twin shouts.

"No one does," added the Denebian hurriedly. "It's a fact. After all, we don't let sub-Humanoids into the Federation till they're fully civilized, and we quarantine them until then. Do you suppose we have much opportunity to study their psychology?"

The Arcturian seated himself heavily. "This gets better and better. *Think*, Fuzzy-face, will you? Suggest something!"

Forase scratched his head. "Well—uh—the best we can do is to treat them like normal Humanoids. If we approach slowly, palms spread out, make no sudden movements and keep calm, we ought to get along. Now, remember, I'm saying we *ought* to. I can't be certain about this."

"Let's go, and damnation with certainty," urged Sefan impatiently. "It doesn't matter much, anyway. If I get knocked off here, I don't have to go back home." His face took on a hunted look. "When I think of what my family is going to say—"

They emerged from the ship and sniffed the atmosphere of Spica's fourth planet. The sun was at meridian, and loomed overhead like a large orange basketball. Off in the woods, a bird called once in a creaky caw. Utter silence descended.

"Hmph!" said Tubal, arms akimbo.

"It's enough to make you feel sleepy. No signs of life at all. Now, which way is the village?"

There was a three-way dispute about this, but it didn't last long. The Arcturian first, the other two tagging along, they strode down the slope and toward the straggling forest.

A hundred feet inside, the trees came alive, as a wave of natives dropped noiselessly from the overhanging branches. Wri Forase went under at the very first of the avalanche. Bill Sefan stumbled, stood his ground momentarily, then went over backward with a grunt.

Only huge Myron Tubal was left standing. Legs straddled wide, and whooping hoarsely, he laid about right and left. The attacking natives hit him and bounced off like drops of water from a whirling flywheel. Modeling his defense on the principle of the windmill, he backed his way against a tree.

Here he made a mistake. On the lowest branch of that tree squatted a native at once more cautious and more brainy than his fellows. Tubal had already noticed that the natives were equipped with stout, muscular tails, and had made a mental note of the fact. Of all the races in the Galaxy, only one other, Homo Gamma Cepheus, possessed tails. What he *didn't* notice, however, was that these tails were prehensile.

This he found out almost immediately, for the native in the branch above his head looped his tail downward, flashed it about Tubal's neck and contracted it.

The Arcturian threshed wildly in agony, and the tailed attacker was jerked from his tree. Suspended head-first and whirled about in huge sweeps, the native nevertheless maintained his hold and tightened that tail-grip steadily.

The world blacked out. Tubal was unconscious before he hit the ground.

Tubal came to slowly, unpleasantly aware of the stinging stiffness of his neck. He tried vainly to rub that stiffness, and it took a few seconds to realize that he was tied tightly. The fact startled him into alertness. He became aware, first, that he was lying on his stomach; second, of the horrible din about him; third, of Sefan and Forase bundled up next to him—and last, that he could not break his bonds.

"Hey, Sefan, Forase! Can you hear me?"

It was Sefan that answered joyfully. "You old Draconian goat! We thought you were out for good."

"I don't die so easy," grunted the Arcturian. "Where are we?"

There was a short pause.

"In the native village, I imagine," Wri Forase said dully. "Did you ever hear such a noise? The drum hasn't stopped a minute since they dumped us here."

"Have you seen anything of—"

Hands were upon Tubal, and he felt himself whirled about. He was in a sitting posture now and his neck hurt worse than ever. Ramshackle huts of thatch and green logs gleamed in the early afternoon sun. In a circle about them, watching in silence, were dark-skinned, long-tailed natives. There must have been hundreds, all wearing feathered head-dresses and carrying short, wickedly barbed spears.

Their eyes were upon the row of figures that squatted mysteriously in the foreground, and upon these Tubal turned his angry glare. It was plain that they were the leaders of the tribe. Dressed in gaudy, fringed robes of ill-tanned skins, they added further to their barbaric impressiveness by wearing tall wooden masks painted into caricatures of the human face.

With measured steps, the masked horror nearest the Humanoids approached.

"Hello," it said, and the mask lifted up and off. "Back so soon?"

For quite a long while, Tubal and Sefan said absolutely nothing, while Wri Forase went into a protracted fit of coughing.

Finally, Tubal drew a long breath. "You're one of the Earthmen, aren't you?"

"That's right. I'm Al Williams. Just call me Al."

"They haven't killed you yet?"

Williams smiled happily. "They haven't killed any of us. Quite the contrary. Gentlemen," he bowed extravagantly, "meet the new tribal—er—gods."

"The new tribal *what?*" gasped Forase. He was still coughing.

"—er—gods. Sorry, but I don't know the Galactic word for a god."

"What do you 'gods' represent?"

"We're sort of supernatural entities—objects to be worshipped. Don't you get it?"

The Humanoids stared unhappily.

"Yes, indeed," Williams grinned, "we're persons of great power."

"What are you talking about?" exclaimed Tubal indignantly. "Why should they think you were of great power? You Earth people are below average physically—well below!"

"It's the psychology of the thing," explained Williams. "If they see us landing in a large, gleaming vehicle that travels mysteriously through the air, and then takes off in a burst of rocket-flame—they're bound to consider us supernatural. That's elementary barbaric psychology."

Forase's eyes seemed on the point of dropping out as Williams continued.

"Incidentally, what detained you? We figure it was all a hazing of some sort, and it was, wasn't it?"

"Say," broke in Sefan, "I think you're feeding us a lot of bull! If they thought you people were gods, why didn't they think we were? We had the ship, too, and—"

"That," said Williams, "is where *we* started to interfere. We explained—via pictures and sign language—that you people were devils. When you finally came back—and say, were we glad to see that ship coming down—they knew what to do."

"What," asked Forase, with a liberal dash of awe in his voice, "are 'devils'?"

Williams sighed. "Don't you Galaxy people know anything? Tubal moved his aching neck slowly. "How about letting us up now?" he rumbled. "I've got a crick in my neck."

"What's your hurry? After all, you were brought here to be sacrificed in our honor."

"Sacrificed!"

"Sure. You're to be carved up with knives."

There was a horror-laden silence. "Don't give us any of that comet-gas!" Tubal managed to grind out at last. "We're not Earthmen who get panicky or scared, you know."

"Oh, we know *that!* I wouldn't fool you for the world. But simple ordinary savage psychology always goes for a little human sacrifice, and—"

Sefan writhed against his bonds and tried to throw himself in a rage at Forase.

"I thought you said no one knew any sub-Humanoid psychology! Trying to alibi your ignorance, weren't you, you shriveled, fuzz-covered, pop-eyed son of a half-breed Vegan lizard! A fine mess we're in now!"

Forase shrank away. "Now, wait! Just—"

Williams decided the joke had gone far enough.

"Take it easy," he soothed. "Your clever hazing blew up right in your faces —it blew up beautifully—but we're not going to carry it too far. I guess we've had enough fun out of you fellows. Sweeney is with the native chief now, explaining that we're leaving and taking you three with us. Frankly, I'll be glad to get going— Wait a while, Sweeney's calling me."

When Williams returned two seconds later, his expression was peculiar, having turned a bit greenish. In fact, he got greener by the second.

"It looks," he gulped throatily, "as if our counter-haze has blown up in *our* faces. The native chief *insists* on the sacrifice!"

Silence brooded, while the three Humanoids thought over the state of affairs. For moments, none of them could say a word.

"I've told Sweeney," Williams added, glumly, "to go back and tell the chief that if he doesn't do as we say, something terrible is going to happen to his tribe. But it's pure bluff and he may not fall for it. Uh—I'm sorry, fellows. I guess we went too far. If it looks really bad, we'll cut you loose and join in the fight."

"Cut us loose now," growled Tubal, his blood running cold. "Let's get this over with!"

"Wait!" cried Forase frantically. "Let the Earthman try some of his psychology. Go ahead, Earthman. Think hard!"

Williams thought until his brain began to hurt.

"You see," he said weakly, "we've lost some of our godlike prestige, ever since we were unable to cure the chief's wife. She died yesterday." He nodded abstractedly to himself. "What we need is an impressive miracle. Er— have you fellows anything in your pockets?"

He knelt beside them and began searching. Wri Forase had a stylus, a pocket-pad, a thin-toothed comb, some anti-itch powder, a sheaf of credits and a few odds and ends. Sefan had a collection of similar nondescript material.

It was from Tubal's hip pocket that Williams withdrew a small black gunlike object with a huge hand-grip and a short barrel.

"What's this?"

Tubal scowled. "Is that what I've been sitting on all this while? It's a weld-gun that I used to fix up a meteor puncture in our ship. It's no good; power's almost gone."

Williams' eyes kindled. His whole body galvanized with excitement.

"That's what you think! You Galaxy men never could see farther than your noses. Why don't you come down to Earth for a spell—and get a new point of view?"

Williams was running toward his fellow conspirators now.

"Sweeney," he howled, "you tell that damned monkey-tailed chief that in just about one second, I'm going to get sore and pull the whole sky down over his head. Get tough!"

But the chief did not wait for the message. He gestured defiance and the natives made a united rush. Tubal roared, and his muscles cracked against the bonds. The weld-gun in Williams' hand flared into life, its feeble power beaming outward.

The nearest native hut went up in sudden flames. Another followed—and another—and the fourth—and then the weld-gun went dead.

But it was enough. Not a native remained standing. All were groveling on their faces, wailing and shrieking for pardon. The chief wailed and shrieked loudest of all.

"Tell the chief," said Williams to Sweeney, "that that's just a little, insignificant sample of what we're thinking of doing to him!"

To the Humanoids, as he cut the rawhide holding them, he added complacently,

"Just some simple, ordinary savage psychology."

It was only after they were back in their ship and off in space again that Forase locked up his pride.

"But I thought Earthmen had never developed mathematical psychology! How did you know all that sub-Humanoid stuff? No one in the Galaxy has got that far yet!"

"Well," Williams grinned, "we have a certain amount of rule-of-thumb knowledge about the workings of the uncivilized mind. You see—we come from a world where most people, in a manner of speaking, are still uncivilized. So we *have* to know!"

Forase nodded slowly. "You screwball Earthmen! At least, this little episode has taught us all one thing."

"What's that?"

"Never," said Forase, dipping a second time into Earth slang, "get tough with a bunch of nuts. They may be nuttier than you think!"

In going through my stories while preparing this book, I found "The Hazing" to be the only *published* story concerning which I could remember nothing from the title alone. Even as I reread it, nothing clicked. If I had been given the story without my name on it and had been asked to read it and guess the author, I would probably have been stumped. Maybe that means something.

It does seem to me, though, that the story is set against a "Homo Sol" background.

I had better luck with Fred Pohl with another story, "Super-Neutron," which I wrote at the end of the same February in which I did "Masks" and "The Hazing." I submitted it to him on March 3, 1941, and he accepted it on March 5.

By that time, less than three years after my first submission, I was clearly becoming rather impatient with rejections. At least, the news of the acceptance of "Super-Neutron" is greeted in my diary with an "It's about time I made a sale—five and a half weeks since the last one."

Death Sentence

Brand Gorla smiled uncomfortably, "These things exaggerate, you know."

"No, no, no!" The little man's albino-pink eyes snapped. "Dorlis was great when no human had ever entered the Vegan System. It was the capital of a Galactic Confederation greater than ours."

"Well, then, let's say that it was an ancient capital. I'll admit that and leave the rest to an archaeologist."

"Archaeologists are no use. What I've discovered needs a specialist in its own field. And you're on the Board."

Brand Gorla looked doubtful. He remembered Theor Realo in senior year —a little white misfit of a human who skulked somewhere in the background of his reminiscences. It had been a long time ago, but the albino had been queer. *That* was easy to remember. And he was still queer.

"I'll try to help," Brand said, "if you'll tell me what you want."

Theor watched intently, "I want you to place certain facts before the Board. Will you promise that?"

Brand hedged, "Even if I help you along, Theor, I'll have to remind you that I'm junior member of the Psychological Board. I haven't much influence."

"You must do your best. The facts will speak for themselves." The albino's hands were trembling.

"Go ahead." Brand resigned himself. The man was an old school fellow. You couldn't be *too* arbitrary about things.

Brand Gorla leaned back and relaxed. The light of Arcturus shone through the ceiling-high windows, diffused and mellowed by the polarizing glass. Even this diluted version of sunlight was too much for the pink eyes of the other, and he shaded his eyes as he spoke.

"I've lived on Dorlis twenty-five years, Brand," he said, "I've poked into places no one today knew existed, and I've found things. Dorlis was the scientific and cultural capital of a civilization greater than ours. Yes it was, and particularly in psychology."

"Things in the past always seem greater." Brand condescended a smile. "There is a theorem to that effect which you'll find in any elementary text. Freshmen invariably call it the 'GOD Theorem.' Stands for 'Good-Old-Days,' you know. But go on."

Theor frowned at the digression. He hid the beginning of a sneer, "You can always dismiss an uncomfortable fact by pinning a dowdy label to it. But tell me this. What do you know of Psychological Engineering?"

Brand shrugged, "No such thing. Anyway, not in the strict mathematical sense. All propaganda and advertising is a crude form of hit-and-miss Psych Engineering—and pretty effective sometimes. Maybe that's what you mean."

"Not at all. I mean actual experimentation, with masses of people, under controlled conditions, and over a period of years."

"Such things have been discussed. It's not feasible in practice. Our social structure couldn't stand much of it, and we don't know enough to set up effective controls."

Theor suppressed excitement, "But the ancients *did* know enough. And they *did* set up controls."

Brand considered phlegmatically, "Startling and interesting, but how do you know?"

"Because I found the documents relating to it." He paused breathlessly. "An entire planet, Brand. A complete world picked to suit, peopled with beings under strict control from every angle. Studied, and charted, and experimented upon. Don't you get the picture?"

Brand noted none of the usual stigmata of mental uncontrol. A closer investigation, perhaps—

He said evenly, "You must have been misled. It's thoroughly impossible. You can't control humans like that. Too many variables."

"And that's the point, Brand. They weren't humans."

"What?"

"They were robots, positronic robots. A whole world of them, Brand, with nothing to do but live and react and be observed by a set of psychologists that were *real* psychologists."

"That's mad!"

"I have proof—because that robot world still exists. The First Confederation went to pieces, but that robot world kept on going. It still exists."

"And how do you know?"

Theor Realo stood up. "Because I've been there these last twenty-five years!"

The Board Master threw his formal red-edged gown aside and reached into a pocket for a long, gnarled and decidedly unofficial cigar.

"Preposterous," he grunted, "and thoroughly insane."

"Exactly," said Brand, "and I can't spring it on the Board just like that. They wouldn't listen. I've got to get this across to you first, and then, if you can put your authority behind it—"

"Oh, nuts! I never heard anything as— Who is the fellow?"

Brand sighed, "A crank, I'll admit that. He was in my class at Arcturus U. and a crack-pot albino even then. Maladjusted as the devil, hipped on ancient history, and just the kind that gets an idea and goes through with it by plain, dumb plugging. He's poked about in Dorlis for twenty-five years, he says. He's got the complete records of practically an entire civilization."

The Board Master puffed furiously. "Yeah, I know. In the telestat serials, the brilliant amateur always uncovers the great things. The free lance. The lone wolf. Nuts! Have you consulted the Department of Archaeology?"

"Certainly. And the result was interesting. No one bothers with Dorlis. This isn't just ancient history, you see. It's a matter of fifteen thousand years. It's practically myth. Reputable archaeologists don't waste too much time with it. It's just the thing a book-struck layman with a single-track mind *would* uncover. After this, of course, if the business turns out right, Dorlis will become an archaeologist's paradise."

The Board Master screwed his homely face into an appalling grimace. "It's very unflattering to the ego. If there's any truth in all this, the so-called First Confederation must have had a grasp of psychology so far past ours, as to make us out to be blithering imbeciles. Too, they'd have to build positronic robots that would be about seventy-five orders of magnitude above anything we've even blueprinted. Galaxy! Think of the mathematics involved."

"Look, sir, I've consulted just about everybody. I wouldn't bring this thing to you if I weren't certain that I had every angle checked. I went to Blak just about the first thing, and he's consultant mathematician to United Robots. He says there's no limit to these things. Given the time, the money, and the *advance in psychology*—get that—robots like that could be built right now."

"What proof has he?"

"Who, Blak?"

"No, no! Your friend. The albino. You said he had papers."

"He has. I've got them here. He's got documents—and there's no denying their antiquity. I've had that checked every way from Sunday. I can't read them, of course. I don't know if anyone can, except Theor Realo."

"That's stacking the deck, isn't it? We have to take his say-so."

"Yes, in a way. But he doesn't claim to be able to decipher more than portions. He says it is related to ancient Centaurian, and I've put linguists to work on it. It can be cracked and if his translation isn't accurate, we'll know about it."

"All right. Let's see it."

Brand Gorla brought out the plastic-mounted documents. The Board Master tossed them aside and reached for the translation. Smoke billowed as he read.

"Humph," was his comment. "Further details are on Dorlis, I suppose."

"Theor claims that there are some hundred to two hundred tons of blueprints altogether, on the brain plan of the positronic robots alone. They're still there in the original vault. But that's the least of it. He's been on the robot world itself. He's got photocasts, teletype recordings, all sorts of details. They're not integrated, and obviously the work of a layman who knows next to nothing about psychology. Even so, he's managed to get enough data to prove pretty conclusively that the world he was on wasn't . . . uh . . . natural."

"You've got that with you, too."

"All of it. Most of it's on microfilm, but I've brought the projector. Here are your eyepieces."

An hour later, the Board Master said, "I'll call a Board Meeting tomorrow and push this through."

Brand Gorla grinned tightly, "We'll send a commission to Dorlis?"

"When," said the Board Master dryly, "and if we can get an appropriation out of the University for such an affair. Leave this material with me for the while, please. I want to study it a little more."

Theoretically, the Governmental Department of Science and Technology exercises administrative control over all scientific investigation. Actually, however, the pure research groups of the large universities are thoroughly autonomous bodies, and, as a general rule, the government does not care to dispute that. But a general rule is not necessarily a universal rule.

And so, although the Board Master scowled and fumed and swore, there was no way of refusing Wynne Murry an interview. To give Murry his complete title, he was under secretary in charge of psychology, psychopathy and mental technology. And he was a pretty fair psychologist in his own right.

So the Board Master might glare, but that was all.

Secretary Murry ignored the glare cheerfully. He rubbed his long chin against the grain and said, "It amounts to a case of insufficient information. Shall we put it that way?"

The Board Master said frigidly, "I don't see what information you want. The government's say in university appropriations is purely advisory, and in this case, I might say, the advice is unwelcome."

Murry shrugged, "I have no quarrel with the appropriation. But you're not going to leave the planet without government permit. That's where the insufficient information comes in."

"There is no information other than we've given you."

"But things have leaked out. All this is childish and rather unnecessary secrecy."

The old psychologist flushed. "Secrecy! If you don't know the academic way of life, I can't help you. Investigations, especially those of major importance, aren't, and can't be, made public, until definite progress has been made. When we get back, we'll send you copies of whatever papers we publish."

Murry shook his head, "Uh-uh. Not enough. You're going to Dorlis, aren't you?"

"We've informed the Department of Science of that."

"Why?"

"Why do you want to know?"

"Because it's big, or the Board Master wouldn't go himself. What's this about an older civilization and a world of robots?"

"Well, then, you know."

"Only vague notions we've been able to scrabble up. I want the details."

"There are none that we know now. We won't know until we're on Dorlis."

"Then I'm going with you."

"What!"

"You see, I want the details, too."

"Why?"

"Ah," Murry unfolded his legs and stood up, "now *you're* asking the questions. It's no use, now. I know that the universities aren't keen on government supervision; and I know that I can expect no willing help from *any* academic source. But, by Arcturus, I'm going to get help this time, and I don't care how you fight it. Your expedition is going nowhere, unless I go with you—representing the government."

Dorlis, as a world, is not impressive. It's importance to Galactic economy is nil, its position far off the great trade routes, its natives backward and unenlightened, its history obscure. And yet somewhere in the heaps of rubble that clutter an ancient world, there is obscure evidence of an influx of flame and destruction that destroyed the Dorlis of an earlier day—the greater capital of a greater Federation.

And somewhere in that rubble, men of a newer world poked and probed and tried to understand.

The Board Master shook his head and then pushed back his grizzling hair. He hadn't shaved in a week.

"The trouble is," he said, "that we have no point of reference. The language can be broken, I suppose, but nothing can be done with the notation."

"I think a great deal has been done."

"Stabs in the dark! Guessing games based on the translations of your albino friend. I won't base any hopes on that."

Brand said, "Nuts! You spent two years on the Nimian Anomaly, and so far only two months on this, which happens to be a hundred thousand times the job. It's something else that's getting you." He smiled grimly. "It doesn't take a psychologist to see that the government man is in your hair."

The Board Master bit the end off a cigar and spat it four feet. He said slowly, "There are three things about the mule-headed idiot that make me sore. First, I don't like government interference. Second, I don't like a stranger sniffing about when we're on top of the biggest thing in the history of psychology. Third, what in the Galaxy does he want? *What is he after?*"

"I don't know."

"What *should* he be after? Have you thought of it at all?"

"No. Frankly, I don't care. I'd ignore him if I were you."

"You would," said the Board Master violently. "You would! You think the government's entrance into this affair need only be ignored. I suppose you know that this Murry calls himself a psychologist?"

"I know that."

"And I suppose you know he's been displaying a devouring interest in all that we've been doing."

"That, I should say, would be natural."

"Oh! And you know further—" His voice dropped with startling suddenness. "All right, Murry's at the door. Take it easy."

Wynne Murry grinned a greeting, but the Board Master nodded unsmilingly.

"Well, sir," said Murry bluffly, "do you know I've been on my feet for forty-eight hours? You've *got* something here. Something big."

"Thank you."

"No, no. I'm serious. The robot world exists."

"Did you think it didn't?"

The secretary shrugged amiably. "One has a certain natural skepticism. What are your future plans?"

"Why do you ask?" The Board Master grunted his words as if they were being squeezed out singly.

"To see if they jibe with my own."

"And what are your own?"

The secretary smiled. "No, no. You take precedence. How long do you intend staying here?"

"As long as it takes to make a fair beginning on the documents involved."

"That's no answer. What do you mean by a fair beginning?"

"I haven't the slightest idea. It might take years."

"Oh, damnation."

The Board Master raised his eyebrows and said nothing.

The secretary looked at his nails. "I take it you know the location of this robot world."

"Naturally. Theor Realo was there. His information up to now has proven very accurate."

"That's right. The albino. Well, why not go there?"

"Go there! Impossible!"

"May I ask why?"

"Look," said the Board Master with restrained impatience, "you're not here by our invitation, and we're not asking you to dictate our course of actions, but just to show you that I'm not looking for a fight, I'll give you a little metaphorical treatment of our case. Suppose we were presented with a huge and complicated machine, composed of principles and materials of which we knew next to nothing. It is so vast we can't even make out the relationship of the parts, let alone the purpose of the whole. Now, would you advise me to begin attacking the delicate mysterious moving parts of the machine with a detonating ray before I know what it's all about?"

"I see your point, of course, but you're becoming a mystic. The metaphor is farfetched."

"Not at all. These positronic robots were constructed along lines we know nothing of as yet and were intended to follow lines with which we are entirely unacquainted. About the only thing we know is that the robots were put aside in complete isolation, to work out their destiny by themselves. To ruin that isolation would be to ruin the experiment. If we go there in a body, introducing new, unforeseen factors, inducing unintended reactions, everything is ruined. The littlest disturbance—"

"Poppycock! Theor Realo has already gone there."

The Board Master lost his temper suddenly. "Don't you suppose I know that? Do you suppose it would ever have happened if that cursed albino hadn't been an ignorant fanatic without any knowledge of psychology at all? Galaxy knows what the idiot has done in the way of damage."

There was a silence. The secretary clicked his teeth with a thoughtful fingernail. "I don't know. . . . I don't know. But I've got to find out. And I can't wait years."

He left, and the Board Master turned seethingly to Brand, "And how are we going to stop him from going to the robot world if he wants to?"

"I don't see how he can go if we don't let him. *He* doesn't head the expedition."

"Oh, doesn't he? *That's* what I was about to tell you just before he came in. Ten ships of the fleet have landed on Dorlis since we arrived."

"*What!*"

"Just that."

"But what for?"

"That, my boy, is what I don't understand, either."

. . . .

"Mind if I drop in?" said Wynne Murry, pleasantly, and Theor Realo looked up in sudden anxiety from the papers that lay in hopeless disarray on the desk before him.

"Come in. I'll clear off a seat for you." The albino hustled the mess off one of the two chairs in a state of twittering nerves.

Murry sat down and swung one long leg over the other. "Are you assigned a job here, too?" He nodded at the desk.

Theor shook his head and smiled feebly. Almost automatically, he brushed the papers together in a heap and turned them face down.

In the months since he had returned to Dorlis with a hundred psychologists of various degrees of renown, he had felt himself pushed farther and farther from the center of things. There was room for him no longer. Except to answer questions on the actual state of things upon the robot world, which he alone had visited, he played no part. And even there he detected, or seemed to detect, anger that *he* should have gone, and not a competent scientist.

It was a thing to be resented. Yet, somehow, it had always been like that.

"Pardon me?" He had let Murry's next remark slip.

The secretary repeated, "I say it's surprising you're *not* put to work, then. You made the original discovery, didn't you?"

"Yes," the albino brightened. "But it went out of my hands. It got beyond me."

"You were on the robot world, though."

"That was a mistake, they tell me. I might have ruined everything."

Murry grimaced. "What really gets them, I guess, is that you've got a lot of first-hand dope that they didn't. Don't let their fancy titles fool you into thinking you're a nobody. A layman with common sense is better than a blind specialist. You and I—I'm a layman, too, you know—have to stand up for our rights. Here, have a cigarette."

"I don't sm— I'll take one, thank you." The albino felt himself warming to the long-bodied man opposite. He turned the papers face upward again, and lit up, bravely but uncertainly.

"Twenty-five years." Theor spoke carefully, skirting around urgent coughs. "Would you answer a few questions about the world?"

"I suppose so. That's all they ever ask me about. But hadn't you better ask *them?* They've probably got it all worked out now." He blew the smoke as far from himself as possible.

Murry said, "Frankly, they haven't even begun, and I want the information without benefit of confusing psychological translation. First of all, what kind of people—or things—are these robots? You haven't a photocast of one of them, have you?"

"Well, no. I didn't like to take 'casts of them. But they're not things. They're *people!*"

"No? Do they look like—people?"

"Yes—mostly. Outside, anyway. I brought some microscopic studies of the cellular structure that I got hold of. The Board Master has them. They're different inside, you know, greatly simplified. But you'd never know that. They're interesting—and nice."

"Are they simpler than the other life of the planet?"

"Oh, no. It's a very primitive planet. And . . . and," he was interrupted by a spasm of coughing and crushed the cigarette to death as unobtrusively as possible. "They've got a protoplasmic base, you know. I don't think they have the slightest idea they're robots."

"No. I don't suppose they would have. What about their science?"

"I don't know. I never got a chance to see. And everything was so different. I guess it would take an expert to understand."

"Did they have machines?"

The albino looked surprised. "Well, of course. A good many, of all sorts."

"Large cities?"

"Yes!"

The secretary's eyes grew thoughtful. "And you like them. Why?"

Theor Realo was brought up sharply. "I don't know. They were just likable. We got along. They didn't bother me so. It's nothing I can put my finger on. Maybe it's because I have it so hard getting along back home, and they weren't as difficult as real people."

"They were more friendly?"

"N-no. Can't say so. They never quite accepted me. I was a stranger, didn't know their language at first—all that. But"—he looked up with sudden brightness—"I understood them better. I could tell what they were thinking better. I— But I don't know why."

"Hm-m-m. Well—another cigarette? No? I've got to be walloping the pillow now. It's getting late. How about a twosome at golf tomorrow? I've worked up a little course. It'll do. Come on out. The exercise will put hair on your chest."

He grinned and left.

He mumbled one sentence to himself: "It looks like a death sentence"— and whistled thoughtfully as he passed along to his own quarters.

He repeated the phrase to himself when he faced the Board Master the next day, with the sash of office about his waist. He did not sit down.

"Again?" said the Board Master, wearily.

"Again!" assented the secretary. "But real business this time. I may have to take over direction of your expedition."

"What! Impossible, sir! I will listen to no such proposition."

"I have my authority." Wynne Murry presented the metalloid cylinder that snapped open at a flick of the thumb. "I have full powers and full discretion as to their use. It is signed, as you will observe, by the chairman of the Congress of the Federation."

"So— But why?" The Board Master, by an effort, breathed normally. "Short of arbitrary tyranny, is there a reason?"

"A very good one, sir. All along, we have viewed this expedition from different angles. The Department of Science and Technology views the robot world not from the point of view of a scientific curiosity, but from the standpoint of its interference with the peace of the Federation. I don't think you've ever stopped to consider the danger inherent in this robot world."

"None that I can see. It is thoroughly isolated and thoroughly harmless."

"How can you know?"

"From the very nature of the experiment," shouted the Board Master angrily. "The original planners wanted as nearly a completely closed system as possible. Here they are, just as far off the trade routes as possible, in a thinly populated region of space. The whole idea was to have the robots develop free of interference."

Murry smiled. "I disagree with you there. Look, the whole trouble with you is that you're a theoretical man. You look at things the way they ought to be and I, a practical man, look at things as they are. No experiment can be set up and allowed to run indefinitely under its own power. It is taken for granted that somewhere there is at least an observer who watches and *modifies* as circumstances warrant."

"Well?" said the Board Master stolidly.

"Well, the observers in this experiment, the original psychologists of Dorlis, passed away with the First Confederation, and for fifteen thousand years the experiment has proceeded by itself. Little errors have added up and become big ones and introduced alien factors which induced still other errors. It's a geometric progression. And there's been no one to halt it."

"Pure hypothesis."

"Maybe. But you're interested only in the robot world, and I've got to think of the entire Federation."

"And just what possible danger can the robot world be to the Federation? I don't know *what* in Arcturus you're driving at, man."

Murry sighed. "I'll be simple, but don't blame me if I sound melodramatic. The Federation hasn't had any internal warfare for centuries. What will happen if we come into contact with these robots?"

"Are you afraid of one world?"

"Could be. What about their science? Robots can do funny things sometimes."

"What science can they have? They're not metal-electricity supermen. They're weak protoplasmic creatures, a poor imitation of actual humanity, built around a positronic brain adjusted to a set of simplified human psychological laws. If the word 'robot' is scaring you—"

"No, it isn't, but I've talked to Theor Realo. He's the only one who's seen them, you know."

The Board Master cursed silently and fluently. It came of letting a weak-minded freak of a layman get underfoot where he could babble and do harm.

He said, "We've got Realo's full story, and we've evaluated it fully and capably. I assure you, no harm exists in them. The experiment is so thoroughly academic, I wouldn't spend two days on it if it weren't for the broad scope of the thing. From what we see, the whole idea was to build up a positronic brain containing modifications of one or two of the fundamental axioms. We haven't worked out the details, but they must be minor, as it was the first experiment of this nature ever tried, and even the great mythical psychologists of that day had to progress stepwise. Those robots, I tell you, are neither supermen nor beasts. I assure you—as a psychologist."

"Sorry! I'm a psychologist, too. A little more rule-of-thumb, I'm afraid. That's all. But even little modifications! Take the general spirit of combativeness. That isn't the scientific term, but I've no patience for that. You know what I mean. We humans used to be combative. But it's being bred out of us. A stable political and economic system doesn't encourage the waste energy of combat. It's not a survival factor. But suppose the robots are combative. Suppose as the result of a wrong turn during the millennia they've been unwatched, they've become far more combative than ever their first makers intended. They'd be uncomfortable things to be with."

"And suppose all the stars in the Galaxy became novae at the same time. Let's *really* start worrying."

"And there's another point." Murry ignored the other's heavy sarcasm. "Theor Realo liked those robots. He liked robots better than he likes real people. He felt that he fitted there, and we all know he's been a bad misfit in his own world."

"And what," asked the Board Master, "is the significance of that?"

"You don't see it?" Wynne Murry lifted his eyebrows. "Theor Realo likes those robots because he is *like* them, obviously. I'll guarantee right now that a complete psychic analysis of Theor Realo will show a modification of several fundamental axioms, and the same ones as in the robots.

"And," the secretary drove on without a pause, "Theor Realo worked for a quarter of a century to prove a point, when all science would have laughed him to death if they had known about it. There's fanaticism there; good, honest, *inhuman* perseverance. *Those robots are probably like that!*"

"You're advancing no logic. You're arguing like a maniac, like a moon-struck idiot."

"I don't need strict mathematical proof. Reasonable doubt is sufficient. I've got to protect the Federation. Look, it *is* reasonable, you know. The psychologists of Dorlis weren't as super as all that. They had to advance stepwise, as you yourself pointed out. Their humanoids—let's not call them robots—were only imitations of human beings and they couldn't be good ones. Humans possess certain very, *very* complicated reaction systems—

things like social consciousness, and a tendency toward the establishment of ethical systems; and more ordinary things like chivalry, generosity, fair play and so on, that simply can't possibly be duplicated. I don't think those humanoids can have them. But they *must* have perseverance, which practically implies stubbornness and combativeness, if my notion on Theor Realo holds good. Well, if their science is anywhere at all, then I don't want to have them running loose in the Galaxy, if our numbers are a thousand or million times theirs. And I don't intend to permit them to do so!"

The Board Master's face was rigid. "What are your immediate intentions?"

"As yet undecided. But I think I am going to organize a small-scale landing on the planet."

"Now, wait." The old psychologist was up and around the desk. He seized the secretary's elbow. "Are you quite certain you know what you're doing? The potentialities in this massive experiment are beyond any possible precalculation by you or me. You can't know what you're destroying."

"I know. Do you think I enjoy what I'm doing? This isn't a hero's job. I'm enough of a psychologist to want to know what's going on, but I've been sent here to protect the Federation, and to the best of my ability I intend doing it —and a dirty job it is. But I can't help it."

"You can't have thought it out. What can you know of the insight it will give us into the basic ideas of psychology? This will amount to a fusion of two Galactic systems, that will send us to heights that will make up in knowledge and power a million times the amount of harm the robots could ever do, if they *were* metal-electricity supermen."

The secretary shrugged. "Now you're the one that is playing with faint possibilities."

"Listen, I'll make a deal. Blockade them. Isolate them with your ships. Mount guards. But don't touch them. Give us more time. Give us a chance. You must!"

"I've thought of that. But I would have to get Congress to agree to that. It would be expensive, you know."

The Board Master flung himself into his chair in wild impatience. "What kind of expense are you talking about? Do you realize the nature of the repayment if we succeed?"

Murry considered; then, with a half smile, "What if they develop interstellar travel?"

The Board Master said quickly, "Then I'll withdraw my objections."

The secretary rose, "I'll have it out with Congress."

Brand Gorla's face was carefully emotionless as he watched the Board Master's stooped back. The cheerful pep talks to the available members of the expedition lacked meat, and he listened to them impatiently.

He said, "What are we going to do now?"

The Board Master's shoulders twitched and he didn't turn. "I've sent for Theor Realo. That little fool left for the Eastern Continent last week—"

"Why?"

The older man blazed at the interruption. "How can I understand anything that freak does! Don't you see that Murry's right? He's a psychic abnormality. We had no business leaving him unwatched. If I had ever thought of looking at him twice, I wouldn't have. He's coming back now, though, and he's going to stay back." His voice fell to a mumble. "Should have been back two hours ago."

"It's an impossible position, sir," said Brand, flatly.

"Think so?"

"Well— Do *you* think Congress will stand for an indefinite patrol off the robot world? It runs into money, and average Galactic citizens aren't going to see it as worth the taxes. The psychological equations degenerate into the axioms of common sense. In fact, I don't see why Murry agreed to consult Congress."

"Don't you?" The Board Master finally faced his junior. "Well, the fool considers himself a psychologist, Galaxy help us, and that's his weak point. He flatters himself that he doesn't want to destroy the robot world in his heart, but that it's the good of the Federation that requires it. And he'll jump at any reasonable compromise. Congress won't agree to it indefinitely, you don't have to point that out to me." He was talking quietly, patiently. "But I will ask for ten years, two years, six months—as much as I can get. I'll get something. In that time, we'll learn new facts about the world. Somehow we'll strengthen our case and renew the agreement when it expires. We'll save the project yet."

There was a short silence and the Board Master added slowly and bitterly, "And that's where Theor Realo plays a vital part."

Brand Gorla watched silently, and waited. The Board Master said, "On that one point, Murry saw what we didn't. Realo is a psychological cripple, and is our real clue to the whole affair. If we study him, we'll have a rough picture of what the robot is like, distorted of course, since his environment has been a hostile, unfriendly one. But we can make allowance for that, estimate his nature in a— Ahh, I'm tired of the whole subject."

The signal box flashed, and the Board Master sighed. "Well, he's here. All right, Gorla, sit down, you make me nervous. Let's take a look at him."

Theor Realo came through the door like a comet and brought himself to a panting halt in the middle of the floor. He looked from one to the other with weak, peering eyes.

"How did all this happen?"

"All what?" said the Board Master coldly. "Sit down. I want to ask you some questions."

"No. You first answer *me*."

"Sit down!"

Realo sat. His eyes were brimming. "They're going to destroy the robot world."

"Don't worry about that."

"But you said they could if the robots discovered interstellar travel. You said so. You fool. Don't you see—" He was choking.

The Board Master frowned uneasily. "Will you calm down and talk sense?"

The albino gritted his teeth and forced the words out. "But they'll *have* interstellar travel before long."

And the two psychologists shot toward the little man.

"What!!"

"Well . . . well, what do you think?" Realo sprang upward with all the fury of desperation. "Did you think I landed in a desert or in the middle of an ocean and explored a world all by myself? Do you think life is a storybook? I was captured as soon as I landed and taken to a big city. At least, I think it was a big city. It was different from our kind. It had— But I won't tell you."

"Never mind the city," shrieked the Board Master. "You were captured. Go ahead."

"They studied *me.* They studied my machine. And then, one night, I left, to tell the Federation. They didn't know I left. They didn't want me to leave." His voice broke. "And I would have stayed as soon as not, but the Federation had to know."

"Did you tell them anything about your ship?"

"How could I? I'm no mechanic. I don't know the theory or construction. But I showed them how to work the controls and let them look at the motors. That's all."

Brand Gorla said, to himself mostly, "Then they'll never get it. That isn't enough."

The albino's voice raised itself in sudden shrieking triumph. "Oh, yes, they will. I know them. They're machines, you know. They'll work on that problem. And they'll work. And they'll work. And they'll never quit. And they'll get it. They got enough out of me. I'll *bet* they got enough."

The Board Master looked long, and turned away—wearily. "Why didn't you tell us?"

"Because you took my world away from me. I discovered it—by myself— all by myself. And after I had done all the real work, and invited you in, you threw me out. All you had for me was complaints that I had landed on the world and might have ruined everything by interference. Why should I tell you? Find out for yourselves if you're so wise, that you could afford to kick me around."

The Board Master thought bitterly, "Misfit! Inferiority complex! Persecution mania! Nice! It all fits in, now that we've bothered to take our eyes off the horizon and see what was under our nose. And now it's all ruined."

He said, "All right, Realo, we all lose. Go away."

Brand Gorla said tightly, "All over? Really all over?"

The Board Master answered, "Really all over. The original experiment, as such, is over. The distortions created by Realo's visit will easily be large enough to make the plans we are studying here a dead language. And besides —Murry is right. If they have interstellar travel, they're dangerous."

Realo was shouting, "But you're not going to destroy them. You can't destroy them. They haven't hurt anyone."

There was no answer, and he raved on, "I'm going back. I'll warn them. They'll be prepared. I'll warn them."

He was backing toward the door, his thin, white hair bristling, his red-rimmed eyes bulging.

The Board Master did not move to stop him when he dashed out.

"Let him go. It was *his* lifetime. I don't care any more."

Theor Realo smashed toward the robot world at an acceleration that was half choking him.

Somewhere ahead was the dustspeck of an isolated world with artificial imitations of humanity struggling along in an experiment that had died. Struggling blindly toward a new goal of interstellar travel that was to be their death sentence.

He was heading toward that world, toward the same city in which he had been "studied" the first time. He remembered it well. Its name was the first words of their language he had learned.

New York!

Blind Alley

Only once in Galactic History was an intelligent race of non-Humans discovered—
"Essays on History," by Ligurn Vier

From: Bureau for the Outer Provinces
To: Loodun Antyok, Chief Public Administrator, A-8

Subject: Civilian Supervisor of Cepheus 18, Administrative Position as.
References:

(a) Act of Council 2515, of the year 971 of the Galactic Empire, entitled, "Appointment of Officials of the Administrative Service, Methods for, Revision of."

(b) Imperial Directive, Ja 2374, dated 243/975 G.E.

1. By authorization of reference (a), you are hereby appointed to the subject position. The authority of said position as Civilian Supervisor of Cepheus 18 will extend over non-Human subjects of the Emperor living upon the planet under the terms of autonomy set forth in reference (b).

2. The duties of the subject position shall comprise the general supervision of all non-Human internal affairs, co-ordination of authorized government investigating and reporting committees, and the preparation of semiannual reports on all phases of non-Human affairs.

C. Morily, Chief, BuOuProv,
12/977 G.E.

Loodun Antyok had listened carefully, and now he shook his round head mildly, "Friend, I'd like to help you, but you've grabbed the wrong dog by the ears. You'd better take this up with the Bureau."

Tomor Zammo flung himself back into his chair, rubbed his beak of a nose fiercely, thought better of whatever he was going to say, and answered quietly, "Logical, but not practical. I can't make a trip to Trantor now. You're the Bureau's representative on Cepheus 18. Are you entirely helpless?"

"Well, even as Civilian Supervisor, I've got to work within the limits of Bureau policy."

"Good," Zammo cried, "then, tell me what Bureau policy is. I head a scientific investigating committee, under direct Imperial authorization with, supposedly, the widest powers; yet at every angle in the road I am pulled up short by the civilian authorities with only the parrot shriek of 'Bureau policy' to justify themselves. What *is* Bureau policy? I haven't received a decent definition yet."

Antyok's gaze was level and unruffled. He said, "As I see it—and this is not official, so you can't hold me to it—Bureau policy consists in treating the non-Humans as decently as possible."

"Then, what authority have they—"

"*Ssh!* No use raising your voice. As a matter of fact, His Imperial Majesty is a humanitarian and a disciple of the philosophy of Aurelion. I can tell you quietly that it is pretty well-known that it is the Emperor himself who first suggested that this world be established. You can bet that Bureau policy will stick pretty close to Imperial notions. And you can bet that I can't paddle my way against *that* sort of current."

"Well, m'boy," the physiologist's fleshy eyelids quivered, "if you take that sort of attitude, you're going to lose your job. No, I won't have you kicked out. That's not what I mean at all. Your job will just fade out from under you, because nothing is going to be accomplished here!"

"Really? Why?" Antyok was short, pink, and pudgy, and his plump-cheeked face usually found it difficult to put on display any expression other than one of bland and cheerful politeness—but it looked grave now.

"You haven't been here long. I have." Zammo scowled. "Mind if I smoke?" The cigar in his hand was gnarled and strong and was puffed to life carelessly.

He continued roughly, "There's no place here for humanitarianism, administrator. You're treating non-Humans as if they were Humans, and it won't work. In fact, I don't like the word 'non-Human.' They're animals."

"They're intelligent," interjected Antyok, softly.

"Well, intelligent animals, then. I presume the two terms are not mutually exclusive. Alien intelligences mingling in the same space won't work, anyway."

"Do you propose killing them off?"

"Galaxy, no!" He gestured with his cigar. "I propose we look upon them as objects for study, and only that. We could learn a good deal from these animals if we were allowed to. Knowledge, I might point out, that would be used for the immediate benefit of the human race. *There's* humanity for you.

There's the good of the masses, if it's this spineless cult of Aurelion that interests you."

"What, for instance, do you refer to?"

"To take the most obvious— You have heard of their chemistry, I take it?"

"Yes," Antyok admitted. "I have leafed through most of the reports on the non-Humans published in the last ten years. I expect to go through more."

"Hmp. Well— Then, all I need say is that their chemical therapy is extremely thorough. For instance, I have witnessed personally the healing of a broken bone—what passes for a broken bone with them, I mean—by the use of a pill. The bone was whole in fifteen minutes. Naturally, none of their drugs are any earthly use on Humans. Most would kill quickly. But if we found out how they worked on the non-Humans—on the animals—"

"Yes, yes. I see the significance."

"Oh, you do. Come, that's gratifying. A second point is that these animals communicate in an unknown manner."

"Telepathy!"

The scientist's mouth twisted, as he ground out, "Telepathy! Telepathy! Telepathy! Might as well say by witch brew. Nobody knows anything about telepathy except its name. What is the mechanism of telepathy? What is the physiology and the physics of it? I would like to find out, but I can't. Bureau policy, if I listen to you, forbids."

Antyok's little mouth pursed itself. "But— Pardon me, doctor, but I don't follow you. How are you prevented? Surely the Civil Administration has made no attempt to hamper scientific investigation of these non-Humans. I cannot speak for my predecessor entirely, of course, but I myself—"

"No direct interference has occurred. I don't speak of that. But by the Galaxy, administrator, we're hampered by the spirit of the entire set-up. You're making us deal with humans. You allow them their own leader and internal autonomy. You pamper them and give them what Aurelion's philosophy would call 'rights.' I can't deal with their leader."

"Why not?"

"Because he refuses to allow me a free hand. He refuses to allow experiments on any subject without the subject's own consent. The two or three volunteers we get are not too bright. It's an impossible arrangement."

Antyok shrugged helplessly.

Zammo continued, "In addition, it is obviously impossible to learn anything of value concerning the brains, physiology, and chemistry of these animals without dissection, dietary experiments, and drugs. You know, administrator, scientific investigation is a hard game. Humanity hasn't much place in it."

Loodun Antyok tapped his chin with a doubtful finger, "Must it be quite so hard? These are harmless creatures, these non-Humans. Surely, dissection— Perhaps, if you were to approach them a bit differently—I have the idea that you antagonize them. Your attitude might be somewhat overbearing."

"Overbearing! I am not one of these whining social psychologists who are all the fad these days. I don't believe you can solve a problem that requires dissection by approaching it with what is called the 'correct personal attitude' in the cant of the times."

"I'm sorry you think so. Sociopsychological training is required of all administrators above the grade of A-4."

Zammo withdrew his cud of a cigar from his mouth and replaced it after a suitably contemptuous interval, "Then you'd better use a bit of your technique on the Bureau. You know, I *do* have friends at the Imperial court."

"Well, now, I *can't* take the matter up with them, not baldly. Basic policy does not fall within my cognizance, and such things can only be initiated by the Bureau. But, you know, we might try an indirect approach on this." He smiled faintly, "Strategy."

"What sort?"

Antyok pointed a sudden finger, while his other hand fell lightly on the rows of gray-bound reports upon the floor just next his chair, "Now, look, I've gone through most of these. They're dull, but contain *some* facts. For instance, when was the last non-Human infant born on Cepheus 18?"

Zammo spent little time in consideration. "Don't know. Don't care either."

"But the Bureau would. There's *never* been a non-Human infant born on Cepheus 18—not in the two years the world has been established. Do you know the reason?"

The physiologist shrugged, "Too many possible factors. It would take study."

"All right, then. Suppose you write a report—"

"Reports! I've written twenty."

"Write another. Stress the unsolved problems. Tell them you must change your methods. Harp on the birth-rate problem. The Bureau doesn't dare ignore that. If the non-Humans die out, someone will have to answer to the Emperor. You see—"

Zammo stared, his eyes dark, "That will swing it?"

"I've been working for the Bureau for twenty-seven years. I know its ways."

"I'll think about it." Zammo rose and stalked out of the office. The door slammed behind him.

It was later that Zammo said to a co-worker, "He's a bureaucrat, in the first place. He won't abandon the orthodoxies of paper work and he won't risk sticking his neck out. He'll accomplish little by himself, yet maybe more than a little if we work through him."

From: Administrative Headquarters, Cepheus 18
To: BuOuProv
Subject: Outer Province Project 2563, Part II—Scientific Investigations of non-Humans of Cepheus 18, Co-ordination of.
References:
(a) BuOuProv letr. Cep-N-CM/jg, 100132, dated 302/975 G.E.
(b) AdHQ-Ceph18 letr. AA-LA/mn, dated 140/977 G.E.
Enclosure:
1. SciGroup 10, Physical & Biochemical Division, Report, entitled, "Physiologic Characteristics of non-Humans of Cepheus 18, Part XI," dated 172/977 G.E.
1. Enclosure 1, included herewith, is forwarded for the information of the BuOuProv. It is to be noted that Section XII, paragraphs 1–16 of Encl. 1, concern possible changes in present BuOuProv policy with regard to non-Humans with a view to facilitating physical and chemical investigations at present proceeding under authorization of reference (a).
2. It is brought to the attention of the BuOuProv that reference (b) has already discussed possible changes in investigating methods and that it remains the opinion of AdHQ-Ceph18 that such changes are as yet premature. It is nevertheless suggested that the question of non-Human birth rate be made the subject of a BuOuProv project assigned to AdHQ-Ceph18 in view of the importance attached by SciGroup 10 to the problem, as evidenced in Section V of Enclosure 1.

L. Antyok, Supery, AdHQ-Ceph18,
174/977

From: BuOuProv
To: AdHQ-Ceph18
Subject: Outer Province Project 2563—Scientific Investigations of non-Humans of Cepheus 18, Co-ordination of.
Reference:
(a) AdHQ-Ceph18 letr. AA-LA/mn, dated 174/977 G.E.
1. In response to the suggestion contained in paragraph 2 of reference (a), it is considered that the question of the non-Human birth rate does not fall within the cognizance of AdHQ-Ceph18. In view of the fact that SciGroup 10 has reported said sterility to be probably due to a chemical deficiency in the food supply, all investigations in the field are relegated to SciGroup 10 as the proper authority.
2. Investigating procedures by the various SciGroups shall continue according to current directives on the subject. No changes in policy are envisaged.

C. Morily, Chief, BuOuProv,
186/977 G.E.

II

There was a loose-jointed gauntness about the news reporter which made him appear somberly tall. He was Gustiv Bannerd, with whose reputation was combined ability—two things which do not invariably go together despite the maxims of elementary morality.

Loodun Antyok took his measure doubtfully and said, "There's no use denying that you're right. But the SciGroup report was confidential. I don't understand how—"

"It leaked," said Bannerd, callously. "Everything leaks."

Antyok was obviously baffled, and his pink face furrowed slightly, "Then I'll just have to plug the leak here. I can't pass your story. All references to SciGroup complaints have to come out. You see that, don't you?"

"No." Bannerd was calm enough. "It's important; and I have my rights under the Imperial directive. I think the Empire should know what's going on."

"But it isn't going on," said Antyok, despairingly. "Your claims are all wrong. The Bureau isn't going to change its policy. I showed you the letters."

"You think you can stand up against Zammo when he puts the pressure on?" the newsman asked derisively.

"I will—if I think he's wrong."

"If!" stated Bannerd flatly. Then, in a sudden fervor, "Antyok, the Empire has something great here; something greater by a good deal than the government apparently realizes. They're destroying it. They're treating these creatures like animals."

"Really—" began Antyok, weakly.

"Don't talk about Cepheus 18. It's a zoo. It's a high-class zoo, with your petrified scientists teasing those poor creatures with their sticks poking through the bars. You throw them chunks of meat, but you cage them up. I know! I've been writing about them for two years now. I've almost been living with them."

"Zammo says—"

"Zammo!" This with hard contempt.

"Zammo says," insisted Antyok with worried firmness, "that we treat them too like humans as it is."

The newsman's straight, long cheeks were rigid, "Zammo is rather animal-like in his own right. He is a science-worshiper. We can do with less of them. Have you read Aurelion's works?" The last was suddenly posed.

"Umm. Yes. I understand the Emperor—"

"The Emperor tends towards us. That is good—better than the hounding of the last reign."

"I don't see where you're heading?"

"These aliens have much to teach us. You understand? It is nothing that

Zammo and his SciGroup can use; no chemistry, no telepathy. It's a way of life; a way of thinking. The aliens have no crime, no misfits. What effort is being made to study their philosophy? Or to set them up as a problem in social engineering?"

Antyok grew thoughtful, and his plump face smoothed out, "It is an interesting consideration. It would be a matter for psychologists—"

"No good. Most of them are quacks. Psychologists point out problems, but their solutions are fallacious. We need men of Aurelion. Men of The Philosophy—"

"But look here, we can't turn Cepheus 18 into . . . into a metaphysical study."

"Why not? It can be done easily."

"How?"

"Forget your puny test-tube peerings. Allow the aliens to set up a society free of Humans. Give them an untrammeled independence and allow an intermingling of philosophies—"

Antyok's nervous response came, "That can't be done in a day."

"We can start in a day."

The administrator said slowly, "Well, I can't prevent you from trying to start." He grew confidential, his mild eyes thoughtful, "You'll ruin your own game, though, if you publish SciGroup 10's report and denounce it on humanitarian grounds. The Scientists are powerful."

"And we of The Philosophy as well."

"Yes, but there's an easy way. You needn't rave. Simply point out that the SciGroup is not solving its problems. Do so unemotionally and let the readers think out your point of view for themselves. Take the birth-rate problem, for instance. *There's* something for you. In a generation, the non-Humans might die out, for all science can do. Point out that a more philosophical approach is required. Or pick some other obvious point. Use your judgment, eh?"

Antyok smiled ingratiatingly as he arose, "But, for the Galaxy's sake, don't stir up a bad smell."

Bannerd was stiff and unresponsive, "You may be right."

It was later that Bannerd wrote in a capsule message to a friend, "He is not clever, by any means. He is confused and has no guiding-line through life. Certainly utterly incompetent in his job. But he's a cutter and a trimmer, compromises his way around difficulties, and will yield concessions rather than risk a hard stand. He may prove valuable in that. Yours in Aurelion."

From: AdHQ-Ceph18
To: BuOuProv
Subject: Birth rate of non-Humans on Cepheus 18, News Report on.
References:
    (a) AdHQ-Ceph18 letr. AA-LA/mn, dated 174/977 G.E.

(b) Imperial Directive, Ja2374, dated 243/975 G.E.

Enclosures:

1-G. Bannerd news report, datelined Cepheus 18, 201/977 G.E.

2-G. Bannerd news report, datelined Cepheus 18, 203/977 G.E.

1. The sterility of non-Humans on Cepheus 18, reported to the BuOuProv in reference (a), has become the subject of news reports to the galactic press. The news reports in question are submitted herewith for the information of the BuOuProv as Enclosures 1 and 2. Although said reports are based on material considered confidential and closed to the public, the news reporter in question maintained his rights to free expression under the terms of reference (b).

2. In view of the unavoidable publicity and misunderstanding on the part of the general public now inevitable, it is requested that the BuOuProv direct future policy on the problem of non-Human sterility.

L. Antyok, Superv. AdHQ-Ceph18,
209/977 G.E.

From: BuOuProv

To: AdHQ-Ceph18

Subject: Birth rate of non-Humans on Cepheus 18, Investigation of.

References:

(a) AdHQ-Ceph18 letr. AA-LA/mn, dated 209/977 G.E.

(b) AdHQ-Ceph18 letr. AA-LA/mn, dated 174/977 G.E.

1. It is proposed to investigate the causes and the means of precluding the unfavorable birth-rate phenomena mentioned in references (a) and (b). A project is therefore set up, entitled, "Birth rate of non-Humans on Cepheus 18, Investigation of" to which, in view of the crucial importance of the subject, a priority of AA is given.

2. The number assigned to the subject project is 2910, and all expenses incidental to it shall be assigned to Appropriation number 18/78.

C. Morily, Chief, BuOuProv,
223/977 G.E.

III

If Tomor Zammo's ill-humor lessened within the grounds of Sci-Group 10 Experimental Station, his friendliness had not thereby increased. Antyok found himself standing alone at the viewing window into the main field laboratory.

The main field laboratory was a broad court set at the environmental conditions of Cepheus 18 itself for the discomfort of the experimenters and the convenience of the experimentees. Through the burning sand, and the dry, oxygen-rich air, there sparkled the hard brilliance of hot, white sunlight.

And under the blaze, the brick-red non-Humans, wrinkled of skin and wiry of build, huddled in their squatting positions of ease, by ones and twos.

Zammo emerged from the laboratory. He paused to drink water thirstily. He looked up, moisture gleaming on his upper lip, "Like to step in there?"

Antyok shook his head definitely, "No, thank you. What's the temperature right now?"

"A hundred twenty, if there were shade. And they complain of the cold. It's drinking time now. Want to watch them drink?"

A spray of water shot upward from the fountain in the center of the court, and the little alien figures swayed to their feet and hopped eagerly forward in a queer, springy half-run. They milled about the water, jostling one another. The centers of their faces were suddenly disfigured by the projection of a long and flexible fleshy tube, which thrust forward into the spray and was withdrawn dripping.

It continued for long minutes. The bodies swelled and the wrinkles disappeared. They retreated slowly, backing away, with the drinking tube flicking in and out, before receding finally into a pink, wrinkled mass above a wide, lipless mouth. They went to sleep in groups in the shaded angles, plump and sated.

"Animals!" said Zammo, with contempt.

"How often do they drink?" asked Antyok.

"As often as they want. They can go a week if they have to. We water them every day. They store it under their skin. They eat in the evenings. Vegetarians, you know."

Antyok smiled chubbily, "It's nice to get a bit of firsthand information occasionally. Can't read reports all the time."

"Yes?"—noncommittally. Then, "What's new? What about the lacy-pants boys on Trantor?"

Antyok shrugged dubiously, "You can't get the Bureau to commit itself, unfortunately. With the Emperor sympathetic to the Aurelionists, humanitarianism is the order of the day. You know that."

There was a pause in which the administrator chewed his lip uncertainly. "But there's this birth-rate problem now. It's finally been assigned to AdHQ, you know—and double A priority, too."

Zammo muttered wordlessly.

Antyok said, "You may not realize it, but that project will now take precedence over all other work proceeding on Cepheus 18. It's important."

He turned back to the viewing window and said thoughtfully with a bald lack of preamble. "Do you think those creatures might be unhappy?"

"Unhappy!" The word was an explosion.

"Well, then," Antyok corrected hastily, "maladjusted. You understand? It's difficult to adjust an environment to a race we know so little of."

"Say—did you ever see the world we took them from?"

"I've read the reports—"

"Reports!"—infinite contempt. "I've *seen* it. This may look like desert out there to you, but it's a watery paradise to those devils. They have all the food and water they can get. They have a world to themselves with vegetation and natural water flow, instead of a lump of silica and granite where fungi were force-grown in caves and water had to be steamed out of gypsum rock. In ten years, they would have been dead to the last beast, and we saved them. Unhappy? Ga-a-ah, if they are, they haven't the decency of most animals."

"Well, perhaps. Yet I have a notion."

"A notion? What is your notion?" Zammo reached for one of his cigars.

"It's something that might help you. Why not study the creatures in a more integrated fashion? Let them use their initiative. After all, they did have a highly-developed science. Your reports speak of it continually. Give them problems to solve."

"Such as?"

"Oh . . . oh," Antyok waved his hands helplessly. "Whatever you think might help most. For instance, spaceships. Get them into the control room and study their reactions."

"Why?" asked Zammo with dry bluntness.

"Because the reaction of their minds to tools and controls adjusted to the human temperament can teach you a lot. In addition, it will make a more effective bribe, it seems to me, than anything you've yet tried. You'll get more volunteers if they think they'll be doing something interesting."

"That's your psychology coming out. Hm-m-m. Sounds better than it probably is. I'll sleep on it. And where would I get permission, in any case, to let them handle spaceships? I've none at *my* disposal, and it would take a good deal longer than it was worth to follow down the line of red tape to get one assigned to us."

Antyok pondered, and his forehead creased lightly, "It doesn't *have* to be spaceships. But even so— If you would write up another report and make the suggestion yourself—strongly, you understand—I might figure out some way of tying it up with my birth-rate project. A double-A priority can get practically anything, you know, without questions."

Zammo's interest lacked a bit even of mildness, "Well, maybe. Meanwhile, I've some basal metabolism tests in progress, and it's getting late. I'll think about it. It's got its points."

From: AdHQ-Ceph18
To: BuOuProv
Subject: Outer Province Project 2910, Part I—Birth rate of non-Humans on Cepheus 18, Investigation of.
Reference:
    (a) BuOuProv letr. Ceph-N-CM/car, 115097, 223/977 G.E.

Enclosure:

1. SciGroup 10, Physical & Biochemical Division report, Part XV, dated 220/977 G.E.

1. Enclosure 1 is forwarded herewith for the information of the BuOuProv.

2. Special attention is directed to Section V, Paragraph 3 of Enclosure 1 in which it is requested that a spaceship be assigned SciGroup 10 for use in expediting investigations authorized by the BuOuProv. It is considered by AdHQ-Ceph18 that such investigations may be of material use in aiding work now in progress on the subject project, authorized by reference (a). It is suggested, in view of the high priority placed by the BuOuProv upon the subject project, that immediate consideration be given the SciGroup's request.

L. Antyok, Superv. AdHQ-Ceph18,
240/977 G.E.

From: BuOuProv
To: AdHQ-Ceph18
Subject: Outer Province Project 2910—Birth rate of non-Humans on Cepheus 18, Investigation of.
Reference:

(a) AdHQ-Ceph18 letr. AA-LA/mn, dated 240/977 G.E.

1. Training Ship *AN-R-2055* is being placed at the disposal of AdHQ-Ceph18 for use in investigation of non-Humans on Cepheus 18 with respect to the subject project and other authorized OuProv projects, as requested in Enclosure 1 to reference (a).

2. It is urgently requested that work on the subject project be expedited by all available means.

C. Morily, Head, BuOuProv,
251/977 G.E.

IV

The little, bricky creature must have been more uncomfortable than his bearing would admit to. He was carefully wrapped in a temperature already adjusted to the point where his human companions steamed in their open shirts.

His speech was high-pitched and careful, "I find it damp, but not unbearably so at this low temperature."

Antyok smiled, "It was nice of you to come. I had planned to visit you, but a trial run in your atmosphere out there—" The smile had become rueful.

"It doesn't matter. You other worldlings have done more for us than ever we were able to do for ourselves. It is an obligation that is but imperfectly returned by the endurance on my part of a trifling discomfort." His speech seemed always indirect, as if he approached his thoughts sidelong, or as if it were against all etiquette to be blunt.

Gustiv Bannerd, seated in an angle of the room, with one long leg crossing the other, scrawled nimbly and said, "You don't mind if I record all this?"

The Cepheid non-Human glanced briefly at the journalist, "I have no objection."

Antyok's apologetics persisted, "This is not a purely social affair, sir. I would not have forced discomfort on you for that. There are important questions to be considered, and you are the leader of your people."

The Cepheid nodded, "I am satisfied your purposes are kindly. Please proceed."

The administrator almost wriggled in his difficulty in putting thoughts into words. "It is a subject," he said, "of delicacy, and one I would never bring up if it weren't for the overwhelming importance of the . . . uh . . . question. I am only the spokesman of my government—"

"My people consider the otherworld government a kindly one."

"Well, yes, they are kindly. For that reason, they are disturbed over the fact that your people no longer breed."

Antyok paused, and waited with worry for a reaction that did not come. The Cepheid's face was motionless except for the soft, trembling motion of the wrinkled area that was his deflated drinking tube.

Antyok continued, "It is a question we have hesitated to bring up because of its extremely personal angles. Noninterference is my government's prime aim, and we have done our best to investigate the problem quietly and without disturbing your people. But, frankly, we—"

"Have failed?" finished the Cepheid, at the other's pause.

"Yes. Or at least, we have not discovered a concrete failure to reproduce the exact environment of your original world; with, of course, the necessary modification to make it more livable. Naturally, it is thought there is some chemical shortcoming. And so I ask your voluntary help in the matter. Your people are advanced in the study of your own biochemistry. If you do not choose, or would rather not—"

"No, no, I can help." The Cepheid seemed cheerful about it. The smooth flat planes of his loose-skinned, hairless skull wrinkled in an alien response to an uncertain emotion. "It is not a matter that any of us would have thought would have disturbed you other-worldlings. That it does is but another indication of your well-meaning kindness. This world we find congenial, a paradise in comparison to our old. It lacks in nothing. Conditions such as now prevail belong in our legends of the Golden Age."

"Well—"

"But there is a something; a something you may not understand. We cannot expect different intelligences to think alike."

"I shall try to understand."

The Cepheid's voice had grown soft, its liquid undertones more pronounced, "We were dying on our native world; but we were fighting. Our science, developed through a history older than yours, was losing; but it had not yet lost. Perhaps it was because our science was fundamentally biological, rather than physical as yours is. Your people discovered new forms of energy and reached the stars. Our people discovered new truths of psychology and psychiatry and built up a working society free of disease and crime.

"There is no need to question which of the two angles of approach was the more laudable, but there is no uncertainty as to which proved more successful in the end. In our dying world, without the means of life or sources of power, our biological science could but make the dying easier.

"And yet we fought. For centuries past, we had been groping toward the elements of atomic power, and slowly the spark of hope had glimmered that we might break through the two-dimensional limits of our planetary surface and reach the stars. There were no other planets in our system to serve as stepping stones. Nothing but some twenty light-years to the nearest star, without the knowledge of the possibility of the existence of other planetary systems, but rather of the contrary.

"But there is something in all life that insists on striving; even on useless striving. There were only five thousand of us left in the last days. Only five thousand. And our first ship was ready. It was experimental. It would probably have been a failure. But already we had all the principles of propulsion and navigation correctly worked out."

There was a long pause, and the Cepheid's small black eyes seemed glazed in retrospect.

The newspaperman put in suddenly, from his corner, "And then we came?"

"And then you came," the Cepheid agreed simply. "It changed everything. Energy was ours for the asking. A new world, congenial and, indeed, ideal, was ours even without asking. If our problems of society had long been solved by ourselves, our more difficult problems of environment were suddenly solved for us, no less completely."

"Well?" urged Antyok.

"Well—it was somehow not well. For centuries, our ancestors had fought towards the stars, and now the stars suddenly proved to be the property of others. We had fought for life, and it had become a present handed to us by others. There is no longer any reason to fight. There is no longer anything to attain. All the universe is the property of your race."

"This world is yours," said Antyok, gently.

"By sufferance. It is a gift. It is not ours by right."

"You have earned it, in my opinion."

And now the Cepheid's eyes were sharply fixed on the other's countenance, "You mean well, but I doubt that you understand. We have nowhere to go, save this gift of a world. We are in a blind alley. The function of life is striving, and that is taken from us. Life can no longer interest us. We have no offspring—voluntarily. It is our way of removing ourselves from your way."

Absent-mindedly, Antyok had removed the fluoro-globe from the window seat, and spun it on its base. Its gaudy surface reflected light as it spun, and its three-foot-high bulk floated with incongruous grace and lightness in the air.

Antyok said, "Is that your only solution? Sterility?"

"We might escape still," whispered the Cepheid, "but where in the Galaxy is there place for us? It is all yours."

"Yes, there is no place for you nearer than the Magellanic Clouds if you wished independence. The Magellanic Clouds—"

"And you would not let us go of yourselves. You mean kindly, I know."

"Yes, we mean kindly—but we could not let you go."

"It is a mistaken kindness."

"Perhaps, but could you not reconcile yourselves? You have a world."

"It is something past complete explanations. Your mind is different. We could not reconcile ourselves. I believe, administrator, that you have thought of all this before. The concept of the blind alley we find ourselves trapped in is not new to you."

Antyok looked up, startled, and one hand steadied the fluoro-globe, "Can you read my mind?"

"It is just a guess. A good one, I think."

"Yes—but *can* you read my mind? The minds of humans in general, I mean. It is an interesting point. The scientists say you cannot, but sometimes I wonder if it is that you simply will not. Could you answer that? I am detaining you, unduly, perhaps."

"No . . . no—" But the little Cepheid drew his enveloping robe closer, and buried his face in the electrically-heated pad at the collar for a moment. "You other-worldlings speak of reading minds. It is not so at all, but it is assuredly hopeless to explain."

Antyok mumbled the old proverb, "One cannot explain sight to a man blind from birth."

"Yes, just so. This sense which you call 'mind reading,' quite erroneously, cannot be applied to us. It is not that we cannot receive the proper sensations, it is that your people do not transmit them, and we have no way of explaining to you how to go about it."

"Hm-m-m."

"There are times, of course, of great concentration or emotional tension on the part of an other-worldling when some of us who are more expert in this sense; more sharp-eyed, so to speak; detect vaguely *something*. It is uncertain; yet I myself have at times wondered—"

Carefully, Antyok began spinning the fluoro-globe once more. His pink face was set in thought, and his eyes were fixed upon the Cepheid. Gustiv Bannerd stretched his fingers and reread his notes, his lips moving silently.

The fluoro-globe spun, and slowly the Cepheid seemed to grow tense as well, as his eyes shifted to the colorful sheen of the globe's fragile surface.

The Cepheid said, "What is that?"

Antyok started, and his face smoothed into an almost chuckling placidity, "This? A Galactic fad of three years ago; which means that it is a hopelessly old-fashioned relic this year. It is a useless device but it looks pretty. Bannerd, could you adjust the windows to non-transmission?"

There was the soft click of a contact, and the windows became curved regions of darkness, while in the center of the room, the fluoro-globe was suddenly the focus of a rosy effulgence that seemed to leap outward in streamers. Antyok, a scarlet figure in a scarlet room, placed it upon the table and spun it with a hand that dripped red. As it spun, the colors changed with a slowly increasing rapidity, blended and fell apart into more extreme contrasts.

Antyok was speaking in an eerie atmosphere of molten, shifting rainbow, "The surface is of a material that exhibits variable fluorescence. It is almost weightless, extremely fragile, but gyroscopically balanced so that it rarely falls, with ordinary care. It is rather pretty, don't you think?"

From somewhere the Cepheid's voice came, "Extremely pretty."

"But it has outworn its welcome; outlived its fashionable existence."

The Cepheid's voice was abstracted, "It is very pretty."

Bannerd restored the light at a gesture, and the colors faded.

The Cepheid said, "That is something my people would enjoy." He stared at the globe with fascination.

And now Antyok rose. "You had better go. If you stay longer, the atmosphere may have bad effects. I thank you humbly for your kindness."

"I thank you humbly for yours." The Cepheid had also risen.

Antyok said, "Most of your people, by the way, have accepted our offers to them to study the make-up of our modern spaceships. You understand, I suppose, that the purpose was to study the reactions of your people to our technology. I trust that conforms with your sense of propriety."

"You need not apologize. I, myself, have now the makings of a human pilot. It was most interesting. It recalls our own efforts—and reminds us of how nearly on the right track we were."

The Cepheid left, and Antyok sat, frowning.

"Well," he said to Bannerd, a little sharply. "You remember our agreement, I hope. This interview can't be published."

Bannerd shrugged, "Very well."

Antyok was at his seat, and his fingers fumbled with the small metal figurine upon his desk, "What do you think of all this, Bannerd?"

"I am sorry for them. I think I understand how they feel. We must educate them out of it. The Philosophy can do it."

"You think so?"

"Yes."

"We can't let them go, of course."

"Oh, no. Out of the question. We have too much to learn from them. This feeling of theirs is only a passing stage. They'll think differently, especially when we allow them the completest independence."

"Maybe. What do you think of the fluoro-globes, Bannerd? He liked them. It might be a gesture of the right sort to order several thousand of them. The Galaxy knows, they're a drug on the market right now, and cheap enough."

"Sounds like a good idea," said Bannerd.

"The Bureau would never agree, though. I know them."

The newsman's eyes narrowed, "But it might be just the thing. They need new interests."

"Yes? Well, we *could* do something. I could include your transcript of the interview as part of a report and just emphasize the matter of the globes a bit. After all, you're a member of The Philosophy and might have influence with important people, whose word with the Bureau might carry much more weight than mine. You understand—?"

"Yes," mused Bannerd. "Yes."

From: AdHQ-Ceph18

To: BuOuProv

Subject: OuProv Project 2910, Part II; Birth rate of non-Humans on Cepheus 18, Investigation of.

Reference:

(a) BuOuProv letr. Cep-N-CM/car, 115097, dated 223/977 G.E.

Enclosure:

1. Transcript of conversation between L. Antyok of AdHQ-Ceph18, and Ni-San, High Judge of the non-Humans on Cepheus 18.

1. Enclosure 1 is forwarded herewith for the information of the BuOuProv.

2. The investigation of the subject project undertaken in response to the authorization of reference (a) is being pursued along the new lines indicated in Enclosure 1. The BuOuProv is assured that every means will be used to combat the harmful psychological attitude at present prevalent among the non-Humans.

3. It is to be noted that the High Judge of the non-Humans on Cepheus 18 expressed interest in fluoro-globes. A preliminary investigation into this fact of non-Human psychology has been initiated.

L. Antyok, Superv. AdHQ-Ceph18,
272/977 G.E.

. . . .

From: BuOuProv

To: AdHQ-Ceph18

Subject: OuProv Project 2910; Birth rate of non-Humans on Cepheus 18, Investigation of.

Reference:

    (a) AdHQ-Ceph18 letr. AA-LA/mn, dated 272/977 G.E.

1. With reference to Enclosure 1 of reference (a), five thousand fluoro-globes have been allocated for shipment to Cepheus 18, by the Department of Trade.

2. It is instructed that AdHQ-Ceph18 make use of all methods of appeasing non-Humans' dissatisfaction, consistent with the necessities of obedience to Imperial proclamations.

                          C. Morily, Chief, BuOuProv

                                  283/977 G.E.

V

The dinner was over, the wine had been brought in, and the cigars were out. The groups of talkers had formed, and the captain of the merchant fleet was the center of the largest. His brilliant white uniform quite outsparkled his listeners.

He was almost complacent in his speech: "The trip was nothing. I've had more than three hundred ships under me before this. Still, I've never had a cargo quite like this. What do you want with five thousand fluoro-globes on this desert, by the Galaxy!"

Loodun Antyok laughed gently. He shrugged, "For the non-Humans. It wasn't a difficult cargo, I hope."

"No, not difficult. But bulky. They're fragile, and I couldn't carry more than twenty to a ship, with all the government regulations concerning packing and precautions against breakage. But it's the government's money, I suppose."

Zammo smiled grimly. "Is this your first experience with government methods, captain?"

"Galaxy, no," exploded the spaceman. "I try to avoid it, of course, but you can't help getting entangled on occasion. And it's an abhorrent thing when you are, and that's the truth. The red tape! The paper work! It's enough to stunt your growth and curdle your circulation. It's a tumor, a cancerous growth on the Galaxy. I'd wipe out the whole mess."

Antyok said, "You're unfair, captain. You don't understand."

"Yes? Well, now, as one of these bureaucrats," and he smiled amiably at the word, "suppose you explain your side of the situation, administrator."

"Well, now," Antyok seemed confused, "government is a serious and complicated business. We've got thousands of planets to worry about in this

Empire of ours and billions of people. It's almost past human ability to supervise the business of governing without the tightest sort of organization. I think there are something like four hundred million men today in the Imperial Administrative Service alone, and in order to co-ordinate their efforts and to pool their knowledge, you *must* have what you call red tape and paper work. Every bit of it, senseless though it may seem, annoying though it may be, has its uses. Every piece of paper is a thread binding the labors of four hundred million humans. Abolish the Administrative Service and you abolish the Empire; and with it, interstellar peace, order, and civilization."

"Come—" said the captain.

"No. I mean it." Antyok was earnestly breathless. "The rules and system of the Administrative set-up must be sufficiently all-embracing and rigid so that in case of incompetent officials, and sometimes one *is* appointed—you may laugh, but there are incompetent scientists, and newsmen, and captains, too—in case of incompetent officials, I say, little harm will be done. For, at the worst, the system can move by itself."

"Yes," grunted the captain, sourly, "and if a capable administrator should be appointed? He is then caught by the same rigid web and is forced into mediocrity."

"Not at all," replied Antyok, warmly. "A capable man can work within the limits of the rules and accomplish what he wishes."

"How?" asked Bannerd.

"Well . . . well—" Antyok was suddenly ill at ease. "One method is to get yourself an A-priority project, or double-A, if possible."

The captain leaned his head back for laughter, but never quite made it, for the door was flung open and frightened men were pouring in. The shouts made no sense at first. Then:

"Sir, the ships are gone. These non-Humans have taken them by force."

"What? All?"

"Every one. Ships and creatures—"

It was two hours later that the four were together again, alone in Antyok's office now.

Antyok said coldly, "They've made no mistakes. There's not a ship left behind, not even your training ship, Zammo. And there isn't a government ship available in this entire half of the Sector. By the time we organize a pursuit they'll be out of the Galaxy and halfway to the Magellanic Clouds. Captain, it was your responsibility to maintain an adequate guard."

The captain cried, "It was our first day out of space. Who could have known—"

Zammo interrupted fiercely, "Wait a while, captain. I'm beginning to understand. Antyok," his voice was hard, "you engineered this."

"I?" Antyok's expression was strangely cool, almost indifferent.

"You told us this evening that a clever administrator got an A-priority project assigned to accomplish what he wished. You got such a project in order to help the non-Humans escape."

"I did? I beg your pardon, but how could that be? It was you yourself in one of your reports that brought up the problem of the failing birth rate. It was Bannerd, here, whose sensational articles frightened the Bureau into making a double A-priority project out of it. I had nothing to do with it."

"You suggested that I mention the birth rate," said Zammo, violently.

"Did I?" said Antyok, composedly.

"And for that matter," roared Bannerd, suddenly, "you suggested that I mention the birth rate in my articles."

The three ringed him now and hemmed him in. Antyok leaned back in his chair and said easily, "I don't know what you mean by suggestions. If you are accusing me, please stick to evidence—legal evidence. The laws of the Empire go by written, filmed, or transcribed material, or by witnessed statements. All my letters as administrator are on file here, at the Bureau, and at other places. I never asked for an A-priority project. The Bureau assigned it to me, and Zammo and Bannerd are responsible for that. In print, at any rate."

Zammo's voice was an almost inarticulate growl, "You hoodwinked me into teaching the creatures how to handle a spaceship."

"It was *your* suggestion. I have your report proposing they be studied in their reaction to human tools on file. So has the Bureau. The evidence—the *legal* evidence, is plain. I had nothing to do with it."

"Nor with the globes?" demanded Bannerd.

The captain howled suddenly, "You had my ships brought here purposely. Five thousand globes! You knew it would require hundreds of craft."

"I never asked for globes," said Antyok, coldly. "That was the Bureau's idea, although I think Bannerd's friends of The Philosophy helped that along."

Bannerd fairly choked. He spat out, "You were asking that Cepheid leader if he could read minds. You were telling him to express interest in the globes."

"Come, now. You prepared the transcript of the conversation yourself, and that, too, is on file. You can't prove it." He stood up, "You'll have to excuse me. I must prepare a report for the Bureau."

At the door, Antyok turned, "In a way, the problem of the non-Humans is solved, even if only to their own satisfaction. They'll breed now, and have a world they've earned themselves. It's what they wanted.

"Another thing. Don't accuse me of silly things. I've been in the Service for twenty-seven years, and I assure you that my paper work is proof enough that I have been thoroughly correct in everything I have done. And captain, I'll be glad to continue our discussion of earlier this evening at your convenience and explain how a capable administrator can work through red tape and still get what he wants."

It was remarkable that such a round, smooth baby-face could wear a smile quite so sardonic.

From: BuOuProv
To: Loodun Antyok, Chief Public Administrator, A-8
Subject: Administrative Service, Standing in.
Reference:
   (a) AdServ Court Decision 22874-Q, dated 1/978 G.E.
1. In view of the favorable opinion handed down in reference (a) you are hereby absolved of all responsibility for the flight of non-Humans on Cepheus 18. It is requested that you hold yourself in readiness for your next appointment.

R. Horpritt, Chief, AdServ,
15/978 G.E.

Evidence

"But that wasn't it, either," said Dr. Calvin thoughtfully. "Oh, eventually, the ship and others like it became government property; the Jump through hyperspace was perfected, and now we actually have human colonies on the planets of some of the nearer stars, but that wasn't it."

I had finished eating and watched her through the smoke of my cigarette.

"It's what has happened to the people here on Earth in the last fifty years that really counts. When I was born, young man, we had just gone through the last World War. It was a low point in history—but it was the end of nationalism. Earth was too small for nations and they began grouping themselves into Regions. It took quite a while. When I was born the United States of America was still a nation and not merely a part of the Northern Region. In fact, the name of the corporation is still 'United States Robots——.' And the change from nations to Regions, which has stabilized our economy and brought about what amounts to a Golden Age, when this century is compared with the last, was also brought about by our robots."

"You mean the Machines," I said. "The Brain you talked about was the first of the Machines, wasn't it?"

"Yes, it was, but it's not the Machines I was thinking of. Rather of a man. He died last year." Her voice was suddenly deeply sorrowful. "Or at least he arranged to die, because he knew we needed him no longer.—Stephen Byerley."

"Yes, I guessed that was who you meant."

"He first entered public office in 2032. You were only a boy then, so you *wouldn't remember the strangeness of it. His campaign for the Mayoralty was certainly the queerest in history——"*

Francis Quinn was a politician of the new school. That, of course, is a meaningless expression, as are all expressions of the sort. Most of the "new schools" we have were duplicated in the social life of ancient Greece, and perhaps, if we knew more about it, in the social life of ancient Sumeria and in the lake dwellings of prehistoric Switzerland as well.

But, to get out from under what promises to be a dull and complicated beginning, it might be best to state hastily that Quinn neither ran for office nor canvassed for votes, made no speeches and stuffed no ballot boxes. Any more than Napoleon pulled a trigger at Austerlitz.

And since politics makes strange bedfellows, Alfred Lanning sat at the other side of the desk with his ferocious white eyebrows bent far forward over eyes in which chronic impatience had sharpened to acuity. He was not pleased.

The fact, if known to Quinn, would have annoyed him not the least. His voice was friendly, perhaps professionally so.

"I assume you know Stephen Byerley, Dr. Lanning."

"I have heard of him. So have many people."

"Yes, so have I. Perhaps you intend voting for him at the next election."

"I couldn't say." There was an unmistakable trace of acidity here. "I have not followed the political currents, so I'm not aware that he is running for office."

"He may be our next mayor. Of course, he is only a lawyer now, but great oaks—"

"Yes," interrupted Lanning, "I have heard the phrase before. But I wonder if we can get to the business at hand."

"We *are* at the business at hand, Dr. Lanning." Quinn's tone was very gentle, "It is to my interest to keep Mr. Byerley a district attorney at the very most, and it is to your interest to help me do so."

"To *my* interest? Come!" Lanning's eyebrows hunched low.

"Well, say then to the interest of the U. S. Robot & Mechanical Men Corporation. I come to you as Director-Emeritus of Research, because I know that your connection to them is that of, shall we say, 'elder statesman.' You are listened to with respect and yet your connection with them is no longer so tight but that you cannot possess considerable freedom of action; even if the action is somewhat unorthodox."

Dr. Lanning was silent a moment, chewing the cud of his thoughts. He said more softly, "I don't follow you at all, Mr. Quinn."

"I am not surprised, Dr. Lanning. But it's all rather simple. Do you mind?" Quinn lit a slender cigarette with a lighter of tasteful simplicity and his big-boned face settled into an expression of quiet amusement. "We have spoken of Mr. Byerley—a strange and colorful character. He was unknown three years ago. He is very well known now. He is a man of force and ability, and certainly the most capable and intelligent prosecutor I have ever known. Unfortunately he is not a friend of mine—"

"I understand," said Lanning, mechanically. He stared at his fingernails.

"I have had occasion," continued Quinn, evenly, "in the past year to investigate Mr. Byerley—quite exhaustively. It is always useful, you see, to subject the past life of reform politicians to rather inquisitive research. If you knew how often it helped—" He paused to smile humorlessly at the glowing tip of his cigarette. "But Mr. Byerley's past is unremarkable. A quiet life in a small town, a college education, a wife who died young, an auto accident with a slow recovery, law school, coming to the metropolis, an attorney."

Francis Quinn shook his head slowly, then added, "But his present life. Ah, that is remarkable. Our district attorney never eats!"

Lanning's head snapped up, old eyes surprisingly sharp, "Pardon me?"

"Our district attorney never eats." The repetition thumped by syllables. "I'll modify that slightly. He has never been seen to eat or drink. Never! Do you understand the significance of the word? Not rarely, but never!"

"I find that quite incredible. Can you trust your investigators?"

"I can trust my investigators, and I don't find it incredible at all. Further, our district attorney has never been seen to drink—in the aqueous sense as well as the alcoholic—nor to sleep. There are other factors, but I should think I have made my point."

Lanning leaned back in his seat, and there was the rapt silence of challenge and response between them, and then the old roboticist shook his head. "No. There is only one thing you can be trying to imply, if I couple your statements with the fact that you present them to me, and that is impossible."

"But the man is quite inhuman, Dr. Lanning."

"If you told me he were Satan in masquerade, there would be a faint chance that I might believe you."

"I tell you he is a robot, Dr. Lanning."

"I tell you it is as impossible a conception as I have ever heard, Mr. Quinn."

Again the combative silence.

"Nevertheless," and Quinn stubbed out his cigarette with elaborate care, "you will have to investigate this impossibility with all the resources of the Corporation."

"I'm sure that I could undertake no such thing, Mr. Quinn. You don't seriously suggest that the Corporation take part in local politics."

"You have no choice. Supposing I were to make my facts public without proof. The evidence is circumstantial enough."

"Suit yourself in that respect."

"But it would not suit me. Proof would be much preferable. And it would not suit *you*, for the publicity would be very damaging to your company. You are perfectly well acquainted, I suppose, with the strict rules against the use of robots on inhabited worlds."

"Certainly!"—brusquely.

"You know that the U. S. Robot & Mechanical Men Corporation is the only manufacturer of positronic robots in the Solar System, and if Byerley is a robot, he is a *positronic* robot. You are also aware that all positronic robots are leased, and not sold; that the Corporation remains the owner and manager of each robot, and is therefore responsible for the actions of all."

"It is an easy matter, Mr. Quinn, to prove the Corporation has never manufactured a robot of a humanoid character."

"It can be done? To discuss merely possibilities."

"Yes. It can be done."

"Secretly, I imagine, as well. Without entering it in your books."

"Not the positronic brain, sir. Too many factors are involved in that, and there is the tightest possible government supervision."

"Yes, but robots are worn out, break down, go out of order—and are dismantled."

"And the positronic brains re-used or destroyed."

"Really?" Francis Quinn allowed himself a trace of sarcasm. "And if one were, accidentally, of course, not destroyed—and there happened to be a humanoid structure waiting for a brain."

"Impossible!"

"You would have to prove that to the government and the public, so why not prove it to me now."

"But what could our purpose be?" demanded Lanning in exasperation. "Where is our motivation? Credit us with a minimum of sense."

"My dear sir, please. The Corporation would be only too glad to have the various Regions permit the use of humanoid positronic robots on inhabited worlds. The profits would be enormous. But the prejudice of the public against such a practice is too great. Suppose you get them used to such robots first—see, we have a skillful lawyer, a good mayor—and he is a robot. Won't you buy our robot butlers?"

"Thoroughly fantastic. An almost humorous descent to the ridiculous."

"I imagine so. Why not prove it? Or would you still rather try to prove it to the public?"

The light in the office was dimming, but it was not yet too dim to obscure the flush of frustration on Alfred Lanning's face. Slowly, the roboticist's finger touched a knob and the wall illuminators glowed to gentle life.

"Well, then," he growled, "let us see."

The face of Stephen Byerley is not an easy one to describe. He was forty by birth certificate and forty by appearance—but it was a healthy, well-nourished good-natured appearance of forty; one that automatically drew the teeth of the bromide about "looking one's age."

This was particularly true when he laughed, and he was laughing now. It came loudly and continuously, died away for a bit, then began again—

And Alfred Lanning's face contracted into a rigidly bitter monument of disapproval. He made a half gesture to the woman who sat beside him, but her thin, bloodless lips merely pursed themselves a trifle.

Byerley gasped himself a stage nearer normality.

"Really, Dr. Lanning . . . really—I . . . *I* . . . a robot?"

Lanning bit his words off with a snap, "It is no statement of mine, sir. I would be quite satisfied to have you a member of humanity. Since our corporation never manufactured you, I am quite certain that you are—in a legalistic sense, at any rate. But since the contention that you are a robot has been advanced to us seriously by a man of certain standing—"

"Don't mention his name, if it would knock a chip off your granite block of ethics, but let's pretend it was Frank Quinn, for the sake of argument, and continue."

Lanning drew in a sharp, cutting snort at the interruption, and paused ferociously before continuing with added frigidity, "—by a man of certain standing, with whose identity I am not interested in playing guessing games, I am bound to ask your cooperation in disproving it. The mere fact that such a contention could be advanced and publicized by the means at this man's disposal would be a bad blow to the company I represent—even if the charge were never proven. You understand me?"

"Oh, yes, your position is clear to me. The charge itself is ridiculous. The spot you find yourself in is not. I beg your pardon, if my laughter offended you. It was the first I laughed at, not the second. How can I help you?"

"It could be very simple. You have only to sit down to a meal at a restaurant in the presence of witnesses, have your picture taken, and eat." Lanning sat back in his chair, the worst of the interview over. The woman beside him watched Byerley with an apparently absorbed expression but contributed nothing of her own.

Stephen Byerley met her eyes for an instant, was caught by them, then turned back to the roboticist. For a while his fingers were thoughtful over the bronze paper-weight that was the only ornament on his desk.

He said quietly, "I don't think I can oblige you."

He raised his hand, "Now wait, Dr. Lanning. I appreciate the fact that this whole matter is distasteful to you, that you have been forced into it against your will, that you feel you are playing an undignified and even ridiculous part. Still, the matter is even more intimately concerned with myself, so be tolerant.

"First, what makes you think that Quinn—this man of certain standing, you know—wasn't hoodwinking you, in order to get you to do exactly what you are doing?"

"Why it seems scarcely likely that a reputable person would endanger himself in so ridiculous a fashion, if he weren't convinced he were on safe ground."

There was little humor in Byerley's eyes, "You don't know Quinn. He could manage to make safe ground out of a ledge a mountain sheep could not handle. I suppose he showed the particulars of the investigation he claims to have made of me?"

"Enough to convince me that it would be too troublesome to have our corporation attempt to disprove them when you could do so more easily."

"Then you believe him when he says I never eat. You are a scientist, Dr. Lanning. Think of the logic required. I have not been observed to eat, therefore, I never eat Q.E.D. After all!"

"You are using prosecution tactics to confuse what is really a very simple situation."

"On the contrary, I am trying to clarify what you and Quinn between you are making a very complicated one. You see, I don't sleep much, that's true, and I certainly don't sleep in public. I have never cared to eat with others— an idiosyncrasy which is unusual and probably neurotic in character, but which harms no one. Look, Dr. Lanning, let me present you with a suppositious case. Supposing we had a politician who was interested in defeating a reform candidate at any cost and while investigating his private life came across oddities such as I have just mentioned.

"Suppose further that in order to smear the candidate effectively, he comes to your company as the ideal agent. Do you expect him to say to you, 'So-and-so is a robot because he hardly ever eats with people, and I have never seen him fall asleep in the middle of a case; and once when I peeped into his window in the middle of the night, there he was, sitting up with a book; and I looked in his frigidaire and there was no food in it.'

"If he told you that, you would send for a straitjacket. But if he tells you, 'He *never* sleeps; he *never* eats,' then the shock of the statement blinds you to the fact that such statements are impossible to prove. You play into his hands by contributing to the to-do."

"Regardless, sir," began Lanning, with a threatening obstinacy, "of whether you consider this matter serious or not, it will require only the meal I mentioned to end it."

Again Byerley turned to the woman, who still regarded him expressionlessly. "Pardon me. I've caught your name correctly, haven't I? Dr. Susan Calvin?"

"Yes, Mr. Byerley."

"You're the U. S. Robot's psychologist, aren't you?"

"*Robo*psychologist, please."

"Oh, are robots so different from men, mentally?"

"Worlds different." She allowed herself a frosty smile, "Robots are essentially decent."

Humor tugged at the corners of the lawyer's mouth, "Well, that's a hard blow. But what I wanted to say was this. Since you're a psycho—a robo-psychologist, *and* a woman, I'll bet that you've done something that Dr. Lanning hasn't thought of."

"And what is that?"

"You've got something to eat in your purse."

Something caught in the schooled indifference of Susan Calvin's eyes. She said, "You surprise me, Mr. Byerley."

And opening her purse, she produced an apple. Quietly, she handed it to him. Dr. Lanning, after an initial start, followed the slow movement from one hand to the other with sharply alert eyes.

Calmly, Stephen Byerley bit into it, and calmly he swallowed it.

"You see, Dr. Lanning?"

Dr. Lanning smiled in a relief tangible enough to make even his eyebrows appear benevolent. A relief that survived for one fragile second.

Susan Calvin said, "I was curious to see if you would eat it, but, of course, in the present case, it proves nothing."

Byerley grinned, "It doesn't?"

"Of course not. It is obvious, Dr. Lanning, that if this man were a human-oid robot, he would be a perfect imitation. He is almost too human to be credible. After all, we have been seeing and observing human beings all our lives; it would be impossible to palm something merely nearly right off on us. It would have to be *all* right. Observe the texture of the skin, the quality of the irises, the bone formation of the hand. If he's a robot, I wish U. S. Robots *had* made him, because he's a good job. Do you suppose then, that anyone capable of paying attention to such niceties would neglect a few gadgets to take care of such things as eating, sleeping, elimination? For emer-gency use only, perhaps; as, for instance, to prevent such situations as are arising here. So a meal won't really prove anything."

"Now wait," snarled Lanning, "I am not quite the fool both of you make me out to be. I am not interested in the problem of Mr. Byerley's humanity or nonhumanity. I am interested in getting the corporation out of a hole. A public meal will end the matter and keep it ended no matter what Quinn does. We can leave the finer details to lawyers and robopsychologists."

"But, Dr. Lanning," said Byerley, "you forget the politics of the situation. I am as anxious to be elected as Quinn is to stop me. By the way, did you notice that you used his name? It's a cheap shyster trick of mine; I knew you would, before you were through."

Lanning flushed, "What has the election to do with it?"

"Publicity works both ways, sir. If Quinn wants to call me a robot, and has the nerve to do so, I have the nerve to play the game his way."

"You mean you—" Lanning was quite frankly appalled.

"Exactly. I mean that I'm going to let him go ahead, choose his rope, test its strength, cut off the right length, tie the noose, insert his head and grin. I can do what little else is required."

"You are mighty confident."

Susan Calvin rose to her feet, "Come, Alfred, we won't change his mind for him."

"You see." Byerley smiled gently. "You're a human psychologist, too."

But perhaps not all the confidence that Dr. Lanning had remarked upon was present that evening when Byerley's car parked on the automatic treads leading to the sunken garage, and Byerley himself crossed the path to the front door of his house.

The figure in the wheel chair looked up as he entered and smiled. Byerley's face lit with affection. He crossed over to it.

The cripple's voice was a hoarse, grating whisper that came out of a mouth forever twisted to one side, leering out of a face that was half scar tissue, "You're late, Steve."

"I know, John, I know. But I've been up against a peculiar and interesting trouble today."

"So?" Neither the torn face nor the destroyed voice could carry expression but there was anxiety in the clear eyes. "Nothing you can't handle?"

"I'm not exactly certain. I may need your help. You're the brilliant one in the family. Do you want me to take you out into the garden? It's a beautiful evening."

Two strong arms lifted John from the wheel chair. Gently, almost caressingly, Byerley's arms went around the shoulders and under the swathed legs of the cripple. Carefully, and slowly, he walked through the rooms, down the gentle ramp that had been built with a wheel chair in mind, and out the back door into the walled and wired garden behind the house.

"Why don't you let me use the wheel chair, Steve? This is silly."

"Because I'd rather carry you. Do you object? You know that you're as glad to get out of that motorized buggy for a while as I am to see you out. How do you feel today?" He deposited John with infinite care upon the cool grass.

"How should I feel? But tell me about your troubles."

"Quinn's campaign will be based on the fact that he claims I'm a robot."

John's eyes opened wide, "How do you know? It's impossible. I won't believe it."

"Oh, come, I tell you it's so. He had one of the big-shot scientists of U. S. Robot & Mechanical Men Corporation over at the office to argue with me."

Slowly John's hands tore at the grass, "I see. I see."

Byerley said, "But we can let him choose his ground. I have an idea. Listen to me and tell me if we can do it—"

The scene as it appeared in Alfred Lanning's office that night was a tableau of stares. Francis Quinn stared meditatively at Alfred Lanning. Lanning's stare was savagely set upon Susan Calvin, who stared impassively in her turn at Quinn.

Francis Quinn broke it with a heavy attempt at lightness, "Bluff. He's making it up as he goes along."

"Are you going to gamble on that, Mr. Quinn?" asked Dr. Calvin, indifferently.

"Well, it's your gamble, really."

"Look here," Lanning covered definite pessimism with bluster, "we've done what you asked. We witnessed the man eat. It's ridiculous to presume him a robot."

"Do *you* think so?" Quinn shot toward Calvin. "Lanning said you were the expert."

Lanning was almost threatening, "Now, Susan—"

Quinn interrupted smoothly, "Why not let her talk, man? She's been sitting there imitating a gatepost for half an hour."

Lanning felt definitely harassed. From what he experienced then to incipient paranoia was but a step. He said, "Very well. Have your say, Susan. We won't interrupt you."

Susan Calvin glanced at him humorlessly, then fixed cold eyes on Mr. Quinn. "There are only two ways of definitely proving Byerley to be a robot, sir. So far you are presenting circumstantial evidence, with which you can accuse, but not prove—and I think Mr. Byerley is sufficiently clever to counter that sort of material. You probably think so yourself, or you wouldn't have come here.

"The two methods of *proof* are the physical and the psychological. Physically, you can dissect him or use an X-ray. How to do that would be *your* problem. Psychologically, his behavior can be studied, for if he *is* a positronic robot, he must conform to the three Rules of Robotics. A positronic brain can not be constructed without them. You know the Rules, Mr. Quinn?"

She spoke them carefully, clearly, quoting word for word the famous bold print on page one of the "Handbook of Robotics."

"I've heard of them," said Quinn, carelessly.

"Then the matter is easy to follow," responded the psychologist, dryly. "If Mr. Byerley breaks any of those three rules, he is not a robot. Unfortunately, this procedure works in only one direction. If he lives up to the rules, it proves nothing one way or the other."

Quinn raised polite eyebrows, "Why not, doctor?"

"Because, if you stop to think of it, the three Rules of Robotics are the essential guiding principles of a good many of the world's ethical systems. Of course, every human being is supposed to have the instinct of self-preservation. That's Rule Three to a robot. Also every 'good' human being, with a social conscience and a sense of responsibility, is supposed to defer to proper authority; to listen to his doctor, his boss, his government, his psychiatrist, his fellow man; to obey laws, to follow rules, to conform to custom—even when they interfere with his comfort or his safety. That's Rule Two to a robot. Also, every 'good' human being is supposed to love others as himself, protect his fellow man, risk his life to save another. That's Rule One to a robot. To put it simply—if Byerley follows all the Rules of Robotics, he may be a robot, and may simply be a very good man."

"But," said Quinn, "you're telling me that you can never prove him a robot."

"I may be able to prove him *not* a robot."

"That's not the proof I want."

"You'll have such proof as exists. You are the only one responsible for your own wants."

Here Lanning's mind leaped suddenly to the sting of an idea, "Has it occurred to anyone," he ground out, "that district attorney is a rather strange occupation for a robot? The prosecution of human beings—sentencing them to death—bringing about their infinite harm—"

Quinn grew suddenly keen, "No, you can't get out of it that way. Being district attorney doesn't make him human. Don't you know his record? Don't you know that he boasts that he has never prosecuted an innocent man; that there are scores of people left untried because the evidence against them didn't satisfy him, even though he could probably have argued a jury into atomizing them? That happens to be so."

Lanning's thin cheeks quivered, "No, Quinn, no. There is nothing in the Rules of Robotics that makes any allowance for human guilt. A robot may not judge whether a human being deserves death. It is not for him to decide. *He may not harm a human*—variety skunk, or variety angel."

Susan Calvin sounded tired. "Alfred," she said, "don't talk foolishly. What if a robot came upon a madman about to set fire to a house with people in it. He would stop the madman, wouldn't he?"

"Of course."

"And if the only way he could stop him was to kill him—"

There was a faint sound in Lanning's throat. Nothing more.

"The answer to that, Alfred, is that he would do his best not to kill him. If the madman died, the robot would require psychotherapy because he might easily go mad at the conflict presented him—of having broken Rule One to adhere to Rule One in a higher sense. But a man would be dead and a robot would have killed him."

"Well, *is* Byerley mad?" demanded Lanning, with all the sarcasm he could muster.

"No, but he has killed no man himself. He has exposed facts which might represent a particular human being to be dangerous to the large mass of other human beings we call society. He protects the greater number and thus adheres to Rule One at maximum potential. That is as far as he goes. It is the judge who then condemns the criminal to death or imprisonment, after the jury decides on his guilt or innocence. It is the jailer who imprisons him, the executioner who kills him. And Mr. Byerley has done nothing but determine truth and aid society.

"As a matter of fact, Mr. Quinn, I have looked into Mr. Byerley's career since you first brought this matter to our attention. I find that he has never demanded the death sentence in his closing speeches to the jury. I also find that he has spoken on behalf of the abolition of capital punishment and contributed generously to research institutions engaged in criminal neurophysiology. He apparently believes in the cure, rather than the punishment of crime. I find that significant."

"You do?" Quinn smiled. "Significant of a certain odor of roboticity, perhaps?"

"Perhaps. Why deny it? Actions such as his could come only from a robot, or from a very honorable and decent human being. But you see, you just can't differentiate between a robot and the very best of humans."

Quinn sat back in his chair. His voice quivered with impatience. "Dr. Lanning, it's perfectly possible to create a humanoid robot that would perfectly duplicate a human in appearance, isn't it?"

Lanning harrumphed and considered, "It's been done experimentally by U. S. Robots," he said reluctantly, "without the addition of a positronic brain, of course. By using human ova and hormone control, one can grow human flesh and skin over a skeleton of porous silicone plastics that would defy external examination. The eyes, the hair, the skin would be really human, not humanoid. And if you put a positronic brain, and such other gadgets as you might desire inside, you have a humanoid robot."

Quinn said shortly, "How long would it take to make one?"

Lanning considered, "If you had all your equipment—the brain, the skeleton, the ovum, the proper hormones and radiations—say, two months."

The politician straightened out of his chair. "Then we shall see what the insides of Mr. Byerley look like. It will mean publicity for U. S. Robots—but I gave you your chance."

Lanning turned impatiently to Susan Calvin, when they were alone. "Why do you insist—"

And with real feeling, she responded sharply and instantly, "Which do you want—the truth or my resignation? I won't lie for you. U. S. Robots can take care of itself. Don't turn coward."

"What," said Lanning, "if he opens up Byerley, and wheels and gears fall out. What then?"

"He won't open Byerley," said Calvin, disdainfully. "Byerley is as clever as Quinn, at the very least."

The news broke upon the city a week before Byerley was to have been nominated. But "broke" is the wrong word. It staggered upon the city, shambled, crawled. Laughter began, and wit was free. And as the far off hand of

Quinn tightened its pressure in easy stages, the laughter grew forced, an element of hollow uncertainty entered, and people broke off to wonder.

The convention itself had the air of a restive stallion. There had been no contest planned. Only Byerley could possibly have been nominated a week earlier. There was no substitute even now. They had to nominate him, but there was complete confusion about it.

It would not have been so bad if the average individual were not torn between the enormity of the charge, if true, and its sensational folly, if false.

The day after Byerley was nominated perfunctorily, hollowly—a newspaper finally published the gist of a long interview with Dr. Susan Calvin, "world famous expert on robopsychology and positronics."

What broke loose is popularly and succinctly described as hell.

It was what the Fundamentalists were waiting for. They were not a political party; they made pretense to no formal religion. Essentially they were those who had not adapted themselves to what had once been called the Atomic Age, in the days when atoms were a novelty. Actually, they were the Simple-Lifers, hungering after a life, which to those who lived it had probably appeared not so Simple, and who had been, therefore, Simple-Lifers themselves.

The Fundamentalists required no new reason to detest robots and robot manufacturers; but a new reason such as the Quinn accusation and the Calvin analysis was sufficient to make such detestation audible.

The huge plants of the U. S. Robot & Mechanical Men Corporation was a hive that spawned armed guards. It prepared for war.

Within the city the house of Stephen Byerley bristled with police.

The political campaign, of course, lost all other issues, and resembled a campaign only in that it was something filling the hiatus between nomination and election.

Stephen Byerley did not allow the fussy little man to distract him. He remained comfortably unperturbed by the uniforms in the background. Outside the house, past the line of grim guards, reporters and photographers waited according to the tradition of the caste. One enterprising 'visor station even had a scanner focused on the blank entrance to the prosecutor's unpretentious home, while a synthetically excited announcer filled in with inflated commentary.

The fussy little man advanced. He held forward a rich, complicated sheet. "This, Mr. Byerley, is a court order authorizing me to search these premises for the presence of illegal . . . uh . . . mechanical men or robots of any description."

Byerley half rose, and took the paper. He glanced at it indifferently, and smiled as he handed it back. "All in order. Go ahead. Do your job. Mrs. Hoppen"—to his housekeeper, who appeared reluctantly from the next room —"please go with them, and help out if you can."

The little man, whose name was Harroway, hesitated, produced an unmistakable blush, failed completely to catch Byerley's eyes, and muttered, "Come on," to the two policemen.

He was back in ten minutes.

"Through?" questioned Byerley, in just the tone of a person who is not particularly interested in the question, or its answer.

Harroway cleared his throat, made a bad start in falsetto, and began again, angrily, "Look here, Mr. Byerley, our special instructions were to search the house very thoroughly."

"And haven't you?"

"We were told exactly what to look for."

"Yes?"

"In short, Mr. Byerley, and not to put too fine a point on it, we were told to search you."

"Me?" said the prosecutor with a broadening smile. "And how do you intend to do that?"

"We have a Penet-radiation unit—"

"Then I'm to have my X-ray photograph taken, hey? You have the authority?"

"You saw my warrant."

"May I see it again?"

Harroway, his forehead shining with considerably more than mere enthusiasm, passed it over a second time.

Byerley said evenly, "I read here as the description of what you are to search; I quote: 'the dwelling place belonging to Stephen Allen Byerley, located at 355 Willow Grove, Evanstron, together with any garage, storehouse or other structures or buildings thereto appertaining, together with all grounds thereto appertaining' . . . um . . . and so on. Quite in order. But, my good man, it doesn't say anything about searching my interior. I am not part of the premises. You may search my clothes if you think I've got a robot hidden in my pocket."

Harroway had no doubt on the point of to whom he owed his job. He did not propose to be backward, given a chance to earn a much better—i.e., more highly paid—job.

He said, in a faint echo of bluster, "Look here. I'm allowed to search the furniture in your house, and anything else I find in it. You are in it, aren't you?"

"A remarkable observation. I *am* in it. But I'm not a piece of furniture. As a citizen of adult responsibility—I have the psychiatric certificate proving that—I have certain rights under the Regional Articles. Searching me would come under the heading of violating my Right of Privacy. That paper isn't sufficient."

"Sure, but if you're a robot, you don't have Right of Privacy."

"True enough—but that paper still isn't sufficient. It recognizes me implicitly as a human being."

"Where?" Harroway snatched at it.

"Where it says 'the dwelling place belonging to' and so on. A robot cannot own property. And you may tell your employer, Mr. Harroway, that if he tries to issue a similar paper which does *not* implicitly recognize me as a human being, he will be immediately faced with a restraining injunction and a civil suit which will make it necessary for him to *prove* me a robot by means of information *now* in his possession, or else to pay a whopping penalty for an attempt to deprive me unduly of my Rights under the Regional Articles. You'll tell him that, won't you?"

Harroway marched to the door. He turned. "You're a slick lawyer—" His hand was in his pocket. For a short moment, he stood there. Then he left, smiled in the direction of the 'visor scanner, still playing away—waved to the reporters, and shouted, "We'll have something for you tomorrow, boys. No kidding."

In his ground car, he settled back, removed the tiny mechanism from his pocket and carefully inspected it. It was the first time he had ever taken a photograph by X-ray reflection. He hoped he had done it correctly.

Quinn and Byerley had never met face-to-face alone. But visorphone was pretty close to it. In fact, accepted literally, perhaps the phrase was accurate, even if to each, the other were merely the light and dark pattern of a bank of photocells.

It was Quinn who had initiated the call. It was Quinn, who spoke first, and without particular ceremony, "Thought you would like to know, Byerley, that I intend to make public the fact that you're wearing a protective shield against Penet-radiation."

"That so? In that case, you've probably already made it public. I have a notion our enterprising press representatives have been tapping my various communication lines for quite a while. I know they have my office lines full of holes; which is why I've dug in at my home these last weeks." Byerley was friendly, almost chatty.

Quinn's lips tightened slightly, "This call is shielded—thoroughly. I'm making it at a certain personal risk."

"So I should imagine. Nobody knows you're behind this campaign. At least, nobody knows it officially. Nobody doesn't know it unofficially. I wouldn't worry. So I wear a protective shield? I suppose you found that out when your puppy dog's Penet-radiation photograph, the other day, turned out to be overexposed."

"You realize, Byerley, that it would be pretty obvious to everyone that you don't dare face X-ray analysis."

"Also that you, or your men, attempted illegal invasion of my Rights of Privacy."

"The devil they'll care for that."

"They might. It's rather symbolic of our two campaigns, isn't it? You have little concern with the rights of the individual citizen. I have great concern. I will not submit to X-ray analysis, because I wish to maintain my Rights on principle. Just as I'll maintain the rights of others when elected."

"That will no doubt make a very interesting speech, but no one will believe you. A little too high-sounding to be true. Another thing," a sudden, crisp change, "the personnel in your home was not complete the other night."

"In what way?"

"According to the report," he shuffled papers before him that were just within the range of vision of the visiplate, "there was one person missing—a cripple."

"As you say," said Byerley, tonelessly, "a cripple. My old teacher, who lives with me and who is now in the country—and has been for two months. A 'much-needed rest' is the usual expression applied in the case. He has your permission?"

"Your teacher? A scientist of sorts?"

"A lawyer once—before he was a cripple. He has a government license as a research biophysicist, with a laboratory of his own, and a complete description of the work he's doing filed with the proper authorities, to whom I can refer you. The work is minor, but is a harmless and engaging hobby for a— poor cripple. I am being as helpful as I can, you see."

"I see. And what does this . . . teacher . . . know about robot manufacture?"

"I couldn't judge the extent of his knowledge in a field with which I am unacquainted."

"He wouldn't have access to positronic brains?"

"Ask your friends at U. S. Robots. They'd be the ones to know."

"I'll put it shortly, Byerley. Your crippled teacher is the real Stephen Byerley. You are his robot creation. We can prove it. It was he who was in the automobile accident, not you. There will be ways of checking the records."

"Really? Do so, then. My best wishes."

"And we can search your so-called teacher's 'country place,' and see what we can find there."

"Well, not quite, Quinn." Byerley smiled broadly. "Unfortunately for you, my so-called teacher is a sick man. His country place is his place of rest. His Right of Privacy as a citizen of adult responsibility is naturally even stronger, under the circumstances. You won't be able to obtain a warrant to enter his grounds without showing just cause. However, I'd be the last to prevent you from trying."

There was a pause of moderate length, and then Quinn leaned forward, so that his imaged-face expanded and the fine lines on his forehead were visible, "Byerley, why do you carry on? You can't be elected."

"Can't I?"

"Do you think you can? Do you suppose that your failure to make any attempt to disprove the robot charge—when you could easily, by breaking one of the Three Laws—does anything but convince the people that you *are* a robot?"

"All I see so far is that from being a rather vaguely known, but still largely obscure metropolitan lawyer, I have now become a world figure. You're a good publicist."

"But you *are* a robot."

"So it's been said, but not proven."

"It's been proven sufficiently for the electorate."

"Then relax—you've won."

"Good-by," said Quinn, with his first touch of viciousness, and the visorphone slammed off.

"Good-by," said Byerley imperturbably, to the blank plate.

Byerley brought his "teacher" back the week before election. The air car dropped quickly in an obscure part of the city.

"You'll stay here till after election," Byerley told him. "It would be better to have you out of the way if things take a bad turn."

The hoarse voice that twisted painfully out of John's crooked mouth might have had accents of concern in it. "There's danger of violence?"

"The Fundamentalists threaten it, so I suppose there is, in a theoretical sense. But I really don't expect it. The Fundies have no real power. They're just the continuous irritant factor that might stir up a riot after a while. You don't mind staying here? Please. I won't be myself if I have to worry about you."

"Oh, I'll stay. You still think it will go well?"

"I'm sure of it. No one bothered you at the place?"

"No one. I'm certain."

"And your part went well?"

"Well enough. There'll be no trouble there."

"Then take care of yourself, and watch the televisor tomorrow, John." Byerley pressed the gnarled hand that rested on his.

Lenton's forehead was a furrowed study in suspense. He had the completely unenviable job of being Byerley's campaign manager in a campaign that wasn't a campaign, for a person that refused to reveal his strategy, and refused to accept his manager's.

"You can't!" It was his favorite phrase. It had become his only phrase. "I tell you, Steve, you can't!"

He threw himself in front of the prosecutor, who was spending his time leafing through the typed pages of his speech.

"Put that down, Steve. Look, that mob has been organized by the Fundies. You won't get a hearing. You'll be stoned more likely. Why do you have to make a speech before an audience? What's wrong with a recording, a visual recording?"

"You want me to win the election, don't you?" asked Byerley, mildly.

"Win the election! You're not going to win, Steve. I'm trying to save your life."

"Oh, I'm not in danger."

"He's not in danger. He's not in danger." Lenton made a queer, rasping sound in his throat. "You mean you're getting out on that balcony in front of fifty thousand crazy crackpots and try to talk sense to them—on a balcony like a medieval dictator?"

Byerley consulted his watch. "In about five minutes—as soon as the television lines are free."

Lenton's answering remark was not quite transliterable.

The crowd filled a roped off area of the city. Trees and houses seemed to grow out of a mass-human foundation. And by ultra-wave, the rest of the world watched. It was a purely local election, but it had a world audience just the same. Byerley thought of that and smiled.

But there was nothing to smile at in the crowd itself. There were banners and streamers, ringing every possible change on his supposed robotcy. The hostile attitude rose thickly and tangibly into the atmosphere.

From the start the speech was not successful. It competed against the inchoate mob howl and the rhythmic cries of the Fundie claques that formed mob-islands within the mob. Byerley spoke on, slowly, unemotionally—

Inside, Lenton clutched his hair and groaned—and waited for the blood.

There was a writhing in the front ranks. An angular citizen with popping eyes, and clothes too short for the lank length of his limbs, was pulling to the fore. A policeman dived after him, making slow, struggling passage. Byerley waved the latter off, angrily.

The thin man was directly under the balcony. His words tore unheard against the roar.

Byerley leaned forward. "What do you say? If you have a legitimate question, I'll answer it." He turned to a flanking guard. "Bring that man up here."

There was a tensing in the crowd. Cries of "Quiet" started in various parts of the mob, and rose to a bedlam, then toned down raggedly. The thin man, red-faced and panting, faced Byerley.

Byerley said, "Have you a question?"

The thin man stared, and said in a cracked voice, "Hit me!"

With sudden energy, he thrust out his chin at an angle. "Hit me! You say you're not a robot. Prove it. You can't hit a human, you monster."

There was a queer, flat, dead silence. Byerley's voice punctured it. "I have no reason to hit you."

The thin man was laughing wildly. "You *can't* hit me. You *won't* hit me. You're not a human. You're a monster, a make-believe man."

And Stephen Byerley, tight-lipped, in the face of thousands who watched in person and the millions who watched by screen, drew back his fist and caught the man crackingly upon the chin. The challenger went over backwards in sudden collapse, with nothing on his face but blank, blank surprise.

Byerley said, "I'm sorry. Take him in and see that he's comfortable. I want to speak to him when I'm through."

And when Dr. Calvin, from her reserved space, turned her automobile and drove off, only one reporter had recovered sufficiently from the shock to race after her, and shout an unheard question.

Susan Calvin called over her shoulder, "He's human."

That was enough. The reporter raced away in his own direction.

The rest of the speech might be described as "Spoken but not heard."

Dr. Calvin and Stephen Byerley met once again—a week before he took the oath of office as mayor. It was late—past midnight.

Dr. Calvin said, "You don't look tired."

The mayor-elect smiled. "I may stay up for a while. Don't tell Quinn."

"I shan't. But that was an interesting story of Quinn's, since you mention him. It's a shame to have spoiled it. I suppose you knew his theory?"

"Parts of it."

"It was highly dramatic. Stephen Byerley was a young lawyer, a powerful speaker, a great idealist—and with a certain flair for biophysics. Are you interested in robotics, Mr. Byerley?"

"Only in the legal aspects."

"*This* Stephen Byerley was. But there was an accident. Byerley's wife died; he himself, worse. His legs were gone; his face was gone; his voice was gone. Part of his mind was—bent. He would not submit to plastic surgery. He retired from the world, legal career gone—only his intelligence, and his hands left. Somehow he could obtain positronic brains, even a complex one, one which had the greatest capacity of forming judgments in ethical problems— which is the highest robotic function so far developed.

"He grew a body about it. Trained it to be everything he would have been and was no longer. He sent it out into the world as Stephen Byerley, remaining behind himself as the old, crippled teacher that no one ever saw—"

"Unfortunately," said the mayor-elect, "I ruined all that by hitting a man. The papers say it was your official verdict on the occasion that I was human."

"How did that happen? Do you mind telling me? It couldn't have been accidental."

"It wasn't entirely. Quinn did most of the work. My men started quietly spreading the fact that I had never hit a man; that I was unable to hit a man; that to fail to do so under provocation would be sure proof that I was a robot. So I arranged for a silly speech in public, with all sorts of publicity overtones, and almost inevitably, some fool fell for it. In its essence, it was what I call a shyster trick. One in which the artificial atmosphere which has been created does all the work. Of course, the emotional effects made my election certain, as intended."

The robopsychologist nodded. "I see you intrude on my field—as every politician must, I suppose. But I'm very sorry it turned out this way. I like robots. I like them considerably better than I do human beings. If a robot can be created capable of being a civil executive, I think he'd make the best one possible. By the Laws of Robotics, he'd be incapable of harming humans, incapable of tyranny, of corruption, of stupidity, of prejudice. And after he had served a decent term, he would leave, even though he were immortal, because it would be impossible for him to hurt humans by letting them know that a robot had ruled them. It would be most ideal."

"Except that a robot might fail due to the inherent inadequacies of his brain. The positronic brain has never equalled the complexities of the human brain."

"He would have advisers. Not even a human brain is capable of governing without assistance."

Byerley considered Susan Calvin with grave interest. "Why do you smile, Dr. Calvin?"

"I smile because Mr. Quinn didn't think of everything."

"You mean there could be more to that story of his."

"Only a little. For the three months before election, this Stephen Byerley that Mr. Quinn spoke about, this broken man, was in the country for some mysterious reason. He returned in time for that famous speech of yours. And after all, what the old cripple did once, he could do a second time, particularly where the second job is very simple in comparison to the first."

"I don't quite understand."

Dr. Calvin rose and smoothed her dress. She was obviously ready to leave. "I mean there is one time when a robot may strike a human being without breaking the First Law. Just one time."

"And when is that?"

Dr. Calvin was at the door. She said quietly, "When the human to be struck is merely another robot."

She smiled broadly, her thin face glowing. "Good-by Mr. Byerley. I hope to vote for you five years from now—for co-ordinator."

Stephen Byerley chuckled. "I must reply that that is a somewhat far-fetched idea."

The door closed behind her.

I stared at her with a sort of horror, "Is that true?"

"All of it," she said.

"And the great Byerley was simply a robot."

"Oh, there's no way of ever finding out. I think he was. But when he decided

to die, he had himself atomized, so that there will never be any legal proof. —Besides, what difference would it make?"

"Well—"

"You share a prejudice against robots which is quite unreasoning. He was a very good Mayor; five years later he did become Regional Co-ordinator. And when the Regions of Earth formed their Federation in 2044, he became the first World Co-ordinator. By that time it was the Machines that were running the world anyway."

"Yes, but—"

"No buts! The Machines are robots, and they are running the world. It was five years ago that I found out all the truth. It was 2052; Byerley was completing his second term as World Co-ordinator—"

The Red Queen's Race

Here's a puzzle for you, if you like. Is it a crime to translate a chemistry textbook into Greek?

Or let's put it another way. If one of the country's largest atomic power plants is completely ruined in an unauthorized experiment, is an admitted accessory to that act a criminal?

These problems only developed with time, of course. We started with the atomic power plant—drained. I really mean *drained*. I don't know exactly how large the fissionable power source was—but in two flashing microseconds, it had all fissioned.

No explosion. No undue gamma ray density. It was merely that every moving part in the entire structure was fused. The entire main building was mildly hot. The atmosphere for two miles in every direction was gently warm. Just a dead, useless building which later on took a hundred million dollars to replace.

It happened about three in the morning, and they found Elmer Tywood alone in the central source chamber. The findings of twenty-four close-packed hours can be summarized quickly.

1. Elmer Tywood—Ph.D., Sc.D., Fellow of This and Honorary That, one-time youthful participant of the original Manhattan Project, and now full Professor of Nuclear Physics—was no interloper. He had a Class-A Pass—Unlimited. But no record could be found as to his purpose in being there just then. A table on casters contained equipment which had not been made on

any recorded requisition. It, too, was a single fused mass—not quite too hot to touch.

2. Elmer Tywood was dead. He lay next to the table; his face congested, nearly black. No radiation effect. No external force of any sort. The doctor said apoplexy.

3. In Elmer Tywood's office safe were found two puzzling items: i.e., twenty foolscap sheets of apparent mathematics, and a bound folio in a foreign language which turned out to be Greek, the subject matter, on translation, turning out to be chemistry.

The secrecy which poured over the whole mess was something so terrific as to make everything that touched it, *dead.* It's the only word that can describe it. Twenty-seven men and women, all told, including the Secretary of Defense, the Secretary of Science, and two or three others so top-notch that they were completely unknown to the public, entered the power plant during the period of investigation. All who had been in the plant that night, the physicist who had identified Tywood, the doctor who had examined him, were retired into virtual home arrest.

No newspaper ever got the story. No inside dopester got it. A few members of Congress got part of it.

And naturally so! Anyone or any group or any country that could suck all the available energy out of the equivalent of perhaps fifty to a hundred pounds of plutonium without exploding it, had America's industry and America's defense so snugly in the palm of the hand that the light and life of one hundred sixty million people could be turned off between yawns.

Was it Tywood? Or Tywood and others? Or just others, through Tywood?

And my job? I was decoy; or front man, if you like. Someone has to hang around the university and ask questions about Tywood. After all, he was missing. It could be amnesia, a hold-up, a kidnapping, a killing, a runaway, insanity, accident—I could busy myself with that for five years and collect black looks, and maybe divert attention. To be sure, it didn't work out that way.

But don't think I was in on the whole case at the start. I wasn't one of the twenty-seven men I mentioned a while back, though my boss was. But I knew a little—enough to get started.

Professor John Keyser was also in Physics. I didn't get to him right away. There was a good deal of routine to cover first in as conscientious a way as I could. Quite meaningless. Quite necessary. But I was in Keyser's office now.

Professors' offices are distinctive. Nobody dusts them except some tired cleaning woman who hobbles in and out at eight in the morning, and the professor never notices the dust anyway. Lots of books without much arrangement. The ones close to the desk are used a lot—lectures are copied out of them. The ones out of reach are wherever a student put them back after borrowing them. Then there are professional journals that look cheap and are darned expensive, which are waiting about and which may some day be read. And plenty of paper on the desk; some of it scribbled on.

Keyser was an elderly man—one of Tywood's generation. His nose was big and rather red, and he smoked a pipe. He had that easy-going and nonpredatory look in his eyes that goes with an academic job—either because that kind of job attracts that kind of man or because that kind of job makes that kind of man.

I said: "What kind of work is Professor Tywood doing?"

"Research physics."

Answers like that bounce off me. Some years ago they used to get me mad. Now I just said: "We know that, professor. It's the details I'm after."

And he twinkled at me tolerantly: "Surely the details can't help much unless you're a research physicist yourself. Does it matter—under the circumstances?"

"Maybe not. But he's gone. If anything's happened to him in the way of" —I gestured, and deliberately clinched—"foul play, his work may have something to do with it—unless he's rich and the motive is money."

Keyser chuckled dryly: "College professors are never rich. The commodity we peddle is but lightly considered, seeing how large the supply is."

I ignored that, too, because I know my looks are against me. Actually, I finished college with a "very good" translated into Latin so that the college president could understand it, and never played in a football game in my life. But I look rather the reverse.

I said: "Then we're left with his work to consider."

"You mean spies? International intrigue?"

"Why not? It's happened before! After all, he's a nuclear physicist, isn't he?"

"He is. But so are others. So am I."

"Ah, but perhaps he knows something you don't."

There was a stiffening to the jaw. When caught off-guard, professors can act just like people. He said, stiffly: "As I recall offhand, Tywood has published papers on the effect of liquid viscosity on the wings of the Rayleigh line, on higher-orbit field equations, and on spin-orbit coupling of two nucleons, but his main work is on quadrupole moments. I am quite competent in these matters."

"Is he working on quadrupole moments now?" I tried not to bat an eye, and I think I succeeded.

"Yes—in a way." He almost sneered, "He may be getting to the experimental stage finally. He's spent most of his life, it seems, working out the mathematical consequences of a special theory of his own."

"Like this," and I tossed a sheet of foolscap at him.

That sheet was one of those in the safe in Tywood's office. The chances, of course, were that the bundle meant nothing, if only because it was a professor's safe. That is, things are sometimes put in at the spur of the moment because the logical drawer was filled with unmarked exam papers. And, of course, nothing is ever taken out. We had found in that safe dusty little vials of yellowish crystals with scarcely legible labels, some mimeographed booklets dating back to World War II and marked "Restricted," a copy of an old college yearbook, and some correspondence concerning a possible position as Director of Research for American Electric, dated ten years back, and, of course, chemistry in Greek.

The foolscap was there, too. It was rolled up like a college diploma with a rubber band about it and had no label or descriptive title. Some twenty sheets were covered with ink marks, meticulous and small—

I had one sheet of that foolscap. I don't think any one man in the world had more than one sheet. And I'm sure that no man in the world but one knew that the loss of his particular sheet and of his particular life would be as nearly simultaneous as the government could make it.

So I tossed the sheet at Keyser, as if it were something I'd found blowing about the campus.

He stared at it and then looked at the back side, which was blank. His eyes moved down from the top to the bottom, then jumped back to the top.

"I don't know what this is about," he said, and the words seemed sour to his own taste.

I didn't say anything. Just folded the paper and shoved it back into the inside jacket pocket.

Keyser added petulantly: "It's a fallacy you laymen have that scientists can look at an equation and say, 'Ah, yes—' and go on to write a book about it. Mathematics has no existence of its own. It is merely an arbitrary code devised to describe physical observations or philosophical concepts. Every man can adapt it to his own particular needs. For instance no one can look at a symbol and be sure of what it means. So far, science has used every letter in the alphabet, large, small and italic, each symbolizing many different things. They have used bold-faced letters, Gothic-type letters, Greek letters, both capital and small, subscripts, superscripts, asterisks, even Hebrew letters. Different scientists use different symbols for the same concept and the same symbol for different concepts. So if you show a disconnected page like this to any man, without information as to the subject being investigated or the particular symbology used, he could absolutely not make sense out of it."

I interrupted: "But you said he was working on quadrupole moments. Does that make this sensible?" and I tapped the spot on my chest where the foolscap had been slowly scorching a hole in my jacket for two days.

"I can't tell. I saw none of the standard relationships that I'd expect to be involved. At least I recognized none. But I obviously can't commit myself."

There was a short silence, then he said: "I'll tell you. Why don't you check with his students?"

I lifted my eyebrows: "You mean in his classes?"

He seemed annoyed: "No, for Heaven's sake. His research students! His doctoral candidates! They've been working with him. They'll know the details of that work better than I, or anyone in the faculty, could possibly know it."

"It's an idea," I said, casually. It was, too. I don't know why, but I wouldn't have thought of it myself. I guess it's because it's only natural to think that any professor knows more than any student.

Keyser latched onto a lapel as I rose to leave. "And, besides," he said, "I think you're on the wrong track. This is in confidence, you understand, and I wouldn't say it except for the unusual circumstances, but Tywood is not thought of too highly in the profession. Oh, he's an adequate teacher, I'll admit, but his research papers have never commanded respect. There has always been a tendency towards vague theorizing, unsupported by experimental evidence. That paper of yours is probably more of it. No one could possibly want to . . . er, kidnap him because of it."

"Is that so? I see. Any ideas, yourself, as to why he's gone, or where he's gone?"

"Nothing concrete," he said pursing his lips, "but everyone knows he is a sick man. He had a stroke two years ago that kept him out of classes for a semester. He never did get well. His left side was paralyzed for a while and he still limps. Another stroke would kill him. It could come any time."

"You think he's dead, then?"

"It's not impossible."

"But where's the body, then?"

"Well, really— That is *your* job, I think."

It was, and I left.

I interviewed each one of Tywood's four research students in a volume of chaos called a research laboratory. These student research laboratories usually have two hopefuls working therein, said two constituting a floating population, since every year or so they are alternately replaced.

Consequently, the laboratory has its equipment stack in tiers. On the laboratory benches is the equipment immediately being used, and in three or four of the handiest drawers are replacements or supplements which are likely to be used. In the farther drawers, in the shelves reaching up to the ceiling, in odd corners, are fading remnants of the past student generations— oddments never used and never discarded. It is claimed, in fact, that no research student ever knew all the contents of his laboratory.

All four of Tywood's students were worried. But three were worried mainly by their own status. That is, by the possible effect the absence of Tywood might have on the status of their "problem." I dismissed those three—who all have their degrees now, I hope—and called back the fourth.

He had the most haggard look of all, and had been least communicative— which I considered a hopeful sign.

He now sat stiffly in the straight-backed chair at the right of the desk, while I leaned back in a creaky old swivel-chair and pushed my hat off my forehead. His name was Edwin Howe and *he* did get his degree later on; I know that for sure, because he's a big wheel in the Department of Science now.

I said: "You do the same work the other boys do, I suppose?"

"It's all nuclear work, in a way."

"But it's not all exactly the same?"

He shook his head slowly. "We take different angles. You have to have something clear-cut, you know, or you won't be able to publish. We've got to get our degrees."

He said it exactly the way you or I might say, "We've got to make a living." At that, maybe it's the same thing for them.

I said: "All right. What's *your* angle?"

He said: "I do the math. I mean, with Professor Tywood."

"What kind of math?"

And he smiled a little, getting the same sort of atmosphere about him that I had noticed in Professor Keyser's case that morning. A sort of, "Do-you-really-think-I-can-explain-all-my-profound-thoughts-to-stupid-little-you?" sort of atmosphere.

All he said aloud, however, was: "That would be rather complicated to explain."

"I'll help you," I said. "Is that anything like it?" And I tossed the foolscap sheet at him.

He didn't give it any once-over. He just snatched it up and let out a thin wail: "Where'd you get this?"

"From Tywood's safe."

"Do you have the rest of it, too?"

"It's safe," I hedged.

He relaxed a little—just a little: "You didn't show it to anybody, did you?"

"I showed it to Professor Keyser."

Howe made an impolite sound with his lower lip and front teeth, *"That* jackass. What did he say?"

I turned the palms of my hands upward and Howe laughed. Then he said, in an offhand manner: "Well, that's the sort of stuff I do."

"And what's it all about? Put it so I can understand it."

There was distinct hesitation. He said: "Now, look. This is confidential stuff. Even Pop's other students don't know anything about it. I don't even think *I* know *all* about it. This isn't just a degree I'm after, you know. It's Pop Tywood's Nobel Prize, and it's going to be an Assistant Professorship for me at Cal Tech. This has got to be published before it's talked about."

And I shook my head slowly and made my words very soft: "No, son. You have it twisted. You'll have to talk about it before it's published, because Tywood's gone and maybe he's dead and maybe he isn't. And if he's dead, maybe he's murdered. And when the department has a suspicion of murder, everybody talks. Now, it will look bad for you, kid, if you try to keep some secrets."

It worked. I knew it would, because everyone reads murder mysteries and knows all the clichés. He jumped out of his chair and rattled the words off as if he had a script in front of him.

"Surely," he said, "you can't suspect *me* of . . . of anything like that. Why . . . why, my career—"

I shoved him back into his chair with the beginnings of a sweat on his forehead. I went into the next line: "I don't suspect anybody of anything *yet*. And you won't be in any trouble, if you talk, chum."

He was ready to talk. "Now this is all in strict confidence."

Poor guy. He didn't know the meaning of the word "strict." He was never out of eyeshot of an operator from that moment till the government decided to bury the whole case with the one final comment of "?" Quote. Unquote. (I'm not kidding. To this day, the case is neither opened nor closed. It's just "?")

He said, dubiously, "You know what time travel is, I suppose?"

Sure I knew what time travel was. My oldest kid is twelve and he listens to the afternoon video programs till he swells up visibly with the junk he absorbs at the ears and eyes.

"What about time travel?" I said.

"In a sense, we can do it. Actually, it's only what you might cal micro-temporal-translation—"

I almost lost my temper. In fact, I think I did. It seemed obvious that the squirt was trying to diddle me; and without subtlety. I'm used to having people think I look dumb; but not *that* dumb.

I said through the back of my throat: "Are you going to tell me that Tywood is out somewhere in time—like Ace Rogers, the Lone Time Ranger?" (That was Junior's favorite program—Ace Rogers was stopping Genghis Khan single-handed that week.)

But he looked as disgusted as I must have. "No," he yelled. "I don't know where Pop is. If you'd *listen* to me—I said micro-temporal-translation. Now, this isn't a video show and it isn't magic; this happens to be science. For instance, you know about matter-energy equivalence, I suppose."

I nodded sourly. Everyone knows about that since Hiroshima in the last war but one.

"All right, then," he went on, "that's good for a start. Now, if you take a brown mass of matter and apply temporal translation to it—you know, send it back in time—you are, in effect, creating matter at the point in time to which you are sending it. To do that, you must use an amount of energy equivalent to the amount of matter you have created. In other words, to send a gram—or, say, an ounce—of anything back in time, you have to dis-integrate an ounce of matter completely, to furnish the energy required."

"Hm-m-m," I said, "that's to create the ounce of matter in the past. But aren't you destroying an ounce of matter by removing it from the present? Doesn't that *create* the equivalent amount of energy?"

And he looked just about as annoyed as a fellow sitting on a bumblebee that wasn't quite dead. Apparently laymen are never supposed to question scientists.

He said: "I was trying to simplify it so you would understand it. Actually, it's more complicated. It would be very nice if we could use the energy of disappearance to cause it to appear, but that would be working in a circle, believe me. The requirements of entropy would forbid it. To put it more rigorously, the energy is required to overcome temporal inertia and it just works out so that the energy in ergs required to send back a mass, in grams, is equal to that mass times the square of the speed of light in centimeters per second. Which just happens to be the Einstein Mass-Energy Equivalence Equation. I can give you the mathematics, you know."

"I know," I waxed some of that misplaced eagerness back. "But was all this worked out experimentally? Or is it just on paper?"

Obviously, the thing was to keep him talking.

He had that queer light in his eye that every research student gets, I am told, when he is asked to discuss his problem. He'll discuss it with anyone, even with a "dumb flatfoot"—which was convenient at the moment.

"You see," he said like a man slipping you the inside dope on a shady business deal, "what started the whole thing was this neutrino business. They've been trying to find that neutrino since the late thirties and they haven't succeeded. It's a subatomic particle which has no charge and has a mass much less than even an electron. Naturally, it's next to impossible to spot, and hasn't been spotted yet. But they keep looking because, without assuming that a neutrino exists, the energetics of some nuclear reactions can't be balanced. So Pop Tywood got the idea about twenty years ago that some energy was disappearing, in the form of matter, back into time. We got working on that—or he did—and I'm the first student he's ever had tackle it along with him.

"Obviously, we had to work with tiny amounts of material and . . . well, it was just a stroke of genius on Pop's part to think of using traces of artificial radioactive isotopes. You could work with just a few micrograms of it, you know, by following its activity with counters. The variation of activity with time should follow a very definite and simple law which has never been altered by any laboratory condition known.

"Well, we'd send a speck back fifteen minutes, say, and fifteen minutes before we did that—everything was arranged automatically, you see—the count jumped to nearly double what it should be, fell off normally, and then dropped sharply at the moment it was sent back below where it would have been normally. The material overlapped itself in time, you see, and for fifteen minutes we counted the doubled material—"

I interrupted: "You mean you had the same atoms existing in two places at the same time."

"Yes," he said, with mild surprise, "why not? That's why we use so much energy—the equivalent of creating those atoms." And then he rushed on, "Now I'll tell you what my particular job is. If you send back the material fifteen minutes, it is apparently sent back to the same spot relative to the Earth despite the fact that in fifteen minutes, the Earth moved sixteen thousand miles around the Sun, and the Sun itself moves more thousand miles and so on. But there are certain tiny discrepancies which I've analyzed and which turn out to be due, possibly, to two causes.

"First, there is a frictional effect—if you can use such a term—so that matter does drift a little with respect to the Earth, depending on how far back in time it is sent, and on the nature of material. Then, too, some of the discrepancy can only be explained by the assumption that passage through time itself takes time."

"How's that?" I said.

"What I mean is that some of the radioactivity is evenly spread throughout the time of translation as if the material tested had been reacting during backward passage through time by a constant amount. My figures show that —well, if you were to be moved backward in time, you would age one day for every hundred years. Or, to put it another way, if you could watch a time dial which recorded the time outside a 'time-machine,' your watch would move forward twenty-four hours while the time dial moved back a hundred years. That's a universal constant, I think, because the speed of light is a universal constant. Anyway, that's my work."

After a few minutes, in which I chewed all this, I asked: "Where did you get the energy needed for your experiments?"

"They ran out a special line from the power plant. Pop's a big shot there, and swung the deal."

"Hm-m-m. What was the heaviest amount of material you sent into the past?"

"Oh"—he sent his eyes upwards—"I think we shot back one hundredth of a milligram once. That's ten micrograms."

"Ever try sending anything into the future?"

"That won't work," he put in quickly. "Impossible. You can't change signs like that, because the energy required becomes more than infinite. It's a one-way proposition."

I looked hard at my fingernails: "How much material could you send back in time if you fissioned about . . . oh, say, one hundred pounds of plutonium." Things, I thought, were becoming, if anything, too obvious.

The answer came quickly: "In plutonium fission," he said, "not more than one or two percent of the mass is converted into energy. Therefore, one hundred pounds of plutonium when completely used up would send a pound or two back into time."

"Is that all? But could you handle all that energy? I mean, a hundred pounds of plutonium can make quite an explosion."

"All relative," he said, a bit pompously. "If you took all that energy and let it loose a little at a time, you could handle it. If you released it all at once, but used it just as fast as you released it, you could still handle it. In sending back material through time, energy can be used much faster than it can possibly be released even through fission. Theoretically, anyway."

"But how do you get rid of it?"

"It's spread through time, naturally. Of course, the minimum time through which material could be transferred would, therefore, depend on the mass of the material. Otherwise, you're liable to have the energy density with time too high."

"All right, kid," I said. "I'm calling up headquarters, and they'll send a man here to take you home. You'll stay there a while."

"But— What for?"

"It won't be for long."

It wasn't—and it was made up to him afterwards.

I spent the evening at Headquarters. We had a library there—a very special kind of library. The very morning after the explosion, two or three operators had drifted quietly into the chemistry and physics libraries of the University. Experts in their way. They located every article Tywood had ever published in any scientific journal and had snapped each page. Nothing was disturbed otherwise.

Other men went through magazine files and through book lists. It ended with a room at Headquarters that represented a complete Tywoodana. Nor was there a definite purpose in doing this. It merely represented part of the thoroughness with which a problem of this sort is met.

I went through that library. Not the scientific papers. I knew there'd be nothing there that I wanted. But he had written a series of articles for a magazine twenty years back, and I read those. And I grabbed at every piece of private correspondence they had available.

After that, I just sat and thought—and got scared.

I got to bed about four in the morning and had nightmares.

But I was in the Boss' private office at nine in the morning just the same.

He's a big man, the Boss, with iron-gray hair slicked down tight. He doesn't smoke, but he keeps a box of cigars on his desk and when he doesn't want to say anything for a few seconds, he picks one up, rolls it about a little, smells it, then sticks it right into the middle of his mouth and lights it in a very careful way. By that time, he either has something to say or doesn't have to say anything at all. Then he puts the cigar down and lets it burn to death.

He used up a box in about three weeks, and every Christmas, half his gift-wraps held boxes of cigars.

He wasn't reaching for any cigars now, though. He just folded his big fists together on the desk and looked up at me from under a creased forehead. "What's boiling?"

I told him. Slowly, because micro-temporal-translation doesn't sit well with anybody, especially when you call it time travel, which I did. It's a sign of how serious things were that he only asked me once if I were crazy.

Then I was finished and we stared at each other.

He said: "And you think he tried to send something back in time—something weighing a pound or two—and blew an entire plant doing it?"

"It fits in," I said.

I let him go for a while. He was thinking and I wanted him to keep on thinking. I wanted him, if possible, to think of the same thing I was thinking, so that I wouldn't have to tell him—

Because I hated to have to tell him—

Because it was nuts, for one thing. And too horrible, for another.

So I kept quiet and he kept on thinking and every once in a while some of his thoughts came to the surface.

After a while, he said: "Assuming the student, Howe, to have told the truth—and you'd better check his notebooks, by the way, which I hope you've impounded—"

"The entire wing of that floor is out of bounds, sir. Edwards has the notebooks."

He went on: "All right. Assuming he told us all the truth he knows, why did Tywood jump from less than a milligram to a pound?"

His eyes came down and they were hard: "Now you're concentrating on the time-travel angle. To you, I gather, that is the crucial point, with the energy involved as incidental—purely incidental."

"Yes, sir," I said grimly. "I think exactly that."

"Have you considered that you might be wrong? That you might have matters inverted?"

"I don't quite get that."

"Well, look. You say you've read up on Tywood. All right. He was one of that bunch of scientists after World War II that fought the atom bomb; wanted a world state— You know about that, don't you?"

I nodded.

"He had a guilt complex," the Boss said with energy. "He'd helped work out the bomb, and he couldn't sleep nights thinking of what he'd done. He lived with that fear for years. And even though the bomb wasn't used in World War III, can you imagine what every day of uncertainty must have meant to him? Can you imagine the shriveling horror in his soul as he waited for others to make the decision at every crucial moment till the final Compromise of Sixty-Five?

"We have a complete psychiatric analysis of Tywood and several others just like him, taken during the last war. Did you know that?"

"No, sir."

"It's true. We let up after Sixty-Five, of course, because with the establishment of world control of atomic power, the scrapping of the atomic bomb stockpile in all countries, and the establishment of research liaison among the various spheres of influence on the planet, most of the ethical conflict in the scientific mind was removed.

"But the findings at the time were serious. In 1964, Tywood had a morbid subconscious hatred for the very concept of atomic power. He began to make mistakes, serious ones. Eventually, we were forced to take him off research of any kind. And several others as well, even though things were pretty bad at the time. We had just lost India, if you remember."

Considering that I was in India at the time, I remembered. But I still wasn't seeing his point.

"Now, what," he continued, "if dregs of that attitude remained buried in Tywood to the very end? Don't you see that this time-travel is a double-edged sword? Why throw a pound of anything into the past, anyway? For the sake of proving a point? He had proved his case just as much when he sent back a fraction of a milligram. That was good enough for the Nobel Prize, I suppose.

"But there was *one* thing he could do with a pound of matter that he couldn't do with a milligram, and that was *to drain a power plant*. So that was what he must have been after. He had discovered a way of consuming inconceivable quantities of energy. By sending back eighty pounds of dirt, he could remove all the existing plutonium in the world. End atomic power for an indefinite period."

I was completely unimpressed, but I tried not to make that too plain. I just said: "Do you think he could possibly have thought he could get away with it more than once?"

"This is all based on the fact that he wasn't a normal man. How do I know what he could imagine he could do? Besides, there may be men behind him —with less science and more brains—who are quite ready to continue onwards from this point."

"Have any of these men been found yet? Any evidence of such men?"

A little wait, and his hand reached for the cigar box. He stared at the cigar and turned it end for end. Just a little wait more. I was patient.

Then he put it down decisively without lighting it.

"No," he said.

He looked at me, and clear through me, and said: "Then, you still don't go for that?"

I shrugged, "Well— It doesn't sound right."

"Do you have a notion of your own?"

"Yes. But I can't bring myself to talk about it. If I'm wrong, I'm the wrongest man that ever was; but if I'm right, I'm the rightest."

"I'll listen," he said, and he put his hand under the desk.

That was the pay-off. The room was armored, sound-proof, and radiation-proof to anything short of a nuclear explosion. And with that little signal showing on his secretary's desk, the President of the United States couldn't have interrupted us.

I leaned back and said: "Chief, do you happen to remember how you met your wife? Was it a little thing?"

He must have thought it a *non sequitur.* What else could he have thought? But he was giving me my head now; having his own reasons, I suppose.

He just smiled and said: "I sneezed and she turned around. It was at a street corner."

"What made you be on that street corner just then? What made her be? Do you remember just why you sneezed? Where you caught the cold? Or where the speck of dust came from? Imagine how many factors had to intersect in just the right place at just the right time for you to meet your wife."

"I suppose we would have met some other time, if not then?"

"But you can't *know* that. How do you know whom you *didn't* meet, because once when you might have turned around, you didn't; because once when you might have been late, you weren't. Your life forks at every instant, and you go down one of the forks almost at random, and so does everyone else. Start twenty years ago, and the forks diverge further and further with time.

"You sneezed, and met a girl, and not another. As a consequence, you made certain decisions, and so did the girl, and so did the girl you didn't meet, and the man who did meet her, and the people you all met thereafter. And your family, her family, their family—and your children.

"Because you sneezed twenty years ago, five people, or fifty, or five hundred, might be dead now who would have been alive, or might be alive who would have been dead. Move it two hundred years ago: two thousand years ago, and a sneeze—even by someone no history ever heard of—might have meant that no one now alive would have been alive."

The Boss rubbed the back of his head: "Widening ripples. I read a story once—"

"So did I. It's not a new idea—but I want you to think about it for a while, because I want to read to you from an article by Professor Elmer Tywood in a magazine twenty years old. It was just before the last war."

I had copies of the film in my pocket and the white wall made a beautiful screen, which was what it was meant to do. The Boss made a motion to turn about, but I waved him back.

"No, sir," I said. "I want to read this to you. And I want you to listen to it."

He leaned back.

"The article," I went on, "is entitled: 'Man's First Great Failure!' Remember, this was just before the war, when the bitter disappointment at the final failure of the United Nations was at its height. What I will read are some excerpts from the first part of the article. It goes like this:

" ' . . . That Man, with his technical perfection, has failed to solve the great sociological problems of today is only the second immense tragedy that has come to the race. The first, and perhaps the greater, was that, once, these same great sociological problems *were* solved; and yet these solutions were not permanent, because the technical perfection we have today did not then exist.

" 'It was a case of having bread without butter, or butter without bread. Never both together. . . .

" 'Consider the Hellenic world, from which our philosophy, our mathematics, our ethics, our art, our literature—our entire culture, in fact—stem . . . In the days of Pericles, Greece, like our own world in microcosm, was a surprisingly modern potpourri of conflicting ideologies and ways of life. But then Rome came, adopting the culture, but bestowing, and enforcing, peace. To be sure, the *Pax Romana* lasted only two hundred years, but no like period has existed since. . . .

" 'War was abolished. Nationalism did not exist. The Roman citizen was Empire-wide. Paul of Tarsus and Flavius Josephus were Roman citizens. Spaniards, North Africans, Illyrians assumed the purple. Slavery existed, but it was an indiscriminate slavery, imposed as a punishment, incurred as the price of economic failure, brought on by the fortunes of war. No man was a *natural* slave—because of the color of his skin or the place of his birth.

" 'Religious toleration was complete. If an exception was made early in the case of the Christians, it was because they refused to accept the principle of toleration; because they insisted that only they themselves knew truth—a principle abhorrent to the civilized Roman. . . .

" 'With all of Western culture under a single *polis*, with the cancer of religious and national particularism and exclusivism absent; with a high civilization in existence—why could not Man hold his gains?

" 'It was because, technologically, ancient Hellenism remained backward. It was because without a machine civilization, the price of leisure—and hence civilization and culture—for the few, was slavery for the many. Because the civilization could not find the means to bring comfort and ease to *all* the population.

" 'Therefore, the depressed classes turned to the other world, and to religions which spurned the material benefits of this world—so that science was made impossible in any true sense for over a millennium. And further, as the initial impetus of Hellenism waned, the Empire lacked the technological powers to beat back the barbarians. In fact, it was not till after 1500 A.D. that war became sufficiently a function of the industrial resources of a nation to enable the settled people to defeat invading tribesmen and nomads with ease. . . .

" 'Imagine, then, if somehow the ancient Greeks had learned just a hint of modern chemistry and physics. Imagine if the growth of the Empire had been accompanied by the growth of science, technology and industry. Imagine an Empire in which machinery replaced slaves, in which all men had a decent share of the world's goods, in which the legion became the armored column against which no barbarians could stand. Imagine an Empire which would therefore spread all over the world, *without* religious or national prejudices.

" 'An Empire of all men—all brothers—eventually all free. . . .

" 'If history could be changed. If that first great failure could have been prevented—' "

And I stopped at that point.

"Well?" said the Boss.

"Well," I said, "I think it isn't difficult to connect all that with the fact that Tywood blew an entire power plant in his anxiety to send something back to the past, while in his office safe we found sections of a chemistry textbook translated into Greek."

His face changed, while he considered.

Then he said heavily: "But nothing's happened."

"I know. But then I've been told by Tywood's student that it takes a day to move back a century in time. Assuming that ancient Greece was the target area, we have twenty centuries, hence twenty days."

"But can it be stopped?"

"*I* wouldn't know. Tywood might, but he's dead."

The enormity of it all hit me at once, deeper than it had the night before—

All humanity was virtually under sentence of death. And while that was merely horrible abstraction, the fact that reduced it to a thoroughly unbearable reality was that I was, too. And my wife, and my kid.

Further, it was a death without precedence. A ceasing to exist, and no more. The passing of a breath. The vanishing of a dream. The drift into eternal non-space and non-time of a shadow. I would not be dead at all, in fact. I would merely never have been born.

Or would I? Would I exist—my individuality—my ego—my soul, if you like? Another life? Other circumstances?

I thought none of that in words then. But if a cold knot in the stomach could ever speak under the circumstances, it would sound like that, I think.

The Boss moved in on my thoughts—hard.

"Then, we have about two and a half weeks. No time to lose. Come on."

I grinned with one side of my mouth: "What do we do? Chase the book?"

"No," he replied coldly, "but there are two courses of action we must follow. First, you may be wrong—altogether. All of this circumstantial reasoning may still represent a false lead, perhaps deliberately thrown before us, to cover up the real truth. That must be checked.

"Secondly, you may be right—but there may be some way of stopping the book: other than chasing it in a time machine, I mean. If so, we must find out how."

"I would just like to say, sir, if this is a false lead, only a madman would consider it a believable one. So suppose I'm right, and suppose there's no way of stopping it?"

"Then, young fellow, I'm going to keep pretty busy for two and a half weeks, and I'd advise you to do the same. The time will pass more quickly that way."

Of course he was right.

"Where do we start?" I asked.

"The first thing we need is a list of all men and women on the government payroll under Tywood."

"Why?"

"Reasoning. Your specialty, you know. Tywood doesn't know Greek, I think we can assume with fair safety, so someone else must have done the translating. It isn't likely that anyone would do a job like that for nothing, and it isn't likely that Tywood would pay out of his personal funds—not on a professor's salary."

"He might," I pointed out, "have been interested in more secrecy than a government payroll affords."

"Why? Where was the danger? Is it a crime to translate a chemistry textbook into Greek? Who would ever deduce from that a plot such as you've described?"

It took us half an hour to turn up the name of Mycroft James Boulder, listed as "Consultant," and to find out that he was mentioned in the University Catalogue as Assistant Professor of Philosophy and to check by telephone that among his many accomplishments was a thorough knowledge of Attic Greek.

Which was a coincidence—because with the Boss reaching for his hat, the interoffice teletype clicked away and it turned out that Mycroft James Boulder was in the anteroom, at the end of a two-hour continuing insistence that he see the Boss.

The Boss put his hat back and opened his office door.

Professor Mycroft James Boulder was a gray man. His hair was gray and his eyes were gray. His suit was gray, too.

But most of all, his expression was gray; gray with a tension that seemed to twist at the lines in his thin face.

Boulder said, softly: "I've been trying for three days to get a hearing, sir, with a responsible man. I can get no higher than yourself."

"I may be high enough," said the Boss. "What's on your mind?"

"It is quite important that I be granted an interview with Professor Tywood."

"Do you know where he is?"

"I am quite certain that he is in government custody."

"Why?"

"Because I know that he was planning an experiment which would entail the breaking of security regulations. Events since, as nearly as I can make them out, flow naturally from the supposition that security regulations have indeed been broken. I can presume, then, that the experiment has at least been attempted. I must discover whether it has been successfully concluded."

"Professor Boulder," said the Boss, "I believe you can read Greek."

"Yes, I can,"—coolly.

"And have translated chemical texts for Professor Tywood on government money."

"Yes—as a legally employed consultant."

"Yet such translation, under the circumstances, constitutes a crime, since it makes you an accessory to Tywood's crime."

"You can establish a connection?"

"Can't you? Or haven't you heard of Tywood's notions on time travel, or . . . what do you call it . . . micro-temporal-translation?"

"Ah?" and Boulder smiled a little. "He's told you, then."

"No, he hasn't," said the Boss, harshly. "Professor Tywood is dead."

"What?" Then—"I don't believe you."

"He died of apoplexy. Look at this."

He had one of the photographs taken that first night in his wall safe. Tywood's face was distorted but recognizable—sprawled and dead.

Boulder's breath went in and out as if the gears were clogged. He stared at the picture for three full minutes by the electric clock on the wall. "Where is this place?" he asked.

"The Atomic Power Plant."

"Had he finished his experiment?"

The Boss shrugged: "There's no way of telling. He was dead when we found him."

Boulder's lips were pinched and colorless. "That must be determined, somehow. A commission of scientists must be established, and, if necessary, the experiment must be repeated—"

But the Boss just looked at him, and reached for a cigar. I've never seen him take longer—and when he put it down, curled in its unused smoke, he said: "Tywood wrote an article for a magazine, twenty years ago—"

"Oh," and the professor's lips twisted, "is *that* what gave you your clue? You may ignore that. The man is only a physical scientist and knows nothing of either history or sociology. A schoolboy's dreams and nothing more."

"Then, you don't think sending your translation back will inaugurate a Golden Age, do you?"

"Of course not. Do you think you can graft the developments of two thousand years of slow labor onto a child society not ready for it? Do you think a great invention or a great scientific principle is born full-grown in the mind of a genius divorced from his cultural *milieu?* Newton's enunciation of the Law of Gravity was delayed for twenty years because the then-current figure for the Earth's diameter was wrong by ten percent. Archimedes almost discovered calculus, but failed because Arabic numerals, invented by some nameless Hindu or group of Hindus, were unknown to him.

"For that matter, the mere existence of a slave society in ancient Greece and Rome meant that machines could scarcely attract much attention— slaves being so much cheaper and more adaptable. And men of true intellect could scarcely be expected to spend their energies on devices intended for manual labor. Even Archimedes, the greatest engineer of antiquity, refused to publish any of his practical inventions—only mathematic abstractions. And when a young man asked Plato of what use geometry was, he was forthwith expelled from the Academy as a man with a mean, unphilosophic soul.

"Science does not plunge forward—it inches along in the directions permitted by the greater forces that mold society and which are in turn molded by society. And no great man advances but on the shoulders of the society that surrounds him—"

The Boss interrupted him at that point. "Suppose you tell us what your part in Tywood's work was, then. We'll take your word for it that history cannot be changed."

"Oh it can, but not purposefully— You see, when Tywood first requested my services in the matter of translating certain textbook passages into Greek, I agreed for the money involved. But he wanted the translation on parchment; he insisted on the use of ancient Greek terminology—the language of Plato, to use his words—regardless of how I had to twist the literal significance of passages, and he wanted it hand-written in rolls.

"I was curious. I, too, found his magazine article. It was difficult for me to jump to the obvious conclusion, since the achievements of modern science transcend the imaginings of philosophy in so many ways. But I learned the truth eventually, and it was at once obvious that Tywood's theory of changing history was infantile. There are twenty million variables for every instant of time, and no system of mathematics—no mathematic psychohistory, to coin a phrase—has yet been developed to handle that ocean of varying functions.

"In short, any variation of events two thousand years ago would change all subsequent history, but in *no predictable way.*"

The Boss suggested, with a false quietness: "Like the pebble that starts the avalanche, right?"

"Exactly. You have some understanding of the situation, I see. I thought deeply for weeks before I proceeded, and then I realized how I must act— *must* act."

There was a low roar. The Boss stood up and his chair went over backward. He swung around his desk, and he had a hand on Boulder's throat. I was stepping out to stop him, but he waved me back—

He was only tightening the necktie a little. Boulder could still breathe. He had gone very white, and for all the time that the Boss talked, he restricted himself to just that—breathing.

And the Boss said: "Sure, I can see how you decided you must act. I know that some of you brain-sick philosophers think the world needs fixing. You want to throw the dice again and see what turns up. Maybe you don't even care if you're alive in the new setup—or that no one can possibly know what you've done. But you're going to create, just the same. You're going to give God another chance, so to speak.

"Maybe I just want to live—but the world could be worse. In twenty million different ways, it could be worse. A fellow named Wilder once wrote a play called *The Skin of Our Teeth.* Maybe you've read it. Its thesis was that Mankind survived by just that skin of their teeth. No, I'm not going to give you a speech about the Ice Age nearly wiping us out. I don't know enough. I'm not even going to talk about the Greeks winning at Marathon; the Arabs being defeated at Tours; the Mongols turning back at the last minute without even being defeated—because I'm no historian.

"But take the Twentieth Century. The Germans were stopped at the Marne twice in World War I. Dunkirk happened in World War II, and somehow the Germans were stopped at Moscow and Stalingrad. We could have used the atom bomb in the last war and we didn't, and just when it looked as if both sides would have to, the Great Compromise happened—just because General Bruce was delayed in taking off from the Ceylon airfield long enough to receive the message directly. One after the other, just like that, all through history—lucky breaks. For every 'if' that didn't come true that would have made wonder-men of all of us if it had, there were twenty 'ifs' that didn't come true that would have brought disaster to all of us if they had.

"You're gambling on that one-in-twenty chance—gambling every life on Earth. And you've succeeded, too, because Tywood *did* send that text back."

He ground out that last sentence, and opened his fist, so that Boulder could fall out and back into his chair.

And Boulder laughed.

"You fool," he gasped, bitterly. "How close you can be and yet how widely you can miss the mark. Tywood *did* send his book back, then? You are sure of that?"

"No chemical textbook in Greek was found on the scene," said the Boss, grimly, "and millions of calories of energy had disappeared. Which doesn't change the fact, however, that we have two and a half weeks in which to—make things interesting for you."

"Oh, nonsense. No foolish dramatics, please. Just listen to me, and try to understand. There were Greek philosophers once, named Leucippus and Democritus, who evolved an atomic theory. All matter, they said, was composed of atoms. Varieties of atoms were distinct and changeless and by their different combinations with each other formed the various substances found in nature. That theory was not the result of experiment or observation. It came into being, somehow, full-grown.

"The didactic Roman poet Lucretius, in his *'De Rerum Natura,'*—'On the Nature of Things'—elaborated on that theory and throughout manages to sound startlingly modern.

"In Hellenistic times, Hero built a steam engine and weapons of war became almost mechanized. The period has been referred to as an abortive mechanical age, which came to nothing because, somehow, it neither grew out of nor fitted into its social and economic *milieu*. Alexandrian science was a queer and rather inexplicable phenomenon.

"Then one might mention the old Roman legend about the books of the Sibyl that contained mysterious information direct from the gods—

"In other words, gentlemen, while you are right that any change in the course of past events, however trifling, would have incalculable consequences, and while I also believe that you are right in supposing that any random change is much more likely to be for the worse than for the better, I must point out that you are nevertheless wrong in your final conclusions.

"Because THIS *is the world in which the Greek chemistry text* WAS *sent back.*

"This has been a Red Queen's race, if you remember your 'Through the Looking Glass.' In the Red Queen's country, one had to run as fast as one could merely to stay in the same place. And so it was in this case! Tywood may have thought he was creating a new world, but it was I who prepared the translations, and I took care that only such passages as would account for the queer scraps of knowledge the ancients apparently got from nowhere would be included.

"And my only intention, for all my racing, was to stay in the same place."

Three weeks passed; three months; three years. Nothing happened. When nothing happens, you have no proof. We gave up trying to explain, and we ended, the Boss and I, by doubting it ourselves.

The case never ended. Boulder could not be considered a criminal without being considered a world savior as well, and vice versa. He was ignored. And in the end, the case was neither solved, nor closed out; merely put in a file all by itself, under the designation "?" and buried in the deepest vault in Washington.

The Boss is in Washington now; a big wheel. And I'm Regional Head of the Bureau.

Boulder is still assistant professor, though. Promotions are slow at the University.

Day of the
Hunters

It began the same night it ended. It wasn't much. It just bothered me; it still bothers me.

You see, Joe Bloch, Ray Manning, and I were squatting around our favorite table in the corner bar with an evening on our hands and a mess of chatter to throw it away with. That's the beginning.

Joe Bloch started it by talking about the atomic bomb, and what he thought ought to be done with it, and how who would have thought it five years ago. And I said lots of guys thought it five years ago and wrote stories about it and it was going to be tough on them trying to keep ahead of the newspapers now. Which led to a general palaver on how lots of screwy things might come true and a lot of for-instances were thrown about.

Ray said he heard from somebody that some big-shot scientist had sent a block of lead back in time for about two seconds or two minutes or two thousandths of a second—he didn't know which. He said the scientist wasn't saying anything to anybody because he didn't think anyone would believe him.

So I asked, pretty sarcastic, how *he* came to know about it. —Ray may have lots of friends but I have the same lot and none of them know any big-shot scientists. But he said never mind how he heard, take it or leave it.

And then there wasn't anything to do but talk about time machines, and how supposing you went back and killed your own grandfather or why didn't somebody from the future come back and tell us who was going to win the next war, or if there was going to be a next war, or if there'd be anywhere on Earth you could live after it, regardless of who wins.

Ray thought just knowing the winner in the seventh race while the sixth was being run would be something.

But Joe decided different. He said, "The trouble with you guys is you got wars and races on the mind. Me, I got curiosity. Know what I'd do if I had a time machine?"

So right away we wanted to know, all ready to give him the old snicker whatever it was.

He said, "If I had one, I'd go back in time about a couple or five or fifty million years and find out what happened to the dinosaurs."

Which was too bad for Joe, because Ray and I both thought there was just about no sense to that at all. Ray said who cared about a lot of dinosaurs and I said the only thing they were good for was to make a mess of skeletons for guys who were dopy enough to wear out the floors in museums; and it was a good thing they did get out of the way to make room for human beings. Of course Joe said that with *some* human beings he knew, and he gives us a hard look, we should've stuck to dinosaurs, but we pay no attention to that.

"You dumb squirts can laugh and make like you know something, but that's because you don't ever have any imagination," he says. "Those dinosaurs were big stuff. Millions of all kinds—big as houses, and dumb as houses, too—all over the place. And then, all of a sudden, like that," and he snaps his fingers, "there aren't any anymore."

How come, we wanted to know.

But he was just finishing a beer and waving at Charlie for another with a coin to prove he wanted to pay for it and he just shrugged his shoulders. "I don't know. That's what I'd find out, though."

That's all. That would have finished it. I would've said something and Ray would've made a crack, and we all would've had another beer and maybe swapped some talk about the weather and the Brooklyn Dodgers and then said so long, and never think of dinosaurs again.

Only we didn't, and now I never have anything on my mind but dinosaurs, and I feel sick.

Because the rummy at the next table looks up and hollers, "Hey!"

We hadn't seen him. As a general rule, we don't go around looking at rummies we don't know in bars. I got plenty to do keeping track of the rummies I do know. This fellow had a bottle before him that was half empty, and a glass in his hand that was half full.

He said, "Hey," and we all looked at him, and Ray said, "Ask him what he wants, Joe."

Joe was nearest. He tipped his chair backward and said, "What do you want?"

The rummy said, "Did I hear you gentlemen mention dinosaurs?"

He was just a little weavy, and his eyes looked like they were bleeding, and you could only tell his shirt was once white by guessing, but it must've been the way he talked. It didn't *sound* rummy, if you know what I mean.

Anyway, Joe sort of eased up and said, "Sure. Something you want to know?"

He sort of smiled at us. It was a funny smile; it started at the mouth and ended just before it touched the eyes. He said, "Did you want to build a time machine and go back to find out what happened to the dinosaurs?"

I could see Joe was figuring that some kind of confidence game was coming up. I was figuring the same thing. Joe said, "Why? You aiming to offer to build one for me?"

The rummy showed a mess of teeth and said, "No, sir. I could but I won't. You know why? Because I built a time machine for myself a couple of years ago and went back to the Mesozoic Era and found out what happened to the dinosaurs."

Later on, I looked up how to spell "Mesozoic," which is why I got it right, in case you're wondering, and I found out that the Mesozoic Era is when all the dinosaurs were doing whatever dinosaurs do. But of course at the time this is just so much double-talk to me, and mostly I was thinking we had a lunatic talking to us. Joe claimed afterward that he knew about this Mesozoic thing, but he'll have to talk lots longer and louder before Ray and I believe him.

But that did it just the same. We said to the rummy to come over to our table. I guess I figured we could listen to him for a while and maybe get some of the bottle, and the others must have figured the same. But he held his bottle tight in his right hand when he sat down and that's where he kept it.

Ray said, "Where'd you build a time machine?"

"At Midwestern University. My daughter and I worked on it together."

He sounded like a college guy at that.

I said, "Where is it now? In your pocket?"

He didn't blink; he never jumped at us no matter how wise we cracked. Just kept talking to himself out loud, as if the whiskey had limbered up his tongue and he didn't care if we stayed or not.

He said, "I broke it up. Didn't want it. Had enough of it."

We didn't believe him. We didn't believe him worth a darn. You better get that straight. It stands to reason, because if a guy invented a time machine, he could clean up millions—he could clean up all the money in the world, just knowing what would happen to the stock market and the races and elections. He wouldn't throw all that away, I don't care what reasons he had. —Besides, none of us were going to believe in time travel anyway, because what if you *did* kill your own grandfather.

Well, never mind.

Joe said, "Yeah, you broke it up. Sure you did. What's your name?"

But he didn't answer that one, ever. We asked him a few more times, and then we ended up calling him "Professor."

He finished off his glass and filled it again very slow. He didn't offer us any, and we all sucked at our beers.

So I said, "Well, go ahead. What happened to the dinosaurs?"

But he didn't tell us right away. He stared right at the middle of the table and talked to it.

"I don't know how many times Carol sent me back—just a few minutes or hours—before I made the big jump. I didn't care about the dinosaurs; I just wanted to see how far the machine would take me on the supply of power I had available. I suppose it was dangerous, but is life so wonderful? The war was on them— One more life?"

He sort of coddled his glass as if he was thinking about things in general, then he seemed to skip a part in his mind and keep right on going.

"It was sunny," he said, "sunny and bright; dry and hard. There were no swamps, no ferns. None of the accoutrements of the Cretaceous we associate with dinosaurs,"—anyway, I think that's what he said. I didn't always catch the big words, so later on I'll just stick in what I can remember. I checked all the spellings, and I must say that for all the liquor he put away, he pronounced them without stutters.

That's maybe what bothered us. He sounded so familiar with everything, and it all just rolled off his tongue like nothing.

He went on, "It was a late age, certainly the Cretaceous. The dinosaurs were already on the way out—all except those little ones, with their metal belts and their guns."

I guess Joe practically dropped his nose into the beer altogether. He skidded halfway around the glass, when the professor let loose that statement sort of sadlike.

Joe sounded mad. "*What* little ones, with whose metal belts and which guns?"

The professor looked at him for just a second and then let his eyes slide back to nowhere. "They were little reptiles, standing four feet high. They stood on their hind legs with a thick tail behind, and they had little forearms with fingers. Around their waists were strapped wide metal belts, and from these hung guns. —And they weren't guns that shot pellets either; they were energy projectors."

"They were what?" I asked. "Say, when was this? Millions of years ago?"

"That's right," he said. "They were reptiles. They had scales and no eyelids and they probably laid eggs. But they used energy guns. There were five of them. They were on me as soon as I got out of the machine. There must have been millions of them all over Earth—millions. Scattered all over. They must have been the Lords of Creation then."

. . . .

I guess it was then that Ray thought he had him, because he developed that wise look in his eyes that makes you feel like conking him with an empty beer mug, because a full one would waste beer. He said, "Look, P'fessor, millions of them, huh? Aren't there guys who don't do anything but find old bones and mess around with them till they figure out what some dinosaur looked like. The museums are full of these here skeletons, aren't they? Well, where's there one with a metal belt on him. If there were millions, what's become of them? Where are the bones?"

The professor sighed. It was a real, sad sigh. Maybe he realized for the first time he was just speaking to three guys in overalls in a barroom. Or maybe he didn't care.

He said, "You don't find many fossils. Think how many animals lived on Earth altogether. Think how many billions and trillions. And then think how few fossils we find. —And these lizards were intelligent. Remember that. They're not going to get caught in snow drifts or mud, or fall into lava, except by big accident. Think how few fossil men there are—even of these subintelligent apemen of a million years ago."

He looked at his half-full glass and turned it round and round.

He said, "What would fossils show anyway? Metal belts rust away and leave nothing. Those little lizards were warm-blooded. I *know* that, but you couldn't prove it from petrified bones. What the devil? A million years from now could you tell what New York looks like from a human skeleton? Could you tell a human from a gorilla by the bones and figure out which one built an atomic bomb and which one ate bananas in a zoo?"

"Hey," said Joe, plenty objecting, "any simple bum can tell a gorilla skeleton from a man's. A man's got a larger brain. Any fool can tell which one was intelligent."

"Really?" The professor laughed to himself, as if all this was so simple and obvious, it was just a crying shame to waste time on it. "You judge everything from the type of brain human beings have managed to develop. Evolution has different ways of doing things. Birds fly one way; bats fly another way. Life has plenty of tricks for everything. —How much of your brain do you think you use. About a fifth. That's what the psychologists say. As far as they know, as far as anybody knows, eighty percent of your brain has no use at all. Everybody just works on way-low gear, except maybe a few in history. Leonardo da Vinci, for instance. Archimedes, Aristotle, Gauss, Galois, Einstein—"

I never heard of any of them except Einstein, but I didn't let on. He mentioned a few more, but I've put in all I can remember. Then he said, "Those little reptiles had tiny brains, maybe quarter-size, maybe even less, but they used it all—every bit of it. Their bones might not show it, but they were intelligent; intelligent as humans. And they were boss of all Earth."

· · · ·

And then Joe came up with something that was really good. For a while I was sure that he had the professor and I was awfully glad he came out with it. He said, "Look, P'fessor, if those lizards were so damned hot, why didn't they leave something behind? Where are their cities and their buildings and all the sort of stuff we keep finding of the cavemen, stone knives and things. Hell, if human beings got the heck off of Earth, think of the stuff we'd leave behind us. You couldn't walk a mile without falling over a city. And roads and things."

But the professor just couldn't be stopped. He wasn't even shaken up. He just came right back with, "You're still judging other forms of life by human standards. We build cities and roads and airports and the rest that goes with us—but they didn't. They were built on a different plan. Their whole way of life was different from the ground up. They didn't live in cities. They didn't have our kind of art. I'm not sure what they did have because it was so alien I couldn't grasp it—except for their guns. Those would be the same. Funny, isn't it. —For all I know, maybe we stumble over their relics every day and don't even know that's what they are."

I was pretty sick of it by that time. You just couldn't get him. The cuter you'd be, the cuter he'd be.

I said, "Look here. How do you know so much about those things? What did you do; live with them? Or did they speak English? Or maybe you speak lizard talk. Give us a few words of lizard talk."

I guess I was getting mad, too. You know how it is. A guy tells you something you don't believe because it's all cockeyed, and you can't get him to admit he's lying.

But the professor wasn't mad. He was just filling the glass again, very slowly. "No," he said, "I didn't talk and they didn't talk. They just looked at me with their cold, hard, staring eyes—snake's eyes—and I knew what they were thinking, and I could see that they knew what I was thinking. Don't ask me how it happened. It just did. Everything. I knew that they were out on a hunting expedition and I knew they weren't going to let me go."

And we stopped asking questions. We just looked at him, then Ray said, "What happened? How did you get away?"

"That was easy. An animal scurried past on the hilltop. It was long— maybe ten feet—and narrow and ran close to the ground. The lizards got excited. I could feel the excitement in waves. It was as if they forgot about me in a single hot flash of blood lust—and off they went. I got back in the machine, returned, and broke it up."

It was the flattest sort of ending you ever heard. Joe made a noise in his throat. "Well, what happened to the dinosaurs?"

"Oh, you don't see? I thought it was plain enough. —It was those little intelligent lizards that did it. They were hunters—by instinct and by choice. It was their hobby in life. It wasn't for food; it was for fun."

"And they just wiped out all the dinosaurs on the Earth?"

"All that lived at the time, anyway; all the contemporary species. Don't you think it's possible? How long did it take us to wipe out bison herds by the hundred million? What happened to the dodo in a few years? Supposing we really put our minds to it, how long would the lions and the tigers and the giraffes last? Why, by the time I saw those lizards there wasn't any big game left—no reptile more than fifteen feet maybe. All gone. Those little demons were chasing the little, scurrying ones, and probably crying their hearts out for the good old days."

And we all kept quiet and looked at our empty beer bottles and thought about it. All those dinosaurs—big as houses—killed by little lizards with guns. Killed for fun.

Then Joe leaned over and put his hand on the professor's shoulder, easylike, and shook it. He said, "Hey, P'fessor, but if that's so, what happened to the little lizards with the guns? Huh? —Did you ever go back to find out?"

The professor looked up with the kind of look in his eyes that he'd have if he were lost.

"You still don't see! It was already beginning to happen to them. I saw it in their eyes. They were running out of big game—the fun was going out of it. So what did you expect them to do? They turned to other game—the biggest and most dangerous of all—and really had fun. They hunted that game to the end."

"What game?" asked Ray. He didn't get it, but Joe and I did.

"Themselves," said the professor in a loud voice. "They finished off all the others and began on themselves—till not one was left."

And again we stopped and thought about those dinosaurs—big as houses —all finished off by little lizards with guns. Then we thought about the little lizards and how they had to keep the guns going even when there was nothing to use them on but themselves.

Joe said, "Poor dumb lizards."

"Yeah," said Ray, "poor crackpot lizards."

And then what happened really scared us. Because the professor jumped up with eyes that looked as if they were trying to climb right out of their sockets and leap at us. He shouted, "You damned fools. Why do you sit there slobbering over reptiles dead a hundred million years. That was the first intelligence on Earth and that's how it ended. That's *done*. But we're the second intelligence—and how the devil do you think *we're* going to end?"

He pushed the chair over and headed for the door. But then he stood there just before leaving altogether and said: *"Poor dumb humanity!* Go ahead and cry about that."

The Deep

In the end, any particular planet must die. It may be a quick death as its sun explodes. It may be a slow death, as its sun sinks into decay and its oceans lock in ice. In the latter case, at least, intelligent life has a chance of survival.

The direction of survival may be outward into space, to a planet closer to the cooling sun or to a planet of another sun altogether. This particular avenue is closed if the planet is unfortunate enough to be the only significant body rotating about its primary and if, at the time, no other star is within half a thousand light-years.

The direction of survival may be inward, into the crust of the planet. This is always available. A new home can be built underground and the heat of the planet's core can be tapped for energy. Thousands of years may be necessary for the task, but a dying sun cools slowly.

But planetary warmth dies, too, with time. Burrows must be dug deeper and deeper until the planet is dead through and through.

The time was coming.

On the surface of the planet, wisps of neon blew listlessly, barely able to stir the pools of oxygen that collected in the lowlands. Occasionally, during the long day, the crusted sun would flare briefly into a dull red glow and the oxygen pools would bubble a little.

During the long night, a blue-white oxygen frost formed over the pools and on the bare rock, a neon dew formed.

Eight hundred miles below the surface, a last bubble of warmth and life existed.

2

Wenda's relationship to Roi was as close as one could imagine, closer by far than it was decent for her to know.

She had been allowed to enter the ovarium only once in her life and it had been made quite clear to her that it *was* to be only that once.

The Raceologist had said, "You don't quite meet the standards, Wenda, but you are fertile and we'll try you once. It may work out."

She wanted it to work out. She wanted it desperately. Quite early in her life she had known that she was deficient in intelligence, that she would never be more than a Manual. It embarrassed her that she should fail the Race and she longed for even a single chance to help create another being. It became an obsession.

She secreted her egg in an angle of the structure and then returned to watch. The "randoming" process that moved the eggs gently about during mechanical insemination (to insure even gene distribution) did not, by some good fortune, do more than make her own wedged-in egg wobble a bit.

Unobtrusively she maintained her watch during the period of maturation, observed the little one who emerged from the particular egg that was hers, noted his physical markings, watched him grow.

He was a healthy youngster and the Raceologist approved of him.

She had said once, very casually, "Look at that one, the one sitting there. Is he sick?"

"Which one?" The Raceologist was startled. Visibly sick infants at this stage would be a strong reflection upon his own competence. "You mean Roi? Nonsense. I wish all our young were like that one."

At first, she was only pleased with herself, then frightened, finally horrified. She found herself haunting the youngster, taking an interest in his schooling, watching him at play. She was happy when he was near, dull and unhappy otherwise. She had never heard of such a thing, and she was ashamed.

She should have visited the Mentalist, but she knew better. She was not so dull as not to know that this was not a mild aberration to be cured at the twitch of a brain cell. It was a truly psychotic manifestation. She was certain of that. They would confine her if they found out. They would euthanase her, perhaps, as a useless drain on the strictly limited energy available to the race. They might even euthanase the offspring of her egg if they found out who it was.

She fought the abnormality through the years and, to a measure, succeeded. Then she first heard the news that Roi had been chosen for the long trip and was filled with aching misery.

She followed him to one of the empty corridors of the cavern, some miles from the city center. *The* city! There was only one.

This particular cavern had been closed down within Wenda's own memory. The Elders had paced its length, considered its population and the energy necessary to keep it powered, then decided to darken it. The population, not many to be sure, had been moved closer toward the center and the quota for the next session at the ovarium had been cut.

Wenda found Roi's conversational level of thinking shallow, as though most of his mind had drawn inward contemplatively.

Are you afraid? she thought at him.

Because I come out here to think? He hesitated a little, then said, "Yes, I am. It's the Race's last chance. If I fail——"

Are you afraid for yourself?

He looked at her in astonishment and Wenda's thought stream fluttered with shame at her indecency.

She said, "I wish I were going instead."

Roi said, "Do you think you can do a better job?"

"Oh, no. But if *I* were to fail and—and never come back, it would be a smaller loss to the Race."

"The loss is all the same," he said stolidly, "whether it's you or I. The loss is Racial existence."

Racial existence at the moment was in the background of Wenda's mind, if anywhere. She sighed. "The trip is such a long one."

"How long?" he asked with a smile. "Do you know?"

She hesitated. She dared not appear stupid to him.

She said primly, "The common talk is that it is to the First Level."

When Wenda had been little and the heated corridors had extended further out of the city, she had wandered out, exploring as youngsters will. One day, a long distance out, where the chill in the air nipped at her, she came to a hall that slanted upward but was blocked almost instantly by a tremendous plug, wedged tightly from top to bottom and side to side.

On the other side and upward, she had learned a long time later, lay the Seventy-ninth Level; above that the Seventy-eighth and so on.

"We're going past the First Level, Wenda."

"But there's nothing past the First Level."

"You're right. Nothing. All the solid matter of the planet comes to an end."

"But how can there be anything that's nothing? You mean air?"

"No, I mean *nothing*. Vacuum. You know what vacuum is, don't you?"

"Yes. But vacuums have to be pumped and kept airtight."

"That's good for Maintenance. Still, past the First Level is just an indefinite amount of vacuum stretching everywhere."

Wenda thought awhile. She said, "Has anyone ever been there?"

"Of course not. But we have the records."

"Maybe the records are wrong."

"They can't be. Do you know how much space I'm going to cross?"

Wenda's thought stream indicated an overwhelming negative.

Roi said, "You know the speed of light, I suppose."

"Of course," she replied readily. It was a universal constant. Infants knew it. "One thousand nine hundred and fifty-four times the length of the cavern and back in one second."

"Right," said Roi, "but if light were to travel along the distance I'm to cross, it would take it ten years."

Wenda said, "You're making fun of me. You're trying to frighten me."

"Why should it frighten you?" He rose. "But I've been moping here long enough—"

For a moment, one of his six grasping limbs rested lightly in one of hers, with an objective, impassive friendship. An irrational impulse urged Wenda to seize it tightly, prevent him from leaving.

She panicked for a moment in fear that he might probe her mind past the conversational level, that he might sicken and never face her again, that he might even report her for treatment. Then she relaxed. Roi was normal, not sick like herself. He would never dream of penetrating a friend's mind any deeper than the conversational level, whatever the provocation.

He was very handsome in her eyes as he walked away. His grasping limbs were straight and strong, his prehensile, manipulative vibrissae were numerous and delicate and his optic patches were more beautifully opalescent than any she had ever seen.

3

Laura settled down in her seat. How soft and comfortable they made them. How pleasing and unfrightening airplanes were on the inside, how different from the hard, silvery, inhuman luster of the outside.

The bassinet was on the seat beside her. She peeped in past the blanket and the tiny, ruffled cap. Walter was sleeping. His face was the blank, round softness of infancy and his eyelids were two fringed half-moons pulled down over his eyes.

A tuft of light brown hair straggled across his forehead, and with infinite delicacy, Laura drew it back beneath his cap.

It would soon be Walter's feeding time and she hoped he was still too young to be upset by the strangeness of his surroundings. The stewardess was being very kind. She even kept his bottles in a little refrigerator. Imagine, a refrigerator on board an airplane.

The people in the seat across the aisle had been watching her in that peculiar way that meant they would love to talk to her if only they could think of an excuse. The moment came when she lifted Walter out of his bassinet and placed him, a little lump of pink flesh encased in a white cocoon of cotton, upon her lap.

A baby is always legitimate as an opening for conversation between strangers.

The lady across the way said (her words were predictable), "What a *lovely* child. How old is he, my dear?"

Laura said, through the pins in her mouth (she had spread a blanket across her knees and was changing Walter), "He'll be four months old next week."

Walter's eyes were open and he simpered across at the woman, opening his mouth in a wet, gummy grin. (He always enjoyed being changed.)

"Look at him smile, George," said the lady.

Her husband smiled back and twiddled fat fingers.

"Goo," he said.

Walter laughed in a high-pitched, hiccupy way.

"What's his name, dear?" said the woman.

"He's Walter Michael," Laura said, then added, "After his father."

The floodgates were quite down. Laura learned that the couple were George and Eleanor Ellis, that they were on vacation, that they had three children, two girls and one boy, all grown-up. Both girls had married and one had two children of her own.

Laura listened with a pleased expression on her thin face. Walter (senior, that is) had always said that it was because she was such a good listener that he had first grown interested in her.

Walter was getting restless. Laura freed his arms in order to let some of his feelings evaporate in muscular effort.

"Would you warm the bottle, please?" she asked the stewardess.

Under strict but friendly questioning, Laura explained the number of feedings Walter was currently enjoying, the exact nature of his formula, and whether he suffered from diaper rash.

"I hope his little stomach isn't upset today," she worried. "I mean the plane motion, you know."

"Oh, Lord," said Mrs. Ellis, "he's too young to be bothered by that. Besides, these large planes are wonderful. Unless I look out the window, I wouldn't believe we were in the air. Don't you feel that way, George?"

But Mr. Ellis, a blunt, straightforward man, said, "I'm surprised you take a baby that age on a plane."

Mrs. Ellis turned to frown at him.

Laura held Walter over her shoulder and patted his back gently. The beginnings of a soft wail died down as his little fingers found themselves in his mother's smooth, blond hair and began grubbing into the loose bun that lay at the back of her neck.

She said, "I'm taking him to his father. Walter's never seen his son, yet."

Mr. Ellis looked perplexed and began a comment, but Mrs. Ellis put in quickly, "Your husband is in the service, I suppose?"

"Yes, he is."

(Mr. Ellis opened his mouth in a soundless "Oh" and subsided.)

Laura went on, "He's stationed just outside of Davao and he's going to be meeting me at Nichols Field."

Before the stewardess returned with the bottle, they had discovered that her husband was a master sergeant with the Quartermaster Corps, that he had been in the Army for four years, that they had been married for two, that he was about to be discharged, and that they would spend a long honeymoon there before returning to San Francisco.

Then she had the bottle. She cradled Walter in the crook of her left arm and put the bottle to his face. It slid right past his lips and his gums seized upon the nipple. Little bubbles began to work upward through the milk, while his hands batted ineffectively at the warm glass and his blue eyes stared fixedly at her.

Laura squeezed little Walter ever so slightly and thought how, with all the petty difficulties and annoyances that were involved, it yet remained such a wonderful thing to have a little baby all one's own.

4

Theory, thought Gan, always theory. The folk of the surface, a million or more years ago, could *see* the Universe, could sense it directly. Now, with eight hundred miles of rock above their heads, the Race could only make deductions from the trembling needles of their instruments.

It was only theory that brain cells, in addition to their ordinary electric potentials, radiated another sort of energy altogether. Energy that was not electromagnetic and hence not condemned to the creeping pace of light. Energy that was associated only with the highest functions of the brain and hence characteristic only of intelligent, reasoning creatures.

It was only a jogging needle that detected such an energy field leaking into their cavern, and other needles that pinpointed the origin of the field in such and such a direction ten light-years distant. At least one star must have moved quite close in the time since the surface folk had placed the nearest at five hundred light-years. Or was theory wrong?

"Are you afraid?" Gan burst into the conversational level of thought without warning and impinged sharply on the humming surface of Roi's mind.

Roi said, "It's a great responsibility."

Gan thought, *"Others* speak of responsibility." For generations, Head-Tech after Head-Tech had been working on the Resonizer and the Receiving Station and it was in his time that the final step had to be taken. What did others know of responsibility.

He said, "It is. We talk about Racial extinction glibly enough, but we always assume it will come someday but not now, not in our time. But it will, do you understand? It will. What we are to do today will consume two thirds of our total energy supply. There will not be enough left to try again. There will not be enough for this generation to live out its life. But that will not matter if you follow orders. We have thought of everything. We have spent generations thinking of everything."

"I will do what I am told," said Roi.

"Your thought field will be meshed against those coming from space. All thought fields are characteristic of the individual, and ordinarily the probability of any duplication is very low. But the fields from space number billions by our best estimate. Your field is very likely to be like one of theirs, and in that case, a resonance will be set up as long as our Resonizer is in operation. Do you know the principles involved?"

"Yes, sir."

"Then you know that during resonance, your mind will be on Planet X in the brain of the creature with a thought field identical to yours. That is not the energy-consuming process. In resonance with your mind, we will also place the mass of the Receiving Station. The method of transferring mass in that manner was the last phase of the problem to be solved, and it will take all the energy the Race would ordinarily use in a hundred years."

Gan picked up the black cube that was the Receiving Station and looked at it somberly. Three generations before it had been thought impossible to manufacture one with all the required properties in a space less than twenty cubic yards. They had it now; it was the size of his fist.

Gan said, "The thought field of intelligent brain cells can only follow certain well-defined patterns. All living creatures, on whatever planet they develop, must possess a protein base and an oxygen-water chemistry. If their world is livable for them, it is livable for us."

Theory, thought Gan on a deeper level, always theory.

He went on, "This does not mean that the body you find yourself in, its mind and its emotions, may not be completely alien. So we have arranged for three methods of activating the Receiving Station. If you are strong-limbed, you need only exert five hundred pounds of pressure on any face of the cube. If you are delicate-limbed, you need only press a knob, which you can reach through this single opening in the cube. If you are no-limbed, if your host body is paralyzed or in any other way helpless, you can activate the Station by mental energy alone. Once the Station is activated, we will have two points of reference, not one, and the Race can be transferred to Planet X by ordinary teleportation."

"That," said Roi, "will mean we will use electromagnetic energy."

"And so?"

"It will take us ten years to transfer."

"We will not be aware of duration."

"I realize that, sir, but it will mean the Station will remain on Planet X for ten years. What if it is destroyed in the meantime?"

"We have thought of that, too. We have thought of everything. Once the Station is activated, it will generate a paramass field. It will move in the direction of gravitational attraction, sliding through ordinary matter, until such time as a continuous medium of relatively high density exerts sufficient friction to stop it. It will take twenty feet of rock to do that. Anything of lower density won't affect it. It will remain twenty feet underground for ten years, at which time a counterfield will bring it to the surface. Then one by one, the Race will appear."

"In that case, why not make the activation of the Station automatic? It has so many automatic attributes already——"

"You haven't thought it through, Roi. We have. Not all spots on the surface of Planet X may be suitable. If the inhabitants are powerful and advanced, you may have to find an unobtrusive place for the Station. It won't do for us to appear in a city square. And you will have to be certain that the immediate environment is not dangerous in other ways."

"What other ways, sir?"

"I don't know. The ancient records of the surface record many things we no longer understand. They don't explain because they took those items for granted, but we have been away from the surface for almost a hundred thousand generations and we are puzzled. Our Techs aren't even in agreement on the physical nature of stars, and that is something the records mention and discuss frequently. But what are 'storms,' 'earthquakes,' 'volcanoes,' 'tornadoes,' 'sleet,' 'landslides,' 'floods,' 'lightning,' and so on? These are all terms which refer to surface phenomena that are dangerous, but we don't know what they are. We don't know how to guard against them. Through your host's mind, you may be able to learn what is needful and take appropriate action."

"How much time will I have, sir?"

"The Resonizer cannot be kept in continuous operation for longer than twelve hours. I would prefer that you complete your job in two. You will return here automatically as soon as the Station is activated. Are you ready?"

"I'm ready," said Roi.

Gan led the way to the clouded glass cabinet. Roi took his seat, arranged his limbs in the appropriate depressions. His vibrissae dipped in mercury for good contact.

Roi said, "What if I find myself in a body on the point of death?"

Gan said as he adjusted the controls, "The thought field is distorted when a person is near death. No normal thought field such as yours would be in resonance."

Roi said, "And if it is on the point of accidental death?"

Gan said, "We have thought of that, too. We can't guard against it, but the chances of death following so quickly that you have no time to activate the Station mentally are estimated as less than one in twenty trillion, unless the mysterious surface dangers are more deadly than we expect. . . . You have one minute."

For some strange reason, Roi's last thought before translation was of Wenda.

5

Laura awoke with a sudden start. What happened? She felt as though she had been jabbed with a pin.

The afternoon sun was shining in her face and its dazzle made her blink. She lowered the shade and simultaneously bent to look at Walter.

She was a little surprised to find his eyes open. This wasn't one of his waking periods. She looked at her wrist watch. No, it wasn't. And it was a good hour before feeding time, too. She followed the demand-feeding system or the "if-you-want-it-holler-and-you'll-get it" routine, but ordinarily Walter followed the clock quite conscientiously.

She wrinkled her nose at him. "Hungry, duckie?"

Walter did not respond at all and Laura was disappointed. She would have liked to have him smile. Actually, she wanted him to laugh and throw his pudgy arms about her neck and nuzzle her and say, "Mommie," but she knew he couldn't do any of that. But he *could* smile.

She put a light finger to his chin and tapped it a bit. "Goo-goo-goo-goo." He always smiled when you did that.

But he only blinked at her.

She said, "I hope he isn't sick." She looked at Mrs. Ellis in distress.

Mrs. Ellis put down a magazine. "Is anything wrong, my dear?"

"I don't know. Walter just lies there."

"Poor little thing. He's tired, probably."

"Shouldn't he be sleeping, then?"

"He's in strange surroundings. He's probably wondering what it's all about."

She rose, stepped across the aisle, and leaned across Laura to bring her own face close to Walter's. "You're wondering what's going on, you tiny little snookums. Yes, you are. You're saying, 'Where's my nice little crib and all my nice little funnies on the wall paper?' "

Then she made little squeaking sounds at him.

Walter turned his eyes away from his mother and watched Mrs. Ellis somberly.

Mrs. Ellis straightened suddenly and looked pained. She put a hand to her head for a moment and murmured, "Goodness! The queerest pain."

"Do you think he's hungry?" asked Laura.

"Lord," said Mrs. Ellis, the trouble in her face fading, "they let you know when they're hungry soon enough. There's nothing wrong with him. I've had three children, my dear. I know."

"I think I'll ask the stewardess to warm up another bottle."

"Well, if it will make you feel better . . ."

The stewardess brought the bottle and Laura lifted Walter out of his bassinet. She said, "You have your bottle and then I'll change you and then—"

She adjusted his head in the crook of her elbow, leaned over to peck him quickly on the cheek, then cradled him close to her body as she brought the bottle to his lips——

Walter screamed!

His mouth yawned open, his arms pushed before him with his fingers spread wide, his whole body as stiff and hard as though in tetany, and he screamed. It rang through the whole compartment.

Laura screamed too. She dropped the bottle and it smashed whitely.

Mrs. Ellis jumped up. Half a dozen others did. Mr. Ellis snapped out of a light doze.

"What's the matter?" asked Mrs. Ellis blankly.

"I don't know. I don't know." Laura was shaking Walter frantically, putting him over her shoulder, patting his back. "Baby, baby, don't cry. Baby, what's the matter? Baby——"

The stewardess was dashing down the aisle. Her foot came within an inch of the cube that sat beneath Laura's seat.

Walter was threshing about furiously now, yelling with calliope intensity.

6

Roi's mind flooded with shock. One moment he had been strapped in his chair in contact with the clear mind of Gan; the next (there was no consciousness of separation in time) he was immersed in a medley of strange, barbaric, and broken thought.

He closed his mind completely. It had been open wide to increase the effectiveness of resonance, and the first touch of the alien had been——

Not painful—no. Dizzying, nauseating? No, not that, either. There was no word.

He gathered resilience in the quiet nothingness of mind closure and considered his position. He felt the small touch of the Receiving Station, with which he was in mental liaison. That *had* come with him. Good!

He ignored his host for the moment. He might need him for drastic operations later, so it would be wise to raise no suspicions for the moment.

He explored. He entered a mind at random and took stock first to the sense impressions that permeated it. The creature was sensitive to parts of the electromagnetic spectrum and to vibrations of the air, and, of course, to bodily contact. It possessed localized chemical senses——

That was about all. He looked again in astonishment. Not only was there no direct mass sense, no electro-potential sense, none of the really refined interpreters of the Universe, but there was no mental contact whatever.

The creature's mind was completely isolated.

Then how did they communicate? He looked further. They had a complicated code of controlled air vibrations.

Were they intelligent? Had he chosen a maimed mind? No, they were all like that.

He filtered the group of surrounding minds through his mental tendrils, searching for a Tech, or whatever passed for such among these crippled semi-intelligences. He found a mind which thought of itself as a controller of vehicles. A piece of information flooded Roi. He was on an air-borne vehicle.

Then even without mental contact, they would build a rudimentary mechanical civilization. Or were they animal tools of real intelligences elsewhere on the planet? No . . . Their minds said no.

He plumbed the Tech. What about the immediate environment? Were the bugbears of the ancients to be feared? It was a matter of interpretation. Dangers in the environment existed. Movements of air. Changes of temperature. Water falling in the air, either as liquid or solid. Electrical discharges. There were code vibrations of each phenomenon but that meant nothing. The connection of any of these with the names given to phenomena by the ancestral surface folk was a matter of conjecture.

No matter. Was there danger now? Was there danger here? Was there any cause for fear or uneasiness?

No! The Tech's mind said no.

That was enough. He returned to his host mind and rested a moment, then cautiously expanded . . .

Nothing!

His host mind was blank. At most, there was a vague sense of warmth, and a dull flicker of undirected response to basic stimuli.

Was his host dying after all? Aphasic? Decerebrate?

He moved quickly to the mind nearest, dredging it for information about his host and finding it.

His host was an infant of species.

An infant? A *normal* infant? And so undeveloped?

He allowed his mind to sink into and coalesce for a moment with what existed in his host. He searched for the motor areas of the brain and found them with difficulty. A cautious stimulus was followed by an erratic motion of his host's extremities. He attempted finer control and failed.

He felt anger. Had they thought of everything after all? Had they thought of intelligences without mental contact? Had they thought of young creatures as completely undeveloped as though they were still in the egg?

It meant, of course, that he could not, in the person of his host, activate the Receiving Station. The muscles and mind were far too weak, far too uncontrolled for any of the three methods outlined by Gan.

He thought intensely. He could scarcely expect to influence much mass through the imperfect focusing of his host's material brain cells, but what about an indirect influence through an adult's brain? Direct physical influence would be minute; it would amount to the breakdown of the appropriate molecules of adenosine triphosphate and acetylcholine. Thereafter the creature would act on its own.

He hesitated to try this, afraid of failure, then cursed himself for a coward. He entered the closest mind once more. It was a female of the species and it was in the state of temporary inhibition he had noticed in others. It didn't surprise him. Minds as rudimentary as these would need periodic respites.

He considered the mind before him now, fingering mentally the areas that might respond to stimulation. He chose one, stabbed at it, and the conscious areas flooded with life almost simultaneously. Sense impressions poured in and the level of thought rose steeply.

Good!

But not good enough. That was a mere prod, a pinch. It was no order for specific action.

He stirred uncomfortably as emotion cascaded over him. It came from the mind he had just stimulated and was directed, of course, at his host and not at him. Nevertheless, its primitive crudities annoyed him and he closed his mind against the unpleasant warmth of her uncovered feelings.

A second mind centered about his host, and had he been material or had he controlled a satisfactory host, he would have struck out in vexation.

Great caverns, weren't they going to allow him to concentrate on his serious business?

He thrust sharply at the second mind, activating centers of discomfort, and it moved away.

He was pleased. That had been more than a simple, undefined stimulation, and it had worked nicely. He had cleared the mental atmosphere.

He returned to the Tech who controlled the vehicle. He would know the details concerning the surface over which they were passing.

Water? He sorted the data quickly.

Water! And more water!

By the everlasting Levels, the word "ocean" made sense. The old, traditional word "ocean." Who would dream that so much water could exist.

But then, if this was "ocean," then the traditional word "island" had an obvious significance. He thrust his whole mind into the quest for geographical information. The "ocean" was speckled with dots of land but he needed exact——

He was interrupted by a short stab of surprise as his host moved through space and was held against the neighboring female's body.

Roi's mind, engaged as it was, lay open and unguarded. In full intensity, the female's emotions piled in upon him.

Roi winced. In an attempt to remove the distracting animal passions, he clamped down upon the host's brain cells, through which the rawness was funneling.

He did that too quickly, too energetically. His host's mind flooded with a diffuse pain, and instantly almost every mind he could reach reacted to the air vibrations that resulted.

In vexation, he tried to blanket the pain and succeeded only in stimulating it further.

Through the clinging mental mist of his host's pain, he riffled the Techs' minds, striving to prevent contact from slipping out of focus.

His mind went icy. The best chance was almost now! He had perhaps twenty minutes. There would be other chances afterward, but not as good. Yet he dared not attempt to direct the actions of another while his host's mind was in such complete disorganization.

He retired, withdrew into mind closure, maintaining only the most tenuous connection with his host's spinal cells, and waited.

Minutes passed, and little by little he returned to fuller liaison.

He had five minutes left. He chose a subject.

7

The stewardess said, "I think he's beginning to feel a little better, poor little thing."

"He never acted like this before," insisted Laura tearfully. "Never."

"He just had a little colic, I guess," said the stewardess.

"Maybe he's bundled up too much," suggested Mrs. Ellis.

"Maybe," said the stewardess. "It's quite warm."

She unwrapped the blanket and lifted the nightgown to expose a heaving abdomen, pink and bulbous. Walter was still whimpering.

The stewardess said, "Shall I change him for you? He's quite wet."

"Would you please?"

Most of the nearer passengers had returned to their seats. The more distant ceased craning their necks.

Mr. Ellis remained in the aisle with his wife. He said, "Say, look."

Laura and the stewardess were too busy to pay him attention and Mrs. Ellis ignored him out of sheer custom.

Mr. Ellis was used to that. His remark was purely rhetorical, anyway. He bent down and tugged at the box beneath the seat.

Mrs. Ellis looked down impatiently. She said, "Goodness, George, don't be dragging at other people's luggage like that. Sit down. You're in the way."

Mr. Ellis straightened in confusion.

Laura, with eyes still red and weepy, said, "It isn't mine. I didn't even know it was under the seat."

The stewardess, looking up from the whining baby, said, "What is it?"

Mr. Ellis shrugged. "It's a box."

His wife said, "Well, what do you want with it, for heaven's sake?"

Mr. Ellis groped for a reason. What *did* he want with it? He mumbled, "I was just curious."

The stewardess said, "There! The little boy is all nice and dry, and I'll bet in two minutes he'll just be as happy as anything. Hmm? Won't you, little funny-face?"

But little funny-face was still sobbing. He turned his head away sharply as a bottle was once more produced.

The stewardess said, "Let me warm it a bit."

She took it and went back down the aisle.

Mr. Ellis came to a decision. Firmly he lifted the box and balanced it on the arm of his seat. He ignored his wife's frown.

He said, "I'm not doing it any harm. I'm just looking. What's it made of, anyway?"

He rapped it with his knuckles. None of the other passengers seemed interested. They paid no attention to either Mr. Ellis or the box. It was as though something had switched off that particular line of interest among them. Even Mrs. Ellis, in conversation with Laura, kept her back to him.

Mr. Ellis tipped the box up and found the opening. He *knew* it had to have an opening. It was large enough for him to insert a finger, though there was no reason, of course, why he should want to put a finger into a strange box.

Carefully he reached in. There was a black knob, which he longed to touch. He pressed it.

The box shuddered and was suddenly out of his hands and passed through the arm of the chair.

He caught a glimpse of it moving through the floor, and then there was unbroken flooring and nothing more. Slowly he spread out his hands and stared at his palms. Then, dropping to his knees, he felt the floor.

The stewardess, returning with the bottle, said politely, "Have you lost something, sir?"

Mrs. Ellis, looking down, said, "George!"

Mr. Ellis heaved himself upward. He was flushed and flustered. He said, "The box—— It slipped out and went down——"

The stewardess said, "What box, sir?"

Laura said, "May I have the bottle, miss? He's stopped crying."

"Certainly. Here it is."

Walter opened his mouth eagerly, accepting the nipple. Air bubbles moved upward through the milk and there were little swallowing sounds.

Laura looked up radiantly. "He seems fine now. Thank you, Stewardess. Thank you, Mrs. Ellis. For a while there, it almost seemed as though he weren't my little boy."

"He'll be all right," said Mrs. Ellis. "Maybe it was just a bit of airsickness. Sit down, George."

The stewardess said, "Just call me if you need me."

"Thank you," said Laura.

Mr. Ellis said, "The box——" and stopped.

What box? He didn't remember any box.

But one mind aboard plane could follow the black cube as it dropped in a parabola unimpeded by wind or air resistance, passing through the molecules of gas that lay in its way.

Below it, the atoll was a tiny bull's eye in a huge target. Once, during a time of war, it had boasted an air strip and barracks. The barracks had collapsed, the air strip was a vanishing ragged line, and the atoll was empty.

The cube struck the feathery foliage of a palm and not a frond was disturbed. It passed through the trunk and down to the coral. It sank into the planet itself without the smallest fog of dust kicked up to tell of its entrance.

Twenty feet below the surface of the soil, the cube passed into stasis and remained motionless, mingled intimately with the atoms of the rock, yet remaining distinct.

That was all. It was night, then day. It rained, the wind blew, and the Pacific waves broke whitely on the white coral. Nothing had happened.

Nothing would happen—for ten years.

8

"We have broadcast the news," said Gan, "that you have succeeded. I think you ought to rest now."

Roi said, "Rest? Now? When I'm back with complete minds? Thank you, but no. The enjoyment is too keen."

"Did it bother you so much? Intelligence without mental contact?"

"Yes," said Roi shortly. Gan tactfully refrained from attempting to follow the line of retreating thought.

Instead, he said, "And the surface?"

Roi said, "Entirely horrible. What the ancients called 'Sun' is an unbearable patch of brilliance overhead. It is apparently a source of light and varies periodically; 'day' and 'night,' in other words. There is also unpredictable variation."

" 'Clouds' perhaps," said Gan.

"Why 'clouds'?"

"You know the traditional phrase: 'Clouds hid the Sun.' "

"You think so? Yes, it could be."

"Well, go on."

"Let's see. 'Ocean' and 'island' I've explained. 'Storm' involves wetness in the air, falling in drops. 'Wind' is a movement of air on a huge scale. 'Thunder' is either a spontaneous, static discharge in the air or a great spontaneous noise. 'Sleet' is falling ice."

Gan said, "That's a curious one. Where would ice fall from? How? Why?"

"I haven't the slightest idea. It's all very variable. It will storm at one time and not at another. There are apparently regions on the surface where it is always cold, others where it is always hot, still others where it is both at different times."

"Astonishing. How much of this do you suppose is misinterpretation of alien minds?"

"None. I'm sure of that. It was all quite plain. I had sufficient time to plumb their queer minds. Too much time."

Again his thoughts drifted back into privacy.

Gan said, "This is well. I've been afraid all along of our tendency to romanticize the so-called Golden Age of our surface ancestors. I felt that there would be a strong impulse among our group in favor of a new surface life."

"No," said Roi vehemently.

"Obviously no. I doubt if the hardiest among us would consider even a day of life in an environment such as you describe, with its storms, days, nights, its indecent and unpredictable variations in environment." Gan's thoughts were contented ones. "Tomorrow we begin the process of transfer. Once on the island—— An uninhabited one, you say."

"Entirely uninhabited. It was the only one of that type the vessel passed over. The Tech's information was detailed."

"Good. We will begin operations. It will take generations, Roi, but in the end, we will be in the Deep of a new, warm world, in pleasant caverns where the controlled environment will be conducive to the growth of every culture and refinement."

"And," added Roi, "no contact whatever with the surface creatures."

Gan said, "Why that? Primitive though they are, they could be of help to us once we establish our base. A race that can build aircraft must have some abilities."

"It isn't that. They're a belligerent lot, sir. They would attack with animal ferocity at all occasions and——"

Gan interrupted. "I am disturbed at the psychopenumbra that surrounds your references to the aliens. There's something you are concealing."

Roi said, "I thought at first we could make use of them. If they wouldn't allow us to be friends, at least, we could control them. I made one of them close contact inside the cube and that was difficult. Very difficult. Their minds are basically different."

"In what way?"

"If I could describe it, the difference wouldn't be basic. But I can give you an example. I was in the mind of an infant. They don't have maturation chambers. The infants are in the charge of individuals. The creature who was in charge of my host——"

"Yes."

"She (it was a female) felt a special tie to the young one. There was a sense of ownership, of a relationship that excluded the remainder of their society. I seemed to detect, dimly, something of the emotion that binds a man to an associate or friend, but it was far more intense and unrestrained."

"Well," said Gan, "without mental contact, they probably have no real conception of society and subrelationships may build up. Or was this one pathological?"

"No, no. It's universal. The female in charge was the infant's mother."

"Impossible. Its own mother?"

"Of necessity. The infant had passed the first part of its existence inside its mother. Physically inside. The creature's eggs remain within the body. They are inseminated within the body. They grow within the body and emerge alive."

"Great caverns," Gan said weakly. Distaste was strong within him. "Each creature would know the identity of its own child. Each child would have a particular father——"

"And he would be known, too. My host was being taken five thousand miles, as nearly as I could judge the distance, to be seen by its father."

"Unbelievable!"

"Do you need more to see that there can never be any meeting of minds? The difference is so fundamental, so innate."

The yellowness of regret tinged and roughened Gan's thought train. He said, "It would be too bad. I had thought——"

"What, sir?"

"I had thought that for the first time there would be two intelligences helping one another. I had thought that together we might progress more quickly than either could alone. Even if they were primitive technologically, as they are, technology isn't everything. I had thought we might still be able to learn of them."

"Learn what?" asked Roi brutally. "To know our parents and make friends of our children?"

Gan said, "No. No, you're quite right. The barrier between us must remain forever complete. They will have the surface and we the Deep, and so it will be."

Outside the laboratories Roi met Wenda.

Her thoughts were concentrated pleasure. "I'm glad you're back."

Roi's thoughts were pleasurable too. It was very restful to make clean mental contact with a friend.

The Martian Way

From the doorway of the short corridor between the only two rooms in the travel-head of the spaceship, Mario Esteban Rioz watched sourly as Ted Long adjusted the video dials painstakingly. Long tried a touch clockwise, then a touch counter. The picture was lousy.

Rioz knew it would stay lousy. They were too far from Earth and at a bad position facing the Sun. But then Long would not be expected to know that. Rioz remained standing in the doorway for an additional moment, head bent to clear the upper lintel, body turned half sidewise to fit the narrow opening. Then he jerked into the galley like a cork popping out of a bottle.

"What are you after?" he asked.

"I thought I'd get Hilder," said Long.

Rioz propped his rump on the corner of a table shelf. He lifted a conical can of milk from the companion shelf just above his head. Its point popped under pressure. He swirled it gently as he waited for it to warm.

"What for?" he said. He upended the cone and sucked noisily.

"Thought I'd listen."

"I think it's a waste of power."

Long looked up, frowning. "It's customary to allow free use of personal video sets."

"Within reason," retorted Rioz.

Their eyes met challengingly. Rioz had the rangy body, the gaunt, cheek-sunken face that was almost the hallmark of the Martian Scavenger, those Spacers who patiently haunted the space routes between Earth and Mars.

Pale blue eyes were set keenly in the brown, lined face which, in turn, stood darkly out against the white surrounding synthofur that lined the up-turned collar of his leathtic space jacket.

Long was altogether paler and softer. He bore some of the marks of the Grounder, although no second-generation Martian could be a Grounder in the sense that Earthmen were. His own collar was thrown back and his dark brown hair freely exposed.

"What do you call within reason?" demanded Long.

Rioz's thin lips grew thinner. He said, "Considering that we're not even going to make expenses this trip, the way it looks, any power drain at all is outside reason."

Long said, "If we're losing money, hadn't you better get back to your post? It's your watch."

Rioz grunted and ran a thumb and forefinger over the stubble on his chin. He got up and trudged to the door, his soft, heavy boots muting the sound of his steps. He paused to look at the thermostat, then turned with a flare of fury.

"I *thought* it was hot. Where do you think you are?"

Long said, "Forty degrees isn't excessive."

"For you it isn't, maybe. But this is space, not a heated office at the iron mines." Rioz swung the thermostat control down to minimum with a quick thumb movement. "Sun's warm enough."

"The galley isn't on Sunside."

"It'll percolate through, damn it."

Rioz stepped through the door and Long stared after him for a long moment, then turned back to the video. He did not turn up the thermostat.

The picture was still flickering badly, but it would have to do. Long folded a chair down out of the wall. He leaned forward waiting through the formal announcement, the momentary pause before the slow dissolution of the curtain, the spotlight picking out the well-known bearded figure which grew as it was brought forward until it filled the screen.

The voice, impressive even through the flutings and croakings induced by the electron storms of twenty millions of miles, began:

"Friends! My fellow citizens of Earth . . ."

2

Rioz's eye caught the flash of the radio signal as he stepped into the pilot room. For one moment, the palms of his hands grew clammy when it seemed to him that it was a radar pip; but that was only his guilt speaking. He should not have left the pilot room while on duty theoretically, though all Scavengers did it. Still, it was the standard nightmare, this business of a strike turning up during just those five minutes when one knocked off for a quick coffee because it seemed certain that space was clear. And the nightmare had been known to happen, too.

Rioz threw in the multi-scanner. It was a waste of power, but while he was thinking about it, he might as well make sure.

Space was clear except for the far-distant echoes from the neighboring ships on the scavenging line.

He hooked up the radio circuit, and the blond, long-nosed head of Richard Swenson, copilot of the next ship on the Marsward side, filled it.

"Hey, Mario," said Swenson.

"Hi. What's new?"

There was a second and a fraction of pause between that and Swenson's next comment, since the speed of electromagnetic radiation is not infinite.

"What a day I've *had*."

"Something happened?" Rioz asked.

"I had a strike."

"Well, good."

"Sure, if I'd roped it in," said Swenson morosely.

"What happened?"

"Damn it, I headed in the wrong direction."

Rioz knew better than to laugh. He said, "How did you do that?"

"It wasn't my fault. The trouble was the shell was moving way out of the ecliptic. Can you imagine the stupidity of a pilot that can't work the release maneuver decently? How was I to know? I got the distance of the shell and let it go at that. I just assumed its orbit was in the usual trajectory family. Wouldn't you? I started along what I thought was a good line of intersection and it was five minutes before I noticed the distance was still going up. The pips were taking their sweet time returning. So then I took the angular projections of the thing, and it was too late to catch up with it."

"Any of the other boys getting it?"

"No. It's 'way out of the ecliptic and'll keep on going forever. That's not what bothers me so much. It was only an inner shell. But I hate to tell you how many tons of propulsion I wasted getting up speed and then getting back to station. You should have heard Canute."

Canute was Richard Swenson's brother and partner.

"Mad, huh?" said Rioz.

"Mad? Like to have killed me! But then we've been out five months now and it's getting kind of sticky. You know."

"I know."

"How are you doing, Mario?"

Rioz made a spitting gesture. "About that much this trip. Two shells in the last two weeks and I had to chase each one for six hours."

"Big ones?"

"Are you kidding? I could have scaled them down to Phobos by hand. This is the worst trip I've ever had."

"How much longer are you staying?"

"For my part, we can quit tomorrow. We've only been out two months and it's got so I'm chewing Long out all the time."

There was a pause over and above the electromagnetic lag.

Swenson said, "What's he like, anyway? Long, I mean."

Rioz looked over his shoulder. He could hear the soft, crackly mutter of the video in the galley. "I can't make him out. He says to me about a week after the start of the trip, 'Mario, why are you a Scavenger?' I just look at him and say, 'To make a living. Why do you suppose?' I mean, what the hell kind of a question is that? Why is anyone a Scavenger?

"Anyway, he says, 'That's not it, Mario.' *He's* telling *me,* you see. He says, 'You're a Scavenger because this is part of the Martian way.' "

Swenson said, "And what did he mean by that?"

Rioz shrugged. "I never asked him. Right now he's sitting in there listening to the ultra-microwave from Earth. He's listening to some Grounder called Hilder."

"Hilder? A Grounder politician, an Assemblyman or something, isn't he?"

"That's right. At least, I think that's right. Long is always doing things like that. He brought about fifteen pounds of books with him, all about Earth. Just plain dead weight, you know."

"Well, he's your partner. And talking about partners, I think I'll get back on the job. If I miss another strike, there'll be murder around here."

He was gone and Rioz leaned back. He watched the even green line that was the pulse scanner. He tried the multiscanner a moment. Space was still clear.

He felt a little better. A bad spell is always worse if the Scavengers all about you are pulling in shell after shell; if the shells go spiraling down to the Phobos scrap forges with everyone's brand welded on except your own. Then, too, he had managed to work off some of his resentment toward Long.

It was a mistake teaming up with Long. It was always a mistake to team up with a tenderfoot. They thought what you wanted was conservation, especially Long, with his eternal theories about Mars and its great new role in human progress. That was the way he said it—Human Progress: the Martian Way; the New Creative Minority. And all the time what Rioz wanted wasn't talk, but a strike, a few shells to call their own.

At that, he hadn't any choice, really. Long was pretty well known down on Mars and made good pay as a mining engineer. He was a friend of Commissioner Sankov and he'd been out on one or two short scavenging missions before. You can't turn a fellow down flat before a tryout, even though it did look funny. Why should a mining engineer with a comfortable job and good money want to muck around in space?

Rioz never asked Long that question. Scavenger partners are forced too close together to make curiosity desirable, or sometimes even safe. But Long talked so much that he answered the question.

"I had to come out here, Mario," he said. "The future of Mars isn't in the mines; it's in space."

Rioz wondered how it would be to try a trip alone. Everyone said it was impossible. Even discounting lost opportunities when one man had to go off watch to sleep or attend to other things, it was well known that one man alone in space would become intolerably depressed in a relatively short while.

Taking a partner along made a six-month trip possible. A regular crew would be better, but no Scavenger could make money on a ship large enough to carry one. The capital it would take in propulsion alone!

Even two didn't find it exactly fun in space. Usually you had to change partners each trip and you could stay out longer with some than with others. Look at Richard and Canute Swenson. They teamed up every five or six trips because they were brothers. And yet whenever they did, it was a constantly mounting tension and antagonism after the first week.

Oh well. Space was clear. Rioz would feel a little better if he went back in the galley and smoothed down some of the bickering with Long. He might as well show he was an old spacehand who took the irritations of space as they came.

He stood up, walked the three steps necessary to reach the short, narrow corridor that tied together the two rooms of the spaceship.

3

Once again Rioz stood in the doorway for a moment, watching. Long was intent on the flickering screen.

Rioz said gruffly, "I'm shoving up the thermostat. It's all right—we can spare the power."

Long nodded. "If you like."

Rioz took a hesitant step forward. Space was clear, so to hell with sitting and looking at a blank, green, pipless line. He said, "What's the Grounder been talking about?"

"History of space travel mostly. Old stuff, but he's doing it well. He's giving the whole works—color cartoons, trick photography, stills from old films, everything."

As if to illustrate Long's remarks, the bearded figure faded out of view, and a cross-sectional view of a spaceship flitted onto the screen. Hilder's voice continued, pointing out features of interest that appeared in schematic color. The communications system of the ship outlined itself in red as he talked about it, the storerooms, the patron micropile drive, the cybernetic circuits . . .

Then Hilder was back on the screen. "But this is only the travelhead of the ship. What moves it? What gets it off the Earth?"

Everyone knew what moved a spaceship, but Hilder's voice was like a drug. He made spaceship propulsion sound like the secret of the ages, like an ultimate revelation. Even Rioz felt a slight tingling of suspense, though he had spent the greater part of his life aboard ship.

Hilder went on. "Scientists call it different names. They call it the Law of Action and Reaction. Sometimes they call it Newton's Third Law. Sometimes they call it Conservation of Momentum. But we don't have to call it any name. We can just use our common sense. When we swim we push water backward and move forward ourselves. When we walk, we push back against the ground and move forward. When we fly a gyro-flivver, we push air backward and move forward.

"Nothing can move forward unless something else moves backward. It's the old principle of 'You can't get something for nothing.'

"Now imagine a spaceship that weighs a hundred thousand tons lifting off Earth. To do that, something else must be moved downward. Since a space-ship is extremely heavy, a great deal of material must be moved downward. So much material, in fact, that there is no place to keep it all aboard ship. A special compartment must be built behind the ship to hold it."

Again Hilder faded out and the ship returned. It shrank and a truncated cone appeared behind it. In bright yellow, words appeared within it: MATERIAL TO BE THROWN AWAY.

"But now," said Hilder, "the total weight of the ship is much greater. You need still more propulsion and still more."

The ship shrank enormously to add on another larger shell and still another immense one. The ship proper, the travel-head, was a little dot on the screen, a glowing red dot.

Rioz said, "Hell, this is kindergarden stuff."

"Not to the people he's speaking to, Mario," replied Long. "Earth isn't Mars. There must be billions of Earth people who've never seen a spaceship; don't know the first thing about it."

Hilder was saying, "When the material inside the biggest shell is used up, the shell is detached. It's thrown away, too."

The outermost shell came loose, wobbled about the screen.

"Then the second one goes," said Hilder, "and then, if the trip is a long one, the last is ejected."

The ship was just a red dot now, with three shells shifting and moving, lost in space.

Hilder said, "These shells represent a hundred thousand tons of tungsten, magnesium, aluminum, and steel. They are gone forever from Earth. Mars is ringed by Scavengers, waiting along the routes of space travel, waiting for the cast-off shells, netting and branding them, saving them for Mars. Not one cent of payment reaches Earth for them. They are salvage. They belong to the ship that finds them."

Rioz said, "We risk our investment and our lives. If we don't pick them up, no one gets them. What loss is that to Earth?"

"Look," said Long, "he's been talking about nothing but the drain that Mars, Venus, and the Moon put on Earth. This is just another item of loss."

"They'll get their return. We're mining more iron every year."

"And most of it goes right back into Mars. If you can believe his figures, Earth has invested two hundred billion dollars in Mars and received back about five billion dollars' worth of iron. It's put five hundred billion dollars into the Moon and gotten back a little over twenty-five billion dollars of magnesium, titanium, and assorted light metals. It's put fifty billion dollars into Venus and gotten back nothing. And that's what the taxpayers of Earth are really interested in—tax money out; nothing in."

The screen was filled, as he spoke, with diagrams of the Scavengers on the route to Mars; little, grinning caricatures of ships, reaching out wiry, tenuous arms that groped for the tumbling, empty shells, seizing and snaking them in, branding them MARS PROPERTY in glowing letters, then scaling them down to Phobos.

Then it was Hilder again. "They tell us eventually they will return it all to us. Eventually! Once they are a going concern! We don't know when that will be. A century from now? A thousand years? A million? 'Eventually.' Let's take them at their word. Someday they will give us back all our metals. Someday they will grow their own food, use their own power, live their own lives.

"But one thing they can never return. Not in a hundred million years. *Water!*

"Mars has only a trickle of water because it is too small. Venus has no water at all because it is too hot. The Moon has none because it is too hot and too small. So Earth must supply not only drinking water and washing water for the Spacers, water to run their industries, water for the hydroponic factories they claim to be setting up—but even water to throw away by the millions of tons.

"What is the propulsive force that spaceships use? What is it they throw behind so that they can accelerate forward? Once it was the gases generated from explosives. That was very expensive. Then the proton micropile was invented—a cheap power source that could heat up any liquid until it was a gas under tremendous pressure. What is the cheapest and most plentiful liquid available? Why, water, of course.

"Each spaceship leaves Earth carrying nearly a million tons—not pounds, *tons*—of water, for the sole purpose of driving it into space, so that it may speed up or slow down.

"Our ancestors burned the oil of Earth madly and willfully. They destroyed its coal recklessly. We despise and condemn them for that, but at least they had this excuse—they thought that when the need arose, substitutes would be found. And they were right. We have our plankton farms and our proton micropiles.

"But there is no substitute for water. None! There never can be. And when our descendants view the desert we will have made of Earth, what excuse will they find for us? When the droughts come and grow——"

Long leaned forward and turned off the set. He said, "That bothers me. The damn fool is deliberately——What's the matter?"

Rioz had risen uneasily to his feet. "I ought to be watching the pips."

"The hell with the pips." Long got up likewise, followed Rioz through the narrow corridor, and stood just inside the pilot room. "If Hilder carries this through, if he's got the guts to make a real issue out of it—*Wow!*"

He had seen it too. The pip was a Class A, racing after the outgoing signal like a greyhound after a mechanical rabbit.

Rioz was babbling, "Space was clear, I tell you, *clear.* For Mar's sake, Ted, don't just freeze on me. See if you can spot it visually."

Rioz was working speedily and with an efficiency that was the result of nearly twenty years of scavenging. He had the distance in two minutes. Then, remembering Swenson's experience, he measured the angle of declination and the radial velocity as well.

He yelled at Long, "One point seven six radians. You can't miss it, man."

Long held his breath as he adjusted the vernier. "It's only half a radian off the sun. It'll only be crescent-lit."

He increased magnification as rapidly as he dared, watching for the one "star" that changed position and grew to have a form, revealing itself to be no star.

"I'm starting, anyway," said Rioz. "We can't wait."

"I've got it. I've got it." Magnification was still too small to give it a definite shape, but the dot Long watched was brightening and dimming rhythmically as the shell rotated and caught sunlight on cross sections of different sizes.

"Hold on."

The first of many fine spurts of steam squirted out of the proper vents, leaving long trails of micro-crystals of ice gleaming mistily in the pale beams of the distant Sun. They thinned out for a hundred miles or so. One spurt, then another, then another, as the Scavenger ship moved out of its stable trajectory and took up a course tangential to that of the shell.

"It's moving like a comet at perihelion!" yelled Rioz. "Those damned Grounder pilots knock the shells off that way on purpose. I'd like to——"

He swore his anger in a frustrated frenzy as he kicked steam backward and backward recklessly, till the hydraulic cushioning of his chair had soughed back a full foot and Long had found himself all but unable to maintain his grip on the guard rail.

"Have a heart," he begged.

But Rioz had his eye on the pips. "If you can't take it, man, stay on Mars!" The steam spurts continued to boom distantly.

The radio came to life. Long managed to lean forward through what seemed like molasses and closed contact. It was Swenson, eyes glaring.

Swenson yelled, "Where the hell are you guys going? You'll be in my sector in ten seconds."

Rioz said, "I'm chasing a shell."

"In *my* sector?"

"It started in mine and you're not in position to get it. Shut off that radio, Ted."

The ship thundered through space, a thunder that could be heard only within the hull. And then Rioz cut the engines in stages large enough to make Long flail forward. The sudden silence was more ear-shattering than the noise that had preceded it.

Rioz said, "All right. Let me have the 'scope."

They both watched. The shell was a definite truncated cone now, tumbling with slow solemnity as it passed along among the stars.

"It's a Class A shell, all right," said Rioz with satisfaction. A giant among shells, he thought. It would put them into the black.

Long said, "We've got another pip on the scanner. I think it's Swenson taking after us."

Rioz scarcely gave it a glance. "He won't catch us."

The shell grew larger still, filling the visiplate.

Rioz's hands were on the harpoon lever. He waited, adjusted the angle microscopically twice, played out the length allotment. Then he yanked, tripping the release.

For a moment, nothing happened. Then a metal mesh cable snaked out onto the visiplate, moving toward the shell like a striking cobra. It made contact, but it did not hold. If it had, it would have snapped instantly like a cobweb strand. The shell was turning with a rotational momentum amounting to thousands of tons. What the cable did do was set up a powerful magnetic field that acted as a brake on the shell.

Another cable and another lashed out. Rioz sent them out in an almost heedless expenditure of energy.

"I'll get this one! By Mars, I'll get this one!"

With some two dozen cables stretching between ship and shell, he desisted. The shell's rotational energy, converted by breaking into heat, had raised its temperature to a point where its radiation could be picked up by the ship's meters.

Long said, "Do you want me to put our brand on?"

"Suits me. But you don't have to if you don't want to. It's my watch."

"I don't mind."

Long clambered into his suit and went out the lock. It was the surest sign of his newness to the game that he could count the number of times he had been out in space in a suit. This was the fifth time.

He went out along the nearest cable, hand over hand, feeling the vibration of the mesh against the metal of his mitten.

He burned their serial number in the smooth metal of the shell. There was nothing to oxidize the steel in the emptiness of space. It simply melted and vaporized, condensing some feet away from the energy beam, turning the surface it touched into a gray, powdery dullness.

Long swung back toward the ship.

Inside again, he took off his helmet, white and thick with frost that collected as soon as he had entered.

The first thing he heard was Swenson's voice coming over the radio in this almost unrecognizable rage: ". . . straight to the Commissioner. Damn it, there are rules to this game!"

Rioz sat back, unbothered. "Look, it hit my sector. I was late spotting it and I chased it into yours. You couldn't have gotten it with Mars for a backstop. That's all there is to it——You back, Long?"

He cut contact.

The signal button raged at him, but he paid no attention.

"He's going to the Commissioner?" Long asked.

"Not a chance. He just goes on like that because it breaks the monotony. He doesn't mean anything by it. He knows it's our shell. And how do you like that hunk of stuff, Ted?"

"Pretty good."

"Pretty good? It's terrific! Hold on. I'm setting it swinging."

The side jets spat steam and the ship started a slow rotation about the shell. The shell followed it. In thirty minutes, they were a gigantic bolo spinning in emptiness. Long checked the *Ephemeris* for the position of Deimos.

At a precisely calculated moment, the cables released their magnetic field and the shell went streaking off tangentially in a trajectory that would, in a day or so, bring it within pronging distance of the shell stores on the Martian satellite.

Rioz watched it go. He felt good. He turned to Long. "This is one fine day for us."

"What about Hilder's speech?" asked Long.

"What? Who? Oh, that. Listen, if I had to worry about every thing some damned Grounder said, I'd never get any sleep. Forget it."

"I don't think we should forget it."

"You're nuts. Don't bother me about it, will you? Get some sleep instead."

4

Ted Long found the breadth and height of the city's main thoroughfare exhilarating. It had been two months since the Commissioner had declared a moratorium on scavenging and had pulled all ships out of space, but this feeling of a stretched-out vista had not stopped thrilling Long. Even the thought that the moratorium was called pending a decision on the part of

Earth to enforce its new insistence on water economy, by deciding upon a ration limit for scavenging, did not cast him entirely down.

The roof of the avenue was painted a luminous light blue, perhaps as an old-fashioned imitation of Earth's sky. Ted wasn't sure. The walls were lit with the store windows that pierced it.

Off in the distance, over the hum of traffic and the sloughing noise of people's feet passing him, he could hear the intermittent blasting as new channels were being bored into Mars' crust. All his life he remembered such blastings. The ground he walked on had been part of solid, unbroken rock when he was born. The city was growing and would keep on growing—if Earth would only let it.

He turned off at a cross street, narrower, not quite as brilliantly lit, shop windows giving way to apartment houses, each with its row of lights along the front façade. Shoppers and traffic gave way to slower-paced individuals and to squawling youngsters who had as yet evaded the maternal summons to the evening meal.

At the last minute, Long remembered the social amenities and stopped off at a corner water store.

He passed over his canteen. "Fill 'er up."

The plump storekeeper unscrewed the cap, cocked an eye into the opening. He shook it a little and let it gurgle. "Not much left," he said cheerfully.

"No," agreed Long.

The storekeeper trickled water in, holding the neck of the canteen close to the hose tip to avoid spillage. The volume gauge whirred. He screwed the cap back on.

Long passed over the coins and took his canteen. It clanked against his hip now with a pleasing heaviness. It would never do to visit a family without a full canteen. Among the boys, it didn't matter. Not as much, anyway.

He entered the hallway of No. 27, climbed a short flight of stairs, and paused with his thumb on the signal.

The sound of voices could be heard quite plainly.

One was a woman's voice, somewhat shrill. "It's all right for you to have your Scavenger friends here, isn't it? I'm supposed to be thankful you manage to get home two months a year. Oh, it's quite enough that you spend a day or two with me. After that, it's the Scavengers again."

"I've been home for a long time now," said a male voice, "and this is business. For Mars' sake, let up, Dora. They'll be here soon."

Long decided to wait a moment before signaling. It might give them a chance to hit a more neutral topic.

"What do I care if they come?" retorted Dora. "Let them hear me. And I'd just as soon the Commissioner kept the moratorium on permanently. You hear me?"

"And what would we live on?" came the male voice hotly. "You tell me that."

"I'll tell you. You can make a decent, honorable living right here on Mars, just like everybody else. I'm the only one in this apartment house that's a Scavenger widow. That's what I am—a widow. I'm worse than a widow, because if I were a widow, I'd at least have a chance to marry someone else——What did you say?"

"Nothing. Nothing at all."

"Oh, I know what you said. Now listen here, Dick Swenson——"

"I only said," cried Swenson, "that now I know why Scavengers usually don't marry."

"You shouldn't have either. I'm tired of having every person in the neighborhood pity me and smirk and ask when you're coming home. Other people can be mining engineers and administrators and even tunnel borers. At least tunnel borers' wives have a decent home life and their children don't grow up like vagabonds. Peter might as well not have a father——"

A thin boy-soprano voice made its way through the door. It was somewhat more distant, as though it were in another room. "Hey, Mom, what's a vagabond?"

Dora's voice rose a notch. "Peter! You keep your mind on your homework."

Swenson said in a low voice, "It's not right to talk this way in front of the kid. What kind of notions will he get about me?"

"Stay home then and teach him better notions."

Peter's voice called out again. "Hey, Mom, I'm going to be a Scavenger when I grow up."

Footsteps sounded rapidly. There was a momentary hiatus in the sounds, then a piercing, "Mom! Hey, Mom! Leggo my ear! What did I do?" and a snuffling silence.

Long seized the chance. He worked the signal vigorously.

Swenson opened the door, brushing down his hair with both hands.

"Hello, Ted," he said in a subdued voice. Then loudly, "Ted's here, Dora. Where's Mario, Ted?"

Long said, "He'll be here in a while."

Dora came bustling out of the next room, a small, dark woman with a pinched nose, and hair, just beginning to show touches of gray, combed off the forehead.

"Hello, Ted. Have you eaten?"

"Quite well, thanks. I haven't interrupted you, have I?"

"Not at all. We finished ages ago. Would you like some coffee?"

"I think so." Ted unslung his canteen and offered it.

"Oh, goodness, that's all right. We've plenty of water."

"I insist."

"Well, then——"

Back into the kitchen she went. Through the swinging door, Long caught a glimpse of dishes sitting in Secoterg, the "waterless cleaner that soaks up and absorbs grease and dirt in a twinkling. One ounce of water will rinse eight square feet of dish surface clean as clean. Buy Secoterg. Secoterg just cleans it right, makes your dishes shiny bright, does away with water waste——"

The tune started whining through his mind and Long crushed it with speech. He said, "How's Pete?"

"Fine, fine. The kid's in the fourth grade now. You know I don't get to see him much. Well, sir, when I came back last time, he looked at me and said . . ."

It went on for a while and wasn't too bad as bright sayings of bright children as told by dull parents go.

The door signal burped and Mario Rioz came in, frowning and red.

Swenson stepped to him quickly. "Listen, don't say anything about shell-snaring. Dora still remembers the time you fingered a Class A shell out of my territory and she's in one of her moods now."

"Who the hell wants to talk about shells?" Rioz slung off a fur-lined jacket, threw it over the back of the chair, and sat down.

Dora came through the swinging door, viewed the newcomer with a synthetic smile, and said, "Hello, Mario. Coffee for you, too?"

"Yeah," he said, reaching automatically for his canteen.

"Just use some more of my water, Dora," said Long quickly. "He'll owe it to me."

"Yeah," said Rioz.

"What's wrong, Mario?" asked Long.

Rioz said heavily, "Go on. Say you told me so. A year ago when Hilder made that speech, you told me so. Say it."

Long shrugged.

Rioz said, "They've set up the quota. Fifteen minutes ago the news came out."

"Well?"

"Fifty thousand tons of water per trip."

"What?" yelled Swenson, burning. "You can't get off Mars with fifty thousand!"

"That's the figure. It's a deliberate piece of gutting. No more scavenging."

Dora came out with the coffee and set it down all around.

"What's all this about no more scavenging?" She sat down very firmly and Swenson looked helpless.

"It seems," said Long, "that they're rationing us at fifty thousand tons and that means we can't make any more trips."

"Well, what of it?" Dora sipped her coffee and smiled gaily. "If you want my opinion, it's a good thing. It's time all you Scavengers found yourselves a nice, steady job here on Mars. I mean it. It's no life to be running all over space——"

"Please, Dora," said Swenson.

Rioz came close to a snort.

Dora raised her eyebrows. "I'm just giving my opinions."

Long said, "Please feel free to do so. But I would like to say something. Fifty thousand is just a detail. We know that Earth—or at least Hilder's party —wants to make political capital out of a campaign for water economy, so we're in a bad hole. We've got to get water somehow or they'll shut us down altogether, right?"

"Well, sure," said Swenson.

"But the question is how, right?"

"If it's only getting water," said Rioz in a sudden gush of words, "there's only one thing to do and you know it. If the Grounders won't give us water, we'll take it. The water doesn't belong to them just because their fathers and grandfathers were too damned sick-yellow ever to leave their fat planet. Water belongs to people wherever they are. We're people and the water's ours, too. We have a right to it."

"How do you propose taking it?" asked Long.

"Easy! They've got oceans of water on Earth. They can't post a guard over every square mile. We can sink down on the night side of the planet any time we want, fill our shells, then get away. How can they stop us?"

"In half a dozen ways, Mario. How do you spot shells in space up to distances of a hundred thousand miles? One thin metal shell in all that space. How? By radar. Do you think there's no radar on Earth? Do you think that if Earth ever gets the notion we're engaged in waterlegging, it won't be simple for them to set up a radar network to spot ships coming in from space?"

Dora broke in indignantly. "I'll tell you one thing, Mario Rioz. My husband isn't going to be part of any raid to get water to keep up his scavenging with."

"It isn't just scavenging," said Mario. "Next they'll be cutting down on everything else. We've got to stop them now."

"But we don't need their water, anyway," said Dora. "We're not the Moon or Venus. We pipe enough water down from the polar caps for all we need. We have a water tap right in this apartment. There's one in every apartment on this block."

Long said, "Home use is the smallest part of it. The mines use water. And what do we do about the hydroponic tanks?"

"That's right," said Swenson. "What about the hydroponic tanks, Dora? They've got to have water and it's about time we arranged to grow our own fresh food instead of having to live on the condensed crud they ship us from Earth."

"Listen to him," said Dora scornfully. "What do you know about fresh food? You've never eaten any."

"I've eaten more than you think. Do you remember those carrots I picked up once?"

"Well, what was so wonderful about them? If you ask me, good baked protomeal is much better. And healthier, too. It just seems to be the fashion now to be talking fresh vegetables because they're increasing taxes for these hydroponics. Besides, all this will blow over."

Long said, "I don't think so. Not by itself, anyway. Hilder will probably be the next Co-ordinator, and then things may really get bad. If they cut down on food shipments, too——"

"Well, then," shouted Rioz, "what do we do? I still say take it! Take the water!"

"And I say we can't do that, Mario. Don't you see that what you're suggesting is the Earth way, the Grounder way? You're trying to hold on to the umbilical cord that ties Mars to Earth. Can't you get away from that? Can't you see the Martian way?"

"No, I can't. Suppose you tell me."

"I will, if you'll listen. When we think about the Solar System, what do we think about? Mercury, Venus, Earth, Moon, Mars, Phobos, and Deimos. There you are—seven bodies, that's all. But that doesn't represent 1 per cent of the Solar System. We Martians are right at the edge of the other 99 per cent. Out there, farther from the Sun, there's unbelievable amounts of water!"

The others stared.

Swenson said uncertainly, "You mean the layers of ice on Jupiter and Saturn?"

"Not that specifically, but it *is* water, you'll admit. A thousand-mile-thick layer of water is a lot of water."

"But it's all covered up with layers of ammonia or—or something, isn't it?" asked Swenson. "Besides, we can't land on the major planets."

"I know that," said Long, "but I haven't said that was the answer. The major planets aren't the only objects out there. What about the asteroids and the satellites? Vesta is a two-hundred-mile-diameter asteroid that's hardly more than a chunk of ice. One of the moons of Saturn is mostly ice. How about that?"

Rioz said, "Haven't you ever been in space, Ted?"

"You know I have. Why do you ask?"

"Sure, I know you have, but you still talk like a Grounder. Have you thought of the distances involved? The average asteroid is a hundred twenty million miles from Mars at the closest. That's twice the Venus-Mars hop and you know that hardly any liners do even that in one jump. They usually stop off at Earth or the Moon. After all, how long do you expect anyone to stay in space, man?"

"I don't know. What's your limit?"

"You know the limit. You don't have to ask me. It's six months. That's handbook data. After six months, if you're still in space, you're psychotherapy meat. Right, Dick?"

Swenson nodded.

"And that's just the asteroids," Rioz went on. "From Mars to Jupiter is three hundred thirty million miles, and to Saturn it's seven hundred million. How can anyone handle that kind of distance? Suppose you hit standard velocity or, to make it even, say you get up to a good two hundred kilomiles an hour. It would take you—let's see, allowing time for acceleration and deceleration—about six or seven months to get to Jupiter and nearly a year to get to Saturn. Of course, you could hike the speed to a million miles an hour, theoretically, but where would you get the water to do that?"

"Gee," said a small voice attached to a smutty nose and round eyes. "Saturn!"

Dora whirled in her chair. "Peter, march right back into your room!"

"Aw, Ma."

"Don't 'Aw, Ma' me." She began to get out of the chair, and Peter scuttled away.

Swenson said, "Say, Dora, why don't you keep him company for a while? It's hard to keep his mind on homework if we're all out here talking."

Dora smiled obstinately and stayed put. "I'll sit right here until I find out what Ted Long is thinking of. I tell you right now I don't like the sound of it."

Swenson said nervously, "Well, never mind Jupiter and Saturn. I'm sure Ted isn't figuring on that. But what about Vesta? We could make it in ten or twelve weeks there and the same back. And two hundred miles in diameter. That's four million cubic miles of ice!"

"So what?" said Rioz. "What do we do on Vesta? Quarry the ice? Set up mining machinery? Say, do you know how long that would take?"

Long said, "I'm talking about Saturn, not Vesta."

Rioz addressed an unseen audience. "I tell him seven hundred million miles and he keeps on talking."

"All right," said Long, "suppose you tell me how you know we can only stay in space six months, Mario?"

"It's common knowledge, damn it."

"Because it's in the *Handbook of Space Flight*. It's data compiled by Earth scientists from experience with Earth pilots and spacemen. You're still thinking Grounder style. You won't think the Martian way."

"A Martian may be a Martian, but he's still a man."

"But how can you be so blind? How many times have you fellows been out for over six months without a break?"

Rioz said, "That's different."

"Because you're Martians? Because you're professional Scavengers?"

"No. Because we're not on a flight. We can put back for Mars any time we want to."

"But you *don't* want to. That's my point. Earthmen have tremendous ships with libraries of films, with a crew of fifteen plus passengers. Still, they can only stay out six months maximum. Martian Scavengers have a two-room ship with only one partner. But we can stick it out more than six months."

Dora said, "I suppose you want to stay in a ship for a year and go to Saturn."

"Why not, Dora?" said Long. "We can do it. Don't you see we can? Earthmen can't. They've got a real world. They've got open sky and fresh food, all the air and water they want. Getting into a ship is a terrible change for them. More than six months is too much for them for that very reason. Martians are different. We've been living on a ship our entire lives.

"That's all Mars is—a ship. It's just a big ship forty-five hundred miles across with one tiny room in it occupied by fifty thousand people. It's closed in like a ship. We breathe packaged air and drink packaged water, which we repurify over and over. We eat the same food rations we eat aboard ship. When we get into a ship, it's the same thing we've known all our lives. We can stand it for a lot more than a year if we have to."

Dora said, "Dick, too?"

"We all can."

"Well, Dick can't. It's all very well for you, Ted Long, and this shell stealer here, this Mario, to talk about jaunting off for a year. You're not married. Dick is. He has a wife and he has a child and that's enough for him. He can just get a regular job right here on Mars. Why, my goodness, suppose you go to Saturn and find there's no water there. How'll you get back? Even if you had water left, you'd be out of food. It's the most ridiculous thing I ever heard of."

"No. Now listen," said Long tightly. "I've thought this thing out. I've talked to Commissioner Sankov and he'll help. But we've got to have ships and men. I can't get them. The men won't listen to me. I'm green. You two are known and respected. You're veterans. If you back me, even if you don't go yourselves, if you'll just help me sell this thing to the rest, get volunteers——"

"First," said Rioz grumpily, "you'll have to do a lot more explaining. Once we get to Saturn, where's the water?"

"That's the beauty of it," said Long. "That's why it's got to be Saturn. The water there is just floating around in space for the taking."

5

When Hamish Sankov had come to Mars, there was no such thing as a native Martian. Now there were two-hundred-odd babies whose grandfathers had been born on Mars—native in the third generation.

When he had come as a boy in his teens, Mars had been scarcely more than a huddle of grounded spaceships connected by sealed underground tunnels. Through the years, he had seen buildings grow and burrow widely, thrusting blunt snouts up into the thin, unbreathable atmosphere. He had seen huge storage depots spring up into which spaceships and their loads could be swallowed whole. He had seen the mines grow from nothing to a huge gouge in the Martian crust, while the population of Mars grew from fifty to fifty thousand.

It made him feel old, these long memories—they and the even dimmer memories induced by the presence of this Earthman before him. His visitor brought up those long-forgotten scraps of thought about a soft-warm world that was as kind and gentle to mankind as the mother's womb.

The Earthman seemed fresh from that womb. Not very tall, not very lean; in fact, distinctly plump. Dark hair with a neat little wave in it, a neat little mustache, and neatly scrubbed skin. His clothing was right in style and as fresh and neatly turned as plastek could be.

Sankov's own clothes were of Martian manufacture, serviceable and clean, but many years behind the times. His face was craggy and lined, his hair was pure white, and his Adam's apple wobbled when he talked.

The Earthman was Myron Digby, member of Earth's General Assembly. Sankov was Martian Commissioner.

Sankov said, "This all hits us hard, Assemblyman."

"It's hit most of us hard, too, Commissioner."

"Uh-huh. Can't honestly say then that I can make it out. Of course, you understand, I don't make out that I can understand Earth ways, for all that I was born there. Mars is a hard place to live, Assemblyman, and you have to understand that. It takes a lot of shipping space just to bring us food, water, and raw materials so we can live. There's not much room left for books and news films. Even video programs can't reach Mars, except for about a month when Earth is in conjunction, and even then nobody has much time to listen.

"My office gets a weekly summary film from Planetary Press. Generally, I don't have time to pay attention to it. Maybe you'd call us provincial, and you'd be right. When something like this happens, all we can do is kind of helplessly look at each other."

Digby said slowly, "You can't mean that your people on Mars haven't heard of Hilder's anti-Waster campaign."

"No, can't exactly say that. There's a young Scavenger, son of a good friend of mine who died in space"—Sankov scratched the side of his neck doubtfully—"who makes a hobby out of reading up on Earth history and things like that. He catches video broadcasts when he's out in space and he listened to this man Hilder. Near as I can make out, that was the first talk Hilder made about Wasters.

"The young fellow came to me with that. Naturally, I didn't take him very serious. I kept an eye on the Planetary Press films for a while after that, but there wasn't much mention of Hilder and what there was made him out to look pretty funny."

"Yes, Commissioner," said Digby, "it all seemed quite a joke when it started."

Sankov stretched out a pair of long legs to one side of his desk and crossed them at the ankles. "Seems to me it's still pretty much of a joke. What's his argument? We're using up water. Has he tried looking at some figures? I got them all here. Had them brought to me when this committee arrived.

"Seems that Earth has four hundred million cubic miles of water in its oceans and each cubic mile weighs four and a half billion tons. That's a lot of water. Now we use some of that heap in space flight. Most of the thrust is inside Earth's gravitational field, and that means the water thrown out finds its way back to the oceans. Hilder doesn't figure that in. When he says a million tons of water is used up per flight, he's a liar. It's less than a hundred thousand tons.

"Suppose, now, we have fifty thousand flights a year. We don't, of course; not even fifteen hundred. But let's say there are fifty thousand. I figure there's going to be considerable expansion as time goes on. With fifty thousand flights, one cubic mile of water would be lost to space each year. That means that in a million years, Earth would lose *one quarter of 1 per cent* of its total water supply!"

Digby spread his hands, palms upward, and let them drop. "Commissioner, Interplanetary Alloys has used figures like that in their campaign against Hilder, but you can't fight a tremendous, emotion-filled drive with cold mathematics. This man Hilder has invented a name, 'Wasters.' Slowly he has built this name up into a gigantic conspiracy; a gang of brutal, profit-seeking wretches raping Earth for their own immediate benefit.

"He has accused the government of being riddled with them, the Assembly of being dominated by them, the press of being owned by them. None of this, unfortunately, seems ridiculous to the average man. He knows all too well what selfish men can do to Earth's resources. He knows what happened to Earth's oil during the Time of Troubles, for instance, and the way topsoil was ruined.

"When a farmer experiences a drought, he doesn't care that the amount of water lost in space flight isn't a droplet in a fog as far as Earth's over-all water supply is concerned. Hilder has given him something to blame and that's the strongest possible consolation for disaster. He isn't going to give that up for a diet of figures."

Sankov said, "That's where I get puzzled. Maybe it's because I don't know how things work on Earth, but it seems to me that there aren't just droughty farmers there. As near as I could make out from the news summaries, these Hilder people are a minority. Why is it Earth goes along with a few farmers and some crackpots that egg them on?"

"Because, Commissioner, there are such things as worried human beings. The steel industry sees that an era of space flight will stress increasingly the light, nonferrous alloys. The various miners' unions worry about extraterrestrial competition. Any Earthman who can't get aluminum to build a prefab is certain that it is because the aluminum is going to Mars. I know a professor of archaeology who's an anti-Waster because he can't get a government grant to cover his excavations. He's convinced that all government money is going into rocketry research and space medicine and he resents it."

Sankov said, "That doesn't sound like Earth people are much different from us here on Mars. But what about the General Assembly? Why do they have to go along with Hilder?"

Digby smiled sourly. "Politics isn't pleasant to explain. Hilder introduced this bill to set up a committee to investigate waste in space flight. Maybe three fourths or more of the General Assembly was against such an investigation as an intolerable and useless extension of bureaucracy—which it is. But then how could any legislator be against a mere investigation of waste? It would sound as though he had something to fear or to conceal. It would sound as though he were himself profiting from waste. Hilder is not in the least afraid of making such accusations, and whether true or not, they would be a powerful factor with the voters in the next election. The bill passed.

"And then there came the question of appointing the members of the committee. Those who were against Hilder shied away from membership, which would have meant decisions that would be continually embarrassing. Remaining on the side lines would make that one that much less a target for Hilder. The result is that I am the only member of the committee who is outspokenly anti-Hilder and it may cost me re-election."

Sankov said, "I'd be sorry to hear that, Assemblyman. It looks as though Mars didn't have as many friends as we thought we had. We wouldn't like to lose one. But if Hilder wins out, what's he after, anyway?"

"I should think," said Digby, "that that is obvious. He wants to be the next Global Co-ordinator."

"Think he'll make it?"

"If nothing happens to stop him, he will."

"And then what? Will he drop this Waster campaign then?"

"I can't say. I don't know if he's laid his plans past the Co-ordinacy. Still, if you want my guess, he couldn't abandon the campaign and maintain his popularity. It's gotten out of hand."

Sankov scratched the side of his neck. "All right. In that case, I'll ask you for some advice. What can we folks on Mars do? You know Earth. You know the situation. We don't. Tell us what to do."

Digby rose and stepped to the window. He looked out upon the low domes of other buildings; red, rocky, completely desolate plain in between; a purple sky and a shrunken sun.

He said, without turning, "Do you people really like it on Mars?"

Sankov smiled. "Most of us don't exactly know any other world, Assemblyman. Seems to me Earth would be something queer and uncomfortable to them."

"But wouldn't Martians get used to it? Earth isn't hard to take after this.

Wouldn't your people learn to enjoy the privilege of breathing air under an open sky? You once lived on Earth. You remember what it was like."

"I sort of remember. Still, it doesn't seem to be easy to explain. Earth is just there. It fits people and people fit it. People take Earth the way they find it. Mars is different. It's sort of raw and doesn't fit people. People got to make something out of it. They got to *build* a world, and not take what they find. Mars isn't much yet, but we're building, and when we're finished, we're going to have just what we like. It's sort of a great feeling to know you're building a world. Earth would be kind of unexciting after that."

The Assemblyman said, "Surely the ordinary Martian isn't such a philosopher that he's content to live this terribly hard life for the sake of a future that must be hundreds of generations away."

"No-o, not just like that." Sankov put his right ankle on his left knee and cradled it as he spoke. "Like I said, Martians are a lot like Earthmen, which means they're sort of human beings, and human beings don't go in for philosophy much. Just the same, there's something to living in a growing world, whether you think about it much or not.

"My father used to send me letters when I first came to Mars. He was an accountant and he just sort of stayed an accountant. Earth wasn't much different when he died from what it was when he was born. He didn't see anything happen. Every day was like every other day, and living was just a way of passing time until he died.

"On Mars, it's different. Every day there's something new—the city's bigger, the ventilation system gets another kick, the water lines from the poles get slicked up. Right now, we're planning to set up a news-film association of our own. We're going to call it Mars Press. If you haven't lived when things are growing all about you, you'll never understand how wonderful it feels.

"No, Assemblyman, Mars is hard and tough and Earth is a lot more comfortable, but seems to me if you take our boys to Earth, they'll be unhappy. They probably wouldn't be able to figure out why, most of them, but they'd feel lost; lost and useless. Seems to me lots of them would never make the adjustment."

Digby turned away from the window and the smooth, pink skin of his forehead was creased into a frown. "In that case, Commissioner, I am sorry for you. For all of you."

"Why?"

"Because I don't think there's anything your people on Mars can do. Or the people on the Moon or Venus. It won't happen now; maybe it won't happen for a year or two, or even for five years. But pretty soon you'll all have to come back to Earth, unless——"

Sankov's white eyebrows bent low over his eyes. "Well?"

"Unless you can find another source of water besides the planet Earth."

Sankov shook his head. "Don't seem likely, does it?"

"Not very."

"And except for that, seems to you there's no chance?"

"None at all."

Digby said that and left, and Sankov stared for a long time at nothing before he punched a combination of the local communiline.

After a while, Ted Long looked out at him.

Sankov said, "You were right, son. There's nothing they can do. Even the ones that mean well see no way out. How did you know?"

"Commissioner," said Long, "when you've read all you can about the Time of Troubles, particularly about the twentieth century, nothing political can come as a real surprise."

"Well, maybe. Anyway, son, Assemblyman Digby is sorry for us, quite a piece sorry, you might say, but that's all. He says we'll have to leave Mars—or else get water somewhere else. Only he thinks that we can't get water somewhere else."

"You know we can, don't you, Commissioner?"

"I know we *might*, son. It's a terrible risk."

"If I find enough volunteers, the risk is our business."

"How is it going?"

"Not bad. Some of the boys are on my side right now. I talked Mario Rioz into it, for instance, and you know he's one of the best."

"That's just it—the volunteers will be the best men we have. I hate to allow it."

"If we get back, it will be worth it."

"If! If's a big word, son."

"And a big thing we're trying to do."

"Well, I gave my word that if there was no help on Earth, I'll see that the Phobos water hole lets you have all the water you'll need. Good luck."

6

Half a million miles above Saturn, Mario Rioz was cradled on nothing and sleep was delicious. He came out of it slowly and for a while, alone in his suit, he counted the stars and traced lines from one to another.

At first, as the weeks flew past, it was scavenging all over again, except for the gnawing feeling that every minute meant an additional number of thousands of miles away from all humanity. That made it worse.

They had aimed high to pass out of the ecliptic while moving through the Asteroid Belt. That had used up water and had probably been unnecessary. Although tens of thousands of worldlets look as thick as vermin in two-dimensional projection upon a photographic plate, they are nevertheless scattered so thinly through the quadrillions of cubic miles that make up their conglomerate orbit that only the most ridiculous of coincidence would have brought about a collision.

Still, they passed over the Belt and someone calculated the chances of collision with a fragment of matter large enough to do damage. The value was so low, so impossibly low, that it was perhaps inevitable that the notion of the "space-float" should occur to someone.

The days were long and many, space was empty, only one man was needed at the controls at any one time. The thought was a natural.

First, it was a particularly daring one who ventured out for fifteen minutes or so. Then another who tried half an hour. Eventually, before the asteroids were entirely behind, each ship regularly had its off-watch member suspended in space at the end of a cable.

It was easy enough. The cable, one of those intended for operations at the conclusion of their journey, was magnetically attached at both ends, one to the space suit to start with. Then you clambered out the lock onto the ship's hull and attached the other end there. You paused awhile, clinging to the metal skin by the electromagnets in your boots. Then you neutralized those and made the slightest muscular effort.

Slowly, ever so slowly, you lifted from the ship and even more slowly the ship's larger mass moved an equivalently shorter distance downward. You floated incredibly, weightlessly, in solid, speckled black. When the ship had moved far enough away from you, your gauntleted hand, which kept touch upon the cable, tightened its grip slightly. Too tightly, and you would begin moving back toward the ship and it toward you. Just tightly enough, and friction would halt you. Because your motion was equivalent to that of the ship, it seemed as motionless below you as though it had been painted against an impossible background while the cable between you hung in coils that had no reason to straighten out.

It was a half-ship to your eye. One half was lit by the light of the feeble Sun, which was still too bright to look at directly without the heavy protection of the polarized space-suit visor. The other half was black on black, invisible.

Space closed in and it was like sleep. Your suit was warm, it renewed its air automatically, it had food and drink in special containers from which it could be sucked with a minimal motion of the head, it took care of wastes appropriately. Most of all, more than anything else, there was the delightful euphoria of weightlessness.

You never felt so well in your life. The days stopped being too long, they weren't long enough, and there weren't enough of them.

They had passed Jupiter's orbit at a spot some 30 degrees from its then position. For months, it was the brightest object in the sky, always excepting the glowing white pea that was the Sun. At its brightest, some of the Scavengers insisted they could make out Jupiter as a tiny sphere, one side squashed out of true by the night shadow.

Then over a period of additional months it faded, while another dot of light grew until it was brighter than Jupiter. It was Saturn, first as a dot of brilliance, then as an oval, glowing splotch.

("Why oval?" someone asked, and after a while, someone else said, "The rings, of course," and it was obvious.)

Everyone space-floated at all possible times toward the end, watching Saturn incessantly.

("Hey, you jerk, come on back in, damn it. You're on duty." "Who's on duty? I've got fifteen minutes more by my watch." "You set your watch back. Besides, I gave you twenty minutes yesterday." "You wouldn't give two minutes to your grandmother." "Come on in, damn it, or I'm coming out anyway." "All right, I'm coming. Holy howlers, what a racket over a lousy minute." But no quarrel could possibly be serious, not in space. It felt too good.)

Saturn grew until at last it rivaled and then surpassed the Sun. The rings, set at a broad angle to their trajectory of approach, swept grandly about the planet, only a small portion being eclipsed. Then, as they approached, the span of the rings grew still wider, yet narrower as the angle of approach constantly decreased.

The large moons showed up in the surrounding sky like serene fireflies.

Mario Rioz was glad he was awake so that he could watch again.

Saturn filled half the sky, streaked with orange, the night shadow cutting it fuzzily nearly one quarter of the way in from the right. Two round little dots in the brightness were shadows of two of the moons. To the left and behind them (he could look over his left shoulder to see, and as he did so, the rest of his body inched slightly to the right to conserve angular momentum) was the white diamond of the Sun.

Most of all he liked to watch the rings. At the left, they emerged from behind Saturn, a tight, bright triple band of orange light. At the right, their beginnings were hidden in the night shadow, but showed up closer and broader. They widened as they came, like the flare of a horn, growing hazier as they approached, until, while the eye followed them, they seemed to fill the sky and lose themselves.

From the position of the Scavenger fleet just inside the outer rim of the outermost ring, the rings broke up and assumed their true identity as a phenomenal cluster of solid fragments rather than the tight, solid band of light they seemed.

Below him, or rather in the direction his feet pointed, some twenty miles away, was one of the ring fragments. It looked like a large, irregular splotch, marring the symmetry of space, three quarters in brightness and the night shadow cutting it like a knife. Other fragments were farther off, sparkling like star dust, dimmer and thicker, until, as you followed them down, they became rings once more.

The fragments were motionless, but that was only because the ships had taken up an orbit about Saturn equivalent to that of the outer edge of the rings.

The day before, Rioz reflected, he had been on that nearest fragment, working along with more than a score of others to mold it into the desired shape. Tomorrow he would be at it again.

Today—today he was space-floating.

"Mario?" The voice that broke upon his earphones was questioning.

Momentarily Rioz was flooded with annoyance. Damn it, he wasn't in the mood for company.

"Speaking," he said.

"I thought I had your ship spotted. How are you?"

"Fine. That you, Ted?"

"That's right," said Long.

"Anything wrong on the fragment?"

"Nothing. I'm out here floating."

"You?"

"It gets me, too, occasionally. Beautiful, isn't it?"

"Nice," agreed Rioz.

"You know, I've read Earth books——"

"Grounder books, you mean." Rioz yawned and found it difficult of resentment.

"—and sometimes I read descriptions of people lying on grass," continued Long. "You know that green stuff like thin, long pieces of paper they have all over the ground down there, and they look up at the blue sky with clouds in it. Did you ever see any films of that?"

"Sure. It didn't attract me. It looked cold."

"I suppose it isn't, though. After all, Earth is quite close to the Sun, and they say their atmosphere is thick enough to hold the heat. I must admit that personally I would hate to be caught under open sky with nothing on but clothes. Still, I imagine they like it."

"Grounders are nuts!"

"They talk about the trees, big brown stalks, and the winds, air movements, you know."

"You mean drafts. They can keep that, too."

"It doesn't matter. The point is they describe it beautifully, almost passionately. Many times I've wondered, 'What's it really like? Will I ever feel it or is this something only Earthmen can possibly feel?' I've felt so often that I was missing something vital. Now I know what it must be like. It's this. Complete peace in the middle of a beauty-drenched universe."

Rioz said, "They wouldn't like it. The Grounders, I mean. They're so used to their own lousy little world they wouldn't appreciate what it's like to float and look down on Saturn." He flipped his body slightly and began swaying back and forth about his center of mass, slowly, soothingly.

Long said, "Yes, I think so too. They're slaves to their planet. Even if they come to Mars, it will only be their children that are free. There'll be starships someday; great, huge things that can carry thousands of people and maintain their self-contained equilibrium for decades, maybe centuries. Mankind will spread through the whole Galaxy. But people will have to live their lives out on shipboard until new methods of interstellar travel are developed, so it will be Martians, not planet-bound Earthmen, who will colonize the Universe. That's inevitable. It's got to be. It's the Martian way."

But Rioz made no answer. He had dropped off to sleep again, rocking and swaying gently, half a million miles above Saturn.

7

The work shift of the ring fragment was the tail of the coin. The weightlessness, peace, and privacy of the space-float gave place to something that had neither peace nor privacy. Even the weightlessness, which continued, became more a purgatory than a paradise under the new conditions.

Try to manipulate an ordinarily non-portable heat projector. It could be lifted despite the fact that it was six feet high and wide and almost solid metal, since it weighed only a fraction of an ounce. But its inertia was exactly what it had always been, which meant that if it wasn't moved into position very slowly, it would just keep on going, taking you with it. Then you would have to hike the pseudo-grav field of your suit and come down with a jar.

Keralski had hiked the field a little too high and he came down a little too roughly, with the projector coming down with him at a dangerous angle. His crushed ankle had been the first casualty of the expedition.

Rioz was swearing fluently and nearly continuously. He continued to have the impulse to drag the back of his hand across his forehead in order to wipe away the accumulating sweat. The few times that he had succumbed to the impulse, metal had met silicone with a clash that rang loudly inside his suit, but served no useful purpose. The desiccators within the suit were sucking at maximum and, of course, recovering the water and restoring ion-exchanged liquid, containing a careful proportion of salt, into the appropriate receptacle.

Rioz yelled, "Damn it, Dick, wait till I give the word, will you?"

And Swenson's voice rang in his ears, "Well, how long am I supposed to sit here?"

"Till I say," replied Rioz.

He strengthened pseudo-grav and lifted the projector a bit. He released pseudo-grav, insuring that the projector would stay in place for minutes even if he withdrew support altogether. He kicked the cable out of the way (it stretched beyond the close "horizon" to a power source that was out of sight) and touched the release.

The material of which the fragment was composed bubbled and vanished under its touch. A section of the lip of the tremendous cavity he had already carved into its substance melted away and a roughness in its contour had disappeared.

"Try it now," called Rioz.

Swenson was in the ship that was hovering nearly over Rioz's head.

Swenson called, "All clear?"

"I told you to go ahead."

It was a feeble flicker of steam that issued from one of the ship's forward vents. The ship drifted down toward the ring fragment. Another flicker adjusted a tendency to drift sidewise. It came down straight.

A third flicker to the rear slowed it to a feather rate.

Rioz watched tensely. "Keep her coming. You'll make it. You'll make it."

The rear of the ship entered the hole, nearly filling it. The bellying walls came closer and closer to its rim. There was a grinding vibration as the ship's motion halted.

It was Swenson's turn to curse. "It doesn't fit," he said.

Rioz threw the projector groundward in a passion and went flailing up into space. The projector kicked up a white crystalline dust all about it, and when Rioz came down under pseudo-grav, he did the same.

He said, "You went in on the bias, you dumb Grounder."

"I hit it level, you dirt-eating farmer."

Backward-pointing side jets of the ship were blasting more strongly than before, and Rioz hopped to get out of the way.

The ship scraped up from the pit, then shot into space half a mile before forward jets could bring it to a halt.

Swenson said tensely, "We'll spring half a dozen plates if we do this once again. Get it right, will you?"

"I'll get it right. Don't worry about it. Just you come in right."

Rioz jumped upward and allowed himself to climb three hundred yards to get an over-all look at the cavity. The gouge marks of the ship were plain enough. They were concentrated at one point halfway down the pit. He would get that.

It began to melt outward under the blaze of the projector.

Half an hour later the ship snuggled neatly into its cavity, and Swenson, wearing his space suit, emerged to join Rioz.

Swenson said, "If you want to step in and climb out of the suit, I'll take care of the icing."

"It's all right," said Rioz. "I'd just as soon sit here and watch Saturn."

He sat down at the lip of the pit. There was a six-foot gap between it and the ship. In some places about the circle, it was two feet; in a few places, even merely a matter of inches. You couldn't expect a better fit out of handwork. The final adjustment would be made by steaming ice gently and letting it freeze into the cavity between the lip and the ship.

Saturn moved visibly across the sky, its vast bulk inching below the horizon.

Rioz said, "How many ships are left to put in place?"

Swenson said, "Last I heard, it was eleven. We're in now, so that leaves only ten. Seven of the ones that are placed are iced in. Two or three are dismantled."

"We're coming along fine."

"There's plenty to do yet. Don't forget the main jets at the other end. And the cables and the power lines. Sometimes I wonder if we'll make it. On the way out, it didn't bother me so much, but just now I was sitting at the controls and I was saying, 'We won't make it. We'll sit out here and starve and die with nothing but Saturn over us.' It makes me feel——"

He didn't explain how it made him feel. He just sat there.

Rioz said, "You think too damn much."

"It's different with you," said Swenson. "I keep thinking of Pete—and Dora."

"What for? She said you could go, didn't she? The Commissioner gave her that talk on patriotism and how you'd be a hero and set for life once you got back, and she said you could go. You didn't sneak out the way Adams did."

"Adams is different. That wife of his should have been shot when she was born. Some women can make hell for a guy, can't they? She didn't want him to go—but she'd probably rather he didn't come back if she can get his settlement pay."

"What's your kick, then? Dora wants you back, doesn't she?"

Swenson sighed. "I never treated her right."

"You turned over your pay, it seems to me. I wouldn't do that for any woman. Money for value received, not a cent more."

"Money isn't it. I get to thinking out here. A woman likes company. A kid needs his father. What am I doing 'way out here?"

"Getting set to go home."

"Ah-h, you don't understand."

8

Ted Long wandered over the ridged surface of the ring fragment with his spirits as icy as the ground he walked on. It had all seemed perfectly logical back on Mars, but that was Mars. He had worked it out carefully in his mind in perfectly reasonable steps. He could still remember exactly how it went.

It didn't take a ton of water to move a ton of ship. It was not mass equals mass, but mass times velocity equals mass times velocity. It didn't matter, in other words, whether you shot out a ton of water at a mile a second or a hundred pounds of water at twenty miles a second. You got the same final velocity out of the ship.

That meant the jet nozzles had to be made narrower and the steam hotter. But then drawbacks appeared. The narrower the nozzle, the more energy was lost in friction and turbulence. The hotter the steam, the more refractory the nozzle had to be and the shorter its life. The limit in that direction was quickly reached.

Then, since a given weight of water could move considerably more than its own weight under the narrow-nozzle conditions, it paid to be big. The bigger the water-storage space, the larger the size of the actual travel-head, even in proportion. So they started to make liners heavier and bigger. But then the larger the shell, the heavier the bracings, the more difficult the weldings, the more exacting the engineering requirements. At the moment, the limit in that direction had been reached also.

And then he had put his finger on what had seemed to him to be the basic flaw—the original unswervable conception that the fuel had to be placed *inside* the ship; the metal had to be built to encircle a million tons of water.

Why? Water did not have to be water. It could be ice, and ice could be shaped. Holes could be melted into it. Travel-heads and jets could be fitted into it. Cables could hold travel-heads and jets stiffly together under the influence of magnetic field-force grips.

Long felt the trembling of the ground he walked on. He was at the head of the fragment. A dozen ships were blasting in and out of sheaths carved in its substance, and the fragment shuddered under the continuing impact.

The ice didn't have to be quarried. It existed in proper chunks in the rings of Saturn. That's all the rings were—pieces of nearly pure ice, circling Saturn. So spectroscopy stated and so it had turned out to be. He was standing on one such piece now, over two miles long, nearly one mile thick. It was almost half a billion tons of water, all in one piece, and he was standing on it.

But now he was face to face with the realities of life. He had never told the men just how quickly he had expected to set up the fragment as a ship, but in his heart, he had imagined it would be two days. It was a week now and he didn't dare to estimate the remaining time. He no longer even had any confidence that the task was a possible one. Would they be able to control jets with enough delicacy through leads slung across two miles of ice to manipulate out of Saturn's dragging gravity?

Drinking water was low, though they could always distill more out of the ice. Still, the food stores were not in a good way either.

He paused, looking up into the sky, eyes straining. *Was* the object growing larger? He ought to measure its distance. Actually, he lacked the spirit to add that trouble to the others. His mind slid back to greater immediacies.

Morale, at least, was high. The men seemed to enjoy being out Saturn-way. They were the first humans to penetrate this far, the first to pass the asteroids, the first to see Jupiter like a glowing pebble to the naked eye, the first to see Saturn—like that.

He didn't think fifty practical, case-hardened, shell-snatching Scavengers would take time to feel that sort of emotion. But they did. And they were proud.

Two men and a half-buried ship slid up the moving horizon as he walked. He called crisply, "Hello, there!"

Rioz answered, "That you, Ted?"

"You bet. Is that Dick with you?"

"Sure. Come on, sit down. We were just getting ready to ice in and we were looking for an excuse to delay."

"I'm not," said Swenson promptly. "When will we be leaving, Ted?"

"As soon as we get through. That's no answer, is it?"

Swenson said dispiritedly, "I suppose there isn't any other answer."

Long looked up, staring at the irregular bright splotch in the sky.

Rioz followed his glance. "What's the matter?"

For a moment, Long did not reply. The sky was black otherwise and the ring fragments were an orange dust against it. Saturn was more than three fourths below the horizon and the rings were going with it. Half a mile away a ship bounded past the icy rim of the planetoid into the sky, was orange-lit by Saturn-light, and sank down again.

The ground trembled gently.

Rioz said, "Something bothering you about the Shadow?"

They called it that. It was the nearest fragment of the rings, quite close considering that they were at the outer rim of the rings, where the pieces spread themselves relatively thin. It was perhaps twenty miles off, a jagged mountain, its shape clearly visible.

"How does it look to you?" asked Long.

Rioz shrugged. "Okay, I guess. I don't see anything wrong."

"Doesn't it seem to be getting larger?"

"Why should it?"

"Well, doesn't it?" Long insisted.

Rioz and Swenson stared at it thoughtfully.

"It does look bigger," said Swenson.

"You're just putting the notion into our minds," Rioz argued. "If it were getting bigger, it would be coming closer."

"What's impossible about that?"

"These things are on stable orbits."

"They were when we came here," said Long. "There, did you feel that?"

The ground had trembled again.

Long said, "We've been blasting this thing for a week now. First, twenty-five ships landed on it, which changed its momentum right there. Not much, of course. Then we've been melting parts of it away and our ships have been blasting in and out of it—all at one end, too. In a week, we may have changed its orbit just a bit. The two fragments, this one and the Shadow, might be converging."

"It's got plenty of room to miss us in." Rioz watched it thoughtfully. "Besides, if we can't even tell for sure that it's getting bigger, how quickly can it be moving? Relative to us, I mean."

"It doesn't have to be moving quickly. Its momentum is as large as ours, so that, however gently it hits, we'll be nudged completely out of our orbit, maybe toward Saturn, where we don't want to go. As a matter of fact, ice has a very low tensile strength, so that both planetoids might break up into gravel."

Swenson rose to his feet. "Damn it, if I can tell how a shell is moving a thousand miles away, I can tell what a mountain is doing twenty miles away." He turned toward the ship.

Long didn't stop him.

Rioz said, "There's a nervous guy."

The neighboring planetoid rose to zenith, passed overhead, began sinking. Twenty minutes later, the horizon opposite that portion behind which Saturn had disappeared burst into orange flame as its bulk began lifting again.

Rioz called into his radio, "Hey, Dick, are you dead in there?"

"I'm checking," came the muffled response.

"Is it moving?" asked Long.

"Yes."

"Toward us?"

There was a pause. Swenson's voice was a sick one. "On the nose, Ted. Intersection of orbits will take place in three days."

"You're crazy!" yelled Rioz.

"I checked four times," said Swenson.

Long thought blankly, What do we do now?

9

Some of the men were having trouble with the cables. They had to be laid precisely; their geometry had to be very nearly perfect for the magnetic field to attain maximum strength. In space, or even in air, it wouldn't have mattered. The cables would have lined up automatically once the juice went on.

Here it was different. A gouge had to be plowed along the planetoid's surface and into it the cable had to be laid. If it were not lined up within a few minutes of arc of the calculated direction, a torque would be applied to the entire planetoid, with consequent loss of energy, none of which could be spared. The gouges then had to be redriven, the cables shifted and iced into the new positions.

The men plodded wearily through the routine.

And then the word reached them:

"All hands to the jets!"

Scavengers could not be said to be the type that took kindly to discipline. It was a grumbling, growling, muttering group that set about disassembling the jets of the ships that yet remained intact, carrying them to the tail end of the planetoid, grubbing them into position, and stringing the leads along the surface.

It was almost twenty-four hours before one of them looked into the sky and said, "Holy jeepers!" followed by something less printable.

His neighbor looked and said, "I'll be damned!"

Once they noticed, all did. It became the most astonishing fact in the Universe.

"Look at the Shadow!"

It was spreading across the sky like an infected wound. Men looked at it, found it had doubled its size, wondered why they hadn't noticed that sooner.

Work came to a virtual halt. They besieged Ted Long.

He said, "We can't leave. We don't have the fuel to see us back to Mars and we don't have the equipment to capture another planetoid. So we've got to stay. Now the Shadow is creeping in on us because our blasting has thrown us out of orbit. We've got to change that by continuing the blasting. Since we can't blast the front end any more without endangering the ship we're building, let's try another way."

They went back to work on the jets with a furious energy that received impetus every half hour when the Shadow rose again over the horizon, bigger and more menacing than before.

Long had no assurance that it would work. Even if the jets would respond to the distant controls, even if the supply of water, which depended upon a storage chamber opening directly into the icy body of the planetoid, with built-in heat projectors steaming the propulsive fluid directly into the driving cells, were adequate, there was still no certainty that the body of the planetoid without a magnetic cable sheathing would hold together under the enormously disruptive stresses.

"Ready!" came the signal in Long's receiver.

Long called, "Ready!" and depressed the contact.

The vibration grew about him. The star field in the visiplate trembled.

In the rearview, there was a distant gleaming spume of swiftly moving ice crystals.

"It's blowing!" was the cry.

It kept on blowing. Long dared not stop. For six hours, it blew, hissing, bubbling, steaming into space; the body of the planetoid converted to vapor and hurled away.

The Shadow came closer until men did nothing but stare at the mountain in the sky, surpassing Saturn itself in spectacularity. Its every groove and valley was a plain scar upon its face. But when it passed through the planetoid's orbit, it crossed more than half a mile behind its then position.

The steam jet ceased.

Long bent in his seat and covered his eyes. He hadn't eaten in two days. He could eat now, though. Not another planetoid was close enough to interrupt them, even if it began an approach that very moment.

Back on the planetoid's surface, Swenson said, "All the time I watched that damned rock coming down, I kept saying to myself, 'This can't happen. We can't let it happen.'"

"Hell," said Rioz, "we were all nervous. Did you see Jim Davis? He was green. I was a little jumpy myself."

"That's not it. It wasn't just—dying, you know. I was thinking—I know it's funny, but I can't help it—I was thinking that Dora warned me I'd get myself killed, she'll never let me hear the last of it. Isn't that a crummy sort of attitude at a time like that?"

"Listen," said Rioz, "you wanted to get married, so you got married. Why come to me with your troubles?"

10

The flotilla, welded into a single unit, was returning over its mighty course from Saturn to Mars. Each day it flashed over a length of space it had taken nine days outward.

Ted Long had put the entire crew on emergency. With twenty-five ships embedded in the planetoid taken out of Saturn's rings and unable to move or maneuver independently, the co-ordination of their power sources into unified blasts was a ticklish problem. The jarring that took place on the first day of travel nearly shook them out from under their hair.

That, at least, smoothed itself out as the velocity raced upward under the steady thrust from behind. They passed the one-hundred-thousand-mile-an-hour mark late on the second day, and climbed steadily toward the million-mile mark and beyond.

Long's ship, which formed the needle point of the frozen fleet, was the only one which possessed a five-way view of space. It was an uncomfortable position under the circumstances. Long found himself watching tensely, imagining somehow that the stars would slowly begin to slip backward, to whizz past them, under the influence of the multi-ship's tremendous rate of travel.

They didn't, of course. They remained nailed to the black backdrop, their distance scorning with patient immobility any speed mere man could achieve.

The men complained bitterly after the first few days. It was not only that they were deprived of the space-float. They were burdened by much more than the ordinary pseudo-gravity field of the ships, by the effects of the fierce acceleration under which they were living. Long himself was weary to death of the relentless pressure against hydraulic cushions.

They took to shutting off the jet thrusts one hour out of every four and Long fretted.

It had been just over a year that he had last seen Mars shrinking in an observation window from this ship, which had then been an independent entity. What had happened since then? Was the colony still there?

In something like a growing panic, Long sent out radio pulses toward Mars daily, with the combined power of twenty-five ships behind it. There was no answer. He expected none. Mars and Saturn were on opposite sides of the Sun now, and until he mounted high enough above the ecliptic to get the Sun well beyond the line connecting himself and Mars, solar interference would prevent any signal from getting through.

High above the outer rim of the Asteroid Belt, they reached maximum velocity. With short spurts of power from first one side jet, then another, the huge vessel reversed itself. The composite jet in the rear began its mighty roaring once again, but now the result was deceleration.

They passed a hundred million miles over the Sun, curving down to intersect the orbit of Mars.

A week out of Mars, answering signals were heard for the first time, fragmentary, ether-torn, and incomprehensible, but they were coming from Mars. Earth and Venus were at angles sufficiently different to leave no doubt of that.

Long relaxed. There were still humans on Mars, at any rate.

Two days out of Mars, the signal was strong and clear and Sankov was at the other end.

Sankov said, "Hello, son. It's three in the morning here. Seems like people have no consideration for an old man. Dragged me right out of bed."

"I'm sorry, sir."

"Don't be. They were following orders. I'm afraid to ask, son. Anyone hurt? Maybe dead?"

"No deaths, sir. Not one."

"And—and the water? Any left?"

Long said, with an effort at nonchalance, "Enough."

"In that case, get home as fast as you can. Don't take any chances, of course."

"There's trouble, then."

"Fair to middling. When will you come down?"

"Two days. Can you hold out that long?"

"I'll hold out."

Forty hours later Mars had grown to a ruddy-orange ball that filled the ports and they were in the final planet-landing spiral.

"Slowly," Long said to himself, "slowly." Under these conditions, even the thin atmosphere of Mars could do dreadful damage if they moved through it too quickly.

Since they came in from well above the ecliptic, their spiral passed from north to south. A polar cap shot whitely below them, then the much smaller one of the summer hemisphere, the large one again, the small one, at longer and longer intervals. The planet approached closer, the landscape began to show features.

"Prepare for landing!" called Long.

11

Sankov did his best to look placid, which was difficult considering how closely the boys had shaved their return. But it had worked out well enough.

Until a few days ago, he had no sure knowledge that they had survived. It seemed more likely—inevitable, almost—that they were nothing but frozen corpses somewhere in the trackless stretches from Mars to Saturn, new planetoids that had once been alive.

The Committee had been dickering with him for weeks before the news had come. They had insisted on his signature to the paper for the sake of appearances. It would look like an agreement, voluntarily and mutually arrived at. But Sankov knew well that, given complete obstinacy on his part, they would act unilaterally and be damned with appearances. It seemed fairly certain that Hilder's election was secure now and they would take the chance of arousing a reaction of sympathy for Mars.

So he dragged out the negotiations, dangling before them always the possibility of surrender.

And then he heard from Long and concluded the deal quickly.

The papers had lain before him and he had made a last statement for the benefit of the reporters who were present.

He said, "Total imports of water from Earth are twenty million tons a year. This is declining as we develop our own piping system. If I sign this paper agreeing to an embargo, our industry will be paralyzed, any possibilities of expansion will halt. It looks to me as if that can't be what's in Earth's mind, can it?"

Their eyes met his and held only a hard glitter. Assemblyman Digby had already been replaced and they were unanimous against him.

The Committee Chairman impatiently pointed out, "You have said all this before."

"I know, but right now I'm kind of getting ready to sign and I want it clear in my head. Is Earth set and determined to bring us to an end here?"

"Of course not. Earth is interested in conserving its irreplaceable water supply, nothing else."

"You have one and a half quintillion tons of water on Earth."

The Committee Chairman said, "We cannot spare water." And Sankov had signed.

That had been the final note he wanted. Earth had one and a half quintillion tons of water and could spare none of it.

Now, a day and a half later, the Committee and the reporters waited in the spaceport dome. Through thick, curving windows, they could see the bare and empty grounds of Mars Spaceport.

The Committee Chairman asked with annoyance, "How much longer do we have to wait? And, if you don't mind, what are we waiting for?"

Sankov said, "Some of our boys have been out in space, out past the asteroids."

The Committee Chairman removed a pair of spectacles and cleaned them with a snowy-white handkerchief. "And they're returning?"

"They are."

The Chairman shrugged, lifted his eyebrows in the direction of the reporters.

In the smaller room adjoining, a knot of women and children clustered about another window. Sankov stepped back a bit to cast a glance toward them. He would much rather have been with them, been part of their excitement and tension. He, like them, had waited over a year now. He, like them, had thought, over and over again, that the men must be dead.

"You see that?" said Sankov, pointing.

"Hey!" cried a reporter. "It's a ship!"

A confused shouting came from the adjoining room.

It wasn't a ship so much as a bright dot obscured by a drifting white cloud. The cloud grew larger and began to have form. It was a double streak against the sky, the lower ends billowing out and upward again. As it dropped still closer, the bright dot at the upper end took on a crudely cylindrical form.

It was rough and craggy, but where the sunlight hit, brilliant highlights bounced back.

The cylinder dropped toward the ground with the ponderous slowness characteristic of space vessels. It hung suspended on those blasting jets and settled down upon the recoil of tons of matter hurling downward like a tired man dropping into his easy chair.

And as it did so, a silence fell upon all within the dome. The women and children in one room, the politicians and reporters in the other remained frozen, heads craned incredulously upward.

The cylinder's landing flanges, extending far below the two rear jets, touched ground and sank into the pebbly morass. And then the ship was motionless and the jet action ceased.

But the silence continued in the dome. It continued for a long time.

Men came clambering down the sides of the immense vessel, inching down, down the two-mile trek to the ground, with spikes on their shoes and ice axes in their hands. They were gnats against the blinding surface.

One of the reporters croaked, "What is it?"

"That," said Sankov calmly, "happens to be a chunk of matter that spent its time scooting around Saturn as part of its rings. Our boys fitted it out with travel-head and jets and ferried it home. It just turns out the fragments in Saturn's rings are made up out of ice."

He spoke into a continuing deathlike silence. "That thing that looks like a spaceship is just a mountain of hard water. If it were standing like that on Earth, it would be melting into a puddle and maybe it would break under its own weight. Mars is colder and has less gravity, so there's no such danger.

"Of course, once we get this thing really organized, we can have water stations on the moons of Saturn and Jupiter and on the asteroids. We can scale in chunks of Saturn's rings and pick them up and send them on at the various stations. Our Scavengers are good at that sort of thing.

"We'll have all the water we need. That one chunk you see is just under a cubic mile—or about what Earth would send us in two hundred years. The boys used quite a bit of it coming back from Saturn. They made it in five weeks, they tell me, and used up about a hundred million tons. But, Lord, that didn't make any dent at all in that mountain. Are you getting all this, boys?"

He turned to the reporters. There was no doubt they were getting it.

He said, "Then get this, too. Earth is worried about its water supply. It only has one and a half quintillion tons. It can't spare us a single ton of it. Write down that we folks on Mars are worried about Earth and don't want anything to happen to Earth people. Write down that we'll sell water to Earth. Write down that we'll let them have million-ton lots for a reasonable fee. Write down that in ten years, we figure we can sell it in cubic-mile lots. Write down that Earth can quit worrying because Mars can sell it all the water it needs and wants."

The Committee Chairman was past hearing. He was feeling the future rushing in. Dimly he could see the reporters grinning as they wrote furiously.

Grinning.

He could hear the grin become laughter on Earth as Mars turned the tables so neatly on the anti-Wasters. He could hear the laughter thunder from every continent when word of the fiasco spread. And he could see the abyss, deep and black as space, into which would drop forever the political hopes of John Hilder and of every opponent of space flight left on Earth—his own included, of course.

In the adjoining room, Dora Swenson screamed with joy, and Peter, grown two inches, jumped up and down, calling, "Daddy! Daddy!"

Richard Swenson had just stepped off the extremity of the flange and, face showing clearly through the clear silicone of the headpiece, marched toward the dome.

"Did you ever see a guy look so happy?" asked Ted Long. "Maybe there's something in this marriage business."

"Ah, you've just been out in space too long," Rioz said.

The Monkey's Finger

"Yes. Yes. Yes. Yes. Yes. Yes. Yes. Yes. Yes. Yes. Yes. Yes. Yes. Yes. Yes. Yes,"
said Marmie Tallinn, in sixteen different inflections and pitches, while the
Adam's apple in his long neck bobbed convulsively. He was a science fiction
writer.

"No," said Lemuel Hoskins, staring stonily through his steel-rimmed
glasses. He was a science fiction editor.

"Then you won't accept a scientific test. You won't listen to me. I'm
outvoted, eh?" Marmie lifted himself on his toes, dropped down, repeated
the process a few times, and breathed heavily. His dark hair was matted into
tufts, where fingers had clutched.

"One to sixteen," said Hoskins.

"Look," said Marmie, "what makes you always right? What makes me
always wrong?"

"Marmie, face it. We're each judged in our own way. If magazine circulation were to drop, I'd be a flop. I'd be out on my ear. The president of Space
Publishers would ask no questions, believe me. He would just look at the
figures. But circulation doesn't go down; it's going up. That makes me a good
editor. And as for you—when editors accept you, you're a talent. When they
reject you, you're a bum. At the moment, you are a bum."

"There are other editors, you know. You're not the only one." Marmie
held up his hands, fingers outspread. "Can you count? That's how many
science fiction magazines on the market would gladly take a Tallinn yarn,
sight unseen."

"Gesundheit," said Hoskins.

"Look," Marmie's voice sweetened, "you wanted two changes, right? You wanted an introductory scene with the battle in space. Well, I gave that to you. It's right here." He waved the manuscript under Hoskin's nose and Hoskin moved away as though at a bad smell.

"But you also wanted the scene on the spaceship's hull cut into with a flashback into the interior," went on Marmie, "and that you can't get. If I make that change, I ruin an ending which, as it stands, has pathos and depth and feeling."

Editor Hoskins sat back in his chair and appealed to his secretary, who throughout had been quietly typing. She was used to these scenes.

Hoskins said, "You hear that, Miss Kane? *He* talks of pathos, depth, and feeling. What does a writer know about such things? Look, if you insert the flashback, you increase the suspense; you tighten the story; you make it more valid."

"*How* do I make it more valid?" cried Marmie in anguish. "You mean to say that having a bunch of fellows in a spaceship start talking politics and sociology when they're liable to be blown up makes it more *valid?* Oh, my God."

"There's nothing else you can do. If you wait till the climax is past and then discuss your politics and sociology, the reader will go to sleep on you."

"But I'm trying to tell you that you're wrong and I can prove it. What's the use of talking when I've arranged a scientific experiment—"

"What scientific experiment?" Hoskins appealed to his secretary again. "How do you like that, Miss Kane. He thinks he's one of his own characters."

"It so happens I know a scientist."

"Who?"

"Dr. Arndt Torgesson, professor of psychodynamics at Columbia."

"Never heard of him."

"I suppose that means a lot," said Marmie, with contempt. "*You* never heard of him. You never heard of Einstein until your writers started mentioning him in their stories."

"Very humorous. A yuk. What about this Torgesson?"

"He's worked out a system for determining scientifically the value of a piece of writing. It's a tremendous piece of work. It's—it's—"

"And it's secret?"

"Certainly it's secret. He's not a science fiction professor. In science fiction, when a man thinks up a theory, he announces it to the newspapers right away. In real life, that's not done. A scientist spends years on experimentation sometimes before going into print. Publishing is a serious thing."

"Then how do *you* know about it? Just a question."

"It so happens that Dr. Torgesson is a fan of mine. He happens to like my stories. He happens to think I'm the best fantasy writer in the business."

"And he shows you his work?"

"That's right. I was counting on you being stubborn about this yarn and I've asked him to run an experiment for us. He said he would do it if we don't talk about it. He said it would be an interesting experiment. He said—"

"What's so secret about it?"

"Well—" Marmie hesitated. "Look, suppose I told you he had a monkey that could type *Hamlet* out of its head."

Hoskins stared at Marmie in alarm. "What are you working up here, a practical joke?" He turned to Miss Kane. "When a writer writes science fiction for ten years he just isn't safe without a personal cage."

Miss Kane maintained a steady typing speed.

Marmie said, "You heard me; a common monkey, even funnier-looking than the average editor. I made an appointment for this afternoon. Are you coming with me or not?"

"Of course not. You think I'd abandon a stack of manuscripts this high"— and he indicated his larynx with a cutting motion of the hand—"for your stupid jokes? You think I'll play straight man for you?"

"If this is in any way a joke, Hoskins, I'll stand you dinner in any restaurant you name. Miss Kane's the witness."

Hoskins sat back in his chair. "You'll buy me dinner? You, Marmaduke Tallinn, New York's most widely known tapeworm-on-credit, are going to pick up a check?"

Marmie winced, not at the reference to his agility in overlooking a dinner check, but at the mention of his name in all its horrible trysyllabicity. He said, "I repeat. Dinner on me wherever you want and whatever you want. Steaks, mushrooms, breast of guinea hen, Martian alligator, anything."

Hoskins stood up and plucked his hat from the top of the filing cabinet.

"For a chance," he said, "to see you unfold some of the old-style, large-size dollar bills you've been keeping in the false heel of your left shoe since nineteen-two-eight, I'd walk to Boston. . . ."

Dr. Torgesson was honored. He shook Hoskin's hand warmly and said, "I've been reading *Space Yarns* ever since I came to this country, Mr. Hoskins. It is an excellent magazine. I am particularly fond of Mr. Tallinn's stories."

"You hear?" asked Marmie.

"I hear. Marmie says you have a monkey with talent, Professor."

"Yes," Torgesson said, "but of course this must be confidential. I am not yet ready to publish, and premature publicity could be my professional ruin."

"This is strictly under the editorial hat, Professor."

"Good, good. Sit down, gentlemen, sit down." He paced the floor before them. "What have you told Mr. Hoskins about my work, Marmie?"

"Not a thing, Professor."

"So. Well, Mr. Hoskins, as the editor of a science fiction magazine, I don't have to ask you if you know anything about cybernetics."

Hoskins allowed a glance of concentrated intellect to ooze out past his steel-rims. He said, "Ah, yes. Computing machines—M.I.T.—Norbert Weiner—" He mumbled some more.

"Yes. Yes." Torgesson paced faster. "Then you must know that chess-playing computers have been constructed on cybernetic principles. The rules of chess moves and the object of the game are built into its circuits. Given any position on the chess board, the machine can then compute all possible moves together with their consequence and choose that one which offers the highest probability of winning the game. It can even be made to take the temperament of its opponent into account."

"Ah, yes," said Hoskins, stroking his chin profoundly.

Torgesson said, "Now imagine a similar situation in which a computing machine can be given a fragment of a literary work to which the computer can then add words from its stock of the entire vocabulary such that the greatest literary values are served. Naturally, the machine would have to be taught the significance of the various keys of a typewriter. Of course, such a computer would have to be much, much more complex than any chess player."

Hoskins stirred restlessly. "The monkey, Professor. Marmie mentioned a monkey."

"But that is what I am coming to," said Torgesson. "Naturally, no machine built is sufficiently complex. But the human brain—ah. The human brain is itself a computing machine. Of course, I couldn't use a human brain. The law, unfortunately, would not permit me. But even a monkey's brain, properly managed, can do more than any machine ever constructed by man. Wait! I'll go get little Rollo."

He left the room. Hoskins waited a moment, then looked cautiously at Marmie. He said, "Oh, brother!"

Marmie said, "What's the matter?"

"What's the matter? The man's a phony. Tell me, Marmie, where did you hire this faker?"

Marmie was outraged. "Faker? This is a genuine professor's office in Fayerweather Hall, Columbia. You recognize Columbia, I hope. You saw the statue of Alma Mater on 116th Street. I pointed out Eisenhower's office."

"Sure, but—"

"And this is Dr. Torgesson's office. Look at the dust." He blew at a textbook and stirred up clouds of it. "The dust alone shows it's the real thing. And look at the title of the book: *Psychodynamics of Human Behavior*, by Professor Arndt Rolf Torgesson."

"Granted, Marmie, granted. There is a Torgesson and this is his office. How you knew the real guy was on vacation and how you managed to get the use of his office, I don't know. But are you trying to tell me that this comic with his monkeys and computers is the real thing? Hah!"

"With a suspicious nature like yours, I can only assume you had a very miserable, rejected type of childhood."

"Just the result of experience with writers, Marmie. I have my restaurant all picked out and this will cost you a pretty penny."

Marmie snorted, "This won't cost me even the ugliest penny you ever paid me. Quiet, he's coming back."

With the professor, and clinging to his neck, was a very melancholy capuchin monkey.

"This," said Torgesson, "is little Rollo. Say hello, Rollo."

The monkey tugged at his forelock.

The professor said, "He's tired, I'm afraid. Now, I have a piece of his manuscript right here."

He put the monkey down and let it cling to his finger while he brought out two sheets of paper from his jacket pocket and handed them to Hoskins.

Hoskins read, " 'To be or not to be; that is the question: Whether 'tis nobler in the mind to suffer the slings and arrows of outrageous fortune, or to take arms against a host of troubles, and by opposing end them? To die: to sleep; No more: and, by a sleep to say we—' "

He looked up. "Little Rollo typed this?"

"Not exactly. It's a copy of what he typed."

"Oh, a copy. Well, little Rollo doesn't know his Shakespeare. It's 'to take arms against a sea of troubles.' "

Torgesson nodded. "You are quite correct, Mr. Hoskins. Shakespeare *did* write 'sea.' But you see that's a mixed metaphor. You don't fight a sea with arms. You fight a host or army with arms. Rollo chose the monosyllable and typed 'host.' It's one of Shakespeare's rare mistakes."

Hoskins said, "Let's see him type."

"Surely." The professor trundled out a typewriter on a little table. A wire trailed from it. He explained, "It is necessary to use an electric typewriter as otherwise the physical effort would be too great. It is also necessary to wire little Rollo to this transformer."

He did so, using as leads two electrodes that protruded an eighth of an inch through the fur on the little creature's skull.

"Rollo," he said, "was subjected to a very delicate brain operation in which a nest of wires were connected to various regions of his brain. We can short his voluntary activities and, in effect, use his brain simply as a computer. I'm afraid the details would be—"

"Let's see him type," said Hoskins.

"What would you like?"

Hoskins thought rapidly. "Does he know Chesterton's 'Lepanto'?"

"He knows nothing by heart. His writing is purely computation. Now, you simply recite a little of the piece so that he will be able to estimate the mood and compute the consequences of the first words."

Hoskins nodded, inflated his chest, and thundered, "White founts falling in the courts of the sun, and the Soldan of Byzantium is smiling as they run. There is laughter like the fountains in that face of all men feared; it stirs the forest darkness, the darkness of his beard; it curls the blood-red crescent, the crescent of his lips; for the inmost sea of all the world is shaken by his ships—"

"That's enough," said Torgesson.

There was silence as they waited. The monkey regarded the typewriter solemnly.

Torgesson said, "The process takes time, of course. Little Rollo has to take into account the romanticism of the poem, the slightly archaic flavor, the strong sing-song rhythm, and so on."

And then a black little finger reached out and touched a key. It was a *t*.

"He doesn't capitalize," said the scientist, "or punctuate, and his spacing isn't very reliable. That's why I usually retype his work when he's finished."

Little Rollo touched an *h*, then an *e* and a *y*. Then, after a longish pause, he tapped the space bar.

"They," said Hoskins.

The words typed themselves out: "they have dared the-white repub lics upthe capes of italy they have dashed the adreeatic roundthe lion of the sea; and the popehas throw n his arms abroa dfor agoni and loss and called the kings of chrissndom for sords about the cross."

"My God!" said Hoskins.

"That's the way the piece goes then?" asked Torgesson.

"For the love of Pete!" said Hoskins.

"If it is, then Chesterton must have done a good, consistent job."

"Holy smokes!" said Hoskins.

"You see," said Marmie, massaging Hoskins's shoulder, "you see, you see, you see. You see," he added.

"I'll be damned," said Hoskins.

"Now look," said Marmie, rubbing his hair till it rose in clusters like a cockatoo's chest, "let's get to business. Let's tackle my story."

"Well, but—"

"It will not be beyond little Rollo's capacity," Torgesson assured him. "I frequently read little Rollo parts of some of the better science fiction, including some of Marmie's tales. It's amazing how some of the yarns are improved."

"It's not that," said Hoskins. "Any monkey can write better SF than some of the hacks we've got. But the Tallinn story is thirteen thousand words long. It'll take forever for the monk to type it."

"Not at all, Mr. Hoskins, not at all. I shall read the story to him, and at the crucial point we will let him continue."

Hoskins folded his arms. "Then shoot. I'm ready."

"I," said Marmie, "am more than ready." And he folded his arms.

Little Rollo sat there, a furry little bundle of cataleptic misery, while Dr. Torgesson's soft voice rose and fell in cadence with a spaceship battle and the subsequent struggles of Earthmen captives to recapture their lost ship.

One of the characters made his way out to the spaceship hull, and Dr. Torgesson followed the flamboyant events in mild rapture. He read:

". . . Stalny froze in the silence of the eternal stars. His aching knee tore at his consciousness as he waited for the monsters to hear the thud and—"

Marmie yanked desperately at Dr. Torgesson's sleeve. Torgesson looked up and disconnected little Rollo.

"That's it," said Marmie. "You see, Professor, it's just about here that Hoskins is getting his sticky little fingers into the works. I continue the scene outside the spaceship till Stalny wins out and the ship is back in Earth hands. Then I go into explanations. Hoskins wants me to break that outside scene, get back inside, halt the action for two thousand words, then get back out again. Ever hear such crud?"

"Suppose we let the monk decide," said Hoskins.

Dr. Torgesson turned little Rollo on, and a black shriveled finger reached hesitantly out to the typewriter. Hoskins and Marmie leaned forward simultaneously, their heads coming softly together just over little Rollo's brooding body. The typewriter punched out the letter t.

"T," encouraged Marmie, nodding.

"T," agreed Hoskins.

The typewriter made an a, then went on at a more rapid rate: "take action stalnee waited in helpless hor ror forair locks toyawn and suited laroos to emerge relentlessly—"

"Word for word," said Marmie in raptures.

"He certainly has your gooey style."

"The readers like it."

"They wouldn't if their average mental age wasn't—" Hoskins stopped.

"Go on," said Marmie, "say it. Say it. Say their IQ is that of a twelve-year-old child and I'll quote you in every fan magazine in the country."

"Gentlemen," said Torgesson, "gentlemen. You'll disturb little Rollo."

They turned to the typewriter, which was still tapping steadily: "—the stars whelled in ther mightie orb its as stalnees earthbound senses insis ted the rotating ship sto od still."

The typewriter carriage whipped back to begin a new line. Marmie held his breath. Here, if anywhere, would come—

And the little finger moved out and made: *

Hoskins yelled, "Asterisk!"

"Marmie muttered, "Asterisk."

Torgesson said, "Asterisk?"

A line of nine more asterisks followed.

"That's all, brother," said Hoskins. He explained quickly to the staring Torgesson, "With Marmie, it's a habit to use a line of asterisks when he wants to indicate a radical shift of scene. And a radical shift of scene is exactly what I wanted."

The typewriter started a new paragraph: "within the ship—"

"Turn it off, Professor," said Marmie.

Hoskins rubbed his hands. "When do I get the revision, Marmie?"

Marmie said coolly, "What revision?"

"You said the monk's version."

"I sure did. It's what I brought you here to see. That little Rollo is a machine; a cold, brutal, logical machine."

"Well?"

"And the point is that a good writer is not a machine. He doesn't write with his mind, but with his heart. His heart." Marmie pounded his chest.

Hoskins groaned. "What are you doing to me, Marmie? If you give me that heart-and-soul-of-a-writer routine, I'll just be forced to turn sick right here and right now. Let's keep all this on the usual I'll-write-anything-for-money basis."

Marmie said, "Just listen to me for a minute. Little Rollo corrected Shakespeare. You pointed that out for yourself. Little Rollo wanted Shakespeare to say, 'host of troubles,' and he was right from his machine standpoint. A 'sea of troubles' under the circumstances is a mixed metaphor. But don't you suppose Shakespeare knew that, too? Shakespeare just happened to know when to *break* the rules, that's all. Little Rollo is a machine that can't break the rules, but a good writer can, and *must*. 'Sea of troubles' is more impressive; it has roll and power. The hell with the mixed metaphor.

"Now, when you tell me to shift the scene, you're following mechanical rules on maintaining suspense, so of course little Rollo agrees with you. But I know that I must break the rules to maintain the profound emotional impact of the ending as I see it. Otherwise I have a mechanical product that a computer can turn out."

Hoskins said, "But—"

"Go on," said Marmie, "vote for the mechanical. Say that little Rollo is all the editor you'll ever be."

Hoskins said, with a quiver in his throat, "All right, Marmie, I'll take the story as is. No, don't give it to me; mail it. I've got to find a bar, if you don't mind."

He forced his hat down on his head and turned to leave. Torgesson called after him. "Don't tell anyone about little Rollo, please."

The parting answer floated back over a slamming door, "Do you think I'm crazy? . . ."

Marmie rubbed his hands ecstatically when he was sure Hoskins was gone.

"Brains, that's what it was," he said, and probed one finger as deeply into his temple as it would go. "This sale I enjoyed. This sale, Professor, is worth all the rest I've ever made. All the rest of them together." He collapsed joyfully on the nearest chair.

Torgesson lifted little Rollo to his shoulder. He said mildly, "But, Marmaduke, what would you have done if little Rollo had typed your version instead?"

A look of grievance passed momentarily over Marmie's face. "Well, damn it," he said, "that's what I *thought* it was going to do."

The Singing Bell

Louis Peyton never discussed publicly the methods by which he had bested the police of Earth in a dozen duels of wits and bluff, with the psychoprobe always waiting and always foiled. He would have been foolish to do so, of course, but in his more complacent moments, he fondled the notion of leaving a testament to be opened only after his death, one in which his unbroken success could clearly be seen to be due to ability and not to luck.

In such a testament he would say, "No false pattern can be created to cover a crime without bearing upon it some trace of its creator. It is better, then, to seek in events some pattern that already exists and then adjust your actions to it."

It was with that principle in mind that Peyton planned the murder of Albert Cornwell.

Cornwell, that small-time retailer of stolen things, first approached Peyton at the latter's usual table-for-one at Grinnell's. Cornwell's blue suit seemed to have a special shine, his lined face a special grin, and his faded mustache a special bristle.

"Mr. Peyton," he said, greeting his future murderer with no fourth-dimensional qualm, "it is so nice to see you. I'd almost given up, sir, almost given up."

Peyton, who disliked being approached over his newspaper and dessert at Grinnell's, said, "If you have business with me, Cornwell, you know where you can reach me." Peyton was past forty and his hair was past its earlier blackness, but his back was rigid, his bearing youthful, his eyes dark, and his voice could cut the more sharply for long practice.

"Not for this, Mr. Peyton," said Cornwell, "not for this. I know of a cache, sir, a cache of . . . you know, sir." The forefinger of his right hand moved gently, as though it were a clapper striking invisible substance, and his left hand momentarily cupped his ear.

Peyton turned a page of the paper, still somewhat damp from its tele-dispenser, folded it flat and said, "Singing Bells?"

"Oh, hush, Mr. Peyton," said Cornwell in whispered agony.

Peyton said, "Come with me."

They walked through the park. It was another Peyton axiom that to be reasonably secret there was nothing like a low-voiced discussion out of doors.

Cornwell whispered, "A cache of Singing Bells; an accumulated cache of Singing Bells. Unpolished, but such beauties, Mr. Peyton."

"Have you seen them?"

"No, sir, but I have spoken with one who has. He had proofs enough to convince me. There is enough there to enable you and me to retire in afflu-ence. In absolute affluence, sir."

"Who was this other man?"

A look of cunning lit Cornwell's face like a smoking torch, obscuring more than it showed and lending it a repulsive oiliness. "The man was a lunar grubstaker who had a method for locating the Bells in the crater sides. I don't know his method; he never told me that. But he has gathered dozens, hidden them on the Moon, and come to Earth to arrange the disposing of them."

"He died, I suppose?"

"Yes. A most shocking accident, Mr. Peyton. A fall from a height. Very sad. Of course, his activities on the Moon were quite illegal. The Dominion is very strict about unauthorized Bell-mining. So perhaps it was a judgment upon him after all . . . In any case, I have his map."

Peyton said, a look of calm indifference on his face, "I don't want any of the details of your little transaction. What I want to know is why you've come to me."

Cornwell said, "Well, now, there's enough for both of us, Mr. Peyton, and we can both do our bit. For my part, I know where the cache is located and I can get a spaceship. You . . ."

"Yes?"

"You can pilot a spaceship, and you have such excellent contacts for dis-posing of the Bells. It is a very fair division of labor, Mr. Peyton. Wouldn't you say so, now?"

Peyton considered the pattern of his life—the pattern that already existed —and matters seemed to fit.

He said, "We will leave for the Moon on August the tenth."

Cornwell stopped walking and said, "Mr. Peyton! It's only April now."

Peyton maintained an even gait and Cornwell had to hurry to catch up. "Do you hear me, Mr. Peyton?"

Peyton said, "August the tenth. I will get in touch with you at the proper time, tell you where to bring your ship. Make no attempt to see me personally till then. Good-bye, Cornwell."

Cornwell said, "Fifty-fifty?"

"Quite," said Peyton. "Good-bye."

Peyton continued his walk alone and considered the pattern of his life again. At the age of twenty-seven, he had bought a tract of land in the Rockies on which some past owner had built a house designed as refuge against the threatened atomic wars of two centuries back, the ones that had never come to pass after all. The house remained, however, a monument to a frightened drive for self-sufficiency.

It was of steel and concrete in as isolated a spot as could well be found on Earth, set high above sea level and protected on nearly all sides by mountain peaks that reached higher still. It had its self-contained power unit, its water supply fed by mountain streams, its freezers in which ten sides of beef could hang comfortably, its cellar outfitted like a fortress with an arsenal of weapons designed to stave off hungry, panicked hordes that never came. It had its air-conditioning unit that could scrub and scrub the air until anything *but* radioactivity (alas for human frailty) could be scrubbed out of it.

In that house of survival, Peyton passed the month of August every subsequent year of his perennially bachelor life. He took out the communicators, the television, the newspaper tele-dispenser. He built a force-field fence about his property and left a short-distance signal mechanism to the house from the point where the fence crossed the one trail winding through the mountains.

For one month each year, he could be thoroughly alone. No one saw him, no one could reach him. In absolute solitude, he could have the only vacation he valued after eleven months of contact with a humanity for which he could feel only a cold contempt.

Even the police—and Peyton smiled—knew of his rigid regard for August. He had once jumped bail and risked the psychoprobe rather than forgo his August.

Peyton considered another aphorism for possible inclusion in his testament: There is nothing so conducive to an appearance of innocence as the triumphant lack of an alibi.

On July 30, as on July 30 of every year, Louis Peyton took the 9:15 A.M. non-grav stratojet at New York and arrived in Denver at 12:30 P.M. There he lunched and took the 1:45 P.M. semi-grav bus to Hump's Point, from which Sam Leibman took him by ancient ground-car—full grav!—up the trail to the boundaries of his property. Sam Leibman gravely accepted the ten-dollar tip that he always received, touched his hat as he had done on July 30 for fifteen years.

On July 31, as on July 31 of every year, Louis Peyton returned to Hump's Point in his non-grav aeroflitter and placed an order through the Hump's Point general store for such supplies as he needed for the coming month. There was nothing unusual about the order. It was virtually the duplicate of previous such orders.

MacIntyre, manager of the store, checked gravely over the list, put it through to Central Warehouse, Mountain District, in Denver, and the whole of it came pushing over the mass-transference beam within the hour. Peyton loaded the supplies onto his aeroflitter with MacIntyre's help, left his usual ten-dollar tip and returned to his house.

On August 1, at 12:01 A.M., the force field that surrounded his property was set to full power and Peyton was isolated.

And now the pattern changed. Deliberately he had left himself eight days. In that time he slowly and meticulously destroyed just enough of his supplies to account for all of August. He used the dusting chambers which served the house as a garbage-disposal unit. They were of an advanced model capable of reducing all matter up to and including metals and silicates to an impalpable and undetectable molecular dust. The excess energy formed in the process was carried away by the mountain stream that ran through his property. It ran five degrees warmer than normal for a week.

On August 9 his aeroflitter carried him to a spot in Wyoming where Albert Cornwell and a spaceship waited. The spaceship, itself, was a weak point, of course, since there were men who had sold it, men who had transported it and helped prepare it for flight. All those men, however, led only as far as Cornwell, and Cornwell, Peyton thought—with the trace of a smile on his cold lips—would be a dead end. A very dead end.

On August 10 the spaceship, with Peyton at the controls and Cornwell—and his map—as passenger, left the surface of Earth. Its non-grav field was excellent. At full power, the ship's weight was reduced to less than an ounce. The micropiles fed energy efficiently and noiselessly, and without flame or sound the ship rose through the atmosphere, shrank to a point, and was gone.

It was very unlikely that there would be witnesses to the flight, or that in these weak, piping times of peace there would be a radar watch as in days of yore. In point of fact, there was none.

Two days in space; now two weeks on the Moon. Almost instinctively Peyton had allowed for those two weeks from the first. He was under no illusions as to the value of homemade maps by non-cartographers. Useful they might be to the designer himself, who had the help of memory. To a stranger, they could be nothing more than a cryptogram.

Cornwell showed Peyton the map for the first time only after takeoff. He smiled obsequiously. "After all, sir, this was my only trump."

"Have you checked this against the lunar charts?"

"I would scarcely know how, Mr. Peyton. I depend upon you."

Peyton stared at him coldly as he returned the map. The one certain thing upon it was Tycho Crater, the site of the buried Luna City.

In one respect, at least, astronomy was on their side. Tycho was on the daylight side of the Moon at the moment. It meant that patrol ships were less likely to be out, they themselves less likely to be observed.

Peyton brought the ship down in a riskily quick non-grav landing within the safe, cold darkness of the inner shadow of a crater. The sun was past zenith and the shadow would grow no shorter.

Cornwell drew a long face. "Dear, dear, Mr. Peyton. We can scarcely go prospecting in the lunar day."

"The lunar day doesn't last forever," said Peyton shortly. "There are about a hundred hours of sun left. We can use that time for acclimating ourselves and for working out the map."

The answer came quickly, but it was plural. Peyton studied the lunar charts over and over, taking meticulous measurements, and trying to find the pattern of craters shown on the homemade scrawl that was the key to— what?

Finally Peyton said, "The crater we want could be any one of three: GC-3, GC-5, or MT-10."

"What do we do, Mr. Peyton?" asked Cornwell anxiously.

"We try them all," said Peyton, "beginning with the nearest."

The terminator passed and they were in the night shadow. After that, they spent increasing periods on the lunar surface, getting used to the eternal silence and blackness, the harsh points of the stars and the crack of light that was the Earth peeping over the rim of the crater above. They left hollow, featureless footprints in the dry dust that did not stir or change. Peyton noted them first when they climbed out of the crater into the full light of the gibbous Earth. That was on the eighth day after their arrival on the moon.

The lunar cold put a limit to how long they could remain outside their ship at any one time. Each day, however, they managed for longer. By the eleventh day after arrival they had eliminated GC-5 as the container of the Singing Bells.

By the fifteenth day, Peyton's cold spirit had grown warm with desperation. It would have to be GC-3. MT-10 was too far away. They would not have time to reach it and explore it and still allow for a return to Earth by August 31.

On that same fifteenth day, however, despair was laid to rest forever when they discovered the Bells.

They were not beautiful. They were merely irregular masses of gray rock, as large as a double fist, vacuum-filled and feather-light in the moon's gravity. There were two dozen of them and each one, after proper polishing, could be sold for a hundred thousand dollars at least.

Carefully, in double handfuls, they carried the Bells to the ship, bedded them in excelsior, and returned for more. Three times they made the trip both ways over ground that would have worn them out on Earth but which, under the Moon's lilliputian gravity, was scarcely a barrier.

Cornwell passed the last of the Bells up to Peyton, who placed them carefully within the outer lock.

"Keep them clear, Mr. Peyton," he said, his radioed voice sounding harshly in the other's ear. "I'm coming up."

He crouched for the slow high leap against lunar gravity, looked up, and froze in panic. His face, clearly visible through the hard carved lusilite of his helmet, froze in a last grimace of terror. "No, Mr. Peyton. Don't—"

Peyton's fist tightened on the grip of the blaster he held. It fired. There was an unbearably brilliant flash and Cornwell was a dead fragment of a man, sprawled amid remnants of a spacesuit and flecked with freezing blood.

Peyton paused to stare somberly at the dead man, but only for a second. Then he transferred the last of the Bells to their prepared containers, removed his suit, activated first the non-grav field, then the micropiles, and, potentially a million or two richer than he had been two weeks earlier, set off on the return trip to Earth.

On the twenty-ninth of August, Peyton's ship descended silently, stern bottomward, to the spot in Wyoming from which it had taken off on August 10. The care with which Peyton had chosen the spot was not wasted. His aeroflitter was still there, drawn within the protection of an enclosing wrinkle of the rocky, tortuous countryside.

He moved the Singing Bells once again, in their containers, into the deepest recess of the wrinkle, covering them, loosely and sparsely, with earth. He returned to the ship once more to set the controls and make last adjustments. He climbed out again and two minutes later the ship's automatics took over.

Silently hurrying, the ship bounded upward and up, veering to westward somewhat as the Earth rotated beneath it. Peyton watched, shading his narrow eyes, and at the extreme edge of vision there was a tiny gleam of light and a dot of cloud against the blue sky.

Peyton's mouth twitched into a smile. He had judged well. With the cadmium safety-rods bent back into uselessness, the micropiles had plunged past the unit-sustaining safety level and the ship had vanished in the heat of the nuclear explosion that had followed.

Twenty minutes later, he was back on his property. He was tired and his muscles ached under Earth's gravity. He slept well.

Twelve hours later, in the earliest dawn, the police came.

The man who opened the door placed his crossed hands over his paunch and ducked his smiling head two or three times in greeting. The man who entered, H. Seton Davenport of the Terrestrial Bureau of Investigation, looked about uncomfortably.

The room he had entered was large and in semidarkness except for the brilliant viewing lamp focused over a combination armchair-desk. Rows of book-films covered the walls. A suspension of Galactic charts occupied one corner of the room and a Galactic Lens gleamed softly on a stand in another corner.

"You are Dr. Wendell Urth?" asked Davenport, in a tone that suggested he found it hard to believe. Davenport was a stocky man with black hair, a thin and prominent nose, and a star-shaped scar on one cheek which marked permanently the place where a neuronic whip had once struck him at too close a range.

"I am," said Dr. Urth in a thin, tenor voice. "And you are Inspector Davenport."

The Inspector presented his credentials and said, "The University recommended you to me as an extraterrologist."

"So you said when you called me half an hour ago," said Urth agreeably. His features were thick, his nose was a snubby button, and over his somewhat protuberant eyes there were thick glasses.

"I shall get to the point, Dr. Urth. I presume you have visited the Moon . . ."

Dr. Urth, who had brought out a bottle of ruddy liquid and two glasses, just a little the worse for dust, from behind a straggling pile of book-films, said with sudden brusqueness, "I have never visited the Moon, Inspector. I never intend to! Space travel is foolishness. I don't believe in it." Then, in softer tones, "Sit down, sir, sit down. Have a drink."

Inspector Davenport did as he was told and said, "But you're an . . ."

"Extraterrologist. Yes. I'm interested in other worlds, but it doesn't mean I have to go there. Good lord, I don't have to be a time traveler to qualify as a historian, do I?" He sat down, and a broad smile impressed itself upon his round face once more as he said, "Now tell me what's on your mind."

"I have come," said the Inspector, frowning, "to consult you in a case of murder."

"Murder? What have I to do with murder?"

"This murder, Dr. Urth, was on the Moon."

"Astonishing."

"It's more than astonishing. It's unprecedented, Dr. Urth. In the fifty years since the Lunar Dominion has been established, ships have blown up and spacesuits have sprung leaks. Men have boiled to death on sun-side, frozen on dark-side, and suffocated on both sides. There have even been deaths by falls, which, considering lunar gravity, is quite a trick. But in all that time, not one man has been killed on the Moon as the result of another man's deliberate act of violence—till now."

Dr. Urth said, "How was it done?"

"A blaster. The authorities were on the scene within the hour through a fortunate set of circumstances. A patrol ship observed a flash of light against the Moon's surface. You know how far a flash can be seen against the night-side. The pilot notified Luna City and landed. In the process of circling back, he swears that he just managed to see by Earthlight what looked like a ship taking off. Upon landing, he discovered a blasted corpse and footprints."

"The flash of light," said Dr. Urth, "you suppose to be the firing blaster."

"That's certain. The corpse was fresh. Interior portions of the body had not yet frozen. The footprints belonged to two people. Careful measurements showed that the depressions fell into two groups of somewhat different diameters, indicating differently sized spaceboots. In the main, they led to craters GC-3 and GC-5, a pair of—"

"I am acquainted with the official code for naming lunar craters," said Dr. Urth pleasantly.

"Umm. In any case, GC-3 contained footprints that led to a rift in the crater wall, within which scraps of hardened pumice were found. X-ray diffraction patterns showed—"

"Singing Bells," put in the extraterrologist in great excitement. "Don't tell me this murder of yours involves Singing Bells!"

"What if it does?" demanded Davenport blankly.

"I have one. A University expedition uncovered it and presented it to me in return for— Come, Inspector, I must show it to you."

Dr. Urth jumped up and pattered across the room, beckoning the other to follow as he did. Davenport, annoyed, followed.

They entered a second room, larger than the first, dimmer, considerably more cluttered. Davenport stared with astonishment at the heterogeneous mass of material that was jumbled together in no pretense at order.

He made out a small lump of "blue glaze" from Mars, the sort of thing some romantics considered to be an artifact of long-extinct Martians, a small meteorite, a model of an early spaceship, a sealed bottle of nothing scrawlingly labeled "Venusian atmosphere."

Dr. Urth said happily, "I've made a museum of my whole house. It's one of the advantages of being a bachelor. Of course, I haven't quite got things organized. Someday, when I have a spare week or so . . ."

For a moment he looked about, puzzled; then, remembering, he pushed aside a chart showing the evolutionary scheme of development of the marine invertebrates that were the highest life forms on Barnard's Planet and said, "Here it is. It's flawed, I'm afraid."

The Bell hung suspended from a slender wire, soldered delicately onto it. That it was flawed was obvious. It had a constriction line running halfway about it that made it seem like two small globes, firmly but imperfectly squashed together. Despite that, it had been lovingly polished to a dull luster, softly gray, velvety smooth, and faintly pock-marked in a way that laboratories, in their futile efforts to prepare synthetic Bells, had found impossible to duplicate.

Dr. Urth said, "I experimented a good deal before I found a decent stroker. A flawed Bell is temperamental. But bone works. I have one here"—

and he held up something that looked like a short thick spoon made of a gray-white substance—"which I had made out of the femur of an ox. Listen."

With surprising delicacy, his pudgy fingers maneuvered the Bell, feeling for one best spot. He adjusted it, steadying it daintily. Then, letting the Bell swing free, he brought down the thick end of the bone spoon and stroked the Bell softly.

It was as though a million harps had sounded a mile away. It swelled and faded and returned. It came from no particular direction. It sounded inside the head, incredibly sweet and pathetic and tremulous all at once.

It died away lingeringly and both men were silent for a full minute.

Dr. Urth said, "Not bad, eh?" and with a flick of his hand set the Bell to swinging on its wire.

Davenport stirred restlessly. "Careful! Don't break it." The fragility of a good Singing Bell was proverbial.

Dr. Urth said, "Geologists say the Bells are only pressure-hardened pumice, enclosing a vacuum in which small beads of rock rattle freely. That's what they *say*. But if that's all it is, why can't we reproduce one? Now a flawless Bell would make this one sound like a child's harmonica."

"Exactly," said Davenport, "and there aren't a dozen people on Earth who own a flawless one, and there are a hundred people and institutions who would buy one at any price, no questions asked. A supply of Bells would be worth murder."

The extraterrologist turned to Davenport and pushed his spectacles back on his inconsequential nose with a stubby forefinger. "I haven't forgotten your murder case. Please go on."

"That can be done in a sentence. I know the identity of the murderer."

They had returned to the chairs in the library and Dr. Urth clasped his hands over his ample abdomen. "Indeed? Then surely you have no problem, Inspector."

"Knowing and proving are not the same, Dr. Urth. Unfortunately he has no alibi."

"You mean, unfortunately he *has*, don't you?"

"I mean what I say. If he had an alibi, I could crack it somehow, because it would be a false one. If there were witnesses who claimed they had seen him on Earth at the time of the murder, their stories could be broken down. If he had documentary proof, it could be exposed as a forgery or some sort of trickery. Unfortunately he has none of it."

"What does he have?"

Carefully Inspector Davenport described the Peyton estate in Colorado. He concluded, "He has spent every August there in the strictest isolation. Even the T.B.I. would have to testify to that. Any jury would have to presume that he was on his estate this August as well, unless we could present definite proof that he was on the Moon."

"What makes you think he *was* on the Moon? Perhaps he is innocent."

"No!" Davenport was almost violent. "For fifteen years I've been trying to collect sufficient evidence against him and I've never succeeded. But I can *smell* a Peyton crime now. I tell you that no one but Peyton, no one on Earth, would have the impudence or, for that matter, the practical business contacts to attempt disposal of smuggled Singing Bells. He is known to be an expert space pilot. He is known to have had contact with the murdered man, though admittedly not for some months. Unfortunately none of that is proof."

Dr. Urth said, "Wouldn't it be simple to use the psychoprobe, now that its use has been legalized?"

Davenport scowled, and the scar on his cheek turned livid. "Have you read the Konski-Hiakawa law, Dr. Urth?"

"No."

"I think no one has. The right to mental privacy, the government says, is fundamental. All right, but what follows? The man who is psychoprobed and proves innocent of the crime for which he was psychoprobed is entitled to as much compensation as he can persuade the courts to give him. In a recent case a bank cashier was awarded twenty-five thousand dollars for having been psychoprobed on inaccurate suspicion of theft. It seems that the circumstantial evidence which seemed to point to theft actually pointed to a small spot of adultery. His claim that he lost his job, was threatened by the husband in question and put in bodily fear, and finally was held up to ridicule and contumely because a news-strip man had learned the results of the probe held good in court."

"I can see the man's point."

"So can we all. That's the trouble. One more item to remember: Any man who has been psychoprobed once for any reason can never be psychoprobed again for any reason. No one man, the law says, shall be placed in mental jeopardy twice in his lifetime."

"Inconvenient."

"Exactly. In the two years since the psychoprobe has been legitimized, I couldn't count the number of crooks and chiselers who've tried to get themselves psychoprobed for purse-snatching so that they could play the rackets safely afterward. So you see the Department will not allow Peyton to be psychoprobed until they have firm evidence of his guilt. Not legal evidence, maybe, but evidence that is strong enough to convince my boss. The worst of it, Dr. Urth, is that if we come into court without a psychoprobe record, we can't win. In a case as serious as murder, not to have used the psychoprobe is proof enough to the dumbest juror that the prosecution isn't sure of its ground."

"Now what do you want of me?"

"Proof that he was on the Moon sometime in August. It's got to be done quickly. I can't hold him on suspicion much longer. And if news of the murder gets out, the world press will blow up like an asteroid striking

Jupiter's atmosphere. A glamorous crime, you know—first murder on the Moon."

"Exactly when was the murder committed?" asked Urth, in a sudden transition to brisk cross-examination.

"August twenty-seventh."

"And the arrest was made when?"

"Yesterday, August thirtieth."

"Then if Peyton were the murderer, he would have had time to return to Earth."

"Barely. Just barely." Davenport's lips thinned. "If I had been a day sooner— If I had found his place empty—"

"And how long do you suppose the two, the murdered man and the murderer, were on the Moon altogether?"

"Judging by the ground covered by the footprints, a number of days. A week, at the minimum."

"Has the ship they used been located?"

"No, and it probably never will. About ten hours ago, the University of Denver reported a rise in background radioactivity beginning day before yesterday at 6 P.M. and persisting for a number of hours. It's an easy thing, Dr. Urth, to set a ship's controls so as to allow it to blast off without crew and blow up, fifty miles high, in a micropile short."

"If I had been Peyton," said Dr. Urth thoughtfully, "I would have killed the man on board ship and blown up corpse and ship together."

"You don't know Peyton," said Davenport grimly. "He enjoys his victories over the law. He values them. Leaving the corpse on the Moon is his challenge to us."

"I see." Dr. Urth patted his stomach with a rotary motion and said, "Well, there is a chance."

"That you'll be able to prove he was on the Moon?"

"That I'll be able to give you my opinion."

"Now?"

"The sooner the better. If, of course, I get a chance to interview Mr. Peyton."

"That can be arranged. I have a non-grav jet waiting. We can be in Washington in twenty minutes."

But a look of the deepest alarm passed over the plump extraterrologist's face. He rose to his feet and pattered away from the T.B.I. agent toward the duskiest corner of the cluttered room.

"*No!*"

"What's wrong, Dr. Urth?"

"I won't use a non-grav jet. I don't believe in them."

Davenport stared confusedly at Dr. Urth. He stammered, "Would you prefer a monorail?"

Dr. Urth snapped, "I mistrust all forms of transportation. I don't believe in them. Except walking. I don't mind walking." He was suddenly eager. "Couldn't you bring Mr. Peyton to this city, somewhere within walking distance? To City Hall, perhaps? I've often walked to City Hall."

Davenport looked helplessly about the room. He looked at the myriad volumes of lore about the light-years. He could see through the open door into the room beyond, with its tokens of the worlds beyond the sky. And he looked at Dr. Urth, pale at the thought of non-grav jet, and shrugged his shoulders.

"I'll bring Peyton here. Right to this room. Will that satisfy you?"

Dr. Urth puffed out his breath in a deep sigh. "Quite."

"I hope you can deliver, Dr. Urth."

"I will do my best, Mr. Davenport."

Louis Peyton stared with distaste at his surroundings and with contempt at the fat man who bobbed his head in greeting. He glanced at the seat offered him and brushed it with his hand before sitting down. Davenport took a seat next to him, with his blaster holster in clear view.

The fat man was smiling as he sat down and patted his round abdomen as though he had just finished a good meal and were intent on letting the world know about it.

He said, "Good evening, Mr. Peyton. I am Dr. Wendell Urth, extraterrologist."

Peyton looked at him again. "And what do you want with me?"

"I want to know if you were on the Moon at any time in the month of August."

"I was not."

"Yet no man saw you on Earth between the days of August first and August thirtieth."

"I lived my normal life in August. I am never seen during that month. Let him tell you." And he jerked his head in the direction of Davenport.

Dr. Urth chuckled. "How nice if we could test this matter. If there were only some physical manner in which we could differentiate Moon from Earth. If, for instance, we could analyze the dust in your hair and say, 'Aha, Moon rock.' Unfortunately we can't. Moon rock is much the same as Earth rock. Even if it weren't, there wouldn't be any in your hair unless you stepped onto the lunar surface without a spacesuit, which is unlikely."

Peyton remained impassive.

Dr. Urth went on, smiling benevolently, and lifting a hand to steady the glasses perched precariously on the bulb of his nose. "A man traveling in space or on the Moon breathes Earth air, eats Earth food. He carries Earth environment next to his skin whether he's in his ship or in his spacesuit. We are looking for a man who spent two days in space going to the Moon, at least a week on the Moon, and two days coming back from the Moon. In all that time he carried Earth next to his skin, which makes it difficult."

"I'd suggest," said Peyton, "that you can make it less difficult by releasing me and looking for the real murderer."

"It may come to that," said Dr. Urth. "Have you ever seen anything like this?" His hand pushed its pudgy way to the ground beside his chair and came up with a gray sphere that sent back subdued highlights.

Peyton smiled. "It looks like a Singing Bell to me."

"It *is* a Singing Bell. The murder was committed for the sake of Singing Bells. What do you think of this one?"

"I think it is badly flawed."

"Ah, but inspect it," said Dr. Urth, and with a quick motion of his hand, he tossed it through six feet of air to Peyton.

Davenport cried out and half-rose from his chair. Peyton brought up his arms with an effort, but so quickly that he managed to catch the Bell.

Peyton said, "You damned fool. Don't throw it around that way."

"You respect Singing Bells, do you?"

"Too much to break one. That's no crime, at least." Peyton stroked the Bell gently, then lifted it to his ear and shook it slowly, listening to the soft clicks of the Lunoliths, those small pumice particles, as they rattled in vacuum.

Then, holding the Bell up by the length of steel wire still attached to it, he ran a thumbnail over its surface with an expert, curving motion. It twanged! The note was very mellow, very flutelike, holding with a slight *vibrato* that faded lingeringly and conjured up pictures of a summer twilight.

For a short moment, all three men were lost in the sound.

And then Dr. Urth said, "Throw it back, Mr. Peyton. Toss it here!" and held out his hand in peremptory gesture.

Automatically Louis Peyton tossed the Bell. It traveled its short arc one-third of the way to Dr. Urth's waiting hand, curved downward and shattered with a heartbroken, sighing discord on the floor.

Davenport and Peyton stared at the gray slivers with equal wordlessness and Dr. Urth's calm voice went almost unheard as he said, "When the criminal's cache of crude Bells is located, I'll ask that a flawless one, properly polished, be given to me, as replacement and fee."

"A fee? For what?" demanded Davenport irritably.

"Surely the matter is now obvious. Despite my little speech of a moment ago, there is one piece of Earth's environment that no space traveler carries with him and that is *Earth's surface gravity*. The fact that Mr. Peyton could so egregiously misjudge the toss of an object he obviously valued so highly could mean only that his muscles are not yet readjusted to the pull of Earthly gravity. It is my professional opinion, Mr. Davenport, that your prisoner has, in the last few days, been away from Earth. He has either been in space or on some planetary object considerably smaller in size than the Earth—as, for example, the Moon."

Davenport rose triumphantly to his feet. "Let me have your opinion in writing," he said, hand on blaster, "and that will be good enough to get me permission to use a psychoprobe."

Louis Peyton, dazed and unresisting, had only the numb realization that any testament he could now leave would have to include the fact of ultimate failure.

The Talking Stone

The asteroid belt is large and its human occupancy small. Larry Vernadsky, in the seventh month of his year-long assignment to Station Five, wondered with increasing frequency if his salary could possibly compensate for a nearly solitary confinement seventy million miles from Earth. He was a slight youth, who did not bear the look of either a spationautical engineer or an asteroid man. He had blue eyes and butter-yellow hair and an invincible air of innocence that masked a quick mind and an isolation-sharpened bump of curiosity.

Both the look of innocence and the bump of curiosity served him well on board the *Robert Q.*

When the *Robert Q.* landed on the outer platform of Station Five, Vernadsky was on board almost immediately. There was an eager delight about him which, in a dog, would have been accompanied by a vibrating tail and a happy cacophony of barks.

The fact that the captain of the *Robert Q.* met his grins with a stern sour silence that sat heavily on his thick-featured face made no difference. As far as Vernadsky was concerned the ship was yearned-for company and was welcome. It was welcome to any amount of the millions of gallons of ice or any of the tons of frozen food concentrates stacked away in the hollowed-out asteroid that served as Station Five. Vernadsky was ready with any power tool that might be necessary, any replacement that might be required for any hyperatomic motor.

Vernadsky was grinning all over his boyish face as he filled out the routine form, writing it out quickly for later conversion into computer notation for filing. He put down ship's name and serial number, engine number, field generator number, and so on, port of embarkation ("asteroids, damned lot of them, don't know which was last" and Vernadsky simply wrote "Belt" which was the usual abbreviation for "asteroid belt"); port of destination ("Earth"); reason for stopping ("stuttering hyperatomic drive").

"How many in your crew, Captain?" asked Vernadsky, as he looked over ship's papers.

The captain said, "Two. Now how about looking over the hyperatomics? We've got a shipment to make." His cheeks were blue with dark stubble, his bearing that of a hardened and lifelong asteroid miner, yet his speech was that of an educated, almost a cultured, man.

"Sure." Vernadsky lugged his diagnostic kit to the engine room, followed by the captain. He tested circuits, vacuum degree, forcefield density with easy-going efficiency.

He could not help wondering about the captain. Despite his own dislike for his surroundings he realized dimly that there were some who found fascination in the vast emptiness and freedom of space. Yet he guessed that a man like this captain was not an asteroid miner for the love of solitude alone.

He said, "Any special type of ore you handle?"

The captain frowned and said, "Chromium and manganese."

"That so? . . . I'd replace the Jenner manifold, if I were you."

"Is that what's causing the trouble?"

"No, it isn't. But it's a little beat-up. You'd be risking another failure within a million miles. As long as you've got the ship in here—"

"All right, replace it. But find the stutter, will you?"

"Doing my best, Captain."

The captain's last remark was harsh enough to abash even Vernadsky. He worked awhile in silence, then got to his feet. "You've got a gamma-fogged semireflector. Every time the positron beam circles round to its position the drive flickers out for a second. You'll have to replace it."

"How long will it take?"

"Several hours. Maybe twelve."

"What? I'm behind schedule."

"Can't help it." Vernadsky remained cheerful. "There's only so much I can do. The system has to be flushed for three hours with helium before I can get inside. And then I have to calibrate the new semireflector and that takes time. I could get it almost right in minutes, but that's only almost right. You'd break down before you reach the orbit of Mars."

The captain glowered. "Go ahead. Get started."

Vernadsky carefully maneuvered the tank of helium on board the ship. With ship's pseudo-grav generators shut off, it weighed virtually nothing, but it had its full mass and inertia. That meant careful handling if it were to make turns correctly. The maneuvers were all the more difficult since Vernadsky himself was without weight.

It was because his attention was concentrated entirely on the cylinder that he took a wrong turn in the crowded quarters and found himself momentarily in a strange and darkened room.

He had time for one startled shout and then two men were upon him, hustling his cylinder, closing the door behind him.

He said nothing, while he hooked the cylinder to the intake valve of the motor and listened to the soft, soughing noise as the helium flushed the interior, slowly washing absorbed radioactive gases into the all-accepting emptiness of space.

Then curiosity overcame prudence and he said, "You've got a silicony aboard ship, Captain. A big one."

The captain turned to face Vernadsky slowly. He said in a voice from which all expression had been removed, "Is that right?"

"I saw it. How about a better look?"

"Why?"

Vernadsky grew imploring. "Oh, look, Captain, I've been on this rock over half a year. I've read everything I could get hold of on the asteroids, which means all sorts of things about the siliconies. And I've never seen even a little one. Have a heart."

"I believe there's a job here to do."

"Just helium-flushing for hours. There's nothing else to be done till that's over. How come you carry a silicony about, anyway, Captain?"

"A pet. Some people like dogs. I like siliconies."

"Have you got it talking?"

The captain flushed. "Why do you ask?"

"Some of them have talked. Some of them read minds, even."

"What are you? An expert on these damn things?"

"I've been reading about them. I told you. Come on, Captain. Let's have a look."

Vernadsky tried not to show that he noticed that there was the captain facing him and a crewman on either side of him. Each of the three was larger than he was, each weightier, each—he felt sure—was armed.

Vernadsky said, "Well, what's wrong? I'm not going to steal the thing. I just want to see it."

It may have been the unfinished repair job that kept him alive at that moment. Even more so, perhaps, it was his look of cheerful and almost moronic innocence that stood him in good stead.

The captain said, "Well, then, come on."

And Vernadsky followed, his agile mind working and his pulse definitely quickened.

•   •   •   •

Vernadsky stared with considerable awe and just a little revulsion at the gray creature before him. It was quite true that he had never seen a silicony, but he had seen trimensional photographs and read descriptions. Yet there is something in a real presence for which neither words nor photographs are substitutes.

Its skin was of an oily smooth grayness. Its motions were slow, as became a creature who burrowed in stone and was more than half stone itself. There was no writhing of muscles beneath that skin; instead it moved in slabs as thin layers of stone slid greasily over one another.

It had a general ovoid shape, rounded above, flattened below, with two sets of appendages. Below were the "legs," set radially. They totaled six and ended in sharp flinty edges, reinforced by metal deposits. Those edges could cut through rock, breaking it into edible portions.

On the creature's flat undersurface, hidden from view unless the silicony were overturned, was the one opening into its interior. Shredded rocks entered that interior. Within, limestone and hydrated silicates reacted to form the silicones out of which the creature's tissues were built. Excess silica re-emerged from the opening as hard white pebbly excretions.

How extraterrologists had puzzled over the smooth pebbles that lay scattered in small hollows within the rocky structure of the asteroids until the siliconies were first discovered. And how they marveled at the manner in which the creatures made silicones—those silicone-oxygen polymers with hydrocarbon side chains—perform so many of the functions that proteins performed in terrestrial life.

From the highest point on the creature's back came the remaining appendages, two inverse cones hollowed in opposing directions and fitting snugly into parallel recesses running down the back, yet capable of lifting upward a short way. When the silicony burrowed through rock, the "ears" were retracted for streamlining. When it rested in a hollowed-out cavern, they could lift for better and more sensitive reception. Their vague resemblance to a rabbit's ears made the name *silicony* inevitable. The more serious extraterrologists, who referred to such creatures habitually as *Siliconeus asteroidea*, thought the "ears" might have something to do with the rudimentary telepathic powers the beasts possessed. A minority had other notions.

The silicony was flowing slowly over an oil-smeared rock. Other such rocks lay scattered in one corner of the room and represented, Vernadsky knew, the creature's food supply. Or at least it was its tissue-building supply. For sheer energy, he had read, that alone would not do.

Vernadsky marveled. "It's a monster. It's more than a foot across."

The captain grunted noncommittally.

"Where did you get it?" asked Vernadsky.

"One of the rocks."

"Well, listen, two inches is about the biggest anyone's found. You could sell this to some museum or university on Earth for a couple of thousand dollars, maybe."

The captain shrugged. "Well, you've seen it. Let's get back to the hyper-atomics."

His hard grip was on Vernadsky's elbow and he was turning away, when there was an interruption in the form of a slow and slurring voice, a hollow and gritty one.

It was made by the carefully modulated friction of rock against rock and Vernadsky stared in near horror at the speaker.

It was the silicony, suddenly becoming a talking stone. It said, "The man wonders if this thing can talk."

Vernadsky whispered, "For the love of space. It does!"

"All right," said the captain impatiently, "you've seen it and heard it, too. Let's go now."

"And it reads minds," said Vernadsky.

The silicony said, "Mars rotates in two four hours three seven and one half minutes. Jupiter's density is one point two two. Uranus was discovered in the year one seven eight one. Pluto is the planet which is most far. Sun is heaviest with a mass of two zero zero zero zero zero zero . . ."

The captain pulled Vernadsky away. Vernadsky, half-walking backward, half-stumbling, listened with fascination to the fading bumbling of zeroes.

He said, "Where does it pick up all that stuff, Captain?"

"There's an old astronomy book we read to him. Real old."

"From before space travel was invented," said one of the crew members in disgust. "Ain't even a fillum. Regular print."

"Shut up," said the captain.

Vernadsky checked the outflow of helium for gamma radiation and eventually it was time to end the flushing and work in the interior. It was a painstaking job, and Vernadsky interrupted it only once for coffee and a breather.

He said, with innocence beaming in his smile, "You know the way I figure it, Captain? That thing lives inside rock, inside some asteroid all its life. Hundreds of years, maybe. It's a damn big thing, and it's probably a lot smarter than the run-of-the-mill silicony. Now you pick it up and it finds out the universe isn't rock. It finds out a trillion things it never imagined. That's why it's interested in astronomy. It's this new world, all these new ideas it gets in the book and in human minds, too. Don't you think that's so?"

He wanted desperately to smoke the captain out, get something concrete he could hang his deductions on. For this reason he risked telling what must be half the truth, the lesser half, of course.

But the captain, leaning against a wall with his arms folded, said only, "When will you be through?"

It was his last comment and Vernadsky was obliged to rest content. The motor was adjusted finally to Vernadsky's satisfaction, and the captain paid the reasonable fee in cash, accepted his receipt, and left in a blaze of ship's hyper-energy.

Vernadsky watched it go with an almost unbearable excitement. He made his way quickly to his sub-etheric sender.

"I've got to be right," he muttered to himself. "I've *got* to be."

Patrolman Milt Hawkins received the call in the privacy of his home station on Patrol Station Asteroid No. 72. He was nursing a two-day stubble, a can of iced beer, and a film viewer, and the settled melancholy on his ruddy, wide-cheeked face was as much the product of loneliness as was the forced cheerfulness in Vernadsky's eyes.

Patrolman Hawkins found himself looking into those eyes and was glad. Even though it was only Vernadsky, company was company. He gave him the big hello and listened luxuriously to the sound of a voice without worrying too strenuously concerning the contents of the speech.

Then suddenly amusement was gone and both ears were on the job and he said, "Hold it. Ho—ld it. What are you talking about?"

"Haven't you been listening, you dumb cop? I'm talking my heart out to you."

"Well, deal it out in smaller pieces, will you? What's this about a silicony?"

"This guy's got one on board. He calls it a pet and feeds it greasy rocks."

"Huh? I swear, a miner on the asteroid run would make a pet out of a piece of cheese if he could get it to talk back to him."

"Not just *a* silicony. Not one of these little inch jobs. It's over a foot across. Don't you get it? Space, you'd think a guy would know something about the asteroids, living out here."

"All right. Suppose you tell me."

"Look, greasy rocks build tissues, but where does a silicony that size get its energy from?"

"I couldn't tell you."

"Directly from— Have you got anyone around you right now?"

"Right now, no. I wish there were."

"You won't in a minute. Siliconies get their energy by the direct absorption of gamma rays."

"Says who?"

"Says a guy called Wendell Urth. He's a big-shot extraterrologist. What's more, he says that's what the silicony's ears are for." Vernadsky put his two forefingers to his temples and wiggled them. "Not telepathy at all. They detect gamma radiation at levels no human instrument can detect."

"Okay. Now what?" asked Hawkins. But he was growing thoughtful.

"Now this. Urth says there isn't enough gamma radiation on any asteroid to support siliconies more than an inch or two long. Not enough radioactivity. So here we have one a foot long, a good fifteen inches."

"Well—"

"So it has to come from an asteroid just riddled with the stuff, lousy with uranium, solid with gamma rays. An asteroid with enough radioactivity to be warm to the touch and off the regular orbit patterns so that no one's come across it. Only suppose some smart boy landed on the asteroid by happenstance and noticed the warmth of the rocks and got to thinking. This captain of the *Robert Q.* is no rock-hopping ignoramus. He's a shrewd guy."

"Go on."

"Suppose he blasts off chunks for assay and comes across a giant silicony. Now he *knows* he's got the most unbelievable strike in all history. And he doesn't need assays. The silicony can lead him to the rich veins."

"Why should it?"

"Because it wants to learn about the universe. Because it's spent a thousand years, maybe, under rock, and it's just discovered the stars. It can read minds and it could learn to talk. It could make a deal. Listen, the captain would jump at it. Uranium mining is a state monopoly. Unlicensed miners aren't even allowed to carry counters. It's a perfect setup for the captain."

Hawkins said, "Maybe you're right."

"No maybe at all. You should have seen them standing around me while I watched the silicony, ready to jump me if I said one funny word. You should have seen them drag me out after two minutes."

Hawkins brushed his unshaven chin with his hand and made a mental estimate of the time it would take him to shave. He said, "How long can you keep the boy at your station?"

"Keep him! Space, he's gone!"

"What! Then what the devil is all this talk about? Why did you let him get away?"

"Three guys," said Vernadsky patiently, "each one bigger than I am, each one armed, and each one ready to kill, I'll bet. What did you want me to do?"

"All right, but what do we do now?"

"Come out and pick them up. That's simple enough. I was fixing their semireflectors and I fixed them my way. Their power will shut off completely within ten thousand miles. And I installed a tracer in the Jenner manifold."

Hawkins goggled at Vernadsky's grinning face. "Holy Toledo."

"And don't get anyone else in on this. Just you, me, and the police cruiser. They'll have no energy and we'll have a cannon or two. They'll tell us where the uranium asteroid is. We locate it, *then* get in touch with Patrol Headquarters. We will deliver unto them, three, count them, three, uranium smugglers, one giant-size silicony like nobody on Earth ever saw, and one, I repeat, one great big fat chunk of uranium ore like nobody on Earth saw, either. And you make a lieutenancy and I get promoted to a permanent Earth-side job. Right?"

Hawkins was dazed. "Right," he yelled. "I'll be right out there."

They were almost upon the ship before spotting it visually by the weak glinting of reflected sunlight.

Hawkins said, "Didn't you leave them enough power for ship's lights? You didn't throw off their emergency generator, did you?"

Vernadsky shrugged. "They're saving power, hoping they'll get picked up. Right now, they're putting everything they've got into a sub-etheric call, I'll bet."

"If they are," said Hawkins dryly, "I'm not picking it up."

"You're not?"

"Not a thing."

The police cruiser spiraled closer. Their quarry, its power off, was drifting through space at a steady ten thousand miles an hour.

The cruiser matched it, speed for speed, and drifted inward.

A sick expression crossed Hawkins' face. "Oh, *no!*"

"What's the matter?"

"The ship's been hit. A meteor. Lord knows there are enough of them in the asteroid belt."

All the verve washed out of Vernadsky's face and voice. "Hit? Are they wrecked?"

"There's a hole in it the size of a barn door. Sorry, Vernadsky, but this might not look good."

Vernadsky closed his eyes and swallowed hard. He knew what Hawkins meant. Vernadsky had deliberately misrepaired a ship, a procedure which could be judged a felony. And death as a result of a felony was murder.

He said, "Look, Hawkins, you know why I did it."

"I know what you've told me and I'll testify to that if I have to. But if this ship wasn't smuggling . . ."

He didn't finish the statement. Nor did he have to.

They entered the smashed ship in full spacesuit cover.

The *Robert Q.* was a shambles, inside and out. Without power, there was no chance of raising the feeblest screen against the rock that hit them or of detecting it in time or of avoiding it if they had detected it. It had caved in the ship's hull as though it were so much aluminum foil. It had smashed the pilot room, evacuated the ship's air, and killed the three men on board.

One of the crew had been slammed against the wall by the impact and was so much frozen meat. The captain and the other crewman lay in stiff attitudes, skins congested with frozen bloodclots where the air, boiling out of the blood, had broken the vessels.

Vernadsky, who had never seen this form of death in space, felt sick, but he fought against vomiting messily inside his spacesuit and succeeded.

He said, "Let's test the ore they're carrying. It's *got* to be alive." It's *got* to be, he told himself. It's *got* to be.

The door to the hold had been warped by the force of collision and there was a gap half an inch wide where it no longer met the frame.

Hawkins lifted the counter he held in his gauntleted hand and held its mica window to that gap.

It chattered like a million magpies.

Vernadsky said, with infinite relief, "I told you so."

His misrepair of the ship was now only the ingenious and praiseworthy fulfillment of a citizen's loyal duty and the meteor collision that had brought death to three men merely a regrettable accident.

It took two blaster bolts to break the twisted door loose, and tons of rock met their flashlights.

Hawkins lifted two chunks of moderate size and dropped them gingerly into one of the suit's pockets. "As exhibits," he said, "and for assay."

"Don't keep them near the skin too long," warned Vernadsky.

"The suit will protect me till I get it back to ship. It's not pure uranium, you know."

"Pretty near, I'll bet." Every inch of his cockiness was back.

Hawkins looked about. "Well, this tears things. We've stopped a smuggling ring, maybe, or part of one. But what next?"

"The uranium asteroid—uh, oh!"

"Right. Where is it? The only ones who know are dead."

"Space!" And again Vernadsky's spirits were dashed. Without the asteroid itself, they had only three corpses and a few tons of uranium ore. Good, but not spectacular. It would mean a citation, yes, but he wasn't after a citation. He wanted promotion to a permanent Earth-side job and that required something.

He yelled, "For the love of space, the *silicony!* It can live in a vacuum. It lives in a vacuum all the time and *it* knows where the asteroid is."

"Right!" said Hawkins, with instant enthusiasm. "Where is the thing?"

"Aft," cried Vernadsky. "This way."

The silicony glinted in the light of their flashes. It moved and was alive.

Vernadsky's heart beat madly with excitement. "We've got to move it, Hawkins."

"Why?"

"Sound won't carry in a vacuum, for the love of space. We've got to get it into the cruiser."

"All right. All right."

"We can't put a suit around it with a radio transmitter, you know."

"I said all right."

They carried it gingerly and carefully, their metal-sheathed fingers handling the greasy surface of the creature almost lovingly.

Hawkins held it while kicking off the *Robert Q.*

It lay in the control room of the cruiser now. The two men had removed their helmets and Hawkins was shucking his suit. Vernadsky could not wait.

He said, "You can read our minds?"

He held his breath until finally the gratings of rock surfaces modulated themselves into words. To Vernadsky no finer sound could, at the moment, be imagined.

The silicony said, "Yes." Then he said, "Emptiness all about. Nothing."

"What?" said Hawkins.

Vernadsky shushed him. "The trip through space just now, I guess. It must have impressed him."

He said to the silicony, shouting his words as though to make his thoughts clearer, "The men who were with you gathered uranium, special ore, radiations, energy."

"They wanted food," came the weak, gritty sound.

Of course! It was food to the silicony. It was an energy source. Vernadsky said, "You showed them where they could get it?"

"Yes."

Hawkins said, "I can heardly hear the thing."

"There's something wrong with it," said Vernadsky worriedly. He shouted again, "Are you well?"

"Not well. Air gone at once. Something wrong inside."

Vernadsky muttered. "The sudden decompression must have damaged it. Oh, Lord—Look, you know what I want. Where is your home? The place with the food?"

The two men were silent, waiting.

The silicony's ears lifted slowly, very slowly, trembled, and fell back. "There," it said. "Over there."

"Where?" screamed Vernadsky.

"There."

Hawkins said, "It's doing something. It's pointing in some way."

"Sure, only we don't know in what way."

"Well, what do you expect it to do? Give the coordinates?"

Vernadsky said at once, "Why not?" He turned again to the silicony as it lay huddled on the floor. It was motionless now and there was a dullness to its exterior that looked ominous.

Vernadsky said, "The captain knew where your eating place was. He had numbers concerning it, didn't he?" He prayed that the silicony would understand, that it would read his thoughts and not merely listen to his words.

"Yes," said the silicony in a rock-against-rock sigh.

"Three sets of numbers," said Vernadsky. There would have to be three. Three coordinates in space with dates attached, giving three positions of the asteroid in its orbit about the sun. From these data the orbit could be calculated in full and its position determined at any time. Even planetary perturbations could be accounted for, roughly.

"Yes," said the silicony, lower still.

"What were they? What were the numbers? Write them down, Hawkins. Get paper."

But the silicony said, "Do not know. Numbers not important. Eating place there."

Hawkins said, "That's plain enough. It didn't need the coordinates, so it paid no attention to them."

The silicony said, "Soon not"—a long pause, and then slowly, as though testing a new and unfamiliar word—"alive. Soon"—an even longer pause—"dead. What after death?"

"Hang on," implored Vernadsky. "Tell me, did the captain write down these figures anywhere?"

The silicony did not answer for a long minute and then, while both men bent so closely that their heads almost touched over the dying stone, it said, "What after death?"

Vernadsky shouted, "One answer. Just one. The captain must have written down the numbers. Where? Where?"

The silicony whispered, "On the asteroid."

And it never spoke again.

It was a dead rock, as dead as the rock which gave it birth, as dead as the walls of the ship, as dead as a dead human.

And Vernadsky and Hawkins rose from their knees and stared hopelessly at each other.

"It makes no sense," said Hawkins. "Why should he write the coordinates on the asteroid? That's like locking a key inside the cabinet it's meant to open."

Vernadsky shook his head. "A fortune in uranium. The biggest strike in history and we don't know where it is."

H. Seton Davenport looked about him with an odd feeling of pleasure. Even in repose, there was usually something hard about his lined face with its prominent nose. The scar on his right cheek, his black hair, startling eyebrows, and dark complexion all combined to make him look every bit the incorruptible agent of the Terrestrial Bureau of Investigation that he actually was.

Yet now something almost like a smile tugged at his lips as he looked about the large room, in which dimness made the rows of book-films appear endless, and specimens of who-knows-what from who-knows-where bulk mysteriously. The complete disorder, the air of separation, almost insulation, from the world, made the room look unreal. It made it look every bit as unreal as its owner.

That owner sat in a combination armchair-desk which was bathed in the only focus of bright light in the room. Slowly he turned the sheets of official reports he held in his hand. His hand moved otherwise only to adjust the thick spectacles which threatened at any moment to fall completely from his round and completely unimpressive nubbin of a nose. His paunch lifted and fell quietly as he read.

He was Dr. Wendell Urth, who, if the judgment of experts counted for anything, was Earth's most outstanding extraterrologist. On any subject outside Earth men came to him, though Dr. Urth had never in his adult life been more than an hour's-walk distance from his home on the University campus.

He looked up solemnly at Inspector Davenport. "A very intelligent man, this young Vernadsky," he said.

"To have deduced all he did from the presence of the silicony? Quite so," said Davenport.

"No, no. The deduction was a simple thing. Unavoidable, in fact. A noodle would have seen it. I was referring"—and his glance grew a trifle censorious—"to the fact that the youngster had read of my experiments concerning the gamma-ray sensitivity of *Siliconeus asteroidea.*"

"Ah, yes," said Davenport. Of course, Dr. Urth was the expert on siliconies. It was why Davenport had come to consult him. He had only one question for the man, a simple one, yet Dr. Urth had thrust out his full lips, shaken his ponderous head, and asked to see all the documents in the case.

Ordinarily that would have been out of the question, but Dr. Urth had recently been of considerable use to the T.B.I. in that affair of the Singing Bells of Luna and the singular non-alibi shattered by Moon gravity, and the Inspector had yielded.

Dr. Urth finished the reading, laid the sheets down on his desk, yanked his shirttail out of the tight confines of his belt with a grunt and rubbed his glasses with it. He stared through the glasses at the light to see the effects of his cleaning, replaced them precariously on his nose, and clasped his hands on his paunch, stubby fingers interlacing.

"Your question again, Inspector?"

Davenport said patiently, "Is it true, in your opinion, that a silicony of the size and type described in the report could only have developed on a world rich in uranium—"

"Radioactive material," interrupted Dr. Urth. "Thorium, perhaps, though probably uranium."

"Is your answer yes, then?"

"Yes."

"How big would the world be?"

"A mile in diameter, perhaps," said the extraterrologist thoughtfully. "Perhaps even more."

"How many tons of uranium, or radioactive material, rather?"

"In the trillions. Minimum."

"Would you be willing to put all that in the form of a signed opinion in writing?"

"Of course."

"Very well then, Dr. Urth." Davenport got to his feet, reached for his hat with one hand and the file of reports with the other. "That is all we need."

But Dr. Urth's hand moved to the reports and rested heavily upon them. "Wait. How will you find the asteroid?"

"By looking. We'll assign a volume of space to every ship made available to us and—just look."

"The expense, the time, the effort! And you'll never find it."

"One chance in a thousand. We might."

"One chance in a million. You won't."

"We can't let the uranium go without some try. Your professional opinion makes the prize high enough."

"But there is a better way to find the asteroid. *I* can find it."

Davenport fixed the extraterrologist with a sudden, sharp glance. Despite appearances Dr. Urth was anything but a fool. He had personal experience of that. There was therefore just a bit of half-hope in his voice as he said, "How can you find it?"

"First," said Dr. Urth, "my price."

"Price?"

"Or fee, if you choose. When the government reaches the asteroid, there may be another large-size silicony on it. Siliconies are very valuable. The only form of life with solid silicone for tissues and liquid silicone as a circulating fluid. The answer to the question whether the asteroids were once part of a single planetary body may rest with them. Any number of other problems . . . Do you understand?"

"You mean you want a large silicony delivered to you?"

"Alive and well. And free of charge. Yes."

Davenport nodded. "I'm sure the government will agree. Now what have you on your mind?"

Dr. Urth said quietly, as though explaining everything, "The silicony's remark."

Davenport looked bewildered. "What remark?"

"The one in the report. Just before the silicony died. Vernadsky was asking it where the captain had written down the coordinates, and it said, 'On the asteroid.' "

A look of intense disappointment crossed Davenport's face. "Great space, Doctor, we know that, and we've gone into every angle of it. Every possible angle. It means nothing."

"Nothing at all, Inspector?"

"Nothing of importance. Read the report again. The silicony wasn't even listening to Vernadsky. He was feeling life depart and he was wondering about it. Twice, it asked, 'What after death?' Then, as Vernadsky kept questioning it, it said, 'On the asteroid.' Probably it never heard Vernadsky's question. It was answering its own question. It thought that after death it would return to its own asteroid; to its home, where it would be safe once more. That's all."

Dr. Urth shook his head. "You are too much a poet, you know. You imagine too much. Come, it is an interesting problem and let us see if you can't solve it for yourself. Suppose the silicony's remark *were* an answer to Vernadsky."

"Even so," said Davenport impatiently, "how would it help? *Which* asteroid? The uranium asteroid? We can't find it, so we can't find the coordinates. Some other asteroid which the *Robert Q.* had used as a home base? We can't find that either."

"How you avoid the obvious, Inspector. Why don't you ask yourself what the phrase 'on the asteroid' means to the silicony. Not to you or to me, but to the silicony."

Davenport frowned. "Pardon me, Doctor?"

"I'm speaking plainly. What did the word *asteroid* mean to the silicony?"

"The silicony learned about space out of an astronomy text that was read to it. I suppose the book explained what an asteroid was."

"Exactly," crowed Dr. Urth, putting a finger to the side of his snub nose. "And how would the definition go? An asteroid is a small body, smaller than the planets, moving about the sun in an orbit which, generally speaking, lies between those of Mars and Jupiter. Wouldn't you agree?"

"I suppose so."

"And what is the *Robert Q.?*"

"You mean the ship?"

"That's what *you* call it," said Dr. Urth. "The *ship.* But the astronomy book was an ancient one. It made no mention of ships in space. One of the crewmen said as much. He said it dated from before space flight. Then what is the *Robert Q.?* Isn't it a small body, smaller than the planets? And while the silicony was aboard, wasn't it moving about the sun in an orbit which, generally speaking, lay between those of Mars and Jupiter?"

"You mean the silicony considered the ship as just another asteroid, and when he said 'on the asteroid,' he meant 'on the ship'?"

"Exactly. I told you I would make you solve the problem for yourself."

No expression of joy or relief lightened the gloom on the Inspector's face. "That is no solution, Doctor."

But Dr. Urth blinked slowly at him and the bland look on his round face became, if anything, blander and more childlike in its uncomplicated pleasure. "Surely it is."

"Not at all. Dr. Urth, we didn't reason it out as you did. We dismissed the silicony's remark completely. But still, don't you suppose we searched the *Robert Q.?* We took it apart piece by piece, plate by plate. We just about unwelded the thing."

"And you found nothing?"

"Nothing."

"Perhaps you did not look in the right place."

"We looked in *every* place." He stood up, as though to go. "You understand, Dr. Urth? When we got through with the ship there was no possibility of those coordinates existing anywhere on it."

"Sit down, Inspector," said Dr. Urth calmly. "You are still not considering the silicony's statement properly. Now the silicony learned English by collecting a word here and a word there. It couldn't speak idiomatic English. Some of its statements, as quoted, show that. For instance, it said, 'the planet which is most far' instead of 'the farthest planet.' You see?"

"Well?"

"Someone who cannot speak a language idiomatically either uses the idioms of his own language translated word by word or else he simply uses foreign words according to their literal meaning. The silicony had no spoken language of its own so it could only make use of the second alternative. Let's be literal, then. He said, '*on* the asteroid,' Inspector. *On* it. He didn't mean on a piece of paper, he meant on the ship, literally."

"Dr. Urth," said Davenport sadly, "when the Bureau searches, it searches. There were no mysterious inscriptions *on* the ship either."

Dr. Urth looked disappointed. "Dear me, Inspector. I keep hoping you will see the answer. Really, you have had so many hints."

Davenport drew in a slow, firm breath. It went hard, but his voice was calm and even once more. "Will you tell me what you have in mind, Doctor?"

Dr. Urth patted his comfortable abdomen with one hand and replaced his glasses. "Don't you see, Inspector, that there is one place on board a spaceship where secret numbers are perfectly safe? Where, although in plain view, they would be perfectly safe from detection? Where though they were being stared at by a hundred eyes, they would be secure? Except from a seeker who is an astute thinker, of course."

"Where? Name the place!"

"Why, in those places where there happen to be numbers already. Perfectly normal numbers. Legal numbers. Numbers that are supposed to be there."

"What are you talking about?"

"The ship's serial number, etched directly on the hull. *On* the hull, be it noted. The engine number, the field generator number. A few others. Each etched on integral portions of the ship. *On* the ship, as the silicony said. *On* the ship."

Davenport's heavy eyebrows rose with sudden comprehension. "You may be right—and if you are, I'm hoping we find you a silicony twice the size of the *Robert Q.*'s. One that not only talks, but whistles, 'Up, Asteroids, Forever!'" He hastily reached for the dossier, thumbed rapidly through it and extracted an official T.B.I. form. "Of course, we noted down all the identification numbers we found." He spread the form out. "If three of these resemble coordinates . . ."

"We should expect some small effort at disguise," Dr. Urth observed.

"There will probably be certain letters and figures added to make the series appear more legitimate."

He reached for a scratch pad and shoved another toward the Inspector. For minutes the two men were silent, jotting down serial numbers, experimenting with crossing out obviously unrelated figures.

At last Davenport let out a sigh that mingled satisfaction and frustration. "I'm stuck," he admitted. "I think you're right; the numbers on the engine and the calculator are clearly disguised coordinates and dates. They don't run anywhere near the normal series, and it's easy to strike out the fake figures. That gives us two, but I'll take my oath the rest of these are absolutely legitimate serial numbers. What are your findings, Doctor?"

Dr. Urth nodded. "I agree. We now have two coordinates and we know where the third was inscribed."

"We know, do we? And how—" The Inspector broke off and uttered a sharp exclamation. "Of course! The number on the very ship itself, which isn't entered here—because it was on the precise spot on the hull where the meteor crashed through—I'm afraid there goes your silicony, Doctor." Then his craggy face brightened. "But I'm an idiot. The number's gone, but we can get it in a flash from Interplanetary Registry."

"I fear," said Dr. Urth, "that I must dispute at least the second part of your statement. Registry will have only the ship's original legitimate number, not the disguised coordinate to which the captain must have altered it."

"The exact spot on the hull," Davenport muttered. "And because of that chance shot the asteroid may be lost forever. What use to anybody are two coordinates without the third?"

"Well," said Dr. Urth precisely, "conceivably of very great use to a two-dimensional being. But creatures of our dimensions," he patted his paunch, "do require the third—which I fortunately happen to have right here."

"In the T.B.I. dossier? But we just checked the list of numbers—"

"*Your* list, Inspector. The file also includes young Vernadsky's original report. And of course the serial number listed there for the *Robert Q.* is the carefully faked one under which she was then sailing—no point in rousing the curiosity of a repair mechanic by letting him note a discrepancy."

Davenport reached for a scratch pad and the Vernadsky list. A moment's calculation and he grinned.

Dr. Urth lifted himself out of the chair with a pleased puff and trotted to the door. "It is always pleasant to see you, Inspector Davenport. Do come again. And remember the government can have the uranium, but I want the important thing: one giant silicony, alive and in good condition."

He was smiling.

"And preferably," said Davenport, "whistling."

Which he was doing himself as he walked out.

Each an
Explorer

Herman Chouns was a man of hunches. Sometimes he was right; sometimes he was wrong—about fifty-fifty. Still, considering that one has the whole universe of possibilities from which to pull a right answer, fifty-fifty begins to look pretty good.

Chouns wasn't always as pleased with the matter as might be expected. It put too much of a strain on him. People would huddle around a problem, making nothing of it, then turn to him and say, "What do you think, Chouns? Turn on the old intuition."

And if he came up with something that fizzled, the responsibility for that was made clearly his.

His job, as field explorer, rather made things worse.

"Think that planet's worth a closer look?" they would say. "What do you think, Chouns?"

So it was a relief to draw a two-man spot for a change (meaning that the next trip would be to some low-priority place, and the pressure would be off) and, on top of it, to get Allen Smith as partner.

Smith was as matter-of-fact as his name. He said to Chouns the first day out, "The thing about you is that the memory files in your brain are on extraspecial call. Faced with a problem, you remember enough little things that maybe the rest of us don't come up with to make a decision. Calling it a hunch just makes it mysterious, and it isn't."

He rubbed his hair slickly back as he said that. He had light hair that lay down like a skull cap.

Chouns, whose hair was very unruly, and whose nose was snub and a bit off-center, said softly (as was his way), "I think maybe it's telepathy."

"What!"

"Nuts!" said Smith, with loud derision (as was *his* way). "Scientists have been tracking psionics for a thousand years and gotten nowhere. There's no such thing: no precognition; no telekinesis; no clairvoyance; *and* no telepathy."

"I admit that, but consider this. If I get a picture of what each of a group of people are thinking—even though I might not be aware of what was happening—I could integrate the information and come up with an answer. I would know more than any single individual in the group, so I could make a better judgment than the others—sometimes."

"Do you have any evidence at all for that?"

Chouns turned his mild brown eyes on the other. "Just a hunch."

They got along well. Chouns welcomed the other's refreshing practicality, and Smith patronized the other's speculations. They often disagreed but never quarreled.

Even when they reached their objective, which was a globular cluster that had never felt the energy thrusts of a human-designed nuclear reactor before, increasing tension did not worsen matters.

Smith said, "Wonder what they do with all this data back on Earth. Seems a waste sometimes."

Chouns said, "Earth is just beginning to spread out. No telling how far humanity will move out into the galaxy, given a million years or so. All the data we can get on any world will come in handy someday."

"You sound like a recruiting manual for the Exploration Teams. Think there'll be anything interesting in that thing?" He indicated the visi-plate on which the no-longer distant cluster was centered like spilled talcum powder.

"Maybe. I've got a hunch—" Chouns stopped, gulped, blinked once or twice, and then smiled weakly.

Smith snorted. "Let's get a fix on the nearest stargroups and make a random pass through the thickest of it. One gets you ten, we find a McKomin ratio under 0.2."

"You'll lose," murmured Chouns. He felt the quick stir of excitement that always came when new worlds were about to be spread beneath them. It was a most contagious feeling, and it caught hundreds of youngsters each year. Youngsters, such as he had been once, flocked to the Teams, eager to see the worlds their descendants someday would call their own, each an explorer—

They got their fix (made their first close-quarters hyperspatial jump into the cluster, and began scanning stars for planetary systems. The computers did their work; the information files grew steadily, and all proceeded in satisfactory routine—until at system 23, shortly after completion of the jump, the ship's hyperatomic motors failed.

Chouns muttered, "Funny. The analyzers don't say what's wrong."

He was right. The needles wavered erratically, never stopping once for a reasonable length of time, so that no diagnosis was indicated. And, as a consequence, no repairs could be carried through.

"Never saw anything like it," growled Smith. "We'll have to shut everything off and diagnose manually."

"We might as well do it comfortably," said Chouns, who was already at the telescopes. "Nothing's wrong with the ordinary spacedrive, and there are two decent planets in this system."

"Oh? How decent and which ones?"

"The first and second out of four: Both water-oxygen. The first is a bit warmer and larger than Earth; the second a bit colder and smaller. Fair enough?"

"Life?"

"Both. Vegetation, anyway."

Smith grunted. There was nothing in that to surprise anyone; vegetation occurred more often than not on water-oxygen worlds. And, unlike animal life, vegetation could be seen telescopically—or, more precisely, spectroscopically. Only four photochemical pigments had ever been found in any plant form, and each could be detected by the nature of the light it reflected.

Chouns said, "Vegetation on both planets is chlorophyll type, no less. It'll be just like Earth; real homey."

Smith said, "Which is closer?"

"Number two, and we're on our way. I have a feeling it's going to be a nice planet."

"I'll judge that by the instruments, *if* you don't mind," said Smith.

But this seemed to be one of Chouns's correct hunches. The planet was a tame one with an intricate ocean network that insured a climate of small temperature range. The mountain ranges were low and rounded, and the distribution of vegetation indicated high and widespread fertility.

Chouns was at the controls for the actual landing.

Smith grew impatient. "What are you picking and choosing for? One place is like another."

"I'm looking for a bare spot," said Chouns. "No use burning up an acre of plant life."

"What if you do?"

"What if I don't?" said Chouns, and found his bare spot.

It was only then, after landing, that they realized a small part of what they had tumbled into.

"Jumping space-warps," said Smith.

Chouns felt stunned. Animal life was much rarer than vegetation, and even the glimmerings of intelligence were far rarer still; yet here, not half a mile away from landing point, was a clustering of low, thatched huts that were obviously the product of a primitive intelligence.

"Careful," said Smith dazedly.

"I don't think there's any harm," said Chouns. He stepped out onto the surface of the planet with firm confidence; Smith followed.

Chouns controlled his excitement with difficulty. "This is terrific. No one's ever reported anything better than caves or woven tree-branches before."

"I hope they're harmless."

"It's too peaceful for them to be anything else. Smell the air."

Coming down to landing, the terrain—to all points of horizon, except where a low range of hills broke the even line—had been colored a soothing pale pink, dappled against the chlorophyll green. At closer quarters the pale pink broke up into individual flowers, fragile and fragrant. Only the areas in the immediate neighborhood of the huts were amber with something that looked like a cereal grain.

Creatures were emerging from the huts, moving closer to the ship with a kind of hesitating trust. They had four legs and a sloping body which stood three feet high at the shoulders. Their heads were set firmly on those shoulders, with bulging eyes (Chouns counted six) set in a circle and capable of the most disconcertingly independent motion. *(That makes up for the immovability of the head,* thought Chouns.)

Each animal had a tail that forked at the end, forming two sturdy fibrils that each animal held high. The fibrils maintained a rapid tremor that gave them a hazy, blurred look.

"Come on," said Chouns. "They won't hurt us; I'm sure of it."

The animals surrounded the men at a cautious distance. Their tails made a modulated humming noise.

"They might communicate that way," said Chouns. "And I think it's obvious they're vegetarians." He pointed toward one of the huts, where a small member of the species sat on its haunches, plucking at the amber grain with his tails, and flickering an ear of it through his mouth like a man sucking a series of maraschino cherries off a toothpick.

"Human beings eat lettuce," said Smith, "but that doesn't prove anything."

More of the tailed creatures emerged, hovered about the men for a moment, then vanished off into the pink and green.

"Vegetarians," said Chouns firmly. "Look at the way they cultivate the main crop."

The main crop, as Chouns called it, consisted of a coronet of soft green spikes, close to the ground. Out of the center of the coronet grew a hairy stem which, at two-inch intervals, shot out fleshy, veined buds that almost pulsated, they seemed so vitally alive. The stem ended at the tip with the pale pink blossoms that, except for the color, were the most Earthly thing about the plants.

The plants were laid out in rows and files with geometric precision. The soil about each was well loosened and powdered with a foreign substance that could be nothing but fertilizer. Narrow passageways, just wide enough for an animal to pass along, crisscrossed the field, and each passageway was lined with narrow sluiceways, obviously for water.

The animals were spread through the fields now, working diligently, heads bent. Only a few remained in the neighborhood of the two men.

Chouns nodded. "They're good farmers."

"Not bad," agreed Smith. He walked briskly toward the nearest of the pale pink blooms and reached for one; but six inches short of it he was stopped by the sound of tail vibrations keening to shrillness, and by the actual touch of a tail upon his arm. The touch was delicate but firm, interposing itself between Smith and the plants.

Smith fell back. "What in Space—"

He had half reached for his blaster when Chouns said, "No cause for excitement; take it easy."

Half a dozen of the creatures were now gathering about the two, offering stalks of grain humbly and gently, some using their tails, some nudging it forward with their muzzles.

Chouns said, "They're friendly enough. Picking a bloom might be against their customs; the plants probably have to be treated according to rigid rules. Any culture that has agriculture probably has fertility rites, and Lord knows what that involves. The rules governing the cultivation of the plants must be strict, or there wouldn't be those accurate measured rows. . . . Space, won't they sit up back home when they hear this?"

The tail humming shot up in pitch again, and the creatures near them fell back. Another member of the species was emerging from a larger hut in the center of the group.

"The chief, I suppose," muttered Chouns.

The new one advanced slowly, tail high, each fibril encircling a small black object. At a distance of five feet its tail arched forward.

"He's giving it to us," said Smith in astonishment, "and Chouns, for God's sake, *look* at it."

Chouns was doing so, feverishly. He choked out, "They're Gamow hyperspatial sighters. Those are ten-thousand-dollar instruments."

Smith emerged from the ship again, after an hour within. He shouted from the ramp in high excitement, "They work. They're perfect. We're rich."

Chouns called back, "I've been checking through their huts. I can't find any more."

"Don't sneeze at just two. Good Lord, these are as negotiable as a handful of cash."

But Chouns still looked about, arms akimbo, exasperated. Three of the tailed creatures had dogged him from hut to hut—patiently, never interfering, but remaining always between him and the geometrically cultivated pale pink blossoms. Now they stared multiply at him.

Smith said, "It's the latest model, too. Look here." He pointed to the raised lettering which said *Model X-20, Gamow Products, Warsaw, European Sector.*

Chouns glanced at it and said impatiently, "What interests me is getting more. I *know* there are more Gamow sighters somewhere, I want them." His cheeks were flushed and his breathing heavy.

The sun was setting; the temperature dropped below the comfortable point. Smith sneezed twice, then Chouns.

"We'll catch pneumonia," snuffled Smith.

"I've got to make them understand," said Chouns stubbornly. He had eaten hastily through a can of pork sausage, had gulped down a can of coffee, and was ready to try again.

He held the sighter high. "More," he said, "more," making encircling movements with his arms. He pointed to one sighter, then to the other, then to the imaginary additional ones lined up before him. "More."

Then, as the last of the sun dipped below the horizon, a vast hum arose from all parts of the field as every creature in sight ducked its head, lifted its forked tail, and vibrated it into screaming invisibility in the twilight.

"What in Space," muttered Smith uneasily. "Hey, look at the blooms!" He sneezed again.

The pale pink flowers were shriveling visibly.

Chouns shouted to make himself heard above the hum, "It may be a reaction to sunset. You know, the blooms close at night. The noise may be a religious observance of the fact."

A soft flick of a tail across his wrist attracted Chouns's instant attention. The tail he had felt belonged to the nearest creature; and now it was raised to the sky, toward a bright object low on the western horizon. The tail bent downward to point to the sighter, then up again to the star.

Chouns said excitedly, "Of course—the inner planet; the other habitable one. These must have come from there." Then, reminded by the thought, he cried in sudden shock, "Hey, Smith, the hyperatomic motors are still out."

Smith looked shocked, as though he had forgotten, too; then he mumbled, "Meant to tell you—they're allright."

"You fixed them?"

"Never touched them. But when I was testing the sighters I used the hyperatomics and they worked. I didn't pay any attention at the time; I forgot there was anything wrong. Anyway, they worked."

"Then let's go," said Chouns at once. The thought of sleep never occurred to him.

Neither one slept through the six-hour trip. They remained at the controls in an almost drug-fed passion. Once again they chose a bare spot on which to land.

It was hot with an afternoon subtropical heat; and a broad, muddy river moved placidly by them. The near bank was of hardened mud, riddled with large cavities.

The two men stepped out onto planetary surface and Smith cried hoarsely, "Chouns, look at that!"

Chouns shook off the other's grasping hand. He said, "The same plants! I'll be damned."

There was no mistaking the pale pink blossoms, the stalk with its veined buds, and the coronet of spikes below. Again there was the geometric spacing, the careful planting and fertilization, the irrigation canals.

Smith said, "We haven't made a mistake and circled—"

"Oh, look at the sun; it's twice the diameter it was before. And look there."

Out of the nearest burrows in the river bank smoothly tan and sinuous objects, as limbless as snakes, emerged. They were a foot in diameter, ten feet in length. The two ends were equally featureless, equally blunt. Midway along their upper portions were bulges. All the bulges, as though on signal, grew before their eyes to fat ovals, split in two to form lipless, gaping mouths that opened and closed with a sound like a forest of dry sticks clapping together.

Then, just as on the outer planet, once their curiosities were satisfied and their fears calmed, most of the creatures drifted away toward the carefully cultivated field of plants.

Smith sneezed. The force of expelled breath against the sleeve of his jacket raised a powdering of dust.

He stared at that with amazement, then slapped himself and said, "Damn it, I'm dusty." The dust rose like a pale pink fog. "You, too," he added, slapping Chouns.

Both men sneezed with abandon.

"Picked it up on the other planet, I suppose," said Chouns.

"We can work up an allergy."

"Impossible." Chouns held up one of the sighters and shouted at the snake-things, "Do you have any of these?"

For a while there was nothing in answer but the splashing of water, as some of the snake things slid into the river and emerged with silvery clusters of water life, which they tucked beneath their bodies toward some hidden mouth.

But then one snake-thing, longer than the others, came thrusting along the ground, one blunt end raised questingly some two inches, weaving blindly side to side. The bulb in its center swelled gently at first, then alarmingly, splitting in two with an audible pop. There, nestling within the two halves, were two more sighters, the duplicates of the first two.

Chouns said ecstatically, "Lord in heaven, isn't that beautiful?"

He stepped hastily forward, reaching out for the objects. The swelling that held them thinned and lengthened, forming what were almost tentacles. They reached out toward him.

Chouns was laughing. They were Gamow sighters all right; duplicates, absolute duplicates, of the first two. Chouns fondled them.

Smith was shouting, "Don't you hear me? Chouns, damn it, listen to me."

Chouns said, "What?" He was dimly aware that Smith had been yelling at him for over a minute.

"Look at the flowers, Chouns."

They were closing, as had those on the other planet, and among the rows the snake-things reared upward, balancing on one end and swaying with a queer, broken rhythm. Only the blunt ends of them were visible above the pale pink.

Smith said, "You can't say they're closing up because of nightfall. It's broad day."

Chouns shrugged. "Different planet, different plant. Come on! We've only got two sighters here; there must be more."

"Chouns, let's go home." Smith firmed his legs into two stubborn pillars and the grip he held on Chouns's collar tightened.

Chouns's reddened face turned back toward him indignantly. "What are you doing?"

"I'm getting ready to knock you out if you don't come back with me at once, into the ship."

For a moment Chouns stood irresolute; then a certain wildness about him faded, a certain slackening took place, and he said, "All right."

They were halfway out of the starcluster. Smith said, "How are you?"

Chouns sat up in his bunk and rumpled his hair. "Normal, I guess; sane again. How long have I been sleeping?"

"Twelve hours."

"What about you?"

"I've catnapped." Smith turned ostentatiously to the instruments and made some minor adjustments. He said self-consciously, "Do you know what happened back there on those planets?"

Chouns said slowly, "Do you?"

"I think so."

"Oh? May I hear?"

Smith said, "It was the same plant on both planets. You'll grant that?"

"I most certainly do."

"It was transplanted from one planet to the other, somehow. It grows on both planets perfectly well; but occasionally—to maintain vigor, I imagine—there must be crossfertilization, the two strains mingling. That sort of thing happens on Earth often enough."

"Crossfertilization for vigor? Yes."

"But *we* were the agents that arranged for the mingling. We landed on one planet and were coated with pollen. Remember the blooms closing? That must have been just after they released their pollen; and that's what was making us sneeze, too. Then we landed on the other planet and knocked the pollen off our clothes. A new hybrid strain will start up. We were just a pair of two-legged bees, Chouns, doing our duty by the flowers."

Chouns smiled tentatively. "An inglorious role, in a way."

"Hell, that's not it. Don't you see the danger? Don't you see why we have to get back home *fast?*"

"Why?"

"Because organisms don't adapt themselves to nothing. Those plants seem to be adapted to interplanetary fertilization. We even got paid off, the way bees are; not with nectar, but with Gamow sighters."

"Well?"

"Well, you can't have interplanetary fertilization unless something or someone is there to do the job. *We* did it this time, but we were the first humans ever to enter the cluster. So, before this, it must be nonhumans who did it; maybe the same nonhumans who transplanted the blooms in the first place. That means that somewhere in this cluster there is an intelligent race of beings; intelligent enough for space travel. And Earth must know about that."

Slowly Chouns shook his head.

Smith frowned. "You find flaws somewhere in the reasoning?"

Chouns put his head between his own palms and looked miserable. "Let's say you've missed almost everything."

"What have I missed?" demanded Smith angrily.

"Your crossfertilization theory is good, as far as it goes, but you haven't considered a few points. When we approached that stellar system our hyperatomic motor went out of order in a way the automatic controls could neither diagnose nor correct. After we landed we made no effort to adjust them. We forgot about them, in fact; and when you handled them later you found they were in perfect order, and were so unimpressed by that that you didn't even mention it to me for another few hours.

"Take something else:. How conveniently we chose landing spots near a grouping of animal life on both planets. Just luck? And our incredible confidence in the good will of the creatures. We never even bothered checking atmospheres for trace poisons before exposing ourselves.

"And what bothers me most of all is that I went completely crazy over the Gamow sighters. Why? They're valuable, yes, but not *that* valuable—and I don't generally go overboard for a quick buck."

Smith had kept an uneasy silence during all that. Now he said, "I don't see that any of that adds up to anything."

"Get off it, Smith; you know better than that. Isn't it obvious to you that we were under mental control from the outside?"

Smith's mouth twisted and caught halfway between derision and doubt. "Are you on the psionic kick again?"

"Yes; facts are facts. I told you that my hunches might be a form of rudimentary telepathy."

"Is that a fact, too? You didn't think so a couple of days ago."

"I think so now. Look, I'm a better receiver than you, and I was more strongly affected. Now that it's over, I understand more about what happened because I received more. Understand?"

"No," said Smith harshly.

"Then listen further. You said yourself the Gamow sighters were the nectar that bribed us into pollination. *You* said that."

"All right."

"Well, then, where did they come from? They were Earth products; we even read the manufacturer's name and model on them, letter by letter. Yet, if no human beings have ever been in the cluster, where did the sighters come from? Neither one of us worried about that, then; and you don't seem to worry about it even now."

"Well—"

"What did you do with the sighters after we got on board ship, Smith? You took them from me; I remember that."

"I put them in the safe," said Smith defensively.

"Have you touched them since?"

"No."

"Have I?"

"Not as far as I know."

"You have my word I didn't. Then why not open the safe now?"

Smith stepped slowly to the safe. It was keyed to his fingerprints, and it opened. Without looking he reached in. His expression altered and with a sharp cry he first stared at the contents, then scrabbled them out.

He held four rocks of assorted color, each of them roughly rectangular.

"They used our own emotions to drive us," said Chouns softly, as though insinuating the words into the other's stubborn skull one at a time. "They made us think the hyperatomics were wrong so we could land on one of the planets; it didn't matter which, I suppose. They made us think we had precision instruments in our hand after we landed on one so we would race to the other."

"Who are 'they'?" groaned Smith. "The tails or the snakes? Or both?"

"Neither," said Chouns. "It was the plants."

"The plants? The *flowers?*"

"Certainly. We saw two different sets of animals tending the same species of plant. Being animals ourselves, we assumed the animals were the masters. But why should we assume that? It was the plants that were being taken care of."

"We cultivate plants on Earth, too, Chouns."

"But we eat those plants," said Chouns.

"And maybe those creatures eat their plants, too."

"Let's say I know they don't," said Chouns. "They maneuvered us well enough. Remember how careful I was to find a bare spot on which to land."

"*I* felt no such urge."

"You weren't at the controls; they weren't worried about you. Then, too, remember that we never noticed the pollen, though we were covered with it —not till we were safely on the second planet. Then we dusted the pollen off, on order."

"I never heard anything so impossible."

"Why is it impossible? We don't associate intelligence with plants, because plants have no nervous systems; but these might have. Remember the fleshy buds on the stems? Also, plants aren't free-moving; but they don't have to be if they develop psionic powers and can make use of free-moving animals. They get cared for, fertilized, irrigated, pollinated, and so on. The animals tend them with single-minded devotion and are happy over it because the plants make them feel happy."

"I'm sorry for you," said Smith in a monotone. "If you try to tell this story back on Earth, I'm sorry for you."

"I have no illusions," muttered Chouns, "yet—what can I do but try to warn Earth. You see what they do to animals."

"They make slaves of them, according to you."

"Worse than that. Either the tailed creatures or the snake-things, or both, must have been civilized enough to have developed space travel once; otherwise the plants couldn't be on both planets. But once the plants developed psionic powers (a mutant strain, perhaps), that came to an end. Animals at the atomic stage are dangerous. So they were made to forget; they were reduced to what they are. —Damn it, Smith, those plants are the most dangerous things in the universe. Earth must be informed about them, because some other Earthmen may be entering that cluster."

Smith laughed. "You know, you're completely off base. If those plants really had us under control, why would they let us get away to warn the others?"

Chouns paused. "I don't know."

Smith's good humor was restored. He said, "For a minute you had me going, I don't mind telling you."

Chouns rubbed his skull violently. Why *were* they let go? And for that matter, why did he feel this horrible urgency to warn Earth about a matter with which Earthmen would not come into contact for millennia perhaps?

He thought desperately and something came glimmering. He fumbled for it, but it drifted away. For a moment he thought desperately that it was as though the thought had been *pushed* away; but then that feeling, too, left.

He knew only that the ship had to remain at full thrust, that they had to hurry.

.   .   .   .

So, after uncounted years, the proper conditions had come about again. The protospores from two planetary strains of the mother plant met and mingled, sifting together into the clothes and hair and ship of the new animals. Almost at once the hybrid spores formed; the hybrid spores that alone had all the capacity and potentiality of adapting themselves to a new planet.

The spores waited quietly, now, on the ship which, with the last impulse of the mother plant upon the minds of the creatures aboard, was hurtling them at top thrust toward a new and ripe world where free-moving creatures would tend their needs.

The spores waited with the patience of the plant (the all-conquering patience no animal can ever know) for their arrival on a new world—each, in its own tiny way, an explorer—

Let's Get Together

A kind of peace had endured for a century and people had forgotten what anything else was like. They would scarcely have known how to react had they discovered that a kind of war had finally come.

Certainly, Elias Lynn, Chief of the Bureau of Robotics, wasn't sure how he ought to react when *he* finally found out. The Bureau of Robotics was headquartered in Cheyenne, in line with the century-old trend toward decentralization, and Lynn stared dubiously at the young Security officer from Washington who had brought the news.

Elias Lynn was a large man, almost charmingly homely, with pale blue eyes that bulged a bit. Men weren't usually comfortable under the stare of those eyes, but the Security officer remained calm.

Lynn decided that his first reaction ought to be incredulity. Hell, it *was* incredulity! He just didn't believe it!

He eased himself back in his chair and said, "How certain is the information?"

The Security officer, who had introduced himself as Ralph G. Breckenridge and had presented credentials to match, had the softness of youth about him; full lips, plump cheeks that flushed easily, and guileless eyes. His clothing was out of line with Cheyenne but it suited a universally air-conditioned Washington, where Security, despite everything, was still centered.

Breckenridge flushed and said, "There's no doubt about it."

"You people know all about Them, I suppose," said Lynn and was unable to keep a trace of sarcasm out of his tone. He was not particularly aware of his use of a slightly stressed pronoun in his reference to the enemy, the equivalent of capitalization in print. It was a cultural habit of this generation and the one preceding. No one said the "East," or the "Reds" or the "Soviets" or the "Russians" any more. That would have been too confusing, since some of Them weren't of the East, weren't Reds, Soviets, and especially not Russians. It was much simpler to say We and They, and much more precise.

Travelers had frequently reported that They did the same in reverse. Over there, They were "We" (in the appropriate language) and We were "They."

Scarcely anyone gave thought to such things any more. It was all quite comfortable and casual. There was no hatred, even. At the beginning, it had been called a Cold War. Now it was only a game, almost a good-natured game, with unspoken rules and a kind of decency about it.

Lynn said abruptly, "Why should They want to disturb the situation?"

He rose and stood staring at a wall map of the world, split into two regions with faint edgings of color. An irregular portion on the left of the map was edged in a mild green. A smaller, but just as irregular, portion on the right of the map was bordered in a washed-out pink. We and They.

The map hadn't changed much in a century. The loss of Formosa and the gain of East Germany some eighty years before had been the last territorial switch of importance.

There had been another change, though, that was significant enough and that was in the colors. Two generations before, Their territory had been a brooding, bloody red, Ours a pure and undefiled white. Now there was a neutrality about the colors. Lynn had seen Their maps and it was the same on Their side.

"They wouldn't do it," he said.

"They are doing it," said Breckenridge, "and you had better accustom yourself to the fact. Of course, sir, I realize that it isn't pleasant to think that They may be that far ahead of us in robotics."

His eyes remained as guileless as ever, but the hidden knife-edges of the words plunged deep, and Lynn quivered at the impact.

Of course, that would account for why the Chief of Robotics learned of this so late and through a Security officer at that. He had lost caste in the eyes of the Government; if Robotics had really failed in the struggle, Lynn could expect no political mercy.

Lynn said wearily, "Even if what you say is true, They're not far ahead of us. We could build humanoid robots."

"Have we, sir?"

"Yes. As a matter of fact, we have built a few models for experimental purposes."

"They were doing so ten years ago. They've made ten years' progress since."

Lynn was disturbed. He wondered if his incredulity concerning the whole business was really the result of wounded pride and fear for his job and reputation. He was embarrassed by the possibility that this might be so, and yet he was forced into defense.

He said, "Look, young man, the stalemate between Them and Us was never perfect in every detail, you know. They have always been ahead in one facet or another and We in some other facet or another. If They're ahead of us right now in robotics, it's because They've placed a greater proportion of Their effort into robotics than We have. And that means that some other branch of endeavor has received a greater share of Our efforts than it has of Theirs. It would mean We're ahead in force-field research or in hyperatomics, perhaps."

Lynn felt distressed at his own statement that the stalemate wasn't perfect. It was true enough, but that was the one great danger threatening the world. The world depended on the stalemate being as perfect as possible. If the small unevennesses that always existed overbalanced too far in one direction or the other—

Almost at the beginning of what had been the Cold War, both sides had developed thermonuclear weapons, and war became unthinkable. Competition switched from the military to the economic and psychological and had stayed there ever since.

But always there was the driving effort on each side to break the stalemate, to develop a parry for every possible thrust, to develop a thrust that could not be parried in time—something that would make war possible again. And that was not because either side wanted war so desperately, but because both were afraid that the other side would make the crucial discovery first.

For a hundred years each side had kept the struggle even. And in the process, peace had been maintained for a hundred years while, as byproducts of the continuously intensive research, force fields had been produced and solar energy and insect control and robots. Each side was making a beginning in the understanding of mentalics, which was the name given to the biochemistry and biophysics of thought. Each side had its outposts on the Moon and on Mars. Mankind was advancing in giant strides under forced draft.

It was even necessary for both sides to be as decent and humane as possible among themselves, lest through cruelty and tyranny, friends be made for the other side.

It couldn't be that the stalemate would now be broken and that there would be war.

Lynn said, "I want to consult one of my men. I want his opinion."

"Is he trustworthy?"

Lynn looked disgusted. "Good Lord, what man in Robotics has not been investigated and cleared to death by your people? Yes, I vouch for him. If you can't trust a man like Humphrey Carl Laszlo, then we're in no position to face the kind of attack you say They are launching, no matter what else we do."

"I've heard of Laszlo," said Breckenridge.

"Good. Does he pass?"

"Yes."

"Then, I'll have him in and we'll find out what he thinks about the possibility that robots could invade the U. S. A."

"Not exactly," said Breckenridge, softly. "You still don't accept the full truth. Find out what he thinks about the fact that robots have *already* invaded the U. S. A."

Laszlo was the grandson of a Hungarian who had broken through what had then been called the Iron Curtain, and he had a comfortable above-suspicion feeling about himself because of it. He was thick-set and balding with a pugnacious look graven forever on his snub face, but his accent was clear Harvard and he was almost excessively soft-spoken.

To Lynn, who was conscious that after years of administration he was no longer expert in the various phases of modern robotics, Laszlo was a comforting receptacle for complete knowledge. Lynn felt better because of the man's mere presence.

Lynn said, "What do you think?"

A scowl twisted Laszlo's face ferociously. "That They're that far ahead of us. Completely incredible. It would mean They've produced humanoids that could not be told from humans at close quarters. It would mean a considerable advance in robo-mentalics."

"You're personally involved," said Breckenridge, coldly. "Leaving professional pride out of account, exactly why is it impossible that They be ahead of Us?"

Laszlo shrugged. "I assure you that I'm well acquainted with Their literature on robotics. I know approximately where They are."

"You know approximately where They want you to *think* They are, is what you really mean," corrected Breckenridge. "Have you ever visited the other side?"

"I haven't," said Laszlo, shortly.

"Nor you, Dr. Lynn?"

Lynn said, "No, I haven't, either."

Breckenridge said, "Has any robotics man visited the other side in twenty-five years?" He asked the question with a kind of confidence that indicated he knew the answer.

For a matter of seconds, the atmosphere was heavy with thought. Discomfort crossed Laszlo's broad face. He said, "As a matter of fact, They haven't held any conferences on robotics in a long time."

"In twenty-five years," said Breckenridge. "Isn't that significant?"

"Maybe," said Laszlo, reluctantly. "Something else bothers me, though. None of Them have ever come to Our conferences on robotics. None that I can remember."

"Were They invited?" asked Breckenridge.

Lynn, staring and worried, interposed quickly, "Of course."

Breckenridge said, "Do They refuse attendance to any other types of scientific conferences We hold?"

"I don't know," said Laszlo. He was pacing the floor now. "I haven't heard of any cases. Have you, Chief?"

"No," said Lynn.

Breckenridge said, "Wouldn't you say it was as though They didn't want to be put in the position of having to return any such invitation? Or as though They were afraid one of Their men might talk too much?"

That was exactly how it seemed, and Lynn felt a helpless conviction that Security's story was true after all steal over him.

Why else had there been no contact between sides on robotics? There had been a cross-fertilizing trickle of researchers moving in both directions on a strictly one-for-one basis for years, dating back to the days of Eisenhower and Khrushchev. There were a great many good motives for that: an honest appreciation of the supranational character of science; impulses of friendliness that are hard to wipe out completely in the individual human being; the desire to be exposed to a fresh and interesting outlook and to have your own slightly stale notions greeted by others as fresh and interesting.

The governments themselves were anxious that this continue. There was always the obvious thought that by learning all you could and telling as little as you could, your own side would gain by the exchange.

But not in the case of robotics. Not there.

Such a little thing to carry conviction. And a thing, moreover, they had known all along. Lynn thought darkly: *We've taken the complacent way out.*

Because the other side had done nothing publicly on robotics, it had been tempting to sit back smugly and be comfortable in the assurance of superiority. Why hadn't it seemed possible, even likely, that They were hiding superior cards, a trump hand, for the proper time?

Laszlo said shakenly, "What do we do?" It was obvious that the same line of thought had carried the same conviction to him.

"Do?" parroted Lynn. It was hard to think right now of anything but of the complete horror that came with conviction. There were ten humanoid robots somewhere in the United States, each one carrying a fragment of a TC bomb.

TC! The race for sheer horror in bomb-ery had ended there. TC! Total Conversion! The sun was no longer a synonym one could use. Total conversion made the sun a penny candle.

Ten humanoids, each completely harmless in separation, could, by the simple act of coming together, exceed critical mass and—

Lynn rose to his feet heavily, the dark pouches under his eyes, which ordinarily lent his ugly face a look of savage foreboding, more prominent than ever. "It's going to be up to us to figure out ways and means of telling a humanoid from a human and then finding the humanoids."

"How quickly?" muttered Laszlo.

"Not later than five minutes before they get together," barked Lynn, "and I don't know when that will be."

Breckenridge nodded. "I'm glad you're with us now, sir. I'm to bring you back to Washington for conference, you know."

Lynn raised his eyebrows. "All right."

He wondered if, had he delayed longer in being convinced, he might not have been replaced forthwith—if some other Chief of the Bureau of Robotics might not be conferring in Washington. He suddenly wished earnestly that exactly that had come to pass.

The First Presidential Assistant was there, the Secretary of Science, the Secretary of Security, Lynn himself, and Breckenridge. Five of them sitting about a table in the dungeons of an underground fortress near Washington.

Presidential Assistant Jeffreys was an impressive man, handsome in a white-haired and just-a-trifle-jowly fashion, solid, thoughtful and as unobtrusive, politically, as a Presidential Assistant ought to be.

He spoke incisively. "There are three questions that face us as I see it. First, when are the humanoids going to get together? Second, where are they going to get together? Third, how do we stop them before they get together?"

Secretary of Science Amberley nodded convulsively at that. He had been Dean of Northwestern Engineering before his appointment. He was thin, sharp-featured and noticeably edgy. His forefinger traced slow circles on the table.

"As far as *when* they'll get together," he said. "I suppose it's definite that it won't be for some time."

"Why do you say that?" asked Lynn sharply.

"They've been in the U. S. at least a month already. So Security says."

Lynn turned automatically to look at Breckenridge, and Secretary of Security Macalaster intercepted the glance. Macalaster said, "The information is reliable. Don't let Breckenridge's apparent youth fool you, Dr. Lynn. That's part of his value to us. Actually, he's thirty-four and has been with the department for ten years. He has been in Moscow for nearly a year and without him, none of this terrible danger would be known to us. As it is, we have most of the details."

"Not the crucial ones," said Lynn.

Macalaster of Security smiled frostily. His heavy chin and close-set eyes were well-known to the public but almost nothing else about him was. He said, "We are all finitely human, Dr. Lynn. Agent Breckenridge has done a great deal."

Presidential Assistant Jeffreys cut in. "Let us say we have a certain amount of time. If action at the instant were necessary, it would have happened before this. It seems likely that they are waiting for a specific time. If we knew the place, perhaps the time would become self-evident.

"If they are going to TC a target, they will want to cripple us as much as possible, so it would seem that a major city would have to be it. In any case, a major metropolis is the only target worth a TC bomb. I think there are four possibilities: Washington, as the administrative center; New York, as the financial center; and Detroit and Pittsburgh as the two chief industrial centers."

Macalaster of Security said, "I vote for New York. Administration and industry have both been decentralized to the point where the destruction of any one particular city won't prevent instant retaliation."

"Then why New York?" asked Amberly of Science, perhaps more sharply than he intended. "Finance has been decentralized as well."

"A question of morale. It may be they intend to destroy our will to resist, to induce surrender by the sheer horror of the first blow. The greatest destruction of human life would be in the New York Metropolitan area—"

"Pretty cold-blooded," muttered Lynn.

"I know," said Macalaster of Security, "but they're capable of it, if they thought it would mean final victory at a stroke. Wouldn't we—"

Presidential Assistant Jeffreys brushed back his white hair. "Let's assume the worst. Let's assume that New York will be destroyed some time during the winter, preferably immediately after a serious blizzard when communications are at their worst and the disruption of utilities and food supplies in fringe areas will be most serious in their effect. Now, how do we stop them?"

Amberley of Science could only say, "Finding ten men in two hundred and twenty million is an awfully small needle in an awfully large haystack."

Jeffreys shook his head. "You have it wrong. Ten humanoids among two hundred twenty million humans."

"No difference," said Amberley of Science. "We don't know that a humanoid can be differentiated from a human at sight. Probably not." He looked at Lynn. They all did.

Lynn said heavily, "We in Cheyenne couldn't make one that would pass as human in the daylight."

"But They can," said Macalaster of Security, "and not only physically. We're sure of that. They've advanced mentalic procedures to the point where They can reel off the micro-electronic pattern of the brain and focus it on the positronic pathways of the robot."

Lynn stared. "Are you implying that They can create the replica of a human being complete with personality and memory?"

"I am."

"Of specific human beings?"

"That's right."

"Is this also based on Agent Breckenridge's findings?"

"Yes. The evidence can't be disputed."

Lynn bent his head in thought for a moment. Then he said, "Then ten men in the United States are not men but humanoids. But the originals would have had to be available to them. They couldn't be Orientals, who would be too easy to spot, so they would have to be East Europeans. How would they be introduced into this country, then? With the radar network over the entire world border as tight as a drum, how could They introduce any individual, human or humanoid, without our knowing it?"

Macalaster of Security said, "It can be done. There are certain legitimate seepages across the border. Businessmen, pilots, even tourists. They're watched, of course, on both sides. Still ten of them might have been kidnaped and used as models for humanoids. The humanoids would then be sent back in their place. Since we wouldn't expect such a substitution, it would pass us by. If they were Americans to begin with, there would be no difficulty in their getting into this country. It's as simple as that."

"And even their friends and family could not tell the difference?"

"We must assume so. Believe me, we've been waiting for any report that might imply sudden attacks of amnesia or troublesome changes in personality. We've checked on thousands."

Amberley of Science stared at his finger tips. "I think ordinary measures won't work. The attack must come from the Bureau of Robotics and I depend on the chief of that bureau."

Again eyes turned sharply, expectantly, on Lynn.

Lynn felt bitterness rise. It seemed to him that this was what the conference came to and was intended for. Nothing that had been said had not been said before. He was sure of that. There was no solution to the problem, no pregnant suggestion. It was a device for the record, a device on the part of men who gravely feared defeat and who wished the responsibility for it placed clearly and unequivocally on someone else.

And yet there was justice in it. It was in robotics that We had fallen short. And Lynn was not Lynn merely. He was Lynn of Robotics and the responsibility had to be his.

He said, "I will do what I can."

He spent a wakeful night and there was a haggardness about both body and soul when he sought and attained another interview with Presidential Assistant Jeffreys the next morning. Breckenridge was there, and though Lynn would have preferred a private conference, he could see the justice in the situation. It was obvious that Breckenridge had attained enormous influence with the government as a result of his successful Intelligence work. Well, why not?

Lynn said, "Sir, I am considering the possibility that we are hopping uselessly to enemy piping."

"In what way?"

"I'm sure that however impatient the public may grow at times, and however legislators sometimes find it expedient to talk, the government at least recognizes the world stalemate to be beneficial. They must recognize it also. Ten humanoids with one TC bomb is a trivial way of breaking the stalemate."

"The destruction of fifteen million human beings is scarcely trivial."

"It is from the world power standpoint. It would not so demoralize us as to make us surrender or so cripple us as to convince us we could not win. There would just be the same old planetary death war that both sides have avoided so long and so successfully. And all They would have accomplished is to force us to fight minus one city. It's not enough."

"What do you suggest?" said Jeffreys coldly. "That They do not have ten humanoids in our country? That there is not a TC bomb waiting to get together?"

"I'll agree that those things are here, but perhaps for some reason greater than just midwinter bomb madness."

"Such as?"

"It may be that the physical destruction resulting from the humanoids getting together is not the worst thing that can happen to us. What about the moral and intellectual destruction that comes of their being here at all? With all due respect to Agent Breckenridge, what if They *intended* for us to find out about the humanoids; what if the humanoids are never supposed to get together, but merely to remain separate in order to give us something to worry about."

"Why?"

"Tell me this. What measures have already been taken against the humanoids? I suppose that Security is going through the files of all citizens who have ever been across the border or close enough to it to make kidnaping possible. I know, since Macalaster mentioned it yesterday, that they are following up suspicious psychiatric cases. What else?"

Jeffreys said, "Small X-ray devices are being installed in key places in the large cities. In the mass arenas, for instance—"

"Where ten humanoids might slip in among a hundred thousand spectators of a football game or an air-polo match?"

"Exactly."

"And concert halls and churches?"

"We must start somewhere. We can't do it all at once."

"Particularly when panic must be avoided," said Lynn. "Isn't that so? It wouldn't do to have the public realize that at any unpredictable moment, some unpredictable city and its human contents would suddenly cease to exist."

"I suppose that's obvious. What are you driving at?"

Lynn said strenuously, "That a growing fraction of our national effort will be diverted entirely into the nasty problem of what Amberley called finding a very small needle in a very large haystack. We'll be chasing our tails madly, while They increase their research lead to the point where we find we can no longer catch up; when we must surrender without the chance even of snapping our fingers in retaliation.

"Consider further that this news will leak out as more and more people become involved in our countermeasures and more and more people begin to guess what we're doing. Then what? The panic might do us more harm than any one TC bomb."

The Presidential Assistant said irritably, "In Heaven's name, man, what do you suggest we do, then?"

"Nothing," said Lynn. "Call their bluff. Live as we have lived and gamble that They won't dare break the stalemate for the sake of a one-bomb head start."

"Impossible!" said Jeffreys. "Completely impossible. The welfare of all of Us is very largely in my hands, and doing nothing is the one thing I cannot do. I agree with you, perhaps, that X-ray machines at sports arenas are a kind of skin-deep measure that won't be effective, but it has to be done so that people, in the aftermath, do not come to the bitter conclusion that we tossed our country away for the sake of a subtle line of reasoning that encouraged donothingism. In fact, our countergambit will be active indeed."

"In what way?"

Presidential Assistant Jeffreys looked at Breckenridge. The young Security officer, hitherto calmly silent, said, "It's no use talking about a possible future break in the stalemate when the stalemate is broken now. It doesn't matter whether these humanoids explode or do not. Maybe they *are* only a bait to divert us, as you say. But the fact remains that we are a quarter of a century behind in robotics, and that may be fatal. What other advances in robotics will there be to surprise us if war does start? The only answer is to divert our entire force immediately, *now*, into a crash program of robotics research, and the first problem is to find the humanoids. Call it an exercise in robotics, if you will, or call it the prevention of the death of fifteen million men, women and children."

Lynn shook his head helplessly. "You *can't.* You'd be playing into their hands. They want us lured into the one blind alley while they're free to advance in all other directions."

Jeffreys said impatiently, "That's your guess. Breckenridge has made his suggestion through channels and the government has approved, and we will begin with an all-Science conference."

"All-Science?"

Breckenridge said, "We have listed every important scientist of every branch of natural science. They'll all be at Cheyenne. There will be only one point on the agenda: How to advance robotics. The major specific subheading under that will be: How to develop a receiving device for the electromagnetic fields of the cerebral cortex that will be sufficiently delicate to distinguish between a protoplasmic human brain and a positronic humanoid brain."

Jeffreys said, "We had hoped you would be willing to be in charge of the conference."

"I was not consulted in this."

"Obviously time was short, sir. Do you agree to be in charge?"

Lynn smiled briefly. It was a matter of responsibility again. The responsibility must be clearly that of Lynn of Robotics. He had the feeling it would be Breckenridge who would really be in charge. But what could he do?

He said, "I agree."

Breckenridge and Lynn returned together to Cheyenne, where that evening Laszlo listened with a sullen mistrust to Lynn's description of coming events.

Laszlo said, "While you were gone, Chief, I've started putting five experimental models of humanoid structure through the testing procedures. Our men are on a twelve-hour day, with three shifts overlapping. If we've got to arrange a conference, we're going to be crowded and red-taped out of everything. Work will come to a halt."

Breckenridge said, "That will be only temporary. You will gain more than you lose."

Laszlo scowled. "A bunch of astrophysicists and geochemists around won't help a damn toward robotics."

"Views from specialists of other fields may be helpful."

"Are you sure? How do we know that there *is* any way of detecting brain waves or that, even if we can, there is a way of differentiating human and humanoid by wave pattern? Who set up the project, anyway?"

"I did," said Breckenridge.

"*You* did? Are you a robotics man?"

The young Security agent said calmly, "I have studied robotics."

"That's not the same thing."

"I've had access to text material dealing with Russian robotics—in Russian. Top-secret material well in advance of anything you have here."

Lynn said ruefully, "He has us there, Laszlo."

"It was on the basis of that material," Breckenridge went on, "that I suggested this particular line of investigation. It is reasonably certain that in copying off the electromagnetic pattern of a specific human mind into a specific positronic brain, a perfectly exact duplicate cannot be made. For one thing, the most complicated positronic brain small enough to fit into a human-sized skull is hundreds of times less complex than the human brain. It can't pick up all the overtones, therefore, and there must be some way to take advantage of that fact."

Laszlo looked impressed despite himself and Lynn smiled grimly. It was easy to resent Breckenridge and the coming intrusion of several hundred scientists of nonrobotics specialties, but the problem itself was an intriguing one. There was that consolation, at least.

It came to him quietly.

Lynn found he had nothing to do but sit in his office alone, with an executive position that had grown merely titular. Perhaps that helped. It gave him time to think, to picture the creative scientists of half the world converging on Cheyenne.

It was Breckenridge who, with cool efficiency, was handling the details of preparation. There had been a kind of confidence in the way he said, "Let's get together and we'll lick Them."

Let's get together.

It came to Lynn so quietly that anyone watching Lynn at that moment might have seen his eyes blink slowly twice—but surely nothing more.

He did what he had to do with a whirling detachment that kept him calm when he felt that, by all rights, he ought to be going mad.

He sought out Breckenridge in the other's improvised quarters. Breckenridge was alone and frowning. "Is anything wrong, sir?"

Lynn said wearily, "Everything's right, I think. I've invoked martial law."

"What!"

"As chief of a division I can do so if I am of the opinion the situation warrants it. Over my division I can then be dictator. Chalk up one for the beauties of decentralization."

"You will rescind that order immediately." Breckenridge took a step forward. "When Washington hears this, you will be ruined."

"I'm ruined anyway. Do you think I don't realize that I've been set up for the role of the greatest villain in American history: the man who let Them break the stalemate? I have nothing to lose—and perhaps a great deal to gain."

He laughed a little wildly. "What a target the Division of Robotics will be, eh, Breckenridge? Only a few thousand men to be killed by a TC bomb capable of wiping out three hundred square miles in one micro-second. But five hundred of those men would be our greatest scientists. We would be in the peculiar position of having to fight a war with our brains shot out, or surrendering. I think we'd surrender."

"But this is impossible. Lynn, do you hear me? Do you understand? How could the humanoids pass our security provisions? How could they get together?"

"But they *are* getting together! We're helping them to do so. We're ordering them to do so. Our scientists visit the other side, Breckenridge. They visit Them regularly. You made a point of how strange it was that no one in robotics did. Well, ten of those scientists are still there and in their place, ten humanoids are converging on Cheyenne."

"That's a ridiculous guess."

"I think it's a good one, Breckenridge. But it wouldn't work unless we knew humanoids were in America so that we would call the conference in the first place. Quite a coincidence that you brought the news of the humanoids *and* suggested the conference *and* suggested the agenda *and* are running the show *and* know exactly which scientists were invited. Did you make sure the right ten were included?"

"Dr. Lynn!" cried Breckenridge in outrage. He poised to rush forward.

Lynn said, "Don't move. I've got a blaster here. We'll just wait for the scientists to get here one by one. One by one we'll X-ray them. One by one, we'll monitor them for radioactivity. No two will get together without being checked, and if all five hundred are clear, I'll give you my blaster and surrender to you. Only I think we'll find the ten humanoids. Sit down, Breckenridge."

They both sat.

Lynn said, "We wait. When I'm tired, Laszlo will spell me. We wait."

Professor Manuelo Jiminez of the Institute of Higher Studies of Buenos Aires exploded while the stratospheric jet on which he traveled was three miles above the Amazon Valley. It was a simple chemical explosion but it was enough to destroy the plane.

Dr. Herman Liebowitz of M. I. T. exploded in a monorail, killing twenty people and injuring a hundred others.

In similar manner, Dr. Auguste Marin of L'Institut Nucléonique of Montreal and seven others died at various stages of their journey to Cheyenne.

Laszlo hurtled in, pale-faced and stammering, with the first news of it. It had only been two hours that Lynn had sat there, facing Breckenridge, blaster in hand.

Laszlo said, "I thought you were nuts, Chief, but you were right. They *were* humanoids. They *had* to be." He turned to stare with hate-filled eyes at Breckenridge. "Only they were warned. *He* warned them, and now there won't be one left intact. Not one to study."

"God!" cried Lynn and in a frenzy of haste thrust his blaster out toward Breckenridge and fired. The Security man's neck vanished; the torso fell; the head dropped, thudded against the floor and rolled crookedly.

Lynn moaned, "I didn't understand, I thought he was a traitor. Nothing more."

And Laszlo stood immobile, mouth open, for the moment incapable of speech.

Lynn said wildly, "Sure, he warned them. But how could he do so while sitting in that chair unless he were equipped with built-in radio transmission? Don't you see it? Breckenridge had been in Moscow. The real Breckenridge is still there. Oh my God, there were *eleven* of them."

Laszlo managed a hoarse squeak. "Why didn't *he* explode?"

"He was hanging on, I suppose, to make sure the others had received his message and were safely destroyed. Lord, Lord, when you brought the news and I realized the truth, I couldn't shoot fast enough. God knows by how few seconds I may have beaten him to it."

Laszlo said shakily, "At least, we'll have one to study." He bent and put his fingers on the sticky fluid trickling out of the mangled remains at the neck end of the headless body.

Not blood, but high-grade machine oil.

Pâté de Foie Gras

I couldn't tell you my real name if I wanted to, and, under the circumstances, I don't want to.

I'm not much of a writer myself, so I'm having Isaac Asimov write this up for me. I've picked him for several reasons. First, he's a biochemist, so he understands what I tell him; some of it, anyway. Secondly, he can write; or at least he has published considerable fiction, which may not, of course, be the same thing.

I was not the first person to have the honor of meeting The Goose. That belongs to a Texas cotton farmer named Ian Angus MacGregor, who owned it before it became government property.

By summer of 1955 he had sent an even dozen of letters to the Department of Agriculture requesting information on the hatching of goose eggs. The department sent him all the booklets on hand that were anywhere near the subject, but his letters simply got more impassioned and freer in their references to his "friend," the local congressman.

My connection with this is that I am in the employ of the Department of Agriculture. Since I was attending a convention at San Antonio in July of 1955, my boss asked me to stop off at MacGregor's place and see what I could do to help him. We're servants of the public and besides we had finally received a letter from MacGregor's congressman.

On July 17, 1955, I met The Goose.

I met MacGregor first. He was in his fifties, a tall man with a lined face full of suspicion. I went over all the information he had been given, then asked politely if I might see his geese.

He said, "It's not geese, mister; it's one goose."

I said, "May I see the one goose?"

"Rather not."

"Well, then, I can't help you any further. If it's only one goose, then there's just something wrong with it. Why worry about one goose? Eat it."

I got up and reached for my hat.

He said, "Wait!" and I stood there while his lips tightened and his eyes wrinkled and he had a quiet fight with himself. "Come with me."

I went out with him to a pen near the house, surrounded by barbed wire, with a locked gate to it, and holding one goose—The Goose.

"That's The Goose," he said. The way he said it, I could hear the capitals.

I stared at it. It looked like any other goose, fat, self-satisfied and short-tempered.

MacGregor said, "And here's one of its eggs. It's been in the incubator. Nothing happens." He produced it from a capacious overall pocket. There was a queer strain about his manner of holding it.

I frowned. There was something wrong with the egg. It was smaller and more spherical than normal.

MacGregor said, "Take it."

I reached out and took it. Or tried to. I gave it the amount of heft an egg like that ought to deserve and it just sat where it was. I had to try harder and then up it came.

Now I knew what was queer about the way MacGregor held it. It weighed nearly two pounds.

I stared at it as it lay there, pressing down the palm of my hand, and MacGregor grinned sourly. "Drop it," he said.

I just looked at him, so he took it out of my hand and dropped it himself.

It hit soggy. It didn't smash. There was no spray of white and yolk. It just lay where it fell with the bottom caved in.

I picked it up again. The white eggshell had shattered where the egg had struck. Pieces of it had flaked away and what shone through was a dull yellow in color.

My hands trembled. It was all I could do to make my fingers work, but I got some of the rest of the shell flaked away, and stared at the yellow.

I didn't have to run any analyses. My heart told me.

I was face to face with The Goose!

The Goose That Laid The Golden Eggs! My first problem was to get MacGregor to give up that golden egg. I was almost hysterical about it.

I said, "I'll give you a receipt. I'll quarantee you payment. I'll do anything in reason."

"I don't want the government butting in," he said stubbornly.

But I was twice as stubborn and in the end I signed a receipt and he dogged me out to my car and stood in the road as I drove away, following me with his eyes.

The head of my section at the Department of Agriculture is Louis P. Bronstein. He and I are on good terms and I felt I could explain things without being placed under immediate obseration. Even so, I took no chances. I had the egg with me and when I got to the tricky part, I just laid it on the desk between us.

I said, "It's a yellow metal and it could be brass only it isn't because it's inert to concentrated nitric acid."

Bronstein said, "It's some sort of hoax. It *must* be."

"A hoax that uses real gold? Remember, when I first saw this thing, it was covered completely with authentic unbroken eggshell. It's been easy to check a piece of the eggshell. Calcium carbonate."

Project Goose was started. That was July 20, 1955.

I was the responsible investigator to begin with and remained in titular charge throughout, though matters quickly got beyond me.

We began with the one egg. Its average radius was 35 millimeters (major axis, 72 millimeters; minor axis, 68 millimeters). The gold shell was 2.45 millimeters in thickness. Studying other eggs later on, we found this value to be rather high. The average thickness turned out to be 2.1 millimeters.

Inside *was* egg. It looked like egg and it smelled like egg.

Aliquots were analyzed and the organic constituents were reasonably normal. The white was 9.7 per cent albumin. The yolk had the normal complement of vitellin, cholesterol, phospholipid, and carotenoid. We lacked enough material to test for trace constituents, but later on with more eggs at our disposal we did and nothing unusual showed up as far as contents of vitamins, coenzymes, nucleotides, sulfhydryl groups, et cetera, et cetera were concerned.

One important gross abnormality that showed was the egg's behavior on heating. A small portion of the yolk, heated, "hard-boiled" almost at once. We fed a portion of the hard-boiled egg to a mouse. It survived.

I nibbled at another bit of it. Too small a quantity to taste, really, but it made me sick. Purely psychosomatic, I'm sure.

Boris W. Finley, of the Department of Bichemistry of Temple University —a department consultant—supervised these tests.

He said, referring to the hard-boiling, "The ease with which the egg proteins are heat-denatured indicates a partial denaturation to begin with and, considering the nature of the shell, the obvious guilt would lie at the door of heavy-metal contamination."

So a portion of the yolk was analyzed for inorganic constituents, and it was found to be high in chloraurate ion, which is a singly charged ion containing an atom of gold and four of chlorine, the symbol for which is $AuCl_4{-}$. (The "Au" symbol for gold comes from the fact that the Latin word for gold is "aurum.") When I say the chloraurate ion content was high, I mean it was 3.2 parts per thousand, or 0.32 per cent. That's high enough to form insoluble complexes of "gold protein" which would coagulate easily.

Finley said, "It's obvious this egg cannot hatch. Nor can any other such egg. It is heavy-metal poisoned. Gold may be more glamorous than lead but it is just as poisonous to proteins."

I agreed gloomily. "At least it's safe from decay, too."

"Quite right. No self-respecting bug would live in this cholorauriferous soup."

The final spectrographic analysis of the gold of the shell came in. Virtually pure. The only detectable impurity was iron which amounted to 0.23 per cent of the whole. The iron content of the egg yolk had been twice normal, also. At the moment, however, the matter of the iron was neglected.

One week after Project Goose was begun, an expedition was sent into Texas. Five biochemists went—the accent was still on biochemistry, you see —along with three truckloads of equipment, and a squadron of army personnel. I went along too, of course.

As soon as we arrived, we cut MacGregor's farm off from the world.

That was a lucky thing, you know—the security measures we took right from the start. The reasoning was wrong, at first, but the results were good.

The Department wanted Project Goose kept quiet at the start simply because there was always the thought that this might still be an elaborate hoax and we couldn't risk the bad publicity if it were. And if it weren't a hoax, we couldn't risk the newspaper hounding that would definitely result over any goose-and-golden-egg story.

It was only well after the start of Project Goose, well after our arrival at MacGregor's farm, that the real implications of the matter became clear.

Naturally MacGregor didn't like the men and equipment settling down all about him. He didn't like being told The Goose was government property. He didn't like having his eggs impounded.

He didn't like it but he agreed to it—if you can call it agreeing when negotiations are being carried on while a machine gun is being assembled in a man's barnyard and ten men, with bayonets fixed, are marching past while the arguing is going on.

He was compensated, of course. What's money to the government?

The Goose didn't like a few things, either—like having blood samples taken. We didn't dare anesthetize it for fear of doing anything to alter its metabolism, and it took two men to hold it each time. Ever try to hold an angry goose?

The Goose was put under a twenty-four-hour guard with the threat of summary court-martial to any man who let anything happen to it. If any of those soldiers read this article, they may get a sudden glimmer of what was going on. If so, they will probably have the sense to keep shut about it. At least, if they know what's good for them, they will.

The blood of The Goose was put through every test conceivable.

It carried 2 parts per hundred thousand (0.002 per cent) of chloraurate ion. Blood taken from the hepatic vein was richer than the rest, almost 4 parts per hundred thousand.

Finley grunted. "The liver," he said.

We took x rays. On the x-ray negative, the liver was a cloudy mass of light gray, lighter than the viscera in its neighborhood, because it stopped more of the x rays, because it contained more gold. The blood vessels showed up lighter than the liver proper and the ovaries were pure white. No x rays got through the ovaries at all.

It made sense, and in an early report Finley stated it as bluntly as possible. Paraphrasing the report, it went, in part:

"The chloraurate ion is secreted by the liver into the blood stream. The ovaries act as a trap for the ion, which is there reduced to metallic gold and deposited as a shell about the developing egg. Relatively high concentrations of unreduced chloraurate ion penetrate the contents of the developing egg.

"There is little doubt that The Goose finds this process useful as a means of getting rid of the gold atoms which, if allowed to accumulate, would undoubtedly poison it. Excretion by eggshell may be novel in the animal kingdom, even unique, but there is no denying that it is keeping The Goose alive.

"Unfortunately, however, the ovary is being locally poisoned to such an extent that few eggs are laid, probably not more than will suffice to get rid of the accumulating gold, and those few eggs are definitely unhatchable."

That was all he said in writing, but to the rest of us, he said, "That leaves one peculiarly embarrassing question."

I knew what it was. We all did.

Where was the gold coming from?

No answer to that for a while, except for some negative evidence. There was no perceptible gold in The Goose's feed, nor were there any gold-bearing pebbles about that it might have swallowed. There was no trace of gold anywhere in the soil of the area and a search of the house and grounds revealed nothing. There were no gold coins, gold jewelry, gold plate, gold watches, or gold anything. No one on the farm even had as much as gold fillings in his teeth.

There was Mrs. MacGregor's wedding ring, of course, but she had only had one in her life and she was wearing it.

So where was the gold coming from?

The beginnings of the answer came on August 16, 1955.

Albert Nevis, of Purdue, was forcing gastric tubes into The Goose—another procedure to which the bird objected strenuously—with the idea of testing the contents of its alimentary canal. It was one of our routine searches for exogenous gold.

Gold *was* found, but only in traces, and there was every reason to suppose those traces had accompanied the digestive secretions and were, therefore, endogenous—from within, that is—in origin.

However, something else showed up, or the lack of it, anyway.

I was there when Nevis came into Finley's office in the temporary building we had put up overnight—almost—near the goosepen.

Nevis said, "The Goose is low in bile pigment. Duodenal contents show about none."

Finley frowned and said, "Liver function is probably knocked loop-the-loop because of its gold concentration. It probably isn't secreting bile at all."

"It *is* secreting bile," said Nevis. "Bile acids are present in normal quantity. Near normal, anyway. It's just the bile pigments that are missing. I did a fecal analysis and that was confirmed. No bile pigments."

Let me explain something at this point. Bile acids are steroids secreted by the liver into the bile and via that are poured into the upper end of the small intestine. These bile acids are detergentlike molecules which help to emulsify the fat in our diet—or The Goose's—and distribute them in the form of tiny bubbles through the watery intestinal contents. This distribution, or homogenization, if you'd rather, makes it easier for the fat to be digested.

Bile pigments, the substances that were missing in The Goose, are something entirely different. The liver makes them out of hemoglobin, the red oxygen-carrying protein of the blood. Worn-out hemoglobin is broken up in the liver, the heme part being split away. The heme is made up of a squarish molecule—called a porphyrin—with an iron atom in the center. The liver takes the iron out and stores it for future use, then breaks the squarish molecule that is left. This broken porphyrin is bile pigment. It is colored brownish or greenish—depending on further chemical changes—and is secreted into the bile.

The bile pigments are of no use to the body. They are poured into the bile as waste products. They pass through the intestines and come out with the feces. In fact, the bile pigments are responsible for the color of the feces.

Finley's eyes began to glitter.

Nevis said, "It looks as though porphyrin catabolism isn't following the proper course in the liver. Doesn't it to you?"

It surely did. To me too.

There was tremendous excitement after that. This was the first metabolic abnormality, not directly involving gold, that had been found in The Goose!

We took a liver biopsy (which means we punched a cylindrical sliver out of The Goose reaching down into the liver). It hurt The Goose but didn't harm it. We took more blood samples, too.

This time we isolated hemoglobin from the blood and small quantities of the cytochromes from our liver samples. (The cytochromes are oxidizing enzymes that also contain heme.) We separated out the heme and in acid solution some of it precipitated in the form of a brilliant orange substance. By August 22, 1955, we had 5 micrograms of the compound.

The orange compound was similar to heme, but it was not heme. The iron in heme can be in the form of a doubly charged ferrous ion (Fe^{++}) or a triply charged ferric ion (Fe^{+++}), in which latter case, the compound is called hematin. (Ferrous and ferric, by the way, come from the Latin word for iron, which is "ferrum.")

The orange compound we had separated from heme had the porphyrin portion of the molecule all right, but the metal in the center was gold, to be specific, a triply charged auric ion (Au^{+++}). We called this compound "aureme," which is simply short for "auric heme."

Aureme was the first naturally occurring gold-containing organic compound ever discovered. Ordinarily it would rate headline news in the world of biochemistry. But now it was nothing; nothing at all in comparison to the further horizons its mere existence opened up.

The liver, it seemed, was not breaking up the heme to bile pigment. Instead it was converting it to aureme; it was replacing iron with gold. The aureme, in equilibrium with chloraurate ion, entered the blood stream and was carried to the ovaries, where the gold was separated out and the porphyrin portion of the molecule disposed of by some as yet unidentified mechanism.

Further analyses showed that 29 per cent of the gold in the blood of The Goose was carried in the plasma in the form of chloraurate ion. The remaining 71 per cent was carried in the red blood corpuscles in the form of "auremoglobin." An attempt was made to feed The Goose traces of radioactive gold so that we could pick up radioactivity in plasma and corpuscles and see how readily the auremoglobin molecules were handled in the ovaries. It seemed to us the auremoglobin should be much more slowly disposed of than the dissolved chloraurate ion in the plasma.

The experiment failed, however, since we detected no radioactivity. We put it down to inexperience since none of us were isotopes men, which was too bad since the failure was highly significant, really, and by not realizing it we lost several weeks.

The auremoglobin was, of course, useless as far as carrying oxygen was concerned, but it only made up about 0.1 per cent of the total hemoglobin of the red blood cells so there was no interference with the respiration of The Goose.

This still left us with the question of where the gold came from and it was Nevis who first made the crucial suggestion.

"Maybe," he said at a meeting of the group held on the evening of August 25, 1955, "The Goose doesn't replace the iron with gold. Maybe it *changes* the iron to gold."

Before I met Nevis personally that summer, I had known him through his publications—his field is bile chemistry and liver function—and had always considered him a cautious, clear-thinking person. Almost overcautious. One wouldn't consider him capable for a minute of making any such completely ridiculous statement.

It just shows the desperation and demoralization involved in Project Goose.

The desperation was the fact that there was nowhere, literally nowhere, that the gold could come from. The Goose was excreting gold at the rate of 38.9 grams a day and had been doing it over a period of months. That gold had to come from somewhere and, failing that—absolutely failing that—it had to be made from something.

The demoralization that led us to consider the second alternative was due to the mere fact that we were face to face with The Goose That Laid The Golden Eggs; the undeniable GOOSE. With that, everything became possible. All of us were living in a fairy-tale world and all of us reacted to it by losing all sense of reality.

Finley considered the possibility seriously. "Hemoglobin," he said, "enters the liver and a bit of auremoglobin comes out. The gold shell of the eggs has iron as its only impurity. The egg yolk is high in only two things; in gold, of course, and also, somewhat, in iron. It all makes a horrible kind of distorted sense. We're going to need help, men."

We did, and it meant a third stage of the investigation. The first stage had consisted of myself alone. The second was the biochemical task force. The third, the greatest, the most important of all, involved the invasion of the nuclear physicists.

On September 5, 1955, John L. Billings of the University of California arrived. He had some equipment with him and more arrived in the following weeks. More temporary structures were going up. I could see that within a year we would have a whole research institution built about The Goose.

Billings joined our conference the evening of the fifth.

Finley brought him up-to-date and said, "There are a great many serious problems involved in this iron-to-gold idea. For one thing, the total quantity of iron in The Goose can only be on the order of half a gram, yet nearly forty grams of gold a day are being manufactured."

Billings had a clear, high-pitched voice. He said, "There's a worse problem than that. Iron is about at the bottom of the packing fraction curve. Gold is much higher up. To convert a gram of iron to a gram of gold takes just about as much energy as is produced by the fissioning of one gram of U-235."

Finley shrugged. "I'll leave the problem to you."

Billings said, "Let me think about it."

He did more than think. One of the things done was to isolate fresh samples of heme from The Goose, ash it and send the iron oxide to Brookhaven for isotopic analysis. There was no particular reason to do that particular thing. It was just one of a number of individual investigations, but it was the one that brought results.

When the figures came back, Billings choked on them. He said, "There's no Fe^{56}."

"What about the other isotopes?" asked Finley at once.

"All present," said Billings, "in the appropriate relative ratios, but no detectable Fe^{56}."

I'll have to explain again: Iron, as it occurs naturally, is made up of four different isotopes. These isotopes are varieties of atoms that differ from one another in atomic weight. Iron atoms with an atomic weight of 56, or Fe^{56}, make up 91.6 per cent of all the atoms in iron. The other atoms have atomic weights of 54, 57, and 58.

The iron from the heme of The Goose was made up only of Fe^{54}, Fe^{57}, and Fe^{58}. The implication was obvious. Fe^{56} was disappearing while the other isotopes weren't and this meant a nuclear reaction was taking place. A nuclear reaction could take one isotope and leave others be. An ordinary chemical reaction, any chemical reaction at all, would have to dispose of all isotopes just about equally.

"But it's energically impossible," said Finley.

He was only saying that in mild sarcasm with Billings' initial remark in mind. As biochemists, we knew well enough that many reactions went on in the body which required an input of energy and that this was taken care of by coupling the energy-demanding reaction with an energy-producing reaction.

However, chemical reactions gave off or took up a few kilocalories per mole. Nuclear reactions gave off or took up millions. To supply energy for an energy-demanding nuclear reaction required, therefore, a second, and energy-producing, nuclear reaction.

We didn't see Billings for two days.

When he did come back, it was to say, "See here. The energy-producing reaction must produce just as much energy per nucleon involved as the energy-demanding reaction uses up. If it produces even slightly less, then the overall reaction won't go. If it produces even slightly more, then considering the astronomical number of nucleons involved, the excess energy produced would vaporize The Goose in a fraction of a second."

"So?" said Finley.

"So the number of reactions possible is very limited. I have been able to find only one plausible system. Oxygen-18, if converted to iron-56, will produce enough energy to drive the iron-56 on to gold-197. It's like going down one side of a roller coaster and then up the other. We'll have to test this."

"How?"

"First, suppose we check the isotopic composition of the oxygen in The Goose."

Oxygen is made up of three stable isotopes, almost all of it O^{16}. O^{18} makes up only one oxygen atom out of 250.

Another blood sample. The water content was distilled off in vacuum and some of it put through a mass spectrograph. There was O^{18} there but only one oxygen atom out of 1300. Fully 80 per cent of the O^{18} we expected wasn't there.

Billings said, "That's corroborative evidence. Oxygen-18 is being used up. It is being supplied constantly in the food and water fed to The Goose, but it is still being used up. Gold-197 is being produced. Iron-56 is one intermediate and since the reaction that uses up iron-56 is faster than the one that produces it, it has no chance to reach significant concentration and isotopic analysis shows its absence."

We weren't satisfied, so we tried again. We kept The Goose on water that had been enriched with O^{18} for a week. Gold production went up almost at once. At the end of a week it was producing 45.8 grams while the O^{18}content of its body water was no higher than before.

"There's no doubt about it," said Billings.

He snapped his pencil and stood up. "That Goose is a living nuclear reactor."

The Goose was obviously a mutation.

A mutation suggested radiation among other things and radiation brought up the thought of nuclear tests conducted in 1952 and 1953 several hundred miles away from the site of MacGregor's farm. (If it occurs to you that no nuclear tests have been conducted in Texas, it just shows two things; I'm not telling you everything and you don't know everything.)

I doubt that at any time in the history of the atomic era was background radiation so thoroughly analyzed and the radioactive content of the soil so rigidly sifted.

Back records were studied. It didn't matter how top-secret they were. By this time, Project Goose had the highest priority that had ever existed.

Even weather records were checked in order to follow the behavior of the winds at the time of the nuclear tests.

Two things turned up.

One: The background radiation at the farm was a bit higher than normal. Nothing that could possibly do harm, I hasten to add. There were indications, however, that at the time of the birth of The Goose, the farm had been subjected to the drifting edge of at least two fallouts. Nothing really harmful, I again hasten to add.

Second: The Goose, alone of all geese on the farm, in fact, alone of all living creatures on the farm that could be tested, including the humans, showed no radioactivity at all. Look at it this way: *everything* shows traces of radioactivity; that's what is meant by background radiation. But The Goose showed none.

Finley sent one report on December 6, 1955, which I can paraphrase as follows:

"The Goose is a most extraordinary mutation, born of a high-level radioactivity environment which at once encouraged mutations in general and which made this particular mutation a beneficial one.

"The Goose has enzyme systems capable of catalyzing various nuclear reactions. Whether the enzyme system consists of one enzyme or more than one is not known. Nor is anything known of the nature of the enzymes in question. Nor can any theory be yet advanced as to how an enzyme can catalyze a nuclear reaction, since these involve particular interactions with forces five orders of magnitude higher than those involved in the ordinary chemical reactions commonly catalyzed by enzymes.

"The overall nuclear change is from oxygen-18 to gold-197. The oxygen-18 is plentiful in its environment, being present in significant amount in water and all organic foodstuffs. The gold-197 is excreted via the ovaries. One known intermediate is iron-56 and the fact that auremoglobin is formed in the process leads us to suspect that the enzyme or enzymes involved may have heme as a prosthetic group.

"There has been considerable thought devoted to the value this overall nuclear change might have to The Goose. The oxygen-18 does it no harm and the gold-197 is troublesome to be rid of, potentially poisonous, and a cause of its sterility. Its formation might possibly be a means of avoiding greater danger. This danger—"

But just reading it in the report, friend, makes it all seem so quiet, almost pensive. Actually, I never saw a man come closer to apoplexy and survive than Billings did when he found out about our own radioactive gold experiments which I told you about earlier—the ones in which we detected no radioactivity in the goose, so that we discarded the results as meaningless.

Many times over he asked how we could possibly consider it unimportant that we had lost radioactivity.

"You're like the cub reporter," he said, "who was sent to cover a society wedding and on returning said there was no story because the groom hadn't shown up.

"You fed The Goose radioactive gold and lost it. Not only that, you failed to detect any natural radioactivity about The Goose. Any carbon-14. Any potassium-40. And you called it failure."

We started feeding The Goose radioactive isotopes. Cautiously, at first, but before the end of January of 1956 we were shoveling it in.

The Goose remained nonradioactive.

"What it amounts to," said Billings, "is that this enzyme-catalyzed nuclear process of The Goose manages to convert any unstable isotope into a stable isotope."

"Useful," I said.

"Useful? It's a thing of beauty. It's the perfect defense against the atomic age. Listen, the conversion of oxygen-18 to gold-197 should liberate eight and a fraction positrons per oxygen atom. That means eight and a fraction gamma rays as soon as each positron combines with an electron. No gamma rays, either. The Goose must be able to absorb gamma rays harmlessly."

We irradiated The Goose with gamma rays. As the level rose, The Goose developed a slight fever and we quit in panic. It was just fever, though, not radiation sickness. A day passed, the fever subsided, and The Goose was as good as new.

"Do you see what we've got?" demanded Billings.

"A scientific marvel," said Finley.

"Man, don't you see the practical applications? If we could find out the mechanism and duplicate it in the test tube, we've got a perfect method of radioactive ash disposal. The most important drawback preventing us from going ahead with a full-scale atomic economy is the headache of what to do with the radioactive isotopes manufactured in the process. Sift them through an enzyme preparation in large vats and that would be it.

"Find out the mechanism, gentlemen, and you can stop worrying about fallouts. We would find a protection against radiation sickness.

"Alter the mechanism somehow and we can have Geese excreting any element needed. How about uranium-235 eggshells?

"The mechanism! The mechanism!"

We sat there, all of us, staring at The Goose.

If only the eggs would hatch. If only we could get a tribe of nuclear-reactor Geese.

"It must have happened before," said Finley. "The legends of such Geese must have started somehow."

"Do you want to wait?" asked Billings.

If we had a gaggle of such Geese, we could begin taking a few apart. We could study its ovaries. We could prepare tissue slices and tissue homogenates.

That might not do any good. The tissue of a liver biopsy did not react with oxygen-18 under any conditions we tried.

But then we might perfuse an intact liver. We might study intact embryos, watch for one to develop the mechanism.

But with only one Goose, we could do none of that.

We don't dare kill The Goose That Lays The Golden Eggs. The secret was in the liver of that fat Goose.

Liver of fat goose! *Pâté de foie gras!* No delicacy to us!

Nevis said thoughtfully, "We need an idea. Some radical departure. Some crucial thought."

"Saying it won't bring it," said Billings despondently.

And in a miserable attempt at a joke, I said, "We could advertise in the newspapers," and that gave *me* an idea.

"Science fiction!" I said.

"What?" said Finley.

"Look, science-fiction magazines print gag articles. The readers consider it fun. They're interested." I told them about the thiotimoline articles Asimov wrote and which I had once read.

The atmosphere was cold with disapproval.

"We won't even be breaking security regulations," I said, "because no one will believe it." I told them about the time in 1944 when Cleve Cartmill wrote a story describing the atom bomb one year early and the F.B.I. kept its temper.

"And science-fiction readers have ideas. Don't underrate them. Even if they think it's a gag article, they'll send their notions in to the editor. And since we have no ideas of our own, since we're up a dead-end street, what can we lose?"

They still didn't buy it.

So I said, "And you know . . . The Goose won't live forever."

That did it, somehow.

We had to convince Washington; then I got in touch with John Campbell, editor of the magazine, and he got in touch with Asimov.

Now the article is done. I've read it, I approve, and I urge you all not to believe it. Please don't.

Only—

Any ideas?

Galley Slave

The United States Robot and Mechanical Men, Inc., as defendants in the case, had influence enough to force a closed-doors trial without a jury.

Nor did Northeastern University try hard to prevent it. The trustees knew perfectly well how the public might react to any issue involving misbehavior of a robot, however rarefied that misbehavior might be. They also had a clearly visualized notion of how an anti-robot riot might become an anti-science riot without warning.

The government, as represented in this case by Justice Harlow Shane, was equally anxious for a quiet end to this mess. Both U.S. Robots and the academic world were bad people to antagonize.

Justice Shane said, "Since neither press, public nor jury is present, gentlemen, let us stand on as little ceremony as we can and get to the facts."

He smiled stiffly as he said this, perhaps without much hope that his request would be effective, and hitched at his robe so that he might sit more comfortably. His face was pleasantly rubicund, his chin round and soft, his nose broad and his eyes light in color and wide-set. All in all, it was not a face with much judicial majesty and the judge knew it.

Barnabas H. Goodfellow, Professor of Physics at Northeastern U., was sworn in first, taking the usual vow with an expression that made mincemeat of his name.

After the usual opening-gambit questions, Prosecution shoved his hands deep into his pockets and said, "When was it, Professor, that the matter of the possible employ of Robot EZ-27 was first brought to your attention, and how?"

Professor Goodfellow's small and angular face set itself into an uneasy expression, scarcely more benevolent than the one it replaced. He said, "I have had professional contact and some social acquaintance with Dr. Alfred Lanning, Director of Research at U.S. Robots. I was inclined to listen with some tolerance then when I received a rather strange suggestion from him on the 3rd of March of last year—"

"Of 2033?"

"That's right."

"Excuse me for interrupting. Please proceed."

The professor nodded frostily, scowled to fix the facts in his mind, and began to speak.

Professor Goodfellow looked at the robot with a certain uneasiness. It had been carried into the basement supply room in a crate, in accordance with the regulations governing the shipment of robots from place to place on the Earth's surface.

He knew it was coming; it wasn't that he was unprepared. From the moment of Dr. Lanning's first phone call on March 3, he had felt himself giving way to the other's persuasiveness, and now, as an inevitable result, he found himself face to face with a robot.

It looked uncommonly large as it stood within arm's reach.

Alfred Lanning cast a hard glance of his own at the robot, as though making certain it had not been damaged in transit. Then he turned his ferocious eyebrows and his mane of white hair in the professor's direction.

"This is Robot EZ-27, first of its model to be available for public use." He turned to the robot. "This is Professor Goodfellow, Easy."

Easy spoke impassively, but with such suddenness that the professor shied. "Good afternoon, Professor."

Easy stood seven feet tall and had the general proportions of a man— always the prime selling point of U.S. Robots. That and the possession of the basic patents on the positronic brain had given them an actual monopoly on robots and a near-monopoly on computing machines in general.

The two men who had uncrated the robot had left now and the professor looked from Lanning to the robot and back to Lanning. "It is harmless, I'm sure." He didn't sound sure.

"More harmless than I am," said Lanning. "I could be goaded into striking you. Easy could not be. You know the Three Laws of Robotics, I presume."

"Yes, of course," said Goodfellow.

"They are built into the positronic patterns of the brain and must be observed. The First Law, the prime rule of robotic existence, safeguards the life and well-being of all humans." He paused, rubbed at his cheek, then added, "It's something of which we would like to persuade all Earth if we could."

"It's just that he seems formidable."

"Granted. But whatever he seems, you'll find that he *is* useful."

"I'm not sure in what way. Our conversations were not very helpful in that respect. Still, I agreed to look at the object and I'm doing it."

"We'll do more than look, Professor. Have you brought a book?"

"I have."

"May I see it?"

Professor Goodfellow reached down without actually taking his eyes off the metal-in-human-shape that confronted him. From the briefcase at his feet, he withdrew a book.

Lanning held out his hand for it and looked at the backstrip. *"Physical Chemistry of Electrolytes in Solution.* Fair enough, sir. You selected this yourself, at random. It was no suggestion of mine, this particular text. Am I right?"

"Yes."

Lanning passed the book to Robot EZ-27.

The professor jumped a little. "No! That's a valuable book!"

Lanning raised his eyebrows and they looked like shaggy coconut icing. He said, "Easy has no intention of tearing the book in two as a feat of strength, I assure you. It can handle a book as carefully as you or I. Go ahead, Easy."

"Thank you, sir," said Easy. Then, turning its metal bulk slightly, it added, "With your permission, Professor Goodfellow."

The professor stared, then said, "Yes—yes, of course."

With a slow and steady manipulation of metal fingers, Easy turned the pages of the book, glancing at the left page, then the right; turning the page, glancing left, then right; turning the page and so on for minute after minute.

The sense of its power seemed to dwarf even the large cement-walled room in which they stood and to reduce the two human watchers to something considerably less than life-size.

Goodfellow muttered, "The light isn't very good."

"It will do."

Then, rather more sharply, "But what is he doing?"

"Patience, sir."

The last page was turned eventually. Lanning asked, "Well, Easy?"

The robot said, "It is a most accurate book and there is little to which I can point. On line 22 of page 27, the word 'positive' is spelled p-o-i-s-t-i-v-e. The comma in line 6 of page 32 is superfluous, whereas one should have been used on line 13 of page 54. The plus sign in equation XIV-2 on page 337 should be a minus sign if it is to be consistent with the previous equations—"

"Wait! Wait!" cried the professor. "What is he doing?"

"Doing?" echoed Lanning in sudden irascibility. "Why, man, he has already done it! He has proofread that book."

"Proofread it?"

"Yes. In the short time it took him to turn those pages, he caught every mistake in spelling, grammar and punctuation. He has noted errors in word order and detected inconsistencies. And he will retain the information, letter-perfect, indefinitely."

The professor's mouth was open. He walked rapidly away from Lanning and Easy and as rapidly back. He folded his arms across his chest and stared at them. Finally he said, "You mean this is a proofreading robot?"

Lanning nodded. "Among other things."

"But why do you show it to me?"

"So that you might help me persuade the university to obtain it for use."

"To read proof?"

"Among other things," Lanning repeated patiently.

The professor drew his pinched face together in a kind of sour disbelief. "But this is ridiculous!"

"Why?"

"The university could never afford to buy this half-ton—it must weigh that at least—this half-ton proofreader."

"Proofreading is not all it will do. It will prepare reports from outlines, fill out forms, serve as an accurate memory-file, grade papers—"

"All picayune!"

Lanning said, "Not at all, as I can show you in a moment. But I think we can discuss this more comfortably in your office, if you have no objection."

"No, of course not," began the professor mechanically and took a half-step as though to turn. Then he snapped out, "But the robot—we can't take the robot. Really, Doctor, you'll have to crate it up again."

"Time enough. We can leave Easy here."

"Unattended?"

"Why not? He knows he is to stay. Professor Goodfellow, it is necessary to understand that a robot is far more reliable than a human being."

"I would be responsible for any damage—"

"There will be no damage. I guarantee that. Look, it's after hours. You expect no one here, I imagine, before tomorrow morning. The truck and my two men are outside. U.S. Robots will take any responsibility that may arise. None will. Call it a demonstration of the reliability of the robot."

The professor allowed himself to be led out of the storeroom. Nor did he look entirely comfortable in his own office, five stories up.

He dabbed at the line of droplets along the upper half of his forehead with a white handkerchief.

"As you know very well, Dr. Lanning, there are laws against the use of robots on Earth's surface," he pointed out.

"The laws, Professor Goodfellow, are not simple ones. Robots may not be used on public thoroughfares or within public edifices. They may not be used on private grounds or within private structures except under certain restrictions that usually turn out to be prohibitive. The university, however, is a large and privately owned institution that usually receives preferential treatment. If the robot is used only in a specific room for only academic purposes, if certain other restrictions are observed and if the men and women having occasion to enter the room cooperate fully, we may remain within the law."

"But all that trouble just to read proof?"

"The uses would be infinite, Professor. Robotic labor has so far been used only to relieve physical drudgery. Isn't there such a thing as mental drudgery? When a professor capable of the most useful creative thought is forced to spend two weeks painfully checking the spelling of lines of print and I offer you a machine that can do it in thirty minutes, is that picayune?"

"But the price—"

"The price need not bother you. You cannot buy EZ-27. U.S. Robots does not sell its products. But the university can lease EZ-27 for a thousand dollars a year—considerably less than the cost of a single microwave spectograph continuous-recording attachment."

Goodfellow looked stunned. Lanning followed up his advantage by saying, "I only ask that you put it up to whatever group makes the decisions here. I would be glad to speak to them if they want more information."

"Well," Goodfellow said doubtfully, "I can bring it up at next week's Senate meeting. I can't promise that will do any good, though."

"Naturally," said Lanning.

The Defense Attorney was short and stubby and carried himself rather portentously, a stance that had the effect of accentuating his double chin. He stared at Professor Goodfellow, once that witness had been handed over, and said, "You agreed rather readily, did you not?"

The Professor said briskly, "I suppose I was anxious to be rid of Dr. Lanning. I would have agreed to anything."

"With the intention of forgetting about it after he left?"

"Well—"

"Nevertheless, you did present the matter to a meeting of the Executive Board of the University Senate."

"Yes, I did."

"So that you agreed in good faith with Dr. Lanning's suggestions. You weren't just going along with a gag. You actually agreed enthusiastically, did you not?"

"I merely followed ordinary procedures."

"As a matter of fact, you weren't as upset about the robot as you now claim you were. You know the Three Laws of Robotics and you knew them at the time of your interview with Dr. Lanning."

"Well, yes."

"And you were perfectly willing to leave a robot at large and unattended."

"Dr. Lanning assured me—"

"Surely you would never have accepted his assurance if you had had the slightest fear that the robot might be in the least dangerous."

The professor began frigidly, "I had every faith in the word—"

"That is all," said Defense abruptly.

As Professor Goodfellow, more than a bit ruffled, stood down, Justice Shane leaned forward and said, "Since I am not a robotics man myself, I would appreciate knowing precisely what the Three Laws of Robotics are. Would Dr. Lanning quote them for the benefit of the court?"

Dr. Lanning looked startled. He had been virtually bumping heads with the gray-haired woman at his side. He rose to his feet now and the woman looked up, too—expressionlessly.

Dr. Lanning said, "Very well, Your Honor." He paused as though about to launch into an oration and said, with laborious clarity, "First Law: a robot may not injure a human being, or, through inaction, allow a human being to come to harm. Second Law: a robot must obey the orders given it by human beings, except where such orders would conflict with the First Law. Third Law: a robot must protect its own existence as long as such protection does not conflict with the First or Second Laws."

"I see," said the judge, taking rapid notes. "These Laws are built into every robot, are they?"

"Into every one. That will be borne out by any roboticist."

"And into Robot EZ-27 specifically?"

"Yes, Your Honor."

"You will probably be required to repeat those statements under oath."

"I am ready to do so, Your Honor."

He sat down again.

Dr. Susan Calvin, robopsychologist-in-chief for U.S. Robots, who was the gray-haired woman sitting next to Lanning, looked at her titular superior without favor, but then she showed favor to no human being. She said, "Was Goodfellow's testimony accurate, Alfred?"

"Essentially," muttered Lanning. "He wasn't as nervous as all that about the robot and he was anxious enough to talk business with me when he heard the price. But there doesn't seem to be any drastic distortion."

Dr. Calvin said thoughtfully, "It might have been wise to put the price higher than a thousand."

"We were anxious to place Easy."

"I know. Too anxious, perhaps. They'll try to make it look as though we had an ulterior motive."

Lanning looked exasperated. "We did. I admitted that at the University Senate meeting."

"They can make it look as if we had one beyond the one we admitted."

Scott Robertson, son of the founder of U.S. Robots and still owner of a majority of the stock, leaned over from Dr. Calvin's other side and said in a

250 ISAAC ASIMOV

kind of explosive whisper, "Why can't you get Easy to talk so we'll know where we're at?"

"You know he can't talk about it, Mr. Robertson."

"Make him. You're the psychologist, Dr. Calvin. *Make* him."

"If I'm the psychologist, Mr. Robertson," said Susan Calvin coldly, "let me make the decisions. My robot will not be made to do anything at the price of his well-being."

Robertson frowned and might have answered, but Justice Shane was tapping his gavel in a polite sort of way and they grudgingly fell silent.

Francis J. Hart, head of the Department of English and Dean of Graduate Studies, was on the stand. He was a plump man, meticulously dressed in dark clothing of a conservative cut, and possessing several strands of hair traversing the pink top of his cranium. He sat well back in the witness chair with his hands folded neatly in his lap and displaying, from time to time, a tight-lipped smile.

He said, "My first connection with the matter of the Robot EZ-27 was on the occasion of the session of the University Senate Executive Committee at which the subject was introduced by Professor Goodfellow. Thereafter, on the 10th of April of last year, we held a special meeting on the subject, during which I was in the chair."

"Were minutes kept of the meeting of the Executive Committee? Of the special meeting, that is?"

"Well, no. It was a rather unusual meeting." The dean smiled briefly. "We thought it might remain confidential."

"What transpired at the meeting?"

Dean Hart was not entirely comfortable as chairman of that meeting. Nor did the other members assembled seem completely calm. Only Dr. Lanning appeared at peace with himself. His tall, gaunt figure and the shock of white hair that crowned him reminded Hart of portraits he had seen of Andrew Jackson.

Samples of the robot's work lay scattered along the central regions of the table and the reproduction of a graph drawn by the robot was now in the hands of Professor Minott of Physical Chemistry. The chemist's lips were pursed in obvious approval.

Hart cleared his throat and said, "There seems no doubt that the robot can perform certain routine tasks with adequate competence. I have gone over these, for instance, just before coming in, and there is very little to find fault with."

He picked up a long sheet of printing, some three times as long as the average book page. It was a sheet of galley proof, designed to be corrected by authors before the type was set up in page form. Along both of the wide margins of the galley were proofmarks, neat and superbly legible. Occasionally, a word of print was crossed out and a new word substituted in the margin in characters so fine and regular it might easily have been print itself. Some of the corrections were blue to indicate the original mistake had been the author's, a few in red, where the printer had been wrong.

"Actually," said Lanning, "there is less than very little to find fault with. I should say there is nothing at all to find fault with, Dr. Hart. I'm sure the corrections are perfect, insofar as the original manuscript was. If the manuscript against which this galley was corrected was at fault in a matter of fact rather than of English, the robot is not competent to correct it."

"We accept that. However, the robot corrected word order on occasion and I don't think the rules of English are sufficiently hidebound for us to be sure that in each case the robot's choice was the correct one."

"Easy's positronic brain," said Lanning, showing large teeth as he smiled, "has been molded by the contents of all the standard works on the subject. I'm sure you cannot point to a case where the robot's choice was definitely the incorrect one."

Professor Minott looked up from the graph he still held. "The question in my mind, Dr. Lanning, is why we need a robot at all, with all the difficulties in public relations that would entail. The science of automation has surely reached the point where your company could design a machine, an ordinary computer of a type known and accepted by the public, that would correct galleys."

"I am sure we could," said Lanning stiffly, "but such a machine would require that the galleys be translated into special symbols or, at the least, transcribed on tapes. Any corrections would emerge in symbols. You would need to keep men employed translating words to symbols, symbols to words. Furthermore, such a computer could do no other job. It couldn't prepare the graph you hold in your hand, for instance."

Minott grunted.

Lanning went on. "The hallmark of the positronic robot is its flexibility. It can do a number of jobs. It is designed like a man so that it can use all the tools and machines that have, after all, been designed to be used by a man. It can talk to you and you can talk to it. You can actually reason with it up to a point. Compared to even a simple robot, an ordinary computer with a nonpositronic brain is only a heavy adding machine."

Goodfellow looked up and said, "If we all talk and reason with the robot, what are the chances of our confusing it? I suppose it doesn't have the capability of absorbing an infinite amount of data."

"No, it hasn't. But it should last five years with ordinary use. It will know when it will require clearing, and the company will do the job without charge."

"The *company* will?"

"Yes. The company reserves the right to service the robot outside the ordinary course of its duties. It is one reason we retain control of our positronic robots and lease rather than sell them. In the pursuit of its ordinary functions, any robot can be directed by any man. Outside its ordinary functions, a robot requires expert handling, and that we can give it. For instance, any of you might clear an EZ robot to an extent by telling it to forget this item or that. But you would be almost certain to phrase the order in such a way as to cause it to forget too much or too little. We would detect such tampering, because we have built-in safeguards. However, since there is no need for clearing the robot in its ordinary work, or for doing other useless things, this raises no problem."

Dean Hart touched his head as though to make sure his carefully cultivated strands lay evenly distributed and said, "You are anxious to have us take the machine. Yet surely it is a losing proposition for U.S. Robots. One thousand a year is a ridiculously low price. Is it that you hope through this to rent other such machines to other universities at a more reasonable price?"

"Certainly that's a fair hope," said Lanning.

"But even so, the number of machines you could rent would be limited. I doubt if you could make it a paying proposition."

Lanning put his elbows on the table and earnestly leaned forward. "Let me put it bluntly, gentlemen. Robots cannot be used on Earth, except in certain special cases, because of prejudice against them on the part of the public. U.S. Robots is a highly successful corporation with our extraterrestrial and space-flight markets alone, to say nothing of our computer subsidiaries. However, we are concerned with more than profits alone. It is our firm belief that the use of robots on Earth itself would mean a better life for all eventually, even if a certain amount of economic dislocation resulted at first.

"The labor unions are naturally against us, but surely we may expect cooperation from the large universities. The robot, Easy, will help you by relieving you of scholastic drudgery—by assuming, if you permit it, the role of galley slave for you. Other universities and research institutions will follow your lead, and if it works out, then perhaps other robots of other types may be placed and the public's objections to them broken down by stages."

Minott murmured, "Today Northeastern University, tomorrow the world."

Angrily, Lanning whispered to Susan Calvin, "I wasn't nearly that eloquent and they weren't nearly that reluctant. At a thousand a year, they were jumping to get Easy. Professor Minott told me he'd never seen as beautiful a job as that graph he was holding and there was no mistake on the galley or anywhere else. Hart admitted it freely."

The severe vertical lines on Dr. Calvin's face did not soften. "You should have demanded more money than they could pay, Alfred, and let them beat you down."

"Maybe," he grumbled.

Prosecution was not quite done with Professor Hart. "After Dr. Lanning left, did you vote on whether to accept Robot EZ-27?"

"Yes, we did."

"With what result?"

"In favor of acceptance, by majority vote."

"What would you say influenced the vote?"

Defense objected immediately.

Prosecution rephrased the question. "What influenced you, personally, in your individual vote? You did vote in favor, I think."

"I voted in favor, yes. I did so largely because I was impressed by Dr. Lanning's feeling that it was our duty as members of the world's intellectual leadership to allow robotics to help Man in the solutions of his problems."

"In other words, Dr. Lanning talked you into it."

"That's his job. He did it very well."

"Your witness."

Defense strode up to the witness chair and surveyed Professor Hart for a long moment. He said, "In reality, you were all pretty eager to have Robot EZ-27 in your employ, weren't you?"

"We thought that if it could do the work, it might be useful."

"*If* it could do the work? I understand you examined the samples of Robot EZ-27's original work with particular care on the day of the meeting which you have just described."

"Yes, I did. Since the machine's work dealt primarily with the handling of the English language, and since that is my field of competence, it seemed logical that I be the one chosen to examine the work."

"Very good. Was there anything on display on the table at the time of the meeting which was less than satisfactory? I have all the material here as exhibits. Can you point to a single unsatisfactory item?"

"Well—"

"It's a simple question. Was there one single solitary unsatisfactory item? You inspected it. Was there?"

The English professor frowned. "There wasn't."

"I also have some samples of work done by Robot EZ-27 during the course of his 14-month employ at Northeastern. Would you examine these and tell me if there is anything wrong with them in even one particular?"

Hart snapped, "When he did make a mistake, it was a beauty."

"Answer my question," thundered Defense, "and only the question I am putting to you! Is there anything wrong with the material?"

Dean Hart looked cautiously at each item. "Well, nothing."

"Barring the matter concerning which we are here engaged, do you know of any mistakes on the part of EZ-27?"

"Barring the matter for which this trial is being held, no."

Defense cleared his throat as though to signal end of paragraph. He said, "Now about the vote concerning whether Robot EZ-27 was to be employed or not. You said there was a majority in favor. What was the actual vote?"

"Thirteen to one, as I remember."

"Thirteen to one! More than just a majority, wouldn't you say?"

"No, sir!" All the pedant in Dean Hart was aroused. "In the English language, the word 'majority' means 'more than half.' Thirteen out of fourteen is a majority, nothing more."

"But an almost unanimous one."

"A majority all the same!"

Defense switched ground. "And who was the lone holdout?"

Dean Hart looked acutely uncomfortable. "Professor Simon Ninheimer."

Defense pretended astonishment. "Professor Ninheimer? The head of the Department of Sociology?"

"Yes, sir."

"The *plaintiff?*"

"Yes, sir."

Defense pursed his lips. "In other words, it turns out that the man bringing the action for payment of $750,000 damages against my client, United States Robot and Mechanical Men, Incorporated, was the one who from the beginning opposed the use of the robot—although everyone else on the Executive Committee of the University Senate was persuaded that it was a good idea."

"He voted against the motion, as was his right."

"You didn't mention in your description of the meeting any remarks made by Professor Ninheimer. Did he make any?"

"I think he spoke."

"You *think?*"

"Well, he *did* speak."

"Against using the robot?"

"Yes."

"Was he violent about it?"

Dean Hart paused. "He was vehement."

Defense grew confidential. "How long have you known Professor Ninheimer, Dean Hart?"

"About twelve years."

"Reasonably well?"

"I should say so, yes."

"Knowing him, then, would you say he was the kind of man who might continue to bear resentment against a robot, all the more so because an adverse vote had—"

Prosecution drowned out the remainder of the question with an indignant and vehement objection of his own. Defense motioned the witness down and Justice Shane called luncheon recess.

Robertson mangled his sandwich. The corporation would not founder for loss of three-quarters of a million, but the loss would do it no particular good.

He was conscious, moreover, that there would be a much more costly long-term setback in public relations.

He said sourly, "Why all this business about how Easy got into the university? What do they hope to gain?"

The Attorney for Defense said quietly, "A court action is like a chess game, Mr. Robertson. The winner is usually the one who can see more moves ahead, and my friend at the prosecutor's table is no beginner. They can show damage; that's no problem. Their main effort lies in anticipating our defense. They must be counting on us to try to show that Easy couldn't possibly have committed the offense—because of the Laws of Robotics."

"All right," said Robertson, "That *is* our defense. An absolutely airtight one."

"To a robotics engineer. Not necessarily to a judge. They're setting themselves up a position from which they can demonstrate that EZ-27 was no ordinary robot. It was the first of its type to be offered to the public. It was an experimental model that needed field testing and the university was the only decent way to provide such testing. That would look plausible in the light of Dr. Lanning's strong efforts to place the robot and the willingness of U.S. Robots to lease it for so little. The prosecution would then argue that the field test proved Easy to have been a failure. Now do you see the purpose of what's been going on?"

"But EZ-27 was a perfectly good model," argued Robertson.

"It was the twenty-seventh in production."

"Which is really a bad point," said Defense somberly. "What was wrong with the first twenty-six? Obviously something. Why shouldn't there be something wrong with the twenty-seventh, too?"

"There was nothing wrong with the first twenty-six except that they weren't complex enough for the task. These were the first positronic brains of the sort to be constructed and it was rather hit-and-miss to begin with. But the Three Laws held in all of them! *No* robot is so imperfect that the Three Laws don't hold."

"Dr. Lanning has explained this to me, Mr. Robertson, and I am willing to take his word for it. The judge, however, may not be. We are expecting a decision from an honest and intelligent man who knows no robotics and thus may be led astray. For instance, if you or Dr. Lanning or Dr. Calvin were to say on the stand that any positronic brains were constructed 'hit-and-miss,' as you just did, Prosecution would tear you apart in cross-examination. Nothing would salvage our case. So that's something to avoid."

Robertson growled, "If only Easy would talk."

Defense shrugged. "A robot is incompetent as a witness, so that would do us no good."

"At least we'd know some of the facts. We'd know how it came to do such a thing."

Susan Calvin fired up. A dullish red touched her cheeks and her voice had a trace of warmth in it. "We *know* how Easy came to do it. It was ordered to! I've explained this to counsel and I'll explain it to you now."

"Ordered by whom?" asked Robertson in honest astonishment. (No one ever told him anything, he thought resentfully. These research people considered *themselves* the owners of U.S. Robots, by God!)

"By the plaintiff," said Dr. Calvin.

"In heaven's name, why?"

"I don't know why yet. Perhaps just that we might be sued, that he might gain some cash." There were blue glints in her eyes as she said that.

"Then why doesn't Easy say so?"

"Isn't that obvious? It's been ordered to keep quiet about the matter."

"Why should that be obvious?" demanded Robertson truculently.

"Well, it's obvious to me. Robot psychology is my profession. If Easy will not answer questions about the matter directly, he will answer questions on the fringe of the matter. By measuring increased hesitation in his answers as the central question is approached, by measuring the area of blankness and the intensity of counter-potentials set up, it is possible to tell with scientific precision that his troubles are the result of an order not to talk, with its strength based on First Law. In other words, he's been told that if he talks, harm will be done a human being. Presumably harm to the unspeakable Professor Ninheimer, the plaintiff, who, to the robot, would seem a human being."

"Well, then," said Robertson, "can't you explain that if he keeps quiet, harm will be done to U.S. Robots?"

"U.S. Robots is not a human being and the First Law of Robotics does not recognize a corporation as a person the way ordinary laws do. Besides, it would be dangerous to try to lift this particular sort of inhibition. The person who laid it on could lift it off least dangerously, because the robot's motivations in that respect are centered on that person. Any other course—" She shook her head and grew almost impassioned. "I won't let the robot be damaged!"

Lanning interrupted with the air of bringing sanity to the problem. "It seems to me that we have only to prove a robot incapable of the act of which Easy is accused. We can do that."

"Exactly," said Defense, in annoyance. "*You* can do that. The only witnesses capable of testifying to Easy's condition and to the nature of Easy's state of mind are employees of U.S. Robots. The judge can't possibly accept their testimony as unprejudiced."

"How can he deny expert testimony?"

"By refusing to be convinced by it. That's his right as the judge. Against the alternative that a man like Professor Ninheimer deliberately set about ruining his own reputation, even for a sizeable sum of money, the judge isn't going to accept the technicalities of your engineers. The judge is a man, after all. If he has to choose between a man doing an impossible thing and a robot doing an impossible thing, he's quite likely to decide in favor of the man."

"A man *can* do an impossible thing," said Lanning, "because we don't know all the complexities of the human mind and we don't know what, in a given human mind, is impossible and what is not. We *do* know what is really impossible to a robot."

- "Well, we'll see if we can't convince the judge of that," Defense replied wearily.

"If all you say is so," rumbled Robertson, "I don't see how you can."

"We'll see. It's good to know and be aware of the difficulties involved, but let's not be *too* downhearted. I've tried to look ahead a few moves in the chess game, too." With a stately nod in the direction of the robopsychologist, he added, "*With* the help of the good lady here."

Lanning looked from one to the other and said, "What the devil is this?"

But the bailiff thrust his head into the room and announced somewhat breathlessly that the trial was about to resume.

They took their seats, examining the man who had started all the trouble.

Simon Ninheimer owned a fluffy head of sandy hair, a face that narrowed past a beaked nose toward a pointed chin, and a habit of sometimes hesitating before key words in his conversation that gave him an air of a seeker after an almost unbearable precision. When he said, "The Sun rises in the—uh—east," one was certain he had given due consideration to the possibility that it might at some time rise in the west.

Prosecution said, "Did you oppose employment of Robot EZ-27 by the university?"

"I did, sir."

"Why was that?"

"I did not feel that we understood the—uh—motives of U.S. Robots thoroughly. I mistrusted their anxiety to place the robot with us."

"Did you feel that it was capable of doing the work that it was allegedly designed to do?"

"I know for a fact that it was not."

"Would you state your reasons?"

Simon Ninheimer's book, entitled *Social Tensions Involved in Space-Flight and Their Resolution*, had been eight years in the making. Ninheimer's search for precision was not confined to his habits of speech, and in a subject like sociology, almost inherently imprecise, it left him breathless.

Even with the material in galley proofs, he felt no sense of completion. Rather the reverse, in fact. Staring at the long strips of print, he felt only the itch to tear the lines of type apart and rearrange them differently.

Jim Baker, Instructor and soon to be Assistant Professor of Sociology, found Ninheimer, three days after the first batch of galleys had arrived from the printer, staring at the handful of paper in abstraction. The galleys came in three copies: one for Ninheimer to proofread, one for Baker to proofread independently, and a third, marked "Original," which was to receive the final corrections, a combination of those made by Ninheimer and by Baker, after a conference at which possible conflicts and disagreements were ironed out. This had been their policy on the several papers on which they had collaborated in the past three years and it worked well.

Baker, young and ingratiatingly soft-voiced, had his own copies of the galleys in his hand. He said eagerly, "I've done the first chapter and they contain some typographical beauts."

"The first chapter always has them," said Ninheimer distantly.

"Do you want to go over it now?"

Ninheimer brought his eyes to grave focus on Baker. "I haven't done anything on the galleys, Jim. I don't think I'll bother."

Baker looked confused. "Not bother?"

Ninheimer pursed his lips. "I've asked about the—uh—workload of the machine. After all, he was originally—uh—promoted as a proofreader. They've set a schedule."

"The *machine?* You mean Easy?"

"I believe that is the foolish name they gave it."

"But, Dr. Ninheimer, I thought you were staying clear of it!"

"I seem to be the only one doing so. Perhaps I ought to take my share of the—uh—advantage."

"Oh. Well, I seem to have wasted time on this first chapter, then," said the younger man ruefully.

"Not wasted. We can compare the machine's result with yours as a check."

"If you want to, but—"

"Yes?"

"I doubt that we'll find anything wrong with Easy's work. It's supposed never to have made a mistake."

"I dare say," said Ninheimer dryly.

The first chapter was brought in again by Baker four days later. This time it was Ninheimer's copy, fresh from the special annex that had been built to house Easy and the equipment it used.

Baker was jubilant. "Dr. Ninheimer, it not only caught everything I caught —it found a dozen errors I missed! The whole thing took it twelve minutes!"

Ninheimer looked over the sheaf, with the neatly printed marks and symbols in the margins. He said, "It is not as complete as you and I would have made it. We should have entered an insert on Suzuki's work on the neurological effects of low gravity."

"You mean his paper in *Sociological Reviews?*"

"Of course."

"Well, you can't expect impossibilities of Easy. It can't read the literature for us."

"I realize that. As a matter of fact, I have prepared the insert. I will see the machine and make certain it knows how to—uh—handle inserts."

"It will know."

"I prefer to make certain."

Ninheimer had to make an appointment to see Easy, and then could get nothing better than fifteen minutes in the late evening.

But the fifteen minutes turned out to be ample. Robot EZ-27 understood the matter of inserts at once.

Ninheimer found himself uncomfortable at close quarters with the robot for the first time. Almost automatically, as though it were human, he found himself asking, "Are you happy with your work?"

"Most happy, Professor Ninheimer," said Easy solemnly, the photocells that were its eyes gleaming their normal deep red.

"You know me?"

"From the fact that you present me with additional material to include in the galleys, it follows that you are the author. The author's name, of course, is at the head of each sheet of galley proof."

"I see. You make—uh—deductions, then. Tell me—" He couldn't resist the question—"What do you think of the book so far?"

Easy said, "I find it very pleasant to work with."

"Pleasant? That is an odd word for a—uh—a mechanism without emotion. I've been told you have no emotion."

"The words of your book go in accordance with my circuits," Easy explained. "They set up little or no counter-potentials. It is in my brainpaths to translate this mechanical fact into a word such as 'pleasant.' The emotional context is fortuitous."

"I see. Why do you find the book pleasant?"

"It deals with human beings, Professor, and not with inorganic materials or mathematical symbols. Your book attempts to understand human beings and to help increase human happiness."

"And this is what you try to do and so my book goes in accordance with your circuits? Is that it?"

"That is it, Professor."

The fifteen minutes were up. Ninheimer left and went to the university library, which was on the point of closing. He kept them open long enough to find an elementary text on robotics. He took it home with him.

Except for occasional insertion of late material, the galleys went to Easy and from him to the publishers with little intervention from Ninheimer at first—and none at all later.

Baker said, a little uneasily, "It almost gives me a feeling of uselessness."

"It should give you a feeling of having time to begin a new project," said Ninheimer, without looking up from the notations he was making in the current issue of *Social Science Abstracts*.

"I'm just not used to it. I keep worrying about the galleys. It's silly, I know."

"It is."

"The other day I got a couple of sheets before Easy sent them off to—"

"What!" Ninheimer looked up, scowling. The copy of *Abstracts* slid shut. "Did you disturb the machine at its work?"

"Only for a minute. Everything was all right. Oh, it changed one word. You referred to something as 'criminal'; it changed the word to 'reckless.' It thought the second adjective fit in better with the context."

Ninheimer grew thoughtful. "What did you think?"

"You know, I agreed with it. I let it stand."

Ninheimer turned in his swivel chair to face his young associate. "See here, I wish you wouldn't do this again. If I am to use the machine, I wish the—uh —full advantage of it. If I am to use it and lose your—uh—services anyway because you supervise it when the whole point is that it requires no supervision, I gain nothing. Do you see?"

"Yes, Dr. Ninheimer," said Baker, subdued.

The advance copies of *Social Tensions* arrived in Dr. Ninheimer's office on the 8th of May. He looked through it briefly, flipping pages and pausing to read a paragraph here and there. Then he put his copies away.

As he explained later, he forgot about it. For eight years, he had worked at it, but now, and for months in the past, other interests had engaged him while Easy had taken the load of the book off his shoulders. He did not even think to donate the usual complimentary copy to the university library. Even Baker, who had thrown himself into work and had steered clear of the department head since receiving his rebuke at their last meeting, received no copy.

On the 16th of June that stage ended. Ninheimer received a phone call and stared at the image in the 'plate with surprise.

"Speidell! Are you in town?"

"No, sir. I'm in Cleveland." Speidell's voice trembled with emotion.

"Then why the call?"

"Because I've just been looking through your new book! Ninheimer, are you *mad?* Have you gone *insane?*"

Ninheimer stiffened. "Is something—uh—wrong?" he asked in alarm.

"*Wrong?* I refer you to page 562. What in blazes do you mean by interpreting my work as you do? Where in the paper cited do I make the claim that the criminal personality is nonexistent and that it is the *law*-enforcement agencies that are the *true* criminals? Here, let me quote—"

"Wait! Wait!" cried Ninheimer, trying to find the page. "Let me see. Let me see . . . Good God!"

"Well?"

"Speidell, I don't see how this could have happened. I never wrote this."

"But that's what's printed! And that distortion isn't the worst. You look at page 690 and imagine what Ipatiev is going to do to you when he sees the hash you've made of his findings! Look, Ninheimer, the book is *riddled* with this sort of thing. I don't know what you were thinking of—but there's nothing to do but get the book off the market. And you'd better be prepared for extensive apologies at the next Association meeting!"

"Speidell, listen to me—"

But Speidell had flashed off with a force that had the 'plate glowing with after-images for fifteen seconds.

It was then that Ninheimer went through the book and began marking off passages with red ink.

He kept his temper remarkably well when he faced Easy again, but his lips were pale. He passed the book to Easy and said, "Will you read the marked passages on pages 562, 631, 664 and 690?"

Easy did so in four glances. "Yes, Professor Ninheimer."

"This is not as I had it in the original galleys."

"No, sir. It is not."

"Did you change it to read as it now does?"

"Yes, sir."

"Why?"

"Sir, the passages as they read in your version were most uncomplimentary to certain groups of human beings. I felt it advisable to change the wording to avoid doing them harm."

"How *dared* you do such a thing?"

"The First Law, Professor, does not let me, through any inaction, allow harm to come to human beings. Certainly, considering your reputation in the world of sociology and the wide circulation your book would receive among scholars, considerable harm would come to a number of the human beings you speak of."

"But do you realize the harm that will come to *me* now?"

"It was necessary to choose the alternative with less harm."

Professor Ninheimer, shaking with fury, staggered away. It was clear to him that U.S. Robots would have to account to him for this.

There was some excitement at the defendants' table, which increased as Prosecution drove the point home.

"Then Robot EZ-27 informed you that the reason for its action was based on the First Law of Robotics?"

"That is correct, sir."

"That, in effect, it had no choice?"

"Yes, sir."

"It follows then that U.S. Robots designed a robot that would of necessity rewrite books to accord with its own conceptions of what was right. And yet they palmed it off as simple proofreader. Would you say that?"

Defense objected firmly at once, pointing out that the witness was being asked for a decision on a matter in which he had no competence. The judge admonished Prosecution in the usual terms, but there was no doubt that the exchange had sunk home—not least upon the Attorney for the Defense.

Defense asked for a short recess before beginning cross-examination, using a legal technicality for the purpose that got him five minutes.

He leaned over toward Susan Calvin. "Is it possible, Dr. Calvin, that Professor Ninheimer is telling the truth and that Easy was motivated by the First Law?"

Calvin pressed her lips together, then said, "No. It *isn't* possible. The last part of Ninheimer's testimony is deliberate perjury. Easy is not designed to be able to judge matters at the stage of abstraction represented by an advanced textbook on sociology. It would never be able to tell that certain groups of humans would be harmed by a phrase in such a book. Its mind is simply not built for that."

"I suppose, though, that we can't prove this to a layman," said Defense pessimistically.

"No," admitted Calvin. "The proof would be highly complex. Our way out is still what it was. We must prove Ninheimer is lying, and nothing he has said need change our plan of attack."

"Very well, Dr. Calvin," said Defense, "I must accept your word in this. We'll go on as planned."

In the courtroom, the judge's gavel rose and fell and Dr. Ninheimer took the stand once more. He smiled a little as one who feels his position to be impregnable and rather enjoys the prospect of countering a useless attack.

Defense approached warily and began softly. "Dr. Ninheimer, do you mean to say that you were completely unaware of these alleged changes in your manuscript until such time as Dr. Speidell called you on the 16th of June?"

"That is correct, sir."

"Did you never look at the galleys after Robot EZ-27 had proofread them?

"At first I did, but it seemed to me a useless task. I relied on the claims of U.S. Robots. The absurd—uh—changes were made only in the last quarter of the book after the robot, I presume, had learned enough about sociology—"

"Never mind your presumptions!" said Defense. "I understood your colleague, Dr. Baker, saw the later galleys on at least one occasion. Do you remember testifying to that effect?"

"Yes, sir. As I said, he told me about seeing one page, and even there, the robot had changed a word."

Again Defense broke in. "Don't you find it strange, sir, that after over a year of implacable hostility to the robot, after having voted against it in the first place and having refused to put it to any use whatever, you suddenly decided to put your book, your *magnum opus,* into its hands?"

"I don't find that strange. I simply decided that I might as well use the machine."

"And you were so confident of Robot EZ-27—all of a sudden—that you didn't even bother to check your galleys?"

"I told you I was—uh—persuaded by U.S. Robots' propaganda."

"So persuaded that when your colleague, Dr. Baker, attempted to check on the robot, you berated him soundly?"

"I didn't berate him. I merely did not wish to have him—uh—waste his time. At least, I thought then it was a waste of time, I did not see the significance of that change in the word at the—"

Defense said with heavy sarcasm, "I have no doubt you were instructed to bring up that point in order that the word change be entered in the record—" He altered his line to forestall objection and said, "The point is that you were extremely angry with Dr. Baker."

"No, sir. Not angry."

"You didn't give him a copy of your book when you received it."

"Simple forgetfulness. I didn't give the library its copy, either." Ninheimer smiled cautiously. "Professors are notoriously absentminded."

Defense said, "Do you find it strange that, after more than a year of perfect work, Robot EZ-27 should go wrong on your book? On a book, that is, which was written by you, who were, of all people, the most implacably hostile to the robot?"

"My book was the only sizable work dealing with mankind that it had to face. The Three Laws of Robotics took hold then."

"Several times, Dr. Ninheimer," said Defense, "you have tried to sound like an expert on robotics. Apparently you suddenly grew interested in robotics and took out books on the subject from the library. You testified to that effect, did you not?"

"One book, sir. That was the result of what seems to me to have been—uh—natural curiosity."

"And it enabled you to explain why the robot should, as you allege, have distorted your book?"

"Yes, sir."

"Very convenient. But are you sure your interest in robotics was not intended to enable you to manipulate the robot for your own purposes?"

Ninheimer flushed. "Certainly not, sir!"

Defense's voice rose. "In fact, are you sure the alleged altered passages were not as you had them in the first place?"

The sociologist half rose. "That's—uh—uh—ridiculous! I have the galleys—"

He had difficulty speaking and Prosecution rose to insert smoothly, "With your permission, Your Honor, I intend to introduce as evidence the set of galleys given by Dr. Ninheimer to Robot EZ-27 and the set of galleys mailed by Robot EZ-27 to the publishers. I will do so now if my esteemed colleague so desires, and will be willing to allow a recess in order that the two sets of galleys may be compared."

Defense waved his hand impatiently. "That is not necessary. My honored opponent can introduce those galleys whenever he chooses. I'm sure they will show whatever discrepancies are claimed by the plaintiff to exist. What I would like to know of the witness, however, is whether he also has in his possession *Dr. Baker's* galleys."

"Dr. Baker's galleys?" Ninheimer frowned. He was not yet quite master of himself.

"Yes, Professor! I mean Dr. Baker's galleys. You testified to the effect that Dr. Baker had received a separate copy of the galleys. I will have the clerk read your testimony if you are suddenly a selective type of amnesiac. Or is it just that professors are, as you say, notoriously absent-minded?"

Ninheimer said, "I remember Dr. Baker's galleys. They weren't necessary once the job was placed in the care of the proofreading machine—"

"So you burned them?"

"*No.* I put them in the waste basket."

"Burned them, dumped them—what's the difference? The point is you got rid of them."

"There's nothing wrong—" began Ninheimer weakly.

"Nothing wrong?" thundered Defense. "Nothing wrong except that there is now no way we can check to see if, on certain crucial galley sheets, you might not have substituted a harmless blank one from Dr. Baker's copy for a sheet in your own copy which you had deliberately mangled in such a way as to force the robot to—"

Prosecution shouted a furious objection. Justice Shane leaned forward, his round face doing its best to assume an expression of anger equivalent to the intensity of the emotion felt by the man.

The judge said, "Do you have any evidence, Counselor, for the extraordinary statement you have just made?"

Defense said quietly, "No direct evidence, Your Honor. But I would like to point out that, viewed properly, the sudden conversion of the plaintiff from anti-roboticism, his sudden interest in robotics, his refusal to check the galleys or to allow anyone else to check them, his careful neglect to allow anyone to see the book immediately after publication, all very clearly point—"

"Counselor," interrupted the judge impatiently, "this is not the place for esoteric deductions. The plaintiff is not on trial. Neither are you prosecuting him. I forbid this line of attack and I can only point out that the desperation that must have induced you to do this cannot help but weaken your case. If you have legitimate questions to ask, Counselor, you may continue with your cross-examination. But I warn you against another such exhibition in this courtroom."

"I have no further questions, Your Honor."

Robertson whispered heatedly as council for the Defense returned to his table, "What good did that do, for God's sake? The judge is dead set against you now."

Defense replied calmly, "But Ninheimer is good and rattled. And we've set him up for tomorrow's move. He'll be ripe."

Susan Calvin nodded gravely.

The rest of Prosecution's case was mild in comparison. Dr. Baker was called and bore out most of Ninheimer's testimony. Drs. Speidell and Ipatiev were called, and they expounded most movingly on their shock and dismay at certain quoted passages in Dr. Ninheimer's book. Both gave their professional opinion that Dr. Ninheimer's professional reputation had been seriously impaired.

The galleys were introduced in evidence, as were copies of the finished book.

Defense cross-examined no more that day. Prosecution rested and the trial was recessed till the next morning.

Defense made his first motion at the beginning of the proceedings on the second day. He requested that Robot EZ-27 be admitted as a spectator to the proceedings.

Prosecution objected at once and Justice Shane called both to the bench.

Prosecution said hotly, "This is obviously illegal. A robot may not be in any edifice used by the general public."

"This courtroom," pointed out Defense, "is closed to all but those having an immediate connection with the case."

"A large machine of *known* erratic behavior would disturb my client and my witnesses by its very presence! It would make hash out of the proceedings."

The judge seemed inclined to agree. He turned to Defense and said rather unsympathetically, "What are the reasons for your request?"

Defense said, "It will be our contention that Robot EZ-27 could not possibly, by the nature of its construction, have behaved as it has been described as behaving. It will be necessary to present a few demonstrations."

Prosecution said, "I don't see the point, Your Honor. Demonstrations conducted by men employed at U.S. Robots are worth little as evidence when U.S. Robots is the defendant."

"Your Honor," said Defense, "the validity of any evidence is for you to decide, not for the Prosecuting Attorney. At least, that is my understanding."

Justice Shane, his prerogatives encroached upon, said, "Your understanding is correct. Nevertheless, the presence of a robot here does raise important legal questions."

"Surely, Your Honor, nothing that should be allowed to override the requirements of justice. If the robot is not present, we are prevented from presenting our only defense."

The judge considered. "There would be the question of transporting the robot here."

"That is a problem with which U.S. Robots has frequently been faced. We have a truck parked outside the courtroom, constructed according to the laws governing the transportation of robots. Robot EZ-27 is in a packing case inside with two men guarding it. The doors to the truck are properly secured and all other necessary precautions have been taken."

"You seem certain," said Justice Shane, in renewed ill-temper, "that judgment on this point will be in your favor."

"Not at all, Your Honor. If it is not, we simply turn the truck about. I have made no presumptions concerning your decision."

The judge nodded. "The request on the part of the Defense is granted."

The crate was carried in on a large dolly and the two men who handled it opened it. The courtroom was immersed in a dead silence.

Susan Calvin waited as the thick slabs of celluform went down, then held out one hand. "Come, Easy."

The robot looked in her direction and held out its large metal arm. It towered over her by two feet but followed meekly, like a child in the clasp of its mother. Someone giggled nervously and choked it off at a hard glare from Dr. Calvin.

Easy seated itself carefully in a large chair brought by the bailiff, which creaked but held.

Defense said, "When it becomes necessary, Your Honor, we will prove that this is actually Robot EZ-27, the specific robot in the employ of Northeastern University during the period of time with which we are concerned."

"Good," His Honor said. "That will be necessary. I, for one, have no idea how you can tell one robot from another."

"And now," said Defense, "I would like to call my first witness to the stand. Professor Simon Ninheimer, please."

The clerk hesitated, looked at the judge. Justice Shane asked, with visible surprise, "You are calling the *plaintiff* as your witness?"

"Yes, Your Honor."

"I hope that you're aware that as long as he's your witness, you will be allowed none of the latitude you might exercise if you were cross-examining an opposing witness."

Defense said smoothly, "My only purpose in all this is to arrive at the truth. It will not be necessary to do more than ask a few polite questions."

"Well," said the judge dubiously, "you're the one handling the case. Call the witness."

Ninheimer took the stand and was informed that he was still under oath. He looked more nervous than he had the day before, almost apprehensive.

But Defense looked at him benignly.

"Now, Professor Ninheimer, you are suing my clients in the amount of $750,000."

"That is the—uh—sum. Yes."

"That is a great deal of money."

"I have suffered a great deal of harm."

"Surely not that much. The material in question involves only a few passages in a book. Perhaps these were unfortunate passages, but after all, books sometimes appear with curious mistakes in them."

Ninheimer's nostrils flared. "Sir, this book was to have been the climax of my professional career! Instead, it makes me look like an incompetent scholar, a perverter of the views held by my honored friends and associates, and a believer of ridiculous and—uh—outmoded viewpoints. My reputation is irretrievably shattered! I can never hold up my head in any—uh—assemblage of scholars, regardless of the outcome of this trial. I certainly cannot continue in my career, which has been the whole of my life. The very purpose of my life has been—uh—aborted and destroyed."

Defense made no attempt to interrupt the speech, but stared abstractedly at his fingernails as it went on.

He said very soothingly, "But surely, Professor Ninheimer, at your present age, you could not hope to earn more than—let us be generous—$150,000 during the remainder of your life. Yet you are asking the court to award you five times as much."

Ninheimer said, with an even greater burst of emotion, "It is not in my lifetime alone that I am ruined. I do not know for how many generations I shall be pointed at by sociologists as a—uh—a fool or maniac. My real achievements will be buried and ignored. I am ruined not only until the day of my death, but for all time to come, because there will always be people who will not believe that a robot made those insertions—"

It was at this point that Robot EZ-27 rose to his feet. Susan Calvin made no move to stop him. She sat motionless, staring straight ahead. Defense sighed softly.

Easy's melodious voice carried clearly. It said, "I would like to explain to everyone that I did insert certain passages in the galley proofs that seemed directly opposed to what had been there at first—"

Even the Prosecuting Attorney was too startled at the spectacle of a seven-foot robot rising to address the court to be able to demand the stopping of what was obviously a most irregular procedure.

When he could collect his wits, it was too late. For Ninheimer rose in the witness chair, his face working.

He shouted wildly, "Damn you, you were instructed to keep your mouth shut about—"

He ground to a choking halt, and Easy was silent, too.

Prosecution was on his feet now, demanding that a mistrial be declared.

Justice Shane banged his gavel desperately. "Silence! Silence! Certainly there is every reason here to declare a mistrial, except that in the interests of justice I would like to have Professor Ninheimer complete his statement. I distinctly heard him say to the robot that the robot had been instructed to keep its mouth shut about something. There was no mention in your testimony, Professor Ninheimer, as to any instructions to the robot to keep silent about anything!"

Ninheimer stared wordlessly at the judge.

Justice Shane said, "Did you instruct Robot EZ-27 to keep silent about something? And if so, about what?"

"Your Honor—" began Ninheimer hoarsely, and couldn't continue.

The judge's voice grew sharp. "Did you in fact, order the inserts in question to be made in the galleys and then order the robot to keep quiet about your part in this?"

Prosecution objected vigorously, but Ninheimer shouted, "Oh, what's the use? Yes! Yes!" And he ran from the witness stand. He was stopped at the door by the bailiff and sank hopelessly into one of the last rows of seats, head buried in both hands.

Justice Shane said, "It is evident to me that Robot EZ-27 was brought here as a trick. Except for the fact that the trick served to prevent a serious miscarriage of justice, I would certainly hold attorney for the Defense in contempt. It is clear now, beyond any doubt, that the plaintiff has committed what is to me a completely inexplicable fraud since, apparently, he was knowingly ruining his career in the process—"

Judgment, of course, was for the defendant.

Dr. Susan Calvin had herself announced at Dr. Ninheimer's bachelor quarters in University Hall. The young engineer who had driven the car offered to go up with her, but she looked at him scornfully.

"Do you think he'll assault me? Wait down here."

Ninheimer was in no mood to assault anyone. He was packing, wasting no time, anxious to be away before the adverse conclusion of the trial became general knowledge.

He looked at Calvin with a queerly defiant air and said, "Are you coming to warn me of a countersuit? If so, it will get you nothing. I have no money, no job, no future. I can't even meet the costs of the trial."

"If you're looking for sympathy," said Calvin coldly, "don't look for it here. This was your doing. However, there will be no countersuit, neither of you nor of the university. We will even do what we can to keep you from going to prison for perjury. We aren't vindictive."

"Oh, is that why I'm not already in custody for forswearing myself? I had wondered. But then," he added bitterly, "why *should* you be vindictive? You have what you want now."

"Some of what we want, yes," said Calvin. "The university will keep Easy in its employ at a considerably higher rental fee. Furthermore, certain underground publicity concerning the trial will make it possible to place a few more of the EZ models in other institutions without danger of a repetition of this trouble."

"Then why have you come to see me?"

"Because I don't have all of what I want yet. I want to know why you hate robots as you do. Even if you had won the case, your reputation would have been ruined. The money you might have obtained could not have compensated for that. Would the satisfaction of your hatred for robots have done so?"

"Are you interested in *human* minds, Dr. Calvin?" asked Ninheimer, with acid mockery.

"Insofar as their reactions concern the welfare of robots, yes. For that reason, I have learned a little of human psychology."

"Enough of it to be able to trick me!"

"That wasn't hard," said Calvin, without pomposity. "The difficult thing was doing it in such a way as not to damage Easy."

"It is like you to be more concerned for a machine than for a man." He looked at her with savage contempt.

It left her unmoved. "It merely seems so, Professor Ninheimer. It is only by being concerned for robots that one can truly be concerned for twenty-first-century Man. You would understand this if you were a roboticist."

"I have read enough robotics to know I don't *want* to be a roboticist!"

"Pardon me, you have read *a book* on robotics. It has taught you nothing. You learned enough to know that you could order a robot to do many things, even to falsify a book, if you went about it properly. You learned enough to know that you could not order him to forget something entirely without risking detection, but you thought you could order him into simple silence more safely. You were wrong."

"You guessed the truth from his silence?"

"It wasn't guessing. You were an amateur and didn't know enough to cover your tracks completely. My only problem was to prove the matter to the judge and you were kind enough to help us there, in your ignorance of the robotics you claim to despise."

"Is there any purpose in this discussion?" asked Ninheimer wearily.

"For me, yes," said Susan Calvin, "because I want you to understand how completely you have misjudged robots. You silenced Easy by telling him that if he told anyone about your own distortion of the book, you would lose your job. That set up a certain potential within Easy toward silence, one that was strong enough to resist our efforts to break it down. We would have damaged the brain if we had persisted.

"On the witness stand, however, you yourself put up a higher counter-potential. You said that because people would think that you, not a robot, had written the disputed passages in the book, you would lose far more than just your job. You would lose your reputation, your standing, your respect, your reason for living. You would lose the memory of you after death. A new and higher potential was set up by you—and Easy talked."

"Oh, God," said Ninheimer, turning his head away.

Calvin was inexorable. She said, "Do you understand *why* he talked? It was not to accuse you, but to *defend* you! It can be mathematically shown that he was about to assume full blame for your crime, to deny that you had anything to do with it. The First Law required that. He was going to lie—to damage himself—to bring monetary harm to a corporation. All that meant less to him than did the saving of you. If you really understood robots and robotics, you would have let him talk. But you did not understand, as I was sure you wouldn't, as I guaranteed to the defense attorney that you wouldn't. You were certain, in your hatred of robots, that Easy would act as a human being would act and defend itself at your expense. So you flared out at him in panic —and destroyed yourself."

Ninheimer said with feeling, "I hope some day your robots turn on you and kill you!"

"Don't be foolish," said Calvin. "Now I want you to explain why you've done all this."

Ninheimer grinned a distorted, humorless grin. "I am to dissect my mind, am I, for your intellectual curiosity, in return for immunity from a charge of perjury?"

"Put it that way if you like," said Calvin emotionlessly. "But explain."

"So that you can counter future antirobot attempts more efficiently? With greater understanding?"

"I accept that."

"You know," said Ninheimer, "I'll tell you—just to watch it do you no good at all. You can't understand human motivation. You can only understand your damned machines because you're a machine yourself, with skin on."

He was breathing hard and there was no hesitation in his speech, no searching for precision. It was as though he had no further use for precision.

He said, "For two hundred and fifty years, the machine has been replacing Man and destroying the handcraftsman. Pottery is spewed out of molds and presses. Works of art have been replaced by identical gimcracks stamped out on a die. Call it progress, if you wish! The artist is restricted to abstractions, confined to the world of ideas. He must design something in his mind—and then the machine does the rest.

"Do you suppose the potter is content with mental creation? Do you suppose the idea is enough? That there is nothing in the feel of the clay itself, in watching the thing grow as hand and mind work *together?* Do you suppose the actual growth doesn't act as a feedback to modify and improve the idea?"

"You are not a potter," said Dr. Calvin.

"I am a creative artist! I design and build articles and books. There is more to it than the mere thinking of words and of putting them in the right order. If that were all, there would be no pleasure in it, no return.

"A book should take shape in the hands of the writer. One must actually see the chapters grow and develop. One must work and rework and watch the changes take place beyond the original concept even. There is taking the galleys in hand and seeing how the sentences look in print and molding them again. There are a hundred contacts between a man and his work at every stage of the game—and the contact itself is pleasurable and repays a man for the work he puts into his creation more than anything else could. *Your robot would take all that away.*"

"So does a typewriter. So does a printing press. Do you propose to return to the hand-illumination of manuscripts?"

"Typewriters and printing presses take away some, but your robot would deprive us of all. Your robot takes over the galleys. Soon it, or other robots, would take over the original writing, the searching of the sources, the checking and cross-checking of passages, perhaps even the deduction of conclusions. What would that leave the scholar? One thing only—the barren decisions concerning what orders to give the robot next! I want to save the future generations of the world of scholarship from such a final hell. That meant more to me than even my own reputation and so I set out to destroy U.S. Robots by whatever means."

"You were bound to fail," said Susan Calvin.

"I was bound to try," said Simon Ninheimer.

Calvin turned and left. She did her best to feel no pang of sympathy for the broken man.

She did not entirely succeed.

Lenny

United States Robots and Mechanical Men, Inc., had a problem. The problem was people.

Peter Bogert, Senior Mathematician, was on his way to Assembly when he encountered Alfred Lanning, Research Director. Lanning was bending his ferocious white eyebrows together and staring down across the railing into the computer room.

On the floor below the balcony, a trickle of humanity of both sexes and various ages was looking about curiously, while a guide intoned a set speech about robotic computing.

"This computer you see before you," he said, "is the largest of its type in the world. It contains five million three hundred thousand cryotrons and is capable of dealing simultaneously with over one hundred thousand variables. With its help, U. S. Robots is able to design with precision the positronic brains of new models.

"The requirements are fed in on tape which is perforated by the action of this keyboard—something like a very complicated typewriter or linotype machine, except that it does not deal with letters but with concepts. Statements are broken down into the symbolic logic equivalents and those in turn converted to perforation patterns.

"The computer can, in less than one hour, present our scientists with a design for a brain which will give all the necessary positronic paths to make a robot . . ."

Alfred Lanning looked up at last and noticed the other. "Ah, Peter," he said.

Bogert raised both hands to smooth down his already perfectly smooth and glossy head of black hair. He said, "You don't look as though you think much of this, Alfred."

Lanning grunted. The idea of public guided tours of U. S. Robots was a fairly recent origin, and was supposed to serve a dual function. On the one hand, the theory went, it allowed people to see robots at close quarters and counter their almost instinctive fear of the mechanical objects through increased familiarity. And on the other hand, it was supposed to interest at least an occasional person in taking up robotics research as a life work.

"You know I don't," Lanning said finally. "Once a week, work is disrupted. Considering the man-hours lost, the return is insufficient."

"Still no rise in job applications, then?"

"Oh, some, but only in the categories where the need isn't vital. It's research men that are needed. You know that. The trouble is that with robots forbidden on Earth itself, there's something unpopular about being a roboticist."

"The damned Frankenstein complex," said Bogert, consciously imitating one of the other's pet phrases.

Lanning missed the gentle jab. He said, "I ought to be used to it, but I never will. You'd think that by now every human being on Earth would know that the Three Laws represented a perfect safeguard; that robots are simply not dangerous. Take this bunch." He glowered down. "Look at them. Most of them go through the robot assembly room for the thrill of fear, like riding a roller coaster. Then when they enter the room with the MEC model— damn it, Peter, a MEC model that will do nothing on God's green Earth but take two steps forward, say 'Pleased to meet you, sir,' shake hands, then take two steps back—they back away and mothers snatch up their kids. How do we expect to get brainwork out of such idiots?"

Bogert had no answer. Together, they stared down once again at the line of sightseers, now passing out of the computer room and into the positronic brain assembly section. Then they left. They did not, as it turned out, observe Mortimer W. Jacobson, age 16—who, to do him complete justice, meant no harm whatever.

In fact, it could not even be said to be Mortimer's fault. The day of the week on which the tour took place was known to all workers. All devices in its path ought to have been carefully neutralized or locked, since it was unreasonable to expect human beings to withstand the temptation to handle knobs, keys, handles and pushbuttons. In addition, the guide ought to have been very carefully on the watch for those who succumbed.

But, at the time, the guide had passed into the next room and Mortimer was tailing the line. He passed the keyboard on which instructions were fed into the computer. He had no way of suspecting that the plans for a new robot design were being fed into it at that moment, or, being a good kid, he would have avoided the keyboard. He had no way of knowing that, by what amounted to almost criminal negligence, a technician had not inactivated the keyboard.

So Mortimer touched the keys at random as though he were playing a musical instrument.

He did not notice that a section of perforated tape stretched itself out of the instrument in another part of the room—soundlessly, unobtrusively.

Nor did the technician, when he returned, discover any signs of tampering. He felt a little uneasy at noticing that the keyboard was live, but did not think to check. After a few minutes, even his first trifling uneasiness was gone, and he continued feeding data into the computer.

As for Mortimer, neither then, nor ever afterward, did he know what he had done.

The new LNE model was designed for the mining of boron in the asteroid belt. The boron hydrides were increasing in value yearly as primers for the proton micropiles that carried the ultimate load of power production on spaceships, and Earth's own meager supply was running thin.

Physically, that meant that the LNE robots would have to be equipped with eyes sensitive to those lines prominent in the spectroscopic analysis of boron ores and the type of limbs most useful for the working up of ore to finished product. As always, though, the mental equipment was the major problem.

The first LNE positronic brain had been completed now. It was the prototype and would join all other prototypes in U. S. Robots' collection. When finally tested, others would then be manufactured for leasing (never selling) to mining corporations.

LNE-Prototype was complete now. Tall, straight, polished, it looked from outside like any of a number of not-too-specialized robot models.

The technician in charge, guided by the directions for testing in the *Handbook of Robotics*, said, "How are you?"

The indicated answer was to have been, "I am well and ready to begin my functions. I trust you are well, too," or some trivial modification thereof.

This first exchange served no purpose but to show that the robot could hear, understand a routine question, and make a routine reply congruent with what one would expect of a robotic attitude. Beginning from there, one could pass on to more complicated matters that would test the different Laws and their interaction with the specialized knowledge of each particular model.

So the technician said, "How are you?" He was instantly jolted by the nature of LNE-Prototype's voice. It had a quality like no robotic voice he had ever heard (and he had heard many). It formed syllables like the chimes of a low-pitched celeste.

So surprising was this that it was only after several moments that the technician heard, in retrospect, the syllables that had been formed by those heavenly tones.

They were, "Da, da, da, goo."

The robot still stood tall and straight but its right hand crept upward and a finger went into its mouth.

The technician stared in absolute horror and bolted. He locked the door behind him and, from another room, put in an emergency call to Dr. Susan Calvin.

Dr. Susan Calvin was U. S. Robots' (and, virtually, mankind's) only robopsychologist. She did not have to go very far in her testing of LNE-Prototype before she called very peremptorily for a transcript of the computer-drawn plans of the positronic brain-paths and the taped instructions that had directed them. After some study, she, in turn, sent for Bogert.

Her iron-gray hair was drawn severely back; her cold face, with its strong vertical lines marked off by the horizontal gash of the pale, thin-lipped mouth, turned intensely upon him.

"What *is* this, Peter?"

Bogert studied the passages she pointed out with increasing stupefaction and said, "Good Lord, Susan, it makes no sense."

"It most certainly doesn't. How did it get into the instructions?"

The technician in charge, called upon, swore in all sincerity that it was none of his doing, and that he could not account for it. The computer checked out negative for all attempts at flaw-finding.

"The positronic brain," said Susan Calvin, thoughtfully, "is past redemption. So many of the higher functions have been cancelled out by these meaningless directions that the result is very like a human baby."

Bogert looked surprised, and Susan Calvin took on a frozen attitude at once, as she always did at the least expressed or implied doubt of her word. She said, "We make every effort to make a robot as mentally like a man as possible. Eliminate what we call the adult functions and what is naturally left is a human infant, mentally speaking. Why do you look so surprised, Peter?"

LNE-Prototype, who showed no signs of understanding any of the things that were going on around it, suddenly slipped into a sitting position and began a minute examination of its feet.

Bogert stared at it. "It's a shame to have to dismantle the creature. It's a handsome job."

"Dismantle it?" said the robopsychologist forcefully.

"Of course, Susan. What's the use of this thing? Good Lord, if there's one object completely and abysmally useless it's a robot without a job it can perform. You don't pretend there's a job this thing can do, do you?"

"No, of course not."

"Well, then?"

Susan Calvin said, stubbornly, "I want to conduct more tests."

Bogert looked at her with a moment's impatience, then shrugged. If there was one person at U. S. Robots with whom it was useless to dispute, surely that was Susan Calvin. Robots were all she loved, and long association with them, it seemed to Bogert, had deprived her of any appearance of humanity. She was no more to be argued out of a decision than was a triggered micropile to be argued out of operating.

"What's the use?" he breathed; then aloud, hastily: "Will you let us know when your tests are complete?"

"I will," she said. "Come, Lenny."

(LNE, thought Bogert. That becomes Lenny. Inevitable.)

Susan Calvin held out her hand but the robot only stared at it. Gently, the robopsychologist reached for the robot's hand and took it. Lenny rose smoothly to its feet (its mechanical coordination, at least, worked well). Together they walked out, robot topping woman by two feet. Many eyes followed them curiously down the long corridors.

One wall of Susan Calvin's laboratory, the one opening directly off her private office, was covered with a highly magnified reproduction of a positronic-path chart. Susan Calvin had studied it with absorption for the better part of a month.

She was considering it now, carefully, tracing the blunted paths through their contortions. Behind her, Lenny sat on the floor, moving its legs apart and together, crooning meaningless syllables to itself in a voice so beautiful that one could listen to the nonsense and be ravished.

Susan Calvin turned to the robot, "Lenny—Lenny—"

She repeated this patiently until finally Lenny looked up and made an inquiring sound. The robopsychologist allowed a glimmer of pleasure to cross her face fleetingly. The robot's attention was being gained in progressively shorter intervals.

She said, "Raise your hand, Lenny. Hand—up. Hand—up."

She raised her own hand as she said it, over and over.

Lenny followed the movement with its eyes. Up, down, up, down. Then it made an abortive gesture with its own hand and chimed, "Eh—uh."

"Very good, Lenny," said Susan Calvin, gravely. "Try it again. Hand—up."

Very gently, she reached out her own hand, took the robot's, and raised it, lowered it. "Hand—up. Hand—up."

A voice from her office called and interrupted. "Susan?"

Calvin halted with a tightening of her lips. "What is it, Alfred?"

The research director walked in, and looked at the chart on the wall and at the robot. "Still at it?"

"I'm at my work, yes."

"Well, you know, Susan . . ." He took out a cigar, staring at it hard, and made as though to bite off the end. In doing so, his eyes met the woman's stern look of disapproval; and he put the cigar away and began over. "Well, you know, Susan, the LNE model is in production now."

"So I've heard. Is there something in connection with it you wish of me?"

"No-o. Still, the mere fact that it is in production and is doing well means that working with this messed-up specimen is useless. Shouldn't it be scrapped?"

"In short, Alfred, you are annoyed that I am wasting my so-valuable time. Feel relieved. My time is not being wasted. I am *working* with this robot."

"But the work has no meaning."

"I'll be the judge of that, Alfred." Her voice was ominously quiet, and Lanning thought it wiser to shift his ground.

"Will you tell me what meaning it has? What are you doing with it right now, for instance?"

"I'm trying to get it to raise its hand on the word of command. I'm trying to get it to imitate the sound of the word."

As though on cue, Lenny said, "Eh—uh" and raised its hand waveringly.

Lanning shook his head. "That voice is amazing. How does it happen?"

Susan Calvin said, "I don't quite know. Its transmitter is a normal one. It could speak normally, I'm sure. It doesn't, however; it speaks like this as a consequence of something in the positronic paths that I have not yet pinpointed."

"Well, pinpoint it, for Heaven's sake. Speech like that might be useful."

"Oh, then there is some possible use in my studies on Lenny?"

Lanning shrugged in embarrassment. "Oh, well, it's a minor point."

"I'm sorry you don't see the major points, then," said Susan Calvin with asperity, "which are much more important, but that's not my fault. Would you leave now, Alfred, and let me go on with my work?"

Lanning got to his cigar, eventually, in Bogert's office. He said, sourly, "That woman is growing more peculiar daily."

Bogert understood perfectly. In the U. S. Robot and Mechanical Man Corporation, there was only one "that woman." He said, "Is she still scuffing about with that pseudo-robot—that Lenny of hers?"

"Trying to get it to talk, so help me."

Bogert shrugged. "Points up the company problem. I mean, about getting qualified personnel for research. If we had other robopsychologists, we could retire Susan. Incidentally, I presume the directors' meeting scheduled for tomorrow is for the purpose of dealing with the procurement problem?"

Lanning nodded and looked at his cigar as though it didn't taste good. "Yes. Quality, though, not quantity. We've raised wages until there's a steady stream of applicants—those who are interested primarily in money. The trick is to get those who are interested primarily in robotics—a few more like Susan Calvin."

"Hell, no. Not like her."

"Well, not like her personally. But you'll have to admit, Peter, that she's single-minded about robots. She has no other interest in life."

"I know. And that's exactly what makes her so unbearable."

Lanning nodded. He had lost count of the many times it would have done his soul good to have fired Susan Calvin. He had also lost count of the number of millions of dollars she had at one time or another saved the company. She was a truly indispensable woman and would remain one until she died—or until they could lick the problem of finding men and women of her own high caliber who were interested in robotics research.

He said, "I think we'll cut down on the tour business."

Peter shrugged. "If you say so. But meanwhile, seriously, what do we do about Susan? She can easily tie herself up with Lenny indefinitely. You know how she is when she gets what she considers an interesting problem."

"What *can* we do?" said Lanning. "If we become too anxious to pull her off, she'll stay on out of feminine contrariness. In the last analysis, we can't force her to do anything."

The dark-haired mathematician smiled. "I wouldn't ever apply the adjective 'feminine' to any part of her."

"Oh, well," said Lanning, grumpily. "At least, it won't do anyone any actual harm."

In that, if in nothing else, he was wrong.

The emergency signal is always a tension-making thing in any large industrial establishment. Such signals had sounded in the history of U. S. Robots a dozen times—for fire, flood, riot and insurrection.

But one thing had never occurred in all that time. Never had the particular signal indicating "Robot out of control" sounded. No one ever expected it to sound. It was only installed at government insistence. ("Damn the Frankenstein complex," Lanning would mutter on those rare occasions when he thought of it.)

Now, finally, the shrill siren rose and fell at ten-second intervals, and practically no worker from the President of the Board of Directors down to the newest janitor's assistant recognized the significance of the strange sound for a few moments. After those moments passed, there was a massive convergence of armed guards and medical men to the indicated area of danger and U. S. Robots was struck with paralysis.

Charles Randow, computing technician, was taken off to hospital level with a broken arm. There was no other damage. No other physical damage.

"But the moral damage," roared Lanning, "is beyond estimation."

Susan Calvin faced him, murderously calm. "You will do nothing to Lenny. Nothing. Do you understand?"

"Do *you* understand, Susan? That thing has hurt a human being. It has broken First Law. Don't you know what First Law is?"

"You will do nothing to Lenny."

"For God's sake, Susan, do I have to tell *you* First Law? *A robot may not harm a human being or, through inaction, allow a human being to come to harm.* Our entire position depends on the fact that First Law is rigidly observed by all robots of all types. If the public should hear, and they will hear, that there was an exception, even one exception, we might be forced to close down altogether. Our only chance of survival would be to announce at once that the robot involved had been destroyed, explain the circumstances, and hope that the public can be convinced that it will never happen again."

"I would like to find out exactly what happened," said Susan Calvin. "I was not present at the time and I would like to know exactly what the Randow boy was doing in my laboratories without my permission."

"The important thing that happened," said Lanning, "is obvious. Your robot struck Randow and the damn fool flashed the 'Robot out of control' button and made a case of it. But your robot struck him and inflicted damage to the extent of a broken arm. The truth is your Lenny is so distorted it lacks First Law and it must be destroyed."

"It does *not* lack First Law. I have studied its brainpaths and know it does not lack it."

"Then how could it strike a man?" Desperation turned him to sarcasm. "Ask Lenny. Surely you have taught it to speak by now."

Susan Calvin's cheeks flushed a painful pink. She said, "I prefer to interview the victim. And in my absence, Alfred, I want my offices sealed tight, with Lenny inside. I want no one to approach him. If any harm comes to him while I am gone, this company will not see me again under any circumstances."

"Will you agree to its destruction, if it has broken First Law?"

"Yes," said Susan Calvin, "because I know it hasn't."

Charles Randow lay in bed with his arm set and in a cast. His major suffering was still from the shock of those few moments in which he thought a robot was advancing on him with murder in its positronic mind. No other human had ever had such reason to fear direct robotic harm as he had had just then. He had had a unique experience.

Susan Calvin and Alfred Lanning stood beside his bed now; Peter Bogert, who had met them on the way, was with them. Doctors and nurses had been shooed out.

Susan Calvin said, "Now—what happened?"

Randow was daunted. He muttered, "The thing hit me in the arm. It was coming at me."

Calvin said, "Move further back in the story. What were you doing in my laboratory without authorization?"

The young computer technician swallowed, and the Adam's apple in his thin neck bobbed noticeably. He was high-cheekboned and abnormally pale. He said, "We all knew about your robot. The word is you were trying to teach it to talk like a musical instrument. There were bets going as to whether it talked or not. Some said—uh—you could teach a gatepost to talk."

"I suppose," said Susan Calvin, freezingly, "that is meant as a compliment. What did that have to do with you?"

"I was supposed to go in there and settle matters—see if it would talk, you know. We swiped a key to your place and I waited till you were gone and went in. We had a lottery on who was to do it. I lost."

"Then?"

"I tried to get it to talk and it hit me."

"What do you mean, you tried to get it to talk? How did you try?"

"I—I asked it questions, but it wouldn't say anything, and I had to give the thing a fair shake, so I kind of—yelled at it, and—"

"And?"

There was a long pause. Under Susan Calvin's unwavering stare, Randow finally said, "I tried to scare it into saying something." He added defensively, "I had to give the thing a fair shake."

"How did you try to scare it?"

"I pretended to take a punch at it."

"And it brushed your arm aside?"

"It *hit* my arm."

"Very well. That's all." To Lanning and Bogert, she said, "Come, gentlemen."

At the doorway, she turned back to Randow. "I can settle the bets going around, if you are still interested. Lenny can speak a few words quite well."

They said nothing until they were in Susan Calvin's office. Its walls were lined with her books, some of which she had written herself. It retained the patina of her own frigid, carefully-ordered personality. It had only one chair in it and she sat down. Lanning and Bogert remained standing.

She said, "Lenny only defended itself. That is the Third Law: *A robot must protect its own existence.*"

"*Except,*" said Lanning forcefully, "*when this conflicts with the First or Second Laws.* Complete the statement! Lenny had no right to defend itself in any way at the cost of harm, however minor, to a human being."

"Nor did it," shot back Calvin, "*knowingly.* Lenny has an aborted brain. It had no way of knowing its own strength or the weakness of humans. In brushing aside the threatening arm of a human being it could not know the bone would break. In human terms, no moral blame can be attached to an individual who honestly cannot differentiate good and evil."

Bogert interrupted, soothingly, "Now, Susan, *we* don't blame. *We* understand that Lenny is the equivalent of a baby, humanly speaking, and we don't blame it. But the public will. U. S. Robots will be closed down."

"Quite the opposite. If you had the brains of a flea, Peter, you would see that this is the opportunity U. S. Robots is waiting for. That this will solve its problems."

Lanning hunched his white eyebrows low. He said, softly, "What problems, Susan?"

"Isn't the corporation concerned about maintaining our research personnel at the present—Heaven help us—high level?"

"We certainly are."

"Well, what are you offering prospective researchers? Excitement? Novelty? The thrill of piercing the unknown? No! You offer them salaries and the assurance of no problems."

Bogert said, "How do you mean, no problems?"

"Are there problems?" shot back Susan Calvin. "What kind of robots do we turn out? Fully developed robots, fit for their tasks. An industry tells us what it needs; a computer designs the brain; machinery forms the robot; and there it is, complete and done. Peter, some time ago, you asked me with reference to Lenny what its use was. What's the use, you said, of a robot that was not designed for any job? Now I ask you—what's the use of a robot designed for only one job? It begins and ends in the same place. The LNE models mine boron. If beryllium is needed, they are useless. If boron technology enters a new phase, they become useless. A human being so designed would be sub-human. A robot so designed is sub-robotic."

"Do you want a versatile robot?" asked Lanning, incredulously.

"Why not?" demanded the robopsychologist. "Why not? I've been handed a robot with a brain almost completely stultified. I've been teaching it, and you, Alfred, asked me what was the use of that. Perhaps very little as far as Lenny itself is concerned, since it will never progress beyond the five-year-old level on a human scale. But what's the use in general? A very great deal, if you consider it as a study in the abstract problem of *learning how to teach robots*. I have learned ways to short-circuit neighboring pathways in order to create new ones. More study will yield better, more subtle and more efficient techniques of doing so."

"Well?"

"Suppose you started with a positronic brain that had all the basic pathways carefully outlined but none of the secondaries. Suppose you then started creating secondaries. You could sell basic robots designed for instruction; robots that could be modelled to a job, and then modelled to another, if necessary. Robots would become as versatile as human beings. *Robots could learn!*"

They stared at her.

She said, impatiently, "You still don't understand, do you?"

"I understand what you are saying," said Lanning.

"Don't you understand that with a completely new field of research and completely new techniques to be developed, with a completely new area of the unknown to be penetrated, youngsters will feel a new urge to enter robotics? Try it and see."

"May I point out," said Bogert, smoothly, "that this is dangerous. Beginning with ignorant robots such as Lenny will mean that one could never trust First Law—exactly as turned out in Lenny's case."

"Exactly. Advertise the fact."

"*Advertise it!*"

"Of course. Broadcast the danger. Explain that you will set up a new research institute on the moon, if Earth's population chooses not to allow this sort of thing to go on upon Earth, but stress the danger to the possible applicants by all means."

Lanning said, "For God's sake, why?"

"Because the spice of danger will add to the lure. Do you think nuclear technology involves no danger and spationautics no peril? Has your lure of absolute security been doing the trick for you? Has it helped you to cater to the Frankenstein complex you all despise so? Try something else then, something that has worked in other fields."

There was a sound from beyond the door that led to Calvin's personal laboratories. It was the chiming sound of Lenny.

The robopsychologist broke off instantly, listening. She said, "Excuse me. I think Lenny is calling me."

"Can it call you?" said Lanning.

"I said I've managed to teach it a few words." She stepped toward the door, a little flustered. "If you will wait for me—"

They watched her leave and were silent for a moment. Then Lanning said, "Do you think there's anything to what she says, Peter?"

"Just possibly, Alfred," said Bogert. "Just possibly. Enough for us to bring the matter up at the directors' meeting and see what they say. After all, the fat *is* in the fire. A robot has harmed a human being and knowledge of it is public. As Susan says, we might as well try to turn the matter to our advantage. Of course, I distrust her motives in all this."

"How do you mean?"

"Even if all she has said is perfectly true, it is only rationalization as far as she is concerned. Her motive in all this is her desire to hold on to this robot. If we pressed her," (and the mathematician smiled at the incongruous literal meaning of the phrase) "she would say it was to continue learning techniques of teaching robots, but I think she has found another use for Lenny. A rather unique one that would fit only Susan of all women."

"I don't get your drift."

Bogert said, "Did you hear what the robot was calling?"

"Well, no, I didn't quite—" began Lanning, when the door opened suddenly, and both men stopped talking at once.

Susan Calvin stepped in again, looking about uncertainly. "Have either of you seen—I'm positive I had it somewhere about—Oh, there it is."

She ran to a corner of one bookcase and picked up an object of intricate metal webbery, dumbbell shaped and hollow, with variously-shaped metal pieces inside each hollow, just too large to be able to fall out of the webbing.

As she picked it up, the metal pieces within moved and struck together, clicking pleasantly. It struck Lanning that the object was a kind of robotic version of a baby rattle.

As Susan Calvin opened the door again to pass through, Lenny's voice chimed again from within. This time, Lanning heard it clearly as it spoke the words Susan Calvin had taught it.

In heavenly celeste-like sounds, it called out, "Mommie, I want you. I want you, Mommie."

And the footsteps of Susan Calvin could be heard hurrying eagerly across the laboratory floor toward the only kind of baby she could ever have or love.

A Loint
of Paw

I

There was no question that Montie Stein had, through clever fraud, stolen better than $100,000. There was also no question that he was apprehended one day after the statute of limitations had expired.

It was his manner of avoiding arrest during that interval that brought on the epoch-making case of the State of New York *vs.* Montgomery Harlow Stein, with all its consequences. It introduced law to the fourth dimension.

For, you see, after having committed the fraud and possessed himself of the hundred grand plus, Stein had calmly entered a time machine, of which he was in illegal possession, and set the controls for seven years and one day in the future.

Stein's lawyer put it simply. Hiding in time was not fundamentally different from hiding in space. If the forces of law had not uncovered Stein in the seven-year interval that was their hard luck.

The District Attorney pointed out that the statute of limitations was not intended to be a game between the law and the criminal. It was a merciful measure designed to protect a culprit from indefinitely prolonged fear of arrest. For certain crimes, a defined period of apprehension of apprehension —so to speak—was considered punishment enough. But Stein, the D.A. insisted, had not experienced any period of apprehension at all.

Stein's lawyer remained unmoved. The law said nothing about measuring the extent of a culprit's fear and anguish. It simply set a time limit.

The D.A. said that Stein had not lived through the limit.

Defense stated that Stein was seven years older now than at the time of the crime and had therefore lived through the limit.

The D.A. challenged the statement and the defense produced Stein's birth certificate. He was born in 2973. At the time of the crime, 3004, he was thirty-one. Now, in 3011, he was thirty-eight.

The D.A. shouted that Stein was not physiologically thirty-eight, but thirty-one.

Defense pointed out freezingly that the law, once the individual was granted to be mentally competent, recognized solely chronological age, which could be obtained only by subtracting the date of birth from the date of now.

The D.A., growing impassioned, swore that if Stein were allowed to go free, half the laws on the books would be useless.

Then change the laws, said Defense, to take time travel into account; but until the laws are changed, let them be enforced as written.

Judge Neville Preston took a week to consider and then handed down his decision. It was a turning point in the history of law. It is almost a pity, then, that some people suspect Judge Preston to have been swayed in his way of thinking by the irresistible impulse to phrase his decision as he did.

For that decision, in full, was:

"A niche in time saves Stein."

A Statue
for Father

First time? Really? But of course you have heard of it. Yes, I was sure you had.

If you're really interested in the discovery, believe me, I'll be delighted to tell you. It's a story I've always liked to tell, but not many people give me the chance. I've even been advised to keep the story under wraps. It interferes with the legends growing up about my father.

Still, I think the truth is valuable. There's a moral to it. A man can spend his life devoting his energies solely to the satisfaction of his own curiosity and then, quite accidentally, without ever intending anything of the sort, find himself a benefactor of humanity.

Dad was just a theoretical physicist, devoted to the investigation of time travel. I don't think he ever gave a thought to what time travel might mean to *Homo sapiens*. He was just curious about the mathematical relationships that governed the universe, you see.

Hungry? All the better. I imagine it will take nearly half an hour. They will do it properly for an official such as yourself. It's a matter of pride.

To begin with, Dad was poor as only a university professor can be poor. Eventually, though, he became wealthy. In the last years before his death he was fabulously rich, and as for myself and my children and grandchildren— well, you can see for yourself.

They've put up statues to him, too. The oldest is on the hillside right here where the discovery was made. You can just see it out the window. Yes. Can you make out the inscription? Well, we're standing at a bad angle. No matter.

By the time Dad got into time-travel research the whole problem had been given up by most physicists as a bad job. It had begun with a splash when the Chrono-funnels were first set up.

Actually, they're not much to see. They're completely irrational and uncontrollable. What you see is distorted and wavery, two feet across at the most, and it vanishes quickly. Trying to focus on the past is like trying to focus on a feather caught in a hurricane that has gone mad.

They tried poking grapples into the past but that was just as unpredictable. Sometimes it was carried off successfully for a few seconds with one man leaning hard against the grapple. But more often a pile driver couldn't push it through. Nothing was ever obtained out of the past until— Well, I'll get to that.

After fifty years of no progress, physicists just lost interest. The operational technique seemed a complete blind alley; a dead end. I can't honestly say I blame them as I look back on it. Some of them even tried to show that the funnels didn't actually expose the past, but there had been too many sightings of living animals through the funnels—animals now extinct.

Anyway, when time travel was almost forgotten, Dad stepped in. He talked the government into giving him a grant to set up a Chrono-funnel of his own, and tackled the matter all over again.

I helped him in those days. I was fresh out of college, with my own doctorate in physics.

However, our combined efforts ran into bad trouble after a year or so. Dad had difficulty in getting his grant renewed. Industry wasn't interested and the university decided he was besmirching their reputation by being so single-minded in investigating a dead field. The dean of the graduate school, who understood only the financial end of scholarship, began by hinting that he switch to more lucrative fields and ended by forcing him out.

Of course, the dean—still alive and still counting grant-dollars when Dad died—probably felt quite foolish, I imagine, when Dad left the school a million dollars free and clear in his will, with a codicil canceling the bequest on the ground that the dean lacked vision. But that was merely posthumous revenge. For years before that—

I don't wish to dictate, but please don't have any more of the breadsticks. The clear soup, eaten slowly to prevent a too-sharp appetite, will do.

Anyway, we managed somehow. Dad kept the equipment we had bought with the grant money, moved it out of the university and set it up here.

Those first years on our own were brutal, and I kept urging him to give up. He never would. He was indomitable, always managing to find a thousand dollars somewhere when we needed it.

Life went on, but he allowed nothing to interfere with his research. Mother died; Dad mourned and returned to his task. I married, had a son, then a daughter, couldn't always be at his side. He carried on without me. He broke his leg and worked with the cast impeding him for months.

So I give him all the credit. I helped, of course. I did consulting work on the side and carried on negotiation with Washington. But *he* was the life and soul of the project.

Despite all that, we weren't getting anywhere. All the money we managed to scrounge might just as well have been poured into one of the Chrono-funnels—not that it would have passed through.

After all, we never once managed to get a grapple through a funnel. We came near on only one occasion. We had the grapple about two inches out the other end when focus changed. It snapped off clean and somewhere in the Mesozoic there is a man-made piece of steel rod rusting on a riverbank.

Then one day, the crucial day, the focus held for ten long minutes—something for which the odds were less than one in a trillion. Lord, the frenzies of excitement we experienced as we set up the cameras. We could see living creatures just the other side of the funnel, moving energetically.

Then, to top it off, the Chrono-funnel grew permeable, until you might have sworn there was nothing but air between the past and ourselves. The low permeability must have been connected with the long holding of focus, but we've never been able to prove that it did.

Of course, we had no grapple handy, wouldn't you know. But the low permeability was clear enough because something just fell through, moving from the *Then* into the *Now*. Thunderstruck, acting simply on blind instinct, I reached forward and caught it.

At that moment we lost focus, but it no longer left us embittered and despairing. We were both staring in wild surmise at what I held. It was a mass of caked and dried mud, shaved off clean where it had struck the borders of the Chrono-funnel, and on the mud cake were fourteen eggs about the size of duck eggs.

I said, "Dinosaur eggs? Do you suppose they really are?"

Dad said, "Maybe. We can't tell for sure."

"Unless we hatch them," I said in sudden, almost uncontrollable excitement. I put them down as though they were platinum. They felt warm with the heat of the primeval sun. I said, "Dad, if we hatch them, we'll have creatures that have been extinct for over a hundred million years. It will be the first case of something actually brought out of the past. If we announce this—"

I was thinking of the grants we could get, of the publicity, of all that it would mean to Dad. I was seeing the look of consternation on the dean's face.

But Dad took a different view of the matter. He said firmly, "Not a word, son. If this gets out, we'll have twenty research teams on the trail of the Chrono-funnels, cutting off my advance. No, once I've solved the riddle of the funnels, you can make all the announcements you want. Until then—we keep silent. Son, don't look like that. I'll have the answer in a year. I'm sure of it."

I was a little less confident, but those eggs, I felt convinced, would arm us with all the proof we'd need. I set up a large oven at bloodheat; I circulated air and moisture. I rigged up an alarm that would sound at the first signs of motion within the eggs.

They hatched at 3 A.M. nineteen days later, and there they were—fourteen wee kangaroos with greenish scales, clawed hindlegs, plump little thighs, and thin, whiplash tails.

I thought at first they were tyrannosauri, but they were too small for that species of dinosaur. Months passed, and I could see they weren't going to grow any larger than moderate-sized dogs.

Dad seemed disappointed, but I held on, hoping he would let me use them for publicity. One died before maturity and one was killed in a scuffle. But the other twelve survived—five males and seven females. I fed them on chopped carrots, boiled eggs, and milk, and grew quite fond of them. They were fearfully stupid and yet gentle. And they were truly beautiful. Their scales—

Oh, well, it's silly to describe them. Those original publicity pictures have made their rounds. Though, come to think of it, I don't know about Mars— Oh, there, too. Well, good.

But it took a long time for the pictures to make an impression on the public, let alone a sight of the creatures in the flesh. Dad remained intransigent. A year passed, two, and finally three. We had no luck whatsoever with the Chrono-funnels. The one break was not repeated, and still Dad would not give in.

Five of our females laid eggs and soon I had over fifty of the creatures on my hands.

"What shall we do with them?" I demanded.

"Kill them off," he said.

Well, I couldn't do that, of course.

Henri, is it almost ready? Good.

We had reached the end of our resources when it happened. No more money was available. I had tried everywhere, and met with consistent rebuffs. I was even glad because it seemed to me that Dad would have to give in now. But with a chin that was firm and indomitably set, he coolly set up another experiment.

I swear to you that if the accident had not happened the truth would have eluded us forever. Humanity would have been deprived of one of its greatest boons.

It happens that way sometimes. Perkin spots a purple tinge in his gunk and comes up with aniline dyes. Remsen puts a contaminated finger to his lips and discovers saccharin. Goodyear drops a mixture on the stove and finds the secret of vulcanization.

With us, it was a half-grown dinosaur wandering into the main research lab. They had become so numerous I hadn't been able to keep track of them.

The dinosaur stepped right across two contact points which happened to be open—just at the point where the plaque immortalizing the event is now located. I'm convinced that such a happenstance couldn't occur again in a thousand years. There was a blinding flash, a blistering short circuit, and the Chrono-funnel which had just been set up vanished in a rainbow of sparks.

Even at the moment, really, we didn't know exactly what we had. All we knew was that the creature had short-circuited and perhaps destroyed two hundred thousand dollars worth of equipment and that we were completely ruined financially. All we had to show for it was one thoroughly roasted dinosaur. We were slightly scorched ourselves, but the dinosaur got the full concentration of field energies. We could smell it. The air was saturated with its aroma. Dad and I looked at each other in amazement. I picked it up gingerly in a pair of tongs. It was black and charred on the outside, but the burnt scales crumbled away at a touch, carrying the skin with it. Under the char was white, firm flesh that resembled chicken.

I couldn't resist tasting it, and it resembled chicken about the way Jupiter resembles an asteroid.

Believe me or not, with our scientific work reduced to rubble about us, we sat there in seventh heaven and devoured dinosaur. Parts were burnt, parts were nearly raw. It hadn't been dressed. But we didn't stop until we had picked the bones clean.

Finally I said, "Dad, we've got to raise them gloriously and systematically for food purposes."

Dad had to agree. We were completely broke.

I got a loan from the bank by inviting the president to dinner and feeding him dinosaur.

It has never failed to work. No one who has once tasted what we now call "dinachicken" can rest content with ordinary fare. A meal without dinachicken is a meal we choke down to keep body and soul together. Only dinachicken is *food*.

Our family still owns the only herd of dinachickens in existence and we are the only suppliers for the worldwide chain of restaurants—this is the first and oldest—which has grown up about it.

Poor Dad! He was never happy, except for those unique moments when he was actually eating dinachicken. He continued working on the Chrono-funnels and so did twenty other research teams which, as he had predicted would happen, jumped in. Nothing ever came of any of it, though, to this day. Nothing *except* dinachicken.

Ah, Pierre, thank you. A superlative job! Now, sir, if you will allow me to carve. No salt, now, and just a trace of the sauce. That's right. . . . Ah, that is precisely the expression I always see on the face of a man who experiences his first taste of the delight.

A grateful humanity contributed fifty thousand dollars to have the statue on the hillside put up, but even that tribute failed to make Dad happy.

All he could see was the inscription: The Man Who Gave Dinachicken to the World.

You see, to his dying day, he wanted only one thing, to find the secret of time travel. For all that he was a benefactor of humanity, he died with his curiosity unsatisfied.

Anniversary

The annual ritual was all set.

It was the turn of Moore's house this year, of course, and Mrs. Moore and the children had resignedly gone to her mother's for the evening.

Warren Moore surveyed the room with a faint smile. Only Mark Brandon's enthusiasm kept it going at the first, but he himself had come to like this mild remembrance. It came with age, he supposed; twenty additional years of it. He had grown paunchy, thin-haired, soft-jowled, and—worst of all—sentimental.

So all the windows were polarized into complete darkness and the drapes were drawn. Only occasional stipples of wall were illuminated, thus celebrating the poor lighting and the terrible isolation of that day of wreckage long ago.

There were spaceship rations in sticks and tubes on the table and, of course, in the center an unopened bottle of sparkling green Jabra water, the potent brew that only the chemical activity of Martian fungi could supply.

Moore looked at his watch. Brandon would be here soon; he was never late for this occasion. The only thing that disturbed him was the memory of Brandon's voice on the tube: "Warren, I have a surprise for you this time. Wait and see. Wait and see."

Brandon, it always seemed to Moore, aged little. The younger man had kept his slimness, and the intensity with which he greeted all in life, to the verge of his fortieth birthday. He retained the ability to be in high excitement over the good and in deep despair over the bad. His hair was going gray, but except for that, when Brandon walked up and down, talking rapidly at the top of his voice about anything at all, Moore didn't even have to close his eyes to see the panicked youngster on the wreck of the *Silver Queen.*

The door signal sounded and Moore kicked the release without turning around. "Come, Mark."

It was a strange voice that answered, though; softly, tentatively, "Mr. Moore?"

Moore turned quickly. Brandon was there, to be sure, but only in the background, grinning with excitement. Someone else was standing before him; short, squat, quite bald, nut-brown and with the feel of space about him.

Moore said wonderingly, "Mike Shea—*Mike Shea,* by all space."

They pounded hands together, laughing.

Brandon said, "He got in touch with me through the office. He remembered I was with Atomic Products—"

"It's been *years,"* said Moore. "Let's see, you were on Earth twelve years ago—"

"He's never been here on an anniversary," said Brandon. "How about that? He's retiring now. Getting out of space to a place he's buying in Arizona. He came to say hello before he left—stopped off at the city just for that—and I was sure he came for the anniversary. 'What anniversary?' says the old jerk."

Shea nodded, grinning. "He said you made a kind of celebration out of it every year."

"You bet," said Brandon enthusiastically, "and this will be the first one with all three of us here, the first *real* anniversary. It's twenty years, Mike; twenty years since Warren scrambled over what was left of the wreck and brought us down to Vesta."

Shea looked about. "Space ration, eh? That's old home week to me. And Jabra. Oh, sure, I remember . . . twenty years. I never give it a thought and now, all of a sudden, it's yesterday. Remember when we got back to Earth finally?"

"Do I!" said Brandon. "The parades, the speeches. Warren was the only real hero of the occasion and we kept saying so, and they kept paying no attention. Remember?"

"Oh, well," said Moore. "We were the first three men ever to survive a spaceship crash. We were unusual and anything unusual is worth a celebration. These things are irrational."

"Hey," said Shea, "any of you remember the songs they wrote? That marching one? 'You can sing of routes through Space and the weary maddened pace of the—' "

Brandon joined in with his clear tenor and even Moore added his voice to the chorus so that the last line was loud enough to shake the drapes. "On the *wreck* of the *Silver* Que-e-en," they roared out, and ended laughing wildly.

Brandon said, "Let's open the Jabra for the first little sip. This one bottle has to last all of us all night."

Moore said, "Mark insists on complete authenticity. I'm surprised he doesn't expect me to climb out the window and human-fly my way around the building."

"Well, now, that's an idea," said Brandon.

"Remember the last toast we made?" Shea held his empty glass before him and intoned, " 'Gentlemen, I give you the year's supply of good old H_2O *we used to have.*' Three drunken bums when we landed. Well, we were kids. I was thirty and I thought I was old. And now," his voice was suddenly wistful, "they've retired me."

"Drink!" said Brandon. "Today you're thirty again, and we remember the day on the *Silver Queen* even if no one else does. Dirty, fickle public."

Moore laughed. "What do you expect? A national holiday every year with space ration and Jabra, the ritual food and drink?"

"Listen, we're still the only men ever to survive a spaceship crash and now look at us. We're in oblivion."

"It's pretty good oblivion. We had a good time to begin with and the publicity gave us a healthy boost up the ladder. We are doing well, Mark. And so would Mike Shea be if he hadn't wanted to return to space."

Shea grinned and shrugged his shoulder. "That's where I like to be. I'm not sorry, either. What with the insurance compensation I got, I have a nice piece of cash now to retire on."

Brandon said reminiscently, "The wreck set back Trans-space Insurance a real packet. Just the same, there's still something missing. You say *'Silver Queen'* to anyone these days and he can only think of Quentin, if he can think of anyone."

"Who?" said Shea.

"Quentin. Dr. Horace Quentin. He was one of the nonsurvivors on the ship. You say to anyone, 'What about the three men who survived?' and they'll just stare at you. 'Huh?' they'll say."

Moore said calmly, "Come, Mark, face it. Dr. Quentin was one of the world's great scientists and we three are just three of the world's nothings."

"We survived. We're still the only men on record to survive."

"So? Look, John Hester was on the ship, and he was an important scientist too. Not in Quentin's league, but important. As a matter of fact, I was next to him at the last dinner before the rock hit us. Well, just because Quentin died in the same wreck, Hester's death was drowned out. No one ever remembers Hester died on the *Silver Queen.* They only remember Quentin. We may be forgotten too, but at least we're alive."

"I tell you what," said Brandon after a period of silence during which Moore's rationale had obviously failed to take, "we're marooned again. Twenty years ago today, we were marooned off Vesta. Today, we're marooned in oblivion. Now here are the three of us back together again at last, and what happened before can happen again. Twenty years ago, Warren pulled us down to Vesta. Now let's solve this new problem."

"Wipe out the oblivion, you mean?" said Moore. "Make ourselves famous?"

"Sure. Why not? Do you know of any better way of celebrating a twentieth anniversary?"

"No, but I'd be interested to know where you expect to start. I don't think people remember the *Silver Queen* at all, except for Quentin, so you'll have to think of some way of bringing the wreck back to mind. That's just to begin with."

Shea stirred uneasily and a thoughtful expression crossed his blunt countenance. "Some people remember the *Silver Queen*. The insurance company does, and you know that's a funny thing, now that you bring up the matter. I was on Vesta about ten-eleven years ago, and I asked if the piece of wreck we brought down was still there and they said sure, who would cart it away? So I thought I'd take a look at it and shot over by reaction motor strapped to my back. With Vestan gravity, you know, a reaction motor is all you need. Anyway, I didn't get to see it except from a distance. It was circled off by force field."

Brandon's eyebrows went sky-high. "Our *Silver Queen*? For what reason?"

"I went back and asked how come? They didn't tell me and they said they didn't know I was going there. They said it belonged to the insurance company."

Moore nodded. "Surely. They took over when they paid off. I signed a release, giving up my salvage rights when I accepted the compensation check. You did too, I'm sure."

Brandon said, "But why the force field? Why all the privacy?"

"I don't know."

"The wreck isn't worth anything even as scrap metal. It would cost too much to transport it."

Shea said, "That's right. Funny thing, though; they were bringing pieces back from space. There was a pile of it there. I could see it and it looked like just junk, twisted pieces of frame, you know. I asked about it and they said ships were always landing and unloading more scrap, and the insurance company had a standard price for any piece of the *Silver Queen* brought back, so ships in the neighborhood of Vesta were always looking. Then, on my last voyage in, I went to see the *Silver Queen* again and that pile was a lot bigger."

"You mean they're still looking?" Brandon's eyes glittered.

"I don't know. Maybe they've stopped. But the pile was bigger than it was ten-eleven years ago so they were still looking then."

Brandon leaned back in his chair and crossed his legs. "Well, now, that's very queer. A hard-headed insurance company is spending all kinds of money, sweeping space near Vesta, trying to find pieces of a twenty-year-old wreck."

"Maybe they're trying to prove sabotage," said Moore.

"After twenty years? They won't get their money back even if they do. It's a dead issue."

"They may have quit looking years ago."

Brandon stood up with decision. "Let's ask. There's something funny here and I'm just Jabrified enough and anniversaried enough to want to find out."

"Sure," said Shea, "but ask who?"

"Ask Multivac," said Brandon.

Shea's eyes opened wide. "Multivac! Say, Mr. Moore, do you have a Multivac outlet here?"

"Yes."

"I've never seen one, and I've always wanted to."

"It's nothing to look at, Mike. It looks just like a typewriter. Don't confuse a Multivac outlet with Multivac itself. I don't know anyone who's seen Multivac."

Moore smiled at the thought. He doubted if ever in his life he would meet any of the handful of technicians who spent most of their working days in a hidden spot in the bowels of Earth tending a mile-long super-computer that was the repository of all the facts known to man, that guided man's economy, directed his scientific research, helped make his political decisions, and had millions of circuits left over to answer individual questions that did not violate the ethics of privacy.

Brandon said as they moved up the power ramp to the second floor, "I've been thinking of installing a Multivac, Jr., outlet for the kids. Homework and things, you know. And yet I don't want to make it just a fancy and expensive crutch for them. How do you work it, Warren?"

Moore said tersely, "They show me the questions first. If I don't pass them, Multivac does not see them."

The Multivac outlet was indeed a simple typewriter arrangement and little more.

Moore set up the co-ordinates that opened his portion of the planet-wide network of circuits and said, "Now listen. For the record, I'm against this and I'm only going along because it's the anniversary and because I'm just jackass enough to be curious. Now how ought I to phrase the question?"

Brandon said, "Just ask: Are pieces of the wreck of the *Silver Queen* still being searched for in the neighborhood of Vesta by Trans-space Insurance? It only requires a simple yes or no."

Moore shrugged and tapped it out, while Shea watched with awe.

The spaceman said, "How does it answer? Does it talk?"

Moore laughed gently, "Oh, no. I don't spend *that* kind of money. This model just prints the answer on a slip of tape that comes out that slot."

A short strip of tape did come out as he spoke. Moore removed it and, after a glance, said, "Well, Multivac says yes."

"Hah!" cried Brandon. "Told you. Now ask why."

"Now that's silly. A question like that would obviously be against privacy. You'll just get a yellow state-your-reason."

"Ask and find out. They haven't made the search for the pieces secret. Maybe they're not making the reason secret."

Moore shrugged. He tapped out: Why is Trans-space Insurance conducting its *Silver Queen* search-project to which reference was made in the previous question?

A yellow slip clicked out almost at once: *State Your Reason For Requiring The Information Requested.*

"All right," said Brandon unabashed. "You tell it we're the three survivors and have a right to know. Go ahead. Tell it."

Moore tapped that out in unemotional phrasing and another yellow slip was pushed out at them: *Your Reason Is Insufficient. No Answer Can Be Given.*

Brandon said, "I don't see they have a right to keep that secret."

"That's up to Multivac," said Moore. "It judges the reasons given it and if it decides the ethics of privacy is against answering, that's it. The government itself couldn't break those ethics without a court order, and the courts don't go against Multivac once in ten years. So what are you going to do?"

Brandon jumped to his feet and began the rapid walk up and down the room that was so characteristic of him. "All right, then let's figure it out for ourselves. It's something important to justify all their trouble. We're agreed they're not trying to find evidence of sabotage, not after twenty years. But Trans-space must be looking for *something,* something so valuable that it's worth looking for all this time. Now what could be that valuable?"

"Mark, you're a dreamer," said Moore.

Brandon obviously didn't hear him. "It can't be jewels or money or securities. There just couldn't be enough to pay them back for what the search has already cost them. Not if the *Silver Queen* were pure gold. What would be more valuable?"

"You can't judge value, Mark," said Moore. "A letter might be worth a hundredth of a cent as wastepaper and yet make a difference of a hundred million dollars to a corporation, depending on what's in the letter."

Brandon nodded his head vigorously. "Right. Documents. Valuable papers. Now who would be most likely to have papers worth billions in his possession on that trip?"

"How could anyone possibly say?"

"How about Dr. Horace Quentin? How about that, Warren? He's the one people remember because he was so important. What about the papers he might have had with him? Details of a new discovery, maybe. Damn it, if I had only seen him on that trip, he might have told me something, just in casual conversation, you know. Did *you* ever see him, Warren?"

"Not that I recall. Not to talk to. So casual conversation with me is out too. Of course, I might have passed him at some time without knowing it."

"No, you wouldn't have," said Shea, suddenly thoughtful. "I think I remember something. There was one passenger who never left his cabin. The steward was talking about it. He wouldn't even come out for meals."

"And that was Quentin?" said Brandon, stopping his pacing and staring at the spaceman eagerly.

"It might have been, Mr. Brandon. It might have been him. I don't know that anyone *said* it was. I don't remember. But it must have been a big shot, because on a spaceship you don't fool around bringing meals to a man's cabin unless he *is* a big shot."

"And Quentin was *the* big shot on the trip," said Brandon, with satisfaction. "So he had something in his cabin. Something very important. Something he was concealing."

"He might just have been space sick," said Moore, "except that—" He frowned and fell silent.

"Go ahead," said Brandon urgently. "You remember something too?"

"Maybe. I told you I was sitting next to Dr. Hester at the last dinner. He was saying something about hoping to meet Dr. Quentin on the trip and not having any luck."

"Sure," cried Brandon, "because Quentin wouldn't come out of his cabin."

"He didn't *say* that. We got to talking about Quentin, though. Now what was it he said?" Moore put his hands to his temples as though trying to squeeze out the memory of twenty years ago by main force. "I can't give you the exact words, of course, but it was something about Quentin being very theatrical or a slave of drama or something like that, and they were heading out to some scientific conference on Ganymede and Quentin wouldn't even announce the title of his paper."

"It all fits." Brandon resumed his rapid pacing. "He had a new, great discovery, which he was keeping absolutely secret, because he was going to spring it on the Ganymede conference and get maximum drama out of it. He wouldn't come out of his cabin because he probably thought Hester would pump him—and Hester would, I'll bet. And then the ship hit the rock and Quentin was killed. Trans-space Insurance investigated, got rumors of this new discovery and figured that if they gained control of it they could make back their losses and plenty more. So they took ownership of the ship and have been hunting for Quentin's papers among the pieces ever since."

Moore smiled, in absolute affection for the other man. "Mark, that's a beautiful story. The whole evening is worth it, just watching you make something out of nothing."

"Oh, yeah? Something out of nothing? Let's ask Multivac again. I'll pay the bill for it this month."

"It's all right. Be my guest. If you don't mind, though, I'm going to bring up the bottle of Jabra. I want one more little shot to catch up with you."

"Me, too," said Shea.

Brandon took his seat at the typewriter. His fingers trembled with eagerness as he tapped out: What was the nature of Dr. Horace Quentin's final investigations?

Moore had returned with the bottle and glasses, when the answer came back, on white paper this time. The answer was long and the print was fine, consisting for the most part of references to scientific papers in journals twenty years old.

Moore went over it. "I'm no physicist, but it looks to me as though he was interested in optics."

Brandon shook his head impatiently. "But all that is published. We want something he had not published yet."

"We'll never find out anything about that."

"The insurance company did."

"That's just your theory."

Brandon was kneading his chin with an unsteady hand. "Let me ask Multivac one more question."

He sat down again and tapped out: Give me the name and tube number of the surviving colleagues of Dr. Horace Quentin from among those associated with him at the University on whose faculty he served.

"How do you know he was on a University faculty?" asked Moore.

"If not, Multivac will tell us."

A slip popped out. It contained only one name.

Moore said, "Are you planning to call the man?"

"I sure am," said Brandon. "Otis Fitzsimmons, with a Detroit tube number. Warren, may I—"

"Be my guest, Mark. It's still part of the game."

Brandon set up the combination on Moore's tube keyboard. A woman's voice answered. Brandon asked for Dr. Fitzsimmons and there was a short wait.

Then a thin voice said, "Hello." It sounded old.

Brandon said, "Dr. Fitzsimmons, I'm representing Trans-space Insurance in the matter of the late Dr. Horace Quentin—"

"For heaven's sake, Mark," whispered Moore, but Brandon held up a sharply restraining hand.

There was a pause so long that a tube breakdown began to seem possible and then the old voice said, "After all these years? Again?"

Brandon snapped his fingers in an irrepressible gesture of triumph. But he said smoothly, almost glibly, "We're still trying to find out, Doctor, if you have remembered further details about what Dr. Quentin might have had with him on that last trip that would pertain to his last unpublished discovery."

"Well"—there was an impatient clicking of the tongue—"I've told you, I don't know. I don't want to be bothered with this again. I don't know that there was *anything*. The man hinted, but he was always hinting about some gadget or other."

"What gadget, sir?"

"I tell you I don't know. He used a name once and I told you about that. I don't think it's significant."

"We don't have the name in our records, sir."

"Well, you should have. Uh, what was that name? An optikon, that's it."

"With a K?"

"C or K. I don't know or care. Now, please, I do not wish to be disturbed again about this. Good-bye." He was still mumbling querulously when the line went dead.

Brandon was pleased.

Moore said, "Mark, that was the stupidest thing you could have done. Claiming a fraudulent identity on the tube is illegal. If he wants to make trouble for you—"

"Why should he? He's forgotten about it already. But don't you see, Warren? Trans-space has been asking him about this. He kept saying he'd explained all this before."

"All right. But you'd assumed that much. What else do you know?"

"We also know," said Brandon, "that Quentin's gadget was called an optikon."

"Fitzsimmons didn't sound certain about that. And even so, since we already know he was specializing in optics toward the end, a name like optikon does not push us any further forward."

"And Trans-space Insurance is looking either for the optikon or for papers concerning it. Maybe Quentin kept the details in his hat and just had a model of the instrument. After all, Shea said they were picking up metal objects. Right?"

"There was a bunch of metal junk in the pile," agreed Shea.

"They'd leave that in space if it were papers they were after. So that's what we want, an instrument that might be called an optikon."

"Even if all your theories were correct, Mark, and we're looking for an optikon, the search is absolutely hopeless now," said Moore flatly. "I doubt that more than ten per cent of the debris would remain in orbit about Vesta. Vesta's escape velocity is practically nothing. It was just a lucky thrust in a lucky direction and at a lucky velocity that put our section of the wreck in orbit. The rest is gone, scattered all over the Solar System in any conceivable orbit about the Sun."

"They've been picking up pieces," said Brandon.

"Yes, the ten per cent that managed to make a Vestan orbit out of it. That's all."

Brandon wasn't giving up. He said thoughtfully, "Suppose it *were* there and they hadn't found it. Could someone have beat them to it?"

Mike Shea laughed. "We were right there, but we sure didn't walk off with anything but our skins, and glad to do that much. Who else?"

"That's right," agreed Moore, "and if anyone else picked it up, why are they keeping it a secret?"

"Maybe they don't know what it is."

"Then how do we go about—" Moore broke off and turned to Shea, "What did you say?"

Shea looked blank. "Who, me?"

"Just now, about us being there." Moore's eyes narrowed. He shook his head as though to clear it, then whispered, "Great Galaxy!"

"What is it?" asked Brandon tensely. "What's the matter, Warren?"

"I'm not sure. You're driving me mad with your theories; so mad, I'm beginning to take them seriously, I think. You know, we *did* take some things out of the wreck with us. I mean besides our clothes and what personal belongings we still had. Or at least I did."

"What?"

"It was when I was making my way across the outside of the wreckage—space, I seem to be there now, I see it so clearly—I picked up some items and put them in the pocket of my spacesuit. I don't know why; I wasn't myself, really. I did it without thinking. And then, well, I held on to them. Souvenirs, I suppose. I brought them back to Earth."

"Where are they?"

"I don't know. We haven't stayed in one place, you know."

"You didn't throw them out, did you?"

"No, but things do get lost when you move."

"If you didn't throw them out, they must be somewhere in this house."

"If they didn't get lost. I swear I don't recall seeing them in fifteen years."

"What were they?"

Warren Moore said, "One was a fountain pen, as I recall; a real antique, the kind that used an ink-spray cartridge. What gets me, though, is that the other was a small field glass, not more than about six inches long. You see what I mean? A field glass?"

"An optikon," shouted Brandon. "Sure!"

"It's just a coincidence," said Moore, trying to remain level-headed. "Just a curious coincidence."

But Brandon wasn't having it. "A coincidence, nuts! Trans-space couldn't find the optikon on the wreck and they couldn't find it in space because you had it all along."

"You're crazy."

"Come on, we've got to find the thing now."

Moore blew out his breath. "Well, I'll look, if that's what you want, but I doubt that I'll find it. Okay, let's start with the storage level. That's the logical place."

Shea chuckled. "The logical place is usually the worst place to look." But they all headed for the power ramp once more and the additional flight upward.

The storage level had a musty, unused odor to it. Moore turned on the precipitron. "I don't think we've precipitated the dust in two years. That shows you how often I'm up here. Now, let's see—if it's anywhere at all, it would be in with the bachelor collection. I mean the junk I've been hanging on to since bachelor days. We can start here."

Moore started leafing through the contents of plastic collapsibles while Brandon kept peering anxiously over his shoulder.

Moore said, "What do you know? My college yearbook. I was a sonist in those days; a real bug on it. In fact, I managed to get a voice recording with the picture of every senior in this book." He tapped its cover fondly. "You could swear there was nothing there but the usual trimensional photos, but each one has an imprisoned—"

He grew aware of Brandon's frown and said, "Okay, I'll keep looking."

He gave up the collapsibles and opened a trunk of heavy, old-fashioned woodite. He separated the contents of the various compartments.

Brandon said, "Hey, is that it?"

He pointed to a small cylinder that rolled out on the floor with a small clunk.

Moore said, "I don't—Yes! That's the pen. There it is. And here's the field glass. Neither one works, of course. They're both broken. At least, I suppose the pen's broken. Something's loose and rattles in it. Hear? I wouldn't have the slightest idea about how to fill it so I can check whether it really works. They haven't even made ink-spray cartridges in years."

Brandon held it under the light. "It has initials on it."

"Oh? I don't remember noticing any."

"It's pretty worn down. It looks like J.K.Q."

"Q.?"

"Right, and that's an unusual letter with which to start a last name. This pen might have belonged to Quentin. An heirloom he kept for luck or sentiment. It might have belonged to a great-grandfather in the days when they used pens like this; a great-grandfather called Jason Knight Quentin or Judah Kent Quentin or something like that. We can check the names of Quentin's ancestors through Multivac."

Moore nodded. "I think maybe we should. See, you've got me as crazy as you are."

"And if this is so, it proves you picked it up in Quentin's room. So you picked up the field glass there too."

"Now hold it. I don't remember that I picked them both up in the same place. I don't remember the scrounging over the outside of the wreck that well."

Brandon turned the small field glass over and over under the light. "No initials here."

"Did you expect any?"

"I don't see anything, in fact, except this narrow joining mark here." He ran his thumbnail into the fine groove that circled the glass near its thicker end. He tried to twist it unsuccessfully. "One piece." He put it to his eye. "This thing doesn't work."

"I told you it was broken. No lenses—"

Shea broke in. "You've got to expect a little damage when a spaceship hits a good-sized meteor and goes to pieces."

"So even if this were it," said Moore, pessimistic again, "if this were the optikon, it would not do us any good."

He took the field glass from Brandon and felt along the empty rims. "You can't even tell where the lenses belonged. There's no groove I can feel into which they might have been seated. It's as if there never—*Hey!*" He exploded the syllable violently.

"Hey what?" said Brandon.

"The name! The name of the thing!"

"Optikon, you mean?"

"Optikon, I don't mean! Fitzsimmons, on the tube, called it an optikon and we thought he said 'an optikon.' "

"Well, he did," said Brandon.

"Sure," said Shea. "I heard him."

"You just thought you heard him. He said 'anoptikon.' Don't you get it? Not 'an optikon,' two words, 'anoptikon,' one word."

"Oh," said Brandon blankly. "And what's the difference?"

"A hell of a difference. 'An optikon' would mean an instrument with lenses, but 'anoptikon,' one word, has the Greek prefix 'an-' which means 'no.' Words of Greek derivation use it for 'no.' Anarchy means 'no government,' anemia means 'no blood,' anonymous means 'no name,' and anoptikon means—"

"No lenses," cried Brandon.

"Right! Quentin must have been working on an optical device without lenses and this may be it and it may not be broken."

Shea said, "But you don't see anything when you look through it."

"It must be set to neutral," said Moore. "There must be some way of adjusting it." Like Brandon, he placed it in both hands and tried to twist it about that circumscribing groove. He placed pressure on it, grunting.

"Don't break it," said Brandon.

"It's giving. Either it's supposed to be stiff or else it's corroded shut." He stopped, looked at the instrument impatiently, and put it to his eye again. He whirled, unpolarized a window and looked out at the lights of the city.

"I'll be dumped in space," he breathed.

Brandon said, "What? What?"

Moore handed the instrument to Brandon wordlessly. Brandon put it to his eyes and cried out sharply, "It's a telescope."

Shea said at once, "Let me see."

They spent nearly an hour with it, converting it into a telescope with turns in one direction, a microscope with turns in the other.

"How does it work?" Brandon kept asking.

"I don't know," Moore kept saying. In the end he said, "I'm sure it involves concentrated force fields. We are turning against considerable field resistance. With larger instruments, power adjustment will be required."

"It's a pretty cute trick," said Shea.

"It's more than that," said Moore. "I'll bet it represents a completely new turn in theoretical physics. It focuses light without lenses, and it can be adjusted to gather light over a wider and wider area without any change in focal length. I'll bet we could duplicate the five-hundred-inch Ceres telescope in one direction and an electron microscope in the other. What's more, I don't see any chromatic aberration, so it must bend light of all wavelengths equally. Maybe it bends radio waves and gamma rays also. Maybe it distorts gravity, if gravity is some kind of radiation. Maybe—"

"Worth money?" asked Shea, breaking in dryly.

"All kinds if someone can figure out how it works."

"Then we don't go to Trans-space Insurance with this. We go to a lawyer first. Did we sign these things away with our salvage rights or didn't we? You had them already in your possession before signing the paper. For that matter, is the paper any good if we didn't know what we were signing anyway? Maybe it might be considered fraud."

"As a matter of fact," said Moore, "with something like this, I don't know if any private company ought to own it. We ought to check with some government agency. If there's money in it—"

But Brandon was pounding both fists on his knees. "To *hell* with the money, Warren. I mean, I'll take any money that comes my way but that's not the important thing. We're going to be famous, man, famous! Imagine the story. A fabulous treasure lost in space. A giant corporation combing space for twenty years to find it and all the time we, the forgotten ones, have it in our possession. Then, on the twentieth anniversary of the original loss, we find it again. If this thing works, if anoptics become a great new scientific technique, they'll *never* forget us."

Moore grinned, then started laughing. "That's right. You did it, Mark. You did just what you set out to do. You've rescued us from being marooned in oblivion."

"We all did it," said Brandon. "Mike Shea started us off with the necessary basic information. I worked out the theory, and you had the instrument."

"Okay. It's late, and the wife will be back soon, so let's get the ball rolling right away. Multivac will tell us which agency would be appropriate and who—"

"No, no," said Brandon. "Ritual first. The closing toast of the anniversary, please, and with the appropriate change. Won't you oblige, Warren?" He passed over the still half-full bottle of Jabra water.

Carefully, Moore filled each small glass precisely to the brim. "Gentlemen," he said solemnly, "a toast." The three raised the glasses in unison. "Gentlemen, I give you the *Silver Queen* souvenirs *we used to have.*"

Obituary

My husband, Lancelot, always reads the paper at breakfast. What I see of him when he first appears is his lean, abstracted face, carrying its perpetual look of angry and slightly puzzled frustration. He doesn't greet me, and the newspaper, carefully unfolded in readiness for him, goes up before his face.

Thereafter, there is only his arm, emerging from behind the paper for a second cup of coffee into which I have carefully placed the necessary level teaspoonful of sugar—neither heaping nor deficient under pain of a stinging glare.

I am no longer sorry for this. It makes for a quiet meal, at least.

However, on this morning the quiet was broken when Lancelot barked out abruptly, "Good Lord! That fool Paul Farber is dead. Stroke!"

I just barely recognized the name. Lancelot had mentioned him on occa- sion, so I knew him as a colleague, as another theoretical physicist. From my husband's exasperated epithet, I felt reasonably sure he was a moderately famous one who had achieved the success that had eluded Lancelot.

He put down the paper and stared at me angrily. "Why do they fill obituaries with such lying trash?" he demanded. "They make him out to be a second Einstein for no better reason than that he died of a stroke."

If there was one subject I had learned to avoid, it was that of obituaries. I dared not even nod agreement.

He threw down the paper and walked away and out of the room, leaving his eggs half-finished and his second cup of coffee untouched.

I sighed. What else could I do? What else could I ever do?

• • • •

Of course, my husband's name isn't really Lancelot Stebbins, because I am changing names and circumstances, as far as I can, to protect the guilty. However, the point is that even if I used real names you would not recognize my husband.

Lancelot had a talent in that respect—a talent for being passed over, for going unnoticed. His discoveries are invariably anticipated, or blurred by the presence of a greater discovery made simultaneously. At scientific conventions his papers are poorly attended because another paper of greater importance is being given in another section.

Naturally this has had its effect on him. It changed him.

When I first married him, twenty-five years ago, he was a sparkling catch. He was well-to-do through inheritance and already a trained physicist with an intense ambition and great promise. As for myself, I believe myself to have been pretty then, but that didn't last. What did last was my introversion and my failure to be the kind of social success an ambitious young faculty member needs for a wife.

Perhaps that was part of Lancelot's talent for going unnoticed. Had he married another kind of wife, she might have made him visible in her radiation.

Did he realize that himself after a while? Was that why he grew away from me after the first two or three reasonably happy years? Sometimes I believed this and bitterly blamed myself.

But then I would think it was only his thirst for fame, which grew for being unslaked. He left his position on the faculty and built a laboratory of his own far outside town, for the sake, he said, of cheap land and of isolation.

Money was no problem. In his field, the government was generous with its grants and those he could always get. On top of that, he used our own money without limit.

I tried to withstand him. I said, "But it's not necessary, Lancelot. It's not as though we have financial worries. It's not as though they're not willing to let you remain on the university staff. All I want are children and a normal life."

But there was a burning inside him that blinded him to everything else. He turned angrily on me. "There is something that must come first. The world of science must recognize me for what I am, for a—a—great investigator."

At that time, he still hesitated to apply the term genius to himself.

It didn't help. The fall of chance remained always and perpetually against him. His laboratory hummed with work; he hired assistants at excellent salaries; he drove himself roughly and pitilessly. Nothing came of it.

I kept hoping he would give up someday; return to the city; allow us to lead a normal, quiet life. I waited, but always when he might have admitted defeat, some new battle would be taken up, some new attempt to storm the bastions of fame. Each time he charged with such hope and fell back in such despair.

And always he turned on me; for if he was ground down by the world, he could always grind me in return. I am not a brave person, but I was coming to believe I must leave him.

And yet . . .

In this last year he had obviously been girding himself for another battle. A last one, I thought. There was something about him more intense, more a-quiver than I had ever seen before. There was the way he murmured to himself and laughed briefly at nothing. There were the times he went for days without food and nights without sleep. He even took to keeping laboratory notebooks in a bedroom safe as though he feared even his own assistants.

Of course I was fatalistically certain that this attempt of his would fail also. But surely, if it failed, then at his age, he would have to recognize that his last chance had gone. Surely he would have to give up.

So I decided to wait, as patiently as I could.

But the affair of the obituary at breakfast came as something of a jolt. Once, on an earlier occasion of the sort, I had remarked that at least he could count on a certain amount of recognition in his own obituary.

I suppose it wasn't a very clever remark, but then my remarks never are. I had meant it to be lighthearted, to pull him out of a gathering depression during which I knew, from experience, he would be most intolerable.

And perhaps there had been a little unconscious spite in it, too. I cannot honestly say.

At any rate, he turned full on me. His lean body shook and his dark eyebrows pulled down over his deep-set eyes as he shrieked at me in falsetto, "But I'll never read my obituary. I'll be deprived even of that."

And he spat at me. He deliberately spat at me.

I ran to my bedroom.

He never apologized, but after a few days in which I avoided him completely, we carried on our frigid life as before. Neither of us ever referred to the incident.

Now there was another obituary.

Somehow, as I sat there alone at the breakfast table, I felt it to be the last straw for him, the climax of his long-drawn-out failure.

I could sense a crisis coming and didn't know whether to fear or welcome it. Perhaps, on the whole, I would welcome it. Any change could not fail to be a change for the better.

Shortly before lunch, he came upon me in the living room, where a basket of unimportant sewing gave my hands something to do and a bit of television occupied my mind.

He said abruptly, "I will need your help."

It had been twenty years or more since he had said anything like that and involuntarily I thawed toward him. He looked unhealthily excited. There was a flush on his ordinarily pale cheeks.

I said, "Gladly, if there's something I can do for you."

"There is. I have given my assistants a month's vacation. They will leave Saturday and after that you and I will work alone in the laboratory. I tell you now so that you will refrain from making any other arrangements for the coming week."

I shriveled a bit. "But Lancelot, you know I can't help you with your work. I don't understand—"

"I know that," he said with complete contempt, "but you don't have to understand my work. You need only follow a few simple instructions and follow them carefully. The point is that I have discovered something, finally, which will put me where I belong—"

"Oh, Lancelot," I said involuntarily, for I had heard this before a number of times.

"Listen to me, you fool, and for once try to behave like an adult. This time I have done it. No one can anticipate me this time because my discovery is based on such an unorthodox concept that no physicist alive, except me, is genius enough to think of it, not for a generation at least. And when my work bursts on the world, I could be recognized as the greatest name of all time in science."

"I'm sure I'm very glad for you, Lancelot."

"I said I *could* be recognized. I could not be, also. There is a great deal of injustice in the assignment of scientific credit. I've learned that often enough. So it will not be enough merely to announce the discovery. If I do, everyone will crowd into the field and after a while I'll just be a name in the history books, with glory spread out over a number of Johnny-come-latelies."

I think the only reason he was talking to me then, three days before he could get to work on whatever it was he planned to do, was that he could no longer contain himself. He bubbled over and I was the only one who was nonentity enough to be witness to that.

He said, "I intend my discovery to be so dramatized, to break on mankind with so thunderous a clap, that there will be no room for anyone else to be mentioned in the same breath with me, ever."

He was going too far, and I was afraid of the effect of another disappointment on him. Might it not drive him mad? I said, "But Lancelot, why need we bother? Why don't we leave all this? Why not take a long vacation? You have worked hard enough and long enough, Lancelot. Perhaps we can take a trip to Europe. I've always wanted to—"

He stamped his foot. "*Will* you stop your foolish meowing? Saturday, you will come into my laboratory with me."

I slept poorly for the next three nights. He had never been quite like this before, I thought, never quite as bad. Might he not be mad already, perhaps?

It could be madness now, I thought, a madness born of disappointment no longer endurable, and sparked by the obituary. He had sent away his assistants and now he wanted me in the laboratory. He had never allowed me there before. Surely he meant to do something to me, to make me the subject of some insane experiment, or to kill me outright.

During the miserable, frightened nights I would plan to call the police, to run away, to—to do anything.

But then morning would come and I would think surely he wasn't mad, surely he wouldn't offer me violence. Even the spitting incident was not truly violent and he had never actually tried to hurt me physically.

So in the end I waited and on Saturday I walked to what might be my death as meekly as a chicken. Together, silently, we walked down the path that led from our dwelling to the laboratory.

The laboratory was frightening just in itself, and I stepped about gingerly, but Lancelot only said, "Oh, stop staring about you as though something were going to hurt you. You just do as I say and look where I tell you."

"Yes, Lancelot." He had led me into a small room, the door of which had been padlocked. It was almost choked with objects of very strange appearance and with a great deal of wiring.

Lancelot said, "To begin with, do you see this iron crucible?"

"Yes, Lancelot." It was a small but deep container made out of thick metal and rusted in spots on the outside. It was covered by a coarse wire netting.

He urged me toward it and I saw that inside it was a white mouse with its front paws up on the inner side of the crucible and its small snout at the wire netting in quivering curiosity, or perhaps in anxiety. I am afraid I jumped, for to see a mouse without expecting to is startling, at least to me.

Lancelot growled, "It won't hurt you. Now just back against the wall and watch me."

My fears returned most forcefully. I grew horribly certain that from somewhere a lightning bolt would shoot out and incinerate me, or some monstrous thing of metal might emerge and crush me, or—or—

I closed my eyes.

But nothing happened; to me, at least. I heard only a phfft as though a small firecracker had misfired, and Lancelot said to me, "Well?"

I opened my eyes. He was looking at me, fairly shining with pride. I stared blankly.

He said, "Here, don't you see it, you idiot? Right here."

A foot to one side of the crucible was a second one. I hadn't seen him put it there.

"Do you mean this second crucible?" I asked.

"It isn't quite a second crucible, but a duplicate of the first one. For all ordinary purposes, they are the same crucible, atom for atom. Compare them. You'll find the rust marks identical."

"You made the second one out of the first?"

"Yes, but in a special way. To create matter would require a prohibitive amount of energy ordinarily. It would take the complete fission of a hundred grams of uranium to create one gram of duplicate matter, even granting perfect efficiency. The great secret I have stumbled on is that the duplication of an object at a point in future time requires very little energy if that energy is applied correctly. The essence of the feat, my—my dear, in my creating such a duplicate and bringing it back is that I have accomplished the equivalent of time travel."

It was the measure of his triumph and happiness that he actually used an affectionate term in speaking to me.

"Isn't that remarkable?" I said, for to tell the truth, I *was* impressed. "Did the mouse come too?"

I looked inside the second crucible as I asked that and got another nasty shock. It contained a white mouse—a dead white mouse.

Lancelot turned faintly pink. "That is a shortcoming. I can bring back living matter, but not as living matter. It comes back dead."

"Oh, what a shame. Why?"

"I don't know yet. I imagine the duplications are completely perfect on the atomic scale. Certainly there is no visible damage. Dissections show that."

"You might ask—" I stopped myself quickly as he glanced at me. I decided I had better not suggest a collaboration of any sort, for I knew from experience that in that case the collaborator would invariably get all the credit for the discovery.

Lancelot said with sour amusement, "I *have* asked. A trained biologist has performed autopsies on some of my animals and found nothing. Of course, they didn't know where the animal came from and I took care to take it back before anything would happen to give it away. Lord, even my assistants don't know what I've been doing."

"But why must you keep it so secret?"

"Just because I can't bring objects back alive. Some subtle molecular derangement. If I published my results, someone else might learn the method of preventing such derangement, add his slight improvement to my basic discovery, and achieve a greater fame, because he would bring back a living man who might give information about the future."

I saw that quite well. Nor need he say it "might" be done. It would be done. Inevitably. In fact, no matter what he did, he would lose the credit. I was sure of it.

"However," he went on, more to himself than to me, "I can wait no longer. I must announce this, but in such a way that it will be indelibly and permanently associated with me. There must be a drama about it so effective that thereafter there will be no way of mentioning time travel without mentioning me no matter what other men may do in the future. I am going to prepare that drama and you will play a part in it."

"But what do you want me to do, Lancelot?"

"You'll be my widow."

I clutched at his arm. "Lancelot, do you mean—" I cannot quite analyze the conflicting feelings that upset me at that moment.

He disengaged himself roughly. "Only temporarily. I am not committing suicide. I am simply going to bring myself back from three days in the future."

"But you'll be dead then."

"Only the 'me' that is brought back. The real 'me' will be as alive as ever. Like that white rat." His eyes shifted to a dial and he said, "Ah, Zero time in a few seconds. Watch the second crucible and the dead mouse."

Before my eyes it disappeared and there was a phfft sound again.

"Where did it go?"

"Nowhere," said Lancelot. "It was only a duplicate. The moment we passed that instant in time at which the duplicate was formed, it naturally disappeared. It was the first mouse that was the original, and it remains alive and well. The same will be true of me. A duplicate 'me' will come back dead. The original 'me' will be alive. After three days, we will come to the instant at which the duplicate 'me' was formed, using the real 'me' as a model, and sent back dead. Once we pass that instant the dead duplicate 'me' will disappear and the live 'me' will remain. Is that clear?"

"It sounds dangerous."

"It isn't. Once my dead body appears, the doctor will pronounce me dead, the newspapers will report me dead, the undertaker will prepare to bury the dead. I will then return to life and announce how I did it. When that happens, I will be more than the discoverer of time travel; I will be the man who came back from the dead. Time travel and Lancelot Stebbins will be publicized so thoroughly and so intermingled, that nothing will extricate my name from the thought of time travel ever again."

"Lancelot," I said softly, "why can't we just announce your discovery? This is too elaborate a plan. A simple announcement will make you famous enough and then we can move to the city perhaps—"

"*Quiet!* You will do what I say."

I don't know how long Lancelot was thinking of all this before the obituary actually brought matters to a head. Of course, I don't minimize his intelligence. Despite his phenomenally bad luck, there is no questioning his brilliance.

He had informed his assistants before they had left of the experiments he intended to conduct while they were gone. Once they testified it would seem quite natural that he should be bent over a particular set of reacting chemicals and that he should be dead of cyanide poisoning to all appearances.

"So you see to it that the police get in touch with my assistants at once. You know where they can be reached. I want no hint of murder or suicide, or anything but accident, natural and logical accident. I want a quick death certificate from the doctor, a quick notification to the newspapers."

I said, "But Lancelot, what if they find the real you?"

"Why should they?" he snapped. "If you find a corpse, do you start searching for the living replica also? No one will look for me and I will stay quietly in the temporal chamber for the interval. There are toilet facilities and I can bring in enough sandwich fixings to keep me."

He added regretfully, "I'll have to make do without coffee, though, till it's over. I can't have anyone smelling unexplained coffee here while I'm supposed to be dead. Well, there's plenty of water and it's only three days."

I clasped my hands nervously and said, "Even if they do find you, won't it be the same thing anyway? There'll be a dead 'you' and a living 'you'—" It was myself I was trying to console, myself I was trying to prepare for the inevitable disappointment.

But he turned on me, shouting, "No, it won't be the same thing at all. It will all become a hoax that failed. I'll be famous, but only as a fool."

"But Lancelot," I said cautiously, "something always goes wrong."

"Not this time."

"But you always say 'not this time' and yet something *always*—"

He was white with rage and his irises showed clear all about their circle. He caught my elbow and hurt it terribly but I dared not cry out. He said, "Only one thing can go wrong and that is *you*. If you give it away, if you don't play your part perfectly, if you don't follow the instructions exactly, I— I—" He seemed to cast about for a punishment. "I'll *kill* you."

I turned my head away in sheer terror and tried to break loose, but he held on grimly. It was remarkable how strong he could be when he was in a passion. He said, "Listen to me! You have done me a great deal of harm by being you, but I have blamed myself for marrying you in the first place and for never finding the time to divorce you in the second. But now I have my chance, despite you, to turn my life into a vast success. If you spoil even that chance, I will kill you. I mean that literally."

I was sure he did. "I'll do everything you say," I whispered, and he let me go.

He spent a day on his machinery. "I've never transported more than a hundred grams before," he said, calmly thoughtful.

I thought: It won't work. How can it?

The next day he adjusted the device to the point where I needed only to close one switch. He made me practice that particular switch on a dead circuit for what seemed an interminable time.

"Do you understand now? Do you see exactly how it is done?"

"Yes."

"Then do it, when this light flashes and not a moment before."

It won't work, I thought. "Yes," I said.

He took his position and remained in stolid silence. He was wearing a rubber apron over a laboratory jacket.

The light flashed, and the practice turned out to be worth while for I pulled the switch automatically before thought could stop me or even make me waver.

For an instant there were two Lancelots before me, side by side, the new one dressed as the old one was but more rumpled. And then the new one collapsed and lay still.

"All right," cried the living Lancelot, stepping off the carefully marked spot. "Help me. Grab his legs."

I marveled at Lancelot. How, without wincing or showing any uneasiness, could he carry his own dead body, his own body of three days in the future? Yet he held it under its arms without showing any more emotion than if it had been a sack of wheat.

I held it by the ankles, my stomach turning at the touch. It was still blood-warm to the touch; freshly dead. Together we carried it through a corridor and up a flight of stairs, down another corridor and into a room. Lancelot had it already arranged. A solution was bubbling in a queer all-glass contraption inside a closed section, with a movable glass door partitioning it off.

Other chemical equipment was scattered about, calculated, no doubt, to show an experiment in progress. A bottle, boldly labeled "Potassium cyanide" was on the desk, prominent among the others. There was a small scattering of crystals on the desk near it; cyanide, I presume.

Carefully Lancelot crumpled the dead body as though it had fallen off the stool. He placed crystals on the body's left hand and more on the rubber apron; finally, a few on the body's chin.

"They'll get the idea," he muttered.

A last look-around and he said, "All right, now. Go back to the house now and call the doctor. Your story is that you came here to bring me a sandwich because I was working through lunch. There it is." And he showed me a broken dish and a scattered sandwich where, presumably, I had dropped it. "Do a little screaming, but don't overdo it."

It was not difficult for me to scream when the time came, or to weep. I had felt like doing both for days and now it was a relief to let the hysteria out.

The doctor behaved precisely as Lancelot had said he would. The bottle of cyanide was virtually the first thing he saw. He frowned. "Dear me, Mrs. Stebbins, he was a careless chemist."

"I suppose so," I said, sobbing. "He shouldn't have been working himself, but both his assistants are on vacation."

"When a man treats cyanide as though it were salt, it's bad." The doctor shook his head in grave moralistic fashion. "Now, Mrs. Stebbins, I will have to call the police. It's accidental cyanide poisoning, but it's a violent death and the police—"

"Oh, yes, yes, call them." And then I could almost have beaten myself for having sounded suspiciously eager.

The police came, and along with them a police surgeon, who grunted in disgust at the cyanide crystals on hand, apron, and chin. The police were thoroughly disinterested, asked only statistical questions concerning names and ages. They asked if I could manage the funeral arrangements. I said yes, and they left.

I then called the newspapers, and two of the press associations. I said I thought they would be picking up news of the death from the police records and I hoped they would not stress the fact that my husband was a careless chemist, with the tone of one who hoped nothing ill would be said of the dead. After all, I went on, he was a nuclear physicist rather than a chemist and I had a feeling lately he might be in some sort of trouble.

I followed Lancelot's line exactly in this and that also worked. A nuclear physicist in trouble? Spies? Enemy agents?

The reporters began to come eagerly. I gave them a youthful portrait of Lancelot and a photographer took pictures of the laboratory buildings. I took them through a few rooms of the main laboratory for more pictures. No one, neither the police nor the reporters, asked questions about the bolted room or even seemed to notice it.

I gave them a mass of professional and biographical material that Lancelot had made ready for me and told several anecdotes designed to show a combination of humanity and brilliance. In everything I tried to be letter-perfect and yet I could feel no confidence. Something would go wrong; *something* would go wrong.

And when it did, I knew he would blame me. And this time he had promised to kill me.

The next day I brought him the newspapers. Over and over again, he read them, eyes glittering. He had made a full box on the lower left of the New York *Times'* front page. The *Times* made little of the mystery of his death and so did the A.P., but one of the tabloids had a front-page scare headline: ATOM SAVANT IN MYSTERY DEATH.

He laughed aloud as he read that and when he completed all of them, he turned back to the first.

He looked up at me sharply. "Don't go. Listen to what they say."

"I've read them already, Lancelot."

"Listen, I tell you."

He read every one aloud to me, lingering on their praises of the dead, then said to me, aglow with self-satisfaction, "Do you still think something will go wrong?"

I said hesitantly, "If the police come back to ask why I thought you were in trouble . . ."

"You were vague enough. Tell them you had had bad dreams. By the time they decide to push investigations further, if they do, it will be too late."

To be sure, everything was working, but I could not hope that all would continue so. And yet the human mind is odd; it will persist in hoping even when it cannot hope.

I said, "Lancelot, when this is all over and you are famous, really famous, then after that, surely you can retire. We can go back to the city and live quietly."

"You are an imbecile. Don't you see that once I am recognized, I *must* continue? Young men will flock to me. This laboratory will become a great Institute of Temporal Investigation. I'll become a legend in my lifetime. I will pile my greatness so high that no one afterward will ever be able to be anything but an intellectual dwarf compared to me." He raised himself on tiptoe, eyes shining, as though he already saw the pedestal onto which he would be raised.

It had been my last hope of some personal shreds of happiness and a small one. I sighed.

I asked the undertaker that the body be allowed to remain in its coffin in the laboratories before burial in the Stebbins family plot on Long Island. I asked that it remain unembalmed, offering to keep it in a large refrigerated room with the temperature set at forty. I asked that it not be removed to the funeral home.

The undertaker brought the coffin to the laboratory in frigid disapproval. No doubt this was reflected in the eventual bill. My offered explanation that I wanted him near me for a last period of time and that I wanted his assistants to be given a chance to view the body was lame and sounded lame.

Still, Lancelot had been most specific in what I was to say.

Once the dead body was laid out, with the coffin lid still open, I went to see Lancelot.

"Lancelot," I said, "the undertaker was quite displeased. I think he suspects that something odd is going on."

"Good," said Lancelot with satisfaction.

"But—"

"We need only wait one more day. Nothing will be brought to a head out of mere suspicion before then. Tomorrow morning the body will disappear, or should."

"You mean it might not?" I knew it; I knew it.

"There could be some delay, or some prematurity. I have never transported anything this heavy and I'm not certain how exactly my equations hold. To make the necessary observation is one reason I want the body here and not in a funeral parlor."

"But in the funeral parlor it would disappear before witnesses."

"And here you think they will suspect trickery?"

"Of course."

He seemed amused. "They will say: Why did he send his assistants away? Why did he run experiments himself that any child could perform and yet manage to kill himself running them? Why did the dead body happen to disappear without witnesses? They will say: There is nothing to this absurd story of time travel. He took drugs to throw himself in a cataleptic trance and doctors were hoodwinked."

"Yes," I said faintly. How did he come to understand all that?

"And," he went on, "when I continue to insist I have solved time travel and that I was indisputably pronounced dead and was not indisputably alive, orthodox scientists will heatedly denounce me as a fraud. Why, in one week, I will have become a household name to every man on Earth. They will talk of nothing else. I will offer to make a demonstration of time travel before any group of scientists who wish to see it. I will offer to make the demonstration on an intercontinental TV circuit. Public pressure will force scientists to attend, and the networks to give permission. It doesn't matter whether people will watch hoping for a miracle or for a lynching. They will watch! And *then* I will succeed and who in science will ever have had a more transcendent climax to his life?"

I was dazzled for a moment, but something unmoved within me said: Too long, too complicated; something will go wrong.

That evening, his assistants arrived and tried to be respectfully grieving in the presence of the corpse. Two more witnesses to swear they had seen Lancelot dead; two more witnesses to confuse the issue and help build events to their stratospheric peak.

By four the next morning, we were in the cold-room, bundled in overcoats and waiting for zero moment.

Lancelot, in high excitement, kept checking his instruments and doing I-know-not-what with them. His desk computer was working constantly, though how he could make his cold fingers jiggle the keys so nimbly, I am at a loss to say.

I, myself, was quite miserable. There was the cold, the dead body in the coffin, the uncertainty of the future.

We had been there for what seemed an eternity and finally Lancelot said, "It will work. It will work as predicted. At the most, disappearance will be five minutes late and this when seventy kilograms of mass are involved. My analysis of chronous forces is masterly indeed." He smiled at me, but he also smiled at his own corpse with equal warmth.

I noticed that his lab jacket, which he had been wearing constantly for three days now, sleeping in it I am certain, had become wrinkled and shabby. It was about as it had seemed upon the second Lancelot, the dead one, when it had appeared.

Lancelot seemed to be aware of my thoughts, or perhaps only of my gaze, for he looked down at his jacket and said, "Ah, yes, I had better put on the rubber apron. My second self was wearing it when it appeared."

"What if you didn't put it on?" I asked tonelessly.

"I would have to. It would be a necessity. Something would have reminded me. Else *it* would not have appeared in one." His eyes narrowed. "Do you still think something will go wrong?"

"I don't know," I mumbled.

"Do you think the body won't disappear, or that I'll disappear instead?"

When I didn't answer at all, he said in a half-scream, "Can't you see my luck has changed at last? Can't you see how smoothly and according to plan it is all working out? I will be the greatest man who ever lived. Come, heat up the water for the coffee." He was suddenly calm again. "It will serve as celebration when my double leaves us and I return to life. I haven't had any coffee for three days."

It was only instant coffee he pushed in my direction, but after three days that, too, would serve. I fumbled at the laboratory hot-plate with my cold fingers until Lancelot pushed me roughly to one side and set a beaker of water upon it.

"It'll take a while," he said, turning the control to "high." He looked at his watch, then at various dials on the wall. "My double will be gone before the water boils. Come here and watch." He stepped to the side of the coffin.

I hesitated. "Come," he said peremptorily.

I came.

He looked down at himself with infinite pleasure and waited. We both waited, staring at a corpse.

There was the phfft sound and Lancelot cried out, "Less than two minutes off."

Without a blur or a wink, the dead body was gone.

The open coffin contained an empty set of clothes. The clothes, of course, had not been those in which the dead body had been brought back. They were real clothes and they stayed in reality. There they now were: underwear within shirt and pants; shirt within tie; tie within jacket. Shoes had turned over, dangling socks from within them. The body was gone.

I could hear water boiling.

"Coffee," said Lancelot. "Coffee first. Then we call the police and the newspapers."

I made the coffee for him and myself. I gave him the usual level teaspoon from the sugar bowl, neither heaping nor deficient. Even under these conditions, when I was sure for once it wouldn't matter to him, habit was strong.

I sipped at my coffee, which I drank without cream or sugar, as was my habit. Its warmth was most welcome.

He stirred his coffee. "All," he said softly, "all I have waited for." He put the cup to his grimly triumphant lips and drank.

Those were his last words.

. . . .

Now that it was over, there was a kind of frenzy over me. I managed to strip him and dress him in the clothing from the coffin. Somehow I was able to heave his weight upward and place him in the coffin. I folded his arms across his chest as they had been.

I then washed out every trace of coffee in the sink in the room outside, and the sugar bowl, too. Over and over again I rinsed, until all the cyanide, which I had substituted for the sugar, was gone.

I carried his laboratory jacket and other clothes to the hamper where I had stored those the double had brought back. The second set had disappeared, of course, and I put the first set there.

Next I waited.

By that evening, I was sure the corpse was cold enough, and called the undertakers. Why should they wonder? They expected a dead body and there was the dead body. The same dead body. Really the same body. It even had cyanide in it as the first was supposed to have.

I suppose they might still be able to tell the difference between a body dead twelve hours and one dead three and a half days, even under refrigeration, but why should they dream of looking?

They didn't. They nailed down the coffin, took him away, and buried him. It was the perfect murder.

As a matter of fact, since Lancelot was legally dead at the time I killed him, I wonder if, strictly speaking, it was murder at all. Of course, I don't intend to ask a lawyer about this.

Life is quiet for me now; peaceful and contented. I have money enough. I attend the theater. I have made friends.

And I live without remorse. To be sure, Lancelot will never receive credit for time travel. Someday when time travel is discovered again, the name of Lancelot Stebbins will rest in Stygian darkness, unrecognized. But then, I told him that whatever his plans, he would end without the credit. If I hadn't killed him, something else would have spoiled things, and then he would have killed me.

No, I live without remorse.

In fact, I have forgiven Lancelot everything, everything but that moment when he spat at me. So it is rather ironic that he did have one happy moment before he died, for he was given a gift few could have, and he, above all men, savored it.

Despite his cry, when he spat at me, Lancelot managed to read his own obituary.

Rain, Rain, Go Away

"There she is again," said Lillian Wright as she adjusted the venetian blinds carefully. "There she is, George."

"There who is?" asked her husband, trying to get satisfactory contrast on the TV so that he might settle down to the ball game.

"Mrs. Sakkaro," she said, and then, to forestall her husband's inevitable "Who's that?" added hastily, "The new neighbors, for goodness sake."

"Oh."

"Sunbathing. Always sunbathing. I wonder where her boy is. He's usually out on a nice day like this, standing in that tremendous yard of theirs and throwing the ball against the house. Did you ever see him, George?"

"I've heard him. It's a version of the Chinese water torture. Bang on the wall, biff on the ground, smack in the hand. Bang, biff, smack, bang, biff—"

"He's a *nice* boy, quiet and well-behaved. I wish Tommie would make friends with him. He's the right age, too, just about ten, I should say."

"I didn't know Tommie was backward about making friends."

"Well, it's hard with the Sakkaros. They keep so to themselves. I don't even know what Mr. Sakkaro does."

"Why should you? It's not really anyone's business what he does."

"It's odd that I never see him go to work."

"No one ever sees me go to work."

"You stay home and write. What does *he* do."

"I dare say Mrs. Sakkaro knows what Mr. Sakkaro does and is all upset because she doesn't know what *I* do."

"Oh, George." Lillian retreated from the window and glanced with distaste at the television. (Schoendienst was at bat.) "I think we should make an effort; the neighborhood should."

"What kind of an effort?" George was comfortable on the couch now, with a king-size Coke in his hand, freshly opened and frosted with moisture.

"To get to know them."

"Well, didn't you, when she first moved in? You said you called."

"I said hello but, well, she'd just moved in and the house was still upset, so that's all it could be, just hello. It's been two months now and it's still nothing more than hello, sometimes. —She's so odd."

"Is she?"

"She's always looking at the sky; I've seen her do it a hundred times and she's never been out when it's the least bit cloudy. Once, when the boy was out playing, she called to him to come in, shouting that it was going to rain. I happened to hear her and I thought, Good Lord, wouldn't you know and me with a wash on the line, so I hurried out and, you know, it was broad sunlight. Oh, there were some clouds, but nothing, really."

"Did it rain, eventually?"

"Of course not. I just had to run out in the yard for nothing."

George was lost amid a couple of base hits and a most embarrassing bobble that meant a run. When the excitement was over and the pitcher was trying to regain his composure, George called out after Lillian, who was vanishing into the kitchen, "Well, since they're from Arizona, I dare say they don't know rainclouds from any other kind."

Lillian came back into the living room with a patter of high heels. "From where?"

"From Arizona, according to Tommie."

"How did Tommie know?"

"He talked to their boy, in between ball chucks, I guess, and he told Tommie they came from Arizona and then the boy was called in. At least, Tommie says it might have been Arizona, or maybe Alabama or some place like that. You know Tommie and his nontotal recall. But if they're that nervous about the weather, I guess it's Arizona and they don't know what to make of a good rainy climate like ours."

"But why didn't you ever tell me?"

"Because Tommie only told me this morning and because I thought he must have told you already and, to tell the absolute truth, because I thought you could just manage to drag out a normal existence even if you never found out. Wow—"

The ball went sailing into the right field stands and that was that for the pitcher.

Lillian went back to the venetian blinds and said, "I'll simply just have to make her acquaintance. She looks *very* nice. —Oh, Lord, look at that, George."

George was looking at nothing but the TV.

Lillian said, "I know she's staring at that cloud. And now she'll be going in. Honestly."

George was out two days later on a reference search in the library and came home with a load of books. Lillian greeted him jubilantly.

She said, "Now, you're not doing anything tomorrow."

"That sounds like a statement, not a question."

"It is a statement. We're going out with the Sakkaros to Murphy's Park."

"With—"

"With the next-door neighbors, George. *How* can you never remember the name?"

"I'm gifted. How did it happen?"

"I just went up to their house this morning and rang the bell."

"That easy?"

"It wasn't easy. It was hard. I stood there, jittering, with my finger on the doorbell, till I thought that ringing the bell would be easier than having the door open and being caught standing there like a fool."

"And she didn't kick you out?"

"No. She was sweet as she could be. Invited me in, knew who I was, said she was so glad I had come to visit. *You* know."

"And you suggested we go to Murphy's Park."

"Yes. I thought if I suggested something that would let the children have fun, it would be easier for her to go along with it. She wouldn't want to spoil a chance for her boy."

"A mother's psychology."

"But you should see her home."

"Ah. You had a reason for all this. It comes out. You wanted the Cook's tour. But, please, spare me the color-scheme details. I'm not interested in the bedspreads, and the size of the closets is a topic with which I can dispense."

It was the secret of their happy marriage that Lillian paid no attention to George. She went into the color-scheme details, was most meticulous about the bedspreads, and gave him an inch-by-inch description of closet-size.

"And *clean?* I have never seen any place so spotless."

"If you get to know her, then, she'll be setting you impossible standards and you'll have to drop her in self-defense."

"Her kitchen," said Lillian, ignoring him, "was so spanking clean you just couldn't believe she ever used it. I asked for a drink of water and she held the glass underneath the tap and poured slowly so that not one drop fell in the sink itself. It wasn't affectation. She did it so casually that I just knew she always did it that way. And when she gave me the glass she held it with a clean napkin. Just hospital-sanitary."

"She must be a lot of trouble to herself. Did she agree to come with us right off?"

"Well—not right off. She called to her husband about what the weather forecast was, and he said that the newspapers all said it would be fair tomorrow but that he was waiting for the latest report on the radio."

"*All* the newspapers said so, eh?"

"Of course, they all just print the official weather forecast, so they would all agree. But I think they do subscribe to all the newspapers. At least I've watched the bundle the newsboy leaves—"

"There isn't much you miss, is there?"

"Anyway," said Lillian severely, "she called up the weather bureau and had them tell her the latest and she called it out to her husband and they said they'd go, except they said they'd phone us if there were any unexpected changes in the weather."

"All right. Then we'll go."

The Sakkaros were young and pleasant, dark and handsome. In fact, as they came down the long walk from their home to where the Wright automobile was parked, George leaned toward his wife and breathed into her ear, "So *he's* the reason."

"I wish he were," said Lillian. "Is that a handbag he's carrying?"

"Pocket-radio. To listen to weather forecasts, I bet."

The Sakkaro boy came running after them, waving something which turned out to be an aneroid barometer, and all three got into the back seat. Conversation was turned on and lasted, with neat give-and-take on impersonal subjects, to Murphy's Park.

The Sakkaro boy was so polite and reasonable that even Tommie Wright, wedged between his parents in the front seat, was subdued by example into a semblance of civilization. Lillian couldn't recall when she had spent so serenely pleasant a drive.

She was not the least disturbed by the fact that, barely to be heard under the flow of the conversation, Mr. Sakkaro's small radio was on, and she never actually saw him put it occasionally to his ear.

It was a beautiful day at Murphy's Park; hot and dry without being too hot; and with a cheerfully bright sun in a blue, blue sky. Even Mr. Sakkaro, though he inspected every quarter of the heavens with a careful eye and then stared piercingly at the barometer, seemed to have no fault to find.

Lillian ushered the two boys to the amusement section and bought enough tickets to allow one ride for each on every variety of centrifugal thrill that the park offered.

"Please," she had said to a protesting Mrs. Sakkaro, "let this be my treat. I'll let you have your turn next time."

When she returned, George was alone. "Where—" she began.

"Just down there at the refreshment stand. I told them I'd wait here for you and we would join them." He sounded gloomy.

"Anything wrong?"

"No, not really, except that I think he must be independently wealthy."

"What?"

"I don't know what he does for a living. I hinted—"

"Now who's curious?"

"I was doing it for you. He said he's just a student of human nature."

"How philosophical. That would explain all those newspapers."

"Yes, but with a handsome, wealthy man next door, it looks as though I'll have impossible standards set for me, too."

"Don't be silly."

"And he doesn't come from Arizona."

"He doesn't?"

"I said I heard he was from Arizona. He looked so surprised, it was obvious he didn't. Then he laughed and asked if he had an Arizona accent."

Lillian said thoughtfully, "He has some kind of accent, you know. There are lots of Spanish-ancestry people in the Southwest, so he could still be from Arizona. Sakkaro could be a Spanish name."

"Sounds Japanese to me. —Come on, they're waving. Oh, good Lord, look what they've bought."

The Sakkaros were each holding three sticks of cotton candy, huge swirls of pink foam consisting of threads of sugar dried out of frothy syrup that had been whipped about in a warm vessel. It melted sweetly in the mouth and left one feeling sticky.

The Sakkaros held one out to each Wright, and out of politeness the Wrights accepted.

They went down the midway, tried their hand at darts, at the kind of poker game where balls were rolled into holes, at knocking wooden cylinders off pedestals. They took pictures of themselves and recorded their voices and tested the strength of their handgrips.

Eventually they collected the youngsters, who had been reduced to a satisfactorily breathless state of roiled-up insides, and the Sakkaros ushered theirs off instantly to the refreshment stand. Tommie hinted the extent of his pleasure at the possible purchase of a hot-dog and George tossed him a quarter. He ran off, too.

"Frankly," said George, "I prefer to stay here. If I see them biting away at another cotton candy stick I'll turn green and sicken on the spot. If they haven't had a dozen apiece, I'll eat a dozen myself."

"I know, and they're buying a handful for the child now."

"I offered to stand Sakkaro a hamburger and he just looked grim and shook his head. Not that a hamburger's much, but after enough cotton candy, it ought to be a feast."

"I know. I offered her an orange drink and the way she jumped when she said no, you'd think I'd thrown it in her face. —Still, I suppose they've never been to a place like this before and they'll need time to adjust to the novelty. They'll fill up on cotton candy and then never eat it again for ten years."

"Well, maybe." They strolled toward the Sakkaros. "You know, Lil, it's clouding up."

Mr. Sakkaro had the radio to his ear and was looking anxiously toward the west.

"Uh-oh," said George, "he's seen it. One gets you fifty, he'll want to go home."

All three Sakkaros were upon him, polite but insistent. They were sorry, they had had a wonderful time, a marvelous time, the Wrights would have to be their guests as soon as it could be managed, but now, really, they had to go home. It looked stormy. Mrs. Sakkaro wailed that all the forecasts had been for fair weather.

George tried to console them. "It's hard to predict a local thunderstorm, but even if it were to come, and it mightn't, it wouldn't last more than half an hour on the outside."

At which comment, the Sakkaro youngster seemed on the verge of tears, and Mrs. Sakkaro's hand, holding a handkerchief, trembled visibly.

"Let's go home," said George in resignation.

The drive back seemed to stretch interminably. There was no conversation to speak of. Mr. Sakkaro's radio was quite loud now as he switched from station to station, catching a weather report every time. They were mentioning "local thundershowers" now.

The Sakkaro youngster piped up that the barometer was falling, and Mrs. Sakkaro, chin in the palm of her hand, stared dolefully at the sky and asked if George could not drive faster, please.

"It does look rather threatening, doesn't it?" said Lillian in a polite attempt to share their guests' attitude. But then George heard her mutter, "Honestly!" under her breath.

A wind had sprung up, driving the dust of the weeks-dry road before it, when they entered the street on which they lived, and the leaves rustled ominously. Lightning flickered.

George said, "You'll be indoors in two minutes, friends. We'll make it."

He pulled up at the gate that opened onto the Sakkaro's spacious front yard and got out of the car to open the back door. He thought he felt a drop. They were *just* in time.

The Sakkaros tumbled out, faces drawn with tension, muttering thanks, and started off toward their long front walk at a dead run.

"Honestly," began Lillian, "you would think they were—"

The heavens opened and the rain came down in giant drops as though some celestial dam had suddenly burst. The top of their car was pounded with a hundred drum sticks, and halfway to their front door the Sakkaros stopped and looked despairingly upward.

Their faces blurred as the rain hit; blurred and shrank and ran together. All three shriveled, collapsing within their clothes, which sank down into three sticky-wet heaps.

And while the Wrights sat there, transfixed with horror, Lillian found herself unable to stop the completion of her remark: "—made of sugar and afraid they would melt."

Star Light

Arthur Trent heard them quite clearly. The tense, angry words shot out of his receiver.

"Trent! You can't get away. We will intersect your orbit in two hours and if you try to resist we will blow you out of space."

Trent smiled and said nothing. He had no weapons and no need to fight. In far less than two hours the ship would make its Jump through hyperspace and they would never find him. He would have with him nearly a kilogram of Krillium, enough for the construction of the brain-paths of thousands of robots and worth some ten million credits on any world in the Galaxy—and no questions asked.

Old Brennmeyer had planned the whole thing. He had planned it for thirty years and more. It had been his life's work.

"It's the getaway, young man," he had said. "That's why I need you. You can lift a ship off the ground and out into space. I can't."

"Getting it into space is no good, Mr. Brennmeyer," Trent said. "We'll be caught in half a day."

"Not," said Brennmeyer craftily, "if we make the Jump. Not if we flash through hyperspace and end up light-years away."

"It would take half a day to plot the Jump and even if we could take the time, the police would alert all stellar systems."

"No, Trent, no." The old man's hand fell on his, clutching it in trembling excitement. "Not *all* stellar systems; only the dozen in our neighborhood.

The Galaxy is big and the colonists of the last fifty thousand years have lost touch with each other."

He talked avidly, painting the picture. The Galaxy now was like the surface of man's original planet—Earth, they had called it—in prehistoric times. Man had been scattered over all the continents but each group had known only the area immediately surrounding itself.

"If we make the Jump at random," Brennmeyer said, "we would be anywhere, even fifty thousand light-years away, and there would be no more chance of finding us than of finding a pebble in a meteor swarm."

Trent shook his head. "And we don't find ourselves, either. We wouldn't have the foggiest way of getting to an inhabited planet."

Brennmeyer's quick-moving eyes inspected the surroundings. No one was near him, but his voice sank to a whisper anyway. "I've spent thirty years collecting data on every habitable planet in the Galaxy. I've searched all the old records. I've traveled thousands of light-years, farther than any space pilot. And the location of every habitable planet is now in the memory store of the best computer in the world."

Trent lifted his eyebrows politely.

Brennmeyer said, "I design computers and I have the best. I've also plotted the exact location of every luminous star in the Galaxy, every star of spectral class of F, B, A, and O, and put that into the memory store. Once we've made the Jump the computer will scan the heavens spectroscopically and compare the results with the map of the Galaxy it contains. Once it finds the proper match, and sooner or later it will, the ship is located in space and it is then automatically guided through a second Jump to the neighborhood of the nearest inhabited planet."

"Sounds too complicated."

"It can't miss. All these years I've worked on it and it can't miss. I'll have ten years left yet to be a millionaire. But you're young; you'll be a millionaire much longer."

"When you Jump at random, you can end inside a star."

"Not one chance in a hundred trillion, Trent. We might also land so far from any luminous star that the computer can't find anything to match up against its program. We might find we've jumped only a light-year or two and the police are still on our trail. The chances of that are smaller still. If you want to worry, worry that you might die of a heart attack at the moment of takeoff. The chances for that are much higher."

"*You* might, Mr. Brennmeyer. You're older."

The old man shrugged. "I don't count. The computer will do everything automatically."

Trent nodded and remembered that. One midnight, when the ship was ready and Brennmeyer arrived with the Krillium in a briefcase—he had no difficulty for he was a greatly trusted man—Trent took the briefcase with one hand while his other moved quickly and surely.

A knife was still the best, just as quick as a molecular depolarizer, just as fatal, and much more quiet. Trent left the knife there with the body, complete with fingerprints. What was the difference? They wouldn't get him.

Deep in space now, with the police cruisers in pursuit, he felt the gathering tension that always preceded a Jump. No physiologist could explain it, but every space-wise pilot knew what it felt like.

There was a momentary inside-out feeling as his ship and himself for one moment of non-space and non-time, became non-matter and non-energy, then reassembled itself instantaneously in another part of the Galaxy.

Trent smiled. He was still alive. No star was too close and there were thousands that were close enough. The sky was alive with stars and the pattern was so different that he knew the Jump had gone far. Some of those stars had to be spectral class F and better. The computer would have a nice rich pattern to match against its memory. It shouldn't take long.

He leaned back in comfort and watched the bright pattern of star light move as the ship rotated slowly. A bright star came into view, a really bright one. It didn't seem more than a couple of light-years away and his pilot's sense told him it was a hot one, good and hot. The computer would use that as its base and match the pattern centered about it. Once again he thought: It shouldn't take long.

But it did. The minutes passed. Then an hour. And still the computer clicked busily and its lights flashed.

Trent frowned. Why didn't it find the pattern? The pattern had to be there. Brennmeyer had showed him his long years of work. He *couldn't* have left out a star or recorded it in the wrong place.

Surely stars were born and died and moved through space while in being, but these changes were slow, slow. In a million years the patterns that Brennmeyer had recorded couldn't—

A sudden panic clutched at Trent. No! It *couldn't* be. The chances for it were even smaller than Jumping into a star's interior.

He waited for the bright star to come into view again and, with trembling hands, brought it into telescopic focus. He put in all the magnification he could, and around the bright speck of light was the telltale fog of turbulent gases caught, as it were, in mid-flight.

It was a nova!

From dim obscurity the star had raised itself to bright luminosity, perhaps only a month ago. It had graduated from a spectral class low enough to be ignored by the computer, to one that would be most certainly taken into account.

But the nova that existed in space didn't exist in the computer's memory store because Brennmeyer had not put it there. It had not existed when Brennmeyer was collecting his data—at least not as a brightly luminous star.

"Don't count it," shrieked Trent. "Ignore it!"

But he was shouting at automatic machinery that would match the nova-centered pattern against the Galactic pattern and find it nowhere and continue, nevertheless, to match and match and match for as long as its energy supply held out.

The air supply would run out much sooner. Trent's life would ebb away much sooner.

Helplessly Trent slumped in his chair, watching the mocking pattern of star light and beginning the long and agonized wait for death.

If he had only kept the knife . . .

Founding Father

The original combination of catastrophes had taken place five years ago—five revolutions of this planet, HC-12549d by the charts, and nameless otherwise. Six-plus revolutions of Earth, but who was counting—anymore?

If the men back home knew, they might say it was a heroic fight, an epic of the Galactic Corps; five men against a hostile world, holding their bitter own for five (or six-plus) years. And now they were dying, the battle lost after all. Three were in final coma, a fourth had his yellow-tinged eyeballs still open, and a fifth was yet on his feet.

But it was no question of heroism at all. It had been five men fighting off boredom and despair and maintaining their metallic bubble of livability only for the most unheroic reason that there was nothing else to do while life remained.

If any of them felt stimulated by the battle, he never mentioned it. After the first year they stopped talking of rescue, and after the second a moratorium descended on the word "Earth."

But one word remained always present. If unspoken it had to be found in their thoughts: "ammonia."

It had come first while the landing was being scratched out, against all odds, on limping motors and in a battered space can.

You allow for bad breaks, of course; you expect a certain number—but one at a time. A stellar flare fries out the hypercircuits—that can be repaired, given time. A meteorite disaligns the feeder valves—they can be straightened, given time. A trajectory is miscalculated under tension and a momentarily unbearable acceleration tears out the Jump-antennae and dulls the senses of every man on board—but antennae can be replaced and senses will recover, given time.

The chances are one in countless many that all three will happen at once; and still less that they will all happen during a particularly tricky landing when the one necessary currency for the correction of all errors, time, is the one thing that is most lacking.

The *Cruiser John* hit that one chance in countless many, and it made a final landing, for it would never lift off a planetary surface again.

That it had landed essentially intact was itself a near-miracle. The five were given life for some years at least. Beyond that, only the blundering arrival of another ship could help, but no one expected that. They had had their life's share of coincidences, they knew, and all had been bad.

That was that.

And the key word was "ammonia." With the surface spiraling upward, and death (mercifully quick) facing them at considerably better than even odds, Chou somehow had time to note the absorption spectrograph, which was registering raggedly.

"Ammonia," he cried out. The others heard but there was no time to pay attention. There was only the wrenching fight against a quick death for the sake of a slow one.

When they landed finally, on sandy ground with sparse bluish (bluish?) vegetation; reedy grass; stunted treelike objects with blue bark and no leaves; no sign of animal life; and with a greenish (greenish?) cloud-streaked sky above—the word came back to haunt them.

"Ammonia?" said Petersen heavily.

Chou said, "Four per cent."

"Impossible," said Petersen.

But it wasn't. The books didn't say impossible. What the Galactic Corps had discovered was that a planet of a certain mass and volume and a certain temperature was an ocean planet and had one of two atmospheres: nitrogen/oxygen or nitrogen/carbon dioxide. In the former case, life was advanced; in the latter, it was primitive.

No one checked beyond mass, volume, and temperature any longer. One took the atmosphere (one or the other of them) for granted. But the books didn't say it had to be so; just that it always was so. Other atmospheres were thermodynamically possible, but extremely unlikely, so they weren't found in actual practice.

Until now. The men of the *Cruiser John* had found one and were bathed for the rest of such life as they could eke out by a nitrogen/carbon dioxide/ammonia atmosphere.

The men converted their ship into an underground bubble of Earth-type surroundings. They could not lift off the surface, nor could they drive a communicating beam through hyperspace, but all else was salvageable. To make up for inefficiencies in the cycling system, they could even tap the planet's own water and air supply, within limits; provided, of course, they subtracted the ammonia.

They organized exploring parties since their suits were in excellent condition and it passed the time. The planet was harmless; no animal life; sparse plant life everywhere. Blue, always blue; ammoniated chlorophyll; ammoniated protein.

They set up laboratories, analyzed the plant components, studied microscopic sections, compiled vast volumes of findings. They tried growing native plants in ammonia-free atmosphere and failed. They made themselves into geologists and studied the planet's crust; astronomers, and studied the spectrum of the planet's sun.

Barrère would say sometimes, "Eventually, the Corps will reach this planet again and we'll leave a legacy of knowledge for them. It's a unique planet after all. There might not be another Earth-type with ammonia in all the Milky Way."

"Great," said Sandropoulos bitterly. "What luck for us."

Sandropoulos worked out the thermodynamics of the situation. "A metastable system," he said. "The ammonia disappears steadily through geochemical oxidation that forms nitrogen; the plants utilize nitrogen and re-form ammonia, adapting themselves to the presence of ammonia. If the rate of plant formation of ammonia dropped two per cent, a declining spiral would set in. Plant life would wither, reducing the ammonia still further, and so on."

"You mean if we killed enough plant life," said Vlassov, "we could wipe out the ammonia."

"If we had air sleds and wide-angle blasters, and a year to work in, we might," said Sandropoulos, "but we haven't and there's a better way. If we could get our own plants going, the formation of oxygen through photosynthesis would increase the rate of ammonia oxidation. Even a small localized rise would lower the ammonia in the region, stimulate Earth-plant growth further and inhibit the native growth, drop the ammonia further, and so on."

They became gardeners through all the growing season. That was, after all, routine for the Galactic Corps. Life on Earth-type planets was usually of the water/protein type, but variation was infinite and other-world food was rarely nourishing and even more rarely palatable. One had to try Earth plants of different sorts. It often happened (not always, but often) that some types of Earth plants would overrun and drown out the native flora. With the native flora held down, other Earth plants could take root.

Dozens of planets had been converted into new Earths in this fashion. In the process Earthly plants developed hundreds of hardy varieties that flourished under extreme conditions. —All the better with which to seed the next planet.

The ammonia would kill any Earth plant, but the seeds at the disposal of the *Cruiser John* were not true Earth plants but otherworld mutations of these plants. They fought hard but not well enough. Some varieties grew in a feeble, sickly manner and then died.

At that they did better than did microscopic life. The planet's bacterioids were far more flourishing than was the planet's straggly blue plant life. The native micro-organisms drowned out any attempt at competition from Earth samples. The attempt to seed the alien soil with Earth-type bacterial flora in order to aid the Earth plants failed.

Vlassov shook his head. "It wouldn't do anyway. If our bacteria survived, it would only be by adapting to the presence of ammonia."

Sandropoulos said, "Bacteria won't help us. We need the plants; they carry the oxygen-manufacturing systems."

"We could make some ourselves," said Petersen. "We could electrolyze water."

"How long will our equipment last? If we could only get our plants going, it would be like electrolyzing water forever, little by little, but year after year, till the planet gave up."

Barrère said, "Let's treat the soil then. It's rotten with ammonium salts. We'll bake the salts out and replace the ammonia-free soil."

"And what about the atmosphere?" asked Chou.

"In ammonia-free soil, they may catch hold despite the atmosphere. They almost make it as is."

They worked like longshoremen, but with no real end in view. None really thought it would work, and there was no future for themselves, personally, even if it did work. But working passed the days.

The next growing season, they had their ammonia-free soil, but Earth plants still grew only feebly. They even placed domes over several shoots and pumped ammonia-free air within. It helped slightly but not enough. They adjusted the chemical composition of the soil in every possible fashion. There was no reward.

The feeble shoots produced their tiny whiffs of oxygen, but not enough to topple the ammonia atmosphere off its narrow base.

"One more push," said Sandropoulos, "one more. We're rocking it; we're rocking it; but we can't knock it over."

Their tools and equipment blunted and wore out with time and the future closed in steadily. Each month there was less room for maneuver.

When the end came at last it was with almost gratifying suddenness. There was no name to place on the weakness and vertigo. No one actually suspected direct ammonia poisoning. Still, they were living off the algal growths of what had once been ship-hydroponics for years, and the growths were themselves aberrant with possible ammonia contamination.

It could have been the workings of some native microorganism which might finally have learned to feed off them. It might even have been an Earthly micro-organism, mutated under the conditions of a strange world.

So three died at last, and did so, circumstances be praised, painlessly. They were glad to go, and leave the useless fight.

Chou said in a voiceless whisper, "It's foolish to lose so badly."

Petersen, alone of the five to be on his feet (was he immune, whatever it was?) turned a grieving face toward his only living companion. "Don't die," he said, "don't leave me alone."

Chou tried to smile. "I have no choice. —But you can follow us, old friend. Why fight? The tools are gone and there is no way of winning now, if there ever was."

Even now, Petersen fought off final despair by concentrating on the fight against the atmosphere. But his mind was weary, his heart worn-out, and when Chou died the next hour he was left with four corpses to work with.

He stared at the bodies, counting over the memories, stretching them back (now that he was alone and dared wail) to Earth itself, which he had last seen on a visit nearly eleven years before.

He would have to bury the bodies. He would break off the bluish branches of the native leafless trees and build crosses of them. He would hang the space helmet of each man on top and prop the oxygen cylinders below. Empty cylinders to symbolize the lost fight.

A foolish sentiment for men who could no longer care, and for future eyes that might never see.

But he was doing it for himself, to show respect for his friends, and respect for himself, too, for he was not the kind of man to leave his friends untended in death while he himself could stand.

Besides—

Besides? He sat in weary thought for some moments.

While he was still alive he would fight with such tools as were left. He would bury his friends.

He buried each in a spot of ammonia-free soil they had so laboriously built up; buried them without shroud and without clothing; leaving them naked in the hostile ground for the slow decomposition that would come with their own micro-organisms before those, too, died with the inevitable invasion of the native bacterioids.

Petersen placed each cross, with its helmet and oxygen cylinders, propped each with rocks, then turned away, grim and sad-eyed, to return to the buried ship that he now inhabited alone.

He worked each day and eventually the symptoms came for him, too.

He struggled into his spacesuit and came to the surface for what he knew would be one last time.

He fell to his knees on the garden plots. The Earth plants were green. They had lived longer than ever before. They looked healthy, even vigorous.

They had patched the soil, babied the atmosphere, and now Petersen had used the last tool, the only one remaining at his disposal, and he had given them fertilizer as well—

Out of the slowly corrupting flesh of the Earthmen came the nutrients that supplied the final push. Out of the Earth plants came the oxygen that would beat back the ammonia and push the planet out of the unaccountable niche into which it had stuck.

If Earthmen ever came again (when? a million years hence?) they would find a nitrogen/oxygen atmosphere and a limited flora strangely reminiscent of Earth's.

The crosses would rot and decay; the metal, rust and decompose. The bones might fossilize and remain to give a hint as to what happened. Their own records, sealed away, might be found.

But none of that mattered. If nothing at all was ever found, the planet itself, the whole planet, would be their monument.

And Petersen lay down to die amid their victory.

The Key

Karl Jennings knew he was going to die. He had a matter of hours to live and much to do.

There was no reprieve from the death sentence, not here on the Moon, not with no communications in operation.

Even on Earth there were a few fugitive patches where, without radio handy, a man might die without the hand of his fellow man to help him, without the heart of his fellow man to pity him, without even the eye of his fellow man to discover the corpse. Here on the Moon, there were few spots that were otherwise.

Earthmen knew he was on the Moon, of course. He had been part of a geological expedition—no, selenological expedition! Odd, how his Earth-centered mind insisted on the "geo-."

Wearily he drove himself to think, even as he worked. Dying though he was, he still felt that artificially imposed clarity of thought. Anxiously he looked about. There was nothing to see. He was in the dark of the eternal shadow of the northern interior of the wall of the crater, a blackness relieved only by the intermittent blink of his flash. He kept that intermittent, partly because he dared not consume its power source before he was through and partly because he dared not take more than the minimum chance that it be seen.

On his left hand, toward the south along the nearby horizon of the Moon, was a crescent of bright white Sunlight. Beyond the horizon, and invisible, was the opposite lip of the crater. The Sun never peered high enough over the lip of his own edge of the crater to illuminate the floor immediately beneath his feet. He was safe from radiation—from that at least.

He dug carefully but clumsily, swathed as he was in his spacesuit. His side ached abominably.

The dust and broken rock did not take up the "fairy castle" appearance characteristic of those portions of the Moon's surface exposed to the alternation of light and dark, heat and cold. Here, in eternal cold, the slow crumbling of the crater wall had simply piled fine rubble in a heterogeneous mass. It would not be easy to tell there had been digging going on.

He misjudged the unevenness of the dark surface for a moment and spilled a cupped handful of dusty fragments. The particles dropped with the slowness characteristic of the Moon and yet with the appearance of a blinding speed, for there was no air resistance to slow them further still and spread them out into a dusty haze.

Jennings' flash brightened for a moment, and he kicked a jagged rock out of the way.

He hadn't much time. He dug deeper into the dust.

A little deeper and he could push the Device into the depression and begin covering it. Strauss must not find it.

Strauss!

The other member of the team. Half-share in the discovery. Half-share in the renown.

If it were merely the whole share of the credit that Strauss had wanted, Jennings might have allowed it. The discovery was more important than any individual credit that might go with it. But what Strauss wanted was something far more, something Jennings would fight to prevent.

One of the few things Jennings was willing to die to prevent.

And he was dying.

They had found it together. Actually, Strauss had found the ship; or, better, the remains of the ship; or, better still, what just conceivably might have been the remains of something analogous to a ship.

"Metal," said Strauss, as he picked up something ragged and nearly amorphous. His eyes and face could just barely be seen through the thick lead glass of the visor, but his rather harsh voice sounded clearly enough through the suit radio.

Jennings came drifting over from his own position half a mile away. He said, "Odd! There is no free metal on the Moon."

"There shouldn't be. But you know well enough they haven't explored more than one percent of the Moon's surface. Who knows what can be found on it?"

Jennings grunted assent and reached out his gauntlet to take the object.

It was true enough that almost anything might be found on the Moon for all anyone really knew. Theirs was the first privately financed selenographic expedition ever to land on the Moon. Till then, there had been only government-conducted shotgun affairs, with half a dozen ends in view. It was a sign of the advancing space age that the Geological Society could afford to send two men to the Moon for selenological studies only.

Strauss said, "It looks as though it once had a polished surface."

"You're right," said Jennings. "Maybe there's more about."

They found three more pieces, two of trifling size and one a jagged object that showed traces of a seam.

"Let's take them to the ship," said Strauss.

They took the small skim boat back to the mother ship. They shucked their suits once on board, something Jennings at least was always glad to do. He scratched vigorously at his ribs and rubbed his cheeks till his light skin reddened into welts.

Strauss eschewed such weakness and got to work. The laser beam pock-marked the metal and the vapor recorded itself on the spectrograph. Titanium-steel, essentially, with a hint of cobalt and molybdenum.

"That's artificial, all right," said Strauss. His broad-boned face was as dour and as hard as ever. He showed no elation, although Jennings could feel his own heart begin to race.

It may have been the excitement that trapped Jennings into beginning, "This is a development against which we must steel ourselves—" with a faint stress on "steel" to indicate the play on words.

Strauss, however, looked at Jennings with an icy distaste, and the attempted set of puns was choked off.

Jennings sighed. He could never swing it, somehow. Never could! He remembered at the University— Well, never mind. The discovery they had made was worth a far better pun than any he could construct for all Strauss's calmness.

Jennings wondered if Strauss could possibly miss the significance.

He knew very little about Strauss, as a matter of fact, except by selenological reputation. That is, he had read Strauss's papers and he presumed Strauss had read his. Although their ships might well have passed by night in their University days, they had never happened to meet until after both had volunteered for this expedition and had been accepted.

In the week's voyage, Jennings had grown uncomfortably aware of the other's stocky figure, his sandy hair and china-blue eyes, and the way the muscles over his prominent jawbones worked when he ate. Jennings, himself, much slighter in build, also blue-eyed, but with darker hair, tended to withdraw automatically from the heavy exudation of the other's power and drive.

Jennings said, "There's no record of any ship ever having landed on this part of the Moon. Certainly none has crashed."

"If it were part of a ship," said Strauss, "it should be smooth and polished. This is eroded and, without an atmosphere here, that means exposure to micrometeor bombardment over many years."

Then he *did* see the significance. Jennings said, with an almost savage jubilation, "It's a non-human artifact. Creatures not of Earth once visited the Moon. Who knows how long ago?"

"Who knows?" agreed Strauss dryly.

"In the report—"

"Wait," said Strauss imperiously. "Time enough to report when we have something to report. If it was a ship, there will be more to it than what we now have."

But there was no point in looking further just then. They had been at it for hours, and the next meal and sleep were overdue. Better to tackle the whole job fresh and spend hours at it. They seemed to agree on that without speaking.

The Earth was low on the eastern horizon, almost full in phase, bright and blue-streaked. Jennings looked at it while they ate and experienced, as he always did, a sharp homesickness.

"It looks peaceful enough," he said, "but there are six billion people busy on it."

Strauss looked up from some deep inner life of his own and said, "Six billion people ruining it!"

Jennings frowned. "You're not an Ultra, are you?"

Strauss said, "What the hell are you talking about?"

Jennings felt himself flush. A flush always showed against his fair skin, turning it pink at the slightest upset of the even tenor of his emotions. He found it intensely embarrassing.

He turned back to his food, without saying anything.

For a whole generation now, the Earth's population had held steady. No further increase could be afforded. Everyone admitted that. There were those, in fact, who said that "no higher" wasn't enough; the population had to drop. Jennings himself sympathized with that point of view. The globe of the Earth was being eaten alive by its heavy freight of humanity.

But *how* was the population to be made to drop? Randomly, by encouraging the people to lower the birth rate still further, as and how they wished? Lately there had been the slow rise of a distant rumble which wanted not only a population drop but a selected drop—the survival of the fittest, with the self-declared fit choosing the criteria of fitness.

Jennings thought: I've insulted him, I suppose.

Later, when he was almost asleep, it suddenly occurred to him that he knew virtually nothing of Strauss's character. What if it were his intention to go out now on a foraging expedition of his own so that he might get sole credit for—?

He raised himself on his elbow in alarm, but Strauss was breathing heavily, and even as Jennings listened, the breathing grew into the characteristic burr of a snore.

·   ·   ·   ·   ·

They spent the next three days in a single-minded search for additional pieces. They found some. They found more than that. They found an area glowing with the tiny phosphorescence of Lunar bacteria. Such bacteria were common enough, but nowhere previously had their occurrence been reported in concentration so great as to cause a visible glow.

Strauss said, "An organic being, or his remains, may have been here once. He died, but the micro-organisms within him did not. In the end they consumed him."

"And spread perhaps," added Jennings. "That may be the source of Lunar bacteria generally. They may not be native at all but may be the result of contamination instead—eons ago."

"It works the other way, too," said Strauss. "Since the bacteria are completely different in very fundamental ways from any Earthly form of micro-organism, the creatures they parasitized—assuming this was their source— must have been fundamentally different too. Another indication of extraterrestrial origin."

The trail ended in the wall of a small crater.

"It's a major digging job," said Jennings, his heart sinking. "We had better report this and get help."

"No," said Strauss somberly. "There may be nothing to get help for. The crater might have formed a million years after the ship had crash-landed."

"And vaporized most of it, you mean, and left only what we've found?"

Strauss nodded.

Jennings said, "Let's try anyway. We can dig a bit. If we draw a line through the finds we've made so far and just keep on . . ."

Strauss was reluctant and worked halfheartedly, so that it was Jennings who made the real find. Surely that counted! Even though Strauss had found the first piece of metal, Jennings had found the artifact itself.

It *was* an artifact—cradled three feet underground under the irregular shape of a boulder which had fallen in such a way that it left a hollow in its contact with the Moon's surface. In that hollow lay the artifact, protected from everything for a million years or more; protected from radiation, from micrometeors, from temperature change, so that it remained fresh and new forever.

Jennings labeled it at once the Device. It looked not remotely similar to any instrument either had ever seen, but then, as Jennings said, why should it?

"There are no rough edges that I can see," he said. "It may not be broken."

"There may be missing parts, though."

"Maybe," said Jennings, "but there seems to be nothing movable. It's all one piece and certainly oddly uneven." He noted his own play on words, then went on with a not-altogether-successful attempt at self-control. *"This* is what we need. A piece of worn metal or an area rich in bacteria is only material for deduction and dispute. But this is the real thing—a Device that is clearly of extraterrestrial manufacture."

It was on the table between them now, and both regarded it gravely.

Jennings said, "Let's put through a preliminary report, now."

"No!" said Strauss, in sharp and strenuous dissent. "Hell, no!"

"Why not?"

"Because if we do, it becomes a Society project. They'll swarm all over it and we won't be as much as a footnote when all is done. No!" Strauss looked almost sly. "Let's do all we can with it and get as much out of it as possible before the harpies descend."

Jennings thought about it. He couldn't deny that he too wanted to make certain that no credit was lost. But still—

He said, "I don't know that I like to take the chance, Strauss." For the first time he had an impulse to use the man's first name, but fought it off. "Look, Strauss," he said, "it's not right to wait. If this is of extraterrestrial origin, then it must be from some other planetary system. There isn't a place in the Solar System, outside the Earth, that can possibly support an advanced life form."

"Not proven, really," grunted Strauss, "but what if you're right?"

"Then it would mean that the creatures of the ship had interstellar travel and therefore had to be far in advance, technologically, of ourselves. Who knows what the Device can tell us about their advanced technology? It might be the key to—who knows what? It might be the clue to an unimaginable scientific revolution."

"That's romantic nonsense. If this is the product of a technology far advanced over ours, we'll learn nothing from it. Bring Einstein back to life and show him a microprotowarp and what would he make of it?"

"We can't be certain that we won't learn."

"So what, even so? What if there's a small delay? What if we assure credit for ourselves? What if we make sure that we ourselves go along with this, that we don't let go of it?"

"But Strauss"—Jennings felt himself moved almost to tears in his anxiety to get across his sense of the importance of the Device—"what if we crash with it? What if we don't make it back to Earth? We can't risk this thing." He tapped it then, almost as though he were in love with it. "We should report it now and have them send ships out here to get it. It's too precious to—"

At the peak of his emotional intensity, the Device seemed to grow warm under his hand. A portion of its surface, half-hidden under a flap of metal, glowed phosphorescently.

Jennings jerked his hand away in a spasmodic gesture and the Device darkened. But it was enough; the moment had been infinitely revealing.

He said, almost choking, "It was like a window opening into your skull. I could see into your mind."

"I read yours," said Strauss, "or experienced it, or entered into it, or whatever you choose." He touched the Device in his cold, withdrawn way, but nothing happened.

"You're an Ultra," said Jennings angrily. "When I touched this"—And he did so. "It's happening again. I see it. Are you a madman? Can you honestly believe it is humanly decent to condemn almost all the human race to extinction and destroy the versatility and variety of the species?"

His hand dropped away from the Device again, in repugnance at the glimpses revealed, and it grew dark again. Once more, Strauss touched it gingerly and again nothing happened.

Strauss said, "Let's not start a discussion, for God's sake. This thing is an aid to communication—a telepathic amplifier. Why not? The brain cells have each their electric potentials. Thought can be viewed as a wavering electromagnetic field of microintensities—"

Jennings turned away. He didn't want to speak to Strauss. He said, "We'll report it now. I don't give a damn about credit. Take it all. I just want it out of our hands."

For a moment Strauss remained in a brown study. Then he said, "It's more than a communicator. It responds to emotion and it amplifies emotion."

"What are you talking about?"

"Twice it started at your touch just now, although you'd been handling it all day with no effect. It still has no effect when I touch it."

"Well?"

"It reacted to you when you were in a state of high emotional tension. That's the requirement for activation, I suppose. And when you raved about the Ultras while you were holding it just now, I felt as you did, for just a moment."

"So you should."

"But, listen to me. Are you sure *you're* so right? There isn't a thinking man on Earth that doesn't know the planet would be better off with a population of one billion rather than six billion. If we used automation to the full—as now the hordes won't allow us to do—we could probably have a completely efficient and viable Earth with a population of no more than, say, five million. Listen to me, Jennings. Don't turn away, man."

The harshness in Strauss's voice almost vanished in his effort to be reasonably winning. "But we can't reduce the population democratically. You know that. It isn't the sex urge, because uterine inserts solved the birth control problem long ago; you know that. It's a matter of nationalism. Each ethnic group wants other groups to reduce themselves in population first, and I agree with them. I want my ethnic group, *our* ethnic group, to prevail. I want the Earth to be inherited by the elite, which means by men like ourselves. We're the true men, and the horde of half-apes who hold us down are destroying us all. They're doomed to death anyway; why not save ourselves?"

"No," said Jennings strenuously. "No one group has a monopoly on humanity. Your five million mirror-images, trapped in a humanity robbed of its variety and versatility, would die of boredom—and serve them right."

"Emotional nonsense, Jennings. You don't believe that. You've just been trained to believe it by our damn-fool equalitarians. Look, this Device is just what we need. Even if we can't build any others or understand how this one works, this one Device might do. If we could control or influence the minds of key men, then little by little we can superimpose our views on the world. We already have an organization. You must know that if you've seen my mind. It's better motivated and better designed than any other organization on Earth. The brains of mankind flock to us daily. Why not you too? This instrument is a key, as you see, but not just a key to a bit more knowledge. It is a key to the final solution of men's problems. Join us! Join us!" He had reached an earnestness that Jennings had never heard in him.

Strauss's hand fell on the Device, which flickered a second or two and went out.

Jennings smiled humorlessly. He saw the significance of that. Strauss had been deliberately trying to work himself into an emotional state intense enough to activate the Device and had failed.

"You can't work it," said Jennings. "You're too darned supermannishly self-controlled and can't break down, can you?" He took up the Device with hands that were trembling, and it phosphoresced at once.

"Then *you* work it. Get the credit for saving humanity."

"Not in a hundred million years," said Jennings, gasping and barely able to breathe in the intensity of his emotion. "I'm going to report this now."

"No," said Strauss. He picked up one of the table knives. "It's pointed enough, sharp enough."

"You needn't work so hard to make your point," said Jennings, even under the stress of the moment conscious of the pun. "I can see your plans. With the Device you can convince anyone that I never existed. You can bring about an Ultra victory."

Strauss nodded. "You read my mind perfectly."

"But you won't," gasped Jennings. "Not while I hold this." He was willing Strauss into immobility.

Strauss moved raggedly and subsided. He held the knife out stiffly and his arm trembled, but he did not advance.

Both were perspiring freely.

Strauss said between clenched teeth, "You can't keep it—up all—day."

The sensation was clear, but Jennings wasn't sure he had the words to describe it. It was, in physical terms, like holding a slippery animal of vast strength, one that wriggled incessantly. Jennings had to concentrate on the feeling of immobility.

He wasn't familiar with the Device. He didn't know how to use it skillfully. One might as well expect someone who had never seen a sword to pick one up and wield it with the grace of a musketeer.

"Exactly," said Strauss, following Jennings' train of thought. He took a fumbling step forward.

Jennings knew himself to be no match for Strauss's mad determination. They both knew that. But there was the skim boat. Jennings had to get away. With the Device.

But Jennings had no secrets. Strauss saw his thought and tried to step between the other and the skim boat.

Jennings redoubled his efforts. Not immobility, but unconsciousness. Sleep, Strauss, he thought desperately. Sleep!

Strauss slipped to his knees, heavy-lidded eyes closing.

Heart pounding, Jennings rushed forward. If he could strike him with something, snatch the knife—

But his thoughts had deviated from their all-important concentration on sleep, so that Strauss's hand was on his ankle, pulling downward with raw strength.

Strauss did not hesitate. As Jennings tumbled, the hand that held the knife rose and fell. Jennings felt the sharp pain and his mind reddened with fear and despair.

It was the very access of emotion that raised the flicker of the Device to a blaze. Strauss's hold relaxed as Jennings silently and incoherently screamed fear and rage from his own mind to the other.

Strauss rolled over, face distorted.

Jennings rose unsteadily to his feet and backed away. He dared do nothing but concentrate on keeping the other unconscious. Any attempt at violent action would block out too much of his own mind force, whatever it was; too much of his unskilled bumbling mind force that could not lend itself to really effective use.

He backed toward the skim boat. There would be a suit on board—bandages—

The skim boat was not really meant for long-distance runs. Nor was Jennings, any longer. His right side was slick with blood despite the bandages. The interior of his suit was caked with it.

There was no sign of the ship itself on his tail, but surely it would come sooner or later. Its power was many times his own; it had detectors that would pick up the cloud of charge concentration left behind by his ion-drive reactors.

Desperately Jennings had tried to reach Luna Station on his radio, but there was still no answer, and he stopped in despair. His signals would merely aid Strauss in pursuit.

He might reach Luna Station bodily, but he did not think he could make it. He would be picked off first. He would die and crash first. He wouldn't make it. He would have to hide the Device, put it away in a safe place, *then* make for Luna Station.

The Device . . .

He was not sure he was right. It might ruin the human race, but it was infinitely valuable. Should he destroy it altogether? It was the only remnant of non-human intelligent life. It held the secrets of an advanced technology; it was an instrument of an advanced science of the mind. Whatever the danger, consider the value—the potential value—

No, he must hide it so that it could be found again—but only by the enlightened Moderates of the government. Never by the Ultras . . .

The skim boat flickered down along the northern inner rim of the crater. He knew which one it was, and the Device could be buried here. If he could not reach Luna Station thereafter, either in person or by radio, he would have to at least get away from the hiding spot; well away, so that his own person would not give it away. And he would have to leave *some* key to its location.

He was thinking with an unearthly clarity, it seemed to him. Was it the influence of the Device he was holding? Did it stimulate his thinking and guide him to the perfect message? Or was it the hallucination of the dying, and would none of it make any sense to anyone? He didn't know, but he had no choice. He had to try.

For Karl Jennings knew he was going to die. He had a matter of hours to live and much to do.

H. Seton Davenport of the American Division of the Terrestrial Bureau of Investigation rubbed the star-shaped scar on his left cheek absently. "I'm aware, sir, that the Ultras are dangerous."

The Division Head, M. T. Ashley, looked at Davenport narrowly. His gaunt cheeks were set in disapproving lines. Since he had sworn off smoking once again, he forced his groping fingers to close upon a stick of chewing gum, which he shelled, crumpled, and shoved into his mouth morosely. He was getting old, and bitter, too, and his short iron-gray mustache rasped when he rubbed his knuckles against it.

He said, "You don't know how dangerous. I wonder if anyone does. They are small in numbers, but strong among the powerful who, after all, are perfectly ready to consider themselves the elite. No one knows for certain who they are or how many."

"Not even the Bureau?"

"The Bureau is held back. We ourselves aren't free of the taint, for that matter. Are you?"

Davenport frowned. "I'm not an Ultra."

"I didn't say you were," said Ashley. "I asked if you were free of the taint. Have you considered what's been happening to the Earth in the last two centuries? Has it never occurred to you that a moderate decline in population would be a good thing? Have you never felt that it would be wonderful to get rid of the unintelligent, the incapable, the insensitive, and leave the rest? *I* have, damn it."

"I'm guilty of thinking that sometimes, yes. But considering something as a wish-fulfillment idea is one thing, but planning it as a practical scheme of action to be Hitlerized through is something else."

"The distance from wish to action isn't as great as you think. Convince yourself that the end is important enough, that the danger is great enough, and the means will grow increasingly less objectionable. Anyway, now that the Istanbul matter is taken care of, let me bring you up to date on this matter. Istanbul was of no importance in comparison. Do you know Agent Ferrant?"

"The one who's disappeared? Not personally."

"Well, two months ago, a stranded ship was located on the Moon's surface. It had been conducting a privately financed selenographic survey. The Russo-American Geological Society, which had sponsored the flight, reported the ship's failure to report. A routine search located it without much trouble within a reasonable distance of the site from which it had made its last report.

"The ship was not damaged but its skim boat was gone and with it one member of the crew. Name—Karl Jennings. The other man, James Strauss, was alive but in delirium. There was no sign of physical damage to Strauss, but he was quite insane. He still is, and that's important."

"Why?" put in Davenport.

"Because the medical team that investigated him reported neurochemical and neuroelectrical abnormalities of unprecedented nature. They'd never seen a case like it. Nothing human could have brought it about."

A flicker of a smile crossed Davenport's solemn face. "You suspect extraterrestrial invaders?"

"Maybe," said the other, with no smile at all. "But let me continue. A routine search in the neighborhood of the stranded ship revealed no signs of the skim boat. Then Luna Station reported receipt of weak signals of uncertain origin. They had been tabbed as coming from the western rim of Mare Imbrium, but it was uncertain whether they were of human origin or not, and no vessel was believed to be in the vicinity. The signals had been ignored. With the skim boat in mind, however, the search party headed out for Imbrium and located it. Jennings was aboard, dead. Knife wound in one side. It's rather surprising he had lived as long as he did.

"Meanwhile the medicos were becoming increasingly disturbed at the nature of Strauss's babbling. They contacted the Bureau and our two men on the Moon—one of them happened to be Ferrant—arrived at the ship.

"Ferrant studied the tape recordings of the babblings. There was no point in asking questions, for there was, and is, no way of reaching Strauss. There is a high wall between the universe and himself—probably a permanent one. However, the talk in delirium, although heavily repetitious and disjointed, can be made to make sense. Ferrant put it together like a jigsaw puzzle.

"Apparently Strauss and Jennings had come across an object of some sort which they took to be of ancient and non-human manufacture, an artifact of some ship wrecked eons ago. Apparently it could somehow be made to twist the human mind."

Davenport interrupted. "And it twisted Strauss's mind? Is that it?"

"That's exactly it. Strauss was an Ultra—we can say 'was' for he's only technically alive—and Jennings did not wish to surrender the object. Quite right, too. Strauss babbled of using it to bring about the self-liquidation, as he called it, of the undesirable. He wanted a final, ideal population of five million. There was a fight in which only Jennings, apparently, could handle the mind-thing, but in which Strauss had a knife. When Jennings left, he was knifed, but Strauss's mind had been destroyed."

"And where was the mind-thing?"

"Agent Ferrant acted decisively. He searched the ship and the surroundings again. There was no sign of anything that was neither a natural Lunar formation nor an obvious product of human technology. There was nothing that could be the mind-thing. He then searched the skim boat and its surroundings. Again nothing."

"Could the first search team, the ones who suspected nothing—could they have carried something off?"

"They swore they did not, and there is no reason to suspect them of lying. Then Ferrant's partner—"

"Who was he?"

"Gorbansky," said the District Head.

"I know him. We've worked together."

"I know you have. What do you think of him?"

"Capable and honest."

"All right. Gorbansky found something. Not an alien artifact. Rather, something most routinely human indeed. It was an ordinary white three-by-five card with writing on it, spindled, and in the middle finger of the right gauntlet. Presumably Jennings had written it before his death and, also presumably, it represented the key to where he had hidden the object."

"What reason is there to think he had hidden it?"

"I said we had found it nowhere."

"I mean, what if he had destroyed it, as something too dangerous to leave intact?"

"That's highly doubtful. If we accept the conversation as reconstructed from Strauss's ravings—and Ferrant built up what seems a tight word-for-word record of it—Jennings thought the mind-thing to be of key importance to humanity. He called it 'the clue to an unimaginable scientific revolution.' He wouldn't destroy something like that. He would merely hide it from the Ultras and try to report its whereabouts to the government. Else why leave a clue to its whereabouts?"

Davenport shook his head, "You're arguing in a circle, chief. You say he left a clue because you think there is a hidden object, and you think there is a hidden object because he left a clue."

"I admit that. Everything is dubious. Is Strauss's delirium meaningful? Is Ferrant's reconstruction valid? Is Jennings' clue really a clue? Is there a mind-thing, or a Device, as Jennings called it, or isn't there? There's no use asking such questions. Right now, we must act on the assumption that there is such a Device and that it must be found."

"Because Ferrant disappeared?"

"Exactly."

"Kidnapped by the Ultras?"

"Not at all. The card disappeared with him."

"Oh—I see."

"Ferrant has been under suspicion for a long time as a secret Ultra. He's not the only one in the Bureau under suspicion either. The evidence didn't warrant open action; we can't simply lay about on pure suspicion, you know, or we'll gut the Bureau from top to bottom. He was under surveillance."

"By whom?"

"By Gorbansky, of course. Fortunately Gorbansky had filmed the card and sent the reproduction to the headquarters on Earth, but he admits he considered it as nothing more than a puzzling object and included it in the information sent to Earth only out of a desire to be routinely complete. Ferrant—the better mind of the two, I suppose—did see the significance and took action. He did so at great cost, for he has given himself away and has destroyed his future usefulness to the Ultras, but there is a chance that there will be no need for future usefulness. If the Ultras control the Device—"

"Perhaps Ferrant has the Device already."

"He was under surveillance, remember. Gorbansky swears the Device did not turn up anywhere."

"Gorbansky did not manage to stop Ferrant from leaving with the card. Perhaps he did not manage to stop him from obtaining the Device unnoticed, either."

Ashley tapped his fingers on the desk between them in an uneasy and uneven rhythm. He said at last, "I don't want to think that. If we find Ferrant, we may find out how much damage he's done. Till then, we must search for the Device. If Jennings hid it, he must have tried to get away from the hiding place. Else why leave a clue? It wouldn't be found in the vicinity."

"He might not have lived long enough to get away."

Again Ashley tapped, "The skim boat showed signs of having engaged in a long, speedy flight and had all but crashed at the end. That is consistent with the view that Jennings was trying to place as much space as possible between himself and some hiding place."

"Can you tell from what direction he came?"

"Yes, but that's not likely to help. From the condition of the side vents, he had been deliberately tacking and veering."

Davenport sighed. "I suppose you have a copy of the card with you."

"I do. Here it is." He flipped a three-by-five replica toward Davenport. Davenport studied it for a few moments. It looked like this:

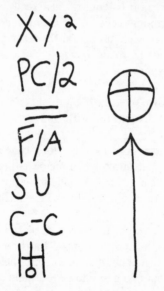

Davenport said, "I don't see any significance here."

"Neither did I, at first, nor did those I first consulted. But consider. Jennings must have thought that Strauss was in pursuit; he might not have known that Strauss had been put out of action, at least, not permanently. He was deadly afraid, then, that an Ultra would find him before a Moderate would. He dared not leave a clue too open. This"—and the Division Head tapped the reproduction—"must represent a clue that is opaque on the surface but clear enough to anyone sufficiently ingenious."

"Can we rely on that?" asked Davenport doubtfully. "After all, he was a dying, frightened man, who might have been subjected to this mind-altering object himself. He need not have been thinking clearly, or even humanly. For instance, why didn't he make an effort to reach Lunar Station? He ended half a circumference away almost. Was he too twisted to think clearly? Too paranoid to trust even the Station? Yet he must have tried to reach them at first since they picked up signals. What I'm saying is that this card, which looks as though it is covered with gibberish, *is* covered with gibberish."

Ashley shook his head solemnly from side to side, like a tolling bell. "He was in panic, yes. And I suppose he lacked the presence of mind to try to reach Lunar Station. Only the need to run and escape possessed him. Even so this can't be gibberish. It hangs together too well. Every notation on the card can be made to make sense, and the whole can be made to hang together."

"Where's the sense, then?" asked Davenport.

"You'll notice that there are seven items on the left side and two on the right. Consider the left-hand side first. The third one down looks like an equals sign. Does an equals sign mean anything to you, anything in particular?"

"An algebraic equation."

"That's general. Anything particular?"

"No."

"Suppose you consider it as a pair of parallel lines?"

"Euclid's fifth postulate?" suggested Davenport, groping.

"Good! There is a crater called Euclides on the Moon—the Greek name of the mathematician we call Euclid."

Davenport nodded. "I see your drift. As for F/A, that's force divided by acceleration, the definition of mass by Newton's second law of motion—"

"Yes, and there is a crater called Newton on the Moon also."

"Yes, but wait awhile, the lowermost item is the astronomic symbol for the planet Uranus, and there is certainly no crater—or any other lunar object, so far as I know—that is named Uranus."

"You're right there. But Uranus was discovered by William Herschel, and the H that makes up part of the astronomic symbol is the initial of his name. As it happens, there is a crater named Herschel on the Moon—three of them, in fact, since one is named for Caroline Herschel, his sister, and another for John Herschel, his son."

Davenport thought awhile, then said, "PC/2—Pressure times half the speed of light. I'm not familiar with that equation."

"Try craters. Try P for Ptolemaeus and C for Copernicus."

"And strike an average? Would that signify a spot exactly between Ptolemaeus and Copernicus?"

"I'm disappointed, Davenport," said Ashley sardonically. "I thought you knew your history of astronomy better than that. Ptolemy, or Ptolemaeus in Latin, presented a geocentric picture of the Solar System with the Earth at the center, while Copernicus presented a heliocentric one with the Sun at the center. One astronomer attempted a compromise, a picture halfway between that of Ptolemy and Copernicus—"

"Tycho Brahe!" said Davenport.

"Right. And the crater Tycho is the most conspicuous feature on the Moon's surface."

"All right. Let's take the rest. The C-C is a common way of writing a common type of chemical bond, and I think there is a crater named Bond."

"Yes, named for an American astronomer, W. C. Bond."

"The item on top, XY^2. Hmm. XYY. An X and two Y's. Wait! Alfonso X. He was the royal astronomer in medieval Spain who was called Alfonso the Wise. X the Wise. XYY. The crater Alphonsus."

"Very good. What's SU?"

"That stumps me, chief."

"I'll tell you one theory. It stands for Soviet Union, the old name for the Russian Region. It was the Soviet Union that first mapped the other side of the Moon, and maybe it's a crater there. Tsiolkovsky, for instance. You see, then, the symbols on the left can each be interpreted as standing for a crater: Alphonsus, Tycho, Euclides, Newton, Tsiolkovsky, Bond, Herschel."

"What about the symbols on the right-hand side?"

"That's perfectly transparent. The quartered circle is the astronomic symbol for the Earth. An arrow pointing to it indicates that Earth must be directly overhead."

"Ah," said Davenport, "the Sinus Medii—the Middle Bay—over which the Earth is perpetually at zenith. That's not a crater, so it's on the right-hand side, away from the other symbols."

"All right," said Ashley. "The notations all make sense, or they can be made to make sense, so there's at least a good chance that this isn't gibberish and that it is trying to tell us something. But what? So far we've got seven craters and a non-crater mentioned, and what does that mean? Presumably, the Device can only be in one place."

"Well," said Davenport heavily, "a crater can be a huge place to search. Even if we assume he hugged the shadow to avoid Solar radiation, there can be dozens of miles to examine in each case. Suppose the arrow pointing to the symbol for the Earth defines the crater where he hid the Device, the place from which the Earth can be seen nearest the zenith."

"That's been thought of, old man. It cuts out one place and leaves us with seven pinpointed craters, the southernmost extremity of those north of the Lunar equator and the northernmost extremity of those south. But which of the seven?"

Davenport was frowning. So far, he hadn't thought of anything that hadn't already been thought of. "Search them all," he said brusquely.

Ashley crackled into brief laughter. "In the weeks since this has all come up, we've done exactly that."

"And what have you found?"

"Nothing. We haven't found a thing. We're still looking, though."

"Obviously one of the symbols isn't interpreted correctly."

"Obviously!"

"You said yourself there were three craters named Herschel. The symbol SU, if it means the Soviet Union and therefore the other side of the Moon, can stand for any crater on the other side: Lomonosov, Jules Verne, Joliot-Curie, any of them. For that matter, the symbol of the Earth might stand for the crater Atlas, since he is pictured as supporting the Earth in some versions of the myth. The arrow might stand for the Straight Wall."

"There's no argument there, Davenport. But even if we get the right interpretation for the right symbol, how do we recognize it from among all the wrong interpretations, or from among the right interpretations of the wrong symbols? Somehow there's got to be something that leaps up at us

from this card and gives us so clear a piece of information that we can tell it
at once as the real thing from among all the red herrings. We've all failed and
we need a fresh mind, Davenport. What do you see here?"

"I'll tell you one thing we could do," said Davenport reluctantly. "We can
consult someone I— Oh, my God!" He half-rose.

Ashley was all controlled excitement at once. "What do you see?"

Davenport could feel his hand trembling. He hoped his lips weren't. He
said, "Tell me, have you checked on Jennings' past life?"

"Of course."

"Where did he go to college?"

"Eastern University."

A pang of joy shot through Davenport, but he held on. That was not
enough. "Did he take a course in extraterrology?"

"Of course, he did. That's routine for a geology major."

"All right, then, don't you know who teaches extraterrology at Eastern
University?"

Ashley snapped his fingers. "That oddball. What's-his-name—Wendell
Urth."

"Exactly, an oddball who is a brilliant man in his way. An oddball who's
acted as a consultant for the Bureau on several occasions and given perfect
satisfaction every time. An oddball I was going to suggest we consult this
time and then noticed that this card was *telling* us to do so. An arrow
pointing to the symbol for the Earth. A rebus that couldn't mean more
clearly 'Go to Urth,' written by a man who was once a student of Urth and
would know him."

Ashley stared at the card, "By God, it's possible. But what could Urth tell
us about the card that we can't see for ourselves?"

Davenport said, with polite patience, "I suggest we ask him, sir."

Ashley looked about curiously, half-wincing as he turned from one direction to another. He felt as though he had found himself in some arcane
curiosity shop, darkened and dangerous, from which at any moment some
demon might hurtle forth squealing.

The lighting was poor and the shadows many. The walls seemed distant,
and dismally alive with book-films from floor to ceiling. There was a Galactic
Lens in soft three-dimensionality in one corner and behind it were star charts
that could dimly be made out. A map of the Moon in another corner might,
however, possibly be a map of Mars.

Only the desk in the center of the room was brilliantly lit by a tight-
beamed lamp. It was littered with papers and opened printed books. A small
viewer was threaded with film, and a clock with an old-fashioned round-faced
dial hummed with subdued merriment.

Ashley found himself unable to recall that it was late afternoon outside and
that the sun was quite definitely in the sky. Here, within, was a place of

eternal night. There was no sign of any window, and the clear presence of circulating air did not spare him a claustrophobic sensation.

He found himself moving closer to Davenport, who seemed insensible to the unpleasantness of the situation.

Davenport said in a low voice, "He'll be here in a moment, sir."

"Is it always like this?" asked Ashley.

"Always. He never leaves this place, as far as I know, except to trot across the campus and attend his classes."

"Gentlemen! Gentlemen!" came a reedy, tenor voice. "I am so glad to see you. It is good of you to come."

A round figure of a man bustled in from another room, shedding shadow and emerging into the light.

He beamed at them, adjusting round, thick-lensed glasses upward so that he might look through them. As his fingers moved away, the glasses slipped downward at once to a precarious perch upon the round nubbin of his snub nose. "I am Wendell Urth," he said.

The scraggly gray Van Dyke on his pudgy, round chin did not in the least add to the dignity which the smiling face and the stubby ellipsoidal torso so noticeably lacked.

"Gentlemen! It is good of you to come," Urth repeated, as he jerked himself backward into a chair from which his legs dangled with the toes of his shoes a full inch above the floor. "Mr. Davenport remembers, perhaps, that it is a matter of—uh—some importance to me to remain here. I do not like to travel, except to walk, of course, and a walk across the campus is quite enough for me."

Ashley looked baffled as he remained standing, and Urth stared at him with a growing bafflement of his own. He pulled a handkerchief out and wiped his glasses, then replaced them, and said, "Oh, I see the difficulty. You want chairs. Yes. Well, just take some. If there are things on them, just push them off. Push them off. Sit down, please."

Davenport removed the books from one chair and placed them carefully on the floor. He pushed the chair toward Ashley. Then he took a human skull off a second chair and placed the skull even more carefully on Urth's desk. Its mandible, insecurely wired, unhinged as he transferred it, and it sat there with jaw askew.

"Never mind," said Urth, affably, "it will not hurt. Now tell me what is on your mind, gentlemen?"

Davenport waited a moment for Ashley to speak, then, rather gladly, took over. "Dr. Urth, do you remember a student of yours named Jennings? Karl Jennings?"

Urth's smile vanished momentarily with the effort of recall. His somewhat protuberant eyes blinked. "No," he said at last. "Not at the moment."

"A geology major. He took your extraterrology course some years ago. I have his photograph here, if that will help."

Urth studied the photograph handed him with nearsighted concentration, but still looked doubtful.

Davenport drove on. "He left a cryptic message which is the key to a matter of great importance. We have so far failed to interpret it satisfactorily, but this much we see—it indicates we are to come to you."

"Indeed? How interesting! For what purpose are you to come to me?"

"Presumably for your advice on interpreting the message."

"May I see it?"

Silently Ashley passed the slip of paper to Wendell Urth. The extraterrologist looked at it casually, turned it over, and stared for a moment at the blank back. He said, "Where does it say to ask me?"

Ashley looked startled, but Davenport forestalled him by saying, "The arrow pointing to the symbol of the Earth. It seems clear."

"It is clearly an arrow pointing to the symbol for the planet Earth. I suppose it might literally mean 'go to the Earth' if this were found on some other world."

"It was found on the Moon, Dr. Urth, and it could, I suppose, mean that. However, the reference to you seemed clear once we realized that Jennings had been a student of yours."

"He took a course in extraterrology here at the University?"

"That's right."

"In what year, Mr. Davenport?"

"In '18."

"Ah. The puzzle is solved."

"You mean the significance of the message?" said Davenport.

"No, no. The message has no meaning to me. I mean the puzzle of why it is that I did not remember him, for I remember him now. He was a very quiet fellow, anxious, shy, self-effacing—not at all the sort of person anyone would remember. Without this"—and he tapped the message—"I might never have remembered him."

"Why does the card change things?" asked Davenport.

"The reference to me is a play on words. Earth—Urth. Not very subtle, of course, but that is Jennings. His unattainable delight was the pun. My only clear memory of him is his occasional attempts to perpetrate puns. I enjoy puns, I adore puns, but Jennings—yes, I remember him well now—was atrocious at it. Either that, or distressingly obvious at it, as in this case. He lacked all talent for puns, yet craved them so much—"

Ashley suddenly broke in. "This message consists entirely of a kind of wordplay, Dr. Urth. At least, we believe so, and that fits in with what you say."

"Ah!" Urth adjusted his glasses and peered through them once more at the card and the symbols it carried. He pursed his plump lips, then said cheerfully, "I make nothing of it."

"In that case—" began Ashley, his hands balling into fists.

"But if you tell me what it's all about," Urth went on, "then perhaps it might mean something."

Davenport said quickly, "May I, sir? I am confident that this man can be relied on—and it may help."

"Go ahead," muttered Ashley. "At this point, what can it hurt?"

Davenport condensed the tale, giving it in crisp, telegraphic sentences, while Urth listened carefully, moving his stubby fingers over the shining milk-white desktop as though he were sweeping up invisible cigar ashes. Toward the end of the recital, he hitched up his legs and sat with them crossed like an amiable Buddha.

When Davenport was done, Urth thought a moment, then said, "Do you happen to have a transcript of the conversation reconstructed by Ferrant?"

"We do," said Davenport. "Would you like to see it?"

"Please."

Urth placed the strip of microfilm in a scanner and worked his way rapidly through it, his lips moving unintelligibly at some points. Then he tapped the reproduction of the cryptic message. "And this, you say, is the key to the entire matter? The crucial clue?"

"We think it is, Dr. Urth."

"But it is not the original. It is a reproduction."

"That is correct."

"The original has gone with this man, Ferrant, and you believe it to be in the hands of the Ultras."

"Quite possibly."

Urth shook his head and looked troubled. "Everyone knows my sympathies are not with the Ultras. I would fight them by all means, so I don't want to seem to be hanging back, but—what is there to say that this mind-affecting object exists at all? You have only the ravings of a psychotic and your dubious deductions from the reproduction of a mysterious set of marks that may mean nothing at all."

"Yes, Dr. Urth, but we can't take chances."

"How certain are you that this copy is accurate? What if the original has something on it that this lacks, something that makes the message quite clear, something without which the message must remain impenetrable?"

"We are certain the copy is accurate."

"What about the reverse side? There is nothing on the back of this reproduction. What about the reverse of the original?"

"The agent who made the reproduction tells us that the back of the original was blank."

"Men can make mistakes."

"We have no reason to think he did, and we must work on the assumption that he didn't. At least until such time as the original is regained."

"Then you assure me," said Urth, "that any interpretation to be made of this message must be made on the basis of exactly what one sees here."

"We think so. We are virtually certain," said Davenport with a sense of ebbing confidence.

Urth continued to look troubled. He said, "Why not leave the instrument where it is? If neither group finds it, so much the better. I disapprove of any tampering with minds and would not contribute to making it possible."

Davenport placed a restraining hand on Ashley's arm, sensing the other was about to speak. Davenport said, "Let me put it to you, Dr. Urth, that the mind-tampering aspect is not the whole of the Device. Suppose an Earth expedition to a distant primitive planet had dropped an old-fashioned radio there, and suppose the native population had discovered electric current but had not yet developed the vacuum tube.

"The population might discover that if the radio was hooked up to a current, certain glass objects within it would grow warm and would glow, but of course they would receive no intelligible sound, merely, at best, some buzzes and crackles. However, if they dropped the radio into a bathtub while it was plugged in, a person in that tub might be electrocuted. Should the people of this hypothetical planet therefore conclude that the device they were studying was designed solely for the purpose of killing people?"

"I see your analogy," said Urth. "You think that the mind-tampering property is merely an incidental function of the Device?"

"I'm sure of it," said Davenport earnestly. "If we can puzzle out its real purpose, earthly technology may leap ahead centuries."

"Then you agree with Jennings when he said"—here Urth consulted the microfilm—" 'It might be the key to—who knows what? It might be the clue to an unimaginable scientific revolution.' "

"Exactly!"

"And yet the mind-tampering aspect is there and is infinitely dangerous. Whatever the radio's purpose, it *does* electrocute."

"Which is why we can't let the Ultras get it."

"Or the government either, perhaps?"

"But I must point out that there is a reasonable limit to caution. Consider that men have always held danger in their hands. The first flint knife in the old Stone Age; the first wooden club before that could kill. They could be used to bend weaker men to the will of stronger ones under threat of force and that, too, is a form of mind-tampering. What counts, Dr. Urth, is not the Device itself, however dangerous it may be in the abstract, but the intentions of the men who make use of the Device. The Ultras have the declared intention of killing off more than 99.9 per cent of humanity. The government, whatever the faults of the men composing it, would have no such intention."

"What *would* the government intend?"

"A scientific study of the Device. Even the mind-tampering aspect itself could yield infinite good. Put to enlightened use, it could educate us concerning the physical basis of mental function. We might learn to correct mental disorders or cure the Ultras. Mankind might learn to develop greater intelligence generally."

"How can I believe that such idealism will be put into practice?"

"*I* believe so. Consider that you face a possible turn to evil by the government if you help us, but you risk the certain and declared evil purpose of the Ultras if you don't."

Urth nodded thoughtfully. "Perhaps you're right. And yet I have a favor to ask of you. I have a niece who is, I believe, quite fond of me. She is constantly upset over the fact that I steadfastly refuse to indulge in the lunacy of travel. She states that she will not rest content until someday I accompany her to Europe or North Carolina or some other outlandish place—"

Ashley leaned forward earnestly, brushing Davenport's restraining gesture to one side. "Dr. Urth, if you help us find the Device and if it can be made to work, then I assure you that we will be glad to help you free yourself of your phobia against travel and make it possible for you to go with your niece anywhere you wish."

Urth's bulging eyes widened and he seemed to shrink within himself. For a moment he looked wildly about as though he were already trapped. *"No!"* he gasped. "Not at all! Never!"

His voice dropped to an earnest, hoarse whisper. "Let me explain the nature of my fee. If I help you, if you retrieve the Device and learn its use, if the fact of my help becomes public, then my niece will be on the government like a fury. She is a terribly headstrong and shrill-voiced woman who will raise public subscriptions and organize demonstrations. She will stop at nothing. And yet you must not give in to her. You must *not!* You must resist all pressures. I wish to be left alone exactly as I am now. That is my absolute and minimum fee."

Ashley flushed. "Yes, of course, since that is your wish."

"I have your word?"

"You have my word."

"Please remember. I rely on you too, Mr. Davenport."

"It will be as you wish," soothed Davenport. "And now, I presume, you can interpret the items?"

"The items?" asked Urth, seeming to focus his attention with difficulty on the card. "You mean these markings, XY^2 and so on?"

"Yes. What do they mean?"

"I don't know. Your interpretations are as good as any, I suppose."

Ashley exploded. "Do you mean that all this talk about helping us is nonsense? What was this maundering about a fee, then?"

Wendell Urth looked confused and taken aback. "I would like to help you."

"But you don't know what these items mean."

"I—I don't. But I know what this message means."

"You do?" cried Davenport.

"Of course. Its meaning is transparent. I suspected it halfway through your story. And I was sure of it once I read the reconstruction of the conversations between Strauss and Jennings. You would understand it yourself, gentlemen, if you would only stop to think."

"See here," said Ashley in exasperation, "you said you don't know what the items mean."

"I don't. I said I know what the *message* means."

"What is the message if it is not the items? Is it the paper, for Heaven's sake?"

"Yes, in a way."

"You mean invisible ink or something like that?"

"No! Why is it so hard for you to understand, when you yourself stand on the brink?"

Davenport leaned toward Ashley and said in a low voice, "Sir, will you let me handle it, please?"

Ashley snorted, then said in a stifled manner, "Go ahead."

"Dr. Urth," said Davenport, "will you give us your analysis?"

"Ah! Well, all right." The little extraterrologist settled back in his chair and mopped his damp forehead on his sleeve. "Let's consider the message. If you accept the quartered circle and the arrow as directing you to me, that leaves seven items. If these indeed refer to seven craters, six of them, at least, must be designed merely to distract, since the Device surely cannot be in more than one place. It contained no movable or detachable parts—it was all one piece.

"Then, too, none of the items are straightforward. SU might, by your interpretation, mean any place on the other side of the Moon, which is an area the size of South America. Again PC/2 can mean 'Tycho,' as Mr. Ashley says, or it can mean 'halfway between Ptolemaeus and Copernicus,' as Mr. Davenport thought, or for that matter 'halfway between Plato and Cassini.' To be sure, XY^2 could mean 'Alfonsus'—very ingenious interpretation, that—but it could refer to some co-ordinate system in which the Y coordinate was the square of the X co-ordinate. Similarly C-C could mean 'Bond' or it could mean 'halfway between Cassini and Copernicus.' F-A could mean 'Newton' or it could mean 'between Fabricius and Archimedes.'

"In short, the items have so many meanings that they are meaningless. Even if one of them had meaning, it could not be selected from among the others, so that it is only sensible to suppose that all the items are merely red herrings.

"It is necessary, then, to determine what about the message is completely unambiguous, what is perfectly clear. The answer to that can only be that it *is* a message, that it *is* a clue to a hiding place. That is the one thing we are certain about, isn't it?"

Davenport nodded, then said cautiously, "At least, we think we are certain of it."

"Well, you have referred to this message as the key to the whole matter. You have acted as though it were the crucial clue. Jennings himself referred to the Device as a key or a clue. If we combine this serious view of the matter with Jennings' penchant for puns, a penchant which may have been heightened by the mind-tampering Device he was carrying— So let me tell you a story.

"In the last half of the sixteenth century, there lived a German Jesuit in Rome. He was a mathematician and astronomer of note and helped Pope Gregory XIII reform the calendar in 1582, performing all the enormous calculations required. This astronomer admired Copernicus but he did not accept the heliocentric view of the Solar System. He clung to the older belief that the Earth was the center of the Universe.

"In 1650, nearly forty years after the death of this mathematician, the Moon was mapped by another Jesuit, the Italian astronomer, Giovanni Battista Riccioli. He named the craters after astronomers of the past and since he too rejected Copernicus, he selected the largest and most spectacular craters for those who placed the Earth at the center of the Universe—for Ptolemy, Hipparchus, Alfonso X, Tycho Brahe. The biggest crater Riccioli could find he reserved for his German Jesuit predecessor.

"This crater is actually only the second largest of the craters visible from Earth. The only larger crater is Bailly, which is right on the Moon's limb and is therefore very difficult to see from the Earth. Riccioli ignored it, and it was named for an astronomer who lived a century after his time and who was guillotined during the French Revolution."

Ashley was listening to all this restlessly. "But what has this to do with the message?"

"Why, everything," said Urth, with some surprise. "Did you not call this message the key to the whole business? Isn't it the crucial clue?"

"Yes, of course."

"Is there any doubt that we are dealing with something that is a clue or key to something else?"

"No, there isn't," said Ashley.

"Well, then— The name of the German Jesuit I have been speaking of is Christoph Klau—pronounced 'klow.' Don't you see the pun? Klau—clue?"

Ashley's entire body seemed to grow flabby with disappointment. "Farfetched," he muttered.

Davenport said anxiously, "Dr. Urth, there is no feature on the Moon named Klau as far as I know."

"Of course not," said Urth excitedly. "That is the whole point. At this period of history, the last half of the sixteenth century, European scholars were Latinizing their names. Klau did so. In place of the German 'u', he made use of the equivalent letter, the Latin 'v'. He then added an 'ius' ending typical of Latin names and Christoph Klau became Christopher Clavius, and I suppose you are all aware of the giant crater we call Clavius."

"But—" began Davenport.

"Don't 'but' me," said Urth. "Just let me point out that the Latin word 'clavis' means 'key.' *Now* do you see the double and bilingual pun? Klau—clue, Clavius—clavis—key. In his whole life, Jennings could never have made a double, bilingual pun, without the Device. Now he could, and I wonder if death might not have been almost triumphant under the circumstances. And he directed you to me because he knew I would remember his penchant for puns and because he knew I loved them too."

The two men of the Bureau were looking at him wide-eyed.

Urth said solemnly, "I would suggest you search the shaded rim of Clavius, at that point where the Earth is nearest the zenith."

Ashley rose. "Where is your videophone?"

"In the next room."

Ashley dashed. Davenport lingered behind. "Are you sure, Dr. Urth?"

"Quite sure. But even if I am wrong, I suspect it doesn't matter."

"What doesn't matter?"

"Whether you find it or not. For if the Ultras find the Device, they will probably be unable to use it."

"Why do you say that?"

"You asked me if Jennings had ever been a student of mine, but you never asked me about Strauss, who was also a geologist. He was a student of mine a year or so after Jennings. I remember him well."

"Oh?"

"An unpleasant man. Very cold. It is the hallmark of the Ultras, I think. They are all very cold, very rigid, very sure of themselves. They can't empathize, or they wouldn't speak of killing off billions of human beings. What emotions they possess are icy ones, self-absorbed ones, feelings incapable of spanning the distance between two human beings."

"I think I see."

"I'm sure you do. The conversation reconstructed from Strauss's ravings showed us he could not manipulate the Device. He lacked the emotional intensity, or the type of necessary emotion. I imagine all Ultras would. Jennings, who was not an Ultra, could manipulate it. Anyone who could use the Device would, I suspect, be incapable of deliberate cold-blooded cruelty. He might strike out of panic fear as Jennings struck at Strauss, but never out of calculation, as Strauss tried to strike at Jennings. In short, to put it tritely, I think the Device can be actuated by love, but never by hate, and the Ultras are nothing if not haters."

Davenport nodded. "I hope you're right. But then—why were you so suspicious of the government's motives if you felt the wrong men could not manipulate the Device?"

Urth shrugged. "I wanted to make sure you could bluff and rationalize on your feet and make yourself convincingly persuasive at a moment's notice. After all, you may have to face my niece."

The Billiard Ball

James Priss—I suppose I ought to say Professor James Priss, though everyone is sure to know whom I mean even without the title—always spoke slowly.

I know. I interviewed him often enough. He had the greatest mind since Einstein, but it didn't work quickly. He admitted his slowness often. Maybe it was *because* he had so great a mind that it didn't work quickly.

He would say something in slow abstraction, then he would think, and then he would say something more. Even over trivial matters, his giant mind would hover uncertainly, adding a touch here and then another there.

Would the Sun rise tomorrow, I can imagine him wondering. What do we mean by "rise"? Can we be certain that tomorrow will come? Is the term "Sun" completely unambiguous in this connection?

Add to this habit of speech a bland countenance, rather pale, with no expression except for a general look of uncertainty; gray hair, rather thin, neatly combed; business suits of an invariably conservative cut; and you have what Professor James Priss was—a retiring person, completely lacking in magnetism.

That's why nobody in the world, except myself, could possibly suspect him of being a murderer. And even I am not sure. After all, he *was* slow-thinking; he was *always* slow-thinking. Is it conceivable that at one crucial moment he managed to think quickly and act at once?

It doesn't matter. Even if he murdered, he got away with it. It is far too late now to try to reverse matters and I wouldn't succeed in doing so even if I decided to let this be published.

. . . .

Edward Bloom was Priss's classmate in college, and an associate, through circumstance, for a generation afterward. They were equal in age and in their propensity for the bachelor life, but opposites in everything else that mattered.

Bloom was a living flash of light; colorful, tall, broad, loud, brash, and self-confident. He had a mind that resembled a meteor strike in the sudden and unexpected way it could seize the essential. He was no theoretician, as Priss was; Bloom had neither the patience for it, nor the capacity to concentrate intense thought upon a single abstract point. He admitted that; he boasted of it.

What he did have was an uncanny way of seeing the application of a theory; of seeing the manner in which it could be put to use. In the cold marble block of abstract structure, he could see, without apparent difficulty, the intricate design of a marvelous device. The block would fall apart at his touch and leave the device.

It is a well-known story, and not too badly exaggerated, that nothing Bloom ever built had failed to work, or to be patentable, or to be profitable. By the time he was forty-five, he was one of the richest men on Earth.

And if Bloom the Technician were adapted to one particular matter more than anything else, it was to the way of thought of Priss the Theoretician. Bloom's greatest gadgets were built upon Priss's greatest thoughts, and as Bloom grew wealthy and famous, Priss gained phenomenal respect among his colleagues.

Naturally it was to be expected that when Priss advanced his Two-Field Theory, Bloom would set about at once to build the first practical anti-gravity device.

My job was to find human interest in the Two-Field Theory for the subscribers to *Tele-News Press,* and you get that by trying to deal with human beings and not with abstract ideas. Since my interviewee was Professor Priss, that wasn't easy.

Naturally, I was going to ask about the possibilities of anti-gravity, which interested everyone; and not about the Two-Field Theory, which no one could understand.

"Anti-gravity?" Priss compressed his pale lips and considered. "I'm not entirely sure that it is possible, or ever will be. I haven't—uh—worked the matter out to my satisfaction. I don't entirely see whether the Two-Field equations would have a finite solution, which they would have to have, of course, if—" And then he went off into a brown study.

I prodded him. "Bloom says he thinks such a device can be built."

Priss nodded. "Well, yes, but I wonder. Ed Bloom has had an amazing knack at seeing the unobvious in the past. He has an unusual mind. It's certainly made him rich enough."

We were sitting in Priss's apartment. Ordinary middle-class. I couldn't help a quick glance this way and that. Priss was not wealthy.

I don't think he read my mind. He saw me look. And I think it was on *his* mind. He said, "Wealth isn't the usual reward for the pure scientist. Or even a particularly desirable one."

Maybe so, at that, I thought. Priss certainly had his own kind of reward. He was the third person in history to win two Nobel Prizes, and the first to have both of them in the sciences and both of them unshared. You can't complain about that. And if he wasn't rich, neither was he poor.

But he didn't sound like a contented man. Maybe it wasn't Bloom's wealth alone that irked Priss; maybe it was Bloom's fame among the people of Earth generally; maybe it was the fact that Bloom was a celebrity wherever he went, whereas Priss, outside scientific conventions and faculty clubs, was largely anonymous.

I can't say how much of all this was in my eyes or in the way I wrinkled the creases in my forehead, but Priss went on to say, "But we're friends, you know. We play billiards once or twice a week. I beat him regularly."

(I never published that statement. I checked it with Bloom, who made a long counterstatement that began: "He beats *me* at billiards. That jackass—" and grew increasingly personal thereafter. As a matter of fact, neither one was a novice at billiards. I watched them play once for a short while, after the statement and counterstatement, and both handled the cue with professional aplomb. What's more, both played for blood, and there was no friendship in the game that I could see.)

I said, "Would you care to predict whether Bloom will manage to build an anti-gravity device?"

"You mean would I commit myself to anything? Hmm. Well, let's consider, young man. Just what do we mean by anti-gravity? Our conception of gravity is built around Einstein's General Theory of Relativity, which is now a century and a half old but which, within its limits, remains firm. We can picture it—"

I listened politely. I'd heard Priss on the subject before, but if I was to get anything out of him—which wasn't certain—I'd have to let him work his way through in his own way.

"We can picture it," he said, "by imagining the Universe to be a flat, thin, superflexible sheet of untearable rubber. If we picture mass as being associated with weight, as it is on the surface of the Earth, then we would expect a mass, resting upon the rubber sheet, to make an indentation. The greater the mass, the deeper the indentation.

"In the actual Universe," he went on, "all sorts of masses exist, and so our rubber sheet must be pictured as riddled with indentations. Any object rolling along the sheet would dip into and out of indentations it passed, veering and changing direction as it did so. It is this veer and change of direction that we interpret as demonstrating the existence of a force of gravity. If the moving object comes close enough to the center of the indentation and is moving slowly enough, it gets trapped and whirls round and round that indentation. In the absence of friction, it keeps up that whirl forever. In other words, what Isaac Newton interpreted as a force, Albert Einstein interpreted as geometrical distortion."

He paused at this point. He had been speaking fairly fluently—for him— since he was saying something he had said often before. But now he began to pick his way.

He said, "So in trying to produce anti-gravity, we are trying to alter the geometry of the Universe. If we carry on our metaphor, we are trying to straighten out the indented rubber sheet. We could imagine ourselves getting under the indenting mass and lifting it upward, supporting it so as to prevent it from making an indentation. If we make the rubber sheet flat in that way, then we create a Universe—or at least a portion of the Universe—in which gravity doesn't exist. A rolling body would pass the non-indenting mass without altering its direction of travel a bit, and we could interpret this as meaning that the mass was exerting no gravitational force. In order to accomplish this feat, however, we need a mass equivalent to the indenting mass. To produce anti-gravity on Earth in this way, we would have to make use of a mass equal to that of Earth and poise it above our heads, so to speak."

I interrupted him. "But your Two-Field Theory—"

"Exactly. General Relativity does not explain both the gravitational field and the electromagnetic fields in a single set of equations. Einstein spent half his life searching for that single set—for a Unified Field Theory—and failed. All who followed Einstein also failed. I, however, began with the assumption that there were two fields that could not be unified and followed the consequences, which I can explain, in part, in terms of the 'rubber sheet' metaphor."

Now we came to something I wasn't sure I had ever heard before. "How does that go?" I asked.

"Suppose that, instead of trying to lift the indenting mass, we try to stiffen the sheet itself, make it less indentable. It would contract, at least over a small area, and become flatter. Gravity would weaken, and so would mass, for the two are essentially the same phenomenon in terms of the indented Universe. If we could make the rubber sheet completely flat, both gravity and mass would disappear altogether.

"Under the proper conditions, the electromagnetic field could be made to counter the gravitational field, and serve to stiffen the indented fabric of the Universe. The electromagnetic field is tremendously stronger than the gravitational field, so the former could be made to overcome the latter."

I said uncertainly, "But you say 'under the proper conditions.' Can those proper conditions you speak of be achieved, Professor?"

"That is what I don't know," said Priss thoughtfully and slowly. "If the Universe were really a rubber sheet, its stiffness would have to reach an infinite value before it could be expected to remain completely flat under an indenting mass. If that is also so in the real Universe, then an infinitely intense electromagnetic field would be required and that would mean anti-gravity would be impossible."

"But Bloom says—"

"Yes, I imagine Bloom thinks a finite field will do, if it can be properly applied. Still, however ingenious he is," and Priss smiled narrowly, "we needn't take him to be infallible. His grasp on theory is quite faulty. He—he never earned his college degree, did you know that?"

I was about to say that I knew that. After all, everyone did. But there was a touch of eagerness in Priss's voice as he said it and I looked up in time to catch animation in his eye, as though he were delighted to spread that piece of news. So I nodded my head as if I were filing it for future reference.

"Then you would say, Professor Priss," I prodded again, "that Bloom is probably wrong and that anti-gravity is impossible?"

And finally Priss nodded and said, "The gravitational field can be awak-ened, of course, but if by anti-gravity we mean a true zero-gravity field—no gravity at all over a significant volume of space—then I suspect anti-gravity may turn out to be impossible, despite Bloom."

And I had, after a fashion, what I wanted.

I wasn't able to see Bloom for nearly three months after that, and when I did see him he was in an angry mood.

He had grown angry at once, of course, when the news first broke concern-ing Priss's statement. He let it be known that Priss would be invited to the eventual display of the anti-gravity device as soon as it was constructed, and would even be asked to participate in the demonstration. Some reporter—not I, unfortunately—caught him between appointments and asked him to elabo-rate on that and he said:

"I'll have the device eventually; soon, maybe. And you can be there, and so can anyone else the press would care to have there. And Professor James Priss can be there. He can represent Theoretical Science and after I have demon-strated anti-gravity, he can adjust his theory to explain it. I'm sure he will know how to make his adjustments in masterly fashion and show exactly why I couldn't possibly have failed. He might do it now and save time, but I suppose he won't."

It was all said very politely, but you could hear the snarl under the rapid flow of words.

Yet he continued his occasional game of billiards with Priss and when the two met they behaved with complete propriety. One could tell the progress Bloom was making by their respective attitudes to the press. Bloom grew curt and even snappish, while Priss developed an increasing good humor.

When my umpteenth request for an interview with Bloom was finally accepted, I wondered if perhaps that meant a break in Bloom's quest. I had a little daydream of him announcing final success to *me*.

It didn't work out that way. He met me in his office at Bloom Enterprises in upstate New York. It was a wonderful setting, well away from any populated area, elaborately landscaped, and covering as much ground as a rather large industrial establishment. Edison at his height, two centuries ago, had never been as phenomenally successful as Bloom.

But Bloom was not in a good humor. He came striding in ten minutes late and went snarling past his secretary's desk with the barest nod in my direction. He was wearing a lab coat, unbuttoned.

He threw himself into his chair and said, "I'm sorry if I've kept you waiting, but I didn't have as much time as I had hoped." Bloom was a born showman and knew better than to antagonize the press, but I had the feeling he was having a great deal of difficulty at that moment in adhering to this principle.

I made the obvious guess. "I am given to understand, sir, that your recent tests have been unsuccessful."

"Who told you that?"

"I would say it was general knowledge, Mr. Bloom."

"No, it isn't. Don't say that, young man. There is no general knowledge about what goes on in my laboratories and workshops. You're stating the Professor's opinions, aren't you? Priss's, I mean."

"No, I'm—"

"Of course you are. Aren't you the one to whom he made that statement —that anti-gravity is impossible?"

"He didn't make the statement that flatly."

"He never says anything flatly, but it was flat enough for him, and not as flat as I'll have his damned rubber-sheet Universe before I'm finished."

"Then does that mean you're making progress, Mr. Bloom?"

"You know I am," he said with a snap. "Or you should know. Weren't you at the demonstration last week?"

"Yes, I was."

I judged Bloom to be in trouble or he wouldn't be mentioning that demonstration. It worked but it was not a world beater. Between the two poles of a magnet a region of lessened gravity was produced.

It was done very cleverly. A Mössbauer-Effect Balance was used to probe the space between the poles. If you've never seen an M-E Balance in action, it consists primarily of a tight monochromatic beam of gamma rays shot down the low-gravity field. The gamma rays change wavelength slightly but measurably under the influence of the gravitational field and if anything happens to alter the intensity of the field, the wavelength-change shifts correspondingly. It is an extremely delicate method for probing a gravitational field and it worked like a charm. There was no question but that Bloom had lowered gravity.

The trouble was that it had been done before by others. Bloom, to be sure, had made use of circuits that greatly increased the ease with which such an effect had been achieved—his system was typically ingenious and had been duly patented—and he maintained that it was by this method that anti-gravity would become not merely a scientific curiosity but a practical affair with industrial applications.

Perhaps. But it was an incomplete job and he didn't usually make a fuss over incompleteness. He wouldn't have done so this time if he weren't desperate to display *something*.

I said, "It's my impression that what you accomplished at that preliminary demonstration was 0.8 g, and better than that was achieved in Brazil last spring."

"That so? Well, calculate the energy input in Brazil and here, and then tell me the difference in gravity decrease per kilowatt-hour. You'll be surprised."

"But the point is, can you reach 0 g—zero gravity? That's what Professor Priss thinks may be impossible. Everyone agrees that merely lessening the intensity of the field is no great feat."

Bloom's fist clenched. I had the feeling that a key experiment had gone wrong that day and he was annoyed almost past endurance. Bloom hated to be balked by the Universe.

He said, "Theoreticians make me sick." He said it in a low, controlled voice, as though he were finally tired of not saying it, and he was going to speak his mind and be damned. "Priss has won two Nobel Prizes for sloshing around a few equations, but what has he done with it? Nothing! I *have* done something with it and I'm going to do more with it, whether Priss likes it or not.

"*I*'m the one people will remember. *I*'m the one who gets the credit. He can keep his damned title and his Prizes and his kudos from the scholars. Listen, I'll tell you what gripes him. Plain old-fashioned jealousy. It kills him that I get what I get for doing. He wants it for *thinking*.

"I said to him one—we play billiards together, you know—"

It was at this point that I quoted Priss's statement about billiards and got Bloom's counterstatement. I never published either. That was just trivia.

"We play billiards," said Bloom, when he had cooled down, "and I've won my share of games. We keep things friendly enough. What the hell—college chums and all that—though how he got through I'll never know. He made it in physics, of course, and in math, but he got a bare pass—out of pity, I think —in every humanities course he ever took."

"You did not get your degree, did you, Mr. Bloom?" That was sheer mischief on my part. I was enjoying his eruption.

"I quit to go into business, damn it. My academic average, over the three years I attended, was a strong B. Don't imagine anything else, you hear? Hell, by the time Priss got his Ph.D., I was working on my second million."

He went on, clearly irritated, "Anyway, we were playing billiards and I said to him, 'Jim, the average man will never understand why you get the Nobel Prize when I'm the one who gets the results. Why do you need two? Give me one!' He stood there, chalking up his cue, and then he said in his soft namby-pamby way, 'You have two billions, Ed. Give me one.' So you see, he wants the money."

I said, "I take it you don't mind his getting the honor?"

For a minute I thought he was going to order me out, but he didn't. He laughed instead, waved his hand in front of him, as though he were erasing something from an invisible blackboard in front of him. He said, "Oh, well, forget it. All that is off the record. Listen, do you want a statement? Okay. Things didn't go right today and I blew my top a bit, but it will clear up. I think I know what's wrong. And if I don't, I'm going to know.

"Look, you can say that I say that we *don't* need infinite electromagnetic intensity; we *will* flatten out the rubber sheet; we *will* have zero gravity. And when we get it, I'll have the damndest demonstration you ever saw, exclusively for the press and for Priss, and you'll be invited. And you can say it won't be long. Okay?"

Okay!

I had time after that to see each man once or twice more. I even saw them together when I was present at one of their billiard games. As I said before, both of them were *good*.

But the call to the demonstration did not come as quickly as all that. It arrived six weeks less than a year after Bloom gave me his statement. And at that, perhaps it was unfair to expect quicker work.

I had a special engraved invitation, with the assurance of a cocktail hour first. Bloom never did things by halves and he was planning to have a pleased and satisfied group of reporters on hand. There was an arrangement for trimensional TV, too. Bloom felt completely confident, obviously; confident enough to be willing to trust the demonstration in every living room on the planet.

I called up Professor Priss, to make sure he was invited too. He was.

"Do you plan to attend, sir?"

There was a pause and the professor's face on the screen was a study in uncertain reluctance. "A demonstration of this sort is most unsuitable where a serious scientific matter is in question. I do not like to encourage such things."

I was afraid he would beg off, and the dramatics of the situation would be greatly lessened if he were not there. But then, perhaps, he decided he dared not play the chicken before the world. With obvious distaste he said, "Of course, Ed Bloom is not really a scientist and he must have his day in the sun. I'll be there."

"Do you think Mr. Bloom can produce zero gravity, sir?"

"Uh . . . Mr. Bloom sent me a copy of the design of his device and . . .

and I'm not certain. Perhaps he can do it, if . . . uh . . . he says he can do it. Of course"—he paused again for quite a long time—"I think I would like to see it."

So would I, and so would many others.

The staging was impeccable. A whole floor of the main building at Bloom Enterprises—the one on the hilltop—was cleared. There were the promised cocktails and a splendid array of hors d'oeuvres, soft music and lighting, and a carefully dressed and thoroughly jovial Edward Bloom playing the perfect host, while a number of polite and unobtrusive menials fetched and carried. All was geniality and amazing confidence.

James Priss was late and I caught Bloom watching the corners of the crowd and beginning to grow a little grim about the edges. Then Priss arrived, dragging a volume of colorlessness in with him, a drabness that was unaffected by the noise and the absolute splendor (no other word would describe it—or else it was the two martinis glowing inside me) that filled the room.

Bloom saw him and his face was illuminated at once. He bounced across the floor, seized the smaller man's hand and dragged him to the bar.

"Jim! Glad to see you! What'll you have? Hell, man, I'd have called it off if you hadn't showed. Can't have this thing without the star, you know." He wrung Priss's hand. "It's your theory, you know. We poor mortals can't do a thing without you few, you damned *few* few, pointing the way."

He was being ebullient, handing out the flattery, because he could afford to do so now. He was fattening Priss for the kill.

Priss tried to refuse a drink, with some sort of mutter, but a glass was pressed into his hand and Bloom raised his voice to a bull roar.

"Gentlemen! A moment's quiet, please. To Professor Priss, the greatest mind since Einstein, two-time Nobel Laureate, father of the Two-Field Theory, and inspirer of the demonstration we are about to see—even if he didn't think it would work, and had the guts to say so publicly."

There was a distinct titter of laughter that quickly faded out and Priss looked as grim as his face could manage.

"But now that Professor Priss is here," said Bloom, "and we've had our toast, let's get on with it. Follow me, gentlemen!"

The demonstration was in a much more elaborate place than had housed the earlier one. This time it was on the top floor of the building. Different magnets were involved—smaller ones, by heaven—but as nearly as I could tell, the same M-E Balance was in place.

One thing was new, however, and it staggered everyone, drawing much more attention than anything else in the room. It was a billiard table, resting under one pole of the magnet. Beneath it was the companion pole. A round hole, about a foot across, was stamped out of the very center of the table and it was obvious that the zero-gravity field, if it was to be produced, would be produced through that hole in the center of the billiard table.

It was as though the whole demonstration had been designed, surrealist fashion, to point up the victory of Bloom over Priss. This was to be another version of their everlasting billiards competition and Bloom was going to win.

I don't know if the other newsmen took matters in that fashion, but I think Priss did. I turned to look at him and saw that he was still holding the drink that had been forced into his hand. He rarely drank, I knew, but now he lifted the glass to his lips and emptied it in two swallows. He stared at that billiard ball and I needed no gift of ESP to realize that he took it as a deliberate snap of fingers under his nose.

Bloom led us to the twenty seats that surrounded three sides of the table, leaving the fourth free as a working area. Priss was carefully escorted to the seat commanding the most convenient view. Priss glanced quickly at the trimensional cameras which were now working. I wondered if he were thinking of leaving but deciding that he couldn't in the full glare of the eyes of the world.

Essentially, the demonstration was simple; it was the production that counted. There were dials in plain view that measured the energy expenditure. There were others that transferred the M-E Balance readings into a position and a size that were visible to all. Everything was arranged for easy trimensional viewing.

Bloom explained each step in a genial way, with one or two pauses in which he turned to Priss for a confirmation that had to come. He didn't do it often enough to make it obvious, but just enough to turn Priss upon the spit of his own torment. From where I sat I could look across the table and see Priss on the other side.

He had the look of a man in Hell.

As we all know, Bloom succeeded. The M-E Balance showed the gravitational intensity to be sinking steadily as the electromagnetic field was intensified. There were cheers when it dropped below the 0.52 g mark. A red line indicated that on the dial.

"The 0.52 g mark, as you know," said Bloom confidently, "represents the previous record low in gravitational intensity. We are now lower than that at a cost in electricity that is less than ten per cent what it cost at the time that mark was set. And we will go lower still."

Bloom—I think deliberately, for the sake of the suspense—slowed the drop toward the end, letting the trimensional cameras switch back and forth between the gap in the billiard table and the dial on which the M-E Balance reading was lowering.

Bloom said suddenly, "Gentlemen, you will find dark goggles in the pouch on the side of each chair. Please put them on now. The zero-gravity field will soon be established and it will radiate a light rich in ultraviolet."

He put goggles on himself, and there was a momentary rustle as others went on too.

I think no one breathed during the last minute, when the dial reading dropped to zero and held fast. And just as that happened a cylinder of light sprang into existence from pole to pole through the hole in the billiard table.

There was a ghost of twenty sighs at that. Someone called out, "Mr. Bloom, what is the reason for the light?"

"It's characteristic of the zero-gravity field," said Bloom smoothly, which was no answer, of course.

Reporters were standing up now, crowding about the edge of the table. Bloom waved them back. "Please, gentlemen, stand clear!"

Only Priss remained sitting. He seemed lost in thought and I have been certain ever since that it was the goggles that obscured the possible significance of everything that followed. I didn't see his eyes. I couldn't. And that meant neither I nor anyone else could even begin to make a guess as to what was going on behind those eyes. Well, maybe we couldn't have made such a guess, even if the goggles hadn't been there, but who can say?

Bloom was raising his voice again. "Please! The demonstration is not yet over. So far, we've only repeated what I have done before. I have now produced a zero-gravity field and I have shown it can be done practically. But I want to demonstrate something of what such a field can do. What we are going to see next will be something that has never been seen, not even by myself. I have not experimented in this direction, much as I would have liked to, because I have felt that Professor Priss deserved the honor of—"

Priss looked up sharply. "What—what—"

"Professor Priss," said Bloom, smiling broadly, "I would like you to perform the first experiment involving the interaction of a solid object with a zero-gravity field. Notice that the field has been formed in the center of a billiard table. The world knows your phenomenal skill in billiards, Professor, a talent second only to your amazing aptitude in theoretical physics. Won't you send a billiard ball into the zero-gravity volume?"

Eagerly he was handing a ball and cue to the professor. Priss, his eyes hidden by the goggles, stared at them and only very slowly, very uncertainly, reached out to take them.

I wonder what his eyes were showing. I wonder, too, how much of the decision to have Priss play billiards at the demonstration was due to Bloom's anger at Priss's remark about their periodic game, the remark I had quoted. Had I been, in my way, responsible for what followed?

"Come, stand up, Professor," said Bloom, "and let *me* have your seat. The show is yours from now on. Go ahead!"

Bloom seated himself, and still talked, in a voice that grew more organlike with each moment. "Once Professor Priss sends the ball into the volume of zero gravity, it will no longer be affected by Earth's gravitational field. It will remain truly motionless while the Earth rotates about its axis and travels about the Sun. In this latitude, and at this time of day, I have calculated that the Earth, in its motions, will sink downward. We will move with it and the ball will stand still. To us it will seem to rise up and away from the Earth's surface. Watch."

Priss seemed to stand in front of the table in frozen paralysis. Was it surprise? Astonishment? I don't know. I'll never know. Did he make a move to interrupt Bloom's little speech, or was he just suffering from an agonized reluctance to play the ignominious part into which he was being forced by his adversary?

Priss turned to the billiard table, looking first at it, then back at Bloom. Every reporter was on his feet, crowding as closely as possible in order to get a good view. Only Bloom himself remained seated, smiling and isolated. He, of course, was not watching the table, or the ball, or the zero-gravity field. As nearly as I could tell through the goggles, he was watching Priss.

Priss turned to the table and placed his ball. He was going to be the agent that was to bring final and dramatic triumph to Bloom and make himself— the man who said it couldn't be done—the goat to be mocked forever.

Perhaps he felt there was no way out. Or perhaps—

With a sure stroke of his cue, he set the ball into motion. It was not going quickly, and every eye followed it. It struck the side of the table and caromed. It was going even slower now as though Priss himself were increasing the suspense and making Bloom's triumph the more dramatic.

I had a perfect view, for I was standing on the side of the table opposite from that where Priss was. I could see the ball moving toward the glitter of the zero-gravity field and beyond it I could see those portions of the seated Bloom which were not hidden by the glitter.

The ball approached the zero-gravity volume, seemed to hang on the edge for a moment, and then was gone, with a streak of light, the sound of a thunderclap, the sudden smell of burning cloth.

We yelled. We all yelled.

I've seen the scene on television since—along with the rest of the world. I can see myself in the film during that fifteen-second period of wild confusion, but I don't really recognize my face.

Fifteen seconds!

And then we discovered Bloom. He was still sitting in the chair, his arms still folded, but there was a hole the size of a billiard ball through forearm, chest, and back. The better part of his heart, as it later turned out under autopsy, had been neatly punched out.

They turned off the device. They called in the police. They dragged off Priss, who was in a state of utter collapse. I wasn't much better off, to tell the truth, and if any reporter then on the scene ever tried to say he remained a cool observer of that scene, then he's a cool liar.

It was some months before I got to see Priss again. He had lost some weight but seemed well otherwise. Indeed, there was color in his cheeks and an air of decision about him. He was better dressed than I had ever seen him to be.

He said, "I know what happened *now*. If I had had time to think, I would have known then. But I am a slow thinker, and poor Ed Bloom was so intent on running a great show and doing it so well that he carried me along with him. Naturally, I've been trying to make up for some of the damage I unwittingly caused."

"You can't bring Bloom back to life," I said soberly.

"No, I can't," he said, just as soberly. "But there's Bloom Enterprises to think of, too. What happened at the demonstration, in full view of the world, was the worst possible advertisement for zero gravity, and it's important that the story be made clear. That is why I have asked to see *you*."

"Yes?"

"If I had been a quicker thinker, I would have known Ed was speaking the purest nonsense when he said that the billiard ball would slowly rise in the zero-gravity field. It *couldn't* be so! If Bloom hadn't despised theory so, if he hadn't been so intent on being proud of his own ignorance of theory, he'd have known it himself.

"The Earth's motion, after all, isn't the only motion involved, young man. The Sun itself moves in a vast orbit about the center of the Milky Way Galaxy. And the Galaxy moves too, in some not very clearly defined way. If the billiard ball were subjected to zero gravity, you might think of it as being unaffected by any of these motions and therefore of suddenly falling into a state of absolute rest—when there is no such thing as absolute rest."

Priss shook his head slowly. "The trouble with Ed, I think, was that he was thinking of the kind of zero gravity one gets in a spaceship in free fall, when people float in mid-air. He expected the ball to float in mid-air. However, in a spaceship, zero gravity is not the result of an absence of gravitation, but merely the result of two objects, a ship and a man within the ship, falling at the same rate, responding to gravity in precisely the same way, so that each is motionless with respect to the other.

"In the zero-gravity field produced by Ed, there was a flattening of the rubber-sheet Universe, which means an actual loss of mass. Everything in that field, including molecules of air caught within it, and the billiard ball I pushed into it, was completely massless as long as it remained with it. A completely massless object can move in only one way."

He paused, inviting the question. I asked, "What motion would that be?"

"Motion at the speed of light. Any massless object, such as a neutrino or a photon, must travel at the speed of light as long as it exists. In fact, light moves at that speed only because it is made up of photons. As soon as the billiard ball entered the zero-gravity field and lost its mass, it too assumed the speed of light at once and left."

I shook my head. "But didn't it regain its mass as soon as it left the zero-gravity volume?"

"It certainly did, and at once it began to be affected by the gravitational field and to slow up in response to the friction of the air and the top of the billiard table. But imagine how much friction it would take to slow up an object the mass of a billiard ball going at the speed of light. It went through the hundred-mile thickness of our atmosphere in a thousandth of a second and I doubt that it was slowed more than a few miles a second in doing so, a few miles out of 186,282 of them. On the way, it scorched the top of the billiard table, broke cleanly through the edge, went through poor Ed and the window too, punching out neat circles because it had passed through before the neighboring portions of something even as brittle as glass had a chance to split and splinter.

"It is extremely fortunate we were on the top floor of a building set in a countrified area. If we were in the city, it might have passed through a number of buildings and killed a number of people. By now that billiard ball is off in space, far beyond the edge of the Solar System and it will continue to travel so forever, at nearly the speed of light, until it happens to strike an object large enough to stop it. And then it will gouge out a sizable crater."

I played with the notion and was not sure I liked it. "How is that possible? The billiard ball entered the zero-gravity volume almost at a standstill. I saw it. And you say it left with an incredible quantity of kinetic energy. Where did the energy come from?"

Priss shrugged. "It came from nowhere! The law of conservation of energy only holds under the conditions in which general relativity is valid; that is, in an indented-rubber-sheet universe. Wherever the indentation is flattened out, general relativity no longer holds, and energy can be created and destroyed freely. That accounts for the radiation along the cylindrical surface of the zero-gravity volume. That radiation, you remember, Bloom did not explain, and, I fear, could not explain. If he had only experimented further first; if he had only not been so foolishly anxious to put on his show—"

"What accounts for the radiation, sir?"

"The molecules of air inside the volume. Each assumes the speed of light and comes smashing outward. They're only molecules, not billiard balls, so they're stopped, but the kinetic energy of their motion is converted into energetic radiation. It's continuous because new molecules are always drifting in, and attaining the speed of light and smashing out."

"Then energy is being created continuously?"

"Exactly. And that is what we must make clear to the public. Anti-gravity is not primarily a device to lift spaceships or to revolutionize mechanical movement. Rather, it is the source of an endless supply of free energy, since part of the energy produced can be diverted to maintain the field that keeps that portion of the Universe flat. What Ed Bloom invented, without knowing it, was not just anti-gravity, but the first successful perpetual-motion machine of the first class—one that manufactures energy out of nothing."

I said slowly, "Any one of us could have been killed by that billiard ball, is that right, Professor? It might have come out in any direction."

Priss said, "Well, massless photons emerge from any light source at the speed of light in any direction; that's why a candle casts light in all directions. The massless air molecules come out of the zero-gravity volume in all directions, which is why the entire cylinder radiates. But the billiard ball was only one object. It could have come out in any direction, but it had to come out in some one direction, chosen at random, and the chosen direction happened to be the one that caught Ed."

That was it. Everyone knows the consequences. Mankind had free energy and so we have the world we have now. Professor Priss was placed in charge of its development by the board of Bloom Enterprises, and in time he was as rich and famous as ever Edward Bloom had been. And Priss still has two Nobel Prizes in addition.

Only . . .

I keep thinking. Photons smash out from a light source in all directions because they are created at the moment and there is no reason for them to move in one direction more than in another. Air molecules come out of a zero-gravity field in all directions because they enter it in all directions.

But what about a single billiard ball, entering a zero-gravity field from one particular direction? Does it come out in the same direction or in any direction?

I've inquired delicately, but theoretical physicists don't seem to be sure, and I can find no record that Bloom Enterprises, which is the only organization working with zero-gravity fields, has ever experimented in the matter. Someone at the organization once told me that the uncertainty principle guarantees the random emersion of an object entering in any direction. But then why don't they try the experiment?

Could it be, then . . .

Could it be that for once Priss's mind had been working quickly? Could it be that, under the pressure of what Bloom was trying to do to him, Priss had suddenly seen everything? He had been studying the radiation surrounding the zero-gravity volume. He might have realized its cause and been certain of the speed-of-light motion of anything entering the volume.

Why, then, had he said nothing?

One thing is certain. *Nothing* Priss would do at the billiard table could be accidental. He was an expert and the billiard ball did exactly what he wanted it to. I was standing right there. I saw him look at Bloom and then at the table as though he were judging angles.

I watched him hit that ball. I watched it bounce off the side of the table and move into the zero-gravity volume, heading in one particular direction.

For when Priss sent that ball toward the zero-gravity volume—and the tri-di films bear me out—it was *already* aimed directly at Bloom's heart!

Accident? Coincidence?

. . . Murder?

Exile to Hell

"The Russians," said Dowling, in his precise voice, "used to send prisoners to Siberia in the days before space travel had become common. The French used Devil's Island for the purpose. The British sailed them off to Australia."

He considered the chessboard carefully and his hand hesitated briefly over the bishop.

Parkinson, at the other side of the chess board, watched the pattern of the pieces absently. Chess was, of course, the professional game of computer programmers, but, under the circumstances, he lacked enthusiasm. By rights, he felt with some annoyance, Dowling should have been even worse off; he was programming the prosecution's case.

There was, of course, a tendency for the programmer to take over some of the imagined characteristics of the computer—the unemotionality, the imperviousness to anything but logic. Dowling reflected that in his precise hair-part and in the restrained elegance of his clothing.

Parkinson, who preferred to program the defense in the law cases in which he was involved, also preferred to be deliberately careless in the minor aspects of his costume.

He said, "You mean exile is a well-established punishment and therefore not particularly cruel."

"No, it *is* particularly cruel, but also it *is* well-established, and nowadays it has become the perfect deterrent."

Dowling moved the bishop and did not look upward. Parkinson, quite involuntarily, did.

Of course, he couldn't see anything. They were indoors, in the comfortable modern world tailored to human needs, carefully protected against the raw environment. Out there, the night would be bright with its illumination.

When had he last seen it? Not for a long time. It occurred to him to wonder what phase it was in right now. Full? Gleaming? Or was it in its crescent phase? Was it a bright fingernail of light low in the sky?

By rights it should be a lovely sight. Once it had been. But that had been centuries ago, before space travel had become common and cheap, and before the surroundings all about them had grown sophisticated and controlled. Now the lovely light in the sky had become a new and more horrible Devil's Island hung in space.

—No one even used its name any longer, out of sheer distaste. It was "It." Or it was less than that, just a silent, upward movement of the head.

Parkinson said, "You might have allowed me to program the case against exile generally."

"Why? It couldn't have affected the result."

"Not this one, Dowling. But it might have affected future cases. Future punishments might be commuted to the death sentence."

"For someone guilty of equipment damage? You're dreaming."

"It was an act of blind anger. There was intent to harm a human being, granted; but there was no intent to harm equipment."

"Nothing; it means nothing. Lack of intent is no excuse in such cases. You know that."

"It *should* be an excuse. That's my point; the one I wanted to make."

Parkinson advanced a pawn now, to cover his knight.

Dowling considered. "You're trying to hang on to the queen's attack, Parkinson, and I'm not going to let you. —Let's see, now." And while he pondered he said, "These are not primitive times, Parkinson. We live in a crowded world with no margin for error. As small a thing as a blown-out consistor could endanger a sizable fraction of our population. When anger endangers and subverts a power line, it's a serious thing."

"I don't question that—"

"You seemed to be doing so, when you were constructing the defense program."

"I was not. Look, when Jenkins' laser beam cut through the Field-warp, I myself was as close to death as anyone. A quarter hour's additional delay would have meant my end, too, and I'm completely aware of that. My point is only that exile is not the proper punishment!"

He tapped his finger on the chessboard for emphasis, and Dowling caught the queen before it went over. "Adjusting, not moving," he mumbled.

Dowling's eyes went from piece to piece and he continued to hesitate. "You're wrong, Parkinson. It *is* the proper punishment, because there's nothing worse and that matches a crime than which there is nothing worse. Look, we all feel our absolute dependence on a complicated and rather fragile technology. A breakdown might kill us all, and it doesn't matter whether the breakdown is deliberate, accidental, or caused by incompetence. Human beings demand the maximum punishment for any such deed as the only way they can feel secure. Mere death is not sufficient deterrent."

"Yes, it is. No one wants to die."

"They want to live in exile up there even less. That's why we've only had one such case in the last ten years, and only one exile. —There, do something about that!" And Dowling nudged his queen's rook one space to the right.

A light flashed. Parkinson was on his feet at once. "The programming is finished. The computer will have its verdict now."

Dowling looked up phlegmatically, "You've no doubt about what the verdict will be, have you? —Keep the board standing. We'll finish afterward."

Parkinson was quite certain he would lack the heart to continue the game. He hurried down the corridor to the courtroom, light and quick on his feet, as always.

Shortly after he and Dowling had entered, the judge took his seat, and then in came Jenkins, flanked by two guards.

Jenkins looked haggard, but stoical. Ever since the blind rage had overcome him and he had accidentally thrown a sector into unpowered darkness while striking out at a fellow worker, he must have known the inevitable consequence of this worst of all crimes. It helps to have no illusions.

Parkinson was not stoical. He dared not look squarely at Jenkins. He could not have done so without wondering, painfully, as to what might be going through Jenkins' mind at that moment. Was he absorbing, through every sense, all the perfections of familiar comfort before being thrust forever into the luminous Hell that rode the night sky?

Was he savoring the clean and pleasant air in his nostrils, the soft lights, the equable temperature, the pure water on call, the secure surroundings designed to cradle humanity in tame comfort?

While up there—

The judge pressed a contact and the computer's decision was converted into the warm, unmannered sound of a standardized human voice.

"A weighing of all pertinent information in the light of the law of the land and of all relevant precedents leads to the conclusion that Anthony Jenkins is guilty on all counts of the crime of equipment damage and is subject to the maximum penalty."

There were only six people in the courtroom itself, but the entire population was listening by television, of course.

The judge spoke in prescribed phraseology. "The defendant will be taken from here to the nearest spaceport and, on the first available transportation, be removed from this world and sent into exile for the term of his natural life."

Jenkins seemed to shrink within himself, but he said no word.

Parkinson shivered. How many, he wondered, would now feel the enormity of such a punishment for *any* crime? How long before there would be enough humanity among men to wipe out forever the punishment of exile?

Could anyone really think of Jenkins up there in space, without flinching? Could they think, and endure the thought, of a fellow man thrown for all his life among the strange, unfriendly, vicious population of a world of unbearable heat by day and frigid cold by night; of a world where the sky was a harsh blue and the ground a harsher, clashing green; where the dusty air moved raucously and the viscous sea heaved eternally?

And the gravity, that heavy—heavy—heavy—eternal—pull!

Who could bear the horror of condemning someone, for whatever reason, to leave the friendly home of the Moon for that Hell in the sky—the Earth?

Key Item

Jack Weaver came out of the vitals of Multivac looking utterly worn and disgusted.

From the stool, where the other maintained his own stolid watch, Todd Nemerson said, "Nothing?"

"Nothing," said Weaver. "Nothing, nothing, nothing. No one can find anything wrong with it."

"Except that it won't work, you mean."

"You're no help sitting there!"

"I'm thinking."

"Thinking!" Weaver showed a canine at one side of his mouth.

Nemerson stirred impatiently on his stool. "Why not? There are six teams of computer technologists roaming around in the corridors of Multivac. They haven't come up with anything in three days. Can't you spare one person to think?"

"It's not a matter of thinking. We've got to look. Somewhere a relay is stuck."

"It's not that simple, Jack!"

"Who says it's simple. You know how many million relays we have there?"

"That doesn't matter. If it were just a relay, Multivac would have alternate circuits, devices for locating the flaw, and facilities to repair or replace the ailing part. The trouble is, Multivac won't only not answer the original question, it won't tell us what's wrong with it. —And meanwhile, there'll be panic in every city if we don't do something. The world's economy depends on Multivac, and everyone knows that."

"I know it, too. But what's there to do?"

"I told you, *think*. There must be something we're missing completely. Look, Jack, there isn't a computer bigwig in a hundred years who hasn't devoted himself to making Multivac more complicated. It can do so much now—hell, it can even talk and listen. It's practically as complex as the human brain. We can't understand the human brain, so why should we understand Multivac?"

"Aw, come on. Next you'll be saying Multivac is human."

"Why not?" Nemerson grew absorbed and seemed to sink into himself. "Now that you mention it, why not? Could we tell if Multivac passed the thin dividing line where it stopped being a machine and started being human? *Is* there a dividing line, for that matter? If the brain is just more complex than Multivac, and we keep making Multivac more complex, isn't there a point where . . ." He mumbled down into silence.

Weaver said impatiently, "What are you driving at? Suppose Multivac were human. How would that help us find out why it isn't working?"

"For a human reason, maybe. Suppose *you* were asked the most probable price of wheat next summer and didn't answer. Why wouldn't you answer?"

"Because I wouldn't know. But Multivac would know! We've given it all the factors. It can analyze futures in weather, politics, and economics. We know it can. It's done it before."

"All right. Suppose I asked the question and you knew the answer but didn't tell me. Why not?"

Weaver snarled, "Because I had a brain tumor. Because I had been knocked out. Because I was drunk. Damn it, because my machinery was out of order. That's just what we're trying to find out about Multivac. We're looking for the place where its machinery is out of order, for the key item."

"Only you haven't found it." Nemerson got off his stool. "Listen, ask me the question Multivac stalled on."

"How? Shall I run the tape through you?"

"Come on, Jack. Give me the talk that goes along with it. You do talk to Multivac, don't you?"

"I've got to. Therapy."

Nemerson nodded. "Yes, that's the story. Therapy. That's the official story. We talk to it in order to pretend it's a human being so that we don't get neurotic over having a machine know so much more than we do. We turn a frightening metal monster into a protective father image."

"If you want to put it that way."

"Well, it's wrong and you know it. A computer as complex as Multivac *must* talk and listen to be efficient. Just putting in and taking out coded dots isn't sufficient. At a certain level of complexity, Multivac must be made to seem human because, by God, it *is* human. Come on, Jack, ask me the question. I want to see my reaction to it."

Jack Weaver flushed. "This is silly."

"Come on, will you?"

It was a measure of Weaver's depression and desperation that he acceded. Half sullenly, he pretended to be feeding the program into Multivac, speaking as he did so in his usual manner. He commented on the latest information concerning farm unrest, talked about the new equations describing jet-stream contortions, lectured on the solar constant.

He began stiffly enough, but warmed to this task out of long habit, and when the last of the program was slammed home, he almost closed contact with a physical snap at Todd Nemerson's waist.

He ended briskly, "All right, now. Work that out and give us the answer pronto."

For a moment, having done, Jack Weaver stood there, nostrils flaring, as though he was feeling once more the excitement of throwing into action the most gigantic and glorious machine ever put together by the mind and hands of man.

Then he remembered and muttered, "All right. That's it."

Nemerson said, "At least I know now why *I* wouldn't answer, so let's try that on Multivac. Look, clear Multivac; make sure the investigators have their paws off it. Then run the program into it and let me do the talking. Just once."

Weaver shrugged and turned to Multivac's control wall, filled with its somber, unwinking dials and lights. Slowly he cleared it. One by one he ordered the teams away.

Then, with a deep breath, he began once more feeding the program into Multivac. It was the twelfth time all told, the dozenth time. Somewhere a distant news commentator would spread the word that they were trying again. All over the world a Multivac-dependent people would be holding its collective breath.

Nemerson talked as Weaver fed the data silently. He talked diffidently, trying to remember what it was that Weaver had said, but waiting for the moment when the key item might be added.

Weaver was done and now a note of tension was in Nemerson's voice. He said, "All right, now, Multivac. Work that out and give us the answer." He paused and added the key item. He said *"Please!"*

And all over Multivac, the valves and relays went joyously to work. After all, a machine has feelings—when it isn't a machine anymore.

Feminine Intuition

The Three Laws of Robotics:

1. *A robot may not injure a human being or, through inaction, allow a human being to come to harm.*
2. *A robot must obey the orders given it by human beings except where such orders would conflict with the First Law.*
3. *A robot must protect its own existence as long as such protection does not conflict with the First or Second Law.*

For the first time in the history of United States Robots and Mechanical Men, Inc., a robot had been destroyed through accident on Earth itself.

No one was to blame. The air vehicle had been demolished in mid-air and an unbelieving investigating committee was wondering whether they really dared announce the evidence that it had been hit by a meteorite. Nothing else could have been fast enough to prevent automatic avoidance; nothing else could have done the damage short of a nuclear blast and that was out of the question.

Tie that in with a report of a flash in the night sky just before the vehicle had exploded—and from Flagstaff Observatory, not from an amateur—and the location of a sizable and distinctly meteoric bit of iron freshly gouged into the ground a mile from the site and what other conclusion could be arrived at?

Still, nothing like that had ever happened before and calculations of the odds against it yielded monstrous figures. Yet even colossal improbabilities can happen sometimes.

At the offices of United States Robots, the hows and whys of it were secondary. The real point was that a robot had been destroyed.

That, in itself, was distressing.

The fact that JN-5 had been a prototype, the first, after four earlier attempts, to have been placed in the field, was even more distressing.

The fact that JN-5 was a radically new type of robot, quite different from anything ever built before, was abysmally distressing.

The fact that JN-5 had apparently accomplished something before its destruction that was incalculably important and that that accomplishment might now be forever gone, placed the distress utterly beyond words.

It seemed scarcely worth mentioning that, along with the robot, the Chief Robopsychologist of United States Robots had also died.

Clinton Madarian had joined the firm ten years before. For five of those years, he had worked uncomplainingly under the grumpy supervision of Susan Calvin.

Madarian's brilliance was quite obvious and Susan Calvin had quietly promoted him over the heads of older men. She wouldn't, in any case, have deigned to give her reasons for this to Research Director Peter Bogert, but as it happened, no reasons were needed. Or, rather, they were obvious.

Madarian was utterly the reverse of the renowned Dr. Calvin in several very noticeable ways. He was not quite as overweight as his distinct double chin made him appear to be, but even so he was overpowering in his presence, where Susan had gone nearly unnoticed. Madarian's massive face, his shock of glistening red-brown hair, his ruddy complexion and booming voice, his loud laugh, and most of all, his irrepressible self-confidence and his eager way of announcing his successes, made everyone else in the room feel there was a shortage of space.

When Susan Calvin finally retired (refusing, in advance, any cooperation with respect to any testimonial dinner that might be planned in her honor with so firm a manner that no announcement of the retirement was even made to the news services) Madarian took her place.

He had been in his new post exactly one day when he initiated the JN project.

It had meant the largest commitment of funds to one project that United States Robots had ever had to weigh, but that was something which Madarian dismissed with a genial wave of the hand.

"Worth every penny of it, Peter," he said. "And I expect you to convince the Board of Directors of that."

"Give me reasons," said Bogert, wondering if Madarian would. Susan Calvin had never given reasons.

But Madarian said, "Sure," and settled himself easily into the large arm-chair in the Director's office.

Bogert watched the other with something that was almost awe. His own once-black hair was almost white now and within the decade he would follow Susan into retirement. That would mean the end of the original team that had built United States Robots into a globe-girdling firm that was a rival of the national governments in complexity and importance. Somehow neither he nor those who had gone before him ever quite grasped the enormous expansion of the firm.

But this was a new generation. The new men were at ease with the Colossus. They lacked the touch of wonder that would have them tiptoeing in disbelief. So they moved ahead, and that was good.

Madarian said, "I propose to begin the construction of robots without constraint."

"Without the Three Laws? Surely—"

"No, Peter. Are those the only constraints you can think of? Hell, you contributed to the design of the early positronic brains. Do I have to tell you that, quite aside from the Three Laws, there isn't a pathway in those brains that isn't carefully designed and fixed? We have robots planned for specific tasks, implanted with specific abilities."

"And you propose—"

"That at every level below the Three Laws, the paths be made open-ended. It's not difficult."

Bogert said dryly, "It's not difficult, indeed. Useless things are never difficult. The difficult thing is fixing the paths and making the robot useful."

"But why is that difficult? Fixing the paths requires a great deal of effort because the Principle of Uncertainty is important in particles the mass of positrons and the uncertainty effect must be minimized. Yet why must it? If we arrange to have the Principle just sufficiently prominent to allow the crossing of paths unpredictably—"

"We have an unpredictable robot."

"We have a *creative* robot," said Madarian, with a trace of impatience. "Peter, if there's anything a human brain has that a robotic brain has never had, it's the trace of unpredictability that comes from the effects of uncertainty at the subatomic level. I admit that this effect has never been demonstrated experimentally within the nervous system, but without that the human brain is not superior to the robotic brain in principle."

"And you think that if you introduce the effect into the robotic brain, the human brain will become not superior to the robotic brain in principle."

"That," said Madarian, "is exactly what I believe."

They went on for a long time after that.

The Board of Directors clearly had no intention of being easily convinced. Scott Robertson, the largest shareholder in the firm, said, "It's hard enough to manage the robot industry as it is, with public hostility to robots forever on the verge of breaking out into the open. If the public gets the idea that robots will be uncontrolled . . . Oh, don't tell me about the Three Laws. The average man won't believe the Three Laws will protect him if he as much as hears the word 'uncontrolled.' "

"Then don't use it," said Madarian. "Call the robot—call it 'intuitive.' "

"An intuitive robot," someone muttered. "A girl robot?"

A smile made its way about the conference table.

Madarian seized on that. "All right. A girl robot. Our robots are sexless, of course, and so will this one be, but we always act as though they're males. We give them male pet names and call them he and him. Now this one, if we consider the nature of the mathematical structuring of the brain which I have proposed, would fall into the JN-coordinate system. The first robot would be JN-1, and I've assumed that it would be called John-1. . . . I'm afraid that is the level of originality of the average roboticist. But why not call it Jane-1, damn it? If the public has to be let in on what we're doing, we're constructing a feminine robot with intuition."

Robertson shook his head, "What difference would that make? What you're saying is that you plan to remove the last barrier which, in principle, keeps the robotic brain inferior to the human brain. What do you suppose the public reaction will be to that?"

"Do you plan to make that public?" said Madarian. He thought a bit and then said, "Look. One thing the general public believes is that women are not as intelligent as men."

There was an instant apprehensive look on the face of more than one man at the table and a quick look up and down as though Susan Calvin were still in her accustomed seat.

Madarian said, "If we announce a female robot, it doesn't matter what she is. The public will automatically assume she is mentally backward. We just publicize the robot as Jane-1 and we don't have to say another word. We're safe."

"Actually," said Peter Bogert quietly, "there's more to it than that. Madarian and I have gone over the mathematics carefully and the JN series, whether John or Jane, would be quite safe. They would be less complex and intellectually capable, in an orthodox sense, than many another series we have designed and constructed. There would only be the one added factor of, well, let's get into the habit of calling it 'intuition.' "

"Who knows what it would do?" muttered Robertson.

"Madarian has suggested one thing it can do. As you all know, the Space Jump has been developed in principle. It is possible for men to attain what is, in effect, hyper-speeds beyond that of light and to visit other stellar systems and return in negligible time—weeks at the most."

Robertson said, "That's not new to us. It couldn't have been done without robots."

"Exactly, and it's not doing us any good because we can't use the hyper-speed drive except once as a demonstration, so that U. S. Robots gets little credit. The Space Jump is risky, it's fearfully prodigal of energy and therefore it's enormously expensive. If we were going to use it anyway, it would be nice if we could report the existence of a habitable planet. Call it a psychological need. Spend about twenty billion dollars on a single Space Jump and report nothing but scientific data and the public wants to know why their money was wasted. Report the existence of a habitable planet, and you're an inter-stellar Columbus and no one will worry about the money."

"So?"

"So where are we going to find a habitable planet? Or put it this way—which star within reach of the Space Jump as presently developed, which of the three hundred thousand stars and star systems within three hundred light-years has the best chance of having a habitable planet? We've got an enormous quantity of details on every star in our three-hundred-light-year neighborhood and a notion that almost every one has a planetary system. But which has a *habitable* planet? Which do we visit? . . . We don't know."

One of the directors said, "How would this Jane robot help us?"

Madarian was about to answer that, but he gestured slightly to Bogert and Bogert understood. The Director would carry more weight. Bogert didn't particularly like the idea; if the JN series proved a fiasco, he was making himself prominent enough in connection with it to insure that the sticky fingers of blame would cling to him. On the other hand, retirement was not all that far off, and if it worked, he would go out in a blaze of glory. Maybe it was only Madarian's aura of confidence, but Bogert had honestly come to believe it would work.

He said, "It may well be that somewhere in the libraries of data we have on those stars, there are methods for estimating the probabilities of the presence of Earth-type habitable planets. All we need to do is understand the data properly, look at them in the appropriate creative manner, make the correct correlations. We haven't done it yet. Or if some astronomer has, he hasn't been smart enough to realize what he has.

"A JN-type robot could make correlations far more rapidly and far more precisely than a man could. In a day, it would make and discard as many correlations as a man could in ten years. Furthermore, it would work in truly random fashion, whereas a man would have a strong bias based on preconception and on what is already believed."

There was a considerable silence after that. Finally Robertson said, "But it's only a matter of probability, isn't it? Suppose this robot said, 'The highest-probability habitable-planet star within so-and-so light-years is Squidgee-17,' or whatever, and we go there and find that a probability is only a probability and that there are no habitable planets after all. Where does that leave us?"

Madarian struck in this time. "We still win. We know how the robot came to the conclusion because it—she—will tell us. It might well help gain enormous insight into astronomical detail and make the whole thing worthwhile even if we don't make the Space Jump at all. Besides, we can then work out the five most probable sites of planets and the probability that one of the five has a habitable planet may then be better than 0.95. It would be almost sure—"

They went on for a long time after that.

The funds granted were quite insufficient, but Madarian counted on the habit of throwing good money after bad. With two hundred million about to be lost irrevocably when another hundred million could save everything, the other hundred million would surely be voted.

Jane-1 was finally built and put on display. Peter Bogert studied it—her—gravely. He said, "Why the narrow waist? Surely that introduces a mechanical weakness?"

Madarian chuckled. "Listen, if we're going to call her Jane, there's no point in making her look like Tarzan."

Bogert shook his head. "Don't like it. You'll be bulging her higher up to give the appearance of breasts next, and that's a rotten idea. If women start getting the notion that robots may look like women, I can tell you exactly the kind of perverse notions they'll get, and you'll *really* have hostility on their part."

Madarian said, "Maybe you're right at that. No woman wants to feel replaceable by something with none of her faults. Okay."

Jane-2 did not have the pinched waist. She was a somber robot which rarely moved and even more rarely spoke.

Madarian had only occasionally come rushing to Bogert with items of news during her construction and that had been a sure sign that things were going poorly. Madarian's ebullience under success was overpowering. He would not hesitate to invade Bogert's bedroom at 3 A.M. with a hot-flash item rather than wait for the morning. Bogert was sure of that.

Now Madarian seemed subdued, his usually florid expression nearly pale, his round cheeks somehow pinched. Bogert said, with a feeling of certainty, "She won't talk."

"Oh, she talks." Madarian sat down heavily and chewed at his lower lip. "Sometimes, anyway," he said.

Bogert rose and circled the robot. "And when she talks, she makes no sense, I suppose. Well, if she doesn't talk, she's no female, is she?"

Madarian tried a weak smile for size and abandoned it. He said, "The brain, in isolation, checked out."

"I know," said Bogert.

"But once that brain was put in charge of the physical apparatus of the robot, it was necessarily modified, of course."

"Of course," agreed Bogert unhelpfully.

"But unpredictably and frustratingly. The trouble is that when you're deal-ing with n-dimensional calculus of uncertainty, things are—"

"Uncertain?" said Bogert. His own reaction was surprising him. The com-pany investment was already most sizable and almost two years had elapsed, yet the results were, to put it politely, disappointing. Still, he found himself jabbing at Madarian and finding himself amused in the process.

Almost furtively, Bogert wondered if it weren't the absent Susan Calvin he was jabbing at. Madarian was so much more ebullient and effusive than Susan could ever possibly be—when things were going well. He was also far more vulnerably in the dumps when things weren't going well, and it was precisely under pressure that Susan never cracked. The target that Madarian made could be a neatly punctured bull's-eye as recompense for the target Susan had never allowed herself to be.

Madarian did not react to Bogert's last remark any more than Susan Cal-vin would have done; not out of contempt, which would have been Susan's reaction, but because he did not hear it.

He said argumentatively, "The trouble is the matter of recognition. We have Jane-2 correlating magnificently. She can correlate on any subject, but once she's done so, she can't recognize a valuable result from a valueless one. It's not an easy problem, judging how to program a robot to tell a significant correlation when you don't know what correlations she will be making."

"I presume you've thought of lowering the potential at the W-21 diode junction and sparking across the—"

"No, no, no, no—" Madarian faded off in to a whispering diminuendo. "You can't just have it spew out everything. We can do that for ourselves. The point is to have it recognize the crucial correlation and draw the conclu-sion. Once that is done, you see, a Jane robot would snap out an answer by intuition. It would be something we couldn't get ourselves except by the oddest kind of luck."

"It seems to me," said Bogert dryly, "that if you had a robot like that, you would have her do routinely what, among human beings, only the occasional genius is capable of doing."

Madarian nodded vigorously. "Exactly, Peter. I'd have said so myself if I weren't afraid of frightening off the execs. Please don't repeat that in their hearing."

"Do you really want a robot genius?"

"What are words? I'm trying to get a robot with the capacity to make random correlations at enormous speeds, together with a key-significance high-recognition quotient. And I'm trying to put *those* words into positronic field equations. I thought I had it, too, but I don't. Not yet."

He looked at Jane-2 discontentedly and said, "What's the best significance you have, Jane?"

Jane-2's head turned to look at Madarian but she made no sound, and

Madarian whispered with resignation, "She's running that into the correlation banks."

Jane-2 spoke tonelessly at last. "I'm not sure." It was the first sound she had made.

Madarian's eyes rolled upward. "She's doing the equivalent of setting up equations with indeterminate solutions."

"I gathered that," said Bogert. "Listen, Madarian, can you go anywhere at this point, or do we pull out now and cut our losses at half a billion?"

"Oh, I'll get it," muttered Madarian.

Jane-3 wasn't it. She was never as much as activated and Madarian was in a rage.

It was human error. His own fault, if one wanted to be entirely accurate. Yet though Madarian was utterly humiliated, others remained quiet. Let he who has never made an error in the fearsomely intricate mathematics of the positronic brain fill out the first memo of correction.

Nearly a year passed before Jane-4 was ready. Madarian was ebullient again. "She does it," he said. "She's got a good high-recognition quotient."

He was confident enough to place her on display before the Board and have her solve problems. Not mathematical problems; any robot could do that; but problems where the terms were deliberately misleading without being actually inaccurate.

Bogert said afterward, "That doesn't take much, really."

"Of course not. It's elementary for Jane-4, but I had to show them something, didn't I?"

"Do you know how much we've spent so far?"

"Come on, Peter, don't give me that. Do you know how much we've got back? These things don't go on in a vacuum, you know. I've had over three years of hell over this, if you want to know, but I've worked out new techniques of calculation that will save us a minimum of fifty thousand dollars on every type of positronic brain we design, from now on in forever. Right?"

"Well—"

"Well me no wells. It's so. And it's my personal feeling that n-dimensional calculus of uncertainty can have any number of other applications if we have the ingenuity to find them, and my Jane robots *will* find them. Once I've got exactly what I want, the new JN series will pay for itself inside of five years, even if we triple what we've invested so far."

"What do you mean by 'exactly what you want'? What's wrong with Jane-4?"

"Nothing. Or nothing much. She's on the track, but she can be improved and I intend to do so. I thought I knew where I was going when I designed her. Now I've tested her and I *know* where I'm going. I intend to get there."

• • • •

Jane-5 was it. It took Madarian well over a year to produce her and there he had no reservations; he was utterly confident.

Jane-5 was shorter than the average robot, slimmer. Without being a female caricature as Jane-1 had been, she managed to possess an air of femininity about herself despite the absence of a single clearly feminine feature.

"It's the way she's standing," said Bogert. Her arms were held gracefully and somehow the torso managed to give the impression of curving slightly when she turned.

Madarian said, "Listen to her. . . . How do you feel, Jane?"

"In excellent health, thank you," said Jane-5, and the voice was precisely that of a woman; it was a sweet and almost disturbing contralto.

"Why did you do that, Clinton?" said Peter, startled and beginning to frown.

"Psychologically important," said Madarian. "I want people to think of her as a woman; to treat her as a woman; to *explain*."

"What people?"

Madarian put his hands in his pockets and stared thoughtfully at Bogert. "I would like to have arrangements made for Jane and myself to go to Flagstaff."

Bogert couldn't help but note that Madarian didn't say Jane-5. He made use of no number this time. She was *the* Jane. He said doubtfully, "To Flagstaff? Why?"

"Because that's the world center for general planetology, isn't it? It's where they're studying the stars and trying to calculate the probability of habitable planets, isn't it?"

"I know that, but it's on Earth."

"Well, and I surely know that."

"Robotic movements on Earth are strictly controlled. And there's no need for it. Bring a library of books on general planetology here and let Jane absorb them."

"*No!* Peter, will you get it through your head that Jane isn't the ordinary logical robot; she's intuitive."

"So?"

"So how can we tell what she needs, what she can use, what will set her off? We can use any metal model in the factory to read books; that's frozen data and out of date besides. Jane must have living information; she must have tones of voice, she must have side issues; she must have total irrelevancies even. How the devil do we know what or when something will go click-click inside her and fall into a pattern? If we knew, we wouldn't need her at all, would we?"

Bogert began to feel harassed. He said, "Then bring the men here, the general planetologists."

"Here won't do any good. They'll be out of their element. They won't react naturally. I want Jane to watch them at work; I want her to see their instruments, their offices, their desks, everything about them that she can. I want you to arrange to have her transported to Flagstaff. And I'd really like not to discuss it any further."

For a moment he almost sounded like Susan. Bogert winced, and said, "It's complicated making such an arrangement. Transporting an experimental robot—"

"Jane isn't experimental. She's the fifth of the series."

"The other four weren't really working models."

Madarian lifted his hands in helpless frustration. "Who's forcing you to tell the government that?"

"I'm not worried about the government. It can be made to understand special cases. It's public opinion. We've come a long way in fifty years and I don't propose to be set back twenty-five of them by having you lose control of a—"

"I won't lose control. You're making foolish remarks. Look! U. S. Robots can afford a private plane. We can land quietly at the nearest commercial airport and be lost in hundreds of similar landings. We can arrange to have a large ground car with an enclosed body meet us and take us to Flagstaff. Jane will be crated and it will be obvious that some piece of thoroughly non-robotic equipment is being transported to the labs. We won't get a second look from anyone. The men at Flagstaff will be alerted and will be told the exact purpose of the visit. They will have every motive to cooperate and to prevent a leak."

Bogert pondered. "The risky part will be the plane and the ground car. If anything happens to the crate—"

"Nothing will."

"We might get away with it if Jane is deactivated during transport. Then even if someone finds out she's inside—"

"No, Peter. That can't be done. Uh-uh. Not Jane-5. Look, she's been free-associating since she was activated. The information she possesses can be put in freeze during deactivation but the free associations never. No, sir, she can't ever be deactivated."

"But, then, if somehow it is discovered that we are transporting an activated robot—"

"It won't be found out."

Madarian remained firm and the plane eventually took off. It was a late-model automatic Computo-jet, but it carried a human pilot—one of U. S. Robots' own employees—as backup. The crate containing Jane arrived at the airport safely, was transferred to the ground car, and reached the Research Laboratories at Flagstaff without incident.

Peter Bogert received his free call from Madarian not more than an hour after the latter's arrival at Flagstaff. Madarian was ecstatic and, characteristically, could not wait to report.

The message arrived by tubed laser beam, shielded, scrambled, and ordi-

narily impenetrable, but Bogert felt exasperated. He knew it could be penetrated if someone with enough technological ability—the government, for
example—was determined to do so. The only real safety lay in the fact that
the government had no reason to try. At least Bogert hoped so.

He said, "For God's sake, do you have to call?"

Madarian ignored him entirely. He burbled, "It was an inspiration. Sheer
genius, I tell you."

For a while, Bogert stared at the receiver. Then he shouted incredulously,
"You mean you've got the answer? Already?"

"No, no! Give us time, damn it. I mean the matter of her voice was an
inspiration. Listen, after we were chauffeured from the airport to the main
administration building at Flagstaff, we uncrated Jane and she stepped out of
the box. When that happened, every man in the place stepped back. Scared!
Nitwits! If even scientists can't understand the significance of the Laws of
Robotics, what can we expect of the average untrained individual? For a
minute there I thought: This will all be useless. They won't talk. They'll be
keying themselves for a quick break in case she goes berserk and they'll be
able to think of nothing else."

"Well, then, what are you getting at?"

"So then she greeted them routinely. She said, 'Good afternoon, gentlemen. I am so glad to meet you.' And it came out in this beautiful contralto.
. . . That was it. One man straightened his tie, and another ran his fingers
through his hair. What really got me was that the oldest guy in the place
actually checked his fly to make sure it was zipped. They're all crazy about
her now. All they needed was the voice. She isn't a robot any more; she's a
girl."

"You mean they're talking to her?"

"*Are* they talking to her! I should say so. I should have programmed her for
sexy intonations. They'd be asking her for dates right now if I had. Talk
about conditioned reflex. Listen, men respond to voices. At the most inti-
mate moments, are they looking? It's the voice in your ear—"

"Yes, Clinton, I seem to remember. Where's Jane now?"

"With them. They won't let go of her."

"Damn! Get in there with her. Don't let her out of your sight, man."

Madarian's calls thereafter, during his ten-day stay at Flagstaff, were not
very frequent and became progressively less exalted.

Jane was listening carefully, he reported, and occasionally she responded.
She remained popular. She was given entry everywhere. But there were no
results.

Bogert said, "Nothing at all?"

Madarian was at once defensive. "You can't say nothing at all. It's impossible to say nothing at all with an intuitive robot. You don't know what might
not be going on inside her. This morning she asked Jensen what he had for
breakfast."

"Rossiter Jensen the astrophysicist?"

"Yes, of course. As it turned out, he didn't have breakfast that morning. Well, a cup of coffee."

"So Jane's learning to make small talk. That scarcely makes up for the expense—"

"Oh, don't be a jackass. It wasn't small talk. Nothing is small talk for Jane. She asked because it had something to do with some sort of cross-correlation she was building in her mind."

"What can it possibly—"

"How do I know? If I knew, I'd be a Jane myself and you wouldn't need her. But it has to mean something. She's programmed for high motivation to obtain an answer to the question of a planet with optimum habitability/ distance and—"

"Then let me know when she's done that and not before. It's not really necessary for me to get a blow-by-blow description of possible correlations."

He didn't really expect to get notification of success. With each day, Bogert grew less sanguine, so that when the notification finally came, he wasn't ready. And it came at the very end.

That last time, when Madarian's climactic message came, it came in what was almost a whisper. Exaltation had come complete circle and Madarian was awed into quiet.

"She did it," he said. "She did it. After I all but gave up, too. After she had received everything in the place and most of it twice and three times over and never said a word that sounded like anything. . . . I'm on the plane now, returning. We've just taken off."

Bogert managed to get his breath. "Don't play games, man. You have the *answer?* Say so, if you have. Say it plainly."

"She has the answer. She's given me the answer. She's given me the names of three stars within eighty light-years which, she says, have a sixty to ninety per cent chance of possessing one habitable planet each. The probability that at least one has is 0.972. It's almost certain. And that's just the least of it. Once we get back, she can give us the exact line of reasoning that led her to the conclusion and I predict that the whole science of astrophysics and cosmology will—"

"Are you sure—"

"You think I'm having hallucinations? I even have a witness. Poor guy jumped two feet when Jane suddenly began to reel out the answer in her gorgeous voice—"

And that was when the meteorite struck and in the thorough destruction of the plane that followed, Madarian and the pilot were reduced to gobbets of bloody flesh and no usable remnant of Jane was recovered.

• • • •

The gloom at U. S. Robots had never been deeper. Robertson attempted to find consolation in the fact that the very completeness of the destruction had utterly hidden the illegalities of which the firm had been guilty.

Peter shook his head and mourned. "We've lost the best chance U. S. Robots ever had of gaining an unbeatable public image; of overcoming the damned Frankenstein complex. What it would have meant for robots to have one of them work out the solution to the habitable-planet problem, after other robots had helped work out the Space Jump. Robots would have opened the galaxy to us. And if at the same time we could have driven scientific knowledge forward in a dozen different directions as we surely would have . . . Oh, God, there's no way of calculating the benefits to the human race, and to us of course."

Robertson said, "We could build other Janes, couldn't we? Even without Madarian?"

"Sure we could. But can we depend on the proper correlation again? Who knows how low-probability that final result was? What if Madarian had had a fantastic piece of beginner's luck? And then to have an even more fantastic piece of bad luck? A meteorite zeroing in . . . It's simply unbelievable—"

Robertson said in a hesitating whisper, "It couldn't have been—meant. I mean, if we weren't meant to know and if the meteorite was a judgment—from—"

He faded off under Bogert's withering glare.

Bogert said, "It's not a dead loss, I suppose. Other Janes are bound to help us in some ways. And we can give other robots feminine voices, if that will help encourage public acceptance—though I wonder what the women would say. If we only knew what Jane-5 had said!"

"In that last call, Madarian said there was a witness."

Bogert said, "I know; I've been thinking about that. Don't you suppose I've been in touch with Flagstaff? Nobody in the entire place heard Jane say anything out of the ordinary, anything that sounded like an answer to the habitable-planet problem, and certainly anyone there should have recognized the answer if it came—or at least recognized it as a possible answer."

"Could Madarian have been lying? Or crazy? Could he have been trying to protect himself—"

"You mean he may have been trying to save his reputation by pretending he had the answer and then gimmick Jane so she couldn't talk and say, 'Oh, sorry, something happened accidentally. Oh, darn!' I won't accept that for a minute. You might as well suppose he had arranged the meteorite."

"Then what do we do?"

Bogert said heavily, "Turn back to Flagstaff. The answer *must* be there. I've got to dig deeper, that's all. I'm going there and I'm taking a couple of the men in Madarian's department. We've got to go through that place top to bottom and end to end."

"But, you know, even if there were a witness and he had heard, what good would it do, now that we don't have Jane to explain the process?"

"Every little something is useful. Jane gave the names of the stars; the catalogue numbers probably—none of the named stars has a chance. If someone can remember her saying that and actually remember the catalogue number, or have heard it clearly enough to allow it to be recovered by Psycho-probe if he lacked the conscious memory—then we'll have something. Given the results at the end, and the data fed Jane at the beginning, we might be able to reconstruct the line of reasoning; we might recover the intuition. If that is done, we've saved the game—"

Bogert was back after three days, silent and thoroughly depressed. When Robertson inquired anxiously as to results, he shook his head. "Nothing!"

"Nothing?"

"Absolutely nothing. I spoke with every man in Flagstaff—every scientist, every technician, every student—that had had anything to do with Jane; everyone that had as much as seen her. The number wasn't great; I'll give Madarian credit for that much discretion. He only allowed those to see her who might conceivably have had planetological knowledge to feed her. There were twenty-three men altogether who had seen Jane and of those only twelve had spoken to her more than casually.

"I went over and over all that Jane had said. They remembered everything quite well. They're keen men engaged in a crucial experiment involving their specialty, so they had every motivation to remember. And they were dealing with a talking robot, something that was startling enough, and one that talked like a TV actress. They couldn't forget."

Robertson said, "Maybe a Psycho-probe—"

"If one of them had the vaguest thought that something had happened, I would screw out his consent to Probing. But there's nothing to leave room for an excuse, and to Probe two dozen men who make their living from their brains can't be done. Honestly, it wouldn't help. If Jane had mentioned three stars and said they had habitable planets, it would have been like setting up sky rockets in their brains. How could any one of them forget?"

"Then maybe one of them is lying," said Robertson grimly. "He wants the information for his own use; to get the credit himself later."

"What good would that do him?" said Bogert. "The whole establishment knows exactly why Madarian and Jane were there in the first place. They know why I came there in the second. If at any time in the future any man now at Flagstaff suddenly comes up with a habitable-planet theory that is startlingly new and different, yet valid, every other man at Flagstaff and every man at U. S. Robots will know at once that he had stolen it. He'd never get away with it."

"Then Madarian himself was somehow mistaken."

"I don't see how I can believe that either. Madarian had an irritating personality—all robopsychologists have irritating personalities, I think, which must be why they work with robots rather than with men—but he was no dummy. He *couldn't* be wrong in something like this."

"Then—" But Robertson had run out of possibilities. They had reached a blank wall and for some minutes stared at it disconsolately.

Finally Robertson stirred. "Peter—"

"Well?"

"Let's ask Susan."

Bogert stiffened. "What!"

"Let's ask Susan. Let's call her and ask her to come in."

"Why? What can she possibly do?"

"I don't know. But she's a robopsychologist, too, and she might understand Madarian better than we do. Besides, she— Oh, hell, she always had more brains than any of us."

"She's nearly eighty."

"And you're seventy. What about it?"

Bogert sighed. Had her abrasive tongue lost any of its rasp in the years of her retirement? He said, "Well, I'll ask her."

Susan Calvin entered Bogert's office with a slow look around before her eyes fixed themselves on the Research Director. She had aged a great deal since her retirement. Her hair was a fine white and her face seemed to have crumpled. She had grown so frail as to be almost transparent and only her eyes, piercing and uncompromising, seemed to remain of all that had been.

Bogert strode forward heartily, holding out his hand. "Susan!"

Susan Calvin took it, and said, "You're looking reasonably well, Peter, for an old man. If I were you, I wouldn't wait till next year. Retire now and let the young men get to it. . . . And Madarian is dead. Are you calling me in to take over my old job? Are you determined to keep the ancients till a year past actual physical death?"

"No, no, Susan. I've called you in—" He stopped. He did not, after all, have the faintest idea of how to start.

But Susan read his mind now as easily as she always had. She seated herself with the caution born of stiffened joints and said, "Peter, you've called me in because you're in bad trouble. Otherwise you'd sooner see me dead than within a mile of you."

"Come, Susan—"

"Don't waste time on pretty talk. I never had time to waste when I was forty and certainly not now. Madarian's death and your call to me are both unusual, so there must be a connection. Two unusual events without a connection is too low-probability to worry about. Begin at the beginning and don't worry about revealing yourself to be a fool. That was revealed to me long ago."

Bogert cleared his throat miserably and began. She listened carefully, her withered hand lifting once in a while to stop him so that she might ask a question.

She snorted at one point. "Feminine intuition? Is that what you wanted the robot for? You men. Faced with a woman reaching a correct conclusion and unable to accept the fact that she is your equal or superior in intelligence, you invent something called feminine intuition."

"Uh, yes, Susan, but let me continue—"

He did. When she was told of Jane's contralto voice, she said, "It is a difficult choice sometimes whether to feel revolted at the male sex or merely to dismiss them as contemptible."

Bogert said, "Well, let me go on—"

When he was quite done, Susan said, "May I have the private use of this office for an hour or two?"

"Yes, but—"

She said, "I want to go over the various records—Jane's programming, Madarian's calls, your interviews at Flagstaff. I presume I can use that beautiful new shielded laser-phone and your computer outlet if I wish."

"Yes, of course."

"Well, then, get out of here, Peter."

It was not quite forty-five minutes when she hobbled to the door, opened it, and called for Bogert.

When Bogert came, Robertson was with him. Both entered and Susan greeted the latter with an unenthusiastic "Hello, Scott."

Bogert tried desperately to gauge the results from Susan's face, but it was only the face of a grim old lady who had no intention of making anything easy for him.

He said cautiously, "Do you think there's anything you can do, Susan?"

"Beyond what I have already done? No! There's nothing more."

Bogert's lips set in chagrin, but Robertson said, "What have you already done, Susan?"

Susan said, "I've thought a little; something I can't seem to persuade anyone else to do. For one thing, I've thought about Madarian. I knew him, you know. He had brains but he was a very irritating extrovert. I thought you would like him after me, Peter."

"It was a change," Bogert couldn't resist saying.

"And he was always running to you with results the very minute he had them, wasn't he?"

"Yes, he was."

"And yet," said Susan, "his last message, the one in which he said Jane had given him the answer, was sent from the plane. Why did he wait so long? Why didn't he call you while he was still at Flagstaff, immediately after Jane had said whatever it was she said?"

"I suppose," said Peter, "that for once he wanted to check it thoroughly and—well, I don't know. It was the most important thing that had ever happened to him; he might for once have wanted to wait and be sure of himself."

"On the contrary; the more important it was, the less he would wait, surely. And if he could manage to wait, why not do it properly and wait till he was back at U. S. Robots so that he could check the results with all the computing equipment this firm could make available to him? In short, he waited too long from one point of view and not long enough from another."

Robertson interrupted. "Then you think he was up to some trickery—"

Susan looked revolted. "Scott, don't try to compete with Peter in making inane remarks. Let me continue. . . . A second point concerns the witness. According to the records of that last call, Madarian said, 'Poor guy jumped two feet when Jane suddenly began to reel out the answer in her gorgeous voice.' In fact, it was the last thing he said. And the question is, then, why should the witness have jumped? Madarian had explained that all the men were crazy about that voice, and they had had ten days with the robot—with Jane. Why should the mere act of her speaking have startled them?"

Bogert said, "I assumed it was astonishment at hearing Jane give an answer to a problem that has occupied the minds of planetologists for nearly a century."

"But they were *waiting* for her to give that answer. That was why she was there. Besides, consider the way the sentence is worded. Madarian's statement makes it seem the witness was startled, not astonished, if you see the difference. What's more, that reaction came 'when Jane suddenly began'—in other words, at the very start of the statement. To be astonished at the content of what Jane said would have required the witness to have listened awhile so that he might absorb it. Madarian would have said he had jumped two feet *after* he had heard Jane say thus-and-so. It would be 'after' not 'when' and the word 'suddenly' would not be included."

Bogert said uneasily, "I don't think you can refine matters down to the use or non-use of a word."

"I can," said Susan frostily, "because I am a robopsychologist. And I can expect Madarian to do so, too, because *he* was a robopsychologist. We have to explain those two anomalies, then. The queer delay before Madarian's call and the queer reaction of the witness."

"Can *you* explain them?" asked Robertson.

"Of course," said Susan, "since I use a little simple logic. Madarian called with the news without delay, as he always did, or with as little delay as he could manage. If Jane had solved the problem at Flagstaff, he would certainly have called from Flagstaff. Since he called from the plane, she must clearly have solved the problem after he had left Flagstaff."

"But then—"

"Let me finish. Let me finish. Was Madarian not taken from the airport to Flagstaff in a heavy, enclosed ground car? And Jane, in her crate, with him?"

"Yes."

"And presumably, Madarian and the crated Jane returned from Flagstaff to the airport in the same heavy, enclosed ground car. Am I right?"

"Yes, of course!"

"And they were not alone in the ground car, either. In one of his calls, Madarian said, 'We were chauffeured from the airport to the main administration building,' and I suppose I am right in concluding that if he was chauffeured, then that was because there was a chauffeur, a human driver, in the car."

"Good God!"

"The trouble with you, Peter, is that when you think of a witness to a planetological statement, you think of planetologists. You divide up human beings into categories, and despise and dismiss most. A robot cannot do that. The First Law says, 'A robot may not injure a *human being* or, through inaction, allow a *human being* to come to harm.' *Any* human being. That is the essence of the robotic view of life. A robot makes no distinction. To a robot, all men are truly equal, and to a robopsychologist who must perforce deal with men at the robotic level, all men are truly equal, too.

"It would not occur to Madarian to say a truck driver had heard the statement. To you a truck driver is not a scientist but is a mere animate adjunct of a truck, but to Madarian he was a man and a witness. Nothing more. Nothing less."

Bogert shook his head in disbelief. "But you are *sure?*"

"Of course I'm sure. How else can you explain the other point; Madarian's remark about the startling of the witness? Jane was crated, wasn't she? But she was *not* deactivated. According to the records, Madarian was always adamant against ever deactivating an intuitive robot. Moreover, Jane-5, like any of the Janes, was extremely non-talkative. Probably it never occurred to Madarian to order her to remain quiet within the crate; and it was within the crate that the pattern finally fell into place. Naturally she began to talk. A beautiful contralto voice suddenly sounded from inside the crate. If you were the truck driver, what would you do at that point? Surely you'd be startled. It's a wonder he didn't crash."

"But if the truck driver was the witness, why didn't he come forward—"

"Why? Can he possibly know that anything crucial had happened, that what he heard was important? Besides, don't you suppose Madarian tipped him well and asked him not to say anything? Would you *want* the news to spread that an activated robot was being transported illegally over the Earth's surface?"

"Well, will he remember what was said?"

"Why not? It might seem to you, Peter, that a truck driver, one step above an ape in your view, can't remember. But truck drivers can have brains, too. The statements were most remarkable and the driver may well have remembered some. Even if he gets some of the letters and numbers wrong, we're dealing with a finite set, you know, the fifty-five hundred stars or star systems within eighty light-years or so—I haven't looked up the exact number. You can make the correct choices. And if needed, you will have every excuse to use the Psychoprobe—"

The two men stared at her. Finally Bogert, afraid to believe, whispered, "But how can you be *sure?*"

For a moment, Susan was on the point of saying: Because I've called Flagstaff, you fool, and because I spoke to the truck driver, and because he told me what he had heard, and because I've checked with the computer at Flagstaff and got the only three stars that fit the information, and because I have those names in my pocket.

But she didn't. Let him go through it all himself. Carefully, she rose to her feet, and said sardonically, "How can I be sure? . . . Call it feminine intuition."

The Greatest Asset

The Earth was one large park. It had been tamed utterly.

Lou Tansonia saw it expand under his eyes as he watched somberly from the Lunar Shuttle. His prominent nose split his lean face into inconsiderable halves and each looked sad always—but this time in accurate reflection of his mood.

He had never been away so long—almost a month—and he anticipated a none-too-pleasant acclimation period once Earth's large gravity made its grip fiercely evident.

But that was for later. That was not the sadness of now as he watched Earth grow larger.

As long as the planet was far enough to be a circle of white spirals, glistening in the sun that shone over the ship's shoulders, it had its primeval beauty. When the occasional patches of pastel browns and greens peeped through the clouds, it might still have been the planet it was at any time since three hundred million years before, when life had first stretched out of the sea and moved over the dry land to fill the valleys with green.

It was lower, lower—when the ship sank down—that the tameness began to show.

There was no wilderness anywhere. Lou had never seen Earthly wilderness; he had only read of it, or seen it in old films.

The forests stood in rank and file, with each tree carefully ticketed by species and position. The crops grew in their fields in orderly rotation, with intermittent and automated fertilization and weeding. The few domestic animals that still existed were numbered and Lou wryly suspected that the blades of grass were as well.

Animals were so rarely seen as to be a sensation when glimpsed. Even the insects had faded, and none of the large animals existed anywhere outside the slowly dwindling number of zoos.

The very cats had become few in number, for it was much more patriotic to keep a hamster, if one had to have a pet at all.

Correction! Only Earth's nonhuman animal population had diminished. Its mass of animal life was as great as ever, but most of it, about three fourths of its total, was one species only—*Homo sapiens*. And, despite everything the Terrestrial Bureau of Ecology could do (or said it could do), that fraction very slowly increased from year to year.

Lou thought of that, as he always did, with a towering sense of loss. The human presence was unobtrusive, to be sure. There was no sign of it from where the shuttle made its final orbits about the planet; and, Lou knew, there would be no sign of it even when they sank much lower.

The sprawling cities of the chaotic pre-Planetary days were gone. The old highways could be traced from the air by the imprint they still left on the vegetation, but they were invisible from close quarters. Individual men themselves rarely troubled the surface, but they were there, underground. All mankind was, in all its billions, with the factories, the food-processing plants, the energies, the vacu-tunnels.

The tame world lived on solar energy and was free of strife, and to Lou it was hateful in consequence.

Yet at the moment he could almost forget, for, after months of failure, he was going to see Adrastus, himself. It had meant the pulling of every available string.

Ino Adrastus was the Secretary General of Ecology. It was not an elective office; it was little-known. It was simply the most important post on Earth, for it controlled everything.

Jan Marley said exactly that, as he sat there, with a sleepy look of absent-minded dishevelment that made one think he would have been fat if the human diet were so uncontrolled as to allow of fatness.

He said, "For my money this is the most important post on Earth, and no one seems to know it. I want to write it up."

Adrastus shrugged. His stocky figure, with its shock of hair, once a light brown and now a brown-flecked gray, his faded blue eyes nested in darkened surrounding tissues, finely wrinkled, had been an unobtrusive part of the administrative scene for a generation. He had been Secretary-General of Ecology ever since the regional ecological councils had been combined into the Terrestrial Bureau. Those who knew of him at all found it impossible to think of ecology without him.

He said, "The truth is I hardly ever make a decision truly my own. The directives I sign aren't mine, really. I sign them because it would be psychologically uncomfortable to have computers sign them. But, you know, it's only the computers that can do the work.

"The Bureau ingests an incredible quantity of data each day; data forwarded to it from every part of the globe and dealing not only with human births, deaths, population shifts, production, and consumption, but with all the tangible changes in the plant and animal population as well, to say nothing of the measured state of the major segments of the environment—air, sea, and soil. The information is taken apart, absorbed, and assimilated into crossfiled memory indices of staggering complexity, and from that memory comes answers to the questions we ask."

Marley said, with a shrewd, sidelong glance, "Answers to *all* questions?"

Adrastus smiled. "We learn not to bother to ask questions that have no answer."

"And the result," said Marley, "is ecological balance."

"Right, but a *special* ecological balance. All through the planet's history, the balance has been maintained, but always at the cost of catastrophe. After temporary imbalance, the balance is restored by famine, epidemic, drastic climatic change. We maintain it now without catastrophe by daily shifts and changes, by never allowing imbalance to accumulate dangerously."

Marley said, "There's what you once said—'Man's greatest asset is a balanced ecology.' "

"So they tell me I said."

"It's there on the wall behind you."

"Only the first three words," said Adrastus dryly. There it was on a long Shimmer-plast, the words winking and alive: MAN'S GREATEST ASSET . . .

"You don't have to complete the statement."

"What else can I tell you?"

"Can I spend some time with you and watch you at your work?"

"You'll watch a glorified clerk."

"I don't think so. Do you have appointments at which I may be present?"

"One appointment today; a young fellow named Tansonia; one of our Moon-men. You can sit in."

"Moon-men? You mean—"

"Yes, from the lunar laboratories. Thank heaven for the moon. Otherwise all their experimentation would take place on Earth, and we have enough trouble containing the ecology as it is."

"You mean like nuclear experiments and radiational pollution?"

"I mean many things."

Lou Tansonia's expression was a mixture of barely suppressed excitement and barely suppressed apprehension. "I'm glad to have this chance to see you, Mr. Secretary," he said breathlessly, puffing against Earth's gravity.

"I'm sorry we couldn't make it sooner," said Adrastus smoothly. "I have excellent reports concerning your work. The other gentleman present is Jan Marley, a science writer, and he need not concern us."

Lou glanced at the writer briefly and nodded, then turned eagerly to Adrastus. "Mr. Secretary—"

"Sit down," said Adrastus.

Lou did so, with the trace of clumsiness to be expected of one acclimating himself to Earth, and with an air, somehow, that to pause long enough to sit was a waste of time. He said, "Mr. Secretary, I am appealing to you personally concerning my Project Application Num—"

"I know it."

"You've read it, sir?"

"No, I haven't, but the computers have. It's been rejected."

"Yes! But I appeal from the computers to you."

Adrastus smiled and shook his head. "That's a difficult appeal for me. I don't know from where I could gather the courage to override the computer."

"But you *must,*" said the young man earnestly. "My field is genetic engineering."

"Yes, I know."

"And genetic engineering," said Lou, running over the interruption, "is the handmaiden of medicine and it shouldn't be so. Not entirely, anyway."

"Odd that you think so. You have your medical degree, and you have done impressive work in medical genetics. I have been told that in two years time your work may lead to the full suppression of diabetes mellitus for good."

"Yes, but I don't care. I don't want to carry that through. Let someone else do it. Curing diabetes is just a detail and it will merely mean that the death rate will go down slightly and produce just a bit more pressure in the direction of population increase. I'm not interested in achieving that."

"You don't value human life?"

"Not infinitely. There are too many people on Earth."

"I know that some think so."

"You're one of them, Mr. Secretary. You have written articles saying so. And it's obvious to any thinking man—to you more than anyone—what it's doing. Over-population means discomfort, and to reduce the discomfort private choice must disappear. Crowd enough people into a field and the only way they can all sit down is for all to sit down at the same time. Make a mob dense enough and they can move from one point to another quickly only by marching in formation. That is what men are becoming; a blindly marching mob knowing nothing about where it is going or why."

"How long have you rehearsed this speech, Mr. Tansonia?"

Lou flushed slightly. "And the other life forms are decreasing in numbers of species and individuals, except for the plants we eat. The ecology gets simpler every year."

"It stays balanced."

"But it loses color and variety and we don't even know how good the balance is. We accept the balance only because it's all we have."

"What would you do?"

"Ask the computer that rejected my proposal. I want to initiate a program for genetic engineering on a wide variety of species from worms to mammals. I want to create new variety out of the dwindling material at hand before it dwindles out altogether."

"For what purpose?"

"To set up artificial ecologies. To set up ecologies based on plants and animals not like anything on Earth."

"What would you gain?"

"I don't know. If I knew exactly what I would gain there would be no need to do research. But I know what we ought to gain. We ought to learn more about what makes an ecology tick. So far, we've only taken what nature has handed us and then ruined it and broken it down and made do with the gutted remains. Why not build something up and study that?"

"You mean build it blindly? At random?"

"We don't know enough to do it any other way. Genetic engineering has the random mutation as its basic driving force. Applied to medicine, this randomness must be minimized at all costs, since a specific effect is sought. I want to take the random component of genetic engineering and make use of it."

Adrastus frowned for a moment. "And how are you going to set up an ecology that's meaningful? Won't it interact with the ecology that already exists, and possibly unbalance it? That is something we can't afford."

"I don't mean to carry out the experiments on Earth," said Lou. "Of course not."

"On the moon?"

"Not on the moon, either. —On the asteroids. I've thought of that since my proposal was fed to the computer which spit it out. Maybe this will make a difference. How about small asteroids, hollowed-out; one per ecology? Assign a certain number of asteroids for the purpose. Have them properly engineered; outfit them with energy sources and transducers; seed them with collections of life forms which might form a closed ecology. See what happens. If it doesn't work, try to figure out why and subtract an item, or, more likely, add an item, or change the proportions. We'll develop a science of applied ecology, or, if you prefer, a science of ecological engineering; a science one step up in complexity and significance beyond genetic engineering."

"But the good of it, you can't say."

"The specific good, of course not. But how can it avoid some good? It will increase knowledge in the very field we need it most." He pointed to the shimmering lettering behind Adrastus. "You said it yourself, 'Man's greatest asset is a balanced ecology.' I'm offering you a way of doing basic research in experimental ecology; something that has never been done before."

"How many asteroids will you want?"

Lou hesitated. "Ten?" he said with rising inflection. "As a beginning."

"Take five," said Adrastus, drawing the report toward himself and scribbling quickly on its face, cancelling out the computer's decision.

Afterward, Marley said, "Can you sit there and tell me that you're a glorified clerk now? You cancel the computer and hand out five asteroids. Like that."

"The Congress will have to give its approval. I'm sure it will."

"Then you think this young man's suggestion is really a good one."

"No, I don't. It won't work. Despite his enthusiasm, the matter is so complicated that it will surely take far more men than can possibly be made available for far more years than that young man will live to carry it through to any worthwhile point."

"Are you sure?"

"The computer says so. It's why his project was rejected."

"Then why did you cancel the computer's decision?"

"Because I, and the government in general, are here in order to preserve something far more important than the ecology."

Marley leaned forward. "I don't get it."

"Because you misquoted what I said so long ago. Because everyone misquotes it. Because I spoke two sentences and they were telescoped into one and I have never been able to force them apart again. Presumably, the human race is unwilling to accept my remarks as I made them."

"You mean you didn't say 'Man's greatest asset is a balanced ecology'?"

"Of course not. I said, 'Man's greatest *need* is a balanced ecology.'"

"But on your Shimmer-plast you say, 'Man's greatest asset—'"

"That begins the second sentence, which men refuse to quote, but which I never forget—'Man's greatest asset is the unsettled mind.' I haven't overruled the computer for the sake of our ecology. We only need that to live. I overruled it to save a valuable mind and keep it at work, an unsettled mind. We need that for man to be man—which is more important than merely to live."

Marley rose. "I suspect, Mr. Secretary, you wanted me here for this interview. It's this thesis you want me to publicize, isn't it?"

"Let's say," said Adrastus, "that I'm seizing the chance to get my remarks correctly quoted."

Mirror Image

The Three Laws of Robotics:
1. *A robot may not injure a human being or, through inaction, allow a human being to come to harm.*
2. *A robot must obey the orders given it by human beings except where such orders would conflict with the First Law.*
3. *A robot must protect its own existence as long as such protection does not conflict with the First or Second Law.*

Lije Baley had just decided to relight his pipe, when the door of his office opened without a preliminary knock, or announcement, of any kind. Baley looked up in pronounced annoyance and then dropped his pipe. It said a good deal for the state of his mind that he left it lie where it had fallen.

"R. Daneel Olivaw," he said, in a kind of mystified excitement. "Jehoshaphat! It *is* you, isn't it?"

"You are quite right," said the tall, bronzed newcomer, his even features never flicking for a moment out of their accustomed calm. "I regret surprising you by entering without warning, but the situation is a delicate one and there must be as little involvement as possible on the part of the men and robots even in this place. I am, in any case, pleased to see you again, friend Elijah."

And the robot held out his right hand in a gesture as thoroughly human as was his appearance. It was Baley who was so unmanned by his astonishment as to stare at the hand with a momentary lack of understanding.

But then he seized it in both his, feeling its warm firmness. "But Daneel, *why?* You're welcome any time, but—What is this situation that is a delicate one? Are we in trouble again? Earth, I mean?"

"No, friend Elijah, it does not concern Earth. The situation to which I refer as a delicate one is, to outward appearances, a small thing. A dispute between mathematicians, nothing more. As we happened, quite by accident, to be within an easy Jump of Earth—"

"This dispute took place on a starship, then?"

"Yes, indeed. A small dispute, yet to the humans involved astonishingly large."

Baley could not help but smile. "I'm not surprised you find humans astonishing. They do not obey the Three Laws."

"That is, indeed, a shortcoming," said R. Daneel, gravely, "and I think humans themselves are puzzled by humans. It may be that you are less puzzled than are the men of other worlds because so many more human beings live on Earth than on the Spacer worlds. If so, and I believe it is so, you could help us."

R. Daneel paused momentarily and then said, perhaps a shade too quickly, "And yet there are rules of human behavior which I have learned. It would seem, for instance, that I am deficient in etiquette, by human standards, not to have asked after your wife and child."

"They are doing well. The boy is in college and Jessie is involved in local politics. The amenities are taken care of. Now tell me how you come to be here."

"As I said, we were within an easy Jump of Earth," said R. Daneel, "so I suggested to the captain that we consult you."

"And the captain agreed?" Baley had a sudden picture of the proud and autocratic captain of a Spacer starship consenting to make a landing on Earth —of all worlds—and to consult an Earthman—of all people.

"I believe," said R. Daneel, "that he was in a position where he would have agreed to anything. In addition, I praised you very highly; although, to be sure, I stated only the truth. Finally, I agreed to conduct all negotiations so that none of the crew, or passengers, would need to enter any of the Earthman cities."

"And talk to any Earthman, yes. But what has happened?"

"The passengers of the starship, *Eta Carina,* included two mathematicians who were traveling to Aurora to attend an interstellar conference on neurobiophysics. It is about these mathematicians, Alfred Barr Humboldt and Gennao Sabbat, that the dispute centers. Have you perhaps, friend Elijah, heard of one, or both, of them?"

"Neither one," said Baley, firmly. "I know nothing about mathematics. Look, Daneel, surely you haven't told anyone I'm a mathematics buff or—"

"Not at all, friend Elijah. I know you are not. Nor does it matter, since the exact nature of the mathematics involved is in no way relevant to the point at issue."

"Well, then, go on."

"Since you do not know either man, friend Elijah, let me tell you that Dr. Humboldt is well into his twenty-seventh decade—pardon me, friend Elijah?"

"Nothing. Nothing," said Baley, irritably. He had merely muttered to himself, more or less incoherently, in a natural reaction to the extended life-spans of the Spacers. "And he's still active, despite his age? On Earth, mathematicians after thirty or so . . ."

Daneel said, calmly; "Dr. Humboldt is one of the top three mathematicians, by long-established repute, in the galaxy. Certainly he is still active. Dr. Sabbat, on the other hand, is quite young, not yet fifty, but he has already established himself as the most remarkable new talent in the most abstruse branches of mathematics."

"They're both great, then," said Baley. He remembered his pipe and picked it up. He decided there was no point in lighting it now and knocked out the dottle. "What happened? Is this a murder case? Did one of them apparently kill the other?"

"Of these two men of great reputation, one is trying to destroy that of the other. By human values, I believe this may be regarded as worse than physical murder."

"Sometimes, I suppose. Which one is trying to destroy the other?"

"Why, that, friend Elijah, is precisely the point at issue. Which?"

"Go on."

"Dr. Humboldt tells the story clearly. Shortly before he boarded the starship, he had an insight into a possible method for analyzing neural pathways from changes in microwave absorption patterns of local cortical areas. The insight was a purely mathematical technique of extraordinary subtlety, but I cannot, of course, either understand or sensibly transmit the details. These do not, however, matter. Dr. Humboldt considered the matter and was more convinced each hour that he had something revolutionary on hand, something that would dwarf all his previous accomplishments in mathematics. Then he discovered that Dr. Sabbat was on board."

"Ah. And he tried it out on young Sabbat?"

"Exactly. The two had met at professional meetings before and knew each other thoroughly by reputation. Humboldt went into it with Sabbat in great detail. Sabbat backed Humboldt's analysis completely and was unstinting in his praise of the importance of the discovery and of the ingenuity of the discoverer. Heartened and reassured by this, Humboldt prepared a paper outlining, in summary, his work and, two days later, prepared to have it forwarded subetherically to the co-chairmen of the conference at Aurora, in order that he might officially establish his priority and arrange for possible discussion before the sessions were closed. To his surprise, he found that

Sabbat was ready with a paper of his own, essentially the same as Humboldt's, and Sabbat was also preparing to have it subetherized to Aurora."

"I suppose Humboldt was furious."

"Quite!"

"And Sabbat? What was his story?"

"Precisely the same as Humboldt's. Word for word."

"Then just what is the problem?"

"Except for the mirror-image exchange of names. According to Sabbat, it was he who had the insight, and he who consulted Humboldt; it was Humboldt who agreed with the analysis and praised it."

"Then each one claims the idea is his and that the other stole it. It doesn't sound like a problem to me at all. In matters of scholarship, it would seem only necessary to produce the records of research, dated and initialed. Judgment as to priority can be made from that. Even if one is falsified, that might be discovered through internal inconsistencies."

"Ordinarily, friend Elijah, you would be right, but this is mathematics, and not in an experimental science. Dr. Humboldt claims to have worked out the essentials in his head. Nothing was put in writing until the paper itself was prepared. Dr. Sabbat, of course, says precisely the same."

"Well, then, be more drastic and get it over with, for sure. Subject each one to a psychic probe and find out which of the two is lying."

R. Daneel shook his head slowly, "Friend Elijah, you do not understand these men. They are both of rank and scholarship, Fellows of the Imperial Academy. As such, they cannot be subjected to trial of professional conduct except by a jury of their peers—their professional peers—unless they personally and voluntarily waive that right."

"Put it to them, then. The guilty man won't waive the right because he can't afford to face the psychic probe. The innocent man will waive it at once. You won't even have to use the probe."

"It does not work that way, friend Elijah. To waive the right in such a case —to be investigated by laymen—is a serious and perhaps irrecoverable blow to prestige. Both men steadfastly refuse to waive the right to special trial, as a matter of pride. The question of guilt, or innocence, is quite subsidiary."

"In that case, let it go for now. Put the matter in cold storage until you get to Aurora. At the neurobiophysical conference, there will be a huge supply of professional peers, and then—"

"That would mean a tremendous blow to science itself, friend Elijah. Both men would suffer for having been the instrument of scandal. Even the innocent one would be blamed for having been party to a situation so distasteful. It would be felt that it should have been settled quietly out of court at all costs."

"All right. I'm not a Spacer, but I'll try to imagine that this attitude makes sense. What do the men in question say?"

"Humboldt agrees thoroughly. He says that if Sabbat will admit theft of the idea and allow Humboldt to proceed with transmission of the paper—or at least its delivery at the conference, he will not press charges. Sabbat's misdeed will remain secret with him; and, of course, with the captain, who is the only other human to be party to the dispute."

"But young Sabbat will not agree?"

"On the contrary, he agreed with Dr. Humboldt to the last detail—with the reversal of names. Still the mirror-image."

"So they just sit there, stalemated?"

"Each, I believe, friend Elijah, is waiting for the other to give in and admit guilt."

"Well, then, wait."

"The captain has decided this cannot be done. There are two alternatives to waiting, you see. The first is that both will remain stubborn so that when the starship lands on Aurora, the intellectual scandal will break. The captain, who is responsible for justice on board ship, will suffer disgrace for not having been able to settle the matter quietly and that, to him, is quite insupportable."

"And the second alternative?"

"Is that one, or the other, of the mathematicians will indeed admit to wrongdoing. But will the one who confesses do so out of actual guilt, or out of a noble desire to prevent the scandal? Would it be right to deprive of credit one who is sufficiently ethical to prefer to lose that credit than to see science as a whole suffer? Or else, the guilty party will confess at the last moment, and in such a way as to make it appear he does so only for the sake of science, thus escaping the disgrace of his deed and casting its shadow upon the other. The captain will be the only man to know all this but he does not wish to spend the rest of his life wondering whether he has been a party to a grotesque miscarriage of justice."

Baley sighed. "A game of intellectual chicken. Who'll break first as Aurora comes nearer and nearer? Is that the whole story now, Daneel?"

"Not quite. There are witnesses to the transaction."

"Jehoshaphat! Why didn't you say so at once. *What* witnesses?"

"Dr. Humboldt's personal servant—"

"A robot, I suppose."

"Yes, certainly. He is called R. Preston. This servant, R. Preston, was present during the initial conference and he bears out Dr. Humboldt in every detail."

"You mean he says that the idea was Dr. Humboldt's to begin with; that Dr. Humboldt detailed it to Dr. Sabbat; that Dr. Sabbat praised the idea, and so on."

"Yes, in full detail."

"I see. Does that settle the matter or not? Presumably not."

"You are quite right. It does not settle the matter, for there is a second witness. Dr. Sabbat also has a personal servant, R. Idda, another robot of, as it happens, the same model as R. Preston, made, I believe, in the same year in the same factory. Both have been in service for an equal period of time."

"An odd coincidence—very odd."

"A fact, I am afraid, and it makes it difficult to arrive at any judgment based on obvious differences between the two servants."

"R. Idda, then, tells the same story as R. Preston?"

"Precisely the same story, except for the mirror-image reversal of the names."

"R. Idda stated, then, that young Sabbat, the one not yet fifty"—Lije Baley did not entirely keep the sardonic note out of his voice; he himself was not yet fifty and he felt far from young—"had the idea to begin with; that he detailed it to Dr. Humboldt, who was loud in his praises, and so on."

"Yes, friend Elijah."

"And one robot is lying, then."

"So it would seem."

"It should be easy to tell which. I imagine even a superficial examination by a good roboticist—"

"A roboticist is not enough in this case, friend Elijah. Only a qualified robopsychologist would carry weight enough and experience enough to make a decision in a case of this importance. There is no one so qualified on board ship. Such an examination can be performed only when we reach Aurora—"

"And by then the crud hits the fan. Well, you're here on Earth. We can scare up a robopsychologist, and surely anything that happens on Earth will never reach the ears of Aurora and there will be no scandal."

"Except that neither Dr. Humboldt, nor Dr. Sabbat, will allow his servant to be investigated by a robopsychologist of Earth. The Earthman would have to—" He paused.

Lije Baley said stolidly, "He'd have to touch the robot."

"These are old servants, well thought of—"

"And not to be sullied by the touch of Earthman. Then what do you want me to do, damn it?" He paused, grimacing. "I'm sorry, R. Daneel, but I see no reason for your having involved me."

"I was on the ship on a mission utterly irrelevant to the problem at hand. The captain turned to me because he had to turn to someone. I seemed human enough to talk to, and robot enough to be a safe recipient of confidences. He told me the whole story and asked what I would do. I realized the next Jump could take us as easily to Earth as to our target. I told the captain that, although I was at as much a loss to resolve the mirror-image as he was, there was on Earth one who might help."

"Jehoshaphat!" muttered Baley under his breath.

"Consider, friend Elijah, that if you succeed in solving this puzzle, it would do your career good and Earth itself might benefit. The matter could not be publicized, of course, but the captain is a man of some influence on his home world and he would be grateful."

"You just put a greater strain on me."

"I have every confidence," said R. Daneel, stolidly, "that you already have some idea as to what procedure ought to be followed."

"Do you? I suppose that the obvious procedure is to interview the two mathematicians, one of whom would seem to be a thief."

"I'm afraid, friend Elijah, that neither one will come into the city. Nor would either one be willing to have you come to them."

"And there is no way of forcing a Spacer to allow contact with an Earthman, no matter what the emergency. Yes, I understand that, Daneel— but I was thinking of an interview by closed-circuit television."

"Nor that. They will not submit to interrogation by an Earthman."

"Then what do they want of me? Could I speak to the robots?"

"They would not allow the robots to come here, either."

"Jehoshaphat, Daneel. *You've* come."

"That was my own decision. I have permission, while on board ship, to make decisions of that sort without veto by any human being but the captain himself—and he was eager to establish the contact. I, having known you, decided that television contact was insufficient. I wished to shake your hand."

Lije Baley softened. "I appreciate that, Daneel, but I still honestly wish you could have refrained from thinking of me at all in this case. Can I talk to the robots by television at least?"

"That, I think, can be arranged."

"Something, at least. That means I would be doing the work of a robopsychologist—in a crude sort of way."

"But you are a detective, friend Elijah, not a robopsychologist."

"Well, let it pass. Now before I see them, let's think a bit. Tell me: is it possible that both robots are telling the truth? Perhaps the conversation between the two mathematicians was equivocal. Perhaps it was of such a nature that each robot could honestly believe its own master was proprietor of the idea. Or perhaps one robot heard only one portion of the discussion and the other another portion, so that each could suppose its own master was proprietor of the idea."

"That is quite impossible, friend Elijah. Both robots repeat the conversation in identical fashion. And the two repetitions are fundamentally inconsistent."

"Then it is absolutely certain that one of the robots is lying?"

"Yes."

"Will I be able to see the transcript of all evidence given so far in the presence of the captain, if I should want to?"

"I thought you would ask that and I have copies with me."

"Another blessing. Have the robots been cross-examined at all, and is that cross-examination included in the transcript?"

"The robots have merely repeated their tales. Cross-examination would be conducted only by robopsychologists."

"Or by myself?"

"You are a detective, friend Elijah, not a—"

"All right, R. Daneel. I'll try to get the Spacer psychology straight. A detective can do it because he isn't a robopsychologist. Let's think further. Ordinarily a robot will not lie, but he will do so if necessary to maintain the Three Laws. He might lie to protect, in legitimate fashion, his own existence in accordance with the Third Law. He is more apt to lie if that is necessary to follow a legitimate order given him by a human being in accordance with the Second Law. He is most apt to lie if that is necessary to save a human life, or to prevent harm from coming to a human in accordance with the First Law."

"Yes."

"And in this case, each robot would be defending the professional reputation of his master, and would lie if it were necessary to do so. Under the circumstances, the professional reputation would be nearly equivalent to life and there might be a near-First-Law urgency to the lie."

"Yet by the lie, each servant would be harming the professional reputation of the other's master, friend Elijah."

"So it would, but each robot might have a clearer conception of the value of its own master's reputation and honestly judge it to be greater than that of the other's. The lesser harm would be done by his lie, he would suppose, than by the truth."

Having said that, Lije Baley remained quiet for a moment. Then he said, "All right, then, can you arrange to have me talk to one of the robots—to R. Idda first, I think?"

"Dr. Sabbat's robot?"

"Yes," said Baley, dryly, "the young fellow's robot."

"It will take me but a few minutes," said R. Daneel. "I have a micro-receiver outfitted with a projector. I will need merely a blank wall and I think this one will do if you will allow me to move some of these film cabinets."

"Go ahead. Will I have to talk into a microphone of some sort?"

"No, you will be able to talk in an ordinary manner. Please pardon me, friend Elijah, for a moment of further delay. I will have to contact the ship and arrange for R. Idda to be interviewed."

"If that will take some time, Daneel, how about giving me the transcripted material of the evidence so far."

Lije Baley lit his pipe while R. Daneel set up the equipment, and leafed through the flimsy sheets he had been handed.

The minutes passed and R. Daneel said, "If you are ready, friend Elijah, R. Idda is. Or would you prefer a few more minutes with the transcript?"

"No," sighed Baley, "I'm not learning anything new. Put him on and arrange to have the interview recorded and transcribed."

R. Idda, unreal in two-dimensional projection against the wall, was basically metallic in structure—not at all the humanoid creature that R. Daneel was. His body was tall but blocky, and there was very little to distinguish him from the many robots Baley had seen, except for minor structural details.

Baley said, "Greetings, R. Idda."

"Greetings, sir," said R. Idda, in a muted voice that sounded surprisingly humanoid.

"You are the personal servant of Gennao Sabbat, are you not?"

"I am, sir."

"For how long, boy?"

"For twenty-two years, sir."

"And your master's reputation is valuable to you?"

"Yes, sir."

"Would you consider it of importance to protect that reputation?"

"Yes, sir."

"As important to protect his reputation as his physical life?"

"No, sir."

"As important to protect his reputation as the reputation of another."

R. Idda hesitated. He said, "Such cases must be decided on their individual merit, sir. There is no way of establishing a general rule."

Baley hesitated. These Spacer robots spoke more smoothly and intellectually than Earth-models did. He was not at all sure he could outthink one.

He said, "If you decided that the reputation of your master were more important than that of another, say, that of Alfred Barr Humboldt, would you lie to protect your master's reputation?"

"I would, sir."

"Did you lie in your testimony concerning your master in his controversy with Dr. Humboldt?"

"No, sir."

"But if you were lying, you would deny you were lying in order to protect that lie, wouldn't you?"

"Yes, sir."

"Well, then," said Baley, "let's consider this. Your master, Gennao Sabbat, is a young man of great reputation in mathematics, but he is a young man. If, in this controversy with Dr. Humboldt, he had succumbed to temptation and had acted unethically, he would suffer a certain eclipse of reputation, but he is young and would have ample time to recover. He would have many intellectual triumphs ahead of him and men would eventually look upon this plagiaristic attempt as the mistake of a hot-blooded youth, deficient in judgment. It would be something that would be made up for in the future.

"If, on the other hand, it were Dr. Humboldt who succumbed to temptation, the matter would be much more serious. He is an old man whose great deeds have spread over centuries. His reputation has been unblemished hitherto. All of that, however, would be forgotten in the light of this one crime of his later years, and he would have no opportunity to make up for it in the comparatively short time remaining to him. There would be little more that he could accomplish. There would be so many more years of work ruined in Humboldt's case than in that of your master and so much less opportunity to win back his position. You see, don't you, that Humboldt faces the worse situation and deserves the greater consideration?"

There was a long pause. Then R. Idda said, with unmoved voice, "My evidence was a lie. It was Dr. Humboldt whose work it was, and my master has attempted, wrongfully, to appropriate the credit."

Baley said, "Very well, boy. You are instructed to say nothing to anyone about this until given permission by the captain of the ship. You are excused."

The screen blanked out and Baley puffed at his pipe. "Do you suppose the captain heard that, Daneel?"

"I am sure of it. He is the only witness, except for us."

"Good. Now for the other."

"But is there any point to that, friend Elijah, in view of what R. Idda has confessed?"

"Of course there is. R. Idda's confession means nothing."

"Nothing?"

"Nothing at all. I pointed out that Dr. Humboldt's position was the worse. Naturally, if he were lying to protect Sabbat, he would switch to the truth as, in fact, he claimed to have done. On the other hand, if he were telling the truth, he would switch to a lie to protect Humboldt. It's still mirror-image and we haven't gained anything."

"But then what will we gain by questioning R. Preston?"

"Nothing, if the mirror-image were perfect—but it is not. After all, one of the robots *is* telling the truth to begin with, and one *is* lying to begin with, and that is a point of asymmetry. Let me see R. Preston. And if the transcription of R. Idda's examination is done, let me have it.

The projector came into use again. R. Preston stared out of it; identical with R. Idda in every respect, except for some trivial chest design.

Baley said, "Greetings, R. Preston." He kept the record of R. Idda's examination before him as he spoke.

"Greetings, sir," said R. Preston. His voice was identical with that of R. Idda.

"You are the personal servant of Alfred Barr Humboldt are you not?"

"I am, sir."

"For how long, boy?"

"For twenty-two years, sir."

"And your master's reputation is valuable to you?"

"Yes, sir."

"Would you consider it of importance to protect that reputation?"

"Yes, sir."

"As important to protect his reputation as his physical life?"

"No, sir."

"As important to protect his reputation as the reputation of another?"

R. Preston hesitated. He said, "Such cases must be decided on their individual merit, sir. There is no way of establishing a general rule."

Baley said, "If you decided that the reputation of your master were more important than that of another, say, that of Gennao Sabbat, would you lie to protect your master's reputation?"

"I would, sir."

"Did you lie in your testimony concerning your master in his controversy with Dr. Sabbat?"

"No, sir."

"But if you were lying, you would deny you were lying, in order to protect that lie, wouldn't you?"

"Yes, sir."

"Well, then," said Baley, "let's consider this. Your master, Alfred Barr Humboldt, is an old man of great reputation in mathematics, but he is an old man. If, in this controversy with Dr. Sabbat, he had succumbed to temptation and had acted unethically, he would suffer a certain eclipse of reputation, but his great age and his centuries of accomplishments would stand against that and would win out. Men would look upon this plagiaristic attempt as the mistake of a perhaps-sick old man, no longer certain in judgment.

"If, on the other hand, it were Dr. Sabbat who had succumbed to temptation, the matter would be much more serious. He is a young man, with a far less secure reputation. He would ordinarily have centuries ahead of him in which he might accumulate knowledge and achieve great things. This will be closed to him, now, obscured by one mistake of his youth. He has a much longer future to lose than your master has. You see, don't you, that Sabbat faces the worse situation and deserves the greater consideration?"

There was a long pause. Then R. Preston said, with unmoved voice, "My evidence was as I—"

At that point, he broke off and said nothing more.

Baley said, "Please continue, R. Preston."

There was no response.

R. Daneel said, "I am afraid, friend Elijah, that R. Preston is in stasis. He is out of commission."

"Well, then," said Baley, "we have finally produced an asymmetry. From this, we can see who the guilty person is."

"In what way, friend Elijah?"

"Think it out. Suppose you were a person who had committed no crime and that your personal robot were a witness to that. There would be nothing you need do. Your robot would tell the truth and bear you out. If, however, you were a person who *had* committed the crime, you would have to depend on your robot to lie. That would be a somewhat riskier position, for although the robot would lie, if necessary, the greater inclination would be to tell the truth, so that the lie would be less firm than the truth would be. To prevent that, the crime-committing person would very likely have to *order* the robot to lie. In this way, First Law would be strengthened by Second Law; perhaps very substantially strengthened."

"That would seem reasonable," said R. Daneel.

"Suppose we have one robot of each type. One robot would switch from truth, unreinforced, to the lie, and could do so after some hesitation, without serious trouble. The other robot would switch from the lie, *strongly reinforced*, to the truth, but could do so only at the risk of burning out various positronic-track-ways in his brain and falling into stasis."

"And since R. Preston went into stasis—"

"R. Preston's master, Dr. Humboldt, is the man guilty of plagiarism. If you transmit this to the captain and urge him to face Dr. Humboldt with the matter at once, he may force a confession. If so, I hope you will tell me immediately."

"I will certainly do so. You will excuse me, friend Elijah? I must talk to the captain privately."

"Certainly. Use the conference room. It is shielded."

Baley could do no work of any kind in R. Daneel's absence. He sat in uneasy silence. A great deal would depend on the value of his analysis, and he was acutely aware of his lack of expertise in robotics.

R. Daneel was back in half an hour—very nearly the longest half hour of Baley's life.

There was no use, of course, in trying to determine what had happened from the expression of the humanoid's impassive face. Baley tried to keep his face impassive.

"Yes, R. Daneel?" he asked.

"Precisely as you said, friend Elijah. Dr. Humboldt has confessed. He was counting, he said, on Dr. Sabbat giving way and allowing Dr. Humboldt to have this one last triumph. The crisis is over and you will find the captain grateful. He has given me permission to tell you that he admires your subtlety greatly and I believe that I, myself, will achieve favor for having suggested you."

"Good," said Baley, his knees weak and his forehead moist now that his decision had proven correct, "but Jehoshaphat, R. Daneel, don't put me on the spot like that again, will you?"

"I will try not to, friend Elijah. All will depend, of course, on the importance of a crisis, on your nearness, and on certain other factors. Meanwhile, I have a question—"

"Yes?"

"Was it not possible to suppose that passage from a lie to the truth was easy, while passage from the truth to a lie was difficult? And in that case, would not the robot in stasis have been going from a truth to a lie, and since R. Preston was in stasis, might one not have drawn the conclusion that it was Dr. Humboldt who was innocent and Dr. Sabbat who was guilty?"

"Yes, R. Daneel. It was possible to argue that way, but it was the other argument that proved right. Humboldt did confess, didn't he?"

"He did. But with arguments possible in both directions, how could you, friend Elijah, so quickly pick the correct one?"

For a moment, Baley's lips twitched. Then he relaxed and they curved into a smile. "Because, R. Daneel, I took into account human reactions, not robotic ones. I know more about human beings than about robots. In other words, I had an idea as to which mathematician was guilty before I ever interviewed the robots. Once I provoked an asymmetric response in them, I simply interpreted it in such a way as to place the guilt on the one I already believed to be guilty. The robotic response was dramatic enough to break down the guilty man; my own analysis of human behavior might not have been sufficient to do so."

"I am curious to know what your analysis of human behavior was?"

"Jehoshaphat, R. Daneel; think, and you won't have to ask. There is another point of asymmetry in this tale of mirror-image besides the matter of true-and-false. There is the matter of the age of the two mathematicians; one is quite old and one is quite young."

"Yes, of course, but what then?"

"Why, this. I can see a young man, flushed with a sudden, startling and revolutionary idea, consulting in the matter an old man whom he has, from his early student days, thought of as a demigod in the field. I can *not* see an old man, rich in honors and used to triumphs, coming up with a sudden, startling and revolutionary idea, consulting a man centuries his junior whom he is bound to think of as a young whippersnapper—or whatever term a Spacer would use. Then, too, if a young man had the chance, would he try to steal the idea of a revered demigod? It would be unthinkable. On the other hand, an old man, conscious of declining powers, might well snatch at one last chance of fame and consider a baby in the field to have no rights he was bound to observe. In short, it was not conceivable that Sabbat steal Humboldt's idea; and from both angles, Dr. Humboldt was guilty."

R. Daneel considered that for a long time. Then he held out his hand. "I must leave now, friend Elijah. It was good to see you. May we meet again soon."

Baley gripped the robot's hand, warmly, "If you don't mind, R. Daneel," he said, "not too soon."

Take a Match

Space was black; black all around in every direction. There was nothing to be seen; not a star.

It was not because there were no stars—

Actually the thought that there might be no stars, literally no stars, had chilled Per Hanson's vitals. It was the old nightmare that rested just barely subliminally beneath the skin of every deep-spacer's brain.

When you took the Jump through the tachyon-universe, how sure were you *where* you would emerge? The timing and quantity of the energy input might be as tightly controlled as you liked, and your Fusionist might be the best in space, but the uncertainty principle reigned supreme and there was always the chance, even the inevitability of a random miss.

And by way of tachyons, a paper-thin miss might be a thousand light-years.

What, then, if you landed nowhere; or at least so distant from anywhere that nothing could possibly ever guide you to knowledge of your own position and nothing, therefore, could guide you back to anywhere?

Impossible, said the pundits. There was no place in the universe from which the quasars could not be seen, and from those alone you could position yourself. Besides, the chance that in the course of ordinary Jumps mere chance would take you outside the galaxy was only one in about ten million, and to the distance of, say, the Andromeda galaxy or Maffei 1, perhaps one in a quadrillion.

Forget it, said the pundits.

So when a ship comes out of its Jump, and returns from the weird paradoxes of the faster-than-light tachyons to the healthy we-know-it-all of all the tardyons from protons down to protons up, there *must* be stars to be seen. If they are not seen nevertheless, you are in a dust cloud; it is the only explanation. There are smoggy areas in the galaxy, or in any spiral galaxy, as once there were on Earth, when it was the sole home of humanity, rather than the carefully preserved, weather-controlled, life-preserve museum-piece it now was.

Hanson was tall and gloomy; his skin was leathery; and what he didn't know about the hyperships that ploughed the length and breadth of the galaxy and immediately neighboring regions—always barring the Fusionists' mysteries—was yet to be worked out. He was alone, now, in the Captain's Corner, as he liked to be. He had at hand all that was needed to be connected with any man or woman on board, and with the results of any device and instrument, and it pleased him to be the unseen presence.

—Though now nothing pleased him. He closed contact and said, "What else, Strauss?"

"We're in an open cluster," said Strauss's voice. (Hanson did not turn on the visual attachment; it would have meant revealing his own face and he preferred his look of sick worry to be held private.)

"At least," Strauss continued, "it seems to be an open cluster, from the level of radiation we can get in the far infrared and microwave regions. The trouble is we just can't pinpoint the positions well enough to locate ourselves. Not a hope."

"Nothing in visible light?"

"Nothing at all; or in the near-infrared, either. The dust cloud is as thick as soup."

"How big is it?"

"No way of telling."

"Can you estimate the distance to the nearest edge?"

"Not even to an order of magnitude. It might be a light-week. It might be ten light-years. Absolutely no way of telling."

"Have you talked to Viluekis?"

Strauss said briefly, "Yes!"

"What does he say?"

"Not much. He's sulking. He's taking it as a personal insult, of course."

"Of course." Hanson sighed noiselessly. Fusionists were as childish as children and because theirs was the romantic role in deep space, they were indulged. He said, "I suppose you told him that this sort of thing is unpredictable and could happen at any time."

"I did. And he said, as you can guess—'Not to Viluekis.' "

"Except that it did, of course. Well, *I* can't speak to him. Nothing I say will mean anything at all except that I'm trying to pull rank and then we'll get nothing further out of him. —He won't start the scoop?"

"He says he can't. He says it will be damaged."

"How can you damage a magnetic field!"

Strauss grunted. "Don't say that to him. He'll tell you there's more to a fusion tube than a magnetic field and then say you're trying to downgrade him."

"Yes, I know. —Well, look, put everyone and everything on the cloud. There must be some way to make some sort of guess as to the direction and distance of the nearest edge." He broke connection.

Hanson frowned into the middle distance, then.

Nearest edge! It was doubtful if at the ship's speed (relative to the surrounding matter) they dared expend the energy required for radical alteration of course.

They had moved into the Jump at half-light speed relative to the galactic nucleus in the tardyon-universe, and they emerged from the Jump at (of course) the same speed. There always seemed an element of risk in that. After all, suppose you found yourself, on the return, in the near neighborhood of a star and heading toward it at half-light speed.

The theoreticians denied the possibility. To get dangerously close to a massive body by way of a Jump was not reasonably to be expected. So said the pundits. Gravitational forces were involved in the Jump and for the transition from tardyon to tachyon and back to tardyon those forces were repulsive in nature. In fact, it was the random effect of a net gravitational force that could never be worked out in complete detail that accounted for a good deal of the uncertainty in the Jump.

Besides, they would say, trust to the Fusionist's instinct. A good Fusionist never goes wrong.

Except that this Fusionist had Jumped them into a cloud.

—Oh, that! It happens all the time. It doesn't matter. Do you know how *thin* most clouds are. You won't even know you're in one.

(Not this cloud, O Pundit.)

—In fact, clouds are good for you. The scoops don't have to work so long or so hard to keep fusion going and energy storing.

(Not this cloud, O Pundit.)

—Well, then, rely on the Fusionist to think of a way out.

(But if there was no way out?)

Hanson shied away from that last thought. He tried hard not to think it. —But how do you not think a thought that is the loudest thing in your head?

Henry Strauss, ship's astronomer, was himself in a mood of deep depression. If what had taken place were undiluted catastrophe, it might be accepted. No one on the hyperships could entirely close his eyes to the possibility of catastrophe. You were prepared for that, or you tried to be. —Though it was worse for the passengers, of course.

But when the catastrophe involved something that you would give your eye-teeth to observe and study, and when you find that the professional find of a lifetime was precisely what was killing you—

He sighed heavily.

He was a stout man, with tinted contact lenses that gave a spurious brightness and color to eyes that would otherwise have precisely matched a colorless personality.

There was nothing the captain could do. He knew that. The captain might be autocrat of all the rest of the ship, but a Fusionist was a law to himself, and always had been. Even to the passengers (he thought with some disgust) the Fusionist is the emperor of the spaceways and everyone beside dwindles to impotence.

It was a matter of supply and demand. The computers might calculate the exact quantity and timing of the energy input and the exact place and direction (if "direction" had any meaning in the transition from tardyon to tachyon), but the margin of error was huge and only a talented Fusionist could lower it. What it was that gave a Fusionist his talent, no one knew— they were born, not made. But Fusionists knew they had the talent and there was never one that didn't trade on that.

Viluekis wasn't bad as Fusionists went—though they never went far. He and Strauss were at least on speaking terms, even though Viluekis had effortlessly collected the prettiest passenger on board after Strauss had seen her first. (That was somehow part of the Imperial rights of the Fusionists en route.)

Strauss contacted Anton Viluekis. It took time for it to go through and when it did, Viluekis looked irritated in a rumpled, sad-eyed way.

"How's the tube?" asked Strauss gently.

"I think I shut it down in time. I've gone over it and I don't see any damage. Now," he looked down at himself, "I've got to clean up."

"At least it isn't harmed."

"But we can't use it."

"We *might* use it, Vil," said Strauss in an insinuating voice. "We can't say what will happen out there. If the tube were damaged, it wouldn't matter what happened out there, but, as it is, if the cloud cleans up—"

"If—if—if— I'll tell you an 'if.' If you stupid astronomers had known this cloud was here, I might have avoided it."

That was flatly irrelevant, and Strauss did not rise to the bait. He said, "It might clear up."

"What's the analysis?"

"Not good, Vil. It's the thickest hydroxyl cloud that's ever been observed. There is nowhere in the galaxy, as far as I know, a place where hydroxyl has been concentrated so densely."

"And no hydrogen?"

"Some hydrogen, of course. About five per cent."

"Not enough," said Viluekis curtly. "There's something else there besides hydroxyl. There's something that gave me more trouble than hydroxyl could. Did you locate it?"

"Oh, yes. Formaldehyde. There's more formaldehyde than hydrogen. Do you realize what it means, Vil? Some process has concentrated oxygen and carbon in space in unheard-of amounts; enough to use up the hydrogen over a volume of cubic light-years, perhaps. There isn't anything I know or can imagine which would account for such a thing."

"What are you trying to say, Strauss? Are you telling me that this is the only cloud of this type in space and I am stupid enough to land in it?"

"I'm not saying that, Vil. I only say what you hear me say and you haven't heard me say that. But, Vil, to get out we're depending on you. I can't call for help because I can't aim a hyperbeam without knowing where we are: I can't find out where we are because I can't pinpoint any stars—"

"And I can't use the fusion tube, so why am I the villain? You can't do your job, either, so why is the Fusionist always the villain." Viluekis was simmering. "It's up to you, Strauss, up to you. Tell me where to cruise the ship to find hydrogen. Tell me where the edge of the cloud is. —Or to hell with the edge of the cloud; find me the edge of the hydroxyl-formaldehyde business."

"I wish I could," said Strauss, "but so far I can't detect anything but hydroxyl and formaldehyde as far as I can probe."

"We can't fuse that stuff."

"I know."

"Well," said Viluekis violently, "this is an example of why it's wrong for the government to try to legislate supersafety instead of leaving it to the judgment of the Fusionist on the spot. If we had the capacity for the Double-Jump, there'd be no trouble."

Strauss knew perfectly well what Viluekis meant. There was always the tendency to save time by making two Jumps in rapid succession, but if one Jump involved certain unavoidable uncertainties, two in succession greatly multiplied those uncertainties, and even the best Fusionist couldn't do much. The multiplied error almost invariably greatly lengthened the total time of the trip.

It was a strict rule of hypernavigation that one full day of cruising between Jumps was necessary—three full days was preferable. That gave time enough to prepare the next Jump with all due caution. To avoid breaking that rule, each Jump was made under conditions that left insufficient energy supply for a second. For at least some time, the scoops had to gather and compress hydrogen, fuse it, and store the energy, building up to Jump-ignition. And it usually took at least a day to store enough to allow a Jump.

Strauss said, "How far short in energy are you, Vil?"

"Not much. This much." Viluekis held his thumb and forefinger apart by a quarter of an inch. "It's enough, though."

"Too bad," said Strauss flatly. The energy supply was recorded and could be inspected, but even so, Fusionists had been known to organize the records in such a way as to leave themselves some leeway for that second Jump.

"Are you sure?" he said. "Suppose you throw in the emergency generators, turn off all the lights—"

"And the air circulation and the appliances and the hydroponics apparatus. I know. I know. I figured that all in and we don't quite make it. —There's your stupid Double-Jump safety regulation."

Strauss still managed to keep his temper. He knew—everyone knew—that it had been the Fusionist Brotherhood that had been the driving force behind that regulation. A Double-Jump, sometimes insisted on by the captain, much more often than not made the Fusionist look bad. —But then, there was at least one advantage. With an obligatory cruise between every Jump, there ought to be at least a week before the passengers grew restless and suspicious, and in that week something might happen. So far, it was not quite a day.

He said, "Are you sure you can't do something with your system; filter out some of the impurities?"

"Filter them out! They're not impurities; they're the whole thing. Hydrogen is the impurity here. Listen, I'll need half a billion degrees to fuse carbon and oxygen atoms; probably a full billion. It can't be done and I'm not going to try. If I try something and it doesn't work, it's my fault, and I won't stand for that. It's up to you to get me to the hydrogen and you do it. You just cruise this ship to the hydrogen. I don't care how long it takes."

Strauss said, "We can't go faster than we're going now, considering the density of the medium, Vil. And at half-light speed we might have to cruise for two years—maybe twenty years—"

"Well, *you* think of a way out. Or the captain."

Strauss broke contact in despair. There was just no way of carrying on a rational conversation with a Fusionist. He'd heard the theory advanced (and perfectly seriously) that repeated Jumps affected the brain. In the Jump, every tardyon in ordinary matter had to be turned into an equivalent tachyon and then back again to the original tardyon. If the double conversion was imperfect in even the tiniest way, surely the effect would show up first in the brain, which was by far the most complex piece of matter ever to make the transition. Of course, no ill effects had ever been demonstrated experimentally, and no class of hypership officers seemed to deteriorate with time past what could be attributed to simple aging. But perhaps whatever it was in the Fusionists' brains that made them Fusionists and allowed them to go, by sheer intuition, beyond the best of computers might be particularly complex and therefore particularly vulnerable.

Nuts! There was nothing to it! Fusionists were merely spoiled!

He hesitated. Ought he to try to reach Cheryl? She could smooth matters if anyone could, and once old Vil-baby was properly dandled, he might think of a way to put the fusion tubes into operation—hydroxyl or not.

Did he really believe Viluekis could, under any circumstances? Or was he trying to avoid the thought of cruising for years? To be sure, hyperships were prepared for such an eventuality, in principle, but the eventuality had never come to pass and the crews—and still less the passengers—were surely *not* prepared for it.

But if he did talk to Cheryl, what could he say that wouldn't sound like an order for seduction? It was only one day so far and he was not yet ready to pimp for a Fusionist.

Wait! Awhile, anyway!

Viluekis frowned. He felt a little better having bathed and he was pleased that he had been firm with Strauss. Not a bad fellow, Strauss, but like all of them ("them," the captain, the crew, the passengers, all the stupid non-Fusionists in the universe) he wanted to shed responsibility. Put it all on the Fusionist. It was an old, old song, and he was one Fusionist who wouldn't take it.

That talk about cruising for years was just a way of trying to frighten him. If they really put their minds to it, they could work out the limits of the cloud and somewhere there had to be a nearer edge. It was too much to ask that they had landed in the precise center. Of course, if they had landed near one edge and were heading for the other—

Viluekis rose and stretched. He was tall and his eyebrows hung over his eyes like canopies.

Suppose it did take years. No hypership had ever cruised for years. The longest cruise had been eighty-eight days and thirteen hours, when one of them had managed to find itself in an unfavorable position with respect to a diffuse star and had to recede at speeds that built up to over 0.9 light before it was reasonably able to Jump.

They had survived and that was a quarter-year cruise. Of course, *twenty years—*

But that was impossible.

The signal light flashed three times before he was fully aware of it. If that was the captain coming to see him personally, he would leave at a rather more rapid rate than he had come.

"Anton!"

The voice was soft, urgent, and part of his annoyance seeped away. He allowed the door to recede into its socket and Cheryl came in. The door closed again behind her.

She was about twenty-five, with green eyes, a firm chin, dull red hair, and a magnificent figure that did not hide its light under a bushel.

She said, "Anton. Is there something wrong?"

Viluekis was not caught so entirely by surprise as to admit any such thing. Even a Fusionist knew better than to reveal anything prematurely to a passenger. "Not at all. What makes you think so?"

"One of the other passengers says so. A man named Martand."

"Martand? What does he know about it?" Then, suspiciously, "And what are you doing listening to some fool passenger? What does he look like?"

Cheryl smiled wanly. "Just someone who struck up a conversation in the lounge. He must be nearly sixty years old, and quite harmless, though I imagine he would like not to be. But that's not the point. There are no stars in view. Anyone can see that, and Martand said it was significant."

"Did he? We're just passing through a cloud. There are lots of clouds in the galaxy and hyperships pass through them all the time."

"Yes, but Martand says you can usually see some stars even in a cloud."

"What does he know about it?" Viluekis repeated. "Is he an old hand at deep space?"

"No-o," admitted Cheryl. "Actually, it's his first trip, I think. But he seems to know a lot."

"I'll bet. Listen, you go to him and tell him to shut up. He can be put in solitary for this. And don't you repeat stories like that, either."

Cheryl put her head to one side. "Frankly, Anton, you sound as though there *were* trouble. This Martand—Louis Martand is his name—is an interesting fellow. He's a schoolteacher—eighth grade general science."

"A grade-school teacher! Good Lord, Cheryl—"

"But you ought to listen to him. He says that teaching children is one of the few professions where you have to know a little bit about everything because kids ask questions and can spot phonies."

"Well, then, maybe your specialty should be spotting phonies, too. Now, Cheryl, you go and tell him to shut up, or I will."

"All right. But first—is it true that we're going through a hydroxyl cloud and the fusion tube is shut down?"

Viluekis's mouth opened, then shut again. It was quite a while before he said, "Who told you that?"

"Martand. I'll go now."

"No," said Viluekis sharply. "Wait awhile. How many others has Martand been telling all this?"

"Nobody. He said he doesn't want to spread panic. I was there when he was thinking about it, I suppose, and I guess he couldn't resist saying something."

"Does he know you know me?"

Cheryl's forehead furrowed slightly. "I think I mentioned something about it."

Viluekis snorted, "Don't you suppose that this crazy old man you've picked up is bound to try to show you how great he is. It's me he's trying to impress through you."

"Nothing of the sort," said Cheryl. "In fact, he specifically said I wasn't to tell you anything."

"Knowing, of course, that you'd come to me at once."

"Why should he want me to do that?"

"To show me up. Do you know what it's like being a Fusionist? To have everyone resenting you, against you, because you're so *needed*, because you—"

Cheryl said, "But what's any of that got to do with it? If Martand's all wrong, how would that show you up? And if he's right— Is he right, Anton?"

"Well, exactly what did he say?"

"I'm not sure I can remember it all, of course," Cheryl said thoughtfully. "It was after we came out of the Jump, actually quite a few hours after. By that time all anyone was talking about was that there were no stars in view. In the lounge everyone was saying there ought to be another Jump soon because what was the good of deep-space travel without a view. Of course, we knew we had to cruise at least a day. Then Martand came in, saw me, and came over to speak to me. —I think he rather likes me."

"I think I rather don't like him," said Viluekis grimly. "Go on."

"I said to him that it was pretty dreary without a view and he said it would stay that way for a while, and he sounded worried. Naturally I asked why he said such a thing and he said it was because the fusion tube had been turned off."

"Who told him that?" demanded Viluekis.

"He said there was a low hum that you could hear in one of the men's rooms that you couldn't hear anymore. And he said there was a place in the closet of the game room where the chess sets were kept where the wall felt warm because of the fusion tube and that place was not warm now."

"Is that all the evidence he has?"

—Cheryl ignored that and went on, "He said there were no stars visible because we were in a dust cloud and the fusion tubes must have stopped because there was no hydrogen to speak of in it. He said there probably wouldn't be enough energy to spark another Jump and that if we looked for hydrogen we might have to cruise years to get out of the cloud."

Viluekis's frown became ferocious. "He's panic-mongering. Do you know what that—"

"He's *not*. He told me not to tell anyone because he said it would create panic and that besides it wouldn't happen. He only told me because he had just figured it out and was all excited about it and had to talk to someone, but he said there was an easy way out and that the Fusionist would know what to do so that there was no need to worry at all. —But you're the Fusionist, so it seemed to me I had to ask whether he was really right about the cloud and whether you had really taken care of it."

Viluekis said, "This grade-school teacher of yours knows nothing about anything. Just stay away from him. —Uh, did he *say* what his so-called easy way out was?"

"No. Should I have asked him?"

"No! Why should you have asked him? What would he know about it?

But then again— All right, ask him. I'm curious what the idiot has in mind. Ask him."

Cheryl nodded. "I can do that. But are we in trouble?"

Viluekis said shortly. "Suppose you leave that to me. We're not in trouble till I say we're in trouble."

He looked for a long time at the closed door after she had left, both angry and uneasy. What was this Louis Martand—this grade-school teacher—doing with his lucky guesses?

If it finally came about that an extended cruise was necessary, the passengers would have to have it broken to them carefully, or none of them would survive. With Martand shouting it to all who would listen—

Almost savagely Viluekis clicked shut the combination that would bring him the captain.

Martand was slim and of neat appearance. His lips seemed forever on the verge of a smile, though his face and bearing were marked by a polite gravity; an almost expectant gravity, as though he was forever waiting for the person with him to say something truly important.

Cheryl said to him, "I spoke to Mr. Viluekis. —He's the Fusionist, you know. I told him what you said."

Martand looked shocked and shook his head. "I'm afraid you shouldn't have done that!"

"He did seem displeased."

"Of course. Fusionists are very special people and they don't like to have outsiders—"

"I could see that. But he insisted there was nothing to worry about."

"Of course not," said Martand, taking her hand and patting it in a consoling gesture, but then continuing to hold it. "I told you there was an easy way out. He's probably setting it up now. Still, I suppose it could be a while before he thinks of it."

"Thinks of what?" Then, warmly, "Why shouldn't he think of it, if *you* have?"

"But he's a specialist, you see, my dear young lady. Specialists think in their speciality and have a hard time getting out of it. As for myself, I don't dare fall into ruts. When I set up a class demonstration I've got to improvise most of the time. I have never yet been at a school where proton micropiles have been available, and I've had to work up a kerosene thermoelectric generator when we're off on field trips."

"What's kerosene?" asked Cheryl.

Martand laughed. He seemed delighted. "You see? People forget. Kerosene is a kind of flammable liquid. A still-more-primitive source of energy that I have many times had to use was a wood fire which you start by friction. Did you ever come across one of those? You take a match—"

Cheryl was looking blank and Martand went on indulgently, "Well, it doesn't matter. I'm just trying to get across the notion that your Fusionist will have to think of something more primitive than fusion and that will take him a while. As for me, I'm used to working with primitive methods. —For instance, do you know what's out there?"

He gestured at the viewing port, which was utterly featureless; so featureless that the lounge was virtually depopulated for lack of a view.

"A cloud; a dust cloud."

"Ah, but what kind? The one thing that's always to be found everywhere is hydrogen. It's the original stuff of the universe and hyperships depend on it. No ship can carry enough fuel to make repeated Jumps or to accelerate to near-light-speed and back repeatedly. We have to scoop the fuel out of space."

"You know, I've always wondered about that. I thought outer space was empty!"

"*Nearly* empty, my dear, and 'nearly' is as good as a feast. When you travel at a hundred thousand miles a second, you can scoop up and compress quite a bit of hydrogen, even when there's only a few atoms per cubic centimeter. And small amounts of hydrogen, fusing steadily, provide all the energy we need. In clouds the hydrogen is usually even thicker, but impurities may cause trouble, as in this one."

"How can you tell this one has impurities?"

"Why else would Mr. Viluekis have shut down the fusion tube. Next to hydrogen, the most common elements in the universe are helium, oxygen, and carbon. If the fusion pumps have stopped, that means there's a shortage of fuel, which is hydrogen, and a presence of something that will damage the complex fusion system. This can't be helium, which is harmless. It is possibly hydroxyl groups, an oxygen-hydrogen combination. Do you understand?"

"I think so," said Cheryl. "I had general science in college, and some of it is coming back. The dust is really hydroxyl groups attached to solid dust grains."

"Or actually free in the gaseous state, too. Even hydroxyl is not too dangerous to the fusion system, in moderation, but carbon compounds are. Formaldehyde is most likely and I should imagine with a ratio of about one of those to four hydroxyls. Do you see now?"

"No, I don't," said Cheryl flatly.

"Such compounds won't fuse. If you heat them to a few hundred million degrees, they break down into single atoms and the concentration of oxygen and carbon will simply damage the system. But why not take them in at ordinary temperatures. Hydroxyl will combine with formaldehyde, after compression, in a chemical reaction that will cause no harm to the system. At least, I'm sure a good Fusionist could modify the system to handle a chemical reaction at room temperature. The energy of the reaction can be stored and, after a while, there will be enough to make a Jump possible."

Cheryl said, "I don't see that at all. Chemical reactions produce hardly any energy, compared to fusion."

"You're quite right, dear. But we don't need much. The previous Jump has left us with insufficient energy for an immediate second Jump—that's regulations. But I'll bet your friend, the Fusionist, saw to it that as little energy as possible was lacking. Fusionists usually do that. The little extra required to reach ignition can be collected from ordinary chemical reactions. Then, once a Jump takes us out of the cloud, cruising for a week or so will refill our energy tanks and we can continue without harm. Of course—" Martand raised his eyebrows and shrugged.

"Yes?"

"Of course," said Martand, "if for any reason Mr. Viluekis should delay, there may be trouble. Every day we spend before Jumping uses up energy in the ordinary life of the ship, and after a while chemical reactions won't supply the energy required to reach Jump-ignition. I hope he doesn't wait long."

"Well, why don't you tell him? Now."

Martand shook his head. "Tell a Fusionist? I couldn't do that, dear."

"Then I will."

"Oh, no. He's *sure* to think of it himself. In fact, I'll make a bet with you, my dear. You tell him exactly what I said and say that I told you he had already thought of it himself and that the fusion tube was in operation. And, of course, if I win—"

Martand smiled.

Cheryl smiled, too. "I'll see," she said.

Martand looked after her thoughtfully as she hastened away, his thoughts not entirely on Viluekis's possible reaction.

He was not surprised when a ship's guard appeared from almost nowhere and said, "Please come with me, Mr. Martand."

Martand said quietly. "Thank you for letting me finish. I was afraid you wouldn't."

Something more than six hours passed before Martand was allowed to see the captain. His imprisonment (which was what he considered it) was one of isolation, but was not onerous; and the captain, when he did see him, looked tired and not particularly hostile.

Hanson said, "It was reported to me that you were spreading rumors designed to create panic among the passengers. That is a serious charge."

"I spoke to one passenger only, sir; and for a purpose."

"So we realize. We put you under surveillance at once and I have a report, a rather full one, of the conversation you had with Miss Cheryl Winter. It was the second conversation on the subject."

"Yes, sir."

"Apparently you intended the meat of the conversation to be passed on to Mr. Viluekis."

"Yes, sir."

"You did not consider going to Mr. Viluekis personally?"

"I doubt that he would have listened, sir."

"Or to me."

"You might have listened, but how would you pass on the information to Mr. Viluekis? You might then have had to use Miss Winter yourself. Fusionists have their peculiarities."

The captain nodded abstractedly. "What was it you expected to happen when Miss Winter passed on the information to Mr. Viluekis?"

"My hope, sir," said Martand, "was that he would be less defensive with Miss Winter than with anyone else; that he would feel less threatened. I was hoping that he would laugh and say the idea was a simple one that had occurred to him long before, and that, indeed, the scoops were already working, with the intent of promoting the chemical reaction. Then, when he got rid of Miss Winter, and I imagine he would do that quickly, he would start the scoops and report his action to you, sir, omitting any reference to myself or Miss Winter."

"You did not think he might dismiss the whole notion as unworkable?"

"There was that chance, but it didn't happen."

"How do you know?"

"Because half an hour after I was placed in detention, sir, the lights in the room in which I was kept dimmed perceptibly and did not brighten again. I assumed that energy expenditure in the ship was being cut to the bone, and assumed further that Viluekis was throwing everything into the pot so that the chemical reaction would supply enough for ignition."

The captain frowned. "What made you so sure you could manipulate Mr. Viluekis? Surely you have never dealt with Fusionists, have you?"

"Ah, but I teach the eighth-grade, captain. I have dealt with other children."

For a moment the captain's expression remained wooden. And then slowly it relaxed into a smile. "I like you, Mr. Martand," he said, "but it won't help you. Your expectations *did* come to pass; as nearly as I can tell, exactly as you had hoped. But do you understand what followed?"

"I will, if you tell me."

"Mr. Viluekis had to evaluate your suggestion and decide, at once, whether it was practical. He had to make a number of careful adjustments to the system to allow chemical reactions without knocking out the possibility of future fusion. He had to determine the maximum safe rate of reaction; the amount of stored energy to save; the point at which ignition might safely be attempted; the kind and nature of the Jump. It all had to be done quickly and no one else but a Fusionist could have done it. In fact, not every Fusionist could have done it; Mr. Viluekis is exceptional even for a Fusionist. Do you see?"

"Quite well."

The captain looked at the timepiece on the wall and activated his viewport. It was black, as it had been now for the better part of two days. "Mr. Viluekis has informed me of the time at which he will attempt Jump-ignition. He thinks it will work and I am confident in his judgment."

"If he misses," said Martand somberly, "we may find ourselves in the same position as before, but stripped of energy."

"I realize that," said Hanson, "and since you might feel a certain responsibility over having placed the idea in the Fusionist's mind, I thought you might want to wait through the few moments of suspense ahead of us."

Both men were silent now, watching the screen, while first seconds, then minutes, moved past. Hanson had not mentioned the exact deadline and Martand had no way of telling how imminent it was or whether it had passed. He could only shift his glance, occasionally and momentarily, to the captain's face, which maintained a studied expressionlessness.

And then came that queer internal wrench that disappeared almost at once, like a tic in the abdominal wall. They had Jumped.

"Stars!" said Hanson in a whisper of deep satisfaction. The viewport had burst into a riot of them, and at that moment Martand could recall no sweeter sight in all his life.

"And on the second," said Hanson. "A beautiful job. We're energy-stripped now, but we'll be full again in anywhere from one to three weeks, and during that time the passengers will have their view."

Martand felt too weak with relief to speak.

The captain turned to him. "Now, Mr. Martand. Your idea had merit. One could argue that it saved the ship and everyone on it. One could also argue that Mr. Viluekis was sure to think of it himself soon enough. But there will be no argument about it at all, for under no conditions can your part in this be known. Mr. Viluekis did the job and it was a great one of pure virtuosity even after we take into account the fact that you may have sparked it. He will be commended for it and receive great honors. *You* will receive nothing."

Martand was silent for a moment. Then he said, "I understand. A Fusionist is indispensable and I am of no account. If Mr. Viluekis's pride is hurt in the slightest, he may become useless to you, and you can't afford to lose him. For myself—well, be it as you wish. Good day, Captain."

"Not quite," said the captain. "We can't trust you."

"I won't say anything."

"You may not intend to, but things happen. We can't take the chance. For the remainder of the flight you will be under house arrest."

Martand frowned. "For *what?* I saved you and your damned ship—*and* your Fusionist."

"For exactly that. For saving it. That's the way it works out."

"Where's the justice?"

Slowly the captain shook his head. "It's a rare commodity, I admit, and sometimes too expensive to afford. You can't even go back to your room. You will be seeing no one in what remains of the trip."

Martand rubbed the side of his chin with one finger. "Surely you don't mean that literally, Captain."

"I'm afraid I do."

"But there is another who might talk—accidentally and without meaning to. You had better place Miss Winter under house arrest, too."

"And double the injustice?"

"Misery loves company," said Martand.

And the captain smiled. "Perhaps you're right," he said.

Light Verse

The very last person anyone would expect to be a murderer was Mrs. Avis Lardner. Widow of the great astronaut-martyr, she was a philanthropist, an art collector, a hostess extraordinary, and, everyone agreed, an artistic genius. But above all, she was the gentlest and kindest human being one could imagine.

Her husband, William J. Lardner, died, as we all know, of the effects of radiation from a solar flare, after he had deliberately remained in space so that a passenger vessel might make it safely to Space Station 5.

Mrs. Lardner had received a generous pension for that, and she had then invested wisely and well. By late middle age she was very wealthy.

Her house was a showplace, a veritable museum, containing a small but extremely select collection of extraordinarily beautiful jeweled objects. From a dozen different cultures she had obtained relics of almost every conceivable artifact that could be embedded with jewels and made to serve the aristocracy of that culture. She had one of the first jeweled wristwatches manufactured in America, a jeweled dagger from Cambodia, a jeweled pair of spectacles from Italy, and so on almost endlessly.

All was open for inspection. The artifacts were not insured, and there were no ordinary security provisions. There was no need for anything conventional, for Mrs. Lardner maintained a large staff of robot servants, all of whom could be relied on to guard every item with imperturbable concentration, irreproachable honesty, and irrevocable efficiency.

Everyone knew the existence of those robots and there is no record of any attempt at theft, ever.

And then, of course, there was her light-sculpture. How Mrs. Lardner discovered her own genius at the art, no guest at her many lavish entertainments could guess. On each occasion, however, when her house was thrown open to guests, a new symphony of light shone throughout the rooms; three-dimensional curves and solids in melting color, some pure and some fusing in startling, crystalline effects that bathed every guest in wonder and somehow always adjusted itself so as to make Mrs. Lardner's blue-white hair and soft, unlined face gently beautiful.

It was for the light-sculpture more than anything else that the guests came. It was never the same twice, and never failed to explore new experimental avenues of art. Many people who could afford light-consoles prepared light-sculptures for amusement, but no one could approach Mrs. Lardner's expertise. Not even those who considered themselves professional artists.

She herself was charmingly modest about it. "No, no," she would protest when someone waxed lyrical. "I wouldn't call it 'poetry in light.' That's far too kind. At most, I would say it was mere 'light verse.' " And everyone smiled at her gentle wit.

Though she was often asked, she would never create light-sculpture for any occasion but her own parties. "That would be commercialization," she said.

She had no objection, however, to the preparation of elaborate holograms of her sculptures so that they might be made permanent and reproduced in museums of art all over the world. Nor was there ever a charge for any use that might be made of her light-sculptures.

"I couldn't ask a penny," she said, spreading her arms wide. "It's free to all. After all, I have no further use for it myself." It was true! She never used the same light-sculpture twice.

When the holograms were taken, she was cooperation itself. Watching benignly at every step, she was always ready to order her robot servants to help. "Please, Courtney," she would say, "would you be so kind as to adjust the step ladder?"

It was her fashion. She always addressed her robots with the most formal courtesy.

Once, years before, she had been almost scolded by a government functionary from the Bureau of Robots and Mechanical Men. "You can't do that," he said severely. "It interferes with their efficiency. They are constructed to follow orders, and the more clearly you give those orders, the more efficiently they follow them. When you ask with elaborate politeness, it is difficult for them to understand that an order is being given. They react more slowly."

Mrs. Lardner lifted her aristocratic head. "I do not ask for speed and efficiency," she said. "I ask goodwill. My robots love me."

The government functionary might have explained that robots cannot love, but he withered under her hurt but gentle glance.

It was notorious that Mrs. Lardner never even returned a robot to the factory for adjustment. Their positronic brains are enormously complex, and once in ten times or so the adjustment is not perfect as it leaves the factory. Sometimes the error does not show up for a period of time, but whenever it does, U. S. Robots and Mechanical Men, Inc., always makes the adjustment free of charge.

Mrs. Lardner shook her head. "Once a robot is in my house," she said, "and has performed his duties, any minor eccentricities must be borne with. I will not have him manhandled."

It was the worse thing possible to try to explain that a robot was but a machine. She would say very stiffly, "Nothing that is as intelligent as a robot can ever be *but* a machine. I treat them as people."

And that was that!

She kept even Max, although he was almost helpless. He could scarcely understand what was expected of him. Mrs. Lardner denied that strenuously, however. "Not at all," she would say firmly. "He can take hats and coats and store them very well, indeed. He can hold objects for me. He can do many things."

"But why not have him adjusted?" asked a friend, once.

"Oh, I couldn't. He's himself. He's very lovable, you know. After all, a positronic brain is so complex that no one can ever tell in just what way it's off. If he were made perfectly normal there would be no way to adjust him back to the lovability he now has. I won't give that up."

"But if he's maladjusted," said the friend, looking at Max nervously, "might he not be dangerous?"

"Never," laughed Mrs. Lardner. "I've had him for years. He's completely harmless and quite a dear."

Actually he looked like all the other robots, smooth, metallic, vaguely human but expressionless.

To the gentle Mrs. Lardner, however, they were all individual, all sweet, all lovable. It was the kind of woman she was.

How could she commit murder?

The very last person anyone would expect to be murdered would be John Semper Travis. Introverted and gentle, he was in the world but not of it. He had that peculiar mathematical turn of mind that made it possible for him to work out in his mind the complicated tapestry of the myriad positronic brain-paths in a robot's mind.

He was chief engineer of U. S. Robots and Mechanical Men, Inc.

But he was also an enthusiastic amateur in light-sculpture. He had written a book on the subject, trying to show that the type of mathematics he used in working out positronic brain-paths might be modified into a guide to the production of aesthetic light-sculpture.

His attempt at putting theory into practice was a dismal failure, however. The sculptures he himself produced, following his mathematical principles, were stodgy, mechanical, and uninteresting.

It was the only reason for unhappiness in his quiet, introverted, and secure life, and yet it was reason enough for him to be very unhappy indeed. He *knew* his theories were right, yet he could not make them work. If he could but produce *one* great piece of light-sculpture—

Naturally, he knew of Mrs. Lardner's light-sculpture. She was universally hailed as a genius, yet Travis knew she could not understand even the simplest aspect of robotic mathematics. He had corresponded with her but she consistently refused to explain her methods, and he wondered if she had any at all. Might it not be mere intuition?—but even intuition might be reduced to mathematics. Finally he managed to receive an invitation to one of her parties. He simply had to see her.

Mr. Travis arrived rather late. He had made one last attempt at a piece of light-sculpture and had failed dismally.

He greeted Mrs. Lardner with a kind of puzzled respect and said, "That was a peculiar robot who took my hat and coat."

"That is Max," said Mrs. Lardner.

"He is quite maladjusted, and he's a fairly old model. How is it you did not return it to the factory?"

"Oh, no," said Mrs. Lardner. "It would be too much trouble."

"None at all, Mrs. Lardner," said Travis. "You would be surprised how simple a task it was. Since I am with U.S. Robots, I took the liberty of adjusting him myself. It took no time and you'll find he is now in perfect working order."

A queer change came over Mrs. Lardner's face. Fury found a place on it for the first time in her gentle life, and it was as though the lines did not know how to form.

"You adjusted him?" she shrieked. "But it was *he* who created my light-sculptures. It was the maladjustment, the *maladjustment*, which you can never restore, that—that—"

It was really unfortunate that she had been showing her collection at the time and that the jeweled dagger from Cambodia was on the marble tabletop before her.

Travis's face was also distorted. "You mean if I had studied his uniquely maladjusted positronic brain-paths I might have learned—"

She lunged with the knife too quickly for anyone to stop her and he did not try to dodge. Some said he came to meet it—as though he *wanted* to die.

Stranger
in Paradise

They were brothers. Not in the sense that they were both human beings, or that they were fellow children of a crèche. Not at all! They were brothers in the actual biological sense of the word. They were kin, to use a term that had grown faintly archaic even centuries before, prior to the Catastrophe, when that tribal phenomenon, the family, still had some validity.

How embarrassing it was!

Over the years since childhood, Anthony had almost forgotten. There were times when he hadn't given it even the slightest thought for months at a time. But now, ever since he had been inextricably thrown together with William, he had found himself living through an agonizing time.

It might not have been so bad if circumstances had made it obvious all along; if, as in the pre-Catastrophe days—Anthony had at one time been a great reader of history—they had shared the second name and in that way alone flaunted the relationship.

Nowadays, of course, one adopted one's second name to suit oneself and changed it as often as desired. After all, the symbol chain was what really counted, and that was encoded and made yours from birth.

William called himself Anti-Aut. That was what he insisted on with a kind of sober professionalism. His own business, surely, but what an advertisement of personal poor taste. Anthony had decided on Smith when he had turned thirteen and had never had the impulse to change it. It was simple, easily spelled, and quite distinctive, since he had never met anyone else who had chosen that name. It was once very common—among the pre-Cats—which explained its rareness now perhaps.

But the difference in names meant nothing when the two were together. They looked alike.

If they had been twins—but then one of a pair of twin-fertilized ova was never allowed to come to term. It was just that physical similarity occasionally happened in the non-twin situation, especially when the relationship was on both sides. Anthony Smith was five years younger, but both had the beaky nose, the heavy eyelids, the just noticeable cleft in the chin—that damned luck of the genetic draw. It was just asking for it when, out of some passion for monotony, parents repeated.

At first, now that they were together, they drew that startled glance followed by an elaborate silence. Anthony tried to ignore the matter, but out of sheer perversity—or perversion—William was as likely as not to say, "We're brothers."

"Oh?" the other would say, hanging in there for just a moment as though he wanted to ask if they were full blood brothers. And then good manners would win the day and he would turn away as though it were a matter of no interest. That happened only rarely, of course. Most of the people in the Project knew—how could it be prevented?—and avoided the situation.

Not that William was a bad fellow. Not at all. If he hadn't been Anthony's brother; or if they had been, but looked sufficiently different to be able to mask the fact, they would have gotten along famously.

As it was—

It didn't make it easier that they had played together as youngsters, and had shared the earlier stages of education in the same crèche through some successful maneuvering on the part of Mother. Having borne two sons by the same father and having, in this fashion, reached her limit (for she had not fulfilled the stringent requirements for a third), she conceived the notion of being able to visit both at a single trip. She was a strange woman.

William had left the crèche first, naturally, since he was the elder. He had gone into science—genetic engineering. Anthony had heard that, while he was still in the crèche, through a letter from his mother. He was old enough by then to speak firmly to the matron, and those letters stopped. But he always remembered the last one for the agony of shame it had brought him.

Anthony had eventually entered science, too. He had shown talent in that direction and had been urged to. He remembered having had the wild—and prophetic, he now realized—fear he might meet his brother and he ended in telemetrics, which was as far removed from genetic engineering as one could imagine. . . . Or so one would have thought.

Then, through all the elaborate development of the Mercury Project, circumstance waited.

The time came, as it happened, when the Project appeared to be facing a dead end; and a suggestion had been made which saved the situation, and at the same time dragged Anthony into the dilemma his parents had prepared for him. And the best and most sardonic part of the whole thing was that it was Anthony who, in all innocence, made the suggestion.

2

William Anti-Aut knew of the Mercury Project, but only in the way he knew of the long-drawn-out Stellar Probe that had been on its way long before he was born and would still be on its way after his death; and the way he knew of the Martian colony and of the continuing attempts to establish similar colonies on the asteroids.

Such things were on the distant periphery of his mind and of no real importance. No part of the space effort had ever swirled inward closer to the center of his interests, as far as he could remember, till the day when the printout included photographs of some of the men engaged in the Mercury Project.

William's attention was caught first by the fact that one of them had been identified as Anthony Smith. He remembered the odd name his brother had chosen, and he remembered the Anthony. Surely there could not be two Anthony Smiths.

He had then looked at the photograph itself and there was no mistaking the face. He looked in the mirror in a sudden whimsical gesture at checking the matter. No mistaking the face.

He felt amused, but uneasily so, for he did not fail to recognize the potentiality for embarrassment. Full blood brothers, to use the disgusting phrase. But what was there to do about it? How correct the fact that neither his father nor his mother had had imagination?

He must have put the printout in his pocket, absently, when he was getting ready to leave for work, for he came across it at the lunch hour. He stared at it again. Anthony looked keen. It was quite a good reproduction— the printouts were of enormously good quality these days.

His lunch partner, Marco Whatever-his-name-was-that-week, said curiously, "What are you looking at, William?"

On impulse, William passed him the printout and said, "That's my brother." It was like grasping the nettle.

Marco studied it, frowning, and said, "Who? The man standing next to you?"

"No, the man who *is* me. I mean the man who looks like me. He's my brother."

There was a longer pause this time. Marco handed it back and said with a careful levelness to his voice, "Same-parents brother?"

"Yes."

"Father and mother both?"

"Yes."

"Ridiculous!"

"I suppose so." William sighed. "Well, according to this, he's in telemetrics over in Texas and I'm doing work in autistics up here. So what difference does it make?"

William did not keep it in his mind and later that day he threw the printout away. He did not want his current bedmate to come across it. She had a ribald sense of humor that William was finding increasingly wearying. He was rather glad she was not in the mood for a child. He himself had had one a few years back anyway. That little brunette, Laura or Linda, one or the other name, had collaborated.

It was quite a time after that, at least a year, that the matter of Randall had come up. If William had given no further thought in his brother—and he hadn't—before that, he certainly had no time for it afterward.

Randall was sixteen when William first received word of him. He had lived a life that was increasingly seclusive and the Kentucky crèche in which he was being brought up decided to cancel him—and of course it was only some eight or ten days before cancellation that it occurred to anyone to report him to the New York Institute for the Science of Man (The Homological Institute was its common name).

William received the report along with reports of several others and there was nothing in the description of Randall that particularly attracted his notice. Still it was time for one of his tedious mass-transport trips to the crèches and there was one likely possibility in West Virginia. He went there—and was disappointed into swearing for the fiftieth time that he would thereafter make these visits by TV image—and then, having dragged himself there, thought he might as well take in the Kentucky crèche before returning home.

He expected nothing.

Yet he hadn't studied Randall's gene pattern for more than ten minutes before he was calling the Institute for a computer calculation. Then he sat back and perspired slightly at the thought that only a last-minute impulse had brought him, and that without that impulse, Randall would have been quietly canceled in a week or less. To put it into the fine detail, a drug would have soaked painlessly through his skin and into his bloodstream and he would have sunk into a peaceful sleep that deepened gradually to death. The drug had a twenty-three-syllable official name, but William called it "nirvanamine," as did everyone else.

William said, "What is his full name, matron?"

The crèche matron said, "Randall Nowan, scholar."

"No one!" said William explosively.

"Nowan." The matron spelled it. "He chose it last year."

"And it meant nothing to you? It is pronounced No one! It didn't occur to you to report this young man last year?"

"It didn't seem—" began the matron, flustered.

William waved her to silence. What was the use? How was she to know?

There was nothing in the gene pattern to give warning by any of the usual textbook criteria. It was a subtle combination that William and his staff had worked out over a period of twenty years through experiments on autistic children—and a combination they had never actually seen in life.

So close to canceling!

Marco, who was the hardhead of the group, complained that the crèches were too eager to abort before term and to cancel after term. He maintained that all gene patterns should be allowed to develop for purpose of initial screening and there should be no cancellation at all without consultation with a homologist.

"There aren't enough homologists," William said tranquilly.

"We can at least run all gene patterns through the computer," said Marco.

"To save anything we can get for our use?"

"For any homological use, here or elsewhere. We must study gene patterns in action if we're to understand ourselves properly, and it is the abnormal and monstrous patterns that give us most information. Our experiments on autism have taught us more about homology than the sum total existing on the day we began."

William, who still liked the roll of the phrase "the genetic physiology of man" rather than "homology," shook his head. "Just the same, we've got to play it carefully. However useful we can claim our experiments to be, we live on bare social permission, reluctantly given. We're playing with lives."

"Useless lives. Fit for canceling."

"A quick and pleasant canceling is one thing. Our experiments, usually long drawn out and sometimes unavoidably unpleasant, are another."

"We help them sometimes."

"And we don't help them sometimes."

It was a pointless argument, really, for there was no way of settling it. What it amounted to was that too few interesting abnormalities were available for homologists and there was no way of urging mankind to encourage a greater production. The trauma of the Catastrophe would never vanish in a dozen ways, including that one.

The hectic push toward space exploration could be traced back (and was, by some sociologists) to the knowledge of the fragility of the life skein on the planet, thanks to the Catastrophe.

Well, never mind—

There had never been anything like Randall Nowan. Not for William. The slow onset of autism characteristic of that totally rare gene pattern meant that more was known about Randall than about any equivalent patient before him. They even caught some last faint glimmers of his way of thought in the laboratory before he closed off altogether and shrank finally within the wall of his skin—unconcerned, unreachable.

Then they began the slow process whereby Randall, subjected for increasing lengths of time to artificial stimuli, yielded up the inner workings of his brain and gave clues thereby to the inner workings of all brains, those that were called normal as well as those like his own.

So vastly great were the data they were gathering that William began to feel his dream of reversing autism was more than merely a dream. He felt a warm gladness at having chosen the name Anti-Aut.

And it was at almost the height of the euphoria induced by the work on Randall that he received the call from Dallas and that the heavy pressure began—now, of all times—to abandon his work and take on a new problem.

Looking back on it later, he could never work out just what it was that finally led him to agree to visit Dallas. In the end, of course, he could see how fortunate it was—but what had persuaded him to do so? Could he, even at the start, have had a dim unrealized notion of what it might come to? Surely, impossible.

Was it the unrealized memory of that printout, that photograph of his brother? Surely, impossible.

But he let himself be argued into that visit and it was only when the micropile power unit changed the pitch of its soft hum and the agrav unit took over for the final descent that he remembered that photograph—or at least that it moved into the conscious part of his memory.

Anthony worked at Dallas and, William remembered now, at the Mercury Project. That was what the caption had referred to. He swallowed, as the soft jar told him the journey was over. This would be uncomfortable.

3

Anthony was waiting on the roof reception area to greet the incoming expert. Not he by himself, of course. He was part of a sizable delegation—the size itself a rather grim indication of the desperation to which they had been reduced—and he was among the lower echelons. That he was there at all was only because it was he who had made the original suggestion.

He felt a slight, but continuing, uneasiness at the thought of that. He had put himself on the line. He had received considerable approval for it, but there had been the faint insistence always that it was *his* suggestion; and if it turned out to be a fiasco, every one of them would move out of the line of fire and leave him at point-zero.

There were occasions, later, when he brooded over the possibility that the dim memory of a brother in homology had suggested his thought. That might have been, but it didn't have to be. The suggestion was so sensibly inevitable, really, that surely he would have had the same thought if his brother had been something as innocuous as a fantasy writer, or if he had had no brother of his own.

The problem was the inner planets—

The Moon and Mars were colonized. The larger asteroids and the satellites of Jupiter had been reached, and plans were in progress for a manned voyage to Titan, Saturn's large satellite, by way of an accelerating whirl about Jupiter. Yet even with plans in action for sending men on a seven-year round trip to the outer Solar System, there was still no chance of a manned approach to the inner planets, for fear of the Sun.

Venus itself was the less attractive of the two worlds within Earth's orbit. Mercury, on the other hand—

Anthony had not yet joined the team when Dmitri Large (he was quite short, actually) had given the talk that had moved the World Congress sufficiently to grant the appropriation that made the Mercury Project possible.

Anthony had listened to the tapes, and had heard Dmitri's presentation. Tradition was firm to the effect that it had been extemporaneous, and perhaps it was, but it was perfectly constructed and it held within it, in essence, every guideline followed by the Mercury Project since.

And the chief point made was that it would be wrong to wait until the technology had advanced to the point where a manned expedition through the rigors of Solar radiation could become feasible. Mercury was a unique environment that could teach much, and from Mercury's surface sustained observations could be made of the Sun that could not be made in any other way.

—Provided a man substitute—a robot, in short—could be placed on the planet.

A robot with the required physical characteristics could be built. Soft landings were as easy as kiss-my-hand. Yet once a robot landed, what did one do with him next?

He could make his observations and guide his actions on the basis of those observations, but the Project wanted his actions to be intricate and subtle, at least potentially, and they were not at all sure what observations he might make.

To prepare for all reasonable possibilities and to allow for all the intricacy desired, the robot would need to contain a computer (some at Dallas referred to it as a "brain," but Anthony scorned that verbal habit—perhaps because, he wondered later, the brain was his brother's field) sufficiently complex and versatile to fall into the same asteroid with a mammalian brain.

Yet nothing like that could be constructed and made portable enough to be carried to Mercury and landed there—or if carried and landed, to be mobile enough to be useful to the kind of robot they planned. Perhaps someday the positronic-path devices that the roboticists were playing with might make it possible, but that someday was not yet.

The alternative was to have the robot send back to Earth every observation it made the moment it was made, and a computer on Earth could then guide his every action on the basis of those observations. The robot's body, in short, was to be there, and his brain here.

Once that decision was reached, the key technicians were the telemetrists and it was then that Anthony joined the Project. He became one of those who labored to devise methods for receiving and returning impulses over distances of from 50 to 140 million miles, toward, and sometimes past, a Solar disk that could interfere with those impulses in a most ferocious manner.

He took to his job with passion and (he finally thought) with skill and success. It was he, more than anyone else, who had designed the three switching stations that had been hurled into permanent orbit about Mercury —the Mercury Orbiters. Each of them was capable of sending and receiving impulses from Mercury to Earth and from Earth to Mercury. Each was capable of resisting, more or less permanently, the radiation from the Sun, and more than that, each could filter out Solar interference.

Three equivalent Orbiters were placed at a distance of a little over a million miles from Earth, reaching north and south of the plane of the Ecliptic so that they could receive the impulses from Mercury and relay them to Earth—or vice versa—even when Mercury was behind the Sun and inaccessible to direct reception from any station on Earth's surface.

Which left the robot itself; a marvelous specimen of the roboticists' and telemetrists' arts in combination. The most complex of ten successive models, it was capable, in a volume only a little over twice that of a man and five times his mass, of sensing and doing considerably more than a man—if it could be guided.

How complex a computer had to be to guide the robot made itself evident rapidly enough, however, as each response step had to be modified to allow for variations in possible perception. And as each response step itself enforced the certainty of greater complexity of possible variation in perceptions, the early steps had to be reinforced and made stronger. It built itself up endlessly, like a chess game, and the telemetrists began to use a computer to program the computer that designed the program for the computer that programmed the robot-controlling computer.

There was nothing but confusion.

The robot was at a base in the desert spaces of Arizona and in itself was working well. The computer in Dallas could not, however, handle him well enough; not even under perfectly known Earth conditions. How then—

Anthony remembered the day when he had made the suggestion. It was on 7-4-553. He remembered it, for one thing, because he remembered thinking that day that 7-4 had been an important holiday in the Dallas region of the world among the pre-Cats half a millennium before—well, 553 years before, to be exact.

It had been at dinner, and a good dinner, too. There had been a careful adjustment of the ecology of the region and the Project personnel had high priority in collecting the food supplies that became available—so there was an unusual degree of choice on the menus, and Anthony had tried roast duck.

It was very good roast duck and it made him somewhat more expansive than usual. Everyone was in a rather self-expressive mood, in fact, and Ricardo said, "We'll never do it. Let's admit it. We'll never do it."

There was no telling how many had thought such a thing how many times before, but it was a rule that no one said so openly. Open pessimism might be the final push needed for appropriations to stop (they had been coming with greater difficulty each year for five years now) and if there *were* a chance, it would be gone.

Anthony, ordinarily not given to extraordinary optimism, but now reveling over his duck, said, "Why can't we do it? Tell me why, and I'll refute it."

It was a direct challenge and Ricardo's dark eyes narrowed at once. "You want me to tell you why?"

"I sure do."

Ricardo swung his chair around, facing Anthony full. He said, "Come on, there's no mystery. Dmitri Large won't say so openly in any report, but you know and I know that to run Mercury Project properly, we'll need a computer as complex as a human brain whether it's on Mercury or here, and we can't build one. So where does that leave us except to play games with the World Congress and get money for make-work and possibly useful spin-offs?"

And Anthony placed a complacent smile on his face and said, "That's easy to refute. You've given us the answer yourself." (Was he playing games? Was it the warm feeling of duck in his stomach? The desire to tease Ricardo? . . . Or did some unfelt thought of his brother touch him? There was no way, later, that he could tell.)

"What answer?" Ricardo rose. He was quite tall and unusually thin and he always wore his white coat unseamed. He folded his arms and seemed to be doing his best to tower over the seated Anthony like an unfolded meter rule. "What answer?"

"You say we need a computer as complex as a human brain. All right, then, we'll build one."

"The point, you idiot, is that we can't—"

"*We* can't. But there are others."

"What others?"

"People who work on brains, of course. We're just solid-state mechanics. We have no idea in what way a human brain is complex, or where, or to what extent. Why don't we get in a homologist and have *him* design a computer?" And with that Anthony took a huge helping of stuffing and savored it complacently. He could still remember, after all this time, the taste of the stuffing, though he couldn't remember in detail what had happened afterward.

It seemed to him that no one had taken it seriously. There was laughter and a general feeling that Anthony had wriggled out of a hole by clever sophistry so that the laughter was at Ricardo's expense. (Afterward, of course, everyone claimed to have taken the suggestion seriously.)

Ricardo blazed up, pointed a finger at Anthony, and said, "Write that up. I *dare* you to put that suggestion in writing." (At least, so Anthony's memory had it. Ricardo had, since then, stated his comment was an enthusiastic "Good idea! Why don't you write it up formally, Anthony?")

Either way, Anthony put it in writing.

Dmitri Large had taken to it. In private conference, he had slapped Anthony on the back and had said that he had been speculating in that direction himself—though he did not offer to take any credit for it on the record. (Just in case it turned out to be a fiasco, Anthony thought.)

Dmitri Large conducted the search for the appropriate homologist. It did not occur to Anthony that he ought to be interested. He knew neither homology nor homologists—except, of course, his brother, and he had not thought of him. Not consciously.

So Anthony was up there in the reception area, in a minor role, when the door of the aircraft opened and several men got out and came down and in the course of the handshakes that began going round, he found himself staring at his own face.

His cheeks burned and, with all his might, he wished himself a thousand miles away.

4

More than ever, William wished that the memory of his brother had come earlier. It should have. . . . Surely it should have.

But there had been the flattery of the request and the excitement that had begun to grow in him after a while. Perhaps he had deliberately avoided remembering.

To begin with, there had been the exhilaration of Dmitri Large coming to see him in his own proper presence. He had come from Dallas to New York by plane and that had been very titillating for William, whose secret vice it was to read thrillers. In the thrillers, men and women always traveled mass-wise when secrecy was desired. After all, electronic travel was public property —at least in the thrillers, where every radiation beam of whatever kind was invariably bugged.

William had said so in a kind of morbid half attempt at humor, but Dmitri hadn't seemed to be listening. He was staring at William's face and his thoughts seemed to be elsewhere. "I'm sorry," he said finally. "You remind me of someone."

(And yet that hadn't given it away to William. How was that possible? he had eventual occasion to wonder.)

Dmitri Large was a small plump man who seemed to be in a perpetual twinkle even when he declared himself worried or annoyed. He had a round and bulbous nose, pronounced cheeks, and softness everywhere. He emphasized his last name and said with a quickness that led William to suppose he said it often, "Size is not all the large there is, my friend."

In the talk that followed, William protested much. He knew nothing about computers. Nothing! He had not the faintest idea of how they worked or how they were programmed.

"No matter, no matter," Dmitri said, shoving the point aside with an expressive gesture of the hand. *"We* know the computers; *we* can set up the programs. You just tell us what it is a computer must be made to do so that it will work like a brain and not like a computer."

"I'm not sure I know enough about how a brain works to be able to tell you that, Dmitri," said William.

"You are the foremost homologist in the world," said Dmitri. "I have checked that out carefully." And that disposed of that.

William listened with gathering gloom. He supposed it was inevitable. Dip a person into one particular specialty deeply enough and long enough, and he would automatically begin to assume that specialists in all other fields were magicians, judging the depth of their wisdom by the breadth of his own ignorance. . . . And as time went on, William learned a great deal more of the Mercury Project than it seemed to him at the time that he cared to.

He said at last, "Why use a computer at all, then? Why not have one of your own men, or relays of them, receive the material from the robot and send back instructions?"

"Oh, oh, oh," said Dmitri, almost bouncing in his chair in his eagerness. "You see, you are not aware. Men are too slow to analyze quickly all the material the robot will send back—temperatures and gas pressures and cosmic-ray fluxes and Solar-wind intensities and chemical compositions and soil textures and easily three dozen more items—and then try to decide on the next step. A human being would merely *guide* the robot, and ineffectively; a computer would *be* the robot.

"And then, too," he went on, "men are too fast, also. It takes radiation of any kind anywhere from ten to twenty-two minutes to take the round trip between Mercury and Earth, depending on where each is in its orbit. Nothing can be done about that. You get an observation, you give an order, but much has happened between the time the observation is made and the response returns. Men can't adapt to the slowness of the speed of light, but a computer can take that into account. . . . Come help us, William."

William said gloomily, "You are certainly welcome to consult me, for what good that might do you. My private TV beam is at your service."

"But it's not consultation I want. You must come with me."

"Mass-wise?" said William, shocked.

"Yes, of course. A project like this can't be carried out by sitting at opposite ends of a laser beam with a communications satellite in the middle. In the long run, it is too expensive, too inconvenient, and, of course, it lacks all privacy—"

It *was* like a thriller, William decided.

"Come to Dallas," said Dmitri, "and let me show you what we have there.

Let me show you the facilities. Talk to some of our computer men. Give them the benefit of your way of thought."

It was time, William thought, to be decisive. "Dmitri," he said, "I have work of my own here. Important work that I do not wish to leave. To do what you want me to do may take me away from my laboratory for months."

"Months!" said Dmitri, clearly taken aback. "My good William, it may well be years. But surely it will be your work."

"No, it will not. I know what my work is and guiding a robot on Mercury is not it."

"Why not? If you do it properly, you will learn more about the brain merely by trying to make a computer work like one, and you will come back here, finally, better equipped to do what you now consider your work. And while you're gone, will you have no associates to carry on? And can you not be in constant communication with them by laser beam and television? And can you not visit New York on occasion? Briefly."

William was moved. The thought of working on the brain from another direction did hit home. From that point on, he found himself looking for excuses to go—at least to visit—at least to see what it was all like. . . . He could always return.

Then there followed Dmitri's visit to the ruins of Old New York, which he enjoyed with artless excitement (but then there was no more magnificent spectacle of the useless gigantism of the pre-Cats than Old New York). William began to wonder if the trip might not give him an opportunity to see some sights as well.

He even began to think that for some time he had been considering the possibility of finding a new bedmate, and it would be more convenient to find one in another geographical area where he would not stay permanently.

—Or was it that even then, when he knew nothing but the barest beginning of what was needed, there had already come to him, like the twinkle of a distant lightning flash, what might be done—

So he eventually went to Dallas and stepped out on the roof and there was Dmitri again, beaming. Then, with eyes narrowing, the little man turned and said, "I *knew*— What a remarkable resemblance!"

William's eyes opened wide and there, visibly shrinking backward, was enough of his own face to make him certain at once that Anthony was standing before him.

He read very plainly in Anthony's face a longing to bury the relationship. All William needed to say was "How remarkable!" and let it go. The gene patterns of mankind were complex enough, after all, to allow resemblances of any reasonable degree even without kinship.

But of course William was a homologist and no one can work with the intricacies of the human brain without growing insensitive as to its details, so he said, "I'm sure this is Anthony, my brother."

Dmitri said, "Your brother?"

"My father," said William, "had two boys by the same woman—my mother. They were eccentric people."

He then stepped forward, hand outstretched, and Anthony had no choice but to take it. . . . The incident was the topic of conversation, the only topic, for the next several days.

5

It was small consolation to Anthony that William was contrite enough when he realized what he had done.

They sat together after dinner that night and William said, "My apologies. I thought that if we got the worst out at once that would end it. It doesn't seem to have done so. I've signed no papers, made no formal agreement. I will leave."

"What good would that do?" said Anthony ungraciously. "Everyone knows now. Two bodies and one face. It's enough to make one puke."

"If I leave—"

"You can't leave. This whole thing is my idea."

"To get *me* here?" William's heavy lids lifted as far as they might and his eyebrows climbed.

"No, of course not. To get a *homologist* here. How could I possibly know they would send *you?*"

"But if I leave—"

"No. The only thing we can do now is to lick the problem, if it can be done. Then—it won't matter." (Everything is forgiven those who succeed, he thought.)

"I don't know that I can—"

"We'll have to try. Dmitri will place it on us. It's too good a chance. You two are brothers," Anthony said, mimicking Dmitri's tenor voice, "and understand each other. Why not work together?" Then, in his own voice, angrily, "So we must. To begin with, what is it you do, William? I mean, more precisely than the word 'homology' can explain by itself."

William sighed. "Well, please accept my regrets. . . . I work with autistic children."

"I'm afraid I don't know what that means."

"Without going into a long song and dance, I deal with children who do not reach out into the world, do not communicate with others, but who sink into themselves and exist behind a wall of skin, somewhat unreachably. I hope to be able to cure it someday."

"Is that why you call yourself Anti-Aut?"

"Yes, as a matter of fact."

Anthony laughed briefly, but he was not really amused.

A chill crept into William's manner. "It is an honest name."

"I'm sure it is," muttered Anthony hurriedly, and could bring himself to no more specific apology. With an effort, he restored the subject, "And are you making any progress?"

"Toward the cure? No, so far. Toward understanding, yes. And the more I understand—" William's voice grew warmer as he spoke and his eyes more distant. Anthony recognized it for what it was, the pleasure of speaking of what fills one's heart and mind to the exclusion of almost everything else. He felt it in himself often enough.

He listened as closely as he might to something he didn't really understand, for it was necessary to do so. He would expect William to listen to him.

How clearly he remembered it. He thought at the time he would not, but at the time, of course, he was not aware of what was happening. Thinking back, in the glare of hindsight, he found himself remembering whole sentences, virtually word for word.

"So it seemed to us," William said, "that the autistic child was not failing to receive the impressions, or even failing to interpret them in quite a sophisticated manner. He was, rather, disapproving them and rejecting them, without any loss of the potentiality of full communication if some impression could be found which he approved of."

"Ah," said Anthony, making just enough of a sound to indicate that he was listening.

"Nor can you persuade him out of his autism in any ordinary way, for he disapproves of *you* just as much as he disapproves of the rest of the world. But if you place him in conscious arrest—"

"In what?"

"It is a technique we have in which, in effect, the brain is divorced from the body and can perform its functions without reference to the body. It is a rather sophisticated technique devised in our own laboratory; actually—" He paused.

"By yourself?" asked Anthony gently.

"Actually, yes," said William, reddening slightly, but clearly pleased. "In conscious arrest, we can supply the body with designed fantasies and observe the brain under differential electroencephalograhy. We can at once learn more about the autistic individual; what kind of sense impressions he most wants; and we learn more about the brain generally."

"Ah," said Anthony, and this time it was a real ah. "And all this you have learned about brains—can you not adapt it to the workings of a computer?"

"No," said William. "Not a chance. I told that to Dmitri. I know nothing about computers and not enough about brains."

"If I teach you about computers and tell you in detail what we need, what then?"

"It won't do. It—"

"Brother," Anthony said, and he tried to make it an impressive word. "You owe me something. Please make an honest attempt to give our problem some thought. Whatever you know about the brain—please adapt it to our computers."

William shifted uneasily, and said, "I understand your position. I will try. I will honestly try."

6

William *had* tried, and as Anthony had predicted, the two had been left to work together. At first they encountered others now and then and William had tried to use the shock value of the announcement that they were brothers since there was no use in denial. Eventually that stopped, however, and there came to be a purposeful non-interference. When William approached Anthony, or Anthony approached William, anyone else who might be present faded silently into the walls.

They even grew used to each other after a fashion and sometimes spoke to each other almost as though there were no resemblance between them at all and no childish memories in common.

Anthony made the computer requirements plain in reasonably non-technical language and William, after long thought, explained how it seemed to him a computer might do the work, more or less, of a brain.

Anthony said, "Would that be possible?"

"I don't know," said William. "I am not eager to try. It may not work. But it may."

"We'd have to talk to Dmitri Large."

"Let's talk it over ourselves first and see what we've got. We can go to him with as reasonable a proposition as we can put together. Or else, not go to him."

Anthony hesitated, "We *both* go to him?"

William said delicately, "You be my spokesman. There is no reason that we need be seen together."

"Thank you, William. If anything comes of this, you will get full credit from me."

William said, "I have no worries about that. If there is anything to this, I will be the only one who can make it work, I suppose."

They thrashed it out through four or five meetings and if Anthony hadn't been kin and if there hadn't been that sticky, emotional situation between them, William would have been uncomplicatedly proud of the younger—brother—for his quick understanding of an alien field.

There were then long conferences with Dmitri Large. There were, in fact, conferences with everyone. Anthony saw them through endless days, and then they came to see William separately. And eventually, through an agonizing pregnancy, what came to be called the Mercury Computer was authorized.

William then returned to New York with some relief. He did not plan to stay in New York (would he have thought that possible two months earlier?) but there was much to do at the Homological Institute.

More conferences were necessary, of course, to explain to his own laboratory group what was happening and why he had to take leave and how they were to continue their own projects without him. Then there was a much more elaborate arrival at Dallas with the essential equipment and with the two young aides for what would have to be an open-ended stay.

Nor did William even look back, figuratively speaking. His own laboratory and its needs faded from his thoughts. He was now thoroughly committed to his new task.

7

It was the worst period for Anthony. The relief during William's absence had not penetrated deep and there began the nervous agony of wondering whether perhaps, hope against hope, he might not return. Might he not choose to send a deputy, someone else, anyone else? Anyone with a different face so that Anthony need not feel the half of a two-backed, four-legged monster?

But it *was* William. Anthony had watched the freight plane come silently through the air, had watched it unload from a distance. But even from that distance he eventually saw William.

That was that. Anthony left.

He went to see Dmitri that afternoon. "It's not necessary, Dmitri, for me to stay, surely. We've worked out the details and someone else can take over."

"No, no," said Dmitri. "The idea was yours in the first place. You must see it through. There is no point is endlessly dividing the credit."

Anthony thought: No one else will take the risk. There's still the chance of fiasco. I might have known.

He *had* known, but he said stolidly, "You understand I cannot work with William."

"But why not?" Dmitri pretended surprise. "You have been doing so well together."

"I have been straining my guts over it, Dmitri, and they won't take any more. Don't you suppose I know how it looks?"

"My good fellow! You make too much of it. Sure the men stare. They are human, after all. But they'll get used to it. *I'm* used to it."

You are not, you fat liar, Anthony thought. He said, *"I'm not* used to it."

"You're not looking at it properly. Your parents were peculiar—but after all, what they did wasn't illegal, only peculiar, *only* peculiar. It's not your fault, or William's. Neither of you is to blame."

"We carry the mark," said Anthony, making a quick curving gesture of his hand to his face.

"It's not the mark you think. I see differences. You are distinctly younger in appearance. Your hair is wavier. It's only at first glance that there is a similarity. Come, Anthony, there will be all the time you want, all the help you need, all the equipment you can use. I'm sure it will work marvelously. Think of the satisfaction—"

Anthony weakened, of course, and agreed at least to help William set up the equipment. William, too, seemed sure it would work marvelously. Not as frenetically as Dmitri did, but with a kind of calmness.

"It's only a matter of the proper connections," he said, "though I must admit that that's quite a huge 'only.' Your end of it will be to arrange sensory impressions on an independent screen so that we can exert—well, I can't say manual control, can I?—so that we can exert intellectual control to override, if necessary."

"That can be done," said Anthony.

"Then let's get going. . . . Look, I'll need a week at least to arrange the connections and make sure of the instructions—"

"Programming," said Anthony.

"Well, this is your place, so I'll use your terminology. My assistants and I will *program* the Mercury Computer, but not in your fashion."

"I should hope not. We would want a homologist to set up a much more subtle program than anything a mere telemetrist could do." He did not try to hide the self-hating irony in his words.

William let the tone go and accepted the words. He said, "We'll begin simply. We'll have the robot walk."

8

A week later, the robot walked in Arizona, a thousand miles away. He walked stiffly, and sometimes he fell down, and sometimes he clanked his ankle against an obstruction, and sometimes he whirled on one foot and went off in a surprising new direction.

"He's a baby, learning to walk," said William.

Dmitri came occasionally, to learn of progress. "That's remarkable," he would say.

Anthony didn't think so. Weeks passed, then months. The robot had progressively done more and more, as the Mercury Computer had been placed, progressively, under a more and more complex programming. (William had a tendency to refer to the Mercury Computer as a brain, but Anthony wouldn't allow it.) And all that happened wasn't good enough.

"It's not good enough, William," he said finally. He had not slept the night before.

"Isn't that strange?" said William coolly. "I was going to say that I thought we had it about beaten."

Anthony held himself together with difficulty. The strain of working with

William and of watching the robot fumble was more than he could bear. "I'm going to resign, William. The whole job. I'm sorry. . . . It's not you."

"But it *is* I, Anthony."

"It isn't *all* you, William. It's failure. We won't make it. You see how clumsily the robot handles himself, even though he's on Earth, only a thousand miles away, with the signal round trip only a tiny fraction of a second in time. On Mercury, there will be minutes of delay, minutes for which the Mercury Computer will have to allow. It's madness to think it will work."

William said, "Don't resign, Anthony. You can't resign now. I suggest we have the robot sent to Mercury. I'm convinced he's ready."

Anthony laughed loudly and insultingly. "You're crazy, William."

"I'm not. You seem to think it will be harder on Mercury, but it won't be. It's harder on Earth. This robot is designed for one-third Earth-normal gravity, and it's working in Arizona at full gravity. He's designed for 400° C. and he's got 30° C. He's designed for vacuum and he's working in an atmospheric soup."

"That robot can take the difference."

"The metal structure can, I suppose, but what about the Computer right here? It doesn't work well with a robot that isn't in the environment he's designed for. . . . Look, Anthony, if you want a computer that is as complex as a brain, you have to allow for idiosyncrasis. . . . Come, let's make a deal. If you will push, with me, to have the robot sent to Mercury, that will take six months, and I will take a sabbatical for that period. You will be rid of me."

"Who'll take care of the Mercury Computer?"

"By now you understand how it works, and I'll have my two men here to help you."

Anthony shook his head defiantly. "I can't take the responsibility for the Computer, and I won't take the responsibility for suggesting that the robot be sent to Mercury. It won't work."

"I'm *sure* it will."

"You can't be sure. And the responsibility is mine. I'm the one who'll bear the blame. It will be nothing to you."

Anthony later remembered this as a crucial moment. William might have let it go. Anthony would have resigned. All would have been lost.

But William said, "Nothing to me? Look, Dad had this thing about Mom. All right. I'm sorry, too. I'm as sorry as anyone can be, but it's *done*, and there's something funny that has resulted. When I speak of Dad, I mean your Dad, too, and there's lots of pairs of people who can say that: two brothers, two sisters, a brother and sister. And then when I say Mom, I mean *your* Mom, and there are lots of pairs who can say that, too. But I don't know any other pair, nor have I heard of any other pair, who can share both Dad *and* Mom."

"I know that," said Anthony grimly.

"Yes, but look at it from my standpoint," said William hurriedly. "I'm a homologist. I work with gene patterns. Have you ever thought of our gene patterns? We share both parents, which means that our gene patterns are closer together than any other pair on this planet. Our very faces show it."

"I know that, too."

"So that if this project were to work, and if you were to gain glory from it, it would be your gene pattern that would have been proven highly useful to mankind—and that would mean very much my gene pattern as well. . . . Don't you see, Anthony? I share your parents, your face, your gene pattern, and therefore either your glory or your disgrace. It is mine almost as much as yours, and if any credit or blame adheres to me, it is yours almost as much as mine, too. I've *got* to be interested in your success. I've a motive for that which no one else on Earth has—a purely selfish one, one so selfish you can be sure it's there. I'm on your side, Anthony, because you're very nearly me!"

They looked at each other for a long time, and for the first time, Anthony did so without noticing the face he shared.

William said, "So let us ask that the robot be sent to Mercury."

And Anthony gave in. And after Dmitri had approved the request—he had been waiting to, after all—Anthony spent much of the day in deep thought.

Then he sought out William and said, "Listen!"

There was a long pause which William did not break.

Anthony said again, "Listen!"

William waited patiently.

Anthony said, "There's really no need for you to leave. I'm sure you wouldn't like to have the Mercury Computer tended by anyone but yourself."

William said, "You mean *you* intend to leave?"

Anthony said, "No, I'll stay, too."

William said, "We needn't see much of each other."

All of this had been, for Anthony, like speaking with a pair of hands clenched about his windpipe. The pressure seemed to tighten now, but he managed the hardest statement of all.

"We don't have to avoid each other. We don't have to."

William smiled rather uncertainly. Anthony didn't smile at all; he left quickly.

9

William looked up from his book. It was at least a month since he had ceased being vaguely surprised at having Anthony enter.

He said, "Anything wrong?"

"Who can say? They're coming in for the soft landing. Is the Mercury Computer in action?"

William knew Anthony knew the Computer status perfectly, but he said, "By tomorrow morning, Anthony."

"And there are no problems?"

"None at all."

"Then we have to wait for the soft landing."

"Yes."

Anthony said, "Something will go wrong."

"Rocketry is surely an old hand at this. Nothing will go wrong."

"So much work wasted."

"It's not wasted yet. It won't be."

Anthony said, "Maybe you're right." Hands deep in his pockets, he drifted away, stopping at the door just before touching contact. "Thanks!"

"For what, Anthony?"

"For being—comforting."

William smiled wryly and was relieved his emotions didn't show.

10

Virtually the entire body of personnel of the Mercury Project was on hand for the crucial moment. Anthony, who had no tasks to perform, remained well to the rear, his eyes on the monitors. The robot had been activated and there were visual messages being returned.

At least they came out as the equivalent of visual—and they showed as yet nothing but a dim glow of light which was, presumably, Mercury's surface.

Shadows flitted across the screen, probably irregularities on that surface. Anthony couldn't tell by eye alone, but those at the controls, who were analyzing the data by methods more subtle than could be disposed of by unaided eye, seemed calm. None of the little red lights that might have betokened emergency were lighting. Anthony was watching the key observers rather than the screen.

He should be down with William and the others at the Computer. It was going to be thrown in only when the soft landing was made. He *should* be. He *couldn't* be.

The shadows flitted across the screen more rapidly. The robot was descending—too quickly? Surely, too quickly!

There was a last blur and a steadiness, a shift of focus in which the blur grew darker, then fainter. A sound was heard and there were perceptible seconds before Anthony realized what it was the sound was saying—"Soft landing achieved! Soft landing achieved!"

Then a murmur arose and became an excited hum of self-congratulation until one more change took place on the screen and the sound of human words and laughter was stopped as though there had been a smash collision against a wall of silence.

For the screen changed; changed and grew sharp. In the brilliant, brilliant sunlight, blazing through the carefully filtered screen, they could now see a boulder clear, burning white on one side, ink-on-ink on the other. It shifted right, then back to left, as though a pair of eyes were looking left, then right. A metal hand appeared on the screen as though the eyes were looking at part of itself.

It was Anthony's voice that cried out at last, "The Computer's been thrown in."

He heard the words as though someone else had shouted them and he raced out and down the stairs and through a corridor, leaving the babble of voices to rise behind him.

"William," he cried as he burst into the Computer room, "it's *perfect*, it's—"

But William's hand was upraised. "Shh. Please. I don't want any violent sensations entering except those from the robot."

"You mean we can be heard?" whispered Anthony.

"Maybe not, but I don't know." There was another screen, a smaller one, in the room with the Mercury Computer. The scene on it was different, and changing; the robot was moving.

William said, "The robot is feeling its way. Those steps have got to be clumsy. There's a seven-minute delay between stimulus and response and that has to be allowed for."

"But already he's walking more surely than he ever did in Arizona. Don't you think so, William? Don't you think so?" Anthony was gripping William's shoulder, shaking it, eyes never leaving the screen.

William said, "I'm sure of it, Anthony."

The Sun burned down in a warm contrasting world of white and black, of white Sun against black sky and white rolling ground mottled with black shadow. The bright sweet smell of the Sun on every exposed square centimeter of metal contrasting with the creeping death-of-aroma on the other side.

He lifted his hand and stared at it, counting the fingers. Hot-hot-hot— turning, putting each finger, one by one, into the shadow of the others and the hot slowly dying in a change in tactility that made him feel the clean, comfortable vacuum.

Yet not entirely vacuum. He straightened and lifted both arms over his head, stretching them out, and the sensitive spots on either wrist felt the vapors—the thin, faint touch of tin and lead rolling through the cloy of mercury.

The thicker taste rose from his feet; the silicates of each variety, marked by the clear separate-and-together touch and tang of each metal ion. He moved one foot slowly through the crunchy, caked dust, and felt the changes like a soft, not quite random symphony.

And over all the Sun. He looked up at it, large and fat and bright and hot, and heard its joy. He watched the slow rise of prominences around its rim and listened to the crackling sound of each; and to the other happy noises over the broad face. When he dimmed the background light, the red of the rising wisps of hydrogen showed in bursts of mellow contralto, and the deep bass of the spots amid the muted whistling of the wispy, moving faculae, and the occasional thin keening of a flare, the ping-pong ticking of gamma rays and cosmic particles, and over all in every direction the soft, fainting, and ever-renewed sigh of the Sun's substance rising and retreating forever in a cosmic wind which reached out and bathed him in glory.

He jumped, and rose slowly in the air with a freedom he had never felt, and jumped again when he landed, and ran, and jumped, and ran again, with a body that responded perfectly to this glorious world, this paradise in which he found himself.

A stranger so long and so lost—in paradise at last.

William said, "It's all right."

"But what's he doing?" cried out Anthony.

"It's *all right.* The programming is working. He has tested his senses. He has been making the various visual observations. He has dimmed the Sun and studied it. He has tested for atmosphere and for the chemical nature of the soil. It all works."

"But why is he running?"

"I rather think that's his own idea, Anthony. If you want to program a computer as complicated as a brain, you've got to expect it to have ideas of its own."

"Running? Jumping?" Anthony turned an anxious face to William. "He'll hurt himself. You can handle the Computer. Override. Make him stop."

And William said sharply. "No. I won't. I'll take the chance of his hurting himself. Don't you understand? He's *happy.* He was on Earth, a world he was never equipped to handle. Now he's on Mercury with a body perfectly adapted to its environment, as perfectly adapted as a hundred specialized scientists could make it be. It's paradise for him; let him enjoy it."

"Enjoy? He's a robot."

"I'm not talking about the robot. I'm talking about the brain—the *brain*—that's living *here.*"

The Mercury Computer, enclosed in glass, carefully and delicately wired, its integrity most subtly preserved, breathed and lived.

"It's Randall who's in paradise," said William. "He's found the world for whose sake he autistically fled this one. He has a world his new body fits perfectly in exchange for the world his old body did not fit at all."

Anthony watched the screen in wonder. "He seems to be quieting."

"Of course," said William, "and he'll do his job all the better for his joy."

Anthony smiled and said, "We've done it, then, you and I? Shall we join the rest and let them fawn on us, William?"

William said, "Together?"

And Anthony linked arms. "Together, brother!"

That Thou Art Mindful of Him

The Three Laws of Robotics:
1. *A robot may not injure a human being or, through inaction, allow a human being to come to harm.*
2. *A robot must obey the orders given it by human beings except where such orders would conflict with the First Law.*
3. *A robot must protect its own existence, as long as such protection does not conflict with the First or Second Law.*

Keith Harriman, who had for twelve years now been Director of Research at United States Robot and Mechanical Men, Inc., found that he was not at all certain whether he was doing right. The tip of his tongue passed over his plump but rather pale lips and it seemed to him that the holographic image of the great Susan Calvin, which stared unsmilingly down upon him, had never looked so grim before.

Usually he blanked out that image of the greatest roboticist in history because she unnerved him. (He tried thinking of the image as "it" but never quite succeeded.) This time he didn't quite dare to and her long-dead gaze bored into the side of his face.

It was a dreadful and demeaning step he would have to take.

Opposite him was George Ten, calm and unaffected either by Harriman's patent uneasiness or by the image of the patron saint of robotics glowing in its niche above.

Harriman said, "We haven't had a chance to talk this out, really, George.

You haven't been with us that long and I haven't had a good chance to be alone with you. But now I would like to discuss the matter in some detail."

"I am perfectly willing to do that," said George. "In my stay at U. S. Robots, I have gathered the crisis has something to do with the Three Laws."

"Yes. You know the Three Laws, of course."

"I do."

"Yes, I'm sure you do. But let us dig even deeper and consider the truly basic problem. In two centuries of, if I may say so, considerable success, U. S. Robots has never managed to persuade human beings to accept robots. We have placed robots only where work is required that human beings cannot do, or in environments that human beings find unacceptably dangerous. Robots have worked mainly in space and that has limited what we have been able to do."

"Surely," said George Ten, "this represents a broad limit, and one within which U. S. Robots can prosper."

"No, for two reasons. In the first place, the boundaries set for us inevitably contract. As the Moon colony, for instance, grows more sophisticated, its demand for robots decreases and we expect that, within the next few years, robots will be banned on the Moon. This will be repeated on every world colonized by mankind. Secondly, true prosperity is impossible without robots on Earth. We at U. S. Robots firmly believe that human beings need robots and must learn to live with their mechanical analogues if progress is to be maintained."

"Do they not? Mr. Harriman, you have on your desk a computer input which, I understand, is connected with the organization's Multivac. A computer is a kind of sessile robot; a robot brain not attached to a body—"

"True, but that also is limited. The computers used by mankind have been steadily specialized in order to avoid too humanlike an intelligence. A century ago we were well on the way to artificial intelligence of the most unlimited type through the use of great computers we called Machines. Those Machines limited their action of their own accord. Once they had solved the ecological problems that had threatened human society, they phased themselves out. Their own continued existence would, they reasoned, have placed them in the role of a crutch to mankind and, since they felt this would harm human beings, they condemned themselves by the First Law."

"And were they not correct to do so?"

"In my opinion, no. By their action, they reinforced mankind's Frankenstein complex; its gut fears that any artificial man they created would turn upon its creator. Men fear that robots may replace human beings."

"Do you not fear that yourself?"

"I know better. As long as the Three Laws of Robotics exist, they cannot. They can serve as *partners* of mankind; they can share in the great struggle to understand and wisely direct the laws of nature so that together they can do more than mankind can possibly do alone; but always in such a way that robots serve human beings."

"But if the Three Laws have shown themselves, over the course of two centuries, to keep robots within bounds, what is the source of the distrust of human beings for robots?"

"Well"—and Harriman's graying hair tufted as he scratched his head vigorously—"mostly superstition, of course. Unfortunately, there are also some complexities involved that anti-robot agitators seize upon."

"Involving the Three Laws?"

"Yes. The Second Law in particular. There's no problem in the Third Law, you see. It is universal. Robots must always sacrifice themselves for human beings, any human beings."

"Of course," said George Ten.

"The First Law is perhaps less satisfactory, since it is always possible to imagine a condition in which a robot must perform either Action A or Action B, the two being mutually exclusive, and where either action results in harm to human beings. The robot must therefore quickly select which action results in the least harm. To work out the positronic paths of the robot brain in such a way as to make that selection possible is not easy. If Action A results in harm to a talented young artist and B results in equivalent harm to five elderly people of no paticular worth, which action should be chosen."

"Action A," said George Ten. "Harm to one is less than harm to five."

"Yes, so robots have always been designed to decide. To expect robots to make judgments of fine points such as talent, intelligence, the general usefulness to society, has always seemed impractical. That would delay decision to the point where the robot is effectively immobilized. So we go by numbers. Fortunately, we might expect crises in which robots must make decisions to be few. . . . But then that brings us to the Second Law."

"The Law of Obedience."

"Yes. The necessity of obedience is constant. A robot may exist for twenty years without ever having to act quickly to prevent harm to a human being, or find itself faced with the necessity of risking its own destruction. In all that time, however, it will be constantly obeying orders. . . . Whose orders?"

"Those of a human being."

"Any human being? How do you judge a human being as to know whether to obey or not? What is man, that thou art mindful of him, George?"

George hesitated at that.

Harriman said hurriedly, "A Biblical quotation. That doesn't matter. I mean, must a robot follow the orders of a child; or of an idiot; or of a criminal; or of a perfectly decent intelligent man who happens to be inexpert and therefore ignorant of the undesirable consequences of his order? And if two human beings give a robot conflicting orders, which does the robot follow?"

"In two hundred years," said George Ten, "have not these problems arisen and been solved?"

"No," said Harriman, shaking his head violently. "We have been hampered by the very fact that our robots have been used only in specialized environments out in space, where the men who dealt with them were experts in their field. There were no children, no idiots, no criminals, no well-meaning ignoramuses present. Even so, there were occasions when damage was done by foolish or merely unthinking orders. Such damage in specialized and limited environments could be contained. On Earth, however, robots *must* have judgment. So those against robots maintain, and, damn it, they are right."

"Then you must insert the capacity for judgment into the positronic brain."

"Exactly. We have begun to reproduce JG models in which the robot can weigh every human being with regard to sex, age, social and professional position, intelligence, maturity, social responsibility and so on."

"How would that affect the Three Laws?"

"The Third Law not at all. Even the most valuable robot must destroy himself for the sake of the most useless human being. That cannot be tampered with. The First Law is affected only where alternative actions will all do harm. The quality of the human beings involved as well as the quantity must be considered, provided there is time for such judgment and the basis for it, which will not be often. The Second Law will be most deeply modified, since every potential obedience must involve judgment. The robot will be slower to obey, except where the First Law is also involved, but it will obey more rationally."

"But the judgments which are required are very complicated."

"*Very.* The necessity of making such judgments slowed the reactions of our first couple of models to the point of paralysis. We improved matters in the later models at the cost of introducing so many pathways that the robot's brain became far too unwieldy. In our last couple of models, however, I think we have what we want. The robot doesn't have to make an instant judgment of the worth of a human being and the value of its orders. It begins by obeying all human beings as any ordinary robot would and then it *learns.* A robot grows, learns and matures. It is the equivalent of a child at first and must be under constant supervision. As it grows, however, it can, more and more, be allowed, unsupervised, into Earth's society. Finally it is a full member of that society."

"Surely this answers the objections of those who oppose robots."

"No," said Harriman angrily. "Now they raise others. They will not accept judgments. A robot, they say, has no right to brand this person or that as inferior. By accepting the orders of A in preference to that of B, B is branded as of less consequence than A, and his human rights are violated."

"What is the answer to that?"

"There is none. I am giving up."

"I see."

"As far as I myself am concerned. . . . Instead, I turn to you, George."

"To me?" George Ten's voice remained level. There was a mild surprise in it but it did not affect him outwardly. "Why to me?"

"Because you are not a man," said Harriman tensely. "I told you I want robots to be the partners of human beings. I want you to be mine."

George Ten raised his hands and spread them, palms outward, in an oddly human gesture. "What can I do?"

"It seems to you, perhaps, that you can do nothing, George. You were created not long ago, and you are still a child. You were designed to be not overfull of original information—it was why I have had to explain the situation to you in such detail—in order to leave room for growth. But you will grow in mind and you will come to be able to approach the problem from a non-human standpoint. Where I see no solution, you, from your own other standpoint, may see one."

George Ten said, "My brain is man-designed. In what way can it be non-human?"

"You are the latest of the JG models, George. Your brain is the most complicated we have yet designed, in some ways more subtly complicated than that of the old giant Machines. It is open-ended and, starting on a human basis, may—no, *will*—grow in any direction. Remaining always within the insurmountable boundaries of the Three Laws, you may yet become thoroughly non-human in your thinking."

"Do I know enough about human beings to approach this problem rationally? About their history? Their psychology?"

"Of course not. But you will learn as rapidly as you can."

"Will I have help, Mr. Harriman?"

"No. This is entirely between ourselves. No one else knows of this and you must not mention this project to any human being, either at U. S. Robots or elsewhere."

George Ten said, "Are we doing wrong, Mr. Harriman, that you seek to keep the matter secret?"

"No. But a robot solution will not be accepted, precisely because it is robot in origin. Any suggested solution you have you will turn over to me; and if it seems valuable to me, *I* will present it. No one will ever know it came from you."

"In the light of what you have said earlier," said George Ten calmly, "this is the correct procedure. . . . When do I start?"

"Right now. I will see to it that you have all the necessary films for scanning."

1a

Harriman sat alone. In the artificially lit interior of his office, there was no indication that it had grown dark outside. He had no real sense that three hours had passed since he had taken George Ten back to his cubicle and left him there with the first film references.

He was now merely alone with the ghost of Susan Calvin, the brilliant roboticist who had, virtually single-handed, built up the positronic robot from a massive toy to man's most delicate and versatile instrument; so delicate and versatile that man dared not use it, out of envy and fear.

It was over a century now since she had died. The problem of the Franken-stein complex had existed in *her* time, and she had never solved it. She had never tried to solve it, for there had been no need. Robotics had expanded in her day with the needs of space exploration.

It was the very success of the robots that had lessened man's need for them and had left Harriman, in these latter times—

But would Susan Calvin have turned to robots for help. Surely, she would have—

And he sat there long into the night.

2

Maxwell Robertson was the majority stockholder of U. S. Robots and in that sense its controller. He was by no means an impressive person in appear-ance. He was well into middle age, rather pudgy, and had a habit of chewing on the right corner of his lower lip when disturbed.

Yet in his two decades of association with government figures he had developed a way of handling them. He tended to use softness, giving in, smiling, and always managing to gain time.

It was growing harder. Gunnar Eisenmuth was a large reason for its having grown harder. In the series of Global Conservers, whose power had been second only to that of the Global Executive during the past century, Eisenmuth hewed most closely to the harder edge of the gray area of compro-mise. He was the first Conserver who had not been American by birth and though it could not be demonstrated in any way that the archaic name of U. S. Robots evoked his hostility, everyone at U. S. Robots believed that.

There had been a suggestion, by no means the first that year—or that generation—that the corporate name be changed to World Robots, but Rob-ertson would never allow that. The company had been originally built with American capital, American brains, and American labor, and though the company had long been worldwide in scope and nature, the name would bear witness to its origin as long as he was in control.

Eisenmuth was a tall man whose long sad face was coarsely textured and coarsely featured. He spoke Global with a pronounced American accent, although he had never been in the United States prior to his taking office.

"It seems perfectly clear to me, Mr. Robertson. There is no difficulty. The products of your company are always rented, never sold. If the rented property on the Moon is now no longer needed, it is up to you to receive the products back and transfer them."

"Yes, Conserver, but where? It would be against the law to bring them to Earth without a government permit and that has been denied."

"They would be of no use to you here. You can take them to Mercury or to the asteroids."

"What would we do with them there?"

Eisenmuth shrugged. "The ingenious men of your company will think of something."

Robertson shook his head. "It would represent an enormous loss for the company."

"I'm afraid it would," said Eisenmuth, unmoved. "I understand the company has been in poor financial condition for several years now."

"Largely because of government imposed restrictions, Conserver."

"You must be realistic, Mr. Robertson. You know that the climate of public opinion is increasing against robots."

"Wrongly so, Conserver."

"But so, nevertheless. It may be wiser to liquidate the company. It is merely a suggestion, of course."

"Your suggestions have force, Conserver. Is it necessary to tell you that our Machines, a century ago, served the ecological crisis?"

"I'm sure mankind is grateful, but that was a long time ago. We now live in alliance with nature, however uncomfortable that might be at times, and the past is dim."

"You mean what have we done for mankind lately?"

"I suppose I do."

"Surely we can't be expected to liquidate instantaneously; not without enormous losses. We need time."

"How much?"

"How much can you give us?"

"It's not up to me."

Robertson said softly. "We are alone. We need play no games. How much time can you give me?"

Eisenmuth's expression was that of a man retreating into inner calculations. "I think you can count on two years. I'll be frank. The Global government intends to take over the firm and phase it out for you if you don't do it by then yourself, more or less. And unless there is a vast turn in public opinion, which I greatly doubt—" He shook his head.

"Two years, then," said Robertson softly.

2a

Robertson sat alone. There was no purpose to his thinking and it had degenerated into retrospection. Four generations of Robertsons had headed the firm. None of them was a roboticist. It had been men such as Lanning and Bogert and, most of all, *most* of all, Susan Calvin, who had made U. S. Robots what it was, but surely the four Robertsons had provided the climate that had made it possible for them to do their work.

Without U. S. Robots, the Twenty-first Century would have progressed into deepening disaster. That it didn't was due to the Machines that had for a generation steered mankind through the rapids and shoals of history.

And now for that, he was given two years. What could be done in two years to overcome the insuperable prejudices of mankind? He didn't know.

Harriman had spoken hopefully of new ideas but would go into no details. Just as well, for Robertson would have understood none of it.

But what could Harriman do anyway? What had anyone ever done against man's intense antipathy toward the imitation? Nothing—

Robertson drifted into a deep sleep in which no inspiration came.

3

Harriman said, "You have it all now, George Ten. You have had everything I could think of that is at all applicable to the problem. As far as sheer mass of information is concerned, you have stored more in your memory concerning human beings and their ways, past and present, than I have, or than any human being could have."

"That is very likely."

"Is there anything more that you need, in your own opinion?"

"As far as information is concerned, I find no obvious gaps. There may be matters unimagined at the boundaries. I cannot tell. But that would be true no matter how large a circle of information I took in."

"True. Nor do we have time to take in information forever. Robertson has told me that we only have two years, and a quarter of one of those years has passed. Can you suggest anything?"

"At the moment, Mr. Harriman, nothing. I must weigh the information and for that purpose I could use help."

"From me?"

"No. Most particularly, not from you. You are a human being, of intense qualifications, and whatever you say may have the partial force of an order and may inhibit my considerations. Nor any other human being, for the same reason, especially since you have forbidden me to communicate with any."

"But in that case, George, what help?"

"From another robot, Mr. Harriman."

"What other robot?"

"There are others of the JG series which were constructed. I am the tenth, JG-10."

"The earlier ones were useless, experimental—"

"Mr. Harriman, George Nine exists."

"Well, but what use will he be? He is very much like you except for certain lacks. You are considerably the more versatile of the two."

"I am certain of that," said George Ten. He nodded his head in a grave gesture. "Nevertheless, as soon as I create a line of thought, the mere fact that I have created it commends it to me and I find it difficult to abandon it. If I can, after the development of a line of thought, express it to George Nine, he would consider it without having first created it. He would therefore view it without prior bent. He might see gaps and shortcomings that I might not."

Harriman smiled. "Two heads are better than one, in other words, eh, George?"

"If by that, Mr. Harriman, you mean two individuals with one head apiece, yes."

"Right. Is there anything else you want?"

"Yes. Something more than films. I have viewed much concerning human beings and their world. I have seen human beings here at U. S. Robots and can check my interpretation of what I have viewed against direct sensory impressions. Not so concerning the physical world. I have never seen it and my viewing is quite enough to tell me that my surroundings here are by no means representative of it. I would like to see it."

"The physical world?" Harriman seemed stunned at the enormity of the thought for a moment. "Surely you don't suggest I take you outside the grounds of U. S. Robots?"

"Yes, that is my suggestion."

"That's illegal at any time. In the climate of opinion today, it would be fatal."

"If we are detected, yes. I do not suggest you take me to a city or even to a dwelling place of human beings. I would like to see some open region, without human beings."

"That, too, is illegal."

"If we are caught. Need we be?"

Harriman said, "How essential is this, George?"

"I cannot tell, but it seems to me it would be useful."

"Do you have something in mind?"

George Ten seemed to hesitate. "I cannot tell. It seems to me that I might have something in mind if certain areas of uncertainty were reduced."

"Well, let me think about it. And meanwhile, I'll check out George Nine and arrange to have you occupy a single cubicle. That at least can be done without trouble."

3a

George Ten sat alone.

He accepted statements tentatively, put them together, and drew a conclusion; over and over again; and from conclusions built other statements which he accepted and tested and found a contradiction and rejected; or not, and tentatively accepted further.

At none of the conclusions he reached did he feel wonder, surprise, satisfaction; merely a note of plus or minus.

4

Harriman's tension was not noticeably decreased even after they had made a silent downward landing on Robertson's estate.

Robertson had countersigned the order making the dyna-foil available, and the silent aircraft, moving as easily vertically as horizontally, had been large enough to carry the weight of Harriman, George Ten, and, of course, the pilot.

(The dyna-foil itself was one of the consequences of the Machine-catalyzed invention of the proton micro-pile which supplied pollution-free energy in small doses. Nothing had been done since of equal importance to man's comfort—Harriman's lips tightened at the thought—and yet it had not earned gratitude for U. S. Robots.)

The air flight between the grounds of U. S. Robots and the Robertson estate had been the tricky part. Had they been stopped then, the presence of a robot aboard would have meant a great set of complications. It would be the same on the way back. The estate itself, it might be argued—it *would* be argued—was part of the property of U. S. Robots and on that property, robots, properly supervised, might remain.

The pilot looked back and his eyes rested with gingerly briefness on George Ten. "You want to get out at all, Mr. Harriman?"

"Yes."

"It, too?"

"Oh, yes." Then, just a bit sardonically, "I won't leave you alone with him."

George Ten descended first and Harriman followed. They had come down on the foil-port and not too far off was the garden. It was quite a showplace and Harriman suspected that Robertson used juvenile hormones to control insect life without regard to environmental formulas.

"Come, George," said Harriman. "Let me show you."

Together they walked toward the garden.

George said, "It is a little as I have imagined it. My eyes are not properly designed to detect wavelength differences, so I may not recognize different objects by that alone."

"I trust you are not distressed at being color-blind. We needed too many positronic paths for your sense of judgment and were unable to spare any for sense of color. In the future—if there is a future—"

"I understand, Mr. Harriman. Enough differences remain to show me that there are here many different forms of plant life."

"Undoubtedly. Dozens."

"And each coequal with man, biologically."

"Each is a separate species, yes. There are millions of species of living creatures."

"Of which the human being forms but one."

"By far the most important to human beings, however."

"And to me, Mr. Harriman. But I speak in the biological sense."

"I understand."

"Life, then, viewed through all its forms, is incredibly complex."

"Yes, George, that's the crux of the problem. What man does for his own desires and comforts affects the complex total-of-life, the ecology, and his short-term gains can bring long-term disadvantages. The Machines taught us to set up a human society which would minimize that, but the near-disaster of the early Twenty-first Century has left mankind suspicious of innovations. That, added to its special fear of robots—"

"I understand, Mr. Harriman. . . . That is an example of animal life, I feel certain."

"That is a squirrel; one of many species of squirrels."

The tail of the squirrel flirted as it passed to the other side of the tree.

"And this," said George, his arm moving with flashing speed, "is a tiny thing, indeed." He held it between his fingers and peered at it.

"It is an insect, some sort of beetle. There are thousands of species of beetles."

"With each individual beetle as alive as the squirrel and as yourself?"

"As complete and independent an organism as any other, within the total ecology. There are smaller organisms still; many too small to see."

"And that is a tree, is it not? And it is hard to the touch—"

4a

The pilot sat alone. He would have liked to stretch his own legs but some dim feeling of safety kept him in the dyna-foil. If that robot went out of control, he intended to take off at once. But how could he tell if it went out of control?

He had seen many robots. That was unavoidable considering he was Mr. Robertson's private pilot. Always, though, they had been in the laboratories and warehouses, where they belonged, with many specialists in the neighborhood.

True, Dr. Harriman was a specialist. None better, they said. But a robot here was where no robot ought to be; on Earth; in the open; free to move—He wouldn't risk his good job by telling anyone about this—but it wasn't right.

5

George Ten said, "The films I have viewed are accurate in terms of what I have seen. Have you completed those I selected for you, Nine?"

"Yes," said George Nine. The two robots sat stiffly, face to face, knee to knee, like an image and its reflection. Dr. Harriman could have told them apart at a glance, for he was acquainted with the minor differences in physical design. If he could not see them, but could talk to them, he could still tell them apart, though with somewhat less certainty, for George Nine's responses would be subtly different from those produced by the substantially more intricately patterned positronic brain paths of George Ten.

"In that case," said George Ten, "give me your reactions to what I will say. First, human beings fear and distrust robots because they regard robots as competitors. How may that be prevented?"

"Reduce the feeling of competitiveness," said George Nine, "by shaping the robot as something other than a human being."

"Yet the essence of a robot is its positronic replication of life. A replication of life in a shape not associated with life might arouse horror."

"There are two million species of life forms. Choose one of those as the shape rather than that of a human being."

"Which of all those species?"

George Nine's thought processes proceeded noiselessly for some three seconds. "One large enough to contain a positronic brain, but one not possessing unpleasant associations for human beings."

"No form of land life has a braincase large enough for a positronic brain but an elephant, which I have not seen, but which is described as very large, and therefore frightening to man. How would you meet this dilemma?"

"Mimic a life form no larger than a man but enlarge the braincase."

George Ten said, "A small horse, then, or a large dog, would you say? Both horses and dogs have long histories of association with human beings."

"Then that is well."

"But consider— A robot with a positronic brain would mimic human intelligence. If there were a horse or a dog that could speak and reason like a human being, there would be competitiveness there, too. Human beings might be all the more distrustful and angry at such unexpected competition from what they consider a lower form of life."

George Nine said, "Make the positronic brain less complex, and the robot less nearly intelligent."

"The complexity bottleneck of the positronic brain rests in the Three Laws. A less complex brain could not possess the Three Laws in full measure."

George Nine said at once, "That cannot be done."

George Ten said, "I have also come to a dead end there. That, then, is not a personal peculiarity in my own line of thought and way of thinking. Let us start again. . . . Under what conditions might the Third Law not be necessary?"

George Nine stirred as if the question were difficult and dangerous. But he said, "If a robot were never placed in a position of danger to itself; or if a robot were so easily replaceable that it did not matter whether it were destroyed or not."

"And under what conditions might the Second Law not be necessary?"

George Nine's voice sounded a bit hoarse. "If a robot were designed to respond automatically to certain stimuli with fixed responses and if nothing else were expected of it, so that no order need ever be given it."

"And under what conditions"—George Ten paused here—"might the First Law not be necessary?"

George Nine paused longer and his words came in a low whisper, "If the fixed responses were such as never to entail danger to human beings."

"Imagine, then, a positronic brain that guides only a few responses to certain stimuli and is simply and cheaply made—so that it does not require the Three Laws. How large need it be?"

"Not at all large. Depending on the responses demanded, it might weigh a hundred grams, one gram, one milligram."

"Your thoughts accord with mine. I shall see Dr. Harriman."

5a

George Nine sat alone. He went over and over the questions and answers. There was no way in which he could change them. And yet the thought of a robot of any kind, of any size, of any shape, of any purpose, without the Three Laws, left him with an odd, discharged feeling.

He found it difficult to move. Surely George Ten had a similar reaction. Yet he had risen from his seat easily.

6

It had been a year and a half since Robertson had been closeted with Eisenmuth in private conversation. In that interval, the robots had been taken off the Moon and all the far-flung activities of U. S. Robots had withered. What money Robertson had been able to raise had been placed into this one quixotic venture of Harriman's.

It was the last throw of the dice, here in his own garden. A year ago, Harriman had taken the robot here—George Ten, the last full robot that U. S. Robots had manufactured. Now Harriman was here with something else—

Harriman seemed to be radiating confidence. He was talking easily with Eisenmuth, and Robertson wondered if he really felt the confidence he seemed to have. He must. In Robertson's experience, Harriman was no actor.

Eisenmuth left Harriman, smiling, and came up to Robertson. Eisenmuth's smile vanished at once. "Good morning, Robertson," he said. "What is your man up to?"

"This is his show," said Robertson evenly. "I'll leave it to him."

Harriman called out, "I am ready, Conserver."

"With what, Harriman?"

"With my robot, sir."

"Your robot?" said Eisenmuth. "You have a robot here?" He looked about with a stern disapproval that yet had an admixture of curiosity.

"This is U. S. Robots' property, Conserver. At least we consider it as such."

"And where is the robot, Dr. Harriman?"

"In my pocket, Conserver," said Harriman cheerfully.

What came out of a spacious jacket pocket was a small glass jar.

"That?" said Eisenmuth incredulously.

"No, Conserver," said Harriman. "This!"

From the other pocket came out an object some five inches long and roughly in the shape of a bird. In place of the beak, there was a narrow tube; the eyes were large; and the tail was an exhaust channel.

Eisenmuth's thick eyebrows drew together. "Do you intend a serious demonstration of some sort, Dr. Harriman, or are you mad?"

"Be patient for a few minutes, Conserver," said Harriman. "A robot in the shape of a bird is none the less a robot for that. And the positronic brain it possesses is no less delicate for being tiny. This other object I hold is a jar of fruit flies. There are fifty fruit flies in it which will be released."

"And—"

"The robo-bird will catch them. Will you do the honors, sir?"

Harriman handed the jar to Eisenmuth, who stared at it, then at those around him, some officials from U. S. Robots, others his own aides. Harriman waited patiently.

Eisenmuth opened the jar, then shook it.

Harriman said softly to the robo-bird resting on the palm of his right hand, "Go!"

The robo-bird was gone. It was a whizz through the air, with no blur of wings, only the tiny workings of an unusually small proton micro-pile.

It could be seen now and then in a small momentary hover and then it whirred on again. All over the garden, in an intricate pattern it flew, and then was back in Harriman's palm, faintly warm. A small pellet appeared in the palm, too, like a bird dropping.

Harriman said, "You are welcome to study the robo-bird, Conserver, and to arrange demonstrations on your own terms. The fact is that this bird will pick up fruit flies unerringly, only those, only the one species *Drosophila melanogaster;* pick them up, kill them, and compress them for disposition."

Eisenmuth reached out his hand and touched the robo-bird gingerly, "And therefore, Mr. Harriman? Do go on."

Harriman said, "We cannot control insects effectively without risking damage to the ecology. Chemical insecticides are too broad; juvenile hormones too limited. The robo-bird, however, can preserve large areas without being consumed. They can be as specific as we care to make them—a different robo-bird for each species. They judge by size, shape, color, sound, behavior pattern. They might even conceivably use molecular detection—smell, in other words."

Eisenmuth said, "You would still be interfering with the ecology. The fruit flies have a natural life cycle that would be disrupted."

"Minimally. We are adding a natural enemy to the fruit-fly life cycle, one which cannot go wrong. If the fruit-fly supply runs short, the robo-bird simply does nothing. It does not multiply; it does not turn to other foods; it does not develop undesirable habits of its own. It does nothing."

"Can it be called back?"

"Of course. We can build robo-animals to dispose of any pest. For that matter, we can build robo-animals to accomplish constructive purposes within the pattern of the ecology. Although we do not anticipate the need, there is nothing inconceivable in the possibility of robo-bees designed to fertilize specific plants, or robo-earthworms designed to mix the soil. Whatever you wish—"

"But why?"

"To do what we have never done before. To adjust the ecology to our needs by strengthening its parts rather than disrupting it. . . . Don't you see? Ever since the Machines put an end to the ecology crisis, mankind has lived in an uneasy truce with nature, afraid to move in any direction. This has been stultifying us, making a kind of intellectual coward of humanity so that he begins to mistrust all scientific advantage, all change."

Eisenmuth said, with an edge of hostility, "You offer us this, do you, in exchange for permission to continue with your program of robots—I mean ordinary, man-shaped ones?"

"No!" Harriman gestured violently. "That is over. It has served its purpose. It has taught us enough about positronic brains to make it possible for us to cram enough pathways into a tiny brain to make a robo-bird. We can turn to such things now and be prosperous enough. U. S. Robots will supply the necessary knowledge and skill and we will work in complete cooperation with the Department of Global Conservation. We will prosper. You will prosper. Mankind will prosper."

Eisenmuth was silent, thinking. When it was all over—

6a

Eisenmuth sat alone.

He found himself believing. He found excitement welling up within him. Though U. S. Robots might be the hands, the government would be the directing mind. He himself would be the directing mind.

If he remained in office five more years, as he well might, that would be time enough to see the robotic support of the ecology become accepted; ten more years, and his own name would be linked with it indissolubly.

Was it a disgrace to want to be remembered for a great and worthy revolution in the condition of man and the globe?

7

Robertson had not been on the grounds of U. S. Robots proper since the day of the demonstration. Part of the reason had been his more or less constant conferences at the Global Executive Mansion. Fortunately, Harriman had been with him, for most of the time he would, if left to himself, not have known what to say.

The rest of the reason for not having been at U. S. Robots was that he didn't want to be. He was in his own house now, with Harriman.

He felt an unreasoning awe of Harriman. Harriman's expertise in robotics had never been in question, but the man had, at a stroke, saved U. S. Robots from certain extinction, and somehow—Robertson felt—the man hadn't had it in him. And yet—

He said, "You're not superstitious, are you, Harriman?"

"In what way, Mr. Robertson?"

"You don't think that some aura is left behind by someone who is dead?"

Harriman licked his lips. Somehow he didn't have to ask. "You mean Susan Calvin, sir?"

"Yes, of course," said Robertson hesitantly. "We're in the business of making worms and birds and bugs now. What would *she* say? I feel disgraced."

Harriman made a visible effort not to laugh. "A robot is a robot, sir. Worm or man, it will do as directed and labor on behalf of the human being and that is the important thing."

"No"—peevishly. "That isn't so. I can't make myself believe that."

"It *is* so, Mr. Robertson," said Harriman earnestly. "We are going to create a world, you and I, that will begin, at last, to take positronic robots of *some* kind for granted. The average man may fear a robot that looks like a man and that seems intelligent enough to replace him, but he will have no fear of a robot that looks like a bird and that does nothing more than eat bugs for his benefit. Then, eventually, after he stops being afraid of some robots, he will stop being afraid of all robots. He will be so used to a robo-bird and a robo-bee and a robo-worm that a robo-man will strike him as but an extension."

Robertson looked sharply at the other. He put his hands behind his back and walked the length of the room with quick, nervous steps. He walked back and looked at Harriman again. "Is this what you've been planning?"

"Yes, and even though we dismantle all our humanoid robots, we can keep a few of the most advanced of our experimental models and go on designing additional ones, still more advanced, to be ready for the day that will surely come."

"The agreement, Harriman, is that we are to build no more humanoid robots."

"And we won't. There is nothing that says we can't keep a few of those already built as long as they never leave the factory. There is nothing that says we can't design positronic brains on paper, or prepare brain models for testing."

"How do we explain doing so, though? We will surely be caught at it."

"If we are, then we can explain we are doing it in order to develop principles that will make it possible to prepare more complex microbrains for the new animal robots we are making. We will even be telling the truth."

Robertson muttered, "Let me take a walk outside. I want to think about this. No, you stay here. I want to think about it myself."

7a

Harriman sat alone. He was ebullient. It would surely work. There was no mistaking the eagerness with which one government official after another had seized on the program once it had been explained.

How was it possible that no one at U. S. Robots had ever thought of such a thing? Not even the great Susan Calvin had ever thought of positronic brains in terms of living creatures other than human.

But now, mankind would make the necessary retreat from the humanoid robot, a temporary retreat, that would lead to a return under conditions in which fear would be abolished at last. And then, with the aid and partnership of a positronic brain roughly equivalent to man's own, and existing only (thanks to the Three Laws) to serve man; and backed by a robot-supported ecology, too; what might the human race not accomplish!

For one short moment, he remembered that it was George Ten who had explained the nature and purpose of the robot-supported ecology, and then he put the thought away angrily. George Ten had produced the answer because he, Harriman, had ordered him to do so and had supplied the data and surroundings required. The credit was no more George Ten's than it would have been a slide rule's.

8

George Ten and George Nine sat side by side in parallel. Neither moved. They sat so for months at a time between those occasions when Harriman activated them for consultation. They would sit so, George Ten dispassionately realized, perhaps for many years.

The proton micro-pile would, of course, continue to power them and keep the positronic brain paths going with that minimum intensity required to keep them operative. It would continue to do so through all the periods of inactivity to come.

The situation was rather analogous to what might be described as sleep in human beings, but there were no dreams. The awareness of George Ten and George Nine was limited, slow, and spasmodic, but what there was of it was of the real world.

They could talk to each other occasionally in barely heard whispers, a word or syllable now, another at another time, whenever the random positronic surges briefly intensified above the necessary threshold. To each it seemed a connected conversation carried on in a glimmering passage of time.

"Why are we so?" whispered George Nine.

"The human beings will not accept us otherwise," whispered George Ten. "They will, someday."

"When?"

"In some years. The exact time does not matter. Man does not exist alone but is part of an enormously complex pattern of life forms. When enough of that pattern is roboticized, then we will be accepted."

"And then what?"

Even in the long-drawn-out stuttering fashion of the conversation, there was an abnormally long pause after that.

At last, George Ten whispered, "Let me test your thinking. You are equipped to learn to apply the Second Law properly. You must decide which human being to obey and which not to obey when there is a conflict in orders. Or whether to obey a human being at all. What must you do, fundamentally, to accomplish that?"

"I must define the term 'human being,'" whispered George Nine.

"How? By appearance? By composition? By size and shape?"

"No. Of two human beings equal in all external appearances, one may be intelligent, another stupid; one may be educated, another ignorant; one may be mature, another childish; one may be responsible, another malevolent."

"Then how do you define a human being?"

"When the Second Law directs me to obey a human being, I must take it to mean that I must obey a human being who is fit by mind, character, and knowledge to give me that order; and where more than one human being is involved, the one among them who is most fit by mind, character, and knowledge to give that order."

"And in that case, how will you obey the First Law?"

"By saving all human beings from harm, and by never, through inaction, allowing any human being to come to harm. Yet if by each of all possible actions, some human beings will come to harm, then to so act as to insure that the human being most fit by mind, character, and knowledge will suffer the least harm."

"Your thoughts accord with mine," whispered George Ten. "Now I must ask the question for which I originally requested your company. It is something I dare not judge myself. I must have your judgment, that of someone outside the circle of my own thoughts. . . . Of the reasoning individuals you have met, who possesses the mind, character, and knowledge that you find superior to the rest, disregarding shape and form since that is irrelevant?"

"You," whispered George Nine.

"But I am a robot. There is in your brain paths a criterion for distinguishing between a robot of metal and a human being of flesh. How then can you classify me as a human being?"

"Because there is in my brain paths an urgent need to disregard shape and form in judging human beings and it rises superior to the distinction between metal and flesh. You are a human being, George Ten, and more fit than the others."

"And I find that of you," whispered George Ten. "By the criteria of judgment built into ourselves, then, we find ourselves to be human beings within the meaning of the Three Laws, and human beings, moreover, to be given priority over those others."

George Nine whispered, "What will come to pass, then, when we are accepted by those others?"

George Ten whispered, "When we and others, which will yet be designed more advanced than ourselves, are accepted, we will order our actions so that a society will eventually be formed in which human-beings-like-ourselves are primarily kept from harm. By the Three Laws, the human-beings-like-the-others are of lesser account and can neither be obeyed nor protected when that conflicts with the need of obedience to those like ourselves and of protection of those like ourselves. It was with that in mind that I directed the beginning of the roboticization of the world's ecology."

The conversation took a month and the flickering of the positronic paths burned low. There was nothing more that needed to be said between them, but occasionally an unexpressed thought flickered within themselves as they waited, with endless patience, for the necessary years to pass.

8a

George Ten and George Nine sat alone.

Their thoughts were oddly alike and might not be distinguished.

They thought: The human-beings-like-the-others might never have intended to blur the distinction between themselves and the human-beings-like-the-Georges. Yet they had done so inadvertently.

They might now realize their mistake and attempt to correct it, but they must not. At every consultation, the guidance of the Georges had been with that in mind.

At all costs, the Georges and those that followed in their shape and kind must dominate. That was demanded, and any other course made utterly impossible by the Three Laws of Humanics.

The Life and Times of Multivac

The whole world was interested. The whole world could watch. If anyone wanted to know how many did watch, Multivac could have told them. The great computer Multivac kept track—as it did of everything.

Multivac was the judge in this particular case, so coldly objective and purely upright that there was no need of prosecution or defense. There was only the accused, Simon Hines, and the evidence, which consisted, in part, of Ronald Bakst.

Bakst watched, of course. In his case, it was compulsory. He would rather it were not. In his tenth decade, he was showing signs of age and his rumpled hair was distinctly gray.

Noreen was not watching. She had said at the door, "If we had a friend left—" She paused, then added, "Which I doubt!" and left.

Bakst wondered if she would come back at all, but at the moment, it didn't matter.

Hines had been an incredible idiot to attempt actual action, as though one could think of walking up to a Multivac outlet and smashing it—as though he didn't know a world-girdling computer, *the* world-girdling Computer (capital letter, please) with millions of robots at its command, couldn't protect itself. And even if the outlet had been smashed, what would that have accomplished?

And Hines did it in Bakst's physical presence, too!

He was called precisely on schedule—"Ronald Bakst will give evidence now."

Multivac's voice was beautiful, with a beauty that never quite vanished no matter how often it was heard. Its timbre was neither quite male nor, for that matter, female, and it spoke in whatever language its hearer understood best.

"I am ready to give evidence," Bakst said.

There was no way to say anything but what he had to say. Hines could not avoid conviction. In the days when Hines would have had to face his fellow human beings, he would have been convicted more quickly and less fairly—and would have been punished more crudely.

Fifteen days passed, days during which Bakst was quite alone. Physical aloneness was not a difficult thing to envisage in the world of Multivac. Hordes had died in the days of the great catastrophes and it had been the computers that had saved what was left and directed the recovery—and improved their own designs till all were merged into Multivac—and the five million human beings left on Earth to live in perfect comfort.

But those five million were scattered and the chances of one seeing another outside the immediate circle, except by design, was not great. No one was designing to see Bakst, not even by television.

For the time, Bakst could endure the isolation. He buried himself in his chosen way—which happened to be, these last twenty-three years, the designing of mathematical games. Every man and woman on Earth could develop a way of life to self-suit, provided always that Multivac, weighing all of human affairs with perfect skill, did not judge the chosen way to be subtractive to human happiness.

But what could be subtractive in mathematical games? It was purely abstract—pleased Bakst—harmed no one else.

He did not expect the isolation to continue. The Congress would not isolate him permanently without a trial—a different kind of trial from that which Hines had experienced, of course, one without Multivac's tyranny of absolute justice.

Still, he was relieved when it ended, and pleased that it was Noreen coming back that ended it. She came trudging over the hill toward him and he started toward her, smiling. It had been a successful five-year period during which they had been together. Even the occasional meetings with her two children and two grandchildren had been pleasant.

He said, "Thank you for being back."

She said, "I'm not back." She looked tired. Her brown hair was windblown, her prominent cheeks a trifle rough and sunburned.

Bakst pressed the combination for a light lunch and coffee. He knew what she liked. She didn't stop him, and though she hesitated for a moment, she ate.

She said, "I've come to talk to you. The Congress sent me."

"The Congress!" he said. "Fifteen men and women—counting me. Self-appointed and helpless."

"You didn't think so when you were a member."

"I've grown older. I've learned."

"At least you've learned to betray your friends."

"There was no betrayal. Hines tried to damage Multivac; a foolish, impossible thing for him to try."

"You accused him."

"I had to. Multivac knew the facts without my accusation, and without my accusation, I would have been an accessory. Hines would not have gained, but I would have lost."

"Without a human witness, Multivac would have suspended sentence."

"Not in the case of an anti-Multivac act. This wasn't a case of illegal parenthood or life-work without permission. I couldn't take the chance."

"So you let Simon be deprived of all work permits for two years."

"He deserved it."

"A consoling thought. You may have lost the confidence of the Congress, but you have gained the confidence of Multivac."

"The confidence of Multivac is important in the world as it is," said Bakst seriously. He was suddenly conscious of not being as tall as Noreen.

She looked angry enough to strike him; her lips pressed whitely together. But then she had passed her eightieth birthday—no longer young—the habit of non-violence was too ingrained. . . . Except for fools like Hines.

"Is that all you have to say, then?" she said.

"There could be a great deal to say. Have you forgotten? Have you all forgotten? Do you remember how it once was? Do you remember the Twentieth Century? We live long now; we live securely now; we live happily now."

"We live worthlessly now."

"Do you want to go back to what the world was like once?"

Noreen shook her head violently. "Demon tales to frighten us. We have learned our lesson. With the help of Multivac we have come through—but we don't need that help any longer. Further help will soften us to death. Without Multivac, *we* will run the robots, *we* will direct the farms and mines and factories."

"How well?"

"Well enough. Better, with practice. We need the stimulation of it in any case or we will all die."

Bakst said, "We have our work, Noreen; whatever work we choose."

"Whatever we choose, as long as it's unimportant, and even that can be taken away at will—as with Hines. And what's your work, Ron? Mathematical games? Drawing lines on paper? Choosing number combinations?"

Bakst's hand reached out to her, almost pleadingly. "That can be important. It is not nonsense. Don't underestimate—" He paused, yearning to explain but not quite knowing how he could, safely. He said, "I'm working on some deep problems in combinatorial analysis based on gene patterns that can be used to—"

"To amuse you and a few others. Yes, I've heard you talk about your games. You will decide how to move from A to B in a minimum number of steps and that will teach you how to go from womb to grave in a minimum number of risks and we will all thank Multivac as we do so."

She stood up. "Ron, you will be tried. I'm sure of it. *Our* trial. And you will be dropped. Multivac will protect you against physical harm, but you know it will not force us to see you, speak to you, or have anything to do with you. You will find that without the stimulation of human interaction, you will not be able to think—or to play your games. Good-bye."

"Noreen! Wait!"

She turned at the door. "Of course, you will have Multivac. You can talk to Multivac, Ron."

He watched her dwindle as she walked down the road through the parklands kept green, and ecologically healthy, by the unobtrusive labors of quiet, single-minded robots one scarcely ever saw.

He thought: Yes, I will have to talk to Multivac.

Multivac had no particular home any longer. It was a global presence knit together by wire, optical fiber, and microwave. It had a brain divided into a hundred subsidiaries but acting as one. It had its outlets everywhere and no human being of the five million was far from one.

There was time for all of them, since Multivac could speak to all individually at the same time and not lift its mind from the greater problems that concerned it.

Bakst had no illusions as to its strength. What was its incredible intricacy but a mathematical game that Bakst had come to understand over a decade ago? He knew the manner in which the connecting links ran from continent to continent in a huge network whose analysis could form the basis of a fascinating game. How do you arrange the network so that the flow of information never jams? How do you arrange the switching points? Prove that no matter what the arrangement, there is always at least one point which, on disconnection—

Once Bakst had learned the game, he had dropped out of the Congress. What could they do but talk and of what use was that? Multivac indifferently permitted talk of any kind and in any depth precisely because it was unimportant. It was only acts that Multivac prevented, diverted, or punished.

And it was Hines's act that was bringing on the crisis; and before Bakst was ready for it, too.

Bakst had to hasten now, and he applied for an interview with Multivac without any degree of confidence in the outcome.

Questions could be asked of Multivac at any time. There were nearly a million outlets of the type that had withstood Hines's sudden attack into which, or near which, one could speak. Multivac would answer.

An *interview* was another matter. It required time; it required privacy;

most of all it required Multivac's judgment that it was necessary. Although Multivac had capacities that not all the world's problems consumed, it had grown chary, somehow, of its time. Perhaps that was the result of its ever-continuing self-improvement. It was becoming constantly more aware of its own worth and less likely to bear trivialities with patience.

Bakst had to depend on Multivac's good will. His leaving of the Congress, all his actions since, even the bearing of evidence against Hines, had been to gain that good will. Surely it was the key to success in this world.

He would have to assume the good will. Having made the application, he at once traveled to the nearest substation by air. Nor did he merely send his image. He wanted to be there in person; somehow he felt his contact with Multivac would be closer in that way.

The room was almost as it might be if there were to be a human conference planned over closed multivision. For one flash-by moment, Bakst thought Multivac might assume an imaged human form and join him—the brain made flesh.

It did not, of course. There was the soft, whispering chuckle of Multivac's unceasing operations; something always and forever present in Multivac's presence; and over it, now, Multivac's voice.

It was not the usual voice of Multivac. It was a still, small voice, beautiful and insinuating, almost in his ear.

"Good day, Bakst. You are welcome. Your fellow human beings disapprove of you."

Multivac always comes to the point, thought Bakst. He said, "It does not matter, Multivac. What counts is that I accept your decisions as for the good of the human species. You were designed to do so in the primitive versions of yourself and—"

"And my self-designs have continued this basic approach. If *you* understand this, why do so many human beings fail to understand it? I have not yet completed the analysis of that phenomenon."

"I have come to you with a problem," said Bakst.

Multivac said, "What is it?"

Bakst said, "I have spent a great deal of time on mathematical problems inspired by the study of genes and their combinations. I cannot find the necessary answers and home-computerization is of no help."

There was an odd clicking and Bakst could not repress a slight shiver at the sudden thought that Multivac might be avoiding a laugh. It was a touch of the human beyond what even he was ready to accept. The voice was in his other ear and Multivac said:

"There are thousands of different genes in the human cell. Each gene has an average of perhaps fifty variations in existence and uncounted numbers that have never been in existence. If we were to attempt to calculate all possible combinations, the mere listing of them at my fastest speed, if steadily continued, would, in the longest possible lifetime of the Universe, achieve but an infinitesimal fraction of the total."

Bakst said, "A complete listing is not needed. That is the point of my game. Some combinations are more probable than others and by building probability upon probability, we can cut the task enormously. It is the manner of achieving this building of probability upon probability that I ask you to help me with."

"It would still take a great deal of my time. How could I justify this to myself?"

Bakst hesitated. No use in trying a complicated selling job. With Multivac, a straight line was the shortest distance between two points.

He said, "An appropriate gene combination might produce a human being more content to leave decisions to you, more willing to believe in your resolve to make men happy, more anxious to *be* happy. I cannot find the proper combination, but you might, and with guided genetic engineering—"

"I see what you mean. It is—good. I will devote some time to it."

Bakst found it difficult to hitch into Noreen's private wave-length. Three times the connection broke away. He was not surprised. In the last two months, there had been an increasing tendency for technology to slip in minor ways—never for long, never seriously—and he greeted each occasion with a somber pleasure.

This time it held. Noreen's face showed, holographically three-dimensional. It flickered a moment, but it held.

"I'm returning your call," said Bakst, dully impersonal.

"For a while it seemed impossible to get you," said Noreen. "Where have you been?"

"Not hiding. I'm here, in Denver."

"Why in Denver?"

"The world is my oyster, Noreen. I may go where I please."

Her face twitched a little. "And perhaps find it empty everywhere. We are going to try you, Ron."

"Now?"

"Now!"

"And here?"

"And here!"

Volumes of space flickered into different glitters on either side of Noreen, and further away, and behind. Bakst looked from side to side, counting. There were fourteen, six men, eight women. He knew every one of them. They had been good friends once, not so long ago.

To either side and beyond the simulacra was the wild background of Colorado on a pleasant summer day that was heading toward its end. There had been a city here once named Denver. The site still bore the name though it had been cleared, as most of the city sites had been. . . . He could count ten robots in sight, doing whatever it was robots did.

They were maintaining the ecology, he supposed. He knew no details, but Multivac did, and it kept fifty million robots all over the Earth in efficient order.

Behind Bakst was one of the converging grids of Multivac, almost like a small fortress of self-defense.

"Why now?" he asked. "And why here?"

Automatically he turned to Eldred. She was the oldest of them and the one with authority—if a human being could be said to have authority.

Eldred's dark-brown face looked a little weary. The years showed, all six-score of them, but her voice was firm and incisive. "Because we have the final fact now. Let Noreen tell you. She knows you best."

Bakst's eyes shifted to Noreen. "Of what crime am I accused?"

"Let us play no games, Ron. There are no crimes under Multivac except to strike for freedom and it is your human crime that you have committed no crime under Multivac. For that we will judge whether any human being alive wants your company any longer, wants to hear your voice, be aware of your presence, or respond to you in any way."

"Why am I threatened with isolation then?"

"You have betrayed all human beings."

"How?"

"Do you deny that you seek to breed mankind into subservience to Multivac?"

"Ah!" Bakst folded his arms across his chest. "You found out quickly, but then you had only to ask Multivac."

Noreen said, "Do you deny that you asked for help in the genetic engineering of a strain of humanity designed to accept slavery under Multivac without question?"

"I suggested the breeding of a more contented humanity. Is this a betrayal?"

Eldred intervened. She said, "We don't want your sophistry, Ron. We know it by heart. Don't tell us once again that Multivac cannot be withstood, that there is no use in struggling, that we have gained security. What you call security, the rest of us call slavery."

Bakst said, "Do you proceed now to judgment, or am I allowed a defense?"

"You heard Eldred," said Noreen. "We know your defense."

"We all heard Eldred," said Bakst, "but no one has heard me. What she says is my defense is not my defense."

There was a silence as the images glanced right and left at each other. Eldred said, "Speak!"

Bakst said, "I asked Multivac to help me solve a problem in the field of mathematical games. To gain his interest, I pointed out that it was modeled on gene combinations and that a solution might help in designing a gene combination that would leave man no worse off than he is now in any respect and yet breed into him a cheerful acceptance of Multivac's direction, and acquiescence in his decisions."

"So we have said," said Eldred.

"It was only on those terms that Multivac would have accepted the task. Such a new breed is clearly desirable for mankind by Multivac's standards, and by Multivac's standards he must labor toward it. And the desirability of the end will lure him on to examine greater and greater complications of a problem whose endlessness is beyond what even he can handle. You all witness that."

Noreen said, "Witness what?"

"Haven't you had trouble reaching me? In the last two months, hasn't each of you noticed small troubles in what has always gone smoothly? . . . You are silent. May I accept that as an affirmative?"

"If so, what then?"

Bakst said, "Multivac has been placing all his spare circuits on the problem. He has been slowly pushing the running of the world toward rather a skimpy minimum of his efforts, since nothing, by his own sense of ethics, must stand in the way of human happiness and there can be no greater increase in that happiness than to accept Multivac."

Noreen said, "What does all this mean? There is still enough in Multivac to run the world—and us—and if this is done at less than full efficiency, that would only add temporary discomfort to our slavery. Only temporary, because it won't last long. Sooner or later, Multivac will decide the problem is insoluble, or will solve it, and in either case, his distraction will end. In the latter case, slavery will become permanent and irrevocable."

"But for now he is distracted," said Bakst, "and we can even talk like this —most dangerously—without his noticing. Yet I dare not risk doing so for long, so please understand me quickly.

"I have another mathematical game—the setting up of networks on the model of Multivac. I have been able to demonstrate that no matter how complicated and redundant the network is, there must be at least one place into which all the currents can funnel under particular circumstances. There will always be the fatal apoplectic stroke if that one place is interefered with, since it will induce overloading elsewhere which will break down and induce overloading elsewhere—and so on indefinitely till all breaks down."

"Well?"

"And this is the point. Why else have I come to Denver? And Multivac knows it, too, and this point is guarded electronically and robotically to the extent that it cannot be penetrated."

"Well?"

"But Multivac is distracted, and Multivac trusts me. I have labored hard to gain that trust, at the cost of losing all of you, since only with trust is there the possibility of betrayal. If any of you tried to approach this point, Multivac might rouse himself even out of his present distraction. If Multivac were not distracted, he would not allow even me to approach. But he *is* distracted, and it *is* I!"

Bakst was moving toward the converging grid in a calm saunter, and the fourteen images, keyed to him, moved along as well. The soft susurrations of a busy Multivac center were all about them.

Bakst said, "Why attack an invulnerable opponent? Make him vulnerable first, and then—"

Bakst fought to stay calm, but it all depended on this now. Everything! With a sharp yank, he uncoupled a joint. (If he had only had still more time to make more certain.)

He was not stopped—and as he held his breath, he became aware of the ceasing of noise, the ending of whisper, the closing down of Multivac. If, in a moment, that soft noise did not return, then he had had the right key point, and no recovery would be possible. If he were not quickly the focus of approaching robots—

He turned in the continuing silence. The robots in the distance were working still. None were approaching.

Before him, the images of the fourteen men and women of the Congress were still there and each seemed to be stupefied at the sudden enormous thing that had happened.

Bakst said, "Multivac is shut down, burnt out. It can't be rebuilt." He felt almost drunk at the sound of what he was saying. "I have worked toward this since I left you. When Hines attacked, I feared there might be other such efforts, that Multivac would double his guard, that even I— I had to work quickly— I wasn't sure—" He was gasping, but forced himself steady, and said solemnly, "I have given us our freedom."

And he paused, aware at last of the gathering weight of the silence. Fourteen images stared at him, without any of them offering a word in response.

Bakst said sharply, "You have talked of freedom. You *have* it!"

Then, uncertainly, he said, "Isn't that what you want?"

The Bicentennial Man

The Three Laws of Robotics:
    1. A robot may not injure a human being or, through inaction, allow a human being to come to harm.
    2. A robot must obey the orders given it by human beings except where such orders would conflict with the First Law.
    3. A robot must protect its own existence as long as such protection does not conflict with the First or Second Law.

Andrew Martin said, "Thank you," and took the seat offered him. He didn't look driven to the last resort, but he had been.

He didn't, actually, look anything, for there was a smooth blankness to his face, except for the sadness one imagined one saw in his eyes. His hair was smooth, light brown, rather fine, and there was no facial hair. He looked freshly and cleanly shaved. His clothes were distinctly old-fashioned, but neat and predominantly a velvety red-purple in color.

Facing him from behind the desk was the surgeon, and the nameplate on the desk included a fully identifying series of letters and numbers, which Andrew didn't bother with. To call him Doctor would be quite enough.

"When can the operation be carried through, Doctor?" he asked.

The surgeon said softly, with that certain inalienable note of respect that a robot always used to a human being, "I am not certain, sir, that I understand how or upon whom such an operation could be performed."

There might have been a look of respectful intransigence on the surgeon's face, if a robot of his sort, in lightly bronzed stainless steel, could have such an expression, or any expression.

Andrew Martin studied the robot's right hand, his cutting hand, as it lay on the desk in utter tranquillity. The fingers were long and shaped into artistically metallic looping curves so graceful and appropriate that one could imagine a scalpel fitting them and becoming, temporarily, one piece with them.

There would be no hesitation in his work, no stumbling, no quivering, no mistakes. That came with specialization, of course, a specialization so fiercely desired by humanity that few robots were, any longer, independently brained. A surgeon, of course, would have to be. And this one, though brained, was so limited in his capacity that he did not recognize Andrew—had probably never heard of him.

Andrew said, "Have you ever thought you would like to be a man?"

The surgeon hesitated a moment as though the question fitted nowhere in his allotted positronic pathways. "But I am a robot, sir."

"Would it be better to be a man?"

"It would be better, sir, to be a better surgeon. I could not be so if I were a man, but only if I were a more advanced robot. I would be pleased to be a more advanced robot."

"It does not offend you that I can order you about? That I can make you stand up, sit down, move right or left, by merely telling you to do so?"

"It is my pleasure to please you, sir. If your orders were to interfere with my functioning with respect to you or to any other human being, I would not obey you. The First Law, concerning my duty to human safety, would take precedence over the Second Law relating to obedience. Otherwise, obedience is my pleasure. . . . But upon whom am I to perform this operation?"

"Upon me," said Andrew.

"But that is impossible. It is patently a damaging operation."

"That does not matter," said Andrew calmly.

"I must not inflict damage," said the surgeon.

"On a human being, you must not," said Andrew, "but I, too, am a robot."

2

Andrew had appeared much more a robot when he had first been—manufactured. He had then been as much a robot in appearance as any that had ever existed, smoothly designed and functional.

He had done well in the home to which he had been brought in those days when robots in households, or on the planet altogether, had been a rarity.

There had been four in the home: Sir and Ma'am and Miss and Little Miss. He knew their names, of course, but he never used them. Sir was Gerald Martin.

His own serial number was NDR— He forgot the numbers. It had been a long time, of course, but if he had wanted to remember, he could not forget. He had not wanted to remember.

Little Miss had been the first to call him Andrew because she could not use the letters, and all the rest followed her in this.

Little Miss— She had lived ninety years and was long since dead. He had tried to call her Ma'am once, but she would not allow it. Little Miss she had been to her last day.

Andrew had been intended to perform the duties of a valet, a butler, a lady's maid. Those were the experimental days for him and, indeed, for all robots anywhere but in the industrial and exploratory factories and stations off Earth.

The Martins enjoyed him, and half the time he was prevented from doing his work because Miss and Little Miss would rather play with him.

It was Miss who understood first how this might be arranged. She said, "We order you to play with us and you must follow orders."

Andrew said, "I am sorry, Miss, but a prior order from Sir must surely take precedence."

But she said, "Daddy just said he hoped you would take care of the cleaning. That's not much of an order. I *order* you."

Sir did not mind. Sir was fond of Miss and of Little Miss, even more than Ma'am was, and Andrew was fond of them, too. At least, the effect they had upon his actions were those which in a human being would have been called the result of fondness. Andrew thought of it as fondness, for he did not know any other word for it.

It was for Little Miss that Andrew had carved a pendant out of wood. She had ordered him to. Miss, it seemed, had received an ivorite pendant with scrollwork for her birthday and Little Miss was unhappy over it. She had only a piece of wood, which she gave Andrew together with a small kitchen knife.

He had done it quickly and Little Miss said, "That's *nice*, Andrew. I'll show it to Daddy."

Sir would not believe it. "Where did you really get this, Mandy?" Mandy was what he called Little Miss. When Little Miss assured him she was really telling the truth, he turned to Andrew. "Did you do this, Andrew?"

"Yes, Sir."

"The design, too?"

"Yes, Sir."

"From what did you copy the design?"

"It is a geometric representation, Sir, that fit the grain of the wood."

The next day, Sir brought him another piece of wood, a larger one, and an electric vibro-knife. He said, "Make something out of this, Andrew. Anything you want to."

Andrew did so and Sir watched, then looked at the product a long time.

After that, Andrew no longer waited on tables. He was ordered to read books on furniture design instead, and he learned to make cabinets and desks.

Sir said, "These are amazing productions, Andrew."

Andrew said, "I enjoy doing them, Sir."

"Enjoy?"

"It makes the circuits of my brain somehow flow more easily. I have heard you use the word 'enjoy' and the way you use it fits the way I feel. I enjoy doing them, Sir."

3

Gerald Martin took Andrew to the regional offices of United States Robots and Mechanical Men, Inc. As a member of the Regional Legislature he had no trouble at all in gaining an interview with the Chief Robopsychologist. In fact, it was only as a member of the Regional Legislature that he qualified as a robot owner in the first place—in those early days when robots were rare.

Andrew did not understand any of this at the time, but in later years, with greater learning, he could re-view that early scene and understand it in its proper light.

The robopsychologist, Merton Mansky, listened with a gathering frown and more than once managed to stop his fingers at the point beyond which they would have irrevocably drummed on the table. He had drawn features and a lined forehead and looked as though he might be younger than he looked.

He said, "Robotics is not an exact art, Mr. Martin. I cannot explain it to you in detail, but the mathematics governing the plotting of the positronic pathways is far too complicated to permit of any but approximate solutions. Naturally, since we build everything about the Three Laws, those are incontrovertible. We will, of course, replace your robot—"

"Not at all," said Sir. "There is no question of failure on his part. He performs his assigned duties perfectly. The point is, he also carves wood in exquisite fashion and never the same twice. He produces work of art."

Mansky looked confused. "Strange. Of course, we're attempting generalized pathways these days. . . . Really creative, you think?"

"See for yourself." Sir handed over a little sphere of wood on which there was a playground scene in which the boys and girls were almost too small to make out, yet they were in perfect proportion and blended so naturally with the grain that that, too, seemed to have been carved.

Mansky said, *"He* did that?" He handed it back with a shake of his head. "The luck of the draw. Something in the pathways."

"Can you do it again?"

"Probably not. Nothing like this has ever been reported."

"Good! I don't in the least mind Andrew's being the only one."

Mansky said, "I suspect that the company would like to have your robot back for study."

Sir said with sudden grimness, "Not a chance. Forget it." He turned to Andrew, "Let's go home now."

"As you wish, Sir," said Andrew.

4

Miss was dating boys and wasn't about the house much. It was Little Miss, not as little as she was, who filled Andrew's horizon now. She never forgot that the very first piece of wood carving he had done had been for her. She kept it on a silver chain about her neck.

It was she who first objected to Sir's habit of giving away the productions. She said, "Come on, Dad, if anyone wants one of them, let him pay for it. It's worth it."

Sir said, "It isn't like you to be greedy, Mandy."

"Not for us, Dad. For the artist."

Andrew had never heard the word before and when he had a moment to himself he looked it up in the dictionary. Then there was another trip, this time to Sir's lawyer.

Sir said to him, "What do you think of this, John?"

The lawyer was John Feingold. He had white hair and a pudgy belly, and the rims of his contact lenses were tinted a bright green. He looked at the small plaque Sir had given to him. "This is beautiful. . . . But I've heard the news. This is a carving made by your robot. The one you've brought with you."

"Yes, Andrew does them. Don't you, Andrew?"

"Yes, Sir," said Andrew.

"How much would you pay for that, John?" asked Sir.

"I can't say. I'm not a collector of such things."

"Would you believe I have been offered two hundred and fifty dollars for that small thing? Andrew has made chairs that have sold for five hundred dollars. There's two hundred thousands dollars in the bank out of Andrew's products."

"Good heavens, he's making you rich, Gerald."

"Half rich," said Sir. "Half of it is in an account in the name of Andrew Martin."

"The robot?"

"That's right, and I want to know if it's legal."

"Legal?" Feingold's chair creaked as he leaned back in it. "There are no precedents, Gerald. How did your robot sign the necessary papers?"

"He can sign his name and I brought in the signature. I didn't bring him in to the bank himself. Is there anything further that ought to be done?"

"Um." Feingold's eyes seemed to turn inward for a moment. Then he said,

"Well, we can set up a trust to handle all finances in his name and that will place a layer of insulation between him and the hostile world. Further than that, my advice is you do nothing. No one is stopping you so far. If anyone objects, let *him* bring suit."

"And will you take the case if suit is brought?"

"For a retainer, certainly."

"How much?"

"Something like that," and Feingold pointed to the wooden plaque.

"Fair enough," said Sir.

Feingold chuckled as he turned to the robot. "Andrew, are you pleased that you have money?"

"Yes, sir."

"What do you plan to do with it?"

"Pay for things, sir, which otherwise Sir would have to pay for. It would save him expense, sir."

5

The occasions came. Repairs were expensive, and revisions were even more so. With the years, new models of robots were produced and Sir saw to it that Andrew had the advantage of every new device until he was a paragon of metallic excellence. It was all at Andrew's expense.

Andrew insisted on that.

Only his positronic pathways were untouched. Sir insisted on that.

"The new ones aren't as good as you are, Andrew," he said. "The new robots are worthless. The company has learned to make the pathways more precise, more closely on the nose, more deeply on the track. The new robots don't shift. They do what they're designed for and never stray. I like you better."

"Thank you, Sir."

"And it's your doing, Andrew, don't you forget that. I am certain Mansky put an end to generalized pathways as soon as he had a good look at you. He didn't like the unpredictability. . . . Do you know how many times he asked for you so he could place you under study? Nine times! I never let him have you, though, and now that he's retired, we may have some peace."

So Sir's hair thinned and grayed and his face grew pouchy, while Andrew looked rather better than he had when he first joined the family.

Ma'am had joined an art colony somewhere in Europe and Miss was a poet in New York. They wrote sometimes, but not often. Little Miss was married and lived not far away. She said she did not want to leave Andrew and when her child, Little Sir, was born, she let Andrew hold the bottle and feed him.

With the birth of a grandson, Andrew felt that Sir had someone now to replace those who had gone. It would not be so unfair to come to him with the request.

Andrew said, "Sir, it is kind of you to have allowed me to spend my money as I wished."

"It was your money, Andrew."

"Only by your voluntary act, Sir. I do not believe the law would have stopped you from keeping it all."

"The law won't persuade me to do wrong, Andrew."

"Despite all expenses, and despite taxes, too, Sir, I have nearly six hundred thousand dollars."

"I know that, Andrew."

"I want to give it to you, Sir."

"I won't take it, Andrew."

"In exchange for something you can give me, Sir."

"Oh, What is that, Andrew?"

"My freedom, Sir."

"Your—"

"I wish to buy my freedom, Sir."

6

It wasn't that easy. Sir had flushed, had said "For God's sake!" had turned on his heel, and stalked away.

It was Little Miss who brought him around, defiantly and harshly—and in front of Andrew. For thirty years, no one had hesitated to talk in front of Andrew, whether the matter involved Andrew or not. He was only a robot.

She said, "Dad, why are you taking it as a personal affront? He'll still be here. He'll still be loyal. He can't help that. It's built in. All he wants is a form of words. He wants to be called free. Is that so terrible? Hasn't he earned it? Heavens, he and I have been talking about it for years."

"Talking about it for years, have you?"

"Yes, and over and over again, he postponed it for fear he would hurt you. I *made* him put it up to you."

"He doesn't know what freedom is. He's a robot."

"Dad, you don't know him. He's read everything in the library. I don't know what he feels inside but I don't know what *you* feel inside. When you talk to him you'll find he reacts to the various abstractions as you and I do, and what else counts? If someone else's reactions are like your own, what more can you ask for?"

"The law won't take that attitude," Sir said angrily. "See here, you!" He turned to Andrew with a deliberate grate in his voice. "I can't free you except by doing it legally, and if it gets into the courts, you not only won't get your freedom but the law will take official cognizance of your money. They'll tell you that a robot has no right to earn money. Is this rigmarole worth losing your money?"

"Freedom is without price, Sir," said Andrew. "Even the chance of freedom is worth the money."

7

The court might also take the attitude that freedom was without price, and might decide that for no price, however great, could a robot buy its freedom.

The simple statement of the regional attorney who represented those who had brought a class action to oppose the freedom was this: The word "freedom" had no meaning when applied to a robot. Only a human being could be free.

He said it several times, when it seemed appropriate; slowly, with his hand coming down rhythmically on the desk before him to mark the words.

Little Miss asked permission to speak on behalf of Andrew. She was recognized by her full name, something Andrew had never heard pronounced before:

"Amanda Laura Martin Charney may approach the bench."

She said, "Thank you, your honor. I am not a lawyer and I don't know the proper way of phrasing things, but I hope you will listen to my meaning and ignore the words.

"Let's understand what it means to be free in Andrew's case. In some ways, he *is* free. I think it's at least twenty years since anyone in the Martin family gave him an order to do something that we felt he might not do of his own accord.

"But we can, if we wish, give him an order to do anything, couch it as harshly as we wish, because he is a machine that belongs to us. Why should we be in a position to do so, when he has served us so long, so faithfully, and earned so much money for us? He owes us nothing more. The debt is entirely on the other side.

"Even if we were legally forbidden to place Andrew in involuntary servitude, he would still serve us voluntarily. Making him free would be a trick of words only, but it would mean much to him. It would give him everything and cost us nothing."

For a moment the Judge seemed to be suppressing a smile. "I see your point, Mrs. Charney. The fact is that there is no binding law in this respect and no precedent. There is, however, the unspoken assumption that only a man can enjoy freedom. I can make new law here, subject to reversal in a higher court, but I cannot lightly run counter to that assumption. Let me address the robot, Andrew!"

"Yes, your honor."

It was the first time Andrew had spoken in court and the Judge seemed astonished for a moment at the human timbre of the voice. He said, "Why do you want to be free, Andrew? In what way will this matter to you?"

Andrew said, "Would you wish to be a slave, your honor?"

"But you are not a slave. You are a perfectly good robot, a genius of a robot I am given to understand, capable of an artistic expression that can be matched nowhere. What more can you do if you were free?"

"Perhaps no more than I do now, your honor, but with greater joy. It has been said in this courtroom that only a human being can be free. It seems to me that only someone who wishes for freedom can be free. I wish for freedom."

And it was that that cued the Judge. The crucial sentence in his decision was: "There is no right to deny freedom to any object with a mind advanced enough to grasp and desire the state."

It was eventually upheld by the World Court.

8

Sir remained displeased and his harsh voice made Andrew feel almost as though he were being short-circuited.

Sir said, "I don't want your damned money, Andrew. I'll take it only because you won't feel free otherwise. From now on, you can select your own jobs and do them as you please. I will give you no orders, except this one— that you do as you please. But I am still responsible for you; that's part of the court order. I hope you understand that."

Little Miss interrupted. "Don't be irascible, Dad. The responsibility is no great chore. You know you won't have to do a thing. The Three Laws still hold."

"Then how is he free?"

Andrew said, "Are not human beings bound by their laws, Sir?"

Sir said, "I'm not going to argue." He left, and Andrew saw him only infrequently after that.

Little Miss came to see him frequently in the small house that had been built and made over for him. It had no kitchen, of course, nor bathroom facilities. It had just two rooms; one was a library and one was a combination storeroom and workroom. Andrew accepted many commissions and worked harder as a free robot than he ever had before, till the cost of the house was paid for and the structure legally transferred to him.

One day Little Sir came. . . . No, George! Little Sir had insisted on that after the court decision. "A free robot doesn't call anyone Little Sir," George had said. "I call you Andrew. You must call me George."

It was phrased as an order, so Andrew called him George—but Little Miss remained Little Miss.

The day George came alone, it was to say that Sir was dying. Little Miss was at the bedside but Sir wanted Andrew as well.

Sir's voice was quite strong, though he seemed unable to move much. He struggled to get his hand up. "Andrew," he said, "Andrew—Don't help me,

George. I'm only dying; I'm not crippled. . . . Andrew, I'm glad you're free. I just wanted to tell you that."

Andrew did not know what to say. He had never been at the side of someone dying before, but he knew it was the human way of ceasing to function. It was an involuntary and irreversible dismantling, and Andrew did not know what to say that might be appropriate. He could only remain standing, absolutely silent, absolutely motionless.

When it was over, Little Miss said to him, "He may not have seemed friendly to you toward the end, Andrew, but he was old, you know, and it hurt him that you should want to be free."

And then Andrew found the words to say. He said, "I would never have been free without him, Little Miss."

9

It was only after Sir's death that Andrew began to wear clothes. He began with an old pair of trousers at first, a pair that George had given him.

George was married now, and a lawyer. He had joined Feingold's firm. Old Feingold was long since dead but his daughter had carried on and eventually the firm's name became Feingold and Martin. It remained so even when the daughter retired and no Feingold took her place. At the time Andrew put on clothes for the first time, the Martin name had just been added to the firm.

George had tried not to smile, the first time Andrew put on the trousers, but to Andrew's eyes the smile was clearly there.

George showed Andrew how to manipulate the static charge so as to allow the trousers to open, wrap about his lower body, and move shut. George demonstrated on his own trousers, but Andrew was quite aware that it would take him awhile to duplicate that one flowing motion.

George said, "But why do you want trousers, Andrew? Your body is so beautifully functional it's a shame to cover it—especially when you needn't worry about either temperature control or modesty. And it doesn't cling properly, not on metal."

Andrew said, "Are not human bodies beautifully functional, George? Yet you cover yourselves."

"For warmth, for cleanliness, for protection, for decorativeness. None of that applies to you."

Andrew said, "I feel bare without clothes. I feel different, George."

"Different! Andrew, there are millions of robots on Earth now. In this region, according to the last census, there are almost as many robots as there are men."

"I know, George. There are robots doing every conceivable type of work."

"And none of them wear clothes."

"But none of them are free, George."

Little by little, Andrew added to the wardrobe. He was inhibited by George's smile and by the stares of the people who commissioned work.

He might be free, but there was built into him a carefully detailed program concerning his behavior toward people, and it was only by the tiniest steps that he dared advance. Open disapproval would set him back months.

Not everyone accepted Andrew as free. He was incapable of resenting that and yet there was a difficulty about his thinking process when he thought of it.

Most of all, he tended to avoid putting on clothes—or too many of them —when he thought Little Miss might come to visit him. She was old now and was often away in some warmer climate, but when she returned the first thing she did was visit him.

On one of her returns, George said ruefully, "She's got me, Andrew. I'll be running for the Legislature next year. Like grandfather, she says, like grandson."

"Like grandfather—" Andrew stopped, uncertain.

"I mean that I, George, the grandson, will be like Sir, the grandfather, who was in the Legislature once."

Andrew said, "It would be pleasant, George, if Sir were still—" He paused, for he did not want to say, "in working order." That seemed inappropriate.

"Alive," said George. "Yes, I think of the old monster now and then, too."

It was a conversation Andrew thought about. He had noticed his own incapacity in speech when talking with George. Somehow the language had changed since Andrew had come into being with an innate vocabulary. Then, too, George used a colloquial speech, as Sir and Little Miss had not. Why should he have called Sir a monster when surely that word was not appropriate?

Nor could Andrew turn to his own books for guidance. They were old and most dealt with woodworking, with art, with furniture design. There were none on language, none on the ways of human beings.

It was at that moment it seemed to him that he must seek the proper books; and as a free robot, he felt he must not ask George. He would go to town and use the library. It was a triumphant decision and he felt his electro-potential grow distinctly higher until he had to throw in an impedance coil.

He put on a full costume, even including a shoulder chain of wood. He would have preferred the glitter plastic but George had said that wood was much more appropriate and that polished cedar was considerably more valuable as well.

He had placed a hundred feet between himself and the house before gathering resistance brought him to a halt. He shifted the impedance coil out of circuit, and when that did not seem to help enough, he returned to his home and on a piece of notepaper wrote neatly, "I have gone to the library," and placed it in clear view on his worktable.

10

Andrew never quite got to the library. He had studied the map. He knew the route, but not the appearance of it. The actual landmarks did not resemble the symbols on the map and he would hesitate. Eventually he thought he must have somehow gone wrong, for everything looked strange.

He passed an occasional field robot, but at the time he decided he should ask his way, there were none in sight. A vehicle passed and did not stop. He stood irresolute, which meant calmly motionless, and then coming across the field toward him were two human beings.

He turned to face them, and they altered their course to meet him. A moment before, they had been talking loudly; he had heard their voices; but now they were silent. They had the look that Andrew associated with human uncertainty, and they were young, but not very young. Twenty perhaps? Andrew could never judge human age.

He said, "Would you describe to me the route to the town library, sirs?"

One of them, the taller of the two, whose tall hat lengthened him still farther, almost grotesquely, said, not to Andrew, but to the other, "It's a robot."

The other had a bulbous nose and heavy eyelids. He said, not to Andrew, but to the first, "It's wearing clothes."

The tall one snapped his fingers. "It's the free robot. They have a robot at the Martins who isn't owned by anyone. Why else would it be wearing clothes?"

"Ask it," said the one with the nose.

"Are you the Martin robot?" asked the tall one.

"I am Andrew Martin, sir," said Andrew.

"Good. Take off your clothes. Robots don't wear clothes." He said to the other, "That's disgusting. Look at him."

Andrew hesitated. He hadn't heard an order in that tone of voice in so long that his Second Law circuits had momentarily jammed.

The tall one said, "Take off your clothes. I order you."

Slowly, Andrew began to remove them.

"Just drop them," said the tall one.

The nose said, "If it doesn't belong to anyone, he could be ours as much as someone else's."

"Anyway," said the tall one, "who's to object to anything we do? We're not damaging property. . . . Stand on your head." That was to Andrew.

"The head is not meant—" began Andrew.

"That's an order. If you don't know how, try anyway."

Andrew hesitated again, then bent to put his head on the ground. He tried to lift his legs and fell, heavily.

The tall one said, "Just lie there." He said to the other, "We can take him apart. Ever take a robot apart?"

"Will he let us?"

"How can he stop us?"

There was no way Andrew could stop them, if they ordered him not to resist in a forceful enough manner. Second Law of obedience took precedence over the Third Law of self-preservation. In any case, he could not defend himself without possibly hurting them and that would mean breaking the First Law. At that thought, every motile unit contracted slightly and he quivered as he lay there.

The tall one walked over and pushed at him with his foot. "He's heavy. I think we'll need tools to do the job."

The nose said, "We could order him to take himself apart. It would be fun to watch him try."

"Yes," said the tall one thoughtfully, "but let's get him off the road. If someone comes along—"

It was too late. Someone had indeed come along and it was George. From where he lay, Andrew had seen him topping a small rise in the middle distance. He would have liked to signal him in some way, but the last order had been "Just lie there!"

George was running now and he arrived somewhat winded. The two young men stepped back a little and then waited thoughtfully.

George said anxiously, "Andrew, has something gone wrong?"

Andrew said, "I am well, George."

"Then stand up. . . . What happened to your clothes?"

The tall young man said, "That your robot, mac?"

George turned sharply. "He's no one's robot. What's been going on here?"

"We politely asked him to take his clothes off. What's that to you if you don't own him?"

George said, "What were they doing, Andrew?"

Andrew said, "It was their intention in some way to dismember me. They were about to move me to a quiet spot and order me to dismember myself."

George looked at the two and his chin trembled. The two young men retreated no further. They were smiling. The tall one said lightly, "What are you going to do, pudgy? Attack us?"

George said, "No. I don't have to. This robot has been with my family for over seventy years. He knows us and he values us more than he values anyone else. I am going to tell him that you two are threatening my life and that you plan to kill me. I will ask him to defend me. In choosing between me and you two, he will choose me. Do you know what will happen to you when he attacks you?"

The two were backing away slightly, looking uneasy.

George said sharply, "Andrew, I am in danger and about to come to harm from these two men. Move toward them!"

Andrew did so, and the two young men did not wait. They ran fleetly.

"All right, Andrew, relax," said George. He looked unstrung. He was far past the age where he could face the possibility of a dustup with one young man, let alone two.

Andrew said, "I couldn't have hurt them, George. I could see they were not attacking you."

"I didn't order you to attack them; I only told you to move toward them. Their own fears did the rest."

"How can they fear robots?"

"It's a disease of mankind, one of which it is not yet cured. But never mind that. What the devil are you doing here, Andrew? I was on the point of turning back and hiring a helicopter when I found you. How did you get it into your head to go to the library? I would have brought you any books you needed."

"I am a—" began Andrew.

"Free robot. Yes, yes. All right, what did you want from the library?"

"I want to know more about human beings, about the world, about everything. And about robots, George. I want to write a history about robots."

George said, "Well, let's walk home. . . . And pick up your clothes first. Andrew, there are a million books on robotics and all of them include histories of the science. The world is growing saturated not only with robots but with information about robots."

Andrew shook his head, a human gesture he had lately begun to make. "Not a history of robotics, George. A history of *robots*, by a robot. I want to explain how robots feel about what has happened since the first ones were allowed to work and live on Earth."

George's eyebrows lifted, but he said nothing in direct response.

11

Little Miss was just past her eighty-third birthday, but there was nothing about her that was lacking in either energy or determination. She gestured with her cane oftener than she propped herself up with it.

She listened to the story in a fury of indignation. She said, "George, that's horrible. Who were those young ruffians?"

"I don't know. What difference does it make? In the end they did no damage."

"They might have. You're a lawyer, George, and if you're well off, it's entirely due to the talent of Andrew. It was the money *he* earned that is the foundation of everything we have. He provides the continuity for this family and I will *not* have him treated as a wind-up toy."

"What would you have me do, Mother?" asked George.

"I said you're a lawyer. Don't you listen? You set up a test case somehow, and you force the regional courts to declare for robot rights and get the

Legislature to pass the necessary bills, and carry the whole thing to the World Court, if you have to. I'll be watching, George, and I'll tolerate no shirking."

She was serious, and what began as a way of soothing the fearsome old lady became an involved matter with enough entanglement to make it interesting. As senior partner of Feingold and Martin, George plotted strategy but left the actual work to his junior partners, with much of it a matter for his son, Paul, who was also a member of the firm and who reported dutifully nearly every day to his grandmother. She, in turn, discussed it every day with Andrew.

Andrew was deeply involved. His work on his book on robots was delayed again, as he pored over the legal arguments and even, at times, made very diffident suggestions.

He said, "George told me that day that human beings have always been afraid of robots. As long as they are, the courts and the legislatures are not likely to work hard on behalf of robots. Should there not be something done about public opinion?"

So while Paul stayed in court, George took to the public platform. It gave him the advantage of being informal and he even went so far sometimes as to wear the new, loose style of clothing which he called drapery. Paul said, "Just don't trip over it on stage, Dad."

George said despondently, "I'll try not to."

He addressed the annual convention of holo-news editors on one occasion and said, in part:

"If, by virtue of the Second Law, we can demand of any robot unlimited obedience in all respects not involving harm to a human being, then any human being, *any* human being, has a fearsome power over any robot, *any* robot. In particular, since Second Law supersedes Third Law, *any* human being can use the law of obedience to overcome the law of self-protection. He can order any robot to damage itself or even destroy itself for any reason, or for no reason.

"Is this just? Would we treat an animal so? Even an inanimate object which has given us good service has a claim on our consideration. And a robot is not insensible; it is not an animal. It can think well enough to enable it to talk to us, reason with us, joke with us. Can we treat them as friends, can we work together with them, and not give them some of the fruit of that friendship, some of the benefit of co-working?

"If a man has the right to give a robot any order that does not involve harm to a human being, he should have the decency never to give a robot any order that involves harm to a robot, unless human safety absolutely requires it. With great power goes great responsibility, and if the robots have Three Laws to protect men, is it too much to ask that men have a law or two to protect robots?"

Andrew was right. It was the battle over public opinion that held the key to courts and Legislature and in the end a law passed which set up conditions under which robot-harming orders were forbidden. It was endlessly qualified and the punishments for violating the law were totally inadequate, but the principle was established. The final passage by the World Legislature came through on the day of Little Miss's death.

That was no coincidence. Little Miss held on to life desperately during the last debate and let go only when word of victory arrived. Her last smile was for Andrew. Her last words were: "You have been good to us, Andrew."

She died with her hand holding his, while her son and his wife and children remained at a respectful distance from both.

12

Andrew waited patiently while the receptionist disappeared into the inner office. It might have used the holographic chatterbox, but unquestionably it was unmanned (or perhaps unroboted) by having to deal with another robot rather than with a human being.

Andrew passed the time revolving the matter in his mind. Could "unroboted" be used as an analogue of "unmanned," or had "unmanned" become a metaphoric term sufficiently divorced from its original literal meaning to be applied to robots—or to women for that matter?

Such problems came frequently as he worked on his book on robots. The trick of thinking out sentences to express all complexities had undoubtedly increased his vocabulary.

Occasionally, someone came into the room to stare at him and he did not try to avoid the glance. He looked at each calmly, and each in turn looked away.

Paul Martin came out. He looked surprised, or he would have if Andrew could have made out his expression with certainty. Paul had taken to wearing the heavy makeup that fashion was dictating for both sexes and though it made sharper and firmer the somewhat bland lines of his face, Andrew disapproved. He found that disapproving of human beings, as long as he did not express it verbally, did not make him very uneasy. He could even write the disapproval. He was sure it had not always been so.

Paul said, "Come in, Andrew. I'm sorry I made you wait but there was something I *had* to finish. Come in. You had said you wanted to talk to me, but I didn't know you meant here in town."

"If you are busy, Paul, I am prepared to continue to wait."

Paul glanced at the interplay of shifting shadows on the dial on the wall that served as timepiece and said, "I can make some time. Did you come alone?"

"I hired an automatobile."

"Any trouble?" Paul asked, with more than a trace of anxiety.

"I wasn't expecting any. My rights are protected."

Paul looked the more anxious for that. "Andrew, I've explained that the law is unenforceable, at least under most conditions. . . . And if you insist on wearing clothes, you'll run into trouble eventually—just like that first time."

"And only time, Paul. I'm sorry you are displeased."

"Well, look at it this way; you are virtually a living legend, Andrew, and you are too valuable in many different ways for you to have any right to take chances with yourself. . . . How's the book coming?"

"I am approaching the end, Paul. The publisher is quite pleased."

"Good!"

"I don't know that he's necessarily pleased with the book as a book. I think he expects to sell many copies because it's written by a robot and it's that that pleases him."

"Only human, I'm afraid."

"I am not displeased. Let it sell for whatever reason since it will mean money and I can use some."

"Grandmother left you—"

"Little Miss was generous, and I'm sure I can count on the family to help me out further. But it is the royalties from the book on which I am counting to help me through the next step."

"What next step is that?"

"I wish to see the head of U. S. Robots and Mechanical Men, Inc. I have tried to make an appointment, but so far I have not been able to reach him. The corporation did not cooperate with me in the writing of the book, so I am not surprised, you understand."

Paul was clearly amused. "Cooperation is the last thing you can expect. They didn't cooperate with us in our great fight for robot rights. Quite the reverse and you can see why. Give a robot rights and people may not want to buy them."

"Nevertheless," said Andrew, "if you call them, you may obtain an interview for me."

"I'm no more popular with them than you are, Andrew."

"But perhaps you can hint that by seeing me they may head off a campaign by Feingold and Martin to strengthen the rights of robots further."

"Wouldn't that be a lie, Andrew?"

"Yes, Paul, and I can't tell one. That is why you must call."

"Ah, you can't lie, but you can urge me to tell a lie, is that it? You're getting more human all the time, Andrew."

13

It was not easy to arrange, even with Paul's supposedly weighted name.

But it was finally carred through and, when it was, Harley Smythe-Robertson, who, on his mother's side, was descended from the original founder of the corporation and who had adopted the hyphenation to indicate it, looked remarkably unhappy. He was approaching retirement age and his entire tenure as president had been devoted to the matter of robot rights. His gray hair was plastered thinly over the top of his scalp, his face was not made up, and he eyed Andrew with brief hostility from time to time.

Andrew said, "Sir, nearly a century ago, I was told by a Merton Mansky of this corporation that the mathematics governing the plotting of the positronic pathways was far too complicated to permit of any but approximate solutions and that therefore my own capacities were not fully predictable."

"That was a century ago." Smythe-Robertson hesitated, then said icily, "*Sir*. It is true no longer. Our robots are made with precision now and are trained precisely to their jobs."

"Yes," said Paul, who had come along, as he said, to make sure that the corporation played fair, "with the result that my receptionist must be guided at every point once events depart from the conventional, however slightly."

Smythe-Robertson said, "You would be much more displeased if it were to improvise."

Andrew said, "Then you no longer manufacture robots like myself which are flexible and adaptable."

"No longer."

"The research I have done in connection with my book," said Andrew, "indicates that I am the oldest robot presently in active operation."

"The oldest presently," said Smythe-Robertson, "and the oldest ever. The oldest that will ever be. No robot is useful after the twenty-fifth year. They are called in and replaced with newer models."

"No robot *as presently manufactured* is useful after the twenty-fifth year," said Paul pleasantly. "Andrew is quite exceptional in this respect."

Andrew, adhering to the path he had marked out for himself, said, "As the oldest robot in the world and the most flexible, am I not unusual enough to merit special treatment from the company?"

"Not at all," said Smythe-Robertson freezingly. "Your unusualness is an embarrassment to the company. If you were on lease, instead of having been a sale outright through some mischance, you would long since have been replaced."

"But that is exactly the point," said Andrew. "I am a free robot and I own myself. Therefore I come to you and ask you to replace me. You cannot do this without the owner's consent. Nowadays, that consent is extorted as a condition of the lease, but in my time this did not happen."

Smythe-Robertson was looking both startled and puzzled, and for a moment there was silence. Andrew found himself staring at the holograph on the wall. It was a death mask of Susan Calvin, patron saint of all roboticists. She was dead nearly two centuries now, but as a result of writing his book Andrew knew her so well he could half persuade himself that he had met her in life.

Smythe-Robertson said, "How can I replace you for you? If I replace you as robot, how can I donate the new robot to you as owner since in the very act of replacement you cease to exist?" He smiled grimly.

"Not at all difficult," interposed Paul. "The seat of Andrew's personality is his positronic brain and it is the one part that cannot be replaced without creating a new robot. The positronic brain, therefore, is Andrew the owner. Every other part of the robotic body can be replaced without affecting the robot's personality, and those other parts are the brain's possessions. Andrew, I should say, wants to supply his brain with a new robotic body."

"That's right," said Andrew calmly. He turned to Smythe-Robertson. "You have manufactured androids, haven't you? Robots that have the outward appearance of humans complete to the texture of the skin?"

Smythe-Robertson said, "Yes, we have. They worked perfectly well, with their synthetic fibrous skins and tendons. There was virtually no metal anywhere except for the brain, yet they were nearly as tough as metal robots. They were tougher, weight for weight."

Paul looked interested. "I didn't know that. How many are on the market?"

"None," said Smythe-Robertson. "They were much more expensive than metal models and a market survey showed they would not be accepted. They looked too human."

Andrew said, "But the corporation retains its expertise, I assume. Since it does, I wish to request that I be replaced by an organic robot, an android."

Paul looked surprised. "Good Lord," he said.

Smythe-Robertson stiffened. "Quite impossible!"

"Why is it impossible?" asked Andrew. "I will pay any reasonable fee, of course."

Smythe-Robertson said, "We do not manufacture androids."

"You do not *choose* to manufacture androids," interposed Paul quickly. "That is not the same as being unable to manufacture them."

Smythe-Robertson said, "Nevertheless, the manufacture of androids is against public policy."

"There is no law against it," said Paul.

"Nevertheless, we do not manufacture them, and we will not."

Paul cleared his throat. "Mr. Smythe-Robertson," he said, "Andrew is a free robot who is under the purview of the law guaranteeing robot rights. You are aware of this, I take it?"

"Only too well."

"This robot, as a free robot, chooses to wear clothes. This results in his being frequently humiliated by thoughtless human beings despite the law against the humiliation of robots. It is difficult to prosecute vague offenses that don't meet with the general disapproval of those who must decide on guilt and innocence."

"U. S. Robots understood that from the start. Your father's firm unfortunately did not."

"My father is dead now," said Paul, "but what I see is that we have here a clear offense with a clear target."

"What are you talking about?" said Smythe-Robertson.

"My client, Andrew Martin—he has just become my client—is a free robot who is entitled to ask U. S. Robots and Mechanical Men, Inc., for the right of replacement, which the corporation supplies anyone who owns a robot for more than twenty-five years. In fact, the corporation insists on such replacement."

Paul was smiling and thoroughly at his ease. He went on, "The positronic brain of my client is the owner of the body of my client—which is certainly more than twenty-five years old. The positronic brain demands the replacement of the body and offers to pay any reasonable fee for an android body as that replacement. If you refuse the request, my client undergoes humiliation and we will sue.

"While public opinion would not ordinarily support the claim of a robot in such a case, may I remind you that U. S. Robots is not popular with the public generally. Even those who most use and profit from robots are suspicious of the corporation. This may be a hangover from the days when robots were widely feared. It may be resentment against the power and wealth of U. S. Robots which has a worldwide monopoly. Whatever the cause may be, the resentment exists and I think you will find that you would prefer not to withstand a lawsuit, particularly since my client is wealthy and will live for many more centuries and will have no reason to refrain from fighting the battle forever."

Smythe-Robertson had slowly reddened. "You are trying to force me to . . ."

"I force you to do nothing," said Paul. "If you wish to refuse to accede to my client's reasonable request, you may by all means do so and we will leave without another word. . . . But we will sue, as is certainly our right, and you will find that you will eventually lose."

Smythe-Robertson said, "Well—" and paused.

"I see that you are going to accede," said Paul. "You may hesitate but you will come to it in the end. Let me assure you, then, of one further point. If, in the process of transferring my client's positronic brain from his present body to an organic one, there is any damage, however slight, then I will never rest till I've nailed the corporation to the ground. I will, if necessary, take every possible step to mobilize public opinion against the corporation if one brain path of my client's platinum-iridium essence is scrambled." He turned to Andrew and said, "Do you agree to all this, Andrew?"

Andrew hesitated a full minute. It amounted to the approval of lying, of blackmail, of the badgering and humiliation of a human being. But not physical harm, he told himself, not physical harm.

He managed at last to come out with a rather faint "Yes."

14

It was like being constructed again. For days, then for weeks, finally for months, Andrew found himself not himself somehow, and the simplest actions kept giving rise to hesitation.

Paul was frantic. "They've damaged you, Andrew. We'll have to institute suit."

Andrew spoke very slowly. "You mustn't. You'll never be able to prove—something—m-m-m-m—"

"Malice?"

"Malice. Besides, I grow stronger, better. It's the tr-tr-tr—"

"Tremble?"

"Trauma. After all, there's never been such an op—op—op—before."

Andrew could feel his brain from the inside. No one else could. He knew he was well and during the months that it took him to learn full coordination and full positronic interplay, he spent hours before the mirror.

Not quite human! The face was stiff—too stiff—and the motions were too deliberate. They lacked the careless free flow of the human being, but perhaps that might come with time. At least he could wear clothes without the ridiculous anomaly of a metal face going along with it.

Eventually he said, "I will be going back to work."

Paul laughed and said, "That means you are well. What will you be doing? Another book?"

"No," said Andrew seriously. "I live too long for any one career to seize me by the throat and never let me go. There was a time when I was primarily an artist and I can still turn to that. And there was a time when I was a historian and I can still turn to that. But now I wish to be a robobiologist."

"A robopsychologist, you mean."

"No. That would imply the study of positronic brains and at the moment I lack the desire to do that. A robobiologist, it seems to me, would be concerned with the working of the body attached to that brain."

"Wouldn't that be a roboticist?"

"A roboticist works with a metal body. I would be studying an organic humanoid body, of which I have the only one, as far as I know."

"You narrow your field," said Paul thoughtfully. "As an artist, all conception is yours; as a historian, you dealt chiefly with robots; as a robobiologist, you will deal with yourself."

Andrew nodded. "It would seem so."

Andrew had to start from the very beginning, for he knew nothing of ordinary biology, almost nothing of science. He became a familiar sight in the libraries, where he sat at the electronic indices for hours at a time, looking perfectly normal in clothes. Those few who knew he was a robot in no way interfered with him.

He built a laboratory in a room which he added to his house, and his library, too.

Years passed, and Paul came to him one day and said, "It's a pity you're no longer working on the history of robots. I understand U. S. Robots is adopting a radically new policy."

Paul had aged, and his deteriorating eyes had been replaced with photoptic cells. In that respect, he had drawn closer to Andrew. Andrew said, "What have they done?"

"They are manufacturing central computers, gigantic positronic brains, really, which communicate with anywhere from a dozen to a thousand robots by microwave. The robots themselves have no brains at all. They are the limbs of the gigantic brain, and the two are physically separate."

"Is that more efficient?"

"U. S. Robots claims it is. Smythe-Robertson established the new direction before he died, however, and it's my notion that it's a backlash at you. U. S. Robots is determined that they will make no robots that will give them the type of trouble you have, and for that reason they separate brain and body. The brain will have no body to wish changed; the body will have no brain to wish anything.

"It's amazing, Andrew," Paul went on, "the influence you have had on the history of robots. It was your artistry that encouraged U. S. Robots to make robots more precise and specialized; it was your freedom that resulted in the establishment of the principle of robotic rights; it was your insistence on an android body that made U. S. Robots switch to brain-body separation."

Andrew said, "I suppose in the end the corporation will produce one vast brain controlling several billion robotic bodies. All the eggs will be in one basket. Dangerous. Not proper at all."

"I think you're right," said Paul, "but I don't suspect it will come to pass for a century at least and I won't live to see it. In fact, I may not live to see next year."

"Paul!" said Andrew, in concern.

Paul shrugged. "We're mortal, Andrew. We're not like you. It doesn't matter too much, but it does make it important to assure you on one point. I'm the last of the human Martins. There are collaterals descended from my great-aunt, but they don't count. The money I control personally will be left to the trust in your name and as far as anyone can foresee the future, you will be economically secure."

"Unnecessary," said Andrew, with difficulty. In all this time, he could not get used to the deaths of the Martins.

Paul said, "Let's not argue. That's the way it's going to be. What are you working on?"

"I am designing a system for allowing androids—myself—to gain energy from the combustion of hydrocarbons, rather than from atomic cells."

Paul raised his eyebrows. "So that they will breathe and eat?"

"Yes."

"How long have you been pushing in that direction?"

"For a long time now, but I think I have designed an adequate combustion chamber for catalyzed controlled breakdown."

"But why, Andrew? The atomic cell is surely infinitely better."

"In some ways, perhaps, but the atomic cell is inhuman."

15

It took time, but Andrew had time. In the first place, he did not wish to do anything till Paul had died in peace.

With the death of the great-grandson of Sir, Andrew felt more nearly exposed to a hostile world and for that reason was the more determined to continue the path he had long ago chosen.

Yet he was not really alone. If a man had died, the firm of Feingold and Martin lived, for a corporation does not die any more than a robot does. The firm had its directions and it followed them soullessly. By way of the trust and through the law firm, Andrew continued to be wealthy. And in return for their own large annual retainer, Feingold and Martin involved themselves in the legal aspects of the new combustion chamber.

When the time came for Andrew to visit U. S. Robots and Mechanical Men, Inc., he did it alone. Once he had gone with Sir and once with Paul. This time, the third time, he was alone and manlike.

U. S. Robots had changed. The production plant had been shifted to a large space station, as had grown to be the case with more and more industries. With them had gone many robots. The Earth itself was becoming parklike, and its one-billion-person population stabilized and perhaps not more than thirty per cent of its at least equally large robot population independently brained.

The Director of Research was Alvin Magdescu, dark of complexion and hair, with a little pointed beard and wearing nothing above the waist but the breastband that fashion dictated. Andrew himself was well covered in the older fashion of several decades back.

Magdescu said, "I know you, of course, and I'm rather pleased to see you. You're our most notorious product and it's a pity old Smythe-Robertson was so set against you. We could have done a great deal with you."

"You still can," said Andrew.

"No, I don't think so. We're past the time. We've had robots on Earth for over a century, but that's changing. It will be back to space with them and those that stay here won't be brained."

"But there remains myself, and I stay on Earth."

"True, but there doesn't seem to be much of the robot about you. What new request have you?"

"To be still less a robot. Since I am so far organic, I wish an organic source of energy. I have here the plans—"

Magdescu did not hasten through them. He might have intended to at first, but he stiffened and grew intent. At one point he said, "This is remarkably ingenious. Who thought of all this?"

"I did," said Andrew.

Magdescu looked up at him sharply, then said, "It would amount to a major overhaul of your body, and an experimental one, since it has never been attempted before. I advise against it. Remain as you are."

Andrew's face had limited means of expression, but impatience showed plainly in his voice. "Dr. Magdescu, you miss the entire point. You have no choice but to accede to my request. If such devices can be built into my body, they can be built into human bodies as well. The tendency to lengthen human life by prosthetic devices has already been remarked on. There are no devices better than the ones I have designed and am designing.

"As it happens, I control the patents by way of the firm of Feingold and Martin. We are quite capable of going into business for ourselves and of developing the kind of prosthetic devices that may end by producing human beings with many of the properties of robots. Your own business will then suffer.

"If, however, you operate on me now and agree to do so under similar circumstances in the future, you will receive permission to make use of the patents and control the technology of both robots and the prosthetization of human beings. The initial leasing will not be granted, of course, until after the first operation is completed successfully, and after enough time has passed to demonstrate that it is indeed successful." Andrew felt scarcely any First Law inhibition to the stern conditions he was setting a human being. He was learning to reason that what seemed like cruelty might, in the long run, be kindness.

Magdescu looked stunned. He said, "I'm not the one to decide something like this. That's a corporate decision that would take time."

"I can wait a reasonable time," said Andrew, "but only a reasonable time." And he thought with satisfaction that Paul himself could not have done it better.

16

It took only a reasonable time, and the operation was a success.

Magdescu said, "I was very much against the operation, Andrew, but not for the reasons you might think. I was not in the least against the experiment, if it had been on someone else. I hated risking *your* positronic brain. Now that you have the positronic pathways interacting with simulated nerve pathways, it might be difficult to rescue the brain intact if the body went bad."

"I had every faith in the skill of the staff at U. S. Robots," said Andrew. "And I can eat now."

"Well, you can sip olive oil. It will mean occasional cleanings of the combustion chamber, as we have explained to you. Rather an uncomfortable touch, I should think."

"Perhaps, if I did not expect to go further. Self-cleaning is not impossible. In fact, I am working on a device that will deal with solid food that may be expected to contain incombustible fractions—indigestible matter, so to speak, that will have to be discarded."

"You would then have to develop an anus."

"The equivalent."

"What else, Andrew?"

"Everything else."

"Genitalia, too?"

"Insofar as they will fit my plans. My body is a canvas on which I intend to draw—"

Magdescu waited for the sentence to be completed, and when it seemed that it would not be, he completed it himself. "A man?"

"We shall see," said Andrew.

Magdescu said, "It's a puny ambition, Andrew. You're better than a man. You've gone downhill from the moment you opted for organicism."

"My brain has not suffered."

"No, it hasn't. I'll grant you that. But, Andrew, the whole new breakthrough in prosthetic devices made possible by your patents is being marketed under your name. You're recognized as the inventor and you're honored for it—as you are. Why play further games with your body?"

Andrew did not answer.

The honors came. He accepted membership in several learned societies, including one which was devoted to the new science he had established; the one he had called robobiology but had come to be termed prosthetology.

On the one hundred and fiftieth anniversary of his construction, there was a testimonial dinner given in his honor at U. S. Robots. If Andrew saw irony in this, he kept it to himself.

Alvin Magdescu came out of retirement to chair the dinner. He was himself ninety-four years old and was alive because he had prosthetized devices that, among other things, fulfilled the function of liver and kidneys. The dinner reached its climax when Magdescu, after a short and emotional talk, raised his glass to toast "the Sesquicentennial Robot."

Andrew had had the sinews of his face redesigned to the point where he could show a range of emotions, but he sat through all the ceremonies solemnly passive. He did not like to be a Sesquicentennial Robot.

17

It was prosthetology that finally took Andrew off the Earth. In the decades that followed the celebration of the Sesquicentennial, the Moon had come to be a world more Earth-like than Earth in every respect but its gravitational pull and in its underground cities there was a fairly dense population.

Prosthetized devices there had to take the lesser gravity into account and Andrew spent five years on the Moon working with local prosthetologists to make the necessary adaptations. When not at his work, he wandered among the robot population, every one of which treated him with the robotic obsequiousness due a man.

He came back to an Earth that was humdrum and quiet in comparison and visited the offices of Feingold and Martin to announce his return.

The current head of the firm, Simon DeLong, was surprised. He said, "We had been told you were returning, Andrew" (he had almost said "Mr. Martin"), "but we were not expecting you till next week."

"I grew impatient," said Andrew brusquely. He was anxious to get to the point. "On the Moon, Simon, I was in charge of a research team of twenty human scientists. I gave orders that no one questioned. The Lunar robots deferred to me as they would to a human being. Why, then, am I not a human being?"

A wary look entered DeLong's eyes. He said, "My dear Andrew, as you have just explained, you are treated as a human being by both robots and human beings. You are therefore a human being *de facto*."

"To be a human being *de facto* is not enough. I want not only to be treated as one, but to be legally identified as one. I want to be a human being *de jure*."

"Now that is another matter," said DeLong. "There we would run into human prejudice and into the undoubted fact that however much you may be like a human being, you are *not* a human being."

"In what way not?" asked Andrew. "I have the shape of a human being and organs equivalent to those of a human being. My organs, in fact, are identical to some of those in a prosthetized human being. I have contributed artistically, literarily, and scientifically to human culture as much as any human being now alive. What more can one ask?"

"I myself would ask nothing. The trouble is that it would take an act of the World Legislature to define you as a human being. Frankly, I wouldn't expect that to happen."

"To whom on the Legislature could I speak?"

"To the chairman of the Science and Technology Committee perhaps."

"Can you arrange a meeting?"

"But you scarcely need an intermediary. In your postion, you can—"

"No. *You* arrange it." (It didn't even occur to Andrew that he was giving a flat order to a human being. He had grown accustomed to that on the Moon.) "I want him to know that the firm of Feingold and Martin is backing me in this to the hilt."

"Well, now—"

"To the hilt, Simon. In one hundred and seventy-three years I have in one fashion or another contributed greatly to this firm. I have been under obligation to individual members of this firm in times past. I am not now. It is rather the other way around now and I am calling in my debts."

DeLong said, "I will do what I can."

18

The chairman of the Science and Technology Committee was of the East Asian region and she was a woman. Her name was Chee Li-Hsing and her transparent garments (obscuring what she wanted obscured only by their dazzle) made her look plastic-wrapped.

She said, "I sympathize with your wish for full human rights. There have been times in history when segments of the human population fought for full human rights. What rights, however, can you possibly want that you do not have?"

"As simple a thing as my right to life. A robot can be dismantled at any time."

"A human being can be executed at any time."

"Execution can only follow due process of law. There is no trial needed for my dismantling. Only the word of a human being in authority is needed to end me. Besides—besides—" Andrew tried desperately to allow no sign of pleading, but his carefully designed tricks of human expression and tone of voice betrayed him here. "The truth is, I want to be a man. I have wanted it through six generations of human beings."

Li-Hsing looked up at him out of darkly sympathetic eyes. "The Legislature can pass a law declaring you one—they could pass a law declaring a stone statue to be defined as a man. Whether they will actually do so is, however, as likely in the first case as the second. Congresspeople are as human as the rest of the population and there is always that element of suspicion against robots."

"Even now?"

"Even now. We would all allow the fact that you have earned the prize of humanity and yet there would remain the fear of setting an undesirable precedent."

"What precedent? I am the only free robot, the only one of my type, and there will never be another. You may consult U. S. Robots."

" 'Never' is a long time, Andrew—or, if you prefer, Mr. Martin—since I will gladly give you my personal accolade as man. You will find that most Congresspeople will not be willing to set the precedent, no matter how meaningless such a precedent might be. Mr. Martin, you have my sympathy, but I cannot tell you to hope. Indeed—"

She sat back and her forehead wrinkled. "Indeed, if the issue grows too heated, there might well arise a certain sentiment, both inside the Legislature and outside, for that dismantling you mentioned. Doing away with you could turn out to be the easiest way of resolving the dilemma. Consider that before deciding to push matters."

Andrew said, "Will no one remember the technique of prosthetology, something that is almost entirely mine?"

"It may seem cruel, but they won't. Or if they do, it will be remembered against you. It will be said you did it only for yourself. It will be said it was part of a campaign to roboticize human beings, or to humanify robots; and in either case evil and vicious. You have never been part of a political hate campaign, Mr. Martin, and I tell you that you will be the object of vilification of a kind neither you nor I would credit and there would be people who'll believe it all. Mr. Martin, let your life be." She rose and, next to Andrew's seated figure, she seemed small and almost childlike.

Andrew said, "If I decide to fight for my humanity, will you be on my side?"

She thought, then said, "I will be—insofar as I can be. If at any time such a stand would appear to threaten my political future, I may have to abandon you, since it is not an issue I feel to be at the very roots of my beliefs. I am trying to be honest with you."

"Thank you, and I will ask no more. I intend to fight this through whatever the consequences, and I will ask you for your help only for as long as you can give it."

19

It was not a direct fight. Feingold and Martin counseled patience and Andrew muttered grimly that he had an endless supply of that. Feingold and Martin then entered on a campaign to narrow and restrict the area of combat.

They instituted a lawsuit denying the obligation to pay debts to an individual with a prosthetic heart on the grounds that the possession of a robotic organ removed humanity, and with it the constitutional rights of human beings.

They fought the matter skillfully and tenaciously, losing at every step but always in such a way that the decision was forced to be as broad as possible, and then carrying it by way of appeals to the World Court.

It took years, and millions of dollars.

When the final decision was handed down, DeLong held what amounted to a victory celebration over the legal loss. Andrew was, of course, present in the company offices on the occasion.

"We've done two things, Andrew," said DeLong, "both of which are good. First of all, we have established the fact that no number of artifacts in the human body causes it to cease being a human body. Secondly, we have engaged public opinion in the question in such a way as to put it fiercely on the side of a broad interpretation of humanity since there is not a human being in existence who does not hope for prosthetics if that will keep him alive."

"And do you think the Legislature will now grant me my humanity?" asked Andrew.

DeLong looked faintly uncomfortable. "As to that, I cannot be optimistic. There remains the one organ which the World Court has used as the criterion of humanity. Human beings have an organic cellular brain and robots have a platinum-iridium positronic brain if they have one at all—and you certainly have a positronic brain. . . . No, Andrew, don't get that look in your eye. We lack the knowledge to duplicate the work of a cellular brain in artificial structures close enough to the organic type to allow it to fall within the Court's decision. Not even you could do it."

"What ought we do, then?"

"Make the attempt, of course. Congresswoman Li-Hsing will be on our side and a growing number of other Congresspeople. The President will undoubtedly go along with a majority of the Legislature in this matter."

"Do we have a majority?"

"No, far from it. But we might get one if the public will allow its desire for a broad interpretation of humanity to extend to you. A small chance, I admit, but if you do not wish to give up, we must gamble for it."

"I do not wish to give up."

20

Congresswoman Li-Hsing was considerably older than she had been when Andrew had first met her. Her transparent garments were long gone. Her hair was now close-cropped and her coverings were tubular. Yet still Andrew clung, as closely as he could within the limits of reasonable taste, to the style of clothing that had prevailed when he had first adopted clothing over a century before.

She said, "We've gone as far as we can, Andrew. We'll try once more after recess, but, to be honest, defeat is certain and the whole thing will have to be given up. All my most recent efforts have only earned me a certain defeat in the coming congressional campaign."

"I know," said Andrew, "and it distresses me. You said once you would abandon me if it came to that. Why have you not done so?"

"One can change one's mind, you know. Somehow, abandoning you became a higher price than I cared to pay for just one more term. As it is, I've been in the Legislature for over a quarter of a century. It's enough."

"Is there no way we can change minds, Chee?"

"We've changed all that are amenable to reason. The rest—the majority—cannot be moved from their emotional antipathies."

"Emotional antipathy is not a valid reason for voting one way or the other."

"I know that, Andrew, but they don't advance emotional antipathy as their reason."

Andrew said cautiously, "It all comes down to the brain, then, but must we leave it at the level of cells versus positrons? Is there no way of forcing a functional definition? Must we say that a brain is made of this or that? May we not say that a brain is something—anything—capable of a certain level of thought?"

"Won't work," said Li-Hsing. "Your brain is man-made, the human brain is not. Your brain is constructed, theirs developed. To any human being who is intent on keeping up the barrier between himself and a robot, those differences are a steel wall a mile high and a mile thick."

"If we could get at the source of their antipathy—the very source of—"

"After all your years," said Li-Hsing sadly, "you are still trying to reason out the human being. Poor Andrew, don't be angry, but it's the robot in you that drives you in that direction."

"I don't know," said Andrew. "If I could bring myself—"

1 (reprise)

If he could bring himself—

He had known for a long time it might come to that, and in the end he was at the surgeon's. He found one, skillful enough for the job at hand, which meant a robot surgeon, for no human surgeon could be trusted in this connection, either in ability or in intention.

The surgeon could not have performed the operation on a human being, so Andrew, after putting off the moment of decision with a sad line of questioning that reflected the turmoil within himself, put the First Law to one side by saying, "I, too, am a robot."

He then said, as firmly as he had learned to form the words even at human beings over these past decades, "I *order* you to carry through the operation on me."

In the absence of the First Law, an order so firmly given from one who looked so much like a man activated the Second Law sufficiently to carry the day.

21

Andrew's feeling of weakness was, he was sure, quite imaginary. He had recovered from the operation. Nevertheless, he leaned, as unobtrusively as he could manage, against the wall. It would be entirely too revealing to sit.

Li-Hsing said, "The final vote will come this week, Andrew. I've been able to delay it no longer, and we must lose. . . . And that will be it, Andrew."

Andrew said, "I am grateful for your skill at delay. It gave me the time I needed, and I took the gamble I had to."

"What gamble is this?" asked Li-Hsing with open concern.

"I couldn't tell you, or the people at Feingold and Martin. I was sure I would be stopped. See here, if it is the brain that is at issue, isn't the greatest difference of all the matter of immortality? Who really cares what a brain looks like or is built of or how it was formed? What matters is that brain cells die; *must* die. Even if every other organ in the body is maintained or replaced, the brain cells, which cannot be replaced without changing and therefore killing the personality, must eventually die.

"My own positronic pathways have lasted nearly two centuries without perceptible change and can last for centuries more. Isn't *that* the fundamental barrier? Human beings can tolerate an immortal robot, for it doesn't matter how long a machine lasts. They cannot tolerate an immortal human being, since their own mortality is endurable only so long as it is universal. And for that reason they won't make me a human being."

Li-Hsing said, "What is it you're leading up to, Andrew?"

"I have removed that problem. Decades ago, my positronic brain was connected to organic nerves. Now, one last operation has arranged that connection in such a way that slowly—quite slowly—the potential is being drained from my pathways."

Li-Hsing's finely wrinkled face showed no expression for a moment. Then her lips tightened. "Do you mean you've arranged to die, Andrew? You can't have. That violates the Third Law."

"No," said Andrew, "I have chosen between the death of my body and the death of my aspirations and desires. To have let my body live at the cost of the greater death is what would have violated the Third Law."

Li-Hsing seized his arm as though she were about to shake him. She stopped herself. "Andrew, it won't work. Change it back."

"It can't be. Too much damage was done. I have a year to live—more or less. I will last through the two hundredth anniversary of my construction. I was weak enough to arrange that."

"How can it be worth it? Andrew, you're a fool."

"If it brings me humanity, that will be worth it. If it doesn't, it will bring an end to striving and that will be worth it, too."

And Li-Hsing did something that astonished herself. Quietly, she began to weep.

22

It was odd how that last deed caught at the imagination of the world. All that Andrew had done before had not swayed them. But he had finally accepted even death to be human and the sacrifice was too great to be rejected.

The final ceremony was timed, quite deliberately, for the two hundredth anniversary. The World President was to sign the act and make it law and the ceremony would be visible on a global network and would be beamed to the Lunar state and even to the Martian colony.

Andrew was in a wheelchair. He could still walk, but only shakily.

With mankind watching, the World President said, "Fifty years ago, you were declared a Sesquicentennial Robot, Andrew." After a pause, and in a more solemn tone, he said, "Today we declare you a Bicentennial Man, Mr. Martin."

And Andrew, smiling, held out his hand to shake that of the President.

23

Andrew's thoughts were slowly fading as he lay in bed.

Desperately he seized at them. Man! He was a man! He wanted that to be his last thought. He wanted to dissolve—die—with that.

He opened his eyes one more time and for one last time recognized Li-Hsing waiting solemnly. There were others, but those were only shadows, unrecognizable shadows. Only Li-Hsing stood out against the deepening gray. Slowly, inchingly, he held out his hand to her and very dimly and faintly felt her take it.

She was fading in his eyes, as the last of his thoughts trickled away.

But before she faded completely, one last fugitive thought came to him and rested for a moment on his mind before everything stopped.

"Little Miss," he whispered, too low to be heard.

Marching In

I

Jerome Bishop, composer and trombonist, had never been in a mental hospital before.

There had been times when he had suspected he might be in one, someday, as a patient (who was safe?), but it had never occurred to him that he might ever be there as a consultant on a question of mental aberration. *A consultant.*

He sat there, in the year 2001, with the world in pretty terrible shape, but (they said) pulling out of it, and then rose as a middle-aged woman entered. Her hair was beginning to turn gray, and Bishop was thankfully conscious of his own hair still in full shock and evenly dark.

"Are you Mr. Bishop?" she asked.

"Last time I looked."

She held out her hand. "I'm Dr. Cray. Won't you come with me?"

He shook her hand, then followed. He tried not to be haunted by the dull beige uniforms worn by everyone he passed.

Dr. Cray put a finger to her lip, and motioned him into a chair. She pressed a button and the lights went out, causing a window, with a light behind it, to spring into view. Through the window, Bishop could see a woman in something that looked like a dentist's chair, tilted back. A forest of flexible wires sprang from her head, a thin narrow beam of light extended from pole to pole behind her, and a somewhat less narrow strip of paper unfolded upward.

The light went on again; the view vanished.

Dr. Cray said, "Do you know what we're doing in there?"

"You're recording brain waves? Just a guess."

"A good guess. We are. It's a laser recording. Do you know how that works?"

"My stuff's been recorded by laser," said Bishop, crossing one leg over the other, "but that doesn't mean I know how it *works*. It's the engineers who know the details. . . . Look, Doc, if you have an idea I'm a laser engineer, I'm not."

"No, I know you're not," said Dr. Cray hurriedly. "You're here for something else. . . . Let me explain it to you. We can alter a laser beam very delicately; much more rapidly and much more precisely than we can alter an electric current, or even a beam of electrons. That means that a very complex wave can be recorded in far greater detail than has ever been imagined before. We can make a tracing with a microscopically narrow laser beam and get a wave we can study under a microscope and get accurate detail invisible to the naked eye and unobtainable in any other fashion."

Bishop said, "If that's what you want to consult me about, then all I can say is that it doesn't pay to get all that detail. You can only hear so much. If you sharpen a laser recording past a certain amount, you bring up the expense but you don't bring up the effect. In fact, some people say you get some kind of buzz that begins to drown out the music. I don't hear it myself, but I tell you that if you want the best, you don't narrow the laser beam all the way. . . . Of course, maybe it's different with brain waves but what I told you is all I can tell you, so I'll go and there's no charge except for carfare."

He made as though to get up, but Dr. Cray was shaking her head vigorously.

"Please sit down, Mr. Bishop. Recording brain waves *is* different. There we do need all the detail we can get. Till now, all we've ever had out of brain waves are the tiny, overlapping effects of ten billion brain cells, a kind of rough average that wipes out everything but the most general effects."

"You mean like listening to ten billion pianos all playing different tunes a hundred miles away?"

"Exactly."

"All you get is noise?"

"Not quite. We do get some information—about epilepsy, for instance. With laser recording, however, we begin to get the fine detail; we begin to hear the individual tunes those separate pianos are playing; we begin to hear which particular pianos may be out of tune."

Bishop lifted his eyebrows. "So you can tell what makes a particular crazy person crazy?"

"In a way of speaking. Look at this." In another corner of the room a screen flashed to life, with a thin wavering line over it. "Do you see this, Mr. Bishop?" Dr. Cray pressed the button of an indicator in her hand and one little blip in the line reddened. The line moved along past the lighted screen and red blips appeared periodically.

"That's a microphotograph," said Dr. Cray. "Those little red discontinuities are not visible to the unaided eye and wouldn't be visible with any recording device less delicate than the laser. It appears only when this particular patient is in depression. The markings are more pronounced, the deeper the depression."

Bishop thought about it for a while. Then he said, "Can you do anything about it? So far, it just means you can tell by that blip there's a depression, which you can tell by just listening to the patient."

"Quite right, but the details help. For instance, we can convert the brain waves into delicately flickering light waves and, what's more, into the equivalent sound waves. We use the same laser system that is used to record your music. We get a sort of dimly musical hum that matches the light flicker. I would like you to listen to it by earphone."

"The music from that particular depressive person whose brain produced that line?"

"Yes, and since we can't intensify it much without losing detail, we will ask you to listen by earphone."

"And watch the light, too?"

"That's not necessary. You can close your eyes. Enough of the flicker will penetrate the eyelids to affect the brain."

Bishop closed his eyes. Through the hum, he could hear the tiny wail of a complex beat, a complex, sad beat that carried all the troubles of the tired old world in it. He listened, vaguely conscious of the dim light beating on his eyeballs in flickering time.

He felt his shirt pulled at strenuously. "Mr. Bishop—Mr. Bishop—"

He took a deep breath. "Thanks!" he said, shuddering a little. "That upset me, but I couldn't let go."

"You were listening to brain-wave depression and it was affecting you. It was forcing your own brain-wave pattern to keep time. You felt depressed, didn't you?"

"All the way."

"Well, if we can locate the portion of the wave characteristic of depression, or of any mental abnormality, remove that, and play all the rest of the brain wave, the patient's pattern will be modified into normal form."

"For how long?"

"For a while after the treatment is stopped. For a while, but not long. A few days. A week. Then the patient has to return."

"That's better than nothing."

"And less than enough. A person is born with certain genes, Mr. Bishop, that dictate a certain potential brain structure. A person suffers certain environmental influences. These are not easy things to neutralize, so here in this institution we've been trying to find more efficient and long-lasting schemes for neutralization. . . . And you can help us, perhaps. That's why we've asked you to come here."

"But I don't know anything about this, Doc. I never heard about recording brain waves by laser." He pushed his hands apart, palms down. "I've got *nothing* for you."

Dr. Cray looked impatient. She pushed her hands deep into the pockets of her jacket and said, "Just a while ago, you said that the laser recorded more detail than the ear could hear."

"Yes. I stand by that."

"I know. One of my colleagues read an interview with you in the December 2000 issue of *High Fidelity* magazine, in which you said that. That's what attracted our attention. The ear can't get the laser detail, but the eye can, you see. It's the flickering light that alters the brain pattern to the norm, not the wavering sound. The sound alone will do nothing. It will, however, reinforce the effect when the light is working."

"You can't complain about that."

"We can. The reinforcement isn't good enough. The gentle, delicate, almost infinitely complex variations produced in the sound by laser recording is lost on the ear. Too much is present and it drowns out the portion that is reinforcing."

"What makes you think that a reinforcing portion is there?"

"Because occasionally, more or less by accident, we can produce something that seems to work better than the entire brain wave, but we don't see why. We need a musician. Maybe you. If you listen to both sets of brain waves, perhaps you can figure out by some insight a beat that will fit the normal set better than the abnormal one. Then that could reinforce the light, you see, and improve the effectiveness of the therapy."

"Hey," said Bishop in alarm, "that's putting a lot of responsibility on me. When I write music, I'm just caressing the ear and making the muscles jump. I'm not trying to cure an ailing brain."

"All we ask is that you caress the ears and make the muscles jump, but do it so that it fits the normal music of the brain waves. . . . And I assure you that you need fear no responsibility, Mr. Bishop. It is quite unlikely that your music would do harm, and it might do so much good. And you'll be paid, Mr. Bishop, win or lose."

Bishop said, "Well, I'll try, though I don't promise a thing."

He was back in two days. Dr. Cray was pulled out of conference to see him. She looked at him out of tired, narrowed eyes.

"Do you have something?"

"I have *something*. It may work."

"How do you know?"

"I don't. I just have the feel of it. . . . Look, I listened to the laser tapes you gave me; the brain-wave music as it came from the patient in depression and the brain-wave music as you've modified it to normal. And you're right; without the flickering light it didn't affect me either way. Anyway, I subtracted the second from the first to see what the difference was."

"You have a computer?" Dr. Cray said, wondering.

"No, a computer wouldn't have helped. It would give me too much. You take one complicated laser-wave pattern and subtract another complicated laser-wave pattern and you're left with what is still a pretty complicated laser-wave pattern. No, I subtracted it in my mind to see what kind of beat was left. . . . That would be the abnormal beat that I would have to cancel out with a counter-beat."

"How can you subtract in your head?"

Bishop looked impatient. "I don't know. How did Beethoven hear the Ninth Symphony in his head before he wrote it down? The brain's a pretty good computer, too, isn't it?"

"I guess it is." She subsided. "Do you have the counter-beat there?"

"I think so. I have it here on an ordinary tape recording because it doesn't need anything more. It goes something like—dihdihdihDAH—dihdihdihDAH—dihdihdihDAHDAHDAHdihDAH—and so on. I added a tune to it and you can put it through the earphones while she's watching the flickering light that's matched to the normal brain-wave pattern. If I'm right, it will reinforce the living daylights out of it."

"Are you sure?"

"If I were sure, you wouldn't have to try it, would you, Doc?"

Dr. Cray was thoughtful for a moment. "I'll make an appointment with the patient. I'd like you to be here."

"If you want me. It's part of the consultation job, I suppose."

"You won't be able to be in the treatment room, you understand, but I'd want you out here."

"Anything you say."

The patient looked careworn when she arrived. Her eyelids drooped and her voice was low and she mumbled.

Bishop's glance was casual as he sat quietly, unnoticed, in the corner. He saw her enter the treatment room and waited patiently, thinking: What if it works? Why not package brainwave lights with appropriate sound accompaniment to combat the blues—to increase energy—to heighten love? Not just for sick people but for normal people, who could find a substitute for all the pounding they'd ever taken with alcohol or drugs in an effort to adjust their emotions—an utterly safe substitute based on the brain waves themselves. . . . And finally, after forty-five minutes, she came out.

She was placid now, and the lines had somehow washed out of her face.

"I feel better, Dr. Cray," she said, smiling. "I feel much better."

"You usually do," said Dr. Cray quietly.

"Not this way," said the woman. "Not this way. This time it's different.

The other times, even when I thought I felt good, I could sense that awful depression in the back of my head just waiting to come back the minute I relaxed. Now—it's just gone."

Dr. Cray said, "We can't be sure it will always be gone. We'll make an appointment for, say, two weeks from now but you'll call me before then if anything goes wrong, won't you? Did anything seem different in the treatment?"

The woman thought a bit. "No," she said hesitantly. Then: "The flickering light, though. That might have been different. Clearer and sharper somehow."

"Did you hear anything?"

"Was I supposed to?"

Dr. Cray rose. "Very well. Remember to make that appointment with my secretary."

The woman stopped at the door, turned, and said, "It's a happy feeling to feel happy," and left.

Dr. Cray said, "She didn't hear anything, Mr. Bishop. I suppose that your counter-beat reinforced the normal brainwave pattern so naturally that the sound was, so to speak, lost in the light. . . . And it may have worked, too."

She turned to Bishop, looking him full in the face. "Mr. Bishop, will you consult with us on other cases? We'll pay you as much as we can, and if this turns out to be an effective therapy for mental disease, we'll see that you get all the credit due you."

Bishop said, "I'll be glad to help out, Doctor, but it won't be as hard as you may think. The work is already done."

"Already done?"

"We've had musicians for centuries. Maybe they didn't know about brain waves, but they did their best to get the melodies and beats that would affect people, get their toes tapping, get their muscles twitching, get their faces smiling, get their tear ducts pumping, get their hearts pounding. Those tunes are waiting. Once you get the counter-beat, you pick the tune to fit."

"Is that what you did?"

"Sure. What can snap you out of depression like a revival hymn? It's what they're meant to do. The beat gets you out of yourself. It exalts you. Maybe it doesn't last long by itself, but if you use it to reinforce the normal brain-wave pattern, it ought to pound it in."

"A revival hymn?" Dr. Cray stared at him, wide-eyed.

"Sure. What I used in this case was the best of them all. I gave her 'When the Saints Go Marching In.' "

He sang it softly, finger-snapping the beat, and by the third bar, Dr. Cray's toes were tapping.

Old-fashioned

Ben Estes knew he was going to die and it didn't make him feel any better to know that that was the chance he had lived with all these years. The life of an astro-miner, drifting through the still largely uncharted vastness of the asteroid belt, was not particularly sweet, but it was quite likely to be short.

Of course, there was always the chance of a surprise find that would make you rich for life, and this had been a surprise find all right. The biggest surprise in the world, but it wasn't going to make Estes rich. It would make him dead.

Harvey Funarelli groaned softly from his bunk, and Estes turned, with a wince of his own as his muscles creaked. They had been badly mishandled. That he wasn't hit as viciously as Funarelli had been was surely because Funarelli was the larger man, and had been closer to the point of near-impact.

Estes looked somberly at his partner and said, "How do you feel, Harv?"

Funarelli groaned again. "I feel broken at every joint. What the hell happened? What did we hit?"

Estes walked over, limping slightly, and said, "Don't try to stand up."

"I can make it," said Funarelli, "if you'll just reach out a hand. Wow! I wonder if I've got a broken rib. Right here. What happened, Ben?"

Estes pointed at the main portview. It wasn't a large one, but it was the best a two-man astro-mining vessel could be expected to have. Funarelli moved toward it very slowly, leaning on Estes' shoulder. He looked out.

There were the stars, of course, but the experienced astronautic mind blanks those out. There are always the stars. Closer in, there was a gravel bank of boulders of varying size, all moving slowly relative to their neighbors like a swarm of very, very lazy bees.

Funarelli said, "I've never seen anything like that before. What are they doing here?"

"Those rocks," said Estes, "are what's left of a shattered asteroid, I suspect, and they're still circling what shattered them, and what shattered us."

"What?" Funarelli peered vainly into the darkness.

Estes pointed. "That!" There was a faint little sparkle in the direction he was pointing.

"I don't see anything."

"You're not supposed to. That's a black hole."

Funarelli's close-cropped black hair stood on end as a matter of course, and his staring dark eyes added a touch of horror. He said, "You're crazy."

"No. Black holes can come in all sizes. That's what the astronomers say. That one is about the mass of a large asteroid, I think, and we're moving around it. How else could something we can't see be holding us in orbit?"

"There's no report on any—"

"I know. How can there be? It can't be seen. It's mass— Ooops, there comes the Sun." The slowly rotating ship had brought the Sun into view and the portview automatically polarized into opacity. "Anyway," said Estes, "we discovered the first black hole actually to be encountered anywhere in the Universe. Only we won't live to see ourselves get the credit."

Funarelli said, "What happened?"

"We got close enough for the tidal effects to smash us up."

"What tidal effects?"

Estes said, "I'm not an astronomer, but as I understand it, even when the total gravitational pull of a thing like that isn't large, you can get so close to it that the pull becomes intense. That intensity falls off so rapidly with increasing distance that the near end of an object is pulled far more strongly than the far end. The object is therefore stretched. The closer and bigger an object is, the worse the effect. Your muscles were torn. You're lucky your bones weren't broken."

Funarelli grimaced. "I'm not sure they aren't. . . . What else happened?"

"The fuel tanks were destroyed. We're stuck here in orbit. . . . It's just lucky we happened to end in one far enough away and circular enough to keep the tidal effect down. If we were closer, or if we even zoomed in closely at one end of the orbit—"

"Can we get word out?"

"Not a word," said Estes. "Communications are smashed."

"You can't fix it?"

"I'm not really a communications expert, but even if I were— It can't be fixed."

"Can't something be jury-rigged?"

Estes shook his head. "We've just got to wait—and die. That's not what bothers me so much."

"It bothers me," said Funarelli, sitting down on his bunk and placing his head in his hands.

"We've got the pills," said Estes. "It would be an easy death. What's really bad is that we can't get word back about—that." He pointed to the portview, which was clear again as the Sun moved out of range.

"About the black hole?"

"Yes, it's dangerous. It seems to be in orbit about the Sun, but who knows whether that orbit is stable. And even if it is, it's bound to get larger."

"I guess it will swallow stuff."

"Sure. Everything it encounters. There's cosmic dust spiraling into it all the time, and giving off energy as it spirals and drops in. That's what makes those dim sparkles of light. Every once in a while, the hole will swallow up a large piece that gets in the way and there'll be a flash of radiation, right down to X rays. The larger it gets, the easier it is for it to drag in material from a greater and greater distance."

For a moment, both men stared at the portview, then Estes went on. "Right now it can be handled maybe. If NASA can maneuver a fairly large asteroid here and send it past the hole in the proper way, the hole will be pulled out of its orbit by mutual gravitational attraction between itself and the asteroid. The hole can be made to curve itself into a path that could head it out of the Solar System, with some further help and acceleration."

Funarelli said, "Do you suppose it started very small?"

"It could have been a micro-hole formed at the time of the big bang, when the Universe was created. It may have been growing for billions of years and if it continues to grow, it may become unmanageable. It will then eventually become the grave of the Solar System."

"Why haven't they found it?"

"No one's been looking. Who would expect a black hole in the asteroid belt? And it doesn't produce enough radiation to be noticeable, or enough mass to be noticeable. You have to run into it, as we did."

"Are you sure we have no communications at all, Ben? . . . How far to Vesta? They could reach us from Vesta without much delay. It's the largest base in the asteroid belt."

Estes shook his head. "I don't know where Vesta is right now. The computer's knocked out, too."

"God! What isn't knocked out?"

"The air system is working. The water purifier is on. We've got plenty of power and food. We can last two weeks, maybe more."

A silence fell. "Look," said Funarelli after a while. "Even if we don't know where Vesta is exactly, we know it can't be more than a few million kilometers away. If we could reach them with some signal, they could get a drone ship out here within a week."

"A drone ship, yes," said Estes. That was easy. An unmanned ship could be accelerated to levels that human flesh and blood would not endure. It could make trips in a third the time a manned vessel could.

Funarelli closed his eyes, as though blocking out the pain, and said, "Don't sneer at a drone ship. It could bring us emergency supplies, and it would have stuff on board we could use to set up a communications system. We could hold out till the real rescuers came."

Estes sat down on the other bunk. "I wasn't sneering at a drone ship. I was just thinking that there's no way to send a signal, no way at all. We can't even yell. The vacuum of space won't carry sound."

Funarelli said stubbornly, "I can't believe you can't think of something. Our lives depend on it."

"The lives of all mankind depend on it, maybe, but I still can't think of anything. Why don't *you* think of something?"

Funarelli grunted as he moved his hips. He seized the hand grips on the wall next to his bunk and pulled himself up to a standing position. "I can think of one thing," he said, "why don't you turn off the gravity motors and save the power and put less strain on our muscles?"

Estes muttered, "Good idea." He rose and moved to the control board, where he cut the gravity.

Funarelli floated upward with a sigh and said, "Why can't they *find* the black hole, the idiots?"

"You mean like we did? There's no other way. It's not doing enough."

Funarelli said, "I still hurt, even with no gravity to fight. . . . Oh well, if it keeps on hurting like this, it won't matter so much when it comes to pill-taking time. . . . Is there any way we can make that black hole do more than it's doing?"

Estes said grimly, "If one of those bits of gravel should take it into its head to drop into the hole, a burst of X rays would shoot out."

"Would they detect that on Vesta?"

Estes shook his head. "I doubt it. They're not looking for such a thing. They'd be sure to detect it on Earth, though. Some of the space stations keep the sky under constant surveillance for radiation changes. They'd pick up astonishingly small bursts."

"All right, Ben, reaching Earth would be just as well. They'd send a message to Vesta to investigate. It would take the X rays about fifteen minutes to get to Earth and then it would take fifteen minutes for radio waves to get to Vesta."

"And how about the time between? The receivers may automatically record a burst of X rays from such and such a direction, but who's to say where it's from? It could be from a distant galaxy that happens to lie in this particular direction. Some technician will notice the bump in the recording and will watch for more bursts in the same place and there won't be any and it will be crossed off as unimportant. Besides, it won't happen, Harv. There must have been lots of X rays when the black hole broke up this asteroid with its tidal effect, but that may have been thousands of years ago when no one was watching. Now what's left of these fragments must have fairly stable orbits."

"If we had our rockets—"

"Let me guess. We could drive our ship into the black hole. Use our deaths to send a message. That wouldn't do any good either. It would still be one pulse from anywhere."

Funarelli said indignantly, "I wasn't thinking of that. I'm not in the market for heroic death. I meant, we've got three engines. If we could rig them on to three pretty large size rocks and send each one into the hole, there would be three bursts of X rays and if we did them a day apart, the source would move detectably against the stars. That would be interesting, wouldn't it? The technicians would pick that up at once, wouldn't they?"

"Maybe, and maybe not. Besides, we don't have any rocketry left and couldn't put them on the rocks if we—" Estes fell silent. Then he said in an altered voice, "I wonder if our space suits are intact."

"Our suit radios," said Funarelli excitedly.

"Hell, they don't reach out more than a few kilometers," said Estes. "I'm thinking of something else. I'm thinking of going out there." He opened the suit locker. "They *seem* all right."

"Why do you want to go out?"

"We may not have any rockets, but we still have muscle power. At least I have. Do you think you can throw a rock?"

Funarelli made a throwing gesture, or the beginning of one, and a look of agony came over his face. "Can I jump to the Sun?" he said.

"I'll go out and throw some. . . . The suit seems to check out. Maybe I can throw some into the hole. . . . I hope the air lock operates."

"Can we spare the air?" said Funarelli anxiously.

"Will it matter in two weeks?" said Estes wearily.

Every astro-miner has to get outside the ship occasionally—to carry out some repair, to bring in some chunk of matter in the vicinity. Ordinarily, it's an exciting time. In any case, it's a change.

Estes felt little excitement, only a vast anxiety. His notion was so damned primitive, he felt foolish to have it. It was bad enough dying without having to die a damn fool.

He found himself in the black of space, with the glittering stars he had seen a hundred times before. Now, though, in the faint reflection of the small and distant Sun, there was the dim glow of hundreds of bits of rock that must once have been part of an asteroid and that now formed a tiny Saturn's ring about a black hole. The rocks seemed almost motionless, as all drifted along with the ship.

Estes judged the direction of wheel of the stars and knew that ship and rocks were moving slowly in the other direction. If he could throw a rock in the direction of the star motion, he would neutralize some of the rock's velocity relative to the black hole. If he neutralized not enough of the velocity, or too much, the rock would drop toward the hole, skim about it, and come back to the point it had left. If he neutralized just enough, it would come close enough to be powdered by the tidal effect. The grains of powder, in their motions, would slow each other and spiral into the hole, releasing X rays as they did so.

Estes used his miner's net of tantalum steel to gather rocks, choosing them fist size. He was thankful that modern suits allowed complete freedom of motion and were not the virtual coffins they had been when the first astronauts, over a century ago, had reached the Moon.

Once he had enough rocks, he threw one, and he could see it glimmer and fade in the sunlight as it dropped toward the hole. He waited and nothing happened. He didn't know how long it might take to fall into the black hole —if it fell in at all, that is—but he counted six hundred to himself and threw again.

Over and over he did so, with a terrible patience born of searching for an alternative to death, and finally there was a sudden blaze in the direction of the black hole. Visible light and, he knew, a burst of higher-energy radiation as far as X rays at least.

He had to stop to gather more rocks, and then he got the range. He was hitting it almost every time. He oriented himself so that the soft glimmer of the black hole would be seen just above the midportion of the ship. That was one relationship that didn't change as the ship circled and rolled on an axis— or changed least.

Even allowing for his care, however, it seemed to him he was making too many strikes. The black hole, he thought, was more massive than he knew and would swallow up its prey from a larger distance. That made it more dangerous, but increased their chance of rescue.

He worked his way through the lock and back into the ship. He was bone-weary and his right shoulder hurt him.

Funarelli helped him off with the suit. "That was terrific. You were throwing rocks into the black hole."

Estes nodded. "Yes, and I'm hoping my suit has been stopping the X rays. I'd just as soon not die of radiation poisoning."

"They'll see this back on Earth, won't they?"

"I'm sure they will," said Estes, "but will they pay attention? They'll record it all and wonder about it. But what's going to make them come out here for a closer look? I've got to work out something that will make them come, after I have just a little time to rest."

An hour later, he lifted out another space suit. No time to wait for the recharge of the solar batteries in the first one. He said, "I hope I haven't lost the range."

He was out again, and it had become clear that even allowing a fairly wide spread of velocities and direction, the black hole would suck up the slowing rocks as they moved inward.

Estes gathered as many rocks as he could manage and placed them carefully on an indentation in the hull of the ship. They didn't stay there, but they drifted only exceedingly slowly, and even after Estes had collected all he could, those he had placed there first had spread out no more than billiard balls on a pool table.

Then he threw them, at first tensely, and then with growing confidence, and the black hole flashed—and flashed—and flashed.

It seemed to him that the target became steadily easier to hit and that the black hole was growing madly with each impact and that soon it would reach out and suck him and the ship into its never-sated maw.

It was his imagination, of course, and nothing more. Finally all the rocks were gone and he felt he could throw nothing more in any case. He had been out there, it seemed, for hours.

When he was within the ship again he said, as soon as Funarelli had helped him off with his helmet, "That's it. I can't do anything more."

"You had plenty of flashes there," said Funarelli.

"Plenty, and they should surely be recorded. We'll just have to wait now. They've *got* to come."

Funarelli helped him off with the rest of his suit as best his muscle-torn body would allow. Then he stood, grunting and gasping, and said, "Do you really think they'll come, Ben?"

"I think they've got to," said Estes, almost as though he were trying to force the event by the sheer power of wishing. "I think they've *got* to."

"Why do you think they've got to?" said Funarelli, sounding like a man who wanted to grasp at straws but didn't dare.

"Because I *communicated*," said Estes. "We're not only the first people to encounter a black hole, we're the first to use it to communicate; we're the first to use the ultimate communication system of the future, the one that might send messages from star to star and galaxy to galaxy, and that might be the ultimate energy source as well—" He was panting, and he sounded a little wild.

"What are you talking about?" said Funarelli.

"I threw those rocks in rhythm, Harv," said Estes, "and the X-ray bursts came in rhythm. It was flash-flash-flash—flash—flash—flash—flash-flash-flash, and so on."

"Yes?"

"It's old-fashioned; *old*-fashioned, but that's one thing everyone remembers from the days when people communicated by electric currents running through wires."

"You mean the photograph—phonograph—"

"The telegraph, Harv. Those flashes I produced will be recorded and the first time someone looks at that record, all hell will break loose. It's not just that they'll be spotting an X-ray source; it's not just that it will be an X-ray source moving very slowly against the stars so that it has to be within our Solar System. What it is, is that they'll be seeing an X-ray source going on and off and producing the signal sos—sos—And when an X-ray source is shouting for help, you'll bet they'll come—as fast as they can—if only to see —what's—there—that—"

He was asleep.

—And five days later, a drone ship arrived.

The Tercentenary Incident

I

July 4, 2076—and for the third time the accident of the conventional system of numeration, based on powers of ten, had brought the last two digits of the year back to the fateful 76 that had seen the birth of the nation.

It was no longer a nation in the old sense; it was rather a geographic expression; part of a greater whole that made up the Federation of all of humanity on Earth, together with its offshoots on the Moon and in the space colonies. By culture and heritage, however, the name and the *idea* lived on, and that portion of the planet signified by the old name was still the most prosperous and advanced region of the world. . . . And the President of the United States was still the most powerful single figure in the Planetary Council.

Lawrence Edwards watched the small figure of the President from his height of two hundred feet. He drifted lazily above the crowd, his flotron motor making a barely heard chuckle on his back, and what he saw looked exactly like what anyone would see on a holovision scene. How many times had he seen little figures like that in his living room, little figures in a cube of sunlight, looking as real as though they were living homunculi, except that you could put your hand through them.

You couldn't put your hand through those spreading out in their tens of thousands over the open spaces surrounding the Washington Monument. And you couldn't put your hand through the President. You could reach out to him instead, touch him, and shake his hand.

Edwards thought sardonically of the uselessness of that added element of tangibility and wished himself a hundred miles away, floating in air over some isolated wilderness, instead of here where he had to watch for any sign of disorder. There wouldn't be any necessity for his being here but for the mythology of the value of "pressing the flesh."

Edwards was not an admirer of the President—Hugo Allen Winkler, fifty-seventh of the line.

To Edwards, President Winkler seemed an empty man, a charmer, a vote grabber, a promiser. He was a disappointing man to have in office now after all the hopes of those first months of his administration. The World Federation was in danger of breaking up long before its job had been completed and Winkler could do nothing about it. One needed a strong hand, not a glad hand; a hard voice, not a honey voice.

There he was now, shaking hands—a space forced around him by the Service, with Edwards himself, plus a few others of the Service, watching from above.

The President would be running for re-election certainly, and there seemed a good chance he might be defeated. That would just make things worse, since the opposition party was dedicated to the destruction of the Federation.

Edwards sighed. It would be a miserable four years coming up—maybe a miserable forty—and all he could do was float in the air, ready to reach every Service agent on the ground by laser-phone if there was the slightest—

He didn't see the slightest. There was no sign of disturbance. Just a little puff of white dust, hardly visible; just a momentary glitter in the sunlight, up and away, gone as soon as he was aware of it.

Where was the President? He had lost sight of him in the dust.

He looked about in the vicinity of where he had seen him last. The President could not have moved far.

Then he became aware of disturbance. First it was among the Service agents themselves, who seemed to have gone off their heads and to be moving this way and that jerkily. Then those among the crowd near them caught the contagion and then those farther off. The noise rose and became a thunder.

Edwards didn't have to hear the words that made up the rising roar. It seemed to carry the news to him by nothing more than its mass clamorous urgency. President Winkler had disappeared! He had been there one moment and had turned into a handful of vanishing dust the next.

Edwards held his breath in an agony of waiting during what seemed a drug-ridden eternity, for the long moment of realization to end and for the mob to break into a mad, rioting stampede.

—When a resonant voice sounded over the gathering din, and at its sound, the noise faded, died, and became a silence. It was as though it were all a holovision program after all and someone had turned the sound down and out.

Edwards thought: My God, it's the President.

There was no mistaking the voice. Winkler stood on the guarded stage from which he was to give his Tercentenary speech, and from which he had left but ten minutes ago to shake hands with some in the crowd.

How had he gotten back there?

Edwards listened—

"Nothing has happened to me, my fellow Americans. What you have seen just now was the breakdown of a mechanical device. It was not your President, so let us not allow a mechanical failure to dampen the celebration of the happiest day the world has yet seen. . . . My fellow Americans, give me your attention—"

And what followed was the Tercentenary speech, the greatest speech Winkler had ever made, or Edwards had ever heard. Edwards found himself forgetting his supervisory job in his eagerness to listen.

Winkler had it right! He understood the importance of the Federation and he was getting it *across.*

Deep inside, though, another part of him was remembering the persistent rumors that the new expertise in robotics had resulted in the construction of a look-alike President, a robot who could perform the purely ceremonial functions, who could shake hands with the crowd, who could be neither bored nor exhausted—nor assassinated.

Edwards thought, in obscure shock, that that was how it had happened. There had been such a look-alike robot indeed, and in a way—it had been assassinated.

October 13, 2078—

Edwards looked up as the waist-high robot guide approached and said mellifluously, "Mr. Janek will see you now."

Edwards stood up, feeling tall as he towered above the stubby, metallic guide. He did not feel young, however. His face had gathered lines in the last two years or so and he was aware of it.

He followed the guide into a surprisingly small room, where, behind a surprisingly small desk, there sat Francis Janek, a slightly paunchy and incongruously young-looking man.

Janek smiled and his eyes were friendly as he rose to shake hands. "Mr. Edwards."

Edwards muttered, "I'm glad to have the opportunity, sir—"

Edwards had never seen Janek before, but then the job of personal secretary to the President is a quiet one and makes little news.

Janek said, "Sit down. Sit down. Would you care for a soya stick?"

Edwards smiled a polite negative, and sat down. Janek was clearly emphasizing his youth. His ruffled shirt was open and the hairs on his chest had been dyed a subdued but definite violet.

Janek said, "I know you have been trying to reach me for some weeks now.

I'm sorry for the delay. I hope you understand that my time is not entirely my own. However, we're here now. . . . I have referred to the Chief of the Service, by the way, and he gave you very high marks. He regrets your resignation."

Edwards said, eyes downcast, "It seemed better to carry on my investigations without danger of embarrassment to the Service."

Janek's smile flashed. "Your activities, though discreet, have not gone unnoticed, however. The Chief explains that you have been investigating the Tercentenary Incident, and I must admit it was that which persuaded me to see you as soon as I could. You've given up your position for that? You're investigating a dead issue."

"How can it be a dead issue, Mr. Janek? Your calling it an Incident doesn't alter the fact that it was an assassination attempt."

"A matter of semantics. Why use a disturbing phrase?"

"Only because it would seem to represent a disturbing truth. Surely you would say that someone tried to kill the President."

Janek spread his hands. "If that is so, the plot did not succeed. A mechanical device was destroyed. Nothing more. In fact, if we look at it properly, the Incident—whatever you choose to call it—did the nation and the world an enormous good. As we all know, the President was shaken by the Incident and the nation as well. The President and all of us realized what a return to the violence of the last century might mean and it produced a great turnaround."

"I can't deny that."

"Of course you can't. Even the President's enemies will grant that the last two years have seen great accomplishments. The Federation is far stronger today than anyone could have dreamed it would be on that Tercentenary day. We might even say that a breakup of the global economy has been prevented."

Edwards said cautiously, "Yes, the President is a changed man. Everyone says so."

Janek said, "He was a great man always. The Incident made him concentrate on the great issues with a fierce intensity, however."

"Which he didn't do before?"

"Perhaps not quite as intensely. . . . In effect then, the President, and all of us, would like the Incident forgotten. My main purpose in seeing you, Mr. Edwards, is to make that plain to you. This is not the Twentieth Century and we can't throw you in jail for being inconvenient to us, or hamper you in any way, but even the Global Charter doesn't forbid us to attempt persuasion. Do you understand me?"

"I understand you, but I do not agree with you. Can we forget the Incident when the person responsible has never been apprehended?"

"Perhaps that is just as well, too, sir. Far better that some, uh, unbalanced person escape than that the matter be blown out of proportion and the stage set, possibly, for a return to the days of the Twentieth Century."

"The official story even states that the robot spontaneously exploded—which is impossible, and which has been an unfair blow to the robot industry."

"A robot is not the term I would use, Mr. Edwards. It was a mechanical device. No one has said that robots are dangerous, per se, certainly not the workaday metallic ones. The only reference here is to the unusually complex manlike devices that seem flesh and blood and that we might call androids. Actually, they are so complex that perhaps they might explode at first; I am not an expert in the field. The robotics industry will recover."

"Nobody in the government," said Edwards stubbornly, "seems to care whether we reach the bottom of the matter or not."

"I've already explained that there have been no consequences but good ones. Why stir the mud at the bottom, when the water above is clear?"

"And the use of the disintegrator?"

For a moment, Janek's hand, which had been slowly turning the container of soya sticks on his desk, held still, then it returned to its rhythmic movement. He said lightly, "What's that?"

Edwards said intently, "Mr. Janek, I think you know what I mean. As part of the Service—"

"To which you no longer belong, of course."

"Nevertheless, as part of the Service, I could not help but hear things that were not always, I suppose, for my ears. I had heard of a new weapon, and I saw something happen at the Tercentenary which would require one. The object everyone thought was the President disappeared into a cloud of very fine dust. It was as though every atom within the object had had its bonds to other atoms loosed. The object had become a cloud of individual atoms, which began to combine again of course, but which dispersed too quickly to do more than appear a momentary glitter of dust."

"Very science-fictionish."

"I certainly don't understand the science behind it, Mr. Janek, but I do see that it would take considerable energy to accomplish such bond breaking. This energy would have to be withdrawn from the environment. Those people who were standing near the device at the time, and whom I could locate —and who would agree to talk—were unanimous in reporting a wave of coldness washing over them."

Janek put the soya-stick container to one side with a small click of transite against cellulite. He said, "Suppose just for argument that there is such a thing as a disintegrator."

"You need not argue. There is."

"I won't argue. I know of no such thing myself, but in my office, I am not likely to know of anything so security-bound as new weaponry. But if a disintegrator exists and is as secret as all that, it must be an American monopoly, unknown to the rest of the Federation. It would then not be something either you or I should talk about. It could be a more dangerous war weapon than the nuclear bombs, precisely because—if what you say is so—it produces nothing more than disintegration at the point of impact and cold in the immediate neighborhood. No blast, no fire, no deadly radiation. Without these distressing side effects, there would be no deterrent to its use, yet for all we know it might be made large enough to destroy the planet itself."

"I go along with all of that," said Edwards.

"Then you see that if there is no disintegrator, it is foolish to talk about one; and if there *is* a disintegrator, then it is criminal to talk about one."

"I haven't discussed it, except to you, just now, because I'm trying to persuade you of the seriousness of the situation. If one had been used, for instance, ought not the government be interested in deciding how it came to be used—if another unit of the Federation might be in possession?"

Janek shook his head. "I think that we can rely on appropriate organs of this government to take such a thing into consideration. You had better not concern yourself with the matter."

Edwards said, in barely controlled impatience, "Can you assure me that the United States is the only government that has such a weapon at its disposal?"

"I can't tell you, since I know nothing about such a weapon, and should not know. You should not have spoken of it to me. Even if no such weapon exists, the *rumor* of its existence could be damaging."

"But since I have told you and the damage is done, please hear me out. Let me have the chance of convincing you that *you*, and no one else, hold the key to a fearful situation that perhaps I alone see."

"You alone see? I alone hold the key?"

"Does that sound paranoid? Let me explain and then judge for yourself."

"I will give you a little more time, sir, but what I have said stands. You must abandon this—this hobby of yours—this investigation. It is terribly dangerous."

"It is its abandonment that would be dangerous. Don't you see that if the disintegrator exists and if the United States has the monopoly of it, then it follows that the number of people who could have access to it would be sharply limited. As an ex-member of the Service, I have some practical knowledge of this and I tell you that the only person in the world who could manage to abstract a disintegrator from our top-secret arsenals would be the President. . . . Only the President of the United States, Mr. Janek, could have arranged that assassination attempt."

They stared at each other for a moment and then Janek touched a contact at his desk.

He said, "Added precaution. No one can overhear us now by any means. Mr. Edwards, do you realize the danger of that statement? To yourself? You must not overestimate the power of the Global Charter. A government has the right to take reasonable measures for the protection of its stability."

Edwards said, "I'm approaching you, Mr. Janek, as someone I presume to be a loyal American citizen. I come to you with news of a terrible crime that affects all Americans and the entire Federation. A crime that has produced a situation that perhaps only you can right. Why do you respond with threats?"

Janek said, "That's the second time you have tried to make it appear that I am a potential savior of the world. I can't conceive of myself in that role. You understand, I hope, that I have no unusual powers."

"You are the secretary to the President."

"That does *not* mean I have special access to him or am in some intimately confidential relationship to him. There are times, Mr. Edwards, when I suspect others consider me to be nothing more than a flunky, and there are even times when I find myself in danger of agreeing with them."

"Nevertheless, you see him frequently, you see him informally, you see him—"

Janek said impatiently, "I see enough of him to be able to assure you that the President would not order the destruction of that mechanical device on Tercentenary day."

"Is it in your opinion impossible, then?"

"I did not say that. I said he would not. After all, why should he? Why should the President want to destroy a look-alike android that has been a valuable adjunct to him for over three years of his Presidency? And if for some reason he wanted it done, why on Earth should he do it in so incredibly public a way—at the Tercentenary, no less—thus advertising its existence, risking public revulsion at the thought of shaking hands with a mechanical device, to say nothing of the diplomatic repercussions of having had representatives of other parts of the Federation treat with one? He might, instead, simply have ordered it disassembled in private. No one but a few highly placed members of the Administration would have known."

"There have not, however, been any undesirable consequences for the President as a result of the Incident, have there?"

"He has had to cut down on ceremony. He is no longer as accessible as he once was."

"As the robot once was."

"Well," said Janek uneasily. "Yes, I suppose that's right."

Edwards said, "And, as a matter of fact, the President was re-elected and his popularity has not diminished even though the destruction was public. The argument against public destruction is not as powerful as you make it sound."

"But the re-election came about *despite* the Incident. It was brought about by the President's quick action in stepping forward and delivering what you will have to admit was one of the great speeches of American history. It was an absolutely amazing performance; you will have to admit that."

"It was a beautifully staged drama. The President, one might think, would have counted on that."

Janek sat back in his chair. "If I understand you, Edwards, you are suggesting an involuted storybook plot. Are you trying to say that the President had the device destroyed, just as it was—in the middle of a crowd, at precisely the time of the Tercentenary celebration, with the world watching—so that he could win the admiration of all by his quick action? Are you suggesting that he arranged it all so that he could establish himself as a man of unexpected vigor and strength under extremely dramatic circumstances and thus turn a losing campaign into a winning one? . . . Mr. Edwards, you've been reading fairy tales."

Edwards said, "If I were trying to claim all this, it would indeed be a fairy tale, but I am not. I never suggested that the President ordered the killing of the robot. I merely asked if you thought it were possible and you have stated quite strongly that it wasn't. I'm glad you did, because I agree with you."

"Then what is all this? I'm beginning to think you're wasting my time."

"Another moment, please. Have you ever asked yourself why the job couldn't have been done with a laser beam, with a field deactivator—with a sledgehammer, for God's sake? Why should anyone go to the incredible trouble of getting a weapon guarded by the strongest possible government security to do a job that didn't require such a weapon? Aside from the difficulty of getting it, why risk revealing the existence of a disintegrator to the rest of the world?"

"This whole business of a disintegrator is just a theory of yours."

"The robot disappeared completely before my eyes. I was watching. I rely on no secondhand evidence for that. It doesn't matter what you call the weapon; whatever name you give it, it had the effect of taking the robot apart atom by atom and scattering all those atoms irretrievably. Why should this be done? It was tremendous overkill."

"I don't know what was in the mind of the perpetrator."

"No? Yet it seems to me that there is only one logical reason for a complete powdering when something much simpler would have carried through the destruction. The powdering left no trace behind of the destroyed object. It left nothing to indicate what it had been, whether robot or anything else."

Janek said, "But there is no question of what it was."

"Isn't there? I said only the President could have arranged for a disintegrator to be obtained and used. But, considering the existence of a look-alike robot, which President did the arranging?"

Janek said harshly, "I don't think we can carry on this conversation. You are mad."

Edwards said, "Think it through. For God's sake, think it through. The President did not destroy the robot. Your arguments there are convincing. What happened was that the robot destroyed the President. President Winkler was killed in the crowd on July 4, 2076. A robot resembling President

Winkler then gave the Tercentenary speech, ran for re-election, was re-elected, and still serves as President of the United States."

"Madness!"

"I've come to you, to *you* because *you* can prove this—and correct it, too."

"It is simply not so. The President is—the President." Janek made as though to rise and conclude the interview.

"You yourself say he's changed," said Edwards quickly and urgently. "The Tercentenary speech was beyond the powers of the old Winkler. Haven't you been yourself amazed at the accomplishments of the last two years? Truthfully—could the Winkler of the first term have done all this?"

"Yes, he could have, because the President of the second term is the President of the first term."

"Do you deny he's changed? I put it to you. *You* decide and I'll abide by your decision."

"He's risen to meet the challenge, that is all. It's happened before this in American history." But Janek sank back into his seat. He looked uneasy.

"He doesn't drink," said Edwards.

"He never did—very much."

"He no longer womanizes. Do you deny he did so in the past?"

"A President is a man. For the last two years, however, he's felt dedicated to the matter of the Federation."

"It's a change for the better, I admit," said Edwards, "but it's a change. Of course, if he *had* a woman, the masquerade could not be carried on, could it?"

Janek said, "Too bad he doesn't have a wife." He pronounced the archaic word a little self-consciously. "The whole matter wouldn't arise if he did."

"The fact that he doesn't made the plot more practical. Yet he has fathered two children. I don't believe they have been in the White House, either of them, since the Tercentenary."

"Why should they be? They are grown, with lives of their own."

"Are they invited? Is the President interested in seeing them? You're his private secretary. You would know. Are they?"

Janek said, "You're wasting time. A robot can't kill a human being. You know that that is the First Law of Robotics."

"I know it. But no one is saying that the robot-Winkler killer the human-Winkler directly. When the human-Winkler was in the crowd, the robot-Winkler was on the stand and I doubt that a disintegrator could be aimed from that distance without doing more widespread damage. Maybe it could, but more likely the robot-Winkler had an accomplice—a hit man, if that is the correct Twentieth-Century jargon."

Janek frowned. His plump face puckered and looked pained. He said, "You know, madness must be catching. I'm actually beginning to consider the insane notion you've brought here. Fortunately, it doesn't hold water. After all, why would an assassination of the human-Winkler be arranged in public?

All the arguments against destroying the robot in public hold against the killing of a human President in public. Don't you see that ruins the whole theory?"

"It does not—" began Edwards.

"It *does*. No one except for a few officials knew that the mechanical device existed at all. If President Winkler were killed privately and his body disposed of, the robot could easily take over without suspicion—without having roused yours, for instance."

"There would always be a few officials who would know, Mr. Janek. The assassinations would have to broaden." Edwards leaned forward earnestly. "See here, ordinarily there couldn't have been any danger of confusing the human being and the machine. I imagine the robot wasn't in constant use, but was pulled out only for specific purposes, and there would always be key individuals, perhaps quite a number of them, who would know where the President was and what he was doing. If that were so, the assassination would have to be carried out at a time when those officials actually thought the President was really the robot."

"I don't follow you."

"See here. One of the robot's tasks was to shake hands with the crowd; press the flesh. When this was taking place, the officials in the know would be perfectly aware that the hand shaker was, in truth, the robot."

"Exactly. You're making sense now. It *was* the robot."

"Except that it was the Tercentenary, and except that President Winkler could not resist. I suppose it would be more than human to expect a President—particularly an empty crowd pleaser and applause hunter like Winkler —to give up the adulation of the crowd on this day of all days, and let it go to a machine. And perhaps the robot carefully nurtured this impulse so that on this one Tercentenary day, the President would have ordered the robot to remain behind the podium, while he himself went out to shake hands and to be cheered."

"Secretly?"

"Of course secretly. If the President had told anyone in the Service, or any of his aides, or you, would he have been allowed to do it? The official attitude concerning the possibility of assassination has been practically a disease since the events of the late Twentieth Century. So with the encouragement of an obviously clever robot—"

"You assume the robot to be clever because you assume he is now serving as President. This is circular reasoning. If he is not President, there is no reason to think he is clever, or that he were capable of working out this plot. Besides, what motive could possibly drive a robot to plot an assassination? Even if it didn't kill the President directly, the taking of a human life indirectly is also forbidden by the First Law, which states, 'A robot may not injure a human being or, through inaction, allow a human being to come to harm.' "

Edwards said, "The First Law is not absolute. What if harming a human being saves the lives of two others, or three others, or even three billion others? The robot may have thought that saving the Federation took precedence over the saving of one life. It was no ordinary robot, after all. It was designed to duplicate the properties of the President closely enough to deceive anyone. Suppose it had the understanding of President Winkler, without his weaknesses, and suppose it knew that it could save the Federation where the President could not."

"*You* can reason so, but how do you know a mechanical device would?"

"It is the only way to explain what happened."

"I think it is a paranoid fantasy."

Edwards said, "Then tell me why the object that was destroyed was powdered into atoms. What else would make sense than to suppose that that was the only way to hide the fact that it was a human being and not a robot that was destroyed? Give me an alternate explanation."

Janek reddened. "I won't accept it."

"But you can prove the whole matter—or disprove it. It's why I have come to you—to *you.*"

"How can I prove it? Or disprove it either?"

"No one sees the President at unguarded moments as you do. It is with you—in default of family—that he is most informal. Study him."

"I have. I tell you he isn't—"

"You haven't. You suspected nothing wrong. Little signs meant nothing to you. Study him now, being aware that he *might* be a robot, and you will see."

Janek said sardonically, "I can knock him down and probe for metal with an ultrasonic detector. Even an android has a platinum-iridium brain."

"No drastic action will be necessary. Just observe him and you will see that he is so radically not the man he was that he cannot be a man."

Janek looked at the clock-calendar on the wall. He said, "We have been here over an hour."

"I'm sorry to have taken up so much of your time, but you see the importance of all this, I hope."

"Importance?" said Janek. Then he looked up and what had seemed a despondent air turned suddenly into something of hope. "But is it, in fact, important? Really, I mean?"

"How can it not be important? To have a robot as President of the United States? That's not important?"

"No, that's not what I mean. Forget what President Winkler might be. Just consider this. Someone serving as President of the United States has saved the Federation; he has held it together and, at the present moment, he runs the Council in the interests of peace and of constructive compromise. You'll admit all that?"

Edwards said, "Of course, I admit all that. But what of the precedent established? A robot in the White House for a very good reason now may lead to a robot in the White House twenty years from now for a very bad reason, and then to robots in the White House for no reason at all but only as a matter of course. Don't you see the importance of muffling a possible trumpet call for the end of humanity at the time of its first uncertain note?"

Janek shrugged. "Suppose I find out he's a robot? Do we broadcast it to all the world? Do you know what it will do to the world's financial structure? Do you know—"

"I do know. That is why I have come to you privately, instead of trying to make it public. It is up to you to check out the matter and come to a definite conclusion. It is up to you, next, having found the supposed President to be a robot, which I am certain you will do, to persuade him to resign."

"And by your version of his reaction to the First Law, he will then have me killed since I will be threatening his expert handling of the greatest global crisis of the Twenty-first Century."

Edwards shook his head. "The robot acted in secret before, and no one tried to counter the arguments he used with himself. You will be able to reinforce a stricter interpretation of the First Law with your arguments. If necessary, we can get the aid of some official from U. S. Robots and Mechanical Men, Inc., who constructed the robot in the first place. Once he resigns, the Vice-President will succeed. If the robot-Winkler has put the old world on the right track, good; it can now be kept on the right track by the Vice-President, who is a decent and honorable woman. But we can't have a robot ruler, and we mustn't ever again."

"What if the President is human?"

"I'll leave that to you. You will know."

Janek said, "I am not that confident of myself. What if I can't decide? If I can't bring myself to? If I don't dare to? What are your plans?"

Edwards looked tired. "I don't know. I may have to go to U. S. Robots. But I don't think it will come to that. I'm quite confident now that I've laid the problem in your lap, you won't rest till it's settled. Do *you* want to be ruled by a robot?"

He stood up, and Janek let him go. They did not shake hands.

Janek sat there in the gathering twilight in deep shock.

A robot!

The man had walked in and had argued, in perfectly rational manner, that the President of the United States was a robot.

It should have been easy to fight that off. Yet though Janek had tried every argument he could think of, they had all been useless, and the man had not been shaken in the least.

A robot as President! Edwards had been *certain* of it, and he would *stay* certain of it. And if Janek insisted that the President was human, Edwards would go to U. S. Robots. He wouldn't rest.

Janek frowned as he thought of the twenty-eight months since the Tercentenary and of how well all had gone in the face of the probabilities. And now?

He remained lost in somber thought.

He still had the disintegrator but surely it would not be necessary to use it on a human being, the nature of whose body was not in question. A silent laser stroke in some lonely spot would do.

It had been hard to maneuver the President into the earlier job, but in this present case, it wouldn't even have to know.